The Harlem Cycle Volume 3

Cotton Comes to Harlem

Blind Man with a Pistol

Plan B

Other books by Chester Himes
published by Payback Press

THE HARLEM CYCLE VOLUME 1

A Rage in Harlem
The Real Cool Killers
The Crazy Kill

THE HARLEM CYCLE VOLUME 2

The Big Gold Dream
All Shot Up
The Heat's On

"Some of the best crime novels ever written - bloody, bawdy and original - handsomely anthologised at a bargain price and as irresistible as the day they first blew into print...I can't imagine them being bettered."

The Literary Review

"The books have lasting value - as thrillers, as streetwise documentaries, as chapters of black writing at its ribald and unaffected best. On every level they are simply - or not simply - terrific."

The Sunday Times

"Chester's writing was no third-hand bullshit gleaned from some secondary source...every sentence of every page reeks of authenticity."

Melvin van Peebles

"The greatest find in American fiction since Raymond Chandler."

The Observer

"violent and funny and shocking...the pace never slows and the narrative grabs you and holds you to the end."

Liverpool Daily Post

"One of the few black writers to have used the thriller genre to express black experience in the USA."
City Limits

"These stories have everything, well developed plots, strong characters, realism, drama, humour, suspense and, of course, biting social comment."
The Alarm

CHESTER HIMES

The Harlem Cycle Volume 3

Cotton Comes to Harlem
Blind Man with a Pistol
Plan B

This edition first published in 1997 by
Payback Press, an imprint of Canongate Books Ltd,
14 High Street, Edinburgh EH1 1TE

British Library Cataloguing-in-Publication Data

A catalogue record for this book is available upon request
from the British Library

ISBN 0 86241 692 2

Typeset in Minion and Serif Modular by
Palimpsest Book Production Limited,
Polmont, Stirlingshire
Print and bound in Scotland by
Caledonian International Book Manufacturing, Bishopbriggs

Contents

Chester Himes
by Lesley Himes

Upon retiring to Southern Spain after Chester had suffered a series of debilitating strokes, I used to shower and dress him before taking him out every day. He would say, 'I'm not staying in.' We would, therefore, get in the car and as I drove, he would fall asleep like a child in a pram. People saw us in the Seat 124 but they did not realise that he was so terribly handicapped. They just saw him sitting in the car with this debonair look.

We were going out on one of our usual outings, driving through Altea towards Alicante. We turned right into Albir, which is now quite a big village but previously had been simply a few houses, and drove down a country road where, unfortunately, we had a flat tyre. Now Chester was such a fanatic about changing tyres that he never let them get into a state when there would be a flat. However now I was driving, we had a flat and I did not know how to change a tyre. I realised no one would stop and help me while Chester was sitting in the car, looking very debonair and quite relaxed, so I opened the boot and took the wheelchair out. I wheeled Chester round so that he could at least start directing me. He said, 'You do this and you do that.' But I was not strong enough to get the bolts undone. I was becoming desperate. Suddenly, while I was struggling with the wheel, I heard tyres screeching and gravel flying up and two cars stopped, one right after the other. I turned around to look at Chester. He had moved his chair back a bit and had fallen into the ditch. All you could see was Chester's feet sticking up in the air. And the people started pouring out of the cars, looking furiously at me and thinking that I had just knocked a man off the road.

I shouted, 'Oh Chester, oh Chester, are you all right?'

'I'm all right. Don't worry, don't worry.'

I did not know whether to laugh or cry.

'Don't cry Lesley, please don't cry.'

'I don't know how I am going to get you up!'

Then the people started shouting at me, '*Señora! señora! que has hecho* – what have you done to this poor man! You ought to be ashamed, you knocked him down.'

So I said, 'Would you please help me get him up and then I'll explain.'

They did before asking, 'How on earth did you do this?'

'I didn't knock him down, he's my husband.'

They must have thought I was trying to kill him, because they began looking at me in a strange manner suggesting disbelief. They tried to ask Chester but he didn't speak Spanish. However, he was laughing by this time, while I was crying *and* laughing. Chester could always see the humorous side of a situation.

'I had a flat tyre. My husband was sitting in the car and, as you see, he looks fine and I figured that no one would help me unless they saw the wheelchair. He cannot walk. He moved the chair too far back and fell into the ditch, which left him with his legs sticking up in the air.'

I eventually managed to convince them and they looked relieved.

'Don't worry senora. Can we do anything for you?'

The wheel was then changed in no time.

All my friends, when hearing the experience, were in hysterics. Both Chester and I laughed about this and many other things. Humour was his last and greatest weapon and maybe this will help to explain why he laughed so much – to relieve the tension he always felt, maybe to keep himself from crying.

I'm often being asked how I met Chester and I will try and explain it once more. I was working at the *International Herald Tribune* in Paris as a photo librarian and one evening all the pictures were coming in from the various agencies: United Press, Reuters, etc. One of the pictures to appear on my desk that evening was of Chester and I saw that he had won first prize for the best detective novel of the year, *Grand Prix de la littérature policière.* It was 1958 and I knew Richard Wright and William Gardner Smith and a lot of other Afro-American writers, painters, jazz musicians, etc. so although I didn't know him, I certainly *knew* of Chester Himes. I went to the editor and suggested that we should run the story and the picture as after all we were an American newspaper and this was the first time this prize had been won by an American, let alone a black American. However my boss replied that although we would run a short story there was no room for the picture.

After work I stopped in to have a drink with a few pals in the Café de Tournon on the rue de Tournon and while I was sitting there talking to William Gardner Smith a car came roaring round the corner at a tremendous speed. Without looking out to see who it was, Bill said to me, 'Well, only one man will come round a corner driving like that . . . Chester Himes.'

Chester then wanders round the corner, comes in with his Irish setter and says, 'Hi Bill.' As Bill introduced me, I said, 'Congratulations, I've just heard you've won a prize for *La Reine des pommes* [*A Rage in Harlem*].' He was very pleased that I knew this as the newspaper had only been off the press an hour before. As a result he said, 'Let's go out and celebrate. We'll paint the town red.'

Well, we most definitely did. We went into one little place after another and had a marvellous time. At the end of the night Chester said, 'Well I won't be able to drive any more. I think it is time to go, so I'd better take you both home.' He asked Bill where they lived and Bill said that it wasn't as simple as that, 'I live at one end of Paris and Lesley lives at the other.' Chester replied, 'Well there's no question about that Bill, I'm going to take you home *first.*' And that's how it all started.

At the *Herald Tribune* I began work at 5 pm and finished at midnight so my days were wonderfully free. I must admit we spent quite a bit of time in bed, talking, making love, laughing and trying to plan our future. Yet I did not see how there could be a future because I was young, attractive, had a good job, in fact two jobs, and was very independent. And while I had no hang-ups, probably due to the very secure environment in which I'd been brought up, Chester was so loaded with anger and complex emotions, all of which surface in his writing. However, I think his short stories really show something that is very much Chester when he is not angry at the world or angry because he felt he couldn't make a living as a writer. America would not let him write the way he wanted to. He was therefore kind to young writers, such as Ishmael Reed, who wanted guidance and he would help them to rewrite pages and introduce them to his editors. There was no envy and he wanted them (usually African-Americans) to succeed and to be proud of them. In a letter to his editor, Chester lamented 'that the American audience will only buy books by Negroes that are either shockingly honest or shockingly hateful. I don't know why this is . . .'

Chester was a straight talker and always told it like it was which probably explains the negative reaction in America, from both blacks and whites, to his work. As Ishmael Reed, in an article for California Magazine, noted:

> *With the creation of Grave Digger and Coffin Ed, Himes risked and received the condemnation of alienated black intellectuals, who were horrified by their values – the values of the working black middle class, of which these characters were products. They are realists. They are family men. They like jazz and know about black Shakespearean actors like Canada Lee, but their methods for dealing with criminals, though repellent to those they would call sob sisters, are effective and often brutal.*

I would like to think Chester had been acknowledged as a writer a bit more before his death but I'm going to make sure that he will not be forgotten. It was a promise that I made to him.

> *Would you . . . keep my books alive? I don't want to feel*

that I have lived without having accomplished something that's going to be remembered and I don't want to leave this world a common shade and I do so hope that my books will be read and that people will remember me.

One French critic, who asserted that Himes would go down in history as the greatest black writer of the century, considered *Plan B* a delicious legacy that explored the implacable hatred existing between Black and White. The critic felt that Himes had benefited greatly from his detective fiction because he used the form so skilfully to explore deeper concerns. Michael Naudy claimed that Chester was the legitimate heir to the nineteenth-century revolutionary theoreticians of Central Europe. In an interview with John A.Williams, Chester insisted:

I can see what a Black revolution would be like. First of all in order for a revolution to be effective, it has to be massively violent; it has to be as violent as the war in Vietnam . . . In any form of uprising, the major objective is to kill as many people as you can, by whatever means, because the act of killing them and killing them in sufficient numbers is supposed to help you gain your objectives.

Although Chester was not against violence, he was against the notion of disorganised violence. With non-organised rioting one was sure to lose against the police and the army. This is what *Plan B* is all about: a rejection of non-organised violence because it degenerates into chaos and turns against whoever starts it.

When mail came it either thrilled him or upset him. It either made him so absolutely furious that he could not write another word or it thrilled him so much that he felt he would have to go out and celebrate. When the news was bad he would write furious letters in reply. The letters that mattered most were the ones that had to do with his career, of course. When a big cheque or an excellent review arrived, we rejoiced. The bad news was when a cheque had not come when it should have or when Chester thought they did not pay him what they owed, believing the publishers always tried to cheat him. Then there was the unfavourable review or when a manuscript was not accepted. This upset him. The real news for him had to do with his work. He was so geared up that his mail was the most important thing to him. It was his means of keeping in contact with the world. I had to write to him quite often when he was away, even when I didn't really have anything to say, because he needed mail. If he didn't get a letter from me, he got in a terrible state. He said, 'I haven't had a letter from you, I haven't had a letter from anyone, not even you.' He did not have a phone at the time and mail was his only means of communication. The only thing I could do was reassure him that I loved him and was always there for him.

I saw him probably angrier than I've ever seen him, though, when French TV showed him the film that he had made with Pierre Gaisseau, who had previously won an Oscar for his documentary, 'The Sky Above and the Mud Below'. Both went to Harlem to do a reportage – Chester would be setting up the interviews and Pierre doing the filming. Chester did his best to ensure that they showed the beauty parlors and one or two schools as he particularly didn't want his fellow Afro-Americans to come out looking like the sort of people who were just wandering the streets, dancing and singing and shaking their bottoms. Chester hadn't seen the film rushes at this time and we were invited to a private showing one evening so that the TV people and the general media could see it before it went on air. The film started and the very first scene was two enormous people (maybe it was a man and woman, I can't remember now) wandering down the street, shaking their bottoms. Chester felt this was not the way he was trying to portray the people of Harlem and he found it derogatory. He was extremely annoyed and I could feel him sitting next to me sizzling with fury and I thought any minute now he's going to grab my hand and say, 'This is it, I won't take any more of this.'

When the film ended, everyone liked it, they thought it was

absolutely marvellous and Chester said to me, 'Take my hand, please don't look left or right, don't look at anyone. I want you to walk out past all these people. I don't want you to say good evening, good night, I don't want you to say anything or try to shake hands.' He continued, 'When I take your hand, we're going to walk right out of here and you're not going to say anything to anyone.' Chester was so angry and of course the next day he wrote to say he wanted his name removed from the film. 'You can keep my reportage but my name is not going to be on this movie.' The French TV people were very upset but Chester ensured his name was taken off.

I could normally sense when Chester was going to have one of his moods and I'd try to be ready for them. There really is no way anyone could explain these swings. However they were never violent towards me and I was always able to ease him out of them, simply by being very quiet and calm, which is in accordance with my general way of behaving anyway. But although I understood the mood swings and the reasons why he was this way, it did not necessarily make it any easier for me.

In one of his many letters, he tried to make me realise that I was going to have to be a strong woman and understand a lot of things that maybe other people wouldn't have to:

> *All you have to give me in return for my love is this world and all other worlds, hope of heaven as you might say, and hope of every other thing. Just for my love you must be willing to starve, be abused, spat on, live in material insecurity, swim in an endless sea of offence, abuse, scorn, be despised, maybe rejected, cast out, and have hope of only one security, one compensation, one reward, and that is me . . . I may run but I cannot hide, I'm in for it. The only thing that is going to let me out of it is death . . . The only lines that Hemingway ever wrote that sounded true to me were, 'If you are strong and brave this world will break you. If you are very strong the break will heal and perhaps be stronger than before but it will break you anyway. But, if you are neither strong nor brave it will kill you. It will*

kill you anyway but it will kill you sooner.' You may have me, all of me, the good and the bad if you want me. Just don't expect not to be crucified . . .

I love you darling, and want to make you happy. What is it, exactly, that you want from me, darling? I think about this and I think about it and I think about it. But what else can I do besides being Chester Himes, the writer, who loves you?

I was very moved by this letter due to its honesty. I fell in love with a handsome American; in my ignorance I did not even stop to think about or even consider that he was black and I white. Things were not always as simple as I thought they might be. However, I had a great deal of fun and I'd do it all over again – I'd take all that – moments of suffering and moments of joy – I wouldn't change one single thing. We were simply two human beings who wanted to be together, enjoyed being together and could never bear to be apart.

Chester was a complex and sensitive man, both patient and impatient. He wanted to be seen as tough but actually he wasn't tough at all. He would get angry very fast and he would then laugh about everything even faster. He would cry if you told him a sad story or hand over the money in his pockets if you gave him a sob story. His change of emotion was absolutely incredible. It was at times quite frightening because you saw this swift change, it was like a big cloud coming over his face and one side was slightly different from the other.

It's very difficult to say why he would overreact so suddenly. This was caused not by jealousy as such but probably more through a sense of insecurity. I know this had created many problems with his first wife, Jean, and with the other women he knew. I understood this and was very much on the alert. But he was also able to swing into a joyous mood and be very kind, wonderful and generous with me and our friends.

As I said, humour was his last weapon. So we laughed a great deal together. It helped those mood swings. I should say that both *Plan B* and *Blind Man with a Pistol* made Chester laugh a great deal. I was typing *Blind Man* in one room and Chester was typing *Plan B* in another and when we'd meet every so often in the lounge to have a really good laugh, we couldn't stop laughing. I didn't understand at the time how he could find *Plan B* so funny but he cracked up when he was writing it. Maybe I never really could *not* find these funny because of Chester's incredible outbursts of mirth. But reading both books again, I cannot laugh, now, alone. I consider them to be very serious indeed and of enormous relevance to the world of today. I have been re-reading both books and now I do not know why I laughed – with Chester around it was all so much easier.

I remember very well the morning Chester was buried. A friend and I realised that journalists would try to open up the coffin to take photographs, therefore we knew we had to hide it. Fortunately the man from the funeral home was a great admirer of Chester's and, realising the prospective problems posed by prying journalists, he asked if I wanted the coffin to be opened. I replied that under no circumstances whatsoever as I had seen pictures of Salvador Dali in his coffin and he looked so horrible. I did not want them to take pictures of Chester the way he looked. The undertaker decided to hide Chester's coffin in an old, unused cemetery in Benissa while the journalists went to the funeral parlor. The man then sent them up to the new cemetery saying the coffin must be there. During their absence, he took the opportunity to return it from the old cemetery to the parlor.

By the time the journalists returned they soon realised that they were not going to find the coffin, nevermind have it opened. All I could think of, however, was that Chester would have loved this story of the hidden coffin as he was quite obsessed by them, either flying around the place or falling out the back of hearses. I thought, 'Well, you must be chuckling, Chester, because you're the one going through it now.' He probably would have been very amused.

Chester had wanted to be buried in a very elegant dark grey pin-stripe suit, believing it was a fitting way to go. But he was so very thin and I was afraid that if we'd tried to struggle him into this suit, we would have just broken his brittle bones. We draped a sheet over him and I threw all the chrysanthemums from our garden in on top. I still have the suit because somehow it will never fit anyone else. It was made to measure.

I have never regretted anything in my life with Chester except that I didn't get the chance to spend even longer with him.

Lesley Himes,
Alicante, December 1996

Cotton Comes to Harlem

1

The voice from the sound truck said:

'Each family, no matter how big it is, will be asked to put up one thousand dollars. You will get your transportation free, five acres of fertile land in Africa, a mule and a plow and all the seed you need, free. Cows, pigs and chickens cost extra, but at the minimum. No profit on this deal.'

A sea of dark faces wavered before the speaker's long table, rapturous and intent.

'Ain't it wonderful, honey?' said a big black woman with eyes like stars. 'We're going back to Africa.'

Her tall lean husband shook his head in awe. 'After all these four hundred years.'

'Here I is been cooking in white folk's kitchens for more than thirty years. Lord, can it be true?' A stooped old woman voiced a lingering doubt.

The smooth brown speaker with the honest eyes and earnest face heard her. 'It's true all right,' he said. 'Just step right up and give us the particulars and deposit your thousand dollars and you'll have a place on the first boat going over.'

A grumpy old man with a head of white hair shuffled forward to fill out a form and deposit his thousand dollars, muttering to himself, 'It sure took long enough.'

The two pretty black girls taking applications looked up with dazzling smiles.

'Look how long it took the Jews to get out of Egypt,' one said.

'The hand of God is slow but sure,' said the other.

It was a big night in the lives of all these assembled colored people. Now at last, after months of flaming denouncements of the injustice and hypocrisy of white people, hurled from the pulpit of his church; after months of eulogy heaped upon the holy land of Africa, young Reverend Deke O'Malley was at last putting words into action. Tonight he was signing up the people to go on his three ships back to Africa. Huge hand-drawings of the ships stood in prominent view behind the speaker's table, appearing to have the size and design of the *SS Queen Elizabeth*. Before them stood Reverend O'Malley, his tall lithe body clad in dark summer worsted, his fresh handsome face exuding benign authority and inspiring total confidence, flanked by his secretaries and the two young men most active in recruiting applicants.

A vacant lot in the 'Valley' of Harlem near the railroad tracks, where slum tenements had been razed for a new housing development, had been taken over for the occasion. More than a thousand people milled about the patches of old, uneven concrete amid the baked, cindery earth littered with stones, piles of rubbish, dog droppings, broken glass, scattered rags and clusters of stinkweed.

The hot summer night was lit by flashes of sheet lightning, threatening rain, and the air was oppressive with dust, density and motor fumes. Stink drifted from the surrounding slums, now more overcrowded than ever due to the relocation of families from the site of the new buildings to be erected to relieve the overcrowding. But nothing troubled the jubilance of these dark people filled with faith and hope.

The meeting was well organized. The speaker's table stood at one end, draped with a banner reading: BACK TO AFRICA – LAST CHANCE!!! Behind it, beside the drawings of the ships, stood an armored truck, its back doors open, flanked by two black guards wearing khaki uniforms and side arms. To the other side stood the sound truck with amplifiers atop. Tee-shirted young men in tight-fitting jeans roamed about with solemn, unsmiling expressions, swelled with a sense of importance ready to eject any doubters.

But for many of these true-believers it was also a picnic. Bottles of wine, beer and whisky were passed about. Here and there a soul-brother cut a dance step. White teeth flashed in black, laughing faces. Eyes spoke. Bodies promised. They were all charged with anticipation.

A pit had been dug in the center of the lot, housing a

charcoal fire covered with an iron grill. Rows of pork ribs were slowly cooking on the grill, dripping fat into the hot coals with a sizzling of pungent smoke, turned from time to time by four 'hook-men' with long iron hooks. A white-uniformed chef with a long-handled ladle basted the ribs with hot sauce as they cooked, supervising the turning, his tall white chef's cap bobbing over his sweating black face. Two matronly women clad in white nurses' uniforms sat at a kitchen table, placing the cooked ribs into paper plates, adding bread and potato salad, and selling them for one dollar a serving.

The tempting, tantalizing smell of barbecued ribs rose in the air above the stink. Shirt-sleeved men, thinly clad women and half-naked children jostled each other good-naturedly, eating the spicy meat and dropping the bones underfoot.

Above the din of transistor radios broadcasting the night's baseball games, and the bursts of laughter, the sudden shrieks, the other loud voices, came the blaring voice of Reverend Deke O'Malley from the sound truck: 'Africa is our native land and we are going back. No more picking cotton for the white folks and living on fatback and corn pone . . .'

'Yea, baby, yea.'

'See that sign,' Reverend O'Malley shouted, pointing to a large wooden sign against the wire fence which proclaimed that the low-rent housing development to be erected on that site would be completed within two and one half years, and listed the prices of the apartments, which no family among those assembled there could afford to pay. 'Two years you have to wait to move into some boxes – if you can get in, and if you can pay the high rent after you get in. By that time you will be harvesting your second crop in Africa, living in warm sunny houses where the only fire you'll ever need will be for cooking, where we'll have our own governments and our own rulers – *black*, like us—'

'I hear you, baby, I hear you.'

The thousand-dollar subscriptions poured in. The starry-eyed black people were putting their chips on hope. One after another they went forward solemnly and put down their thousand dollars and signed on the dotted line. The armed guards took the money and stacked it carefully into an open safe in the armored truck.

'How many?' Reverend O'Malley asked one of his secretaries in a whisper.

'Eighty-seven,' she whispered in reply.

'Tonight might be your last chance,' Reverend O'Malley said over the amplifiers. 'Next week I must go elsewhere and give all of our brothers a chance to return to our native land. God said the meek shall inherit the earth; we have been meek long enough; now we shall come into our inheritance.'

'Amen, Reverend! Amen!'

Sad-eyed Puerto Ricans from nearby Spanish Harlem and the lost and hungry black people from black Harlem who didn't have the thousand dollars to return to their native land congregated outside the high wire fence, smelling the tantalizing barbecue, dreaming of the day when they could also go back home in triumph and contentment.

'Who's that man?' one of them asked.

'Child, he's the young Communist Christian preacher who's going to take our folks back to Africa.'

A police cruiser was parked at the curb. Two white cops in the front seat cast sour looks over the assemblage.

'Where you think they got a permit for this meeting?'

'Search me. Lieutenant Anderson said leave them alone.'

'This country is being run by niggers.'

They lit cigarettes and smoked in sullen silence.

Inside the fence, three colored cops patrolled the assemblage, swapping jokes with their soul-brothers, exchanging grins, relaxed and friendly.

During a lull in the speaker's voice, two big colored men in dark rumpled suits approached the speaker's table. Bulges from pistols in shoulder slings showed beneath their coats. The guards of the armored truck became alert. The two young recruiting agents, flanking the table, pushed back their chairs.

But the two big men were polite and smiled easily.

'We're detectives from the D.A.'s office,' one said to O'Malley apologetically, as both presented their identifications. 'We have orders to bring you in for questioning.'

The two young recruiting agents came to their feet, tense and angry.

'These white mothers can't let us alone,' one said. 'Now they're using our brothers against us.'

Reverend O'Malley waved them down and spoke to the detectives, 'Have you got a warrant?'

'No, but it would save you a lot of trouble if you came peacefully.'

The second detective added, 'You can take your time and finish with your people, but I'd advise you to talk to the D.A.'

'All right,' Reverend O'Malley said calmly. 'Later.'

The detectives moved to one side. Everyone relaxed. One of the recruiting agents ordered a serving of barbecue.

For a moment attention was centered on a meat delivery truck which had entered the lot. It had been passed by the zealous volunteers guarding the gate.

'You're just in time, boy,' the black chef called to the white driver as the truck approached. 'We're running out of ribs.'

A flash of lightning spotlighted the grinning faces of the two white men on the front seat.

'Wait 'til we turn around, boss,' the driver's helper called in a southern voice.

The truck went forward towards the speaker's table. Eyes watched it indifferently. The truck turned, backed, gently plowing a path through the milling mob.

Ignoring the slight commotion, Reverend O'Malley continued speaking from the amplifiers: 'These damn southern white folks have worked us like dogs for four hundred years and when we ask them to pay off, they ship us up to the North . . .'

'Ain't it the truth!' a sister shouted.

'And these damn northern white folks don't want us—' But he never finished. He broke off in mid-sentence at the sight of two masked white men stepping from the back of the meat delivery truck with two black deadly-looking submachine guns in their hands. 'Unh!!!' he grunted as though someone had hit him in the stomach.

For the brief instant following, silence reigned. The scene

became a tableau of suspended motion. Eyes were riveted on the black holes of death at the front ends of the machine guns. Muscles became paralysed. Brains stopped thinking.

Then a voice that sounded as though it had come from the backwoods of Mississippi said thickly: 'Everybody freeze an' nobody'll git hurt.'

The black men guarding the armored truck raised their hands in reflex action. Black faces broke out with a rash of white eyes. Reverend Deke O'Malley slid quickly beneath the table. The two big colored detectives froze as ordered.

But the young recruiting agent at the left end of the table, who was taking a bite of barbecue, saw his dream vanishing and reached towards his hip pocket for his pistol.

There was a burst from a machine gun. A mixture of teeth, barbecued pork ribs, and human brains flew through the air like macabre birds. A woman screamed. The young man, with half a head gone, sank down out of sight.

The Mississippi voice said furiously: 'Goddamn stupid mother-raper!'

The softer southern voice of the gunner said defensively, 'He was drawing.'

'Mother-rape it! Git the money, let's git going.' The big heavy white man with his black mask slowly moved the black-holed muzzle of his submachine gun over the crowd like the nozzle of a fire hose, saying, 'Doan git daid.'

Bodies remained rigid, eyes riveted, necks frozen, heads stationary, but there was a general movement away from the gun as though the earth itself were moving. Behind, among the people at the rear, panic began exploding like Chinese firecrackers.

The driver's helper got out from the front seat, waving another submachine gun, and the black people melted away.

The two sullen cops in the police cruiser jumped out and rushed to the fence, trying to see what was happening. But all they could see was a strange milling movement of black people.

The three colored cops inside, pistols drawn, were struggling forward against a tide of human flesh, but being slowly washed away.

The second machine-gunner, who had fired the burst, slung his gun over his shoulder, rushed towards the armored truck and began scooping money into a 'gunny-sack'.

'Merciful Jesus,' a woman wailed.

The black guards backed away, arms elevated, and let the white men take the money. Deke remained unseen beneath the table. All that was seen of the dead young man were some teeth still bleeding on the table, before the horrified eyes of the two young secretaries. The colored detectives hadn't breathed.

Outside the fence the cops rushed back to their cruiser. The motor caught, roared; the siren coughed, groaned, began screaming as the car went into a U-turn in the middle of the block heading back towards the gate.

The colored cops on the inside began shooting into the air, trying to clear a path, but only increased the pandemonium. A black tidal wave went over them as from a hurricane.

The white machine-gunner got all of the money – all $87,000 – and jumped into the back of the delivery truck. The motor roared. The other machine-gunner followed the first and slammed shut the back door. The driver's helper climbed in just as the car took off.

The police cruiser came in through the gate, siren screaming, as though black people were invisible. A fat black man flew through the air like an over-inflated football. A fender bumped a woman's bottom and started her spinning like a whirling dervish. People scattered, split, diving, jumping, running to get out of the cruiser's path, colliding and knocking one another down.

But a path was made for the rapidly accelerating meat delivery truck. The cops looked at the driver and his helper as they passed. The two white men looked back, exchanging white looks. The cops went ahead, looking for colored criminals. The white machine-gunners got away.

The two black guards climbed into the front seat of the armored truck. The two colored detectives jumped on the running-boards, pistols in their hands. Deke came out from underneath the table and climbed into the back, beside the empty safe. The motor came instantly to life, sounding for all the world like a big Cadillac engine with four hundred horsepower. The armored truck backed, filled, pointed towards the gate, then hesitated.

'You want I should follow them?' the driver asked.

'Get 'em, goddammit. Run 'em down!' one of the colored detectives grated.

The driver hesitated a moment longer. 'They're armed for bear.'

'Bear ass!' the detective shouted. 'They're getting away, mother!'

There was a glimpse of gray paint as the meat delivery truck went past a taxi on Lexington Avenue, headed north.

The big engine of the armored truck roared; the truck jumped. The police cruiser wheeled to head it off. A woman wild with fright ran in front of it. The car slewed to miss her and ran head-on into the barbecue pit. Steam rose from the bursted radiator pouring on to the hot coals. A sudden flash of lightning lit the wild stampede of running people, seen through the cloud of steam.

'Great Godamighty, the earth's busted open,' a voice cried.

'An' let out all hell,' came the reply.

'Halt or I'll shoot,' a cop cried, climbing from the smoking ruins.

It was the same as talking to the lightning.

The armored truck bulldozed a path to the gate, urged on by a voice shouting, 'Go get 'em, go get 'em.'

It turned into Lexington on screaming tyres. The off-side detective fell off to the street, but they didn't stop for him. A roll of thunder blended with the motor sound as the big engine gathered speed, and another police cruiser fell in behind.

O'Malley tapped on the window separating the front seat from the rear compartment and passed an automatic rifle and a sawed-off shotgun to the guard. The remaining detective on the inside running-board was squatting low, holding on with his left hand and gripping a Colt .45 automatic in his right.

The armored truck was going faster than any armored truck ever seen before or since. The red light showed at 125th Street and a big diesel truck was coming from the west. The armored truck went through the red and passed in front of that big truck as close as a barber's shave.

A joker standing on the corner shouted jubilantly, 'Gawawwwed damn! Them mothers got it.'

The police cruiser stopped for the truck to pass.

'And gone!' the joker added.

The driver urged greater speed from the big laboring motor, 'Get your ass to moving.' But the meat delivery truck had got out of sight. The scream of the police siren was fading in the past.

The meat delivery truck turned left on 137th Street. In turning the back door was flung open and a bale of cotton slid slowly from the clutching hands of the two white machine-gunners and fell into the street. The truck dragged to a screaming sidewise stop and began backing up. But at that moment the armored truck came roaring around the corner like destiny coming on. The meat delivery truck reversed directions without a break in motion and took off again as though it had wings.

From inside the delivery truck came a red burst of machine-gun fire and the bullet-proof windshield of the armored truck was suddenly filled with stars, partly obscuring the driver's vision. He narrowly missed the bale of cotton, thinking he must have d.t.'s.

The guard was trying to get the muzzle of his rifle through a gun slot in the windshield when another burst of machine-gun fire came from the delivery truck and its back doors were slammed shut. No one noticed the detective on the running-board of the armored truck suddenly disappear. One moment he was there, the next he was gone.

The colored people on the tenement stoops, seeking relief from the hot night, began running over one another to get indoors. Some dove into the basement entrances beneath the stairs.

One loudmouthed comic shouted from the safety below the level of the sidewalk, 'Harlem Hospital straight ahead.'

From across the street another loudmouth shouted back, 'Morgue comes first.'

The meat delivery truck was gaining on the armored truck. It must have been powered to keep meat fresh from Texas.

From far behind came the faint sound of the scream of the siren from the police cruiser, seeming to cry, 'Wait for me!'

Lightning flashed. Before the sound of thunder was heard, rain came down in torrents.

2

'Well, kiss my foot if it isn't Jones,' Lieutenant Anderson exclaimed, rising from behind the captain's desk to extend his hand to his ace detectives. Slang sounded as phony as a copper's smile coming from his lips, but the warm smile lighting his thin pale face and the twinkle in his deep-set blue eyes squared it. 'Welcome home.'

Grave Digger Jones squeezed the small white hand in his own big, calloused paw and grinned. 'You need to get out in the sun, Lieutenant, 'fore someone takes you for a ghost,' he said as though continuing a conversation from the night before instead of a six months' interim.

The lieutenant eased back into his seat and stared at Grave Digger appraisingly. The upward glow from the green-shaded desk lamp gave his face a gangrenous hue.

'Same old Jones,' he said. 'We've been missing you, man.'

'Can't keep a good man down,' Coffin Ed Johnson said from behind.

It was Grave Digger's first night back on duty since he had been shot up by one of Benny Mason's hired guns in the caper resulting from the loss of a shipment of heroin. He had been in the hospital for three months fighting a running battle with death, and he had spent three months at home convalescing. Other than for the bullet scars hidden beneath his clothes and the finger-size scar obliterating the hairline at the base of his skull where the first bullet had burned off the hair, he looked much the same. Same dark brown lumpy face with the slowly smoldering reddish-brown eyes; same big, rugged, loosely knit frame of a day laborer in a steel mill; same dark, battered felt hat worn summer and winter perched on the back of his head; same rusty black alpaca suit showing the bulge of the long-barreled, nickel-plated, brass-lined .38 revolver on a .44 frame made to his own specifications resting in its left-side shoulder sling. As far back as Lieutenant Anderson could remember, both of them, his two ace detectives with their identical big hard-shooting, head-whipping pistols, had always looked like two hog farmers on a weekend in the Big Town.

'I just hope it hasn't left you on the quick side,' Lieutenant Anderson said softly.

Coffin Ed's acid-scarred face twitched slightly, the patches of grafted skin changing shape. 'I dig you, Lieutenant,' he said gruffly. 'You mean on the quick side like me.' His jaw knotted as he paused to swallow. 'Better to be quick than dead.'

The lieutenant turned to stare at him, but Grave Digger looked straight ahead. Four years previous a hoodlum had thrown a glass of acid into Coffin Ed's face. Afterwards he had earned the reputation of being quick on the trigger.

'You don't have to apologize,' Grave Digger said roughly. 'You're not getting paid to get killed.'

In the green light Lieutenant Anderson's face turned slightly purple. 'Well, hell,' he said defensively. 'I'm on your side. I know what you're up against here in Harlem. I know your beat. It's my beat too. But the commissioner feels you've killed too many people in this area—' He held up his hand to ward off an interruption. 'Hoodlums, I know – dangerous hoodlums – and you killed in self-defense. But you've been on the carpet a number of times and a short time ago you had three months' suspensions. Newspapers have been yapping about police brutality in Harlem and now various civic bodies have taken up the cry.'

'It's the white men on the force who commit the pointless brutality,' Coffin Ed grated. 'Digger and me ain't trying to play tough.'

'We are tough,' Grave Digger said.

Lieutenant Anderson shifted the papers on the desk and

looked down at his hands. 'Yes, I know, but they're going to drop it on you two – if they can. You know that as well as I do. All I'm asking is to play it safe, from the police side. Don't take any chances, don't make any arrests until you have the evidence, don't use force unless in self-defense, and above all don't shoot anyone unless it's the last resort.'

'And let the criminals go,' Coffin Ed said.

'The commissioner feels there must be some other way to curtail crime besides brute force,' the lieutenant said, his blush deepening.

'Well, tell him to come up here and show us,' Coffin Ed said.

The arteries stood out in Grave Digger's swollen neck and his voice came out cotton dry. 'We got the highest crime rate on earth among the colored people in Harlem. And there ain't but three things to do about it: Make the criminals pay for it – you don't want to do that; pay the people enough to live decently – you ain't going to do that; so all that's left is let 'em eat one another up.'

A sudden blast of noise poured in from the booking room – shouts, curses, voices lifted in anger, women screaming, whines of protest, the scuffling of many feet – as a wagon emptied its haul from a raid on a whorehouse where drugs were peddled.

The intercom on the desk spoke suddenly: 'Lieutenant, you're wanted out here on the desk; they've knocked over Big Liz's circus house.'

The lieutenant flicked the switch. 'In a few minutes, and for Christ's sake keep them quiet.'

He then looked from one detective to the other. 'What the hell's going on today? It's only ten o'clock in the evening and judging from the reports it's been going on like this since morning.' He leafed through the reports, reading charges: 'Man kills his wife with an ax for burning his breakfast pork chop . . . man shoots another man demonstrating a recent shooting he had witnessed . . . man stabs another man for spilling beer on his new suit . . . man kills self in a bar playing Russian roulette with a .32 revolver . . . woman stabs man in stomach fourteen times, no reason given . . . woman scalds neighboring woman with pot of boiling water for speaking to her husband . . . man arrested for threatening to blow up subway train because he entered wrong station and couldn't get his token back—'

'All colored citizens,' Coffin Ed interrupted.

Anderson ignored it. 'Man sees stranger wearing his own new suit, slashes him with a razor,' he read on. 'Man dressed as Cherokee Indian splits white bartender's skull with homemade tomahawk . . . man arrested on Seventh Avenue for hunting cats with hound dog and shotgun . . . twenty-five men arrested for trying to chase all the white people out of Harlem—'

'It's Independence Day,' Grave Digger interrupted.

'*Independence Day!*' Lieutenant Anderson echoed, taking a long, deep breath. He pushed away the reports and pulled a memo from the corner clip of the blotter. 'Well, here's your assignment – from the captain.'

Grave Digger perched a ham on the edge of the desk and cocked his head; but Coffin Ed backed against the wall into the shadow to hide his face, as was his habit when he expected the unexpected.

'You're to cover Deke O'Hara,' Anderson read.

The two colored detectives stared at him, alert but unquestioning, waiting for him to go on and give the handle to the joke.

'He was released ten months ago from the federal prison in Atlanta.'

'As who in Harlem doesn't know,' Grave Digger said drily.

'Many people don't know that ex-con Deke O'Hara is Reverend Deke O'Malley, leader of the new Back-to-Africa movement.'

'All right, omit the squares.'

'He's on the spot; the syndicate has voted to kill him,' Anderson said as if imparting information.

'Bullshit,' Grave Digger said bluntly. 'If the syndicate had wanted to kill him, he'd be decomposed by now.'

'Maybe.'

'What *maybe?* You could find a dozen punks in Harlem who'd kill him for a C-note.'

'O'Malley's not that easy to kill.'

'Anybody's easy to kill,' Coffin Ed stated. 'That's why we police wear pistols.'

'I don't dig this,' Grave Digger said, slapping his right thigh absentmindedly. 'Here's a rat who stooled on his former policy racketeer bosses, got thirteen indicted by the federal grand jury – even one of us, Lieutenant Brandon over in Brooklyn—'

'There's always one black bean,' Lieutenant Anderson said unwittingly.

Grave Digger stared at him. 'Damn right,' he said flatly.

Anderson blushed. 'I didn't mean it the way you're thinking.'

'I know how you meant it, but you don't know how I'm thinking.'

'Well, how are you thinking?'

'I'm thinking do you know why he did it?'

'For the reward,' Anderson said.

'Yeah, that's why. This world is full of people who will do anything for enough money. He thought he was going to get a half million bucks as the ten per cent reward for exposing tax cheats. He told how they'd swindled the government out of over five million in taxes. Seven out of thirteen went to prison; even the rat himself. He was doing so much squealing he confessed he hadn't paid any taxes either. So he got sent down too. He did thirty-one months and now he's out. I don't know how much Judas money he got.'

'About fifty grand,' Lieutenant Anderson said. 'He's put it all in his setup.'

'Digger and me could use fifty G's, but we're cops. If we squeal it all goes on the old pay cheque,' Coffin Ed said from the shadows.

'Let's not worry about that,' Lieutenant Anderson said impatiently. 'The point is to keep him alive.'

'Yeah, the syndicate's out to kill him, poor little rat,' Grave Digger said. 'I heard all about it. They were saying, "O'Malley may run but he can't hide." O'Malley didn't run and all the hiding he's been doing is behind the Bible. But he isn't dead. So what I would like to know is how all of a sudden he got important enough for a police cover when the syndicate had ten months to make the hit if they had wanted to.'

'Well, for one thing, the people here in Harlem, responsible people, the pastors and race leaders and politicians and such, believe he's doing a lot of good for the community. He paid off the mortgage on an old church and started this new Back-to-Africa movement—'

'The original Back-to-Africa movement denies him,' Coffin Ed interrupted.

'—and people have been pestering the commissioner to give him police protection because of his following. They've convinced the commissioner that there'll be a race riot if any white gunmen from downtown come up here and kill him.'

'Do you believe that, Lieutenant? Do you believe they've convinced the commissioner of that crap? That the syndicate's out to kill him after ten months?'

'Maybe it took these citizens that long to find out how useful he is to the community,' Anderson said.

'That's one thing,' Grave Digger conceded. 'What are some other things?'

'The commissioner didn't say. He doesn't always take me and the captain into his confidence,' the lieutenant said with slight sarcasm.

'Only when he's having nightmares about Digger and me shooting down all these innocent people,' Coffin Ed said.

'"*Ours not to reason why, ours but to do or die,*"' Anderson quoted.

'Those days are gone forever,' Grave Digger said. 'Wait until the next war and tell somebody that.'

'Well, let's get down to business,' Lieutenant Anderson said. 'O'Malley is co-operating with us.'

'Why shouldn't he? It's not costing him anything and it might save his life. O'Malley's a rat, but he's not a fool.'

'I'm going to feel downright ashamed nursemaiding that ex-con,' Coffin Ed said.

'Orders are orders,' Anderson said. 'And maybe it's not going to be like you think.'

'I just don't want anybody to tell me that crime doesn't pay,' Grave Digger said and stood up.

'You know the story about the prodigal son,' Anderson said.

'Yeah, I know it. But do you know the story about the fatted calf?'

'What about the fatted calf?'

'When the prodigal son returned, they couldn't find the fatted calf. They looked high and low and finally had to give up. So they went to the prodigal son to apologize, but when they saw how fat he'd gotten to be, they killed him and ate him in the place of the fatted calf.'

'Yes, but just don't let that happen to our prodigal son,' Anderson warned them unsmilingly.

At that instant the telephone rang. Lieutenant Anderson picked up the receiver.

A big happy voice said, '*Captain?*'

'*Lieutenant.*'

'Well, who ever you is, I just want to tell you that the earth has busted open and all hell's got loose over here,' and he gave the address where the Back-to-Africa rally had taken place.

3

'And then Jesus say, "John, the only thing worse than a two-timing woman is a two-timing man."'

'Jesus say that? Ain't it the truth?'

They were standing in the dim light directly in front of the huge brick front of the Abyssinian Baptist Church. The man was telling the woman about a dream he'd had the night before. In this dream he'd had a long conversation with Jesus Christ.

He was a nondescript-looking man with black and white striped suspenders draped over a blue sport shirt and buttoned to old-fashioned wide-legged dark brown pants. He looked like the born victim of a cheating wife.

But one could tell she was strictly a church sister by the prissy way she kept pursing up her mouth. One could tell right off that her soul was really saved. She was wearing a big black skirt and a lavender blouse and her lips pursed and her face shone with righteous indignation when he said:

'So I just out and asked Jesus who was the biggest sinner; my wife going with this man, or this man going with my wife, and Jesus say: "How come you ask me that, John? You ain't thinking 'bout doing nothing to them, is you?" I say, "No, Jesus, I ain't gonna bother 'em, but this man, he's married just like my wife, and I ain't going to be responsible for what might break out between him and his wife," and Jesus say, "Don't you worry, John, there's always going to be some left."'

Suddenly they were lit by a flash of lightning, which showed up a second man on his knees directly in back of the fascinated church sister. He held a safety razor blade between his right thumb and forefinger and he was cutting away the back of her skirt with such care and silence she didn't suspect a thing. First, holding the skirt firmly by the hem with his left hand, he split it in a straight line up to the point where it began to tighten over her buttocks. Then he split her slip in the same manner. After which, holding the right halves of both skirt and slip firmly but gently between the thumb and forefinger of his left hand, he cut out a wide half-circle down through the hem and carefully removed the cutout section and threw it carelessly against the wall of the church behind him. The operation revealed one black buttock encased in rose-colored rayon pants and the bare back of one thick black thigh showing above the rolled top of a beige rayon stocking. She hadn't felt a thing.

'"Anyone who commits adultery, makes no difference whether it be man or woman, breaks one of my Father's commandments," Jesus say: "Makes no difference how good it is,"' John said.

'Amen!' the church sister said. Her buttocks began to tremble as she contemplated this enormous sin.

Behind her, the kneeling man had begun to cut away the left side of her skirt, but the trembling of her buttocks forced him to exercise greater caution.

'I say to Jesus, "That's the trouble with Christianity, the good things is always sinful,"' John said.

'Lawd, ain't it the truth,' the church sister said, leaning forward to slap John on the shoulder in a spontaneous gesture of rising joy. The cutout left side section of the skirt and slip came off in the kneeling man's hand.

Now revealed was all the lower part of the big wide rose-encased buttocks and the backs of two thick black thighs above beige stockings. The black thighs bulged in all directions so that just below the crotch, where the torso began, there was a sort of pocket in which one could visualize the buttocks of some man gripped as in a vice. But now, in that pocket, hung a waterproof purse suspended from elastic bands passing up through the pants and encircling the waist.

With breathless delicacy but a sure touch and steady hand, as though performing a major operation on the brain, the kneeling man reached into the pocket and began cutting the elastic band which held the purse.

John leaned forward and touched her on the shoulder like a spontaneous caress. His voice thickened with suggestion. 'But Jesus say, "Commit all the 'dultry you want to, John. Just be prepared to roast in hell for it."'

'He-he-he,' laughed the church sister and slapped him again on the shoulder. 'He was just kidding you. He'd forgive us for just *one* time,' and she suddenly switched her trembling buttocks, no doubt to demonstrate Jesus's mercy.

In so doing she felt the hand easing the purse from between her legs. She slapped back automatically before she could begin to turn her body, and struck the kneeling man across the face.

'Mother-raper, you is trying to steal my money,' she screamed, turning on the thief.

Lightning flashed, revealing the thief leaping to one side and the big broad buttocks in rose-colored pants twitching in fury. And before the sound of thunder was heard, the rain came down.

The thief leapt blindly into the street. Before the church sister could follow, a meat delivery truck coming at blinding speed hit the thief head-on and knocked the body somersaulting ten yards down the street before running over it. The driver lost control as the truck went over the body. The truck jumped the curb and knocked down a telephone pole at the corner of Seventh Avenue; it slewed across the wet asphalt and crashed against the concrete barrier enclosing the park down the middle of the avenue.

The church sister ran toward the mangled body and snatched her purse still clutched in the dead man's hand, unmindful of the bright lights of the armored truck rushing towards her like twin comets out of the night, unmindful of the rain pouring down in torrents.

The driver of the armored car saw the rose-encased buttocks of a large black woman as she bent over to snatch something from what looked like a dead man lying in the middle of the street. He was convinced he had d.t.'s. But he tried desperately to avoid them at the speed he was going on that wet street, d.t.'s or not. The armored truck skidded, then began wobbling as though doing the shimmy. The brakes meant nothing on the wet asphalt of Seventh Avenue and the car skidded straight on across the avenue and was hit broadside by a big truck going south.

The church sister hurried down the street in the opposite direction, holding the purse clutched tightly in her hand. Near Lexington Avenue, men, women and children crowded about the body of another dead colored man lying in the street, being washed for the grave by the rain. It lay in a grotesque position on its stomach at right angle to the curb, one arm outflung, the other beneath it. The side of the face turned up had been shot away. If there had been a pistol anywhere, now it was gone.

A police cruiser was parked nearby, crosswise to the street. One of the policemen was standing beside the body in the rain. The other one sat in the cruiser, phoning the precinct station.

The church sister was hurrying past on the opposite side of the street, trying to remain unnoticed. But a big colored laborer, wearing the overalls in which he had worked all day, saw her. His eyes popped and his mouth opened in his slack face.

'Lady,' he called tentatively. She didn't look around. 'Lady,' he called again. 'I just wanted to say, your ass is out.'

She turned on him furiously. 'Tend to your own mother-raping business.'

He backed away, touching his cap politely, 'I didn't mean no harm, lady. It's *your* ass.'

She hurried on down the street, worrying more about her hair in the rain than about her behind showing.

At the corner of Lexington Avenue, an old junk man of the kind who haunt the streets at night collecting old paper and discarded junk was struggling with a bale of cotton, trying to get it into his cart. Rain was pouring off his sloppy hat and wetting his ragged overalls to dark blue. His small dried face was framed with thick kinky white hair, giving him a benevolent look. No one else was in sight; everybody who was out on the street in all that rain was looking at the body of the dead man. So when he saw this big strapping lady coming towards him he stopped struggling with the wet bale of cotton and asked politely, 'Ma'am, would you please help me get this bale of cotton into my cart, please, ma'am?'

He hadn't seen her from the rear so he was slightly surprised by her sudden hostility.

'What kind of trick is you playing?' she challenged, giving him an evil look.

'Ain't no trick, ma'am. I just tryna get this bale of cotton into my cart.'

'Cotton!' she shouted indignantly, looking at the bale of cotton with outright suspicion. 'Old and evil as you is you ought to be ashamed of yourself tryna trick me out my money with what you calls a bale of cotton. Does I look like that kinda fool?'

'No, ma'am, but if you was a Christian you wouldn't carry on like that just 'cause an old man asked you to help him lift a bale of cotton.'

'I is a Christian, you wicked bastard,' she shouted. 'That's why all you wicked bastards is tryna steal my money. But I ain't the kind of Christian fool enough not to know there ain't no bales of cotton lying in the street in New York

City. If it weren't for my hair, I'd beat your ass, you old con-man.'

It had been a rough night for the old junk man. First he and a crony had found a half-filled whisky bottle with what they thought was whisky and had sat on a stoop to enjoy themselves, passing the bottle back and forth, when suddenly his crony had said, 'Man, dis ain't whisky; dis is piss.' Then after he'd spent his last money for a bottle of 'smoke' to settle his stomach, it had started to rain. And here was this evil bitch calling him a con-man, as broke as he was.

'You touch me and I'll mark you,' he threatened, reaching in his pocket.

She backed away from him and he turned his back to her, muttering to himself. He didn't see her wet red buttocks above her shining black legs when she hurried down the street and disappeared into a tenement.

Four minutes later, when the first of the police cruisers sent to bottle up the street screamed around the corner from Lexington Avenue, he was still struggling with the bale of cotton in the rain.

The cruiser stopped for the white cops to put the routine question to a colored man: 'Say, uncle, you didn't see any suspicious-looking person pass this way, did you?'

'Nawsuh, just an evil lady mad 'cause her hair got wet.'

The driver grinned, but the cop beside him looked at the bale of cotton curiously and asked, 'What you got there, uncle, a corpse bundled up?'

'Cotton, suh.'

Both cops straightened up and the driver leaned over to look at it too.

'*Cotton?*'

'Yassuh, this is cotton – a bale of cotton.'

'Where the hell did you get a bale of cotton in this city?'

'I found it, suh.'

'Found it? What the hell kind of double-talk is that? Found it where?'

'Right here, suh.'

'Right here?' the cop repeated incredulously. Slowly and

deliberately he got out of the car. His attitude was threatening. He looked closely at the bale of cotton. He bent over and felt the cotton poking through the seams of the burlap wrapping. 'By God, it *is* cotton,' he said straightening up. 'A bale of cotton! What the hell's a bale of cotton doing here in the street?'

'I dunno, boss, I just found it here is all.'

'Probably fell from some truck,' the driver said from within the cruiser. 'Let somebody else take care of it, it ain't our business.'

The cop in the street said, 'Now, uncle, you take this cotton to the precinct station and turn it in. The owner will be looking for it.'

'Yassuh, boss, but I can't get it into my waggin.'

'Here, I'll help you,' the cop said, and together they got it onto the cart.

The junk man set off in the direction of the precinct station, pushing the cart in the rain, and the cop got back into the cruiser and they went on down the street in the direction of the dead man.

4

When Grave Digger and Coffin Ed arrived at the lot where the Back-to-Africa rally had taken place, they found it closed off by a police cordon and the desolate black people, surrounded by policemen, standing helpless in the rain. The police cruiser was still smoking in the barbecue pit and the white cops in their wet black slickers looked mean and dangerous. Coffin Ed's acid-burned face developed a tic and Grave Digger's neck began swelling with rage.

The dead body of the young recruiting agent lay face up in the rain, waiting for the medical examiner to come and pronounce it dead so the men from Homicide could begin their investigation. But the men from Homicide had not arrived, and nothing had been done.

Grave Digger and Coffin Ed stood over the body and looked down at all that was left of the young black face which a few short minutes ago had been so alive with hope. At that moment they felt the same as all the other helpless black people standing in the rain.

'Too bad O'Malley didn't get it instead of this young boy,' Grave Digger said, rain dripping from his black slouch hat over his wrinkled black suit.

'This is what happens when cops get soft on hoodlums,' Coffin Ed said.

'Yeah, we know O'Malley got him killed, but our job is to find out who pulled the trigger.'

They walked over to the herded people and Grave Digger asked, 'Who's in charge here?'

The other young recruiting agent came forward. He was hatless and his solemn black face was shining in the rain. 'I guess I am; the others have gone.'

They walked him over to one side and got the story of what had happened as he saw it. It wasn't much help.

'We were the whole organization,' the young man said. 'Reverend O'Malley, the two secretaries and me and John Hill who was killed. There were volunteers but we were the staff.'

'How about the guards?'

'The two guards with the armored truck? Why, they were sent with the truck from the bank.'

'What bank?'

'The African Bank in Washington, D.C.'

The detectives exchanged glances but didn't comment.

'What's your name, son?' Grave Digger asked.

'Bill Davis.'

'How far did you get in school?'

'I went to college, sir. In Greensboro, North Carolina.'

'And you still believe in the devil?' Coffin Ed asked.

'Let him alone,' Grave Digger said. 'He's telling us all he knows.' Turning to Bill he asked, 'And these two colored detectives from the D.A.'s office. Did you know them?'

'I never saw them before. I was suspicious of them from the

first. But Reverend O'Malley didn't seem perturbed and he made the decisions.'

'Didn't seem perturbed,' Grave Digger echoed. 'Did you suspect it might be a plant?'

'Sir?'

'Did it occur to you they might have been in cahoots with O'Malley to help him get away with the money?'

At first the young man didn't understand. Then he was shocked. 'How could you think that, sir? Reverend O'Malley is absolutely honest. He is very dedicated, sir.'

Coffin Ed sighed.

'Did you ever see the ships which were supposed to take you people back to Africa?' Grave Digger asked.

'No, but all of us have seen the correspondence with the steamship company – The Afro-Asian Line – verifying the year's lease he had negotiated.'

'How much did he pay?'

'It was on a per head basis; he was going to pay one hundred dollars per person. I don't believe they are really as large as they look in these pictures, but we were going to fill them to capacity.'

'How much money had you collected?'

'Eighty-seven thousand dollars from the . . . er . . . subscribers, but we had taken in quite a bit from other things, church socials and this barbecue deal, for instance.'

'And these four white men in the delivery truck got all of it?'

'Well, just the eighty-seven thousand dollars we had taken in tonight. But there were five of them. One stayed inside the truck behind a barricade all the time.'

The detectives became suddenly alert. 'What kind of barricade?' Grave Digger asked.

'I don't know exactly. I couldn't see inside the truck very well. But it looked like some kind of a box covered with burlap.'

'What provision company supplied your meat?' Coffin Ed asked.

'I don't know, sir. That wasn't part of my duties. You'll have to ask the chef.'

They sent for the chef and he came wet and bedraggled, his white cap hanging over one ear like a rag. He was mad at everything – the bandits, the rain, and the police cruiser that had fallen into his barbecue pit. His eyes were bright red and he took it as a personal insult when they asked about the provision company.

'I don't know where the ribs come from after they left the hog,' he said angrily. 'I was just hired to superintend the cooking. I ain't had nothing to do with them white folks and I don't know how many they was – 'cept too many.'

'Leave this soul-brother go,' Coffin Ed said. 'Pretty soon he wouldn't have been here.'

Grave Digger wrote down O'Malley's official address, which he already knew, then as a last question asked, 'What was your connection with the original Back-to-Africa movement, the one headed by Mr Michaux?'

'None at all. Reverend O'Malley didn't have anything at all to do with Mr Michaux's group. In fact he didn't even like Lewis Michaux; I don't think he ever spoke to him.'

'Did it ever occur to you that Mr Michaux might not have had anything to do with Reverend O'Malley? Did you ever think that he might have known something about O'Malley that made him distrust O'Malley?'

'I don't think it was anything like that,' Bill contended. 'What reason could he have to distrust O'Malley? I just think he was envious, that's all. Reverend O'Malley thought he was too slow; he didn't see any reason for waiting any longer; we've waited long enough.'

'And you were intending to go back to Africa too?'

'Yes, sir, still intend to – as soon as we get the money back. You'll get the money back for us, won't you?'

'Son, if we don't, we're gonna raise so much hell they're gonna send us all back to Africa.'

'And for free, too,' Coffin Ed added grimly.

The young man thanked them and went back to stand with the others in the rain.

'Well, Ed, what do you think about it?' Grave Digger asked.

'One thing is for sure, it wasn't the syndicate pulled this caper – not the crime syndicate, anyway.'

'What other kinds of syndicates are there?'

'Don't ask me, I ain't the FBI.'

They were silent for a moment with the rain pouring over them, thinking of these eighty-seven families who had put down their thousand-dollar grubstakes on a dream. They knew that these families had come by their money the hard way. To many, it represented the savings of a lifetime. To most it represented long hours of hard work at menial jobs. None could afford to lose it.

They didn't consider these victims as squares or suckers. They understood them. These people were seeking a home – just the same as the Pilgrim Fathers. Harlem is a city of the homeless. These people had deserted the South because it could never be considered their home. Many had been sent north by the white southerners in revenge for the desegregation ruling. Others had fled, thinking the North was better. But they had not found a home in the North. They had not found a home in America. So they looked across the sea to Africa, where other black people were both the ruled and the rulers. Africa to them was a big free land which they could proudly call home, for there were buried the bones of their ancestors, there lay the roots of their families, and it was inhabited by the descendants of those same ancestors – which made them related by both blood and race. Everyone has to believe in something; and the white people of America had left them nothing to believe in. But that didn't make a black man any less criminal than a white; and they had to find the criminals who hijacked the money, black or white.

'Anyway, the first thing is to find Deke,' Grave Digger put voice to their thoughts. 'If he ain't responsible for this caper he'll sure as hell know who is.'

'He had better know,' Coffin Ed said grimly.

But Deke didn't know any more than they did. He had worked a long time to set up his movement and it had been expensive. At first he had turned to the church to hide from the syndicate. He had figured if he set himself up as a preacher and used his reward money for civil improvement, the syndicate would hesitate about rubbing him out.

But the syndicate hadn't shown any interest in him. That had worried him until he figured out that the syndicate simply didn't want to get involved in the race issue; he had already done all the harm he could do, so they left him to the soul-brothers.

Then he'd gotten the idea for his Back-to-Africa movement from reading a biography of Marcus Garvey, the Negro who had organized the first Back-to-Africa movement. It was said that Garvey had collected over a million dollars. He had been sent to prison, but most of his followers had contended that he was innocent and had still believed in him. Whether he had been innocent or not was not the question; what appealed to him was the fact his followers had still believed in him. That was the con-man's real genius, to keep the suckers always believing.

So he had started his own Back-to-Africa movement, the only difference being when he had got his million, he was going to cut out – he might go back to Africa, himself. He'd heard that people with money could live good in certain places there. The way he had planned it he would use two goons impersonating detectives to impound the money as he collected it; in that way he wouldn't have to bank it and could always keep it on hand.

He didn't know where these white hijackers fitted in. At the first glimpse he thought they were guns from the syndicate. That was why he had hidden beneath the table. But when he discovered they'd just come to grab the money, he had known it was something else again. So he had decided to chase them down and get the money back.

But when they had finally caught up with the meat delivery truck, the white men had disappeared. Perhaps it was just as well; by then he was outgunned anyway. Neither of his guards had been seriously hurt, but he'd lost one of his detectives. The wrecked truck hadn't told him anything and the driver of the truck that had run into them kept getting in the way.

He hadn't had much time so he had ordered them to split

and assemble again every morning at 3 a.m. in the back room of a pool hall on Eighth Avenue and he would contact his other detective himself.

'I've got to see which way this mother-raping cat is jumping,' he said.

He had enough money on him to operate, over five hundred dollars. And he had a five-grand bank account under an alias in an all-night bank in midtown for his getaway money in case of an emergency. But he didn't know yet where to start looking for his eighty-seven grand. Some kind of lead would come. This was Harlem where all black folks were against the whites, and somebody would tell him something. What worried him most was how much information the police had. He knew that in any event they'd be rough on him because of his record; and he knew he'd better keep away from them if he wanted to get his money back.

First, however, he had to get into his house. He needed his pistol; and there were certain documents hidden there – the forged leases from the steamship line and the forged credentials of the Back-to-Africa movement – that would send him back to prison.

He walked down Seventh Avenue to Small's bar, on the pretense of going to call the police, and got into a taxi without attracting any attention. He had the driver take him over to Saint Mark's Church, paid the fare and walked up the stairs. The church door was closed and locked, as he had expected, but he could stand in the shadowed recess and watch the entrance to the Dorrence Brooks apartment house across the street where he lived.

He stood there for a long time casing the building. It was a V-shaped building at the corner of 138th Street and St Nicholas Avenue and he could see the entrance and the streets on both sides. He didn't see any strange cars parked nearby, no police cruisers, no gangster-type limousines. He didn't see any strange people, nothing and no one who looked suspicious. He could see through the glass doors into the front hall and there was not a soul about. The only thing was it was too damn empty.

He circled the church and entered the ark on the west side

of St Nicholas Avenue and approached the building from across the street. He hid in the park beside a tool shed from which he had a full view of the windows of his fourth-floor apartment. Light showed in the windows of the living-room and dining-room. He watched for a long time. But not once did a shadow pass before one of the lighted windows. He got dripping wet in the rain.

His sixth sense told him to telephone, and from some phone booth in the street where the call couldn't be traced. So he walked up to 145th Street and phoned from the box on the corner.

'Hellooo,' she answered. He thought she sounded strange.

'Iris,' he whispered.

Standing beside her, Grave Digger's hand tightened warningly on her arm. He had already briefed her what to say when O'Malley called and the pressure meant he wasn't playing.

'Oh, Betty,' she cried. 'The police are here looking for—'

Grave Digger slapped her with such sudden violence she caromed off the center table and went sprawling on her hands and knees; her dress hiked up showing black lace pants above the creamy yellow skin of her thighs.

Coffin Ed came up and stood over her, the skin of his face jumping like a snake's belly over fire. 'You're so goddamn cute—'

Grave Digger was speaking urgently into the telephone: 'O'Malley, we just want some information, that's—' but the line had gone dead.

His neck swelled as he jiggled the hook to get the precinct station.

At the same moment Iris came up from the floor with the smooth vicious motion of a cat and slapped Coffin Ed across the face, thinking he was Grave Digger in her blinding fury.

She was a hard-bodied high-yellow woman with a perfect figure. She never wore a girdle and her jiggling buttocks gave all men amorous ideas. She had a heart-shaped face with the high cheekbones, big wide red painted mouth, and long-lashed speckled brown eyes of a sexpot and she was thirty-three years old, which gave her the experience. But she was strong as an ox and it was a solid pop she laid on Coffin Ed's cheek.

With pure reflex action he reached out and caught her around the throat with his two huge hands and bent her body backward.

'Easy, man, easy!' Grave Digger shouted, realizing instantly that Coffin Ed was sealed in such a fury he couldn't hear. He dropped the telephone and wheeled, hitting Coffin Ed across the back of the neck with the edge of his hand just a fraction of a second before he'd have crushed her windpipe.

Coffin Ed slumped forward, carrying Iris down with him, beneath him, and his hands slackened from her throat. Grave Digger picked him up by the armpits and propped him on the sofa, then he picked up Iris and dropped her into a chair. Her eyes were huge and limpid with fear and her throat was going black and blue.

Grave Digger stood looking down at them, listening to the phone click frantically, thinking, *Now we're in for it*; then thinking bitterly, *These half-white bitches.* Then he turned back to the telephone and answered the precinct station and asked for the telephone call to be traced. Before he could hang up, Lieutenant Anderson was on the wire.

'Jones, you and Johnson get over to 137th Street and Seventh Avenue. Both trucks are smashed up and everyone gone, but there are two bodies DOA and there might be a lead.' He paused for a moment, then asked, 'How's it going?'

Grave Digger looked from the slumped figure of Coffin Ed into the now blazing eyes of Iris and said, 'Cool, Lieutenant, everything's cool.'

'I'm sending over a man to keep her on ice. He ought to be there any moment.'

'Right.'

'And remember my warning – no force. We don't want anyone hurt if we can help it.'

'Don't worry, Lieutenant, we're like shepherds with newborn lambs.'

The lieutenant hung up.

Coffin Ed had come around and he looked at Grave Digger with a sheepish expression. No one spoke.

Then Iris said in a thick, throat-hurting voice, 'I'm going to get you coppers fired if it's the last thing I do.'

Coffin Ed looked as though he was going to reply, but Grave Digger spoke first: 'You weren't very smart, but neither were we. So we'd better call it quits and start all over.'

'Start over shit,' she flared. 'You break into my house without a search warrant, hold me prisoner, attack me physically, and say let's call it quits. You must think I'm a moron. Even if I'm guilty of a murder, you can't get away with that shit.'

'Eight-seven colored families – like you and me—'

'Not like me!'

'—have lost their life's savings in this caper.'

'So what? You two are going to lose your mother-raping jobs.'

'So if you co-operate and help us get it back you'll get a ten per cent reward – eight thousand, seven hundred dollars.'

'You chickenshit cop, what can I do with that chicken feed? Deke is worth ten times that much to me.'

'Not any more. His number's up and you'd better get on the winning side.'

She gave a short, harsh laugh. 'That ain't your side, big and ugly.'

Then she got up and went and stood directly in front of Coffin Ed where he sat on the sofa. Suddenly her fist flew out and hit him squarely on the nose. His eyes filled with tears as blood spurted from his nostrils. But he didn't move.

'That makes us even,' he said and reached for his handkerchief.

Someone rapped on the door and Grave Digger let in the white detective who had come to take over. Neither of them spoke; they kept the record straight.

'Come on, Ed,' Grave Digger said.

Coffin Ed stood up and the two of them walked to the door, Coffin Ed holding the bloodstained handkerchief to his nose. Just before they went out, Grave Digger turned and said, 'Chances go around, baby.'

5

The rain had stopped when they got outside and people were back on the wet sidewalks, strolling aimlessly and looking about as if to see what might have been washed from heaven. They walked up a couple of blocks where their little black battered sedan with the supercharged motor was parked. It had got much cleaner from the rain.

'You've got to take it easy, Ed man,' Grave Digger said. 'One more second and you'd have killed her.'

Coffin Ed took away the handkerchief and found that his nose had stopped bleeding. He got into the car without replying. He felt guilty for fear he might have gotten Digger into trouble, but for his part he didn't care.

Grave Digger understood. Ever since the hoodlum had thrown acid into his face, Coffin Ed had had no tolerance for crooks. He was too quick to blow up and too dangerous for safety in his sudden rages. But hell, Grave Digger thought, what can one expect? These colored hoodlums had no respect for colored cops unless you beat it into them or blew them away. He just hoped these slick boys wouldn't play it too cute.

The trucks were still where they had been wrecked, guarded by harness cops and surrounded by the usual morbid crowd; but they drove on down to where the bodies lay. They found Sergeant Wiley of Homicide beside the body of the bogus detective, talking to a precinct sergeant and looking bored. He was a quiet, gray-haired, scholarly-looking man dressed in a dark summer suit.

'Everything is wrapped up,' he said to them. 'We're just waiting for the wagon to take them away.' He pointed at the body. 'Know him?'

They looked him over carefully. 'He must be from out of town, eh, Ed?' Grave Digger said.

Coffin Ed nodded.

Sergeant Wiley gave them a rundown: No real identification of any kind, just a phony ID card from the D.A.'s office and a bogus detective shield from headquarters. He had been a big man but now he looked small and forlorn on the wet street and very dead.

They went up and looked at the other body and exchanged looks.

Wiley noticed. 'Run over by the delivery truck,' he said. 'Mean anything?'

'No, he was just a sneak thief. Must have got in the way is all. True monicker was Early Gibson but he was called Early Riser. Worked with a partner most of the time. We'll try to find his partner. He might give us a lead.'

'Sure as hell ain't got no other,' Coffin Ed added.

'Do that,' Wiley said. 'And let me know what you find out.'

'We're going to take a look at the trucks.'

'Right-o, there's nothing more here. We took a statement from the driver of the truck that smashed the armored job and let him go. All he knew was what the three of them looked like and we know what they look like.'

'Any other witness?' Grave Digger asked.

'Hell, you know these people, Jones. All stone blind.'

'What you expect from people who're invisible themselves?' Coffin Ed said roughly.

Wiley let it pass. 'By the way,' he said, 'you'll find those heaps hopped up. The armored truck has an old Cadillac engine and the delivery truck the engine of a Chrysler 300. I've taken the numbers and put out tracers. You don't have to worry about that.'

They left Sergeant Wiley to wait for the wagon and went over to examine the trucks. The tonneau of the armored truck had been built on to the chassis of a 1957 Cadillac, but it didn't tell them anything. The Chrysler engine had been installed in the delivery truck, and it might be traced. They copied the license and engine numbers on the off-chance of finding some garage that had serviced it, but they knew it was unlikely.

The curious crowd that had collected had begun to drift away. The harness cops guarding the wrecks until the police tow trucks carried them off looked extremely bored. The rain hadn't slackened the heat; it had only increased the density. The detectives could feel the sweat trickling down their bodies beneath their wet clothes.

It was getting late and they were impatient to get on to the trail of Deke, but they didn't want to overlook anything so they examined the truck inside and out with their hand torches.

The indistinct lettering: FREYBROS. INC. *Quality Meats, 173 West 116th Street*, showed faintly on the outside panels. They knew there wasn't any such thing as a meat provision firm at that address.

Then suddenly, as he was flashing his light inside, Coffin Ed said, 'Look at this.'

From the tone of his voice Grave Digger knew it was something curious before he looked. 'Cotton,' he said. He and Coffin Ed looked at each other, swapping thoughts.

Caught on a loose screw on the side panel were several strands of cotton. Both of them climbed into the truck and examined it carefully at close range.

'Unprocessed,' Grave Digger said. 'It's been a long time since I've seen any cotton like that.'

'Hush, man, you ain't never seen any cotton like that. You were born and raised in New York.'

Grave Digger chuckled. 'It was when I was in high school. We were studying the agricultural products of America.'

'Now what can a meat provision company use cotton for?'

'Hell, man, the way this car is powered, you'd think meat spoiled on the way to the store – if you want to think like that.'

'Cotton,' Coffin Ed ruminated. 'A mob of white bandits and cotton – in Harlem. Figure that one out.'

'Leave it to the fingerprinters and the other experts,' Grave Digger said, jumping down to the pavement. 'One thing is for sure, I ain't going to spend all night looking for a mother-raping sack of cotton – or a cotton picker either.'

'Let's go get Early Riser's buddy,' Coffin Ed said following him.

* * *

Grave Digger and Coffin Ed were realists. They knew they didn't have second sight. So they had stool pigeons from all walks of life: criminals, straight men and squares. They had their time and places for contacting their pigeons well organized; no pigeon knew another; and only a few of those who were really pigeons were known as pigeons. But without them most crimes would never be solved.

Now they began contacting their pigeons, but only those on the petty-larceny circuit. They knew they wouldn't find Deke through stool pigeons; not that night. But they might find a witness who saw the white men leave.

First they stopped in Big Wilt's Small's Paradise Inn at 135th Street and Seventh Avenue and stood for a moment at the front of the circular bar. They drank two whiskies each and talked to each other about the caper.

The barstools and surrounding tables were filled with the flashily dressed people of many colors and occupations who could afford the price for air-conditioned atmosphere and the professional smiles of the light-bright chicks tending bar. The fat black manager waved the bill on the house and they accepted; they could afford to drink freebies at Small's, it was a straight joint.

Afterwards they sauntered towards the back and stood beside the bandstand, watching the white and black couples dancing the twist in the cabaret. The horns were talking and the saxes talking back.

'Listen to that,' Grave Digger said when the horn took eight on a frenetic solo. 'Talking under their clothes, ain't it?'

Then the two saxes started swapping fours with the rhythm always in the back. 'Somewhere in that jungle is the solution to the world,' Coffin Ed said. 'If we could only find it.'

'Yeah, it's like the sidewalks trying to speak in a language never heard. But they can't spell it either.'

'Naw,' Coffin Ed said. 'Unless there's an alphabet for emotion.'

'The emotion that comes out of experience. If we could read that language, man, we would solve all the crimes in the world.'

'Let's split,' Coffin Ed said. 'Jazz talks too much to me.'

'It ain't so much what it says,' Grave Digger agreed. 'It's what you can't do about it.'

They left the white and black couples in their frenetic embrace, guided by the talking of the jazz, and went back to their car.

'Life could be great but there are hoodlums abroad,' Grave Digger said, climbing beneath the wheel.

'You just ain't saying it, Digger; hoodlums high, and hoodlums low.'

They turned off on 132nd Street beside the new housing development and parked in the darkest spot in the block, cut the motor and doused the lights and waited.

The stool pigeon came in about ten minutes. He was the shiny-haired pimp wearing a white silk shirt and green silk pants who had sat beside them at the bar, with his back turned, talking to a tan-skinned blonde. He opened the door quickly and got into the back seat in the dark.

Coffin Ed turned around to face him. 'You know Early Riser?'

'Yeah. He's a snatcher but I don't know no sting he's made recently.'

'Who does he work with?'

'Work with? I never heard of him working no way but alone.'

'Think hard,' Grave Digger said harshly without turning around.

'I dunno, boss. That's the honest truth. I swear 'fore God.'

'You know about the rumble on '37th Street?' Coffin Ed continued.

'I heard about it but I didn't go see it. I heard the syndicate robbed Deke O'Hara out of a hundred grand he'd just collected from his Back-to-Africa pitch.'

That sounded straight enough so Coffin Ed just said, 'Okay. Do some dreaming about Early Riser,' and let him go.

'Let's try lower Eighth,' Grave Digger said. 'Early was on shit.'

'Yeah, I saw the marks,' Coffin Ed agreed.

Their next stop was a dingy bar on Eighth Avenue near

the corner of 112th Street. This was the neighborhood of the cheap addicts, whiskey-heads, stumblebums, the flotsam of Harlem; the end of the line for the whores, the hard squeeze for the poor honest laborers and a breeding ground for crime. Blank-eyed whores stood on the street corners swapping obscenities with twitching junkies. Muggers and thieves slouched in dark doorways waiting for someone to rob; but there wasn't anyone but each other. Children ran down the street, the dirty street littered with rotting vegetables, uncollected garbage, battered garbage cans, broken glass, dog offal – always running, ducking and dodging. God help them if they got caught. Listless mothers stood in the dark entrances of tenements and swapped talk about their men, their jobs, their poverty, their hunger, their debts, their Gods, their religions, their preachers, their children, their aches and pains, their bad luck with the numbers and the evilness of white people. Workingmen staggered down the sidewalks filled with aimless resentment, muttering curses, hating to go to their hotbox hovels but having nowhere else to go.

'All I wish is that I was God for just one mother-raping second,' Grave Digger said, his voice cotton-dry with rage.

'I know,' Coffin Ed said. 'You'd concrete the face of the mother-raping earth and turn white folks into hogs.'

'But I ain't God,' Grave Digger said, pushing into the bar.

The bar stools were filled with drunken relics, shabby men, ancient whores draped over tired laborers drinking ruckus juice to get their courage up. The tables were filled with the already drunk sleeping on folded arms.

No one recognized the two detectives. They looked prosperous and sober. A wave of vague alertness ran through the joint; everyone thought fresh money was coming in. This sudden greed was indefinably communicated to the sleeping drunks. They stirred in their sleep and awakened, waiting for the moment to get up and cadge another drink.

Grave Digger and Coffin Ed leaned against the bar at the front and waited for one of the two husky bartenders to serve them.

Coffin Ed nodded to a sign over the bar. 'Do you believe that?'

Grave Digger looked up and read: NO JUNKIES SERVED HERE! He said, 'Why not? Poor and raggedy as these junkies are, they ain't got no money for whisky.'

The fat bald-headed bartender with shoulders like a woodchopper came up. 'What's yours, gentlemen?'

Coffin Ed said sourly, 'Hell, man, you expecting any gentlemen in here?'

The bartender didn't have a sense of humor. 'All my customers is gentlemen,' he said.

'Two bourbons on the rocks,' Grave Digger said.

'Doubles,' Coffin Ed added.

The bartender served them with the elaborate courtesy he reserved for all well-paying customers. He rang up the bill and slapped down the change. His eyes flickered at the fifty-cent tip. 'Thank you, gentlemen,' he said, and strolled casually down the bar, winking at a buxom yellow whore at the other end clad in a tight red dress.

Casually she detached herself from the asbestos joker she was trying to kindle and strolled to the head of the bar. Without preamble she squeezed in between Grave Digger and Coffin Ed and draped a big bare yellow arm about the shoulders of each. She smelled like unwashed armpits bathed in dime-store perfume and overpowering bed odor. 'You wanna see a girl?' she asked, sharing her stale whisky breath between them.

'Where's any girl?' Coffin Ed said.

She snatched her arm from about his shoulder and gave her full attention to Grave Digger. Everyone in the joint had seen the obvious play and were waiting eagerly for the result.

'Later,' Grave Digger said. 'I got a word first for Early Riser's gunsel.'

Her eyes flashed. 'Loboy! He ain't no gunsel, he the boss.'

'Gunsel or boss, I got word for him.'

'See me first, honey. I'll pass him the word.'

'No, business first.'

'Don't be like that, honey,' she said, touching his leg. 'There's no time like bedtime.' She fingered his ribs, promising pleasure.

Her fingers touched something hard; they stiffened, paused, and then she plainly felt the big .38 revolver in the shoulder sling. Her hand came off as though it had touched something red hot; her whole body stiffened; her eyes widened and her flaccid face looked twenty years older. 'You from the syndicate?' she asked in a strained whisper.

Grave Digger fished out a leather folder from his right coat pocket, opened it. His shield flashed in the light. 'No, I'm the man.'

Coffin Ed stared at the two bartenders.

Every eye in the room watched tensely. She backed further away; her mouth came open like a scar. 'Git away from me,' she almost screamed. 'I'm a respectable lady.'

All eyes looked down into shot glasses as though reading the answers to all the problems in the world; ears closed up like safe doors, hands froze.

'I'll believe it if you tell me where he's at,' Grave Digger said.

A bartender moved and Coffin Ed's pistol came into his hand. The bartender didn't move again.

'Where who at?' the whore screamed. 'I don't know where nobody at. I'm in here, tending to my own business, ain't bothering nobody, and here you come in here and start messing with me. I ain't no criminal, I'm a church lady—' she was becoming hysterical from her load of junk.

'Let's go,' Coffin Ed said. One of the sleeping drunks staggered out a few minutes later. He found the detectives parked in the black dark in the middle of the slum block on 113th Street. He got quickly into the back and sat in the dark as had the other pigeon.

'I thought you were drunk, Cousin,' Coffin Ed said.

Cousin was an old man with unkempt, dirty, gray-streaked, kinky hair, washed-out brown eyes slowly fading to blue, and skin the color and texture of a dried prune. His wrinkled old thrown-away summer suit smelled of urine, vomit and offal. He was strictly a wino. He looked harmless. But he was one of their ace stool pigeons because no one thought he had the sense for it.

'Nawsah, boss, jes' waitin',' he said in a whining, cowardly-sounding voice.

'Just waiting to get drunk.'

'Thass it, boss, thass jes' what.'

'You know Loboy?' Grave Digger said.

'Yassah, boss, knows him when I sees him.'

'Know who he works with?'

'Early Riser mostly, boss. Leasewise they's together likes as if they's working.'

'Stealing,' Grave Digger said harshly. 'Snatching purses. Robbing women.'

'Yassah, boss, that's what they calls working.'

'What's their pitch? Snatching and running or just mugging?'

'All I knows is what I hears, boss. Folks say they works the *holy dream*.'

'*Holy dream!* What's that?'

'Folks say they worked it out themselves. They gits a church sister what carries her money twixt her legs. Loboy charms her lak a snake do a bird telling her this holy dream whilst Early Riser kneel behind her and cut out the back of her skirt and nip off de money sack. Must work, they's always flush.'

'Live and learn,' Coffin Ed said and Grave Digger asked: 'You seen either one of them tonight?'

'Jes' Loboy. I seen him 'bout an hour ago looking wild and scairt going into Hijenks to get a shot and when he come out he stop in the bar for a glass of sweet wine and then he cut out in a hurry. Looked worried and movin' fast.'

'Where does Loboy live?'

'I dunno, boss, 'round here sommers. Hijenks oughta know.'

'How 'bout that whore who makes like he's hers?'

'She just big-gatin', boss, tryna run up de price. Loboy got a fay chick sommers.'

'All right, where can we find Hijenks?'

'Back there on the corner, boss. Go through the bar an' you come to a door say "Toilet". Keep on an' you see a door say "Closet". Go in an' you see a nail with a cloth hangin' on it. Push the nail twice, then once, then three times an' a invisible door open in the back of the closet. Then you go up some stairs an' you come to 'nother door. Knock three times, then once, then twice.'

'All that? He must be a connection.'

'Got a shooting gallery's all I knows.'

'All right, Cousin, take this five dollars and get drunk and forget what we asked you,' Coffin Ed said, passing him a bill.

'Bless you, boss, bless you.' Cousin shuffled about in the darkness, hiding the bill in his clothes, then he said in his whining cowardly voice, 'Be careful, boss, be careful.'

'Either that or dead,' Grave Digger said.

Cousin chuckled and got out and melted in the dark.

'This is going to be a lot of trouble,' Grave Digger said. 'I hope it ain't for nothing.'

6

Reverend Deke O'Malley didn't know it was Grave Digger's voice over the telephone, but he knew it was the voice of a cop. He got out of the booth as though it had caught on fire. It was still raining but he was already wet and it just obscured his vision. Just the same he saw the light of the taxi coming down the hill on St Nicholas Avenue and hailed it. He climbed in and leaned forward and said, 'Penn Station and goose it.'

He straightened up to wipe the rain out of his eyes and his back hit the seat with a thud. The broad-shouldered young black driver had taken off as though he were powering a rocket ship to heaven.

Deke didn't mind. Speed was what he needed. He had got so far behind everyone the speed gave him a sense of catching up. He figured he could trust Iris. Anyway, he didn't have any choice. As long as she kept his documents hidden, he was relatively safe. But he knew the police would keep her under surveillance and there'd be no way to reach her for a time. He didn't know what the police had on him and that worried him as much as the loss of the money.

He had to admit the robbery had been a cute caper, well organized, bold, even risky. Perhaps it had succeeded just because it was risky. But it had been too well organized for a crime of that dimension, for $87,000, or so it seemed to him; it couldn't have been any better organized for a million dollars. But there seemed a lot of easier ways to get $87,000. One interpretation, of course, was that the syndicate had staged it not only to break him but to frame him. But if it had been the syndicate, why hadn't they just hit him?

Penn Station came before he had finished thinking.

He found a long line of telephone booths and telephoned Mrs John Hill, the wife of the young recruiting agent who had been killed. He didn't remember her but he knew she was a member of his church.

'Are you alone, Mrs Hill?' he asked in a disguised voice.

'Yes,' she replied tentatively, fearfully. 'That is – who's speaking, please?'

'This is Reverend O'Malley,' he announced in his natural voice.

He heard the relief in hers. 'Oh, Reverend O'Malley, I'm so glad you called.'

'I want to offer my sympathy and condolences. I cannot find the words to express my infinite sorrow for this unfortunate accident which has deprived you of your husband—' He knew he sounded like an ass but she'd understand that kind of proper talk.

'Oh, Reverend O'Malley, you are so kind.'

He could tell that she was crying. *Good!* he thought. 'May I be of help to you in any way whatsoever?'

'I just want you to preach his funeral.'

'Of course I shall, Mrs Hill, of course. You may set your mind at peace on that score. But, well, if you will forgive my asking, are you in need of money?'

'Oh, Reverend O'Malley, thank you, but he had life insurance and we have a little saved up – and, well we haven't any children.'

'Well, if you have any need you must let me know. Tell me, have the police been bothering you?'

'Oh, they were here but they just asked questions about our life – where we worked and that kind of thing – and they asked about our Back-to-Africa movement. I was proud to tell them all I knew . . .' Thank God that was nothing, he thought. 'Then, well, they left. They were – well, they were white and I knew they were unsympathetic – I could just feel it – and I was glad when they left.'

'Yes, my dear, we must be prepared for their attitude, that is why our movement was born. And I must confess I have no idea who the vicious white bandits are who murdered your fine . . . er . . . upstanding husband. But I am going to find them and God will punish them. But I have to do it alone. I can't depend on the white police.'

'Oh, don't I know it.'

'In fact, they will do everything to stop me.'

'What makes white folks like that?'

'We must not think *why* they are like that. We must accept it as a fact and go ahead and outwit them and beat them at their own game. And I might need your help, Mrs Hill.'

'Oh, Reverend O'Malley, I'm so glad to hear you say that. I understand just what you mean and I'll do everything in my power to help you track down those foul murderers and get our money back.'

Thank God for squares, O'Malley thought as he said, 'I have utmost confidence in you, Mrs Hill. We both have the same aim in view.'

'Oh, Reverend O'Malley, your confidence is not misplaced.'

He smiled at her stilted speech but he knew she meant it.

'The main thing is for me to stay free of the police while we conduct our own investigation. The police must not know of my whereabouts or that we are working together to bring these foul murderers to justice. They must not know that I have communicated with you or that I will see you.'

'I won't mention your name,' she promised solemnly.

'Do you expect them to return tonight?'

'I'm sure they're not coming back.'

'In that case I will come to your house in an hour and we will make that our headquarters to launch our investigation. Will that bc all right?'

'Oh, Reverend O'Malley, I'm thrilled to be doing something to get revenge – I mean to see those white murderers punished – instead of just sitting here grieving.'

'Yes, Mrs Hill, we shall hunt down the killers for God to punish and perhaps you will draw your shades before I come.'

'And I'll turn out the lights too so you won't have to worry about anyone seeing you.'

'Turn out the lights?' For a moment he was startled. He envisioned himself walking into a pitch-dark ambush and being seized by the cops. Then he realized he had nothing to fear from Mrs Hill. 'Yes, very good,' he said. 'That will be fine. I will telephone you shortly before arriving and if the police are there you must say, "Come on up," but if you are alone, say, "Reverend O'Malley, it's all right."'

'I'll do just that,' she promised. He could hear the excitement in her voice. 'But I'm sure they won't be here.'

'Nothing in life is certain,' he said. 'Just remember what to say when I telephone – in about an hour.'

'I will remember; and good-bye now, until then.'

He hung up. Sweat was streaming down his face. He hadn't realized until then it was so hot in the booth.

He found the big men's room and ordered a shower. Then he undressed and gave his suit to the black attendant to be pressed while he was taking his shower. He luxuriated in the warm needles of water washing away the fear and panic, then he turned on cold and felt a new life and exhilaration replace the fatigue . . . *The indestructible Deke O'Hara,* he thought gloatingly. *What do I care about eighty-seven grand as long as there are squares?*

'Your suit's ready, daddy,' the attendant called, breaking off his reverie.

'Right-o, my man.'

Deke dried, dressed, paid and tipped the attendant and sat on the stand for a shoeshine, reading about the robbery and himself in the morning *Daily News.* The clock on the wall read 2.21 a.m.

Mrs Hill lived uptown in the Riverton Apartments near the Harlem River north of 135th Street. He knew she would be waiting impatiently. He was very familiar with her type: young, thought herself good-looking with the defensive conceit with which they convinced themselves they were more beautiful than all white women; ambitious to get ahead and subconsciously desired white men, hating them at the same time because they frustrated her attempts to get ahead and refused to recognize her innate superiority over white women. More than anything she wanted to escape her drab existence; if she couldn't be middle-class and live in a big house in the suburbs she wanted to leave it all and go back to Africa, where she just *knew* she would be important. He didn't care for the type, but he knew for these reasons he could trust her.

He went out to the ramp to get a taxi. Two empty taxis with white drivers passed him; then a colored driver, seeing his predicament, passed some white people to pick him up. The white policeman supervising the loading saw nothing.

'You know ain't no white cabby gonna take you to Harlem, man,' the colored driver said.

'Hell, they're just losing money and ain't making me mad at all,' Deke said.

The colored driver chuckled.

Deke had him wait at the 125th Street Station while he phoned. The coast was clear. She buzzed the downstairs door the moment he touched the bell and he went up to the seventh floor and found her waiting in her half-open doorway. Behind her the apartment was pitch dark.

'Oh, Reverend O'Malley, I was worried,' she greeted him. 'I thought the police had got you.'

He smiled warmly and patted her hand as he passed to go inside. She closed the door and followed him and for a moment they stood in the pitch dark of the small front hall, their bodies slightly touching.

'We can have some light,' he said. 'I'm sure it's safe enough.'

She clicked switches and the rooms sprang into view. The

shades were drawn and the curtains closed and the apartment was just as he had imagined it. A living-room opening through a wide archway to a small dining room with the closed door of the kitchen beyond. On the other side a door opening to the bedroom and bath. The furniture was the polished oak veneer featured in the credit stores that tried to look expensive, and to one side of the living-room was a long sofa that could be let out into a bed. It had already been let out and the bed made up.

She saw him looking and said apologetically, 'I thought you might want to sleep first.'

'That was very thoughtful of you,' he said. 'But first we must talk.'

'Oh, yesss,' she agreed jubilantly.

The only surprise was herself. She was a really beautiful woman with a smooth brown oval face topped by black curly hair that came in natural ringlets. She had sloe eyes and a petite turned-up nose with very faint black down on her upper lip. Her mouth was wide, generous, with rose-tinted lips and a sudden smile showing even white teeth. Wrapped in a bright blue silk negligee which showed all her curves, her body looked adorable.

He sat at the small round table which had been pushed to one side when the bed was made and indicated her to sit opposite. Then he began speaking to her with pontifical solemnity and seriousness.

'Have you prepared for John's funeral?'

'No, the morgue still has his body but I'm hoping to get Mr Clay for the undertaker and have the funeral in your – our church – and for you to preach the funeral sermon.'

'Of course, Mrs Hill, and I hope by then to have our money back and turn an occasion of deep sorrow also into one of thanksgiving.'

'You can call me Mabel, that's my name,' she said.

'Yes, Mabel, and tomorrow I want you to go to the police and find out what they know so we can use it for our own investigation.' He smiled winningly. 'You're going to be my Mata Hari, Mabel – but one on the side of God.'

Her face lit up with her own brilliant, trusting smile. 'Yes,

Reverend O'Malley, oh, I'm so thrilled,' she said delightedly, involuntarily leaning towards him.

Her whole attitude portrayed such devotion he blinked. My God, he thought, this bitch has already forgotten her dead husband and he isn't even in his coffin.

'I'm so glad, Mabel.' He reached across the table and took one of her hands and held it while he looked deeply into her eyes. 'You don't know how much I depend on you.'

'Oh, Reverend O'Malley, I'll do anything for you,' she vowed.

He had to exercise great restraint. 'Now we will kneel and pray to God for the salvation of the soul of your poor dead husband.'

She suddenly sobered and knelt beside him on the floor.

'O Lord, our Saviour and our Master, receive the soul of our dear departed brother, John Hill, who gave his life in support of our humble aspiration to return to our home in Africa.'

'Amen,' she said. 'He was a good husband.'

'You hear, O Lord, a good husband and a good, upright and honest man. Take him and keep him, O Lord, and have mercy and kindness to his poor wife who must remain longer in this vale of tears without the benefit of a husband to fulfil her desires and quench the flames of her body.'

'Amen,' she whispered.

'And grant her a new lease on life, and yes, O Lord, a new man, for life must go on even out of the depths of death, for life is everlasting, O Lord, and we are but human, all of us.'

'Yes,' she cried. 'Yes.'

He figured it was time to cut that shit out before he found himself in bed with her and he didn't want to confuse the issue – he just wanted his money back. So he said, 'Amen.'

'Amen,' she repeated, disappointedly.

They arose and she asked him if she could fix him anything to eat. He said he wouldn't mind some scrambled eggs, toast and coffee, so she took him into the kitchen and made him sit on one of the padded tubular chairs to the spotless masonite tubular table while she went about preparing his snack. It was a kitchen that went along with the rest of the apartment – electric stove, refrigerator, coffee maker, eggbeater, potato whipper and the like; all electric – compactly arranged, brightly painted and superbly hygienic. But he was entranced by the curves of her body beneath the blue silk negligee as she moved about, bent over to get cream and eggs from the refrigerator, turned quickly here and there to do several things at once; and the swinging of her hips when she moved from stove to table.

But when she sat down opposite him she was too self-conscious to talk. A slow blush rose beneath her smooth brown skin, giving her a sun-kissed look. The snack was excellent, crip bacon, soft scrambled eggs, firm brown toast with a veneer of butter. English marmalade and strong black espresso coffee with thick cream.

He kept the conversation going on the merits of her late husband and how much he would be missed by the Back-to-Africa movement; but he was slowly getting impatient for her to go to bed. It was a relief when she stacked the dishes in the sink and retired to her bedroom with a shy good-night and a wish that he sleep well.

He waited until he felt she was asleep and cracked her door soundlessly. He listened to the even murmur of her breathing. Then he turned on the light in the living-room so he could see her better. If she had awakened he would have pretended to be searching for the bathroom, but she was sleeping soundly with her left hand tight between her legs and her right flung across her exposed breasts. He closed the door and went to the telephone and dialed a number.

'Let me speak to Barry Waterfield, please,' he said when he got an answer.

A sleepy male voice said evilly, 'It's too damn late to be calling roomers. Call in the morning.'

'I just got in town,' Deke said. 'Just passing through – I'm leaving on the 5.45 for Atlanta. I got an important message for him that won't keep.'

'Jussa minute,' the voice said.

Finally another voice came on the line, harsh and heavy with suspicion. 'Who's there?'

'Deke.'

'Oh!'

'Just listen and say nothing. The police are after me. I'm holed up with the wife of our boy, John Hill, who got croaked.' He gave the telephone number and address. 'Nobody knows I'm here but you. And don't call me unless you have to. If she answers tell her your name is James. I'll brief her. Stay out of sight today. Now hang up.'

He listened to the click as the phone was hung up, then waited to see if the line was still open and someone was eavesdropping. Satisfied, he hung up and went back to bed. He turned out the light and lay on his back. A thousand thoughts ran through his mind. He banished them all and finally went to sleep.

He dreamed he was running through a pitch-dark forest and he was terrified and suddenly he saw the moon through the trees and the trees had the shapes of women with breasts hanging like coconuts and suddenly he fell into a pit and it was warm and engulfed him in a warm wet embrace and he felt the most exquisite ecstasy—

'Oh, Reverend O'Malley!' she cried. Light from the bedroom shone across her body, clad only in a frilly nightgown, one ripe brown breast hanging out. She was trembling violently and her face was streaked with tears.

He was so shocked seeing her like this after his dream he leapt from bed and put his arm about her trembling body, wondering if he had attacked her in his sleep. He could feel the warm firm flesh move beneath his hand as she sobbed hysterically.

'Oh, Reverend O'Malley, I've had the most terrible dream.'

'There, there,' he soothed, pulling her body to his. 'Dreams don't mean anything.'

She drew away from him and sat on his bed with her face cupped in her hands, muffling her voice. 'Oh, Reverend O'Malley, I dreamed that you were hurt terribly and when I came to your rescue you looked at me as though you thought I had betrayed you.'

He sat down beside her and began gently stroking her arm. 'I would never think you had betrayed me,' he said soothingly, counting the soft gentle strokes of his hand on the smooth bare flesh of her arm, thinking, any woman will surrender within a hundred strokes. 'I believe in you utterly. You would never be the cause of hurt to me. You will always bring me joy and happiness.'

'Oh, Reverend O'Malley, I feel so inadequate,' she said.

Gently, still counting the strokes of his hand on her arm, he pushed her back and said, 'Now lie down and try not to blame yourself for a silly dream. If I get hurt it will be God's will. We must all bow to God's will. Now repeat after me: If Reverend O'Malley gets hurt, it will be God's will.'

'If Reverend O'Malley gets hurt, it will be God's will,' she repeatedly dutifully in a low voice.

'We must all bow to God's will.'

'We must all bow to God's will.'

With his free hand he opened her legs.

'God's will must be served,' he said.

'God's will must be served,' she repeated.

'This is God's will,' he said hypnotically.

'This is God's will,' she repeated trance-like.

When he penetrated her she believed it was God's will and she cried, 'Oh-oh! I think you're wonderful!'

7

Grave Digger drove east on 113th Street to Seventh Avenue and Harlem showed another face. A few blocks south was the north end of Central Park and the big kidney-shaped lagoon; north of 116th Street was the 'Avenue' – the lush bars and night clubs, Shalimar, Sugar Ray's, Dickie Well's, Count Basie's, Small's, The Red Rooster; the Hotel Theresa; the National Memorial Book Store (*World History Book Outlet on 600,000,000 Colored People*); the beauty parlors (hairdressers); the hash joints (home cooking); the undertakers and the churches. But here, at 113th Street, Seventh Avenue was deserted at this late hour of the night and the old well-kept stone apartment buildings were dark.

Coffin Ed telephoned the station from the car and got Lieutenant Anderson. 'Anything new?'

'Homicide got a colored taxi driver who picked up three white men and a colored woman outside of Small's and drove them to an address far out on Bedford Avenue in Brooklyn. He said the men didn't look like people who go to Small's and the woman was just a common prostitute.'

'Give me his address and the firm he works for.'

Anderson gave him the information but said, 'That's Homicide's baby. We got nothing on O'Hara. What's your score?'

'We're going to Hijenks' shooting gallery looking for a junkie called Loboy who might know something.'

'Hijenks. That's up on Edgecombe at the Roger Morris, isn't it?'

'He's moved down on Eight. Why don't the Feds knock him off? Who's he paying?'

'Don't ask me; I'm a precinct lieutenant.'

'Well, look for us when we get there.'

They drove down to 110th Street and turned back to Eighth Avenue and filled in the square. Near 112th Street they passed an old junk man pushing his cart piled high with the night's load.

'Old Uncle Bud,' said Coffin Ed. 'Shall we dig him a little?'

'What for? He won't co-operate; he wants to keep on living.'

They parked the car and walked to the bar on the corner of 113th Street. A man and a woman stood at the head of the bar, drinking beer and swapping chatter with the bartender. Grave Digger kept on through to the door marked 'Toilet' and went inside. Coffin Ed stopped at the middle of the bar. The bartender looked quickly towards the toilet door and hastened towards Coffin Ed and began wiping the spotless bar with his damp towel.

'What's yours, sir?' he asked. He was a thin tall, stooped-shouldered, light-complexioned man with a narrow moustache and thinning straight hair. He looked neat in a white jacket and black tie; far too neat for that neck of the woods, Coffin Ed thought.

'Bourbon on the rocks.' The bartender hesitated for an instant and Coffin Ed added, 'Two.' The bartender looked relieved.

Grave Digger came back from the toilet as the bartender was serving the drinks.

'You gentlemen are new around here, aren't you?' the bartender asked conversationally.

'We aren't, but you are,' Grave Digger said.

The bartender smiled noncommittally.

'You see that mark down there on the bar?' Grave Digger said. 'I made it ten years ago.'

The bartender looked down the bar. The wooden bar was covered with marks – names, drawings, signatures. 'What mark?'

'Come here, I'll show you,' Grave Digger said, going down to the end of the bar.

The bartender followed slowly, curiosity overcoming caution. Coffin Ed followed him. Grave Digger pointed at the only unmarked spot on the entire bar. The bartender looked. The couple at the front of the bar had stopped talking and stared curiously.

'I don't see nothing,' the bartender said.

'Look closer,' Grave Digger said, reaching inside his coat.

The bartender bent over to look more closely. 'I still don't see nothing.'

'Look up then,' Grave Digger said.

The bartender looked up into the muzzle of Grave Digger's long-barreled, nickel-plated .38. His eyes popped from their sockets and he turned yellow-green.

'Keep looking,' Grave Digger said.

The bartender gulped but couldn't find his voice. The couple at the head of the bar, thinking it was a stickup, melted into the night. It was like magic, one instant they were there, the next instant they were gone.

Chuckling, Coffin Ed went through the 'Toilet' and opened the 'Closet' and gave the signal on the nail holding a dirty rag. The nail was a switch and a light flashed in the entrance hallway upstairs where the lookout sat, reading a comic book. The lookout glanced at the red bulb which should flash the bartender's signal that strangers were downstairs. It didn't flash. He pushed a button and the back door in the closet opened with a soft buzzing sound. Coffin Ed opened the door to the bar and beckoned to Grave Digger, then jumped back to the door upstairs to keep it from closing.

'Good night,' Grave Digger said to the bartender.

The bartender was about to reply but lights went on in his head and briefly he saw the Milky Way before the sky turned black. A junkie was coming from outside when he saw Grave Digger hit the bartender alongside the head and without putting down his foot turned on his heel and started to run. The bartender slumped down behind the bar, unconscious. Grave Digger had only hit him hard enough to knock him out. Without another look, he leapt towards the 'Toilet' and followed Coffin Ed through the concealed door in the 'Closet' up the narrow stairs.

There was no landing at the top of the stairs and the door was the width of the stairway. There was no place to hide.

Halfway up, Grave Digger took Coffin Ed by the arm. 'This is too dangerous for guns; let's play it straight,' he whispered.

Coffin Ed nodded.

They walked up the stairs and Grave Digger knocked out the signal and stood in front of the peephole so he could be seen.

Inside was a small front hallway furnished with a table littered with comic books; above hung a rack containing numerous pigeonholes where weapons were placed before the addicts were allowed into the shooting gallery. A padded chair was drawn up to the table where the lookouts spent their days. On the left side of the door there were several loose nails in the doorframe. The top nail was the switch that blinked the lights in the shooting gallery in case of a raid. The lookout peered at Grave Digger with a finger poised over the the blinker. He didn't recognize him.

'Who're you?' he asked.

Grave Digger flashed his shield and said, 'Detectives Jones and Johnson from the precinct.'

'What you want?'

'We want to talk to Hijenks.'

'Beat it, coppers, there ain't nobody here by that name.'

'You want me to shoot this door open?' Coffin Ed flared.

'Don't make me laugh,' the lookout said. 'This door is bullet-proof and you can't butt it down.'

'Easy, Ed,' Grave Digger cautioned, then to the lookout: 'All right, son, we'll wait.'

'We're just having a little prayer meeting, with the Lord's consent,' the lookout said, but he sounded a little worried.

'Who's the Lord in this case?' Coffin Ed asked harshly.

'Ain't you,' the lookout said.

After that there was silence. Then they heard him moving around inside. Finally they heard another voice ask, 'What is it, Joe?'

'Some nigger cops out there from the precinct.'

'I'll see you sometime, Joe; see who's the niggermost,' Coffin Ed grated.

'You can see me now—' Joe began to bluster, grown brave in the presence of his boss.

'Shut up, Joe,' the voice said. Then they heard the slight sound of the peephole being opened.

'It's Jones and Johnson, Hijenks,' Grave Digger said. 'We just want some information.'

'There's no one here by that name,' Hijenks said.

'By whatever name,' Grave Digger conceded. 'We're looking for Loboy.'

'For what?'

'He might have seen something on that caper where Deke O'Hara's Back-to-Africa group got hijacked.'

'You don't think he was involved?'

'No, he's not involved,' Grave Digger stated flatly. 'But he was in the vicinity of 137th Street and Seventh Avenue when the trucks were wrecked.'

'How do you know that?'

'His sidekick was run over and killed by the hijackers' truck.'

'Well—' Hijenks began, but the lookout cut him off.

'Don't tell those coppers nothing, boss.'

'Shut up, Joe; when I want your advice I'll ask it.'

'We're going to find him anyway, even if we have to get the Feds to break in here to look for him. So if he's here, you'd be doing yourself a favor as well as us if you send him out.'

'At this hour of the night you might find him in Sarah's crib on 105th Street in Spanish Harlem. Do you know where it is?'

'Sarah is an old friend of ours.'

'I'll bet,' Hijenks said. 'Anyway, I don't know where he lives.'

That ended the conversation. No one expected any gratitude for the information; it was strictly business.

They drove across town on 110th Street, past the well-kept old apartment houses overlooking the north end of Central Park and the lagoon where the more affluent colored people lived. It was a quiet street, renamed Cathedral Parkway in honor of the Cathedral of St John the Divine, New York's most beautiful church, which fronted on it – a street of change. The west end, in the vicinity of the cathedral, was still inhabited by whites; but the colored people had taken over that section of Morningside which fronts on the park.

At Fifth Avenue they came to the circle where Spanish Harlem begins. Suddenly the street goes squalid, dirty, teeming with the many colors of Puerto Ricans – so many packed into the incredible slums it seems as though the rotten walls are bursting with human flesh. The English language gives way to Spanish, colored Americans give way to colored Puerto Ricans. By the time they reached Madison Avenue, they were in a Puerto Rican city with Puerto Rican customs, Puerto Rican food; with all stores, restaurants, professional offices, business establishments and such bearing signs and notices in Spanish, offering Puerto Rican services and Puerto Rican goods.

'People talk about Harlem,' Grave Digger said. 'These slums are many times worse.'

'Yeah, but when a Puerto Rican becomes white enough he's accepted as white, but no matter how white a spook might become he's still a nigger,' Coffin Ed replied.

'Hell, man, leave that for the anthropologists,' Grave Digger said, turning south on Lexington towards 105th Street.

Sarah had the top flat in an old-fashioned brick apartment building that had seen better days. Directly beneath her top-floor crib lived a Puerto Rican clan of so many families the apartments on the floor could not hold them all; therefore eating, sleeping, cooking and making love was done in turns while the others stayed outside in the street until those inside were finished. Radios blared at top volume all day and night. Combined with the natural sounds of Spanish speech, laughter and quarreling, the din drowned all sounds that might come from Sarah's above. How the families below fared was of no concern.

Grave Digger and Coffin Ed parked down the street and walked. No one gave them a second look. They were men and that's all that interested Sarah: white men, black men, yellow men, brown men, straight men, crooked men and squares. Sarah said she only barred women; she didn't run a joint for 'freaks'. She paid for protection. Everyone knew she was a stool pigeon; but she pigeoned on the police too.

The first thing that hit the detectives when they entered the dimly lit downstairs hallway was the smell of urine.

'What American slums need is toilets,' Coffin Ed said.

Smelling odors of cooking, loving, hair frying, dogs farting, cats pissing, boys masturbating and the stale fumes of stale wine and black tobacco, Grave Digger said, 'That wouldn't help much.'

Next they noticed the graffiti on the walls.

'Hell, no wonder they make so many babies; that's all they think about,' Coffin Ed concluded.

'If you lived here, what else would you think about?'

They ascended in silence. The stink lessened as they climbed the six flights, the walls became less tattooed. The whorehouse floor was practically clean.

They knocked at a red-painted door at the front. It was opened by a grinning Puerto Rican girl who didn't bother to look through the peephole. 'Welcome, señors,' she said. 'You're at the right place.'

They entered a vestibule and looked at the hooks on the walls.

'We want to talk to Sarah,' Grave Digger said.

The girl waved towards a door. 'Come on in. You don't have to see her.'

'We want to see her. You go in like a good little girl and send her out.'

The girl stopped grinning. 'Who're you?'

Both detectives flashed their shields. 'We're the law.'

The girl sneered and turned quickly into the big front room, leaving the door ajar. They could see into what Sarah called her 'reception room'. The floor was covered with polished red linoleum. Chairs lined the walls: overstuffed chairs for the Johns, straight-backed chairs for the girls; but most of the time the girls were either sitting in the laps of the Johns or bringing them food and drink.

The girls were all dressed alike in one-piece shifts showing their shapes, and high-heeled shoes of different colors. They were all light-complexioned Puerto Rican girls with hair shades ranging from blonde to black; all were young. They looked gay and natural and picturesque flitting about the room, peddling their bodies.

Against the back wall a brilliantly lighted jukebox was playing Spanish music and two couples were dancing. The others were sitting, drinking whisky highballs and eating, saving their energy for the real thing.

Alongside the jukebox was a long, dimly lit hallway, flanked by the small bedrooms for business. The bathroom and the kitchen were at the rear. A dark brown motherly-type woman fried the chicken, dished out the potato salad and mixed the drinks, keeping a sharp eye on the money.

Two apartments had been put together to make Sarah's crib and the back apartment was her private residence.

Grave Digger said, 'If our people were ever let loose they'd be a sensation in the business world, with the flair they got for crooked organizing.'

'That's what the white folks is scared of,' Coffin Ed said.

They watched Sarah come from the back and cross the big

room. The girls treated her as though she were the queen. She was a buxom black woman with snow-white hair done in curls as tight as springs. She had a round face, broad flat nose, thick, dark, unpainted lips and a dazzling white-toothed smile. She wore a black satin gown with long sleeves and a high décolleté; on one wrist was a small platinum watch with a diamond-studded band; on the ring finger a wedding ring set with a diamond the size of an acorn. Several keys dangled on a gold chain about her neck.

She came towards them smiling only with her teeth; her dark eyes were stone cold behind rimless lenses. She closed the door behind her.

'Hello, boys,' she said, shaking hands in turn. 'How are you?'

'Fine, Sarah, business is booming; how's your business?' Grave Digger said.

'Booming too, Digger. Only the criminals got money, and all they do with it is buy pussy. You know how it is, runs hand in hand; girls sell when cotton and corn are a drag on the market. What do you boys want?'

'We want Loboy, Sarah,' Grave Digger said harshly, souring at this landprop's philosophy.

Her smile went out. 'What's he done, Digger?' she asked in a toneless voice.

'None of your mother-raping business,' Coffin Ed flared.

She looked at him. 'Be careful, Edward,' she warned.

'It's not what he's done this time, Sarah,' Grave Digger said soothingly. 'We're curious about what he's seen. We just want to talk to him.'

'I know what that means. But he's kinda nervous and upset now—'

'High, you mean,' Coffin Ed said.

She looked at him again. 'Don't get tough with me, Edward. I'll have you thrown out here on your ass.'

'Look, Sarah, let's level,' Grave Digger said. 'It's not like you think. You know Deke O'Hara got hijacked tonight.'

'I heard it on the radio. But you ain't stupid enough to think Loboy was on that caper.'

'Not that stupid, Sarah. And we don't give a damn about Deke either. But eighty-seven grand of colored people's hard-earned money got lost in the caper; and we want to get it back.'

'How's Loboy fit that act?'

'Chances are he saw the hijackers. He was working in the neighborhood when their getaway truck crashed and they had to split.'

She studied his face impassively; finally she said, 'I dig.' Suddenly her smile came on again. 'I'll do anything to help our poor colored people.'

'I believe you,' Coffin Ed said.

She turned back into the reception room without another word and closed the door behind her. A few minutes later she brought out Loboy.

They took him to 137th Street and told him to reconstruct his activities and tell everything he saw before he got out of the vicinity.

At first Loboy protested, 'I ain't done nothing and I ain't seen nothing and you ain't got nothing against me. I been sick all day, at home and in bed.' He was so high his speech was blurred and he kept dozing off in the middle of each sentence.

Coffin Ed slapped him with his open palm a half-dozen times. Tears came to his eyes.

'You ain't got no right to hit me like that. I'm gonna tell Sarah. You ain't got nothing against me.'

'I'm just trying to get your attention is all,' Coffin Ed said.

He got Loboy's attention, but that was all. Loboy admitted getting a glimpse of the driver of the delivery truck that hit Early Riser, but he didn't remember what he looked like. 'He was white is all I remember. All white folks look alike to me,' he said.

He hadn't seen the white men when they had got from the wrecked truck. He hadn't seen the armored truck at all. By the time it had passed he had jumped the iron fence beside the church and was running down the passageway to 136th Street, headed towards Lenox.

‘Which way did the woman go?’ Grave Digger asked.

‘I didn’t stop to see,’ Loboy confessed.

‘What did she look like?’

‘I don’t remember; big and strong is all.’

They let him go. By then it was past four in the morning. They drove to the precinct station to check out. They were frustrated and dead beat, and no nearer the solution than at the start. Lieutenant Anderson said nothing new had come in; he had put a tap on Deke’s private telephone line but no one had called.

‘We should have talked to the driver who took those three white men to Brooklyn, instead of wasting time on Loboy,’ Grave Digger said.

‘There’s no point in second-guessing,’ Anderson said. ‘Go home and get some sleep.’

He looked white about the gills himself. It had been a hot, raw night – Independence night, he thought – filled with big and little crime. He was sick of crime and criminals; sick of both cops and robbers; sick of Harlem and colored people. He liked colored people all right; they couldn’t help it because they were colored. He was quite attached to his two ace colored detectives; in fact he depended on them. They probably kept his job for him. He was second in command to the precinct captain, and had charge of the night shift. His was the sole responsibility when the captain went home, and without his two aces he might not have been able to carry it. Harlem was a mean rough city and you had to be meaner and rougher to keep any kind of order. He understood why colored people were mean and rough; he’d be mean and rough himself if he was colored. He understood all the evils of segregation. He sympathized with the colored people in his precinct, and with colored people in general. But right now he was good and goddamned sick of them. All he wanted was to go home to his quiet house in Queens in a quiet white neighborhood and kiss his white wife and look in on his two sleeping white children and crawl into bed between two white sheets and go to hell to sleep.

So when the telephone rang and a big happy colored voice

sang, '. . . O where de cotton and de corn grow . . .' he turned purple with anger.

'Go on the stage, clown!' he shouted and banged down the receiver.

The detectives grinned sympathetically. They hadn't heard the voice but they knew it had been some lunatic talking in jive.

'You'll get used to it if you live long enough,' Grave Digger said.

'I doubt it,' Anderson muttered.

Grave Digger and Coffin Ed started home. They both lived on the same street in Astoria, Long Island, and they only used one of their private cars to travel back and forth to work. They kept their official car, the little battered black sedan with the hopped-up engine, in the precinct garage.

But tonight when they went to put it away, they found it had been stolen.

'Well, that's the bitter end,' Coffin Ed said.

'One thing is for sure,' Grave Digger said. 'I ain't going in and report it.'

'Damn right,' Coffin Ed agreed.

8

The next morning, at eight o'clock, an open bed truck pulled up before a store on Seventh Avenue that was being remodeled. Formerly, there had been a notion goods store with a shoeshine parlor serving as a numbers drop on the site. But it had been taken over by a new tenant and a high board wall covering the entire front had been erected during the remodeling.

There had been much speculation in the neighborhood concerning the new business. Some said it would be a bar, others a nightclub. But Small's Paradise Inn was only a short distance away, and the cognoscenti ruled those out. Others said it was an ideal spot for a barbershop or a hairdresser, or even a bowling alley; some half-wits opted for another funeral parlor, as though colored folks weren't dying fast enough as it is. Those in the know claimed they had seen office furnishings moved in during the night and they had it at first hand that it was going to be the headquarters for the Harlem political committee of the Republican Party. But those with the last word said that Big Wilt Chamberlain, the professional basketball player who had bought Small's Cabaret, was going to open a bank to store all the money he was making hand over fist.

By the time the workmen began taking down the wall, a small crowd had collected. But when they had finished, the crowd overflowed into the street. Harlemites, big and little, old and young, strong and feeble, the halt and the blind, male and female, boys and girls, stared in pop-eyed amazement.

'Great leaping Jesus!' said the fat black barber from down the street, expressing the opinion of all.

Plate-glass windows, trimmed with stainless steel, formed a glass front above a strip of shining steel along the sidewalk. Across the top, above the glass, was a big wooden sign glistening with spotless white paint upon which big, bold, black letters announced:

HEADQUARTERS OF
B.T.S. BACK-TO-THE-SOUTHLAND
MOVEMENT B.T.S.
Sign Up Now!!! Be a 'FIRST NEGRO!'
$1,000 Bonus to First Families Signing!

The entire glass front was plastered with bright-colored paintings of conk-haired black cotton-pickers, clad in overalls that resembled Italian-tailored suits, delicately lifting enormous snow-white balls of cotton from rose-colored cotton bolls that looked for all the world like great cones of ice cream, and grinning happily with even whiter teeth; others showed darkies, clad in the same Italian fashion, hoeing corn as though doing the cakewalk, their heads lifted in song that must surely be spirituals. One scene showed these happy darkies at the end of the day celebrating in a clearing in front of ranch-type cabins, dancing the twist, their teeth gleaming in the setting sun, their hips rolling in the playful shadows to the music of a banjo player in a candy-striped suit; while the elders looked on with approval, bobbing their nappy white heads and clapping their manicured hands. Another showed a tall white man with a white mane of hair, a white moustache and white goatee, wearing a black frock coat and shoestring tie, his pink face bubbling with brotherly love, passing out fantastic bundles of bank notes to a row of grinning darkies, above the caption: *Paid by the week.* Lodged between the larger scenes were smaller paintings identified as ALL GOOD THINGS TO EAT: grotesquely oversized animals and edibles with the accompanying captions: *Big-legged Chickens . . . Chitterling Bred Shoats . . . Yams! What Am . . . O! Possum! . . . Lasses In The Jug . . . Grits and Gravy . . . Pappy's Bar-B-Q and Mammy's Hog Maw Stew . . . Corn Whisky . . . Buttermilk . . . Hoppin John.*

In the center of all this jubilation of good food, good times and good pay, were a blown-up photomontage beside a similarly sized drawing: one showing pictures of famine in the Congo, tribal wars, mutilations, depravities, hunger and disease, above the caption, *Unhappy Africa;* the other depicting fat, grinning colored people sitting at tables laden with food, driving about in cars as big as Pullman coaches, black children entering modernistic schools equipped with stadiums and swimming-pools, elderly people clad in Brooks Brothers suits and Saks Fifth Avenue dresses filing into a church that looked astonishingly like Saint Peter's Cathedral in Rome, with its caption: *The Happy South.*

At the bottom was another big white-painted, black-lettered banner reading:

FARE PAID . . . HIGH WAGES . . .
ACCOMMODATIONS FOR COTTON PICKERS
$1,000 Bonus for Each Family of Five Able-Bodied Persons

The small notice in one lower corner which read, *Wanted, a bale of cotton,* went unnoticed.

On the inside, the walls were decorated with more slogans

and pictures of the same papier-mâché cotton plants and bamboo corn stalks were scattered about the floor, in the center of which was an artificial bale of cotton bearing the etched brass legend: *Our Front Line of Defense.*

At the front to one side was a large flat-topped desk with a nameplate stating: Colonel Robert L. Calhoun. Colonel Calhoun in the flesh sat behind the desk, smoking a long, thin cheroot and looking out the window at the crowd of Harlemites with a benign expression. He looked like the model who had posed for the portrait of the colonel in the window, paying off the happy darkies. He had the same narrow, hawklike face crowned by the same mane of snow-white hair, the same wide, drooping white moustache, the same white goatee. There the resemblance stopped. His narrow-set eyes were ice-cold blue and his back was ramrod straight. But he was clad in a similar black frock coat and black shoestring tie, and on the ring finger of his long pale hand was a solid gold signet ring with the letters CSA.

A young blond white man in a seersucker suit, who looked as though he might be an alumnus of Ole Miss, sat on the edge of the Colonel's desk, swinging his leg.

'Are you going to talk to them?' he asked in a college-trained voice with a slight southern accent.

The Colonel removed his cheroot and studied the ash on the tip. His actions were deliberate; his expression impassive. He spoke in a voice that was slow and calculated, with a southern accent as thick as molasses in the winter.

'Not yet, son, let's let it simmer a bit. You can't rush these darkies; they'll come around in their own good time.'

The young man peered through a clear crack in the plastered window. He looked anxious. 'We haven't got all the time in the world,' he said.

The Colonel looked up at him, smiling with perfect white dentures, but his eyes remained cold. 'What's your hurry, son, you got a gal waiting?'

The young man blushed and looked down sullenly. 'All these niggers make me nervous,' he confessed.

'Now don't start feeling guilty, son,' the Colonel said.

'Remember it's for their own good. You got to learn to think of niggers with love and charity.'

The young man smiled sardonically and remained silent.

At the back of the room were two desks side by side, bearing the legend: *Applications*. They were presided over by two neat young colored men who shuffled application forms to look occupied. From time to time the Colonel looked at them approvingly, as though to say, 'See how far you've come.' But they had the expressions of guilty fathers who've been caught robbing their babies' banks.

Outside, on the sidewalk and in the street, black people were expressing righteous indignation.

'Ain't it a scandal, Lord, right up here in Harlem?'

'God ought to strike 'em daid, that's whut.'

'These peckerwoods don't know what they want. One day they's sending us north to get rid of us, and the next they's up here tryna con us into going back.'

'Man, trust white folks and go from Cadillacs to cotton sacks.'

'Ain't it the truth! I'd sooner trust a white-mouthed moccasin sucking at my tiddy.'

'Man, I ought to go in there and say to that ol' colonel, "You wants me to go back south, eh?" and he says, "That's right, boy," and I says, "You gonna let me vote?" and he says, "That's right, boy, vote all you want, just so long you don't cast no ballots," and I says, "You gonna let me marry you' daughter—"'

His audience fell out laughing. But one joker didn't think it was funny; he said, 'There he is, what's stopping you?'

Everyone stopped laughing.

The comedian said shamefacedly, 'Hell, man, I don't do everything I oughta do, you knows that.'

A big matronly woman said, 'Just you wait 'til Reverend O'Malley hears 'bout all this, and then you'll see some action.'

Reverend O'Malley had already heard. Barry Waterfield, the phoney detective in his employ, had telephoned him and given him the lowdown. Reverend O'Malley had sent him to see the Colonel with implicit instructions.

Barry was a big, clean-shaven man with hair cropped short

and a nose flattened in the ring. His dark brown face bore other lumps it had taken during his career as bodyguard, bouncer, mugger and finally killer. He had small brown eyes partly obscured by scar tissue, and two gold teeth in front. He was easily identifiable, which limited his usefulness, but Deke didn't have any other choice.

Barry shaved, carefully brushed his hair, dressed in a dark business suit, but couldn't resist the hand-painted tie depicting an orange sunset on a green background.

When he pushed through the crowd and entered the office of the Back-to-the-Southland movement, talk stopped momentarily and people stared at him. No one knew him, but no one would forget him.

He walked straight to the colonel's desk and said, 'Colonel Calhoun, I'm Mr Waterfield from the Back-to-Africa movement.'

Colonel Calhoun looked up through cold blue eyes and appraised him from head to foot. Colonel Calhoun dug him instantly. The Colonel removed the cheroot from his white moustache and his dentures gleamed whitely.

'What can I do for you . . . er . . . what did you say your name was?'

'Barry Waterfield.'

'Barry. What can I do for you, boy?'

'Well, you see, we have a group of good people we're going to send back to Africa.'

'Back to Africa!' the Colonel exclaimed in horror. 'My boy, you must be raving mad. Uprooting these people from their native land. Don't do it, boy, don't do it.'

'Well, sir, you see, it's going to cost a lot—' He remained standing, as the Colonel had not invited him to be seated.

'A fortune, my boy, a veritable fortune,' the Colonel agreed, rearing back in his chair. 'And who's going to pay for this costly nonsense?'

'Well, sir, you see, that's the trouble. You see, last night we were having a big rally to sign up the families who were going to leave first, and then some bandits robbed us of their money. Eighty-seven thousand dollars.'

The Colonel whistled softly.

'You must have heard about it, sir.'

'No, I can't say that I have, my boy; but I've been pretty busy with this philanthropy of ours. But I'm sorry for those misguided people, even though their misfortune might turn out to be a blessing in disguise. I'm ashamed of you, my boy, an honest-looking American nigra like you, leading your people astray. If you knew what we know, you wouldn't dream of sending your poor people to Africa. Only pestilence and starvation await them there, in those foreign lands. The South is the place for them, the good old reliable Southland. We love and take care of our darkies.'

'Well, you see, sir, that's what I want to talk to you about. These poor people have got ready to go somewhere, and now since they can't go back to Africa it might be best they go back south.'

'Right you are, my boy. You just send them to me and we'll do right by them. The Happy Southland is the only home of your people.'

The two young colored clerks who had been eavesdropping on the conversation were downright shocked to hear Barry say, 'Well, sir, I'm inclined to agree with you, sir.'

The blond young man was standing at the front window, peering out at the milling black mob which he now began to see in a different light. They didn't look dangerous any longer; now they appeared innocent and gullible and he could barely suppress a smile as he thought of how easy it was going to be. Then he frowned at a sudden memory and turned back to stare at Barry with searching suspicion. This nigger sounded too good to be true, he thought.

But the Colonel didn't seem to entertain a doubt. 'You just trust me, my boy,' he went on, 'and we'll take care of your people.'

'Well, you see, sir, I trust you,' Barry said. 'I know you'll do the right thing by us. But our leader, Reverend O'Malley, won't like it, my giving you my confidence. You see, sir, he's a dangerous man.'

A line of white dentures peeped from beneath the Colonel's white moustache, and Barry had a fleeting thought that this mother-raping white man looked too mother-raping white. But the Colonel continued unsuspectingly, 'Don't worry about that nigra, my boy, we're going to take care of him and put an end to his un-American activities.'

Barry leaned a little forward and lowered his voice. 'You see, sir, the point is we have the eighty-seven families of able-bodied people all packed and ready to go; and I've got to tell them if you're ready to pay them their bonuses.'

'My boy, their bonuses is as good as in the bank. You tell them that,' the Colonel said and rolled the cheroot between his lips only to find it had gone out.

He tossed it carelessly on the floor and carefully selected another from a silver case in his breast pocket. Then he clipped the end with a cigar cutter from his vest pocket, stuck the clipped cheroot between his lips and rolled it over and over until the outer leaves of the lip-end were agreeably wet. Both Barry and the blond young man snapped their lighters to offer a light, but the Colonel preferred Barry's flame.

Barry said, 'Well, that is fine of you, sir, that's all I want to know. We got more than a thousand families recruited and I'll sell you the whole list.'

For an instant both the Colonel and the blond young man became immobile. Then the Colonel's dentures showed. 'If I heard you correctly, my boy,' he said smoothly, 'you said *sell.*'

'Well, sir, you see, sir, it's like this,' Barry began, his voice pitched low and grown husky. 'Naturally I would want a little something for myself, taking all this risk. You see, sir, the list is highly confidential and it has taken us months to select and recruit all these able-bodied people. And if they knew I was turning this list over to you, they might make trouble, sir – even though it is for their own good. And I'd want to be able to get away for a while, sir. You understand, sir.'

'My boy, nothing could be plainer,' the Colonel said and puffed his cheroot. 'Plain talk suits me fine. Now how much do you want for your list?'

'Well, sir. I was thinking fifty dollars a family would be about fair, sir.'

'You're a boy after my own heart, even though you do

belong to the nigra race,' the Colonel said. The blond young man frowned and opened his mouth as though to speak, but the Colonel ignored him. 'Now, my boy, I understand your predicament and I don't want to jeopardize your position and usefulness by permitting you to come back here and be seen and suspected by all your people. So I'm going to tell you what I want you to do. You bring the list to me at midnight. I'll be waiting down by the Harlem River underneath the subway extension to the Polo Grounds in my cah, and I'll pay you right then and there. It will be dark and deserted at that time of night and nobody'll see you.'

Barry hesitated, looking torn between fear and greed. 'Well, frankly, sir, that's a good sound idea, but I'm scared of the dark, sir,' he confessed.

The Colonel chuckled. 'There's nothing about the dark to fear, my boy. That's just nigra superstition. The dark never hurt anyone. You'll be as safe as in the arms of Jesus. I give you my word.'

Barry looked relieved at this. 'Well, sir, if you give me your word I know can't nothing happen to me. I'll be there at midnight sharp.'

Without further ado, the Colonel waved a hand, dismissing him.

'Are you going to trust that—' the blond young man began.

For the first time the Colonel showed displeasure in a frown. The blond young man shut up.

As he was leaving, Barry noticed the small sign in the window through the corners of his eyes: *Wanted, a bale of cotton.* What for? he wondered.

9

No one knew where Uncle Bud slept. He could be found any night somewhere on the streets of Harlem, pushing his cart, his eyes searching the darkness for anything valuable enough to sell. He had an exceptional divination of anything of value, because in Harlem no one ever threw anything away valuable enough to sell, if they knew it. But he managed to collect enough saleable junk to exist, and when day broke he was to be seen at one of those run-down junkyards where scrawny-necked, beady-eyed white men paid a few cents for the rags, paper, glass and iron he had collected. Actually he slept in his cart during the summer. He would wheel it to some shady spot on some slum street where no one thought it strange to find a junk man sleeping in his cart, and curl up on the burlap rags covering his load and sleep, undisturbed by the sounds of motor-cars and trucks, children screaming, men cursing and fighting, women gossiping, police sirens wailing, or even by the dead awakening. Nothing troubled his sleep.

On this night, because his cart was filled with the bale of cotton, he wheeled it towards a street beneath the 125th Street approach to the Triborough Bridge, where he would be near Mr Goodman's junkyard when he woke up.

A police cruiser containing two white cops pulled up beside him. 'What you got there, boy?' the one on the inside asked.

Uncle Bud stopped and scratched his head and ruminated. 'Wal, boss, I'se got some cahdbo'd and papuh an' I'se got some bedsprings an' some bottles an' some rags an'—'

'You ain't got no money, have you?' the cop cracked. 'You ain't got no eighty-seven thousand dollars?'

'Nawsuh, wish I did.'

'What would you do with eighty-seven grand?'

Uncle Bud scratched his head again. 'Wal, suh, I'd buy me a brand new waggin. An' then I reckon I'd go to Africa,' he said, adding underneath his breath: 'Where wouldn't any white mother-rapers like you be fucking with me all the time.'

Naturally the cops didn't hear the last, but they laughed at the first and drove on.

Uncle Bud found a spot beside an abandoned truck down by the river and went to sleep. When he awakened the sun was high. At about the same time Barry Waterfield was approaching Colonel Calhoun on Seventh Avenue, he was approaching the junkyard alongside the river south of the bridge.

It was a fenced-in enclosure about piles of scrap iron and dilapidated wooden sheds housing other kinds of junk. Uncle Bud stopped before a small gate at one side of the main office building, a one-storey wooden box fronting on the street. A big black hairless dog the size of a Great Dane came silently to the gate and stared at him through yellow eyes.

'Nice doggie,' Uncle Bud said through the wire gate.

The dog didn't blink.

A shabbily dressed, unshaven white man came from the office and led the dog away and chained it up. Then he returned and said, 'All right, Uncle Bud, what you got there?'

Uncle Bud looked at the white man through the corners of his eyes. 'A bale of cotton, Mr Goodman.'

Mr Goodman was startled. 'A bale of cotton?'

'Yassuh,' Uncle Bud said proudly as he uncovered the bale. 'Genuwine Mississippi cotton.'

Mr Goodman unlocked the gate and came outside to look at it. Most of the cotton was obscured by the burlap covering. But he pulled out a few shreds from the seams and smelled it. 'How do you know it's *Mississippi* cotton?'

'I'd know Mississippi cotton anywhere I seed it,' Uncle Bud stated flatly. 'Much as I has picked.'

'Ain't much of this to be seen,' Mr Goodman observed.

'I can smell it,' Uncle Bud said. 'It smell like nigger-sweat.'

Mr Goodman sniffed at the cotton again. 'Anything special about that?'

'Yassuh, makes it stronger.'

Two colored workmen in overalls came up. 'Cotton!' one exclaimed. 'Lord, lord.'

'Makes you homesick, don't it?' the other one said.

'Homesick for your mama,' the first one said, looking at him sidewise.

'Watch out, man, I don't play the dozzens,' the second one said.

Mr Goodman knew they were just kidding. 'All right, get it on the scales,' he ordered.

The bale weighed four hundred and eighty-seven pounds.

'I'll give you five dollars for it,' Mr Goodman said.

'Five bones!' Uncle Bud exclaimed indignantly. 'Why, dis cotton is worth thirty-nine cents a pound.'

'You're thinking about the First World War,' Mr Goodman said. 'Nowadays they're giving cotton away.'

The two workmen exchanged glances silently.

'I ain't giving dis away,' Uncle Bud said.

'Where can I sell a bale of cotton?' Mr Goodman said. 'Who wants unprocessed cotton? Not even good for bullets no more. Nowadays they shoot atoms. It ain't like as if it was drugstore cotton.'

Uncle Bud was silent.

'All right, ten dollars then,' Mr Goodman said.

'Fifty dollars,' Uncle Bud countered.

'*Mein Gott*, he wants fifty dollars yet!' Mr Goodman appealed to his colored workmen. 'That's more than I'd pay for brass.'

The colored workmen stood with their hands in their pockets, blank-faced and silent. Uncle Bud kept a stubborn silence. All three colored men were against Mr Goodman. He felt trapped and guilty, as though he'd been caught taking advantage of Uncle Bud.

'Since it's you, I'll give you fifteen dollars.'

'Forty,' Uncle Bud muttered.

Mr Goodman gestured eloquently. 'What am I, your father, to give you money for nothing?' the three colored men stared at him accusingly. 'You think I am Abraham Lincoln instead of Abraham Goodman?' The colored men didn't think he was funny. 'Twenty,' Mr Goodman said desperately and turned towards the office.

'Thirty,' Uncle Bud said.

The colored workmen shifted the bale of cotton as though asking whether to take it in or put it back.

'Twenty-five,' Mr Goodman said angrily. 'And I should have my head examined.'

'Sold,' Uncle Bud said.

About that time the Colonel had finished his interview with Barry and was having his breakfast. It had been sent from a 'home-cooking' restaurant down the street. The Colonel seemed to be demonstrating to the colored people outside, many of whom were now peeking through the cracks between the posters covering most of the window, what they could be eating for breakfast if they signed up with him and went back south.

He had a bowl of grits, swimming with butter; four fried eggs sunny side up; six fried home-made sausages; six down-home biscuits, each an inch thick, with big slabs of butter stuck between the halves; and a pitcher of sorghum molasses. The Colonel had brought his own food with him and merely paid the restaurant to cook it. Alongside his heaping plate stood a tall bourbon whisky highball.

The colored people, watching the Colonel shovel grits, eggs and sausage into his mouth and chomp off a hunk of biscuit, felt nostalgic. But when they saw him cover all his food with a thick layer of sorghum molasses, many felt absolutely homesick.

'I wouldn't mind going down home for dinner ever day,' one joker said. 'But I wouldn't want to stay overnight.'

'Baby, seeing that scoff makes my stomach feel lak my throat is cut,' another replied.

Bill Davis, the clean-cut young man who was Reverend O'Malley's recruiting agent, entered the Back-to-the-Southland office as Colonel Calhoun was taking an oversize mouthful of grits, eggs and sausage mixed with molasses. He paused before the Colonel's desk, erect and purposeful.

'Colonel Calhoun, I am Mister Davis,' he said. 'I represent the Back-to-Africa movement of Reverend O'Malley's. I want a word with you.'

The Colonel looked up at Bill Davis through cold blue eyes, continuing to chew slowly and deliberately like a camel chewing its cud. But he took much longer in his appraisal than he had done with Barry Waterfield. When he had finished chewing, he washed his mouth with a sip from his bourbon highball, cleared his throat and said, 'Come back in half an hour, after I've et my breakfast.'

'What I have to say to you I'm going to say now,' Bill Davis said.

The Colonel looked up at him again. The blond young man

who had been standing in the background moved closer. The young colored men at their desks in the rear became nervous.

'Well, what can I do for you . . . er . . . what did you say your name was?' the Colonel said.

'My name is *Mister* Davis, and I'll make it short and sweet. *Get out of town!*'

The blond young man started around the desk and Bill Davis got set to hit him, but the Colonel waved him back.

'Is that all you got to say, my boy?'

'That's all, and I'm not your boy,' Bill Davis said.

'Then you've said it,' the Colonel said and deliberately began eating again.

When Bill emerged, the black people parted to let him pass. They didn't know what he had said to the Colonel, but whatever it was they were for him. He had stood right up to that ol' white man and tol' him something to his teeth. They respected him.

A half-hour later the pickets moved in. They marched up and down Seventh Avenue, holding aloft a Back-to-Africa banner and carrying placards reading: *Goddamn White Man GO! GO! GO! Black Man STAY! STAY! STAY!* There were twenty-five in the picket line and two or three hundred followers. The pickets formed a circle in front of the Back-to-the-Southland office and chanted as they marched, 'Go, white man, go while you can . . . Go, white man, go while you can . . .' Bill Davis stood to one side between two elderly colored men.

Colored people poured into the vicinity from far and wide, overflowed the sidewalks and spilled into the street. Traffic was stopped. The atmosphere grew tense, pregnant with premonition. A black youth ran forward with a brick to hurl through the plate-glass window. A Back-to-Africa follower grabbed him and took it away. 'None of that, son, we're peaceful,' he said.

'What for?' the youth asked.

The man couldn't answer.

Suddenly the air was filled with the distant wailing of the sirens, sounding at first like the faint wailing of banshees, growing ever louder as the police cruisers roared nearer, like souls escaped from hell.

The first cruiser ploughed through the mob and shrieked to a stop on the wrong side of the street. Two uniformed white cops hit the pavement with pistols drawn, shouting, 'Get back! Get off the street! Clear the street!' Then another cruiser plowed through the mob and shrieked to a stop . . . Then a third . . . Then a fourth . . . Then a fifth. Out came the white cops, brandishing their pistols, like trained performers in a macabre ballet entitled 'If You're Black Get Back'.

The mood of the mob became dangerous. A cop pushed a black man. The black man got set to hit the cop. Another cop quickly intervened.

A woman fell down and was trampled. 'Help! Murder!' she screamed.

The mob moved in her direction, taking the cops with it.

'Goddamned mother-raping shit! Here it is!' a young black man shouted, whipping out his switch-blade knife.

Then the precinct captain arrived in a sound truck. 'All officers back to your cars,' he ordered, his voice loud and clear from the amplifiers. 'Back to your cars. And, folks, let's have some order.'

The cops retreated to their cars. The danger passed. Some people cheered. Slowly the people returned to the sidewalks. Passenger cars that had been lined up for more than ten blocks began to move along, curious faces peering out at the black people crowding the sidewalks.

The captain went over and talked to Bill Davis and the two men with him. 'Only nine persons are permitted on a picket line by New York law,' he said. 'Will you thin these pickets down to nine?'

Bill looked at the elderly men. They nodded. He said, 'All right,' to the captain and thinned out the picket line.

Then the captain went inside the office and approached Colonel Calhoun; he asked to see his license. The Colonel's papers were in order; he had a New York City permit to recruit farm labor as the agent of the Back-to-the-Southland movement, which was registered in Birmingham, Alabama.

The captain returned to the street and stationed ten policemen in front of the office to keep order, and two police cruisers to keep the street clear. Then he shook hands with Bill Davis and got back into the sound truck and left.

The mob began to disperse.

'I knew we'd get some action from Reverend O'Malley, soon as he heard about all this,' the church sister said.

Her companion looked bewildered. 'What I wants to know,' she asked, 'is we won or lost?'

Inside, the blond young man asked Colonel Calhoun, 'Aren't we pretty well finished now?'

Colonel Calhoun lit a fresh cheroot and took a puff. 'It's just good publicity, son,' he said.

By then it was noon, and the two young colored clerks slipped out the back door to go to lunch.

Later that afternoon one of Mr Goodman's workmen stood in the crowd surrounding the Back-to-Africa pickets, admiring the poster art on the windows of the Back-to-the-Southland office. He had bathed and shaved and dressed up for a big Saturday night and he was just killing time until his date. Suddenly his gaze fell on the small sign in the corner reading: *Wanted, a bale of cotton.* He started inside. A Back-to-Africa sympathizer grabbed his arm.

'Don't go in there, friend. You don't believe that crap, do you?'

'Baby, I ain't thinking 'bout going south. I ain't never been south. I just wanna talk to the man.'

''Bout what?'

'I just wanna ask the man if them chicken really got legs that big,' he said, pointing to the picture of the chicken.

The man bent over laughing. 'You go 'head and ast him, man, and you tell me what he say.'

The workman went inside and walked up to Colonel Calhoun's desk and took off his cap. 'Colonel,' he said, 'I'm just the man you wanna see. My name is Josh.'

The Colonel gave him the customary cold-eyed appraisal, sitting reared back in his chair as though he hadn't moved. The blond young man stood beside him.

'Well, Josh, what can you do for me?' the Colonel asked, showing his dentures in a smile.

'I can get you a bale of cotton,' Josh said.

The tableau froze. The Colonel was caught in the act of returning the cheroot to his lips. The blond young man was caught in the act of turning to look out towards the street. Then, deliberately, without a change of expression, the Colonel put the cheroot between his lips and puffed. The blond young man turned back to stare wordlessly at Josh, leaning slightly forward.

'You want a bale of cotton, don't you?' Josh asked.

'Where would you get a bale of cotton, my boy?' the Colonel asked casually.

'We got one in the junkyard where I work.'

The blond young man let out his breath in a disappointed sigh.

'A junk man sold it to us just this morning,' Josh went on, hoping to get an offer.

The blond young man tensed again.

But the Colonel continued to appear relaxed and amiable. 'He didn't steal it, did he? We don't want to buy any stolen goods.'

'Oh, Uncle Bud didn't steal it, I'm sure,' Josh said. 'He must of found it somewheres.'

'Found a bale of cotton?' The Colonel sounded skeptical.

'Must have,' Josh contended. 'He spends every night traveling 'bout the streets, picking up junk what's been lost or thrown away. Where could he steal a bale of cotton?'

'And he sold it to you this morning?'

'Yassuh, to Mr Goodman, that is; he owns the junkyard, I just work there. But I can get it for you.'

'When?'

'Well, ain't nobody there now. We close at noon on Sat'day and Mr Goodman go home; but I can get it for you tonight if you wants it right away.'

'How?'

'Well, suh, I got a key, and we don't have to bother Mr Goodman; I can just sell it to you myself.'

'Well,' the Colonel said and puffed his cheroot. 'We'll pick you up in my cah at the 125th Street railroad station at ten o'clock tonight. Can you be there?'

'Oh, yassuh, I can be there!' Josh declared, then hesitated. 'That's all right, but how much you going to pay me?'

'Name your own price,' the Colonel said.

'A hundred dollars,' Josh said, holding his breath.

'Right,' the Colonel said.

10

Iris lay on her sofa in the sitting-room reading *Ebony* magazine and eating chocolate candy. She had been under twenty-four-hour surveillance since the hijacking. A police matron had spent the night in her bedroom while a detective had sat up in the sitting-room. Now there was another detective there alone. He had orders not to let her out of his sight. He had followed her from room to room, even keeping the bathroom door in view after having removed the razor blades and all other instruments by which she might injure herself.

He sat facing her in an overstuffed chair, leafing through a book called *Sex and Race* by W. G. Rogers. The only other books in the house were the Bible and *The Life of Marcus Garvey*. *Sex and Race* didn't interest him. Garvey didn't interest him either. He had read the Bible, at least all he needed to read.

He was bored. He didn't like his assignment. But the captain thought that sooner or later Deke was going to try to contact her, or she him, and he was taking every precaution. The telephone was bugged and the operators alerted to trace all incoming calls; and there was a police cruiser with a radio-telephone parked within thirty seconds' distance down the street, manned by four detectives.

The captain wanted Deke as bad as people in hell want ice water.

Iris threw down the magazine and sat up. She was wearing a silk print dress and the skirt hiked up, showing smooth yellow thighs above tan nylon stockings.

The book fell from the detective's hands.

'Why the hell don't you just arrest me and have it done with?' she flared in her vulgar husky voice.

Her voice grated on the detective's nerves. And her vulgar sensuality bothered him. He was a home-loving man with a wife and three children, and her perfumed voluptuous body with its effluvium of sex outraged his sensibilities. His puritanical soul felt affronted by this aura of sex and his perverse imagination filled him with a sense of guilt. But he had himself well under control.

'I just take orders, ma'am,' he said mildly. 'Any time you want to go to the station of your own accord I'll take you.'

'Shit,' she said, looking at him with disgust.

He was a tall, balding, redheaded, middle-aged man with a slight stoop. A small dried face between huge red ears gave him a monkeyish look and his white skin was blotched with large brown freckles. He was a plain-clothes precinct detective and he looked underpaid.

Iris examined him appraisingly. 'If you weren't such an ugly mother-raper at least we could pass time making love,' she said.

He was beginning to suspect that was the reason the captain had chosen him for the assignment and he felt slightly piqued. But he just grinned and said, jokingly, 'I'll put a sack over my head.'

She started to grin and then looked suddenly caught. Her face mirrored her thoughts. 'All right,' she said, getting up.

He looked alarmed. 'I was just joking,' he said foolishly.

'I'll go undress and you come in with nothing showing but your eyes and mouth.'

He grinned shamefacedly. 'You know I couldn't do that.'

'Why not?' she said. 'You ain't never had nobody like me.'

Red came out in his face as though it had caught fire. He looked like a small boy caught in a guilty act. 'Now, ma'am, you got to be sensible; this surveillance ain't going to last for ever—'

She turned quickly on her high heels and started towards the kitchen. Her walk was exaggerated, like that of a prostitute soliciting trade. But he had to follow her, cursing his instincts which kept defying his will.

She searched in the pantry, paying him no attention. He felt a slight trace of trepidation, fearing she might come out with a gun. But she found what she wanted, a brown paper sack. She turned and tried to put it over his head, but he jumped back and warded her off as though she held a live rattlesnake.

'I just wanted to try it for size,' she said, trying it on her own head instead. 'What are you anyway, a pansy?'

He was incensed by her allusion to his masculinity, but he consoled himself with the thought that in different circumstances he'd ride that yellow bitch until she yelled quits.

She switched past him, looking at him through the corners of her eyes and brushing him lightly with her hips. Then she deliberately shook her buttocks and waved the sack over her head like a dare and went into the bedroom.

He debated whether to follow her. This bitch was getting on his nerves, he told himself. She wasn't the only one who could make love, hell, his wife – He stopped that thought; that wasn't going to get him anywhere. Finally he gave in and followed her. Orders were orders, he told himself.

He found her with a pair of nail scissors in her hand, cutting eyeholes in the paper sack. He felt his ears burning. He looked about the room for a telephone extension, but didn't see any. Against his will he watched her cut out a place for his mouth. Unconsciously his vision strayed to her wide luscious mouth. She licked her lips and stuck out the tip of her tongue.

'Now, ma'am, this has gone far enough,' he protested.

She acted as though she hadn't heard, measuring his head with her eyes. Then she cut out a place for his ears, saying, 'Big ears, big you-know-what.' His ears burned as though on fire. For a moment she stood looking at her handiwork. He looked too.

'You've got to breathe, haven't you, baby?' she cooed and cut out a place for his nose.

'Now you come out of here and sit down and behave

yourself,' he said, trying to sound stern, but his voice was thick with tongue.

She went over to the small record player against the wall and put on a slow sexy blues number and stood for a moment weaving her body tantalizingly, snapping her fingers.

'I'll have to use force,' he warned.

She swung around and threw open her arms and advanced on him. 'Come on and force me, daddy,' she said.

He turned his back and stood in the doorway. She stood before the mirror and took off her ear-rings and necklace and ran her fingers through her hair, whistling a low accompaniment to the music, seemingly paying him no attention. Then she took off her dress.

He turned around to see what she was doing and damn near jumped out of his skin. 'Don't do that!' he shouted.

'You can't stop me from undressing in my own bedroom,' she said.

He went over and snatched up the dressing-table chair and planted it in the doorway and plopped himself down with an air of determination. 'All right, go ahead,' he said, turning his profile towards her so he could watch her for mischief through the corners of his eyes.

She tilted the dressing-table mirror so he could see her reflection, then pulled up her slip over her head. Now her creamy yellow body was clad only in a thin black strapless bra and tiny black pants trimmed with lace, over a garter belt.

'If you're scared, go home,' she taunted.

He gritted his teeth and continued to look away.

She took off her bra and pants and stood facing the mirror, cupping her breasts in her hands and gently caressing her teaties. With only the garter belt and nylon stockings and high-heeled shoes, she looked more nude than were she stark-naked. She saw him peeping at her reflection in the mirror, and began doing things with her stomach and hips.

He swallowed. From the neck up he was blindly furious; but from the neck down he was on a live wire edge. His insides were a battleground for his will and his lust, with his organs suffering the consequences. Whole areas of his body seemed on fire. The fire seemed breaking through his skin. Centipedes were crawling over his testicles and ants were attacking his phallus. He squirmed in his seat as it became more and more unbearable; his pants were too tight; his coat was too small; his head was too hot; his mouth was too dry.

With a flourish like a stripteaser removing her G-string, she took off one shoe and tossed it into his lap. He knocked it violently aside. She took off the other shoe and tossed it into his lap. He caught himself just in time to keep from grabbing it and biting it. She stripped off her stockings and garter belt and approached him to drape them about his neck.

He came to his feet like a Jack-in-the-box, saying in a squeaky voice, 'This has gone far enough.'

'No, it hasn't,' she said and moved into him.

He tried to push her away but she clung to him with all strength, pushing her stomach into him and wrapping her legs about his body. The odor of hot-bodied woman, wet cunt and perfume came up from her and drowned him.

'Goddamned whore!' he grated, and backed her to the bed. He tore off his coat, mouthing, 'I'll show you who's a pansy, you hot-ass slut.'

But at the last moment he regained enough composure to go hang his holstered pistol on the outside doorknob out of her reach, then he turned back towards her.

'Come and get it, pansy,' she taunted, lying on the bed with her legs open and her brown-nippled teats pointing at him like the vision of the great whore who lives in the minds of all puritanical men.

He stripped the zipper of his pants getting them off; popped the buttons from his shirt. When he was nude he tried to dive into her like into the sea, but she fought him off.

'You got to put on your sack first,' she said, snatching it up from the floor and pulling it down over his head backwards by mistake. 'Oop!' she cried.

Blinded momentarily, his hands flew up to tear it off, but she snatched it off first and slipped it on him the right way, so that only his eyes, mouth, nose and ears were showing.

'Now, baby, now,' she cried.

At that moment the telephone rang.

He jumped out of bed as though the furies had attacked him, his lust going out like a light. In his haste he knocked over the chair in the doorway, bruising his shins, and slammed into the doorjamb. Curses spewed from his gasping mouth like geysers of profanity. His lank white body with stooped shoulders and reddish hair moved awkwardly and looked as though it had just come from the grave.

With a quick lithe motion she opened a secret compartment in the bed-table, snatched up the receiver of the telephone extension, and cried, 'Help!' then quickly hung up.

In his haste he didn't hear her. He reached the telephone in the sitting-room and said breathlessly, 'Henderson speaking,' but the connection had been broken. She could hear him jiggling the receiver as she slipped on a sport coat and snatched up a pair of shoes. 'Hello, hello,' he was still shouting when she went bare-footed from the bedroom, locking the door behind her and taking the key, on back to the kitchen and went barefooted out of the house by the service door.

'Your party has hung up,' came the cool voice of the telephone operator.

He realized instantly the call had come from the police cruiser parked down the street. Panic exploded in his head as he realized he didn't even have his pistol. He ran naked back to the bedroom, snatched his pistol from the doorknob and tried to open the door. He found it locked. He became frantic. He couldn't risk shooting off the lock, he might hit her. The detectives from the cruiser would be there any instant and he'd catch hell. He had to get into the goddamned room. He tried breaking in, but it was a strong door with a good lock and his shoulder was taking a beating. He had forgotten the paper sack over his head.

The detectives from the cruiser had rushed there post-haste and had let themselves in with a pass-key. Over the telephone they had heard a woman cry for help. God only knew what was going on in there, but they were ready for it. They went into the apartment and spread out, their pistols in their hands. The sitting-room was empty.

They started through towards the rear. They drew up as though they had run into an invisible wall.

Down the hall was a buck-naked white man with a paper sack over his head and a holstered pistol in his hand, trying to break down the bedroom door with his bare shoulder.

No one ever knew who was the first one to explode with laughter.

Iris went down the service stairway barefooted. The sport coat was a belted wraparound of tan gaberdine and no one could tell she was naked underneath it. At the service exit on St Nicholas Avenue, she slipped into her shoes and peeped out into the street.

A car stood at the kerb in front of the apartment next door with the motor idling. A smartly dressed woman got out and ran towards the entrance. Iris cased her as an afternoon prostitute or a cheating wife. The man behind the wheel called softly, 'Bye now, baby,' and the woman fluttered her fingers and ducked out of sight.

Iris walked rapidly to the car, opened the door and got into the seat the other woman had just vacated. The man looked at her and said, ''Lo, baby,' as though she was the same woman he'd just told good-bye. He was a nice-looking chocolate-brown man dressed in a beautiful gray silk suit, but Iris just glanced at him.

'Drive on, daddy,' she said.

He steered from the curb and climbed St Nicholas Avenue. 'Running to or *from*?' he asked.

'Neither,' she said and when they came to the church at 142nd Street she said: 'Turn left here up to Convent.'

He left-turned up the steep hill past Hamilton Terrace to the quiet stretch of Convent Avenue north of City College.

'Right here,' she directed.

He right-turned north on Convent and when he came opposite the big apartment house she said, 'This is good, daddy.'

'Could be better,' he said.

'Later,' she said and got out.

'Coming back?' he called but she didn't hear him.

She was already running across the street, up the steps and into the foyer of a big well-kept apartment house with two automatic elevators. One was waiting and she took it to the fourth floor and turned towards the apartment at the back of the hall. A serious-looking man wearing black suspenders, a white collarless shirt, and sagging black pants opened the door. He took himself as seriously as a deacon in a solvent church.

'And what can I do for you, young lady?'

'I want to see Barry Waterfield.'

'He don't want to see you, he's already got company,' he leered. 'How 'bout me?'

'Stand aside, buster,' she said, pushing past him. 'And quit peeping through keyholes.'

She went straight to Barry's room but the door was locked and she had to knock.

'Who is it?' asked a woman's voice.

'Iris. Tell Barry to let me in.'

The door was unlocked and Barry stood to one side wearing only a purple silk dressing-gown. He closed the door behind her. A naked high-yellow woman lay in the bed with the sheet drawn up to her neck.

Clothes were draped over the only chair so Iris sat on the bed and ignored the naked woman. 'Where's Deke?' she asked Barry.

He hesitated before replying, 'He's all right, he's holed up safe.'

'If you're scared of talking then write it,' she said.

He looked uncomfortable. 'How'd you get away?'

'None of your business,' she snapped.

'You're sure you weren't tailed?'

'Don't make me laugh. If the cops wanted you they'd have had you long ago, stupid as you are. Just tell me where Deke is and let others do the thinking.'

'I'll call him,' he said, going towards the door.

She started to go with him but pressure on her hip stopped her, and she said only, 'Tell him I'm coming to see him.'

He went out and locked the door from the outside without answering.

The woman in the bed whispered quickly, 'He's with Mabel Hill in the Riverton Apartments,' and gave the street, number and telephone. 'I heard Barry talking.'

Iris looked blank. 'Mabel Hill. The only Mabel Hill I know vaguely is the Mabel Hill who was married to the John Hill who got croaked.'

'That's the cutie,' the woman whispered.

Iris couldn't control the rage that distorted her face.

Barry came in at that moment and looked at her, 'What's the matter with you?'

'Did you get Deke?' she countered.

He wasn't clever enough to dissemble and she knew he was lying when he said, 'Deke's cut out but he left word he would call me. He's changing his hideout.'

'Thanks for nothing,' Iris said, getting up to go.

The naked woman underneath the sheet said, 'Wait a minute and I'll give you a lift. I got my car downstairs.'

'No, you ain't,' Barry said roughly, pushing her down.

Iris unlocked the door and opened it, then turned and said, 'Go to hell, you big mother-raping square,' and slammed the door behind her.

11

Deke hadn't left Mabel's apartment but he'd had some close shaves. Two Homicide detectives had shown up at ten o'clock to question her again. He had hid in the closet, feeling defenseless and stark-naked without a gun, listening to every word with his heart in his mouth for fear he might have left something incriminating in the room, sweating blood from fear they might decide to search the house, and literally sweating in the close dusty heat. The dust had tickled his nose and he'd had to bite his lip to keep from sneezing.

Later, Mr Clay, the undertaker, had come and caught him in the bedroom and he'd had to hide under the bed. They had talked so interminably about money he had begun to wonder whether they intended to bury John Hill or hold his body for ransom.

Then Mabel had again turned into the weeping widow and bemoaned her fate with buckets of tears and enough hysterics for a revival meeting and nothing turned them off but to console her in bed. He had consoled her in bed so many times he'd concluded that if John Hill hadn't been shot she'd have loved him to death. Or was she like that because her mother-raping husband was dead? he asked himself. Was this some kind of freakishness that came out in her? Whore complex or something? But if she had to wait for her mother-raping husband to get killed before she could get her nuts off, hadn't he better take care himself? Or was he the exception being her minister; a minister is supposed to minister. Or was it that she thought if she sinned with her minister, God would forgive her; and the more she sinned, the greater would be God's forgiveness? Or did this bitch just have a hot ass? Anyway, he was goddamned tired of her everlasting urge and he was mentally damning John Hill to hell for getting himself killed.

But finally just before he'd had to holler calf-rope she'd calmed down enough to keep her appointment with the undertaker to go get John's body from the morgue.

It gave him a chance to contact Barry and his other two guns and arrange the caper with the Colonel for that night. So when she came home hysterical again he was ready for her.

Afterwards he was just lounging around in his shorts, drinking bourbon highballs, and she was in the kitchen doing he didn't know what – probably taking an aphrodisiac – when the telephone rang.

It was Barry, telling him that Iris had got loose and was looking for him. He didn't want to see Iris and he didn't want her to find him for fear she might be tailed. So he had given Barry his answer. He figured if the police picked her up it was better she didn't know where he was, then they couldn't get it out of her. Furthermore, she was too damn jealous, and one hitch at a time was enough.

To his annoyance he saw that Mabel had been listening to

his conversation. She made herself a lemon coke with ice and sat down beside him on the sofa.

'I'm glad she's not coming here,' she said.

'Jealousy is one of the seven cardinal sins,' he said.

For a moment he thought she was going to become hysterical again, but she just looked at him possessively and said, 'Oh, Reverend O'Malley, pray with me.'

'Later,' he snapped and got up to get a refill.

He was in the kitchen getting ice from the tray when the doorbell rang. Ice cubes flew into the air like startled birds. He didn't have time to retrieve them. He shoved the tray back, slammed the door shut and dumped his drink into the sink. Then he rushed into the closet in the back hall opposite the bathroom where his clothes were hung, waving a signal to Mabel as he passed through the sitting-room. He had found an old .32 revolver of John Hill's and he snatched it from the shelf where he had hidden it and held it in his shaking hand.

Mabel was flustered. She didn't know whether he had meant she should answer the door or not answer it.

The bell rang again, long and insistently, as though whoever it was must know she was at home. She decided to answer it. There was a chain on the door; and anyway, even if the police did catch Reverend O'Malley there, he hadn't done anything really wrong, she thought. He was just trying to get their money back.

She unlocked the door and someone tried to push it open but the chain caught it. Then through the crack she saw the face of Iris, distorted with rage.

'Open this mother-raping door,' Iris grated in her throaty voice, her lips popping wetly.

'He's not here,' Mabel said smugly from behind the chained door. 'Reverend O'Malley, I mean.'

'I'll start screaming and get the police here and then you tell them that,' Iris threatened.

'If that's all he means to you . . .' Mabel began and flung wide the door. 'Come in.' And she chained and locked the door after her.

Iris went through the house like a gun dog looking for a game bird.

'He heard what you said,' Mabel called after her.

'These mother-raping bitches!' Deke muttered to himself and came out of the closet, covered with a film of sweat, still holding the pistol in his hand. 'Why don't you have some sense?' he said to Iris's back as she was looking into the bathroom.

She wheeled, and her eyes widened and went pitch-black when she saw him in his shorts. Her face convulsed with uncontrollable jealousy. All she thought of then was him in bed with this other woman.

'You chickenshit cheat,' she mouthed, spittle flying from her popping lips. 'You sneaking pimp. You get me out of the way and shack up with some chippy whore.'

'Shut up,' he said dangerously. 'I had to hide out.'

'Hide out? Between this slut's legs!'

From the doorway into the sitting-room Mabel said, 'Reverend O'Malley is just trying to get our money back; he doesn't want it all bungled by the police.'

Iris turned on her. 'I suppose you call him Reverend O'Malley in bed,' she stormed. 'If your mouth isn't too full.'

'I'm not like you,' Mabel said angrily. 'I do it the way God intended.'

Iris rushed at her and tried to scratch her face. Her coat flew open, showing her naked body. Mabel grabbed her by the wrists and shouted tauntingly, 'I'm going to have his baby.' Iris couldn't have a baby and it was the worst thing Mabel could have said. Iris went berserk; she spat in Mabel's face and kicked her shins and struggled to break free. But Mabel was the stronger and she spat back in Iris's face and let go her hands to grab her hair. Iris scratched her on the neck and shoulders and tore her negligee, but Mabel was pulling her hair out by the roots and pain filled her eyes with tears, blinding her.

Deke grabbed Iris by the coat collar with his left hand, still holding the revolver in his right. He hadn't had time to put it away and he was afraid to drop it on the floor. Iris's coat came off in his hand and she was naked except for shoes and there was nothing else to clutch. So he tried to break Mabel's grip on her hair. But Mabel was so infuriated she wouldn't turn loose.

'Break loose, you mother-raping whores!' Deke grated and hit at Mabel's hands with his pistol.

He mashed her fingers against Iris's skull. Iris screamed and scratched eight red lines across his ribs. He hit her in the stomach with his free left hand, then grabbed Mabel's negligee to pull her away. The negligee came off in his hand and she was naked too. Iris clawed her like a cat, streaking her body, and the blood began to flow. Mabel couldn't use her hands but she bent Iris's head down with her arms and bit her in the shoulder. Screaming in pain, with her head bent down, Iris saw the pistol in Deke's hand. She snatched it and shot Mabel in the body until it was empty.

It happened so fast it didn't register on Deke's brain. He heard the thunder of shots; he saw the surprised look of anguish on Mabel's face as she loosened her grip on Iris's head and slowly began to crumble. But it was like a horrifying nightmare before the horror comes.

Then awareness hit him like a time bomb exploding in his head. His body erupted into action as his brain went rattled with panic. He hit Iris in the breast with his left fist, rocking her back, and crossed a right to her neck, knocking her off-balance. He kicked her in the stomach with his bare foot and, when she doubled over, hit her on the back of the head with the side of his fist, knocking her face downward to the floor.

Suddenly the panic started going off in his head like a chain of explosions, each one bigger than the ones before. He leapt over Iris's prostrate figure, started towards the closet to get his clothes, then wheeled and snatched up the pistol from the floor where Iris had dropped it. He didn't look at Mabel; his mind knew she was dead but he tried not to think of it. Somewhere in his head he knew he didn't have any more bullets for the pistol which wasn't his. He dropped it to the floor as though it was burning his hand.

Wheeling, he leapt into the hall, rushed to the closet. The

knob slipped in his hand and one half of his brain began cursing, the other half praying.

In the front of all other thoughts was the sure knowledge that in a few minutes the police would come. Before the shooting, there had been enough screaming to raise the dead; and he knew in this nigger-proper house someone would have called the police. He knew his only hope was flight. To get away before the police got there. It was his life. And these mother-raping seconds were running out. But he knew he'd never get away looking half-dressed. Some meddling mother-raper in this nigger-heaven house would stop him on suspicion and he didn't have a gun.

He tried to dress fast. Quick-quick-quick, urged his brain. But his mother-raping fingers had turned to thumbs. It seemed as though it took him seven hundred mother-raping years to button up his shirt; and some more mother-raping centuries to lace his shoes.

He leapt to the mirror to tie his tie and search for tell-tale scratches. His dark face was powder gray, his stretched eyes like black eight-balls, but there were no scratches showing. He was trying to decide whether to take the elevator down five floors and walk the remaining two, or take the fire-escape and try the roof. He didn't know how these buildings were made, whether the roofs were on the same level and he could get from one to another. In the back of his head he kept thinking there was something he was leaving. Then he realized it was Iris's life. Fear urged him to go back and take the pistol and beat her to death; stop her from talking forever.

He turned from the bathroom, turned towards the sitting-room, and was caught in midstep by the hammering on the door. He ran on his toes to the back window in the bedroom that let onto the outside fire-escape. He opened it quickly, went out and down without hesitation. He didn't have time to decide; he was committed. His feet felt nothing as they touched the iron steps of the steep ladder. His eyes searched the windows he passed.

The fire-escape was on one of the private streets of the housing development. He could only be seen by people across the street or in the windows he passed. Halfway down he saw the hem of a curtain fluttering from a half-open bedroom window. He didn't hesitate. He stopped at the window, opened it and went in. The apartment was arranged the same as the one he had just quit. There was no one in the bedroom. He went through on his toes, praying the house was empty, but with no intention of stopping if it was filled with wedding guests. He came out into the back hall. He could hear a woman singing in the kitchen at the front of the sitting-room. He got to the front door, found it locked and chained. He tried to open it silently; he held his breath as he turned the lock and took off the chain. Time was drowning him in a whirlpool of flying seconds. He got the door unlocked, the chain off. He heard the singing stop. He closed the door quickly behind him and ran down the hall towards the service stairway. He got onto the landing and closed the door just before he heard a faint woman's voice call, 'Henry, where are you, Henry?'

He went down the stairway like a dive-bomber, didn't stop until he was in the basement. He heard footsteps coming his way. He froze behind the closed door, assembling his face, making up his story. But the footsteps went on past him into silence. Cautiously he looked out into the basement. No one was in sight. He went in the direction opposite the one the footsteps had taken and found a door. It opened onto a short flight of stairs. He went up the stairs and found a heavy iron door locked with a Yale snap lock. He unlocked it and pushed the door open a crack and looked out.

He saw 135th Street. Colored people were out in numbers, walking about in their summertime rags. Two men were eating watermelon from a wagon. In the wagon the melons were kept on ice to keep them cool. Children were gathered around a small pushcart, eating cones of shaved ice flavored with colored syrups from bottles. Others were playing stickball in the street. Women were conversing in loud voices; a drunken man weaved down the sidewalk, cursing the world; a blind beggar tapped a path with his white stick, rattling a penny in his tin cup; a dog was messing on the sidewalk; a line of men was sitting in the shade on the steps of a church, talking about the white folks and the Negro problem.

He stepped from the doorway and crossed the street, and soon he was lost in that big turbulent sea of black humanity which is Harlem.

12

When Grave Digger and Coffin Ed came on duty at 8 p.m., Lieutenant Anderson said, 'Your car was found abandoned up at 163rd Street and Edgecombe Drive. Does that tell you anything?'

Coffin Ed backed against the wall in the shadows where Anderson couldn't see his expression, but Anderson heard him make some kind of sound that sounded like a snort. Grave Digger perched a ham on the edge of the desk and massaged his chin. The curve of his back concealed the bulge of the .38 revolver over his heart but made his shoulders look wider. He thought about it and chuckled.

'Tell me it was stolen,' he said finally. 'What you think, Ed?'

'Either that or it drove itself.'

Anderson looked quizzically from one to the other. 'Well, was it stolen?'

Grave Digger chuckled again. 'Think we're going to admit it if it was?'

'It was them chickens, boss?' Coffin Ed said.

Lieutenant Anderson reddened slightly and shook his head. He didn't always dig the private humor of his two ace detectives and sometimes it made him feel uncomfortable. But he realized they attached no significance to the fact their car had been stolen. Whenever they got a clue of importance the air around them became electric.

It became electric now when he said, 'We're holding Deke O'Hara's woman Iris on a homicide rap.'

Both detectives froze in that immobility which denotes full

attention. But neither spoke; they knew a story went with it. They waited.

'She was arrested in the apartment of the man killed in the Back-to-Africa hijack, John Hill. John Hill's wife Mabel had been shot five times; she was dead when the police arrived. Both women were nude and badly mauled – scratched and beaten as though they'd had a furious go with each other. Tenants had called the police before the shooting to report what sounded like a woman fight in the apartment. A gun was found on the floor – a .32 revolver. It had been recently fired and there's no doubt it is the murder gun; but it has gone to ballistics. Her fingerprints were on the stock and smeared on the trigger but are partly obliterated by a clear set of prints by a man. Homicide figures a man handled the gun afterwards; maybe Deke. They're checking against his Bertillon card and we'll soon know.'

Grave Digger and Coffin Ed exchanged looks but said nothing.

'Iris contends Deke wasn't there. An hour earlier she had escaped from her own apartment. She admits going there looking for him but swears he hadn't been there. She had escaped on a ruse – you'll hear all about it. She admits that she and the Hill woman had a fight and she says she took the gun away from the Hill woman and it went off accidentally. She says it was a private fight and had nothing to do with the Back-to-Africa hijacking, but she won't give any reason for it.'

Both detectives turned and looked at him as though guided by the same impulse.

'Do you want to talk to her?' Anderson asked.

The detectives exchanged looks.

'How long after the shooting before the car crew arrived?' Grave Digger asked.

'About two and a half minutes.'

'What floor?'

'Seventh, but there's a fast elevator and he would have had time to get down and away before the police arrived,' he said, reading their thoughts.

'Not if they were naked,' Coffin Ed said.

Anderson blushed. He hadn't gotten to be a lieutenant by being a square but he was always slightly embarrassed by their bald way of stating the facts of life.

'And he'd have to dress well in that neighborhood,' Grave Digger added.

'And completely,' Coffin Ed concluded.

'There was an open window on the fire-escape at the back,' Anderson said. 'But no one has been found who saw him leave.' He looked through the reports on his desk. 'A woman on the fourth floor directly below telephoned to report that she thought she heard her front door being opened and when she went to look found the chain off. But nothing was missing from the house. Homicide found the window open onto the fire-escape but she said she had left it open. Any prints that might have been left on the doorknob were smeared by her son coming and going afterwards, and she wiped whatever prints there may have been from the windowsill when dusting.'

'They believe in keeping spick and span in those apartments,' Grave Digger said.

'So clean that even Deke gets away clean,' Coffin Ed said.

'Who knows?' Grave Digger said. 'Let's go talk to her.'

They had her taken from the cell where she was held, awaiting magistrate's court Monday morning, to the interrogation room in the basement known to the Harlem underworld as the 'Pigeons' Nest'. It was claimed that more pigeons were hatched there than beneath all the eaves in Harlem.

It was a soundproof, windowless room with a stool in the center bolted to the floor and surrounded by floodlights bright enough to make the blackest man transparent.

But only the overhead light was on when the jailer brought her in. She saw Grave Digger standing beside the stool, waiting for her. The door was closed and locked behind her. She had a sudden feeling of being taken from the earth. Then she saw the vague outline of Coffin Ed backed against the wall in the shadows. His acid-burned face looked like a Mardi Gras masque to scare little children. She shuddered.

Grave Digger said, 'Sit down, baby, and tell us how you are.'

She stood defiantly. 'I'm not talking in this hole. You've got it bugged.'

'What for? Ed and me are going to remember anything you say.'

Coffin Ed stepped forward. He looked like the dead killer in the play *Winterset*, coming up out of East River. 'Sit down anyway,' he said.

She sat down. He stepped towards her. Grave Digger switched on the floodlights. She blinked. Coffin Ed had intended to slap her. But now he saw her. He caught his hand. 'Well, well, well,' he said. 'Ain't you beautiful.'

Her smooth, yellow, creamed and perfumed flesh of the day before now ran through all the colors of the spectrum, from black to bright orange; her neck was swollen, one breast was twice the size of the other; red, raw scratches ran down her face, over her neck and shoulders, to disappear beneath her dress; and her hair looked like it had been doused in the river Styx.

'It could have been worse,' Grave Digger said.

'How?' she asked, squinting at the bright lights. The bruises and scratches looked painted on her transparent skin.

'You could be dead.'

She shrugged faintly. 'You call that worse?'

'Well, hell, you're still alive,' Coffin Ed said. 'And you can get eight thousand and seven hundred dollars' reward money if you help us.'

'How about this chickenshit rap they're holding me on?' she bargained.

'That's your baby,' Grave Digger said.

She winced at the word *baby*; that was what had started it all.

'And it ain't chickenshit,' Coffin Ed added.

'It's a rap,' she said.

'Where's Deke?' Grave Digger asked.

'If I knew where the mother-raper was, I'd sure tell you.'

'But you went there to see him.'

She sat thinking for a time, then seemingly she made up her mind. 'He was there,' she admitted. 'In his drawers. Why else would I be mad enough to shoot the chippy whore. But I don't remember him getting away. He had knocked me unconscious.' After a moment she added, 'I wonder why he didn't kill me.'

'How did you get away from the detective guarding you?' he asked.

She laughed suddenly and her marks formed another pattern, like one of those innocuous pictures revealing shocking obscenities at certain angles. 'That was a beauty,' she said. 'It could only happen to a white man.'

Grave Digger looked sardonic. 'As long as it's got nothing to do with this caper, let's skip it.'

'It was just between me and him.'

'What we want to know, baby, is what was the set-up of Deke's Back-to-Africa pitch.'

'Where have you been all your life, you don't know that?' she said.

'We know it. We just want you to confirm it.'

Some of her flippancy returned. 'What's in it for me?' she asked.

Coffin Ed stepped forward. 'Try it on, anyway,' he grated. 'Just for size.'

She looked towards his voice but she couldn't see him through the light and that made it sound more frightening.

'Well, you know he was going to take the money and blow,' she began. 'But not until he'd played other cities too. He had the armored car made. The guards were his. Only the agents and other personnel were squares. The detectives were to come in and get him off the hook by confiscating the money until an investigation could be made. Since all the suckers thought he was honest, there was nothing to fear. He borrowed the idea from the Marcus Garvey movement.'

'We know all that,' Grave Digger said. 'We want some names and descriptions.'

She gave him the name and address of Barry Waterfield, alias Baby Jack Johnson, alias Big Papa Domore. She said the two guns who had guarded the truck were known as Four-Four and Freddy; she had never heard them called by their real monickers and she didn't know where they were staying. They were Deke's men, he probably got them from prison; and he kept them out of sight. The dead man who had impersonated the other detective had been called Elmer Sanders. They were all from Chicago.

That was what they wanted and Coffin Ed relaxed.

But Grave Digger asked, 'He wasn't putting the double-cross on his own men by having himself hijacked?'

She thought for a moment, then said, 'No, I don't think so. I'm reckoning on the way he's acted afterwards.'

'Any idea who they were?'

'I keep thinking of the Syndicate. Just because I can't think of anyone else, I guess.'

'It wasn't the Syndicate,' Grave Digger stated flatly.

'Then I don't know. He never seemed scared of anybody else – Of course he never told me everything.'

Grave Digger smiled sourly at the understatement.

'What you got on Deke?' Coffin Ed asked.

She looked towards the voice behind the lights and felt a tremor run through her body. Why did that mother-raper scare her so? she wondered. Finally she said simply, 'The proof.'

Both detectives froze as though listening for an echo. It didn't come.

'You want us to take him, don't you?' Grave Digger said.

'Take him,' she said.

'Be ready,' he said.

'I'm ready,' she said.

On their way out they stopped again to see Lieutenant Anderson and have him put a tail on Barry Waterfield.

Then Grave Digger said, 'We're going to put our pigeons on Deke. If they get anything they'll phone it to you and you call us in the car.'

'Right,' Anderson said. 'I'll have a couple of cars on alert for an emergency.'

'There ain't going to be any emergency,' Coffin Ed said and they left.

They began contacting all the stool pigeons they could reach. They got many tips on unsolved crimes and wanted criminals but nothing on Deke O'Hara. They filed away the information for later use, but for all of their stool pigeons they had only one instruction: 'Find Deke O'Hara. He's loose on the town. Telephone Lieutenant Anderson at the precinct station, drop the message and hang up. And disappear.'

It was a slow, tedious process, but they had no other. There were five hundred thousand colored people in Harlem and so many holes in which to hide that sewer rats have been known to get lost.

Barry telephoned Deke at Mabel's from Bowman's Bar at the corner of St Nicholas Place and 155th Street on the dot of 10 p.m. as he had been instructed. The phone rang once, twice, three times. Abruptly a warning sounded in his head; his sixth sense told him the police were there and were tracing the call. He hung up as though letting go a snake and headed towards the exit. The bar girl looked at him as he passed, eyebrows raised, wondering what had spurred him so suddenly. He tossed fifty cents on the bar to pay for his thirty-five-cent beer and went out fast, looking for a taxi.

He caught one headed downtown and said, 'Drop me at 145th and Broadway.' When they turned west on 145th he heard the faint whine of a siren headed towards Bowman's and sweat filmed his upper lip.

Broadway is a fringe street. Black Harlem has moved solidly to its east side but its west side is still mixed with Puerto Ricans and leftover whites. He got out on the north-east corner, crossed the street, walked rapidly up to 149th and went down towards the Hudson River. He turned into a small neat apartment house halfway down the block and climbed three flights of stairs.

The light-bright-damn-near-white woman who had been naked in his bed when Iris had called opened the door for him. She was talking before she closed it: 'Iris killed Mabel Hill right after she left us. Ain't that something? They got her in jail. It just came over the radio.' Her voice was strident with excitement.

'Deke?' he asked tensely.

'Oh, he got away. They're looking for him. Let me fix you a drink.'

His gaze swept the three-room apartment, reading every sign. It was a nice place but he didn't see it. He was thinking that Deke must have tried to contact him while he was out.

'Drive me home,' he said.

She began to pout but one look at his face cooled her.

Five minutes later, the young colored detective Paul Robinson, assigned with his partner Ernie Fisher to tail Barry, saw him get out of the closed convertible in front of the apartment where he lived and run quickly up the stairs. Paul was sitting in a black Ford sedan with regular Manhattan plates, parked across the street, pointed uptown. He got Lieutenant Anderson on the radio-telephone and said, 'He just came in.'

'Keep on him,' Anderson said.

When Barry got off at the fourth floor there was a young man standing in the hall waiting to go down. He was Ernie Fisher. For two hours he had been standing there, waiting to descend every time the elevator stopped. But this time he went. When he came out on the street he got into a two-toned Chevrolet sedan parked in front of the entrance, pointed downtown.

Paul got out of the Ford sedan, crossed the street and entered the apartment without glancing at his partner. He took the stand on the fourth floor, waiting to descend.

The deacon-looking landlord told Barry he had had several urgent calls from a Mr Bloomfield who had left a message saying if he didn't want the car he had found another buyer. Barry went immediately to the telephone and called Mr Bloomfield.

'Bloomfield,' replied a voice having no affinity to such a name.

'Mr Bloomfield, I want the car,' Barry said. 'I'm ready right now to close the deal. I've been out raising the money.'

'Come to my office right away,' Mr Bloomfield said and hung up.

'Right away, Mr Bloomfield,' Barry said into the dead phone for the landlord's ears.

He stopped in his room on his way out, strapped on a shoulder holster with a .45 Colt automatic, and changed into a loose black silk sport jacket made to accommodate the gun.

When he came out into the hall he saw a young man standing by the elevator, jabbing the button impatiently. There was nothing about the young man to incur suspicion or jog his memory. He stood beside him and they rode down together. The young man walked rapidly ahead of him and ran down the stairs and across the street without looking back. Barry didn't give him another thought.

A Chevrolet sedan parked at the curb was just moving off and Barry hailed a taxi that drew up in the place vacated. The taxi went downtown, through City College, past the convent from which the street derives its name, and down the hill towards 125th Street. The Chevrolet stayed ahead. The Ford had made a U-turn and was following the taxi a block to the rear.

Convent came to an end at 125th Street. Taking a chance, Ernie turned his Chevrolet left, towards Eighth Avenue. The taxi turned sharply right. The Ford closed in behind it.

Barry had seen the Ford through the rear window. He had his driver stop suddenly in front of a bar. The Ford whizzed past, the driver looking the other way, and turned left where the street splits.

Barry had his driver make a U-turn and head back towards the east side. He didn't see anything unusual about the Chevrolet pulling out from the curb near Eighth Avenue; it looked just like any other hundreds of Chevrolets in Harlem – a poor man's Cadillac. He had the taxi turn right at the Theresa Hotel on Seventh Avenue and pull to the curb. The Chevrolet kept on down 125th Street.

Barry dismissed his taxi and entered the hotel lobby, then suddenly turned about and went outside and had the doorman hail another taxi. He didn't even notice the black Ford sedan parked near the entrance to Sugar Ray's bar. This street was always lined with parked cars. The taxi kept straight on down to 116th Street and turned sharp right. The Ford kept straight ahead. There were a number of cars coming cross town from Lenox on 116th Street, among which were several Chevrolet sedans.

The red light caught the taxi at Eighth Avenue and among

the stream of cars going north was a black Ford sedan. Harlem was full of Ford sedans – the poor man's Lincoln – and Barry didn't give it a look. When the light changed he had the taxi turn right and stop in the middle of the block. The black Ford sedan was nowhere in sight. The Chevrolet sedan kept on across Eighth Avenue.

Paul double-parked the Ford around the corner on 117th Street and quickly walked back to Eighth Avenue. He saw Barry enter a poolroom down the street. He crossed Eighth Avenue, keeping the poolroom in sight, and stood on the opposite sidewalk. Hundreds of Saturday-night drunks and hopheads were standing about, weaving in and out the joints, putting forth their voices. There was nothing to set him apart other than he was better dressed than most and the whores started buzzing around him.

Within a minute a Chevrolet sedan turned south on Eighth from 119th Street and double-parked near 116th Street behind two other double-parked cars.

Paul crossed the street and made as though to enter the poolroom, then seemed to think better of it and turned aimlessly towards 117th Street, collecting whores from all directions.

The Chevrolet sedan moved off, turned the corner on 116th Street and double-parked out of sight. Ernie called Lieutenant Anderson and reported, 'He went into a poolroom on Eighth Avenue,' and gave the name of the poolroom and number.

'Stay with him,' Anderson said, and got Grave Digger and Coffin Ed on the radio-telephone.

13

They were talking to a blind man when they got the call.

The blind man was saying, 'There were five white men in this tank. That in itself was enough to make me suspicious. Then when it stopped, the white man with the goatee who was sitting in the front seat leaned across the driver and beckoned to this colored boy who had been loitering around the station. I turned like I was alarmed when I heard the door click and took a picture. I think I got a clear shot.'

Coffin Ed answered the radio-phone and heard Anderson say, 'They got him stationed for the time being in a pool hall on Eighth Avenue,' and gave the name and number.

'We're on the way,' Coffin Ed said. 'Just play it easy.'

'It's your baby,' Anderson said. 'Holler if you need help.'

Grave Digger said to the blind man, 'Keep it until later, Henry.'

'Nothing ever spoils,' Henry said and got out, putting on his dark glasses at the same time.

It was five minutes by right from where they were parked on Third Avenue, but Grave Digger made it in three and one half without using the horn.

They found Paul in the Ford across the street from the poolroom. He said Barry was inside and Ernie was bottling up the back.

'You go and help him,' Grave Digger said. 'We'll take care of this end.'

They pulled into the spot he had vacated and settled down to wait.

'You think he's contacting Deke in there?' Coffin Ed said.

'I ain't thinking,' Grave Digger said.

Time passed.

'If I had a dollar an hour for all the time I've spent waiting for criminals to come and get themselves caught, I'd take some time off and go fishing,' Coffin Ed said.

Grave Digger chuckled. 'You're a glutton for punishment, man. That's the only thing I don't like about fishing, the waiting.'

'Yeah, but there ain't any danger at the end of that kind of waiting.'

'Hell, Ed, if you were scared of danger you'd have been a bill collector.'

It was Coffin Ed's turn to chuckle. 'Naw I wouldn't,' he said.

'Not in Harlem, Digger, not in Harlem. There ain't any more dangerous a job in Harlem than collecting bills.'

They lapsed into silence, thinking of all the reasons folks in Harlem didn't pay bills. And they thought about the eighty-seven thousand dollars taken from those people who were already so poor they dreamed hungry. 'If I had the mother-raper who got it I'd work his ass at fifty cents an hour shoveling shit until he paid it off,' Coffin Ed said.

'There ain't that much shit,' Grave Digger said drily. 'What with all this newfangled shitless food.'

Men came from the poolroom and others entered. Some they knew, others they didn't, but none they wanted.

An hour passed.

'Think they've lammed?' Coffin Ed ventured.

'How the hell would I know?' Grave Digger said. 'Maybe they're waiting like us.'

A car pulled up before the poolroom and double-parked. Suddenly they sat up. It was a black, chauffeur-driven Lincoln Mark IV, as out of place in that neighborhood as the Holy Virgin.

A uniformed colored chauffeur got out and hastened into the poolroom. Within a matter of seconds he came back and got behind the wheel and started the motor. Suddenly Barry came out. For a moment he stood on the sidewalk, looking up and down, casing the street. He looked across the street. Coffin Ed had ducked out of sight and Grave Digger was studiously searching for an acquaintance among the bums lounging in the doorways on their side of the street, and all Barry saw of him was the back of his head. It looked like the back of any other big black man's head. Satisfied, Barry turned and rapped on the door and another man came out and went straight to the limousine and got in beside the driver. Then Deke came out and went fast between two parked cars and got into the back of the limousine and Barry followed. The limousine took off like a streak, but had to slow for the lights at 125th Street.

Grave Digger had to make a U-turn and by the time he got straightened out, the limousine was out of sight.

'We ought to have got some help,' Coffin Ed said.

'Too late now,' Grave Digger said, gunning the hopped-up car past the slow-moving traffic. 'We ought to've had second sight, too.'

He went straight north on Eighth Avenue without pausing to reconnoiter.

'Where the hell are we going?' Coffin Ed asked.

'Damned if I know,' Grave Digger confessed.

'Hell,' Coffin Ed said disgustedly. 'One day we lose our car and the next day we lose our man.'

'Just let's don't lose our lives,' Grave Digger shouted above the roar of the traffic they were passing.

'Pull down,' Coffin Ed shouted back. 'At this rate we'll be in Albany.'

Grave Digger pulled up to the curb at 145th Street. 'All right, let's give this some thought,' he said.

'What kind of mother-raping thought?' Coffin Ed said.

He was near enough to the scene where the acid had been thrown into his face to evoke the memory. The tic started in his face and his nerves got on edge.

Grave Digger looked at him and looked away. He knew how he was feeling but this wasn't the time for it, he thought. 'Listen,' he said. 'They were driving a stolen car. What does that mean?'

Coffin Ed came back. 'A rendezvous or a getaway.'

'Getaway for what? If they had the money they'd already be gone.'

'Well, where the hell would you rendezvous, if you weren't scared?' Coffin Ed said.

'That's right,' Grave Digger said. 'Underneath the bridge.'

'Anyway, we ain't scared,' Coffin Ed said.

The two guns who had handled Deke's armored car were on the front seat, the same one driving. He was also a car thief specialist, and had stolen this one. He doused the lights when they came to the end of Bradhurst Avenue and eased the big car off the road that led to the Polo Grounds, stopping between two stanchions underneath the 155th Street bridge.

'You two guys spot the car,' Deke ordered. 'We'll wait here.'

The gunmen got out, careful of the rifles on the floor, and split in the darkness.

Deke took a large manila envelope from his inside coat pocket and handed it to Barry. 'Here's the list,' he said. He had had it made weeks before from the telephone directories of Manhattan, the Bronx and Brooklyn by a public stenographer in the Theresa Hotel. 'You let him do the talking. We're going to have you covered every second.'

'I don't like this,' Barry confessed. He was scared and nervous and he couldn't see the Colonel giving any clues away. 'He ain't going to pay no fifty grand for this,' he said, taking it gingerly and sticking it into his inside pocket above his pistol.

'Naturally not,' Deke said. 'But don't argue with him. Answer his questions and take whatever he gives you.'

'Hell, Deke, I don't dig this,' Barry protested. 'What's this cracker outfit got to do with our eighty-seven grand?'

'Let me do the thinking,' Deke said coldly. 'And give me that rod.'

'Hell, you want me to go with my bare ass to see that nut? You're asking me a lot.'

'What the hell can happen to you? We're all going to have you covered. Man, goddammit, you're going to be as safe as in the arms of Jesus Christ.'

As Barry was handing over the gun he remembered, 'That's what the Colonel said.'

'He was right,' Deke said, taking the pistol from the holster and sticking it into his right coat pocket. 'Just his reasons are wrong.'

They were silent with their thoughts until the gunmen materialized out of the darkness and took their places on the front seat. 'They're over by the El,' the driver said, easing the big car soundlessly through the dark as though he had eyes of infra-red.

The trucks and cars manned by the workers cleaning the stadium were moving about in the black dark area beneath the subway extensions and the bridge, which was used by day as a parking space, their bright lights lancing the darkness. Once the black limousine of the Colonel was picked up in a beam of light, but it didn't look out of place in that area where architects and bankers came at night to plan the construction of new buildings when the old stadium was razed. The Lincoln kept to the edge of the area, avoiding the lights, and stopped behind a big trailer truck parked for the night.

The gunmen picked their rifles from the floor and got out on each side and took stations at opposite ends of the truck. They had .303 automatic Savage rifles loaded with .190-point brass-nosed shells, equipped with telescopic sights.

'All right,' Deke said. 'Play it cool.'

Barry shook his head once like shaking off a premonition. 'My mama taught me more sense than this,' he said and got out. Deke got out on the other side. Barry walked around the front of the truck and kept on ahead. His black coat and dark gray trousers were swallowed by the darkness. Deke stopped beside one of his gunmen.

'How does it look?' he asked.

In the telescopic sight Barry looked like the silhouette of half a man neatly quartered, the sight lines crossing in the center of his back as the gunman tracked him through the dark.

'All right,' the gunman said. 'Black on black, but it'll do.'

'Don't let him get hurt,' Deke said.

'He ain't gonna get hurt,' the gunman said.

When Barry stopped walking, two other silhouettes came into the sights, close together like three wise monkeys.

The gunmen widened their sights to take in the limousine and its occupants. Their eyes had become accustomed to the dark. In the faint glow of reflected light, the scene was clearly visible. The Colonel sat in the front seat beside the blond young man in the driver's seat. A white man stood on each side of Barry and a third, standing in front of him, shook him down and took the envelope from his inside pocket and passed it to the Colonel. The Colonel put it into his pocket without looking at it. Suddenly the two men flanking Barry seized his arms and twisted them behind him.

The third man moved up close in front of him.

Grave Digger cut off his lights when they approached the

dark sinister area underneath the bridge. In the faint light reflected from the lights of the trucks and filtering down from above, the area looked like a jungle of iron stanchions, standing like giant sentinels in the eerie dark. The skin on Coffin Ed's face was jumping with a life of its own and Grave Digger felt his collar choking as his neck swelled.

He pulled the car over into the darkness and let the engine idle soundlessly. 'Let's load some light,' he said.

'I got light,' Coffin Ed said.

Grave Digger nodded in the dark and took out his long-barreled, nickelplated .38-caliber revolver and replaced the first three shells with tracer bullets. Coffin Ed drew his revolver, identical to the special made job of Grave Digger's, and spun the cylinder once. Then he held it in his lap. Grave Digger slipped his into his side coat pocket. Then they sat in the dark, listening for the sound that might never come.

'Where's the cotton?' the Colonel asked Barry so abruptly it hit him like a slap.

'Cotton!' he echoed with astonishment.

Then something clicked in his brain. He remembered the small sign advertising for a bale of cotton in the window of the Back-to-the-Southland office. His eyes stretched. *Good God!* he thought. Then he felt the danger of the instant squeeze him like an iron vise. His body turned ice cold as though the blood had been squeezed out; his head exploded with terror. His mind sought an answer that would save his life, but he could only think of one that might satisfy the Colonel. 'Deke's got it!' he blurted out.

Everything happened at once. The Colonel made a gesture. The white men tightened their grips on Barry's arms. The third man in front of Barry drew a hunting knife from his belt. Barry lunged to one side, throwing the man holding his right arm around behind him. And the big hard unmistakable sound of a high-powered rifle shot exploded in the night, followed so quickly by another it sounded like an echo.

The gunman beside Deke had shot the white man behind Barry dead through the heart. But the high-powered big-game bullet had gone through the white man's body and penetrated Barry just above the heart and lodged in his breastbone. The gunman at the other end of the truck had taken the white man holding Barry's left arm, the bullet going through one lung, ricocheting off a rib and ending up in his hip. All three fell together.

The third man with the knife wheeled and ran blindly. The big limousine sprang forward like a big cat, knocked him down, and ran over his body as though it were a bump in the road.

'Take the car!' Deke yelled, meaning, 'Take out the car.'

His gunmen thought he meant take their car and they wheeled and ran towards the Lincoln.

'Mother-rapers,' Deke mouthed and followed them.

Grave Digger was coming from three hundred yards' distance, his bright lights stabbing the darkness from where he'd heard the shots. Coffin Ed was shouting into the radio-telephone: 'All cars! The Polo Grounds. Seal it!'

The Lincoln was turning past the head of the trailer truck on two wheels when Grave Digger caught it in his lights. Coffin Ed leaned out the window and snapped a tracer bullet. It made a long incandescent streak, missing the rear of the disappearing Lincoln and sloping off towards the innocent earth. Then the truck was between them.

'Stop for Barry!' Deke yelled to his driver.

The driver tamped the brakes and the car skidded straight to a stop. Deke leaped out and rushed towards the grotesque pile of bodies. The white man who'd been run over was writhing in agony and Deke hit him with the .45 in passing and crushed his brain. Then he tried to pull Barry from beneath the other bodies.

'No!' Barry screamed in pain.

'For God's sake, the key!' Deke cried.

'Cotton . . .' Barry whispered, blood coming from his mouth and nose as his big body relaxed in death.

Grave Digger came around the truck so fast the little car slewed sideways and Coffin Ed's tracer bullet intended for the gasoline tank shattered the rear window of the Lincoln Mark

IV and set fire to the lining of the roof. The Lincoln went off in a hard straight line like a missile being fired and began zigzagging perilously in the dark. He threw another tracer and punctured the back door. Then he was shooting at the dark and the Lincoln kept going faster.

Grave Digger dragged the little car down and was out and running towards Deke, gun leveled, before it stopped moving. Coffin Ed hit the ground flat-footed on the other side, prepared to add his one remaining bullet. But it wasn't necessary. Deke saw them coming towards him. He had seen the Lincoln drive away. He dropped the pistol and raised his hands. He wanted to live.

'Well, well, look who's here,' Grave Digger said as he went forward to snap on the handcuffs.

'Ain't this a pleasant surprise?' Coffin Ed echoed.

'I want to phone my lawyer,' Deke said.

'All in good time, lover boy, all in good time,' Grave Digger said.

14

Now it was 1 a.m. Homicide had been there and gone. The medical examiner had pronounced all four bodies 'Dead On Arrival'. The bodies were on their way to the morgue. Both the Colonel's limousine and the Lincoln had gotten away. A search was being made. The seventeen police cruisers that had bottled up the area to keep them from escaping had been returned to regular duty. The workmen cleaning the Polo Grounds had returned to their work. The city lived and breathed and slept as usual. People were lying, stealing, cheating, murdering; people were praying, singing, laughing, loving and being loved; and people were being born and people were dying. Its pulse remained the same. New York City. The Big Town.

But the heads, the mothers and fathers, of those eighty-seven families who had sunk their savings on a dream of going back to

Africa lay awake, worrying, wondering if they'd ever get their money back.

Deke was in the 'Pigeons' Nest' in the precinct station, sitting on the wooden stool bolted to the floor, facing the barrage of spotlights. He looked fragile and translucent in the bright light; his smooth black face was more the purplish-orange color of an overpowdered whore than the normal gray of a black man terrified.

'I want to see my lawyer,' he was saying for the hundredth time.

'Your lawyer is asleep at this time of night,' Coffin Ed said with a straight face.

'He'd be mad if we woke him,' Grave Digger added.

Lieutenant Anderson had let them have him first. They were in a jovial mood. They had Deke where they wanted him.

It wasn't funny to Deke. 'Don't get your britches torn,' he warned. 'All you got against me is suspicion of homicide; and I have a perfect right to see my lawyer.'

Coffin Ed slapped him with his cupped palm. It was a light slap but it sounded like a firecracker and rocked Deke's head.

'Who's talking about homicide?' Grave Digger said as though he hadn't noticed it.

'Hell, all we want to know is who's got the money,' Coffin Ed said.

Deke straightened up and took a deep breath.

'So we can go and get it and give it back to those poor people you swindled,' Grave Digger added.

'Swindled my ass,' Deke said. 'It was all legitimate.'

Grave Digger slapped him so hard his body bent one-sided like a rubber man, and Coffin Ed slapped him back. They slapped him back and forth until his brains were addled, but left no bruises.

They let him get his breath back and gave him time for his brains to settle. Then Grave Digger said, 'Let's start over.'

Deke's eyes had turned bright orange in the glaring light. He closed his lids. A trickle of blood flowed from the corner of his mouth. He licked his lips and wiped his hand across his mouth.

'You're hurting me,' he said. His voice sounded as though

his tongue had thickened. 'But you ain't killing me. And that's all that counts.'

Coffin Ed drew back to hit him but Grave Digger caught his arm. 'Easy, Ed,' he said.

'Easy on this mother-raping scum?' Coffin Ed raved. 'Easy on this incestuous sister-raping thief?'

'We're cops,' Grave Digger reminded him. 'Not judges.'

Coffin Ed restrained himself. 'The law was made to protect the innocent,' he said.

Grave Digger chuckled. 'You heard the man,' he said to Deke.

Deke looked as though he might reply to that but thought better of it. 'You're wasting your time on me,' he said instead. 'My Back-to-Africa movement was on the square and all I know about this shooting caper is what I saw in passing. I saw the man was dying and tried to save his life.'

Coffin Ed turned and walked into the shadow. He slapped the wall with the palm of his hand so hard it sounded like a shot. It was all Grave Digger could do to keep from breaking Deke's jaw. His neck swelled and veins sprouted like ropes along his temples.

'Deke, don't try us,' he said. His voice had turned light and cotton-dry. 'We'll take you out of here and pistol-whip you slowly to death – and take the charge.'

It showed on Deke's face he believed him. He didn't speak.

'We know the set-up of the Back-to-Africa movement. We got the FBI records on Four-Four and Freddy. We got the Cook County Bertillon report on Barry and Elmer. We got your prison record too. We know you haven't got the money or you wouldn't still have been around. But you got the key.'

'Got what key?' Deke asked.

'The key to the door that leads to the money.'

Deke shook his head. 'I'm clean,' he said.

'Punk, listen,' Grave Digger said. 'You're going up any way. We got the proof.'

'Got it from where?' Deke asked.

'We got it from Iris,' Grave Digger said.

'If she said the Back-to-Africa movement was crooked she's a lying bitch, and I'll tell her to her teeth.'

'All right,' Grave Digger said.

Three minutes later they had Iris in the room. Lieutenant Anderson and two white detectives had come with her.

She stood in front of Deke and looked him dead in the eyes. 'He killed Mabel Hill,' she said.

Deke's face distorted with rage and he tried to leap at her but the white detectives held him.

'Mabel found out that the Back-to-Africa movement was crooked and she was going to the police. Her husband had been killed and she had lost her money and she was going to get him.' She sounded as if it was good to her.

'You lying whore!' Deke screamed.

'When I stood up for him, she attacked me,' Iris continued. 'I was struggling to defend myself. He grabbed me from behind and put the pistol in my hand and shot her. When I tried to wrestle the pistol away from him, he knocked me down and took it.'

Deke looked sick. He knew it was a good story. He knew if she took it to court, dressed in black, her eyes downcast in sorrow, and spoke in a halting manner – with his record – she could make it stick. She didn't have any kind of a criminal record. He could see the chair in Sing Sing and himself sitting in it.

He stared at her with resignation. 'How much are they paying you?' he asked.

She ignored the question. 'The forged documents which prove the Back-to-Africa movement is crooked are hidden in our apartment in the binding of a book called *Sex and Race.*' She smiled sweetly at Deke. 'Good-bye, big shit,' she said and turned towards the door.

The white detectives looked at one another, then looked at Deke. Anderson was embarrassed.

'How does that feel?' Coffin Ed asked Deke in a grating voice.

Grave Digger walked with Iris to the door. When he turned her over to the jailer he winked at her. She looked surprised for an instant, then winked back, and the jailer took her away.

Deke had wilted. He didn't look hurt, or even frightened; he looked beat, like a condemned man waiting for the electric chair. All he needed was the priest.

Anderson and the two white detectives left without looking at him again.

When the three of them were again alone, Grave Digger said. 'Give us the key and we'll strike off the murder.'

Deke looked up at him as though from a great distance. He looked as though he didn't care about anything any more. 'Frig you,' he said.

'Then give us the eighty-seven grand and we'll drop the whole thing,' Grave Digger persisted.

'Frig you twice,' Deke said.

They turned him over to the jailer to be taken back to his cell.

'I got a feeling we're overlooking something,' Grave Digger said.

'That is for sure,' Coffin Ed agreed. 'But what?'

They were in Anderson's office, talking about Iris. As usual, Grave Digger sat with a ham perched on the edge of the desk and Coffin Ed was backed against the wall in the shadow.

'She'll never get away with it,' Lieutenant Anderson said.

'Maybe not,' Grave Digger conceded. 'But she sure scared the hell out of him.'

'How much did it help?'

Grave Digger looked chagrined.

'None,' Coffin Ed admitted ruefully. 'She put it on too thick. We didn't expect her to accuse him of the murder.'

Grave Digger chuckled at that. 'She didn't hold anything back. I thought for a moment she was going to accuse him of rape.'

Anderson colored slightly. 'Then how far have you got?'

'Nowhere,' Grave Digger confessed.

Anderson sighed. 'I hate to see people tearing at one another like rapacious animals.'

'Hell, what do you expect?' Grave Digger said. 'As long as there are jungles there'll be rapacious animals.'

'Remember the colored taxi driver who picked up the three

white men and the colored woman in front of Small's, right after the trucks were wrecked?' Anderson asked, changing the conversation.

'Took them to Brooklyn. Maybe we ought to talk to him.'

'No use now. Homicide took him down to the morgue. On a hunch. And he identified the bodies of the three white men as the same ones.'

Grave Digger shifted his weight and Coffin Ed leaned forward. For a moment they were silent, lost in thought, then Grave Digger said, 'That ought to tell me something,' adding, 'but it don't.'

'It tells me they ain't got the money either,' Coffin Ed said.

'What they?'

'How the hell do I know? I didn't see the ones who got away,' Coffin Ed said.

Anderson thumbed through the report sheets on his desk. 'The Lincoln was found abandoned on Broadway, where the subway trestle passes over 125th Street, with the two rifles still inside,' he noted. 'It showed where you hit it.'

'So what?'

'The gunmen haven't been found but Homicide has got leaders out. Anyway, we know who they are and they won't get far.'

'Don't worry about those birds, they'll never fly,' Coffin Ed said.

'Those are not the flying kind,' Grave Digger added. 'Those are jailbirds, headed for home.'

'And we're headed for food,' Coffin Ed said. 'My stomach is sending up emergency calls.'

'Damn right,' Grave Digger agreed. 'As Napoleon said, "A woman thinks with her heart but a man with his stomach." And we've got some heavy thinking to do.'

Anderson laughed. 'What Napoleon was that?'

'Napoleon Jones,' Grave Digger said.

'All right, Napoleon Jones, don't forget crime,' Anderson said.

'Crime is what pays us,' Coffin Ed said.

They went to Mammy Louise's. She had changed her pork store with the tiny restaurant in back into a fancy all-night barbecue joint. Mr Louise was dead and a slick young black man with shiny straightened hair and fancy clothes had taken his place. The English bulldog who used to keep Mr Louise at home was still there, but his usefulness was gone and he looked lonely for the short fat figure of Mr Louise, whom he delighted in scaring. The new young man didn't look like the type anything could keep home, bulldog or whatnot.

They sat at a rear table facing the front. The barbecue grill was to their right, presided over by a white-clad chef. To their left was the jukebox, blaring out a Ray Charles number.

Mammy Louise's slick young man came personally to take their orders, playing the role of Patron with mincing arrogance.

'Good evening, gentlemen, what will you gentlemen have tonight?'

Grave Digger looked up. 'What have you got?'

'Barbecued ribs, barbecued feet, barbecued chicken, and we got some chitterlings and hog maws and some collard greens with ears and tails—'

'You'd go out of business if hogs had only loins,' Coffin Ed interrupted.

The young man flashed his teeth. 'We got some ham and succotash and some hog head and black-eyed peas—'

'What do you do with the bristles?' Grave Digger asked.

The young man was becoming irritated. 'Anything you want, gentlemen,' he said with a strained smile.

'Don't brag,' Coffin Ed muttered.

The smile went out.

'Just bring us two double orders of ribs,' Grave Digger said quickly. 'With side dishes of black-eyed peas, rice, okra, collard greens with fresh tomatoes and onions, and top it off with some deep-dish apple pie and vanilla ice cream. Okay?'

The young man smiled again. 'Just a light snack.'

'Yeah, we want to think,' Coffin Ed said.

They watched the young man walk away with a switch.

'Mr Louise must be turning over in his grave,' Coffin Ed said.

'Hell, he's more likely running after some chippy angel, now that he's got away from that bulldog.'

'If he went in that direction.'

'All chippies were angels to Mr Louise,' Grave Digger said.

The place was filled mostly with young people who peeped at them through the corners of their eyes when they came back to play the jukebox. Everyone knew them. They looked at these young people, thinking they didn't know what it was all about yet.

Suddenly they were listening.

'Pres,' Grave Digger recognized, cocking his ear. 'And Sweets.'

'Roy Eldridge too,' Coffin Ed added. 'Who's on the bass?'

'I don't know him or the guitar either,' Grave Digger confessed. 'I guess I'm an old pappy.'

'What's that platter?' Coffin Ed asked the youth standing by the jukebox who had played the number.

His girl looked at them through wide dark eyes, as though they'd escaped from the zoo, but the boy replied self-consciously, '"Laughing to Keep from Crying." It's foreign.'

'No, it ain't,' Coffin Ed said.

No one contradicted him. They were silent with their thoughts until a waiter brought the food. The table was loaded. Grave Digger chuckled. 'Looks like a famine is coming on.'

'We're going to head it off,' Coffin Ed said.

The waiter brought three kinds of hot sauce – Red Devil, Little Sister's Big Brother, West Virginia Coke Oven – vinegar, a plate of yellow corn bread and a dish of country butter.

'Bone apperteet,' he said.

'*Merci, m'sieu,*' Coffin Ed replied.

'Black Frenchman,' Grave Digger commented when the waiter had left.

'Good old war,' Coffin Ed said. 'It got us out of the South.'

'Yeah, now the white folks want to start another war to get us back.'

That was the last of that conversation. The food claimed their attention. They sloshed the succulent pork barbecue with Coke Oven hot sauce and gnawed it from the bones with noisy relish. It made the chef feel good all over to watch them eat.

When they had finished, Mammy Louise came from the

kitchen. She was shaped like a weather balloon on two feet, with a pilot balloon serving as a head. The round black face beneath the bandanna which encased her head was shiny with sweat, but still she wore a heavy sweater over a black woollen dress. She claimed she had never been warm since coming north. Her ancestors were runaway slaves who had joined a tribe of southern Indians and formed a new race known as 'Geechies'. Her native language was a series of screeches punctuated by grunts, but she spoke American with an accent. She smelled like stewed goat.

'How's y'all, nasty 'licemen?' she greeted them jovially.

'Fine, Mammy Louise, how's yourself?'

'Cold,' she confessed.

'Don't your new love keep you warm?' Coffin Ed asked.

She cast a look at the mincing dandy flashing his teeth at two women at a front table. ''Oman lak me tikes w'ut de good Lawd send 'thout question, I'se 'fied.'

'If you are satisfied, who're we to complain?' Grave Digger said.

A man poked his head in the door and said something to her fine young man and he hurried back to their table and said, 'Your car's calling.'

They jumped up and hurried out without paying.

15

Lieutenant Anderson said, 'A man was found dead in a junkyard underneath 125th Street approach to the Triborough Bridge.'

'What about it?' Coffin Ed replied.

'*What about it?*' Anderson flared. 'Have you guys quit the force? Go over and look at it. You might learn that killing is a crime. Just the same as robbery.'

Coffin Ed felt his ears burning. 'Right away,' he said respectfully.

'What about it?' he heard Anderson muttering as he switched off.

Grave Digger was chuckling as he wheeled the car into the traffic. 'Got your ass torn, eh, buddy?'

'Yeah, the boss man got salty.'

'Let that be a lesson to you. Don't play murder cheap.'

'All right, I'm outnumbered,' Coffin Ed said.

They found Sergeant Wiley in charge of the crew from Homicide. His men were casting footprints, dusting for fingerprints, and taking photographs. A young pink-faced assistant medical examiner was tagging the body DOA and whistling cheerfully.

'My old friends, the lion tamers,' Sergeant Wiley greeted them. 'Have no fear, the dog is dead.'

They looked at the dead dog, then glanced casually about.

'What've you got here?' Grave Digger asked.

'Just another corpse,' Wiley said. 'My fifth for the night.'

'So you covered the caper at the Polo Grounds?'

'Caper! Hell, when I arrived there were only four stiffs. You men got the live one.'

'You can have him.'

'For what? If he wasn't any good for you what the hell I want him for?'

'Who knows? Maybe he'll like you better.'

Wiley smiled. He looked more like a professor of political science at the New School than a homicide detective-sergeant but Grave Digger and Coffin Ed knew him for a cool clever cop. 'Let's look around,' he said, leading the way into the shed where the body was found. 'Here's the score. We got a social security card from his wallet which gives his name as Joshua Peavine and an address on West 121st Street. He was stabbed once in the heart. That's all we know.'

The detectives looked carefully over the junk-filled shed. Three aisles, flanked by junk stacked to the corrugated-iron ceiling, branched off from the main aisle that led in from the door. All available space was filled except an empty spot at the end of the main aisle beside the back wall.

'Somebody got something,' Coffin Ed remarked.

'What the hell would anybody want from here?' Wiley asked, gesturing towards the stacks of flattened cardboard, old books and magazines, rags, radios, sewing-machines, rusty tools, battered mannequins and unidentifiable scraps of metal.

'The man got killed for something, much less the dog,' Coffin Ed maintained.

'Might have been a sex crime,' Grave Digger ventured. 'Suppose he came here with a white man. It's happened before.'

'I thought of that,' Wiley said. 'But the dead dog contradicts it.'

'He'd kill the dog if it was worth it,' Coffin Ed said.

Wiley raised his eyebrows. 'All that secrecy in Harlem?'

'He'd do what was necessary if the pay was right.'

'Maybe,' Wiley conceded. 'But here's the twist. We found a ball of meat that looks as though it might be poisoned in his pocket – we'll have it analysed of course. So the dog was already poisoned by someone else. Unless he had two balls of poisoned meat – which wouldn't seem necessary.'

'This empty space bothers me,' Grave Digger confessed. 'This empty space in all this conglomeration of junk. Was there anything knocked off the hijack truck the other night that might identify it? Something that might wind up in a junkyard. A spare wheel?'

Wiley shook his head. 'Maybe a gun could have been lost, but nothing I can think of that would be sold here. Nothing at least to fill this empty space. I think we're on the wrong track there.'

'There's only one way to find out,' Grave Digger said.

Wiley nodded. The door to the office had been forced by Wiley's men but nothing had been found to draw attention. The three of them went in and Wiley telephoned Mr Goodman at his home in Brooklyn.

Mr Goodman was horrified. 'Everything happens to me,' he cried. 'Such a good boy, so honest. He wouldn't hurt a fly yet.'

'We want you to come over and tell us what is missing.'

'Missing!' Mr Goodman screamed. 'You're not thinking Josh was killed protecting my place? He wasn't a nitwit.'

'We're not thinking anything. We just want you to tell us what's missing.'

'You think thieves have stolen something from my junkyard? Diamonds, maybe. Bricks of gold. Necklaces of rubies. Have you seen my junk? Only another junk man would want anything from my junkyard and he'd need a truck to take away ten dollars' worth.'

'We just want you to come over and take a look, Mr Goodman,' Wiley said patiently.

'*Mein Gott*, at this hour of the morning! You say Josh is dead. Poor boy. My heart bleeds. But can I bring him back to life, at two o'clock in the morning? Can I raise the dead? If there is junk missing you can see it for yourself. Do you think I can identify my junk? How can anyone identify junk? Junk is junk; that's what makes it junk. If someone has taken some of my junk he is welcome. There will be signs where he has taken truck-loads, unless he is a lunatic. Look you for a lunatic, there is your man. And my Reba is awake and worrying should I go over in that place full of lunatic murderers at this time of night. She is a lunatic too. You just put Josh in the morgue and I will come Monday morning and identify his body.'

'This is important, Mr Goodman—' The line went dead. Wiley jiggled the hook. 'Mr Goodman, Mr Goodman—' The voice of the operator came on. Wiley looked about and said, 'He hung up,' and hung up himself.

'Send for him,' Coffin Ed said.

Wiley looked at him. 'On what charge? I'd have to get a court order to get him out of Brooklyn.'

'There's more ways than one to skin a cat,' Grave Digger said.

'Don't tell me,' Wiley said, leading the way back to the yard. 'Let me stay ignorant.'

They stood for a moment looking at the carcass of the dead dog. The ruddy-faced assistant medical examiner passed them, singing cheerfully, '*I'll be glad when you're dead, you rascal you; I'll be standing at Broad and High when they bring your dead ass by, I'll be glad when you're dead . . .*'

Grave Digger and Coffin Ed exchanged looks.

Wiley noticed and said, 'It's a living.'

'More bodies, more babies,' Grave Digger agreed.

The morgue wagon came and took away the body of the man and the carcass of the dog. Wiley called his men and prepared to leave. 'I'm going to let you have it,' he said.

'We got it,' Coffin Ed said. 'Sleep tight.'

Left to themselves they went back over the ground in detail. 'Anywhere else it would figure something was stolen,' Coffin Ed said. 'Here it don't make any sense.'

'Let's quit guessing, let's go get Goodman.'

Coffin Ed nodded. 'Right.'

They closed the shed and turned out the lights and went slowly through the yard to the gate. When they started to cross the street to where their car was parked, a dark shape came from beneath the bridge like a juggernaut. They couldn't see what it was but they ran because years of police work had taught them that nothing moves in the dark but danger. When they saw it was a black car moving at incredible speed they dove face downward on the pavement on the other side. A burst of flame lit the night as the silence exploded; machine-gun bullets sprayed over them as the black car passed. It was over. For a brief instant there was the diminishing whine of a high-powered engine, then silence again. The black shape had disappeared as though it had never been.

By now they had their pistols in their hands, but they still lay cautiously flat to the pavement, searching the night for a moving target. Nothing moved. Finally they crawled to the protection of their little car and stood up, still searching the shadows for movement. They eased into the car like wary shadows themselves. Their breathing was audible. They still looked around.

Car lights had slowed in the moving chain on the bridge overhead, but the deserted, off-beat street below remained dark.

'Report it,' Grave Digger said as they sat in the dark.

Coffin Ed called the precinct from the car and got Lieutenant Anderson. He gave it just like it happened.

'Why, for God's sake?' Anderson said.

'I don't figure it,' Coffin Ed confessed. 'We got nothing, no description, no license number – and no ideas.'

'I don't know what you're on to, but be careful,' Anderson warned.

'How much more careful can a cop be?'

'You could use some help.'

'Help to get killed,' Coffin Ed grumbled and felt a warning pressure from Grave Digger's hand. 'We're going to Brooklyn now to get the owner of this junkyard.'

'Well, if you have to, but for God's sake go easy; you don't have any jurisdiction in Brooklyn and you can get us all in a jam.'

'Easy does it,' Coffin Ed said and cut off.

Grave Digger mashed the starter and they went down the dark street. He was frowning from his thoughts. 'Ed, we're just missing something,' he said.

'Goddamned right,' Coffin Ed agreed. 'Just missing getting killed.'

'I mean, doesn't this tell you something?'

'Tells me to get the hell off the Force while I'm still alive.'

'What I mean is, so much nonsense must make sense,' Grave Digger persisted as he entered the approach to the East Side throughway.

'Do you believe that shit?' Coffin Ed said.

'I was thinking why would anyone want to rub us out because a junkyard laborer was murdered?'

'You tell me.'

'What's so important about this killing? It smells like some kind of double-cross.'

'I don't see it. Unless you're trying to tie this to the hijack caper. And that sure don't make any sense. People are getting killed in Harlem all the time. Why not you and me?'

'I got to think something,' Grave Digger said and entered the stream of traffic on the throughway without stopping.

Mr Goodman was still awake when they arrived. The news of Josh's murder had upset him. He was clad in bathrobe and nightgown and looked as though he'd been raiding the kitchen.

But he still protested against going back to Harlem just to look over his junkyard.

'What good can it do? How can it help you? No one steals junk. I only kept the dog to keep bums from sleeping in the yard, and cart pushers like Uncle Bud from filling his cart with my junk to sell to another junk man.'

'Listen, Mr Goodman, the other night eighty-seven poor colored families lost their life savings in a robbery—'

'Yes, yes, I read in the papers. They wanted to go back to Africa. I want to get back to Israel where I've never been either. It comes to no good, this looking for bigger apples on foreign trees. Here every man is free—'

'Yes, Mr Goodman,' Grave Digger interrupted with feigned patience. 'But we're cops, not philosophers. And we just want to find out what is missing from your junkyard and we can't wait until Monday morning because by then someone else might be killed. Even us. Even you.'

'If I must, I must, to keep some other poor colored man from being killed, about some junk,' Mr Goodman said resignedly, adding bitterly: 'What this world is coming to nobody knows, when people are killed about some junk – not to speak of a poor innocent dog.'

He led them into the parlor to wait while he dressed. When he returned ready to go, he said, 'My Reba don't like it.'

The detectives didn't comment on his Reba's dislikes.

At first Mr Goodman did not see where anything was missing. It looked exactly as he had left it.

'All this trouble, getting up and dressing and coming all this distance in the dark hours of morning, for nothing,' he complained.

'But there must have been something in this empty space,' Coffin Ed insisted. 'What are you keeping this space for?'

'Is that a crime? Always I keep space for what might come in. Did poor Josh get killed for this empty space? Just who is the lunatic, I ask you?' Then he remembered. 'A bale of cotton,' he said.

Grave Digger and Coffin Ed froze. Their nostrils quivered

like hound dogs on a scent. Thoughts churned through their heads like sheets of lightning.

'Uncle Bud brought in a bale of cotton this morning,' Mr Goodman went on. 'I had it put out here. I haven't thought of it since. With income taxes and hydrogen bombs and black revolutions, who thinks of a bale of cotton? Uncle Bud is one of the cart men—'

'We know Uncle Bud,' Coffin Ed said.

'Then you know he must have found this bale of cotton on his nightly rounds.' Mr Goodman shrugged and spread his hands. 'I can't ask every cart man for a bill of sale.'

'Mr Goodman, that's all we want to know,' Grave Digger said. 'We'll drive you to a taxi and pay for your time.'

'Pay I want none,' Mr Goodman said. 'But curious I am. Who would kill a man about a bale of cotton? Cotton, *mein Gott.*'

'That's what we want to find out,' Grave Digger said and led the way to their car.

Now it was three-thirty in the morning and they were back at the precinct station talking it over with Lieutenant Anderson. Anderson had already alerted all cars to pick up Uncle Bud for questioning and they were trying to fix the picture.

'You're certain this bale of cotton was carried by the meat delivery truck used by the jackers?' Anderson said.

'We found fibers of raw cotton in the truck. Uncle Bud finds a bale of cotton on 137th Street and sells it to the junkyard. The bale of cotton is missing. A junkyard laborer has been killed. We're certain of that much,' Grave Digger said.

'But what could make this bale of cotton that important?'

'Identification. Maybe it points directly to the hijackers,' Grave Digger said.

'Yes, but remember the dog was dead before Josh and his murderer arrived. Maybe the cotton was gone by then too.'

'Maybe. But that doesn't change the fact that somebody wanted the cotton and didn't let him live to tell whether they got it, or somebody got it before.'

'Let's quit guessing and go find the cotton,' Coffin Ed said.

Grave Digger looked at him as though he felt like saying, 'Go find it then.'

During the silence the phone rang and Anderson picked up the receiver and said, 'Yes . . . yes . . . yes, 119th Street and Lenox . . . yes . . . well, keep looking.' He hung up.

'They found the junk cart,' Grave Digger said more than asked.

Anderson nodded. 'But Uncle Bud wasn't with it.'

'It figures,' Coffin Ed said. 'He's probably in the river by now.'

'Yeah,' Grave Digger said angrily. 'This mother-raping cotton punished the colored man down south and now it's killing them up north.'

'Which reminds me,' Anderson said. 'Dan Sellers of Car 90 says he saw an old colored junk man who'd found a bale of cotton on 137th Street right after the trucks crashed the night of the hijack. The old man was trying to get it into his cart – probably Uncle Bud – and they stopped to question him. Then he got out and helped him load it and ordered him to bring it to the station. But he never came.'

'Now you tell us,' Grave Digger said bitterly.

Anderson colored. 'I'd forgotten it until now. After all, we hadn't thought of cotton.'

'You hadn't,' Coffin Ed said.

'Speaking of cotton, what do you know about a Colonel Calhoun who's opened a store-front office on Seventh Avenue to recruit people to go south and pick cotton? Calls it the Back-to-the-Southland movement,' Grave Digger asked.

Anderson looked at him curiously. 'Lay off him,' he warned. 'I admit it's a stupid pitch, but it's strictly on the legitimate. The captain has questioned him and checked his license and credentials; they're all in order. And he's got influential friends.'

'I don't doubt it,' Grave Digger said drily. 'All southern crackers got influential friends up north.'

Anderson looked down.

'The Back-to-Africa members are picketing him,' Coffin Ed said. 'They don't want that crap in Harlem.'

'The Muslims haven't bothered him,' Anderson said defensively.

'Hell, they're just giving him enough rope.'

'Just his timing is bad,' Coffin Ed argued. 'Right after this Back-to-Africa movement is hijacked he opens this go-south-and-pick-cotton pitch. If you ask me, he's looking for trouble.'

Anderson thumbed through the reports on his desk. 'Last night at ten p.m. he phoned and reported that his car had been stolen from in front of his office on Seventh Avenue. Gave his home address as Hotel Dixie on 42nd Street. A cruiser stopped by but the office was closed for the night. We gave it a routine check at midnight. The desk said he had come home at ten thirty-five p.m. and hadn't left his suite. His nephew was with him.'

'What kind of car?' Grave Digger asked.

'Black limousine. Special body. Ferrari chassis. Birmingham, Alabama plates. And just lay off of him. We got enough trouble as it is.'

'I'm just thinking that cotton grows in the South,' Grave Digger said.

'And tobacco grows in Cuba,' Anderson said. 'Go home and get some sleep. Whatever's going to happen has happened by now.'

'We're going, boss,' Grave Digger said. 'No more we can do tonight anyway. But don't hand us that crap. This caper has just begun.'

16

Everything happens in Harlem six days a week, but Sunday morning, people worship God. Those who are not religious stay in bed. The whores, pimps, gamblers, criminals and racketeers catch up on their sleep or their love. But the religious get up and put on their best clothes and go to church. The bars are closed. The stores are closed. The streets are deserted save for the families on their way to church. A drunk better not be caught molesting them; he'll get all the black beat off him.

All of the Sunday newspapers had carried the story of the arrest of Reverend D. O'Malley, leader of the Back-to-Africa movement, on suspicion of fraud and homicide. The accounts of the hijacking had been rehashed and pictures of O'Malley and his wife, Iris, and Mabel Hill added to the sensationalism.

As a consequence Reverend O'Malley's interdenominational church, 'The Star of Ham', on 121st Street between Seventh and Lenox Avenues, was crowded with the Back-to-Africa followers and the curious. A scattering of Irish people who had read the story in *The New York Times*, which didn't carry pictures, had made their way uptown, thinking Reverend O'Malley was one of them.

Reverend T. Booker Washington (no relation to the great Negro educator), the assistant minister, led the services. At first he led the congregation in prayer. He prayed for the Back-to-Africa followers, and he prayed that their money be returned; and he prayed for sinners and for good people who had been falsely accused, and for all black people who had suffered the wages of injustice.

Then he began his sermon, speaking quietly and with dignity and understanding of the unfortunate robbery, and of the tragic deaths of young Mr and Mrs Hill, members of the church and active participants in the Back-to-Africa movement. The congregation sat in hushed silence. Then Reverend Washington spoke openly and frankly of the inexplicable tragedy which seemed to haunt the life of that saintly man, Reverend O'Malley, as though God were trying him.

'It is as though God was testing this man with the trials of Job to ascertain the strength of his faith and his endurance and courage for some great task ahead.'

'Amen,' a sister said tentatively.

Reverend Washington moved carefully, sampling the reaction of his audience before proceeding to controversial ground.

'All of his life this noble and selfless man has been subjected to the cruel and biased judgement of the white people whom he defies for you.'

'Amen,' the sister cried louder and with more confidence. A few timid 'amens' echoed.

'I know Reverend O'Malley is innocent of any crime,' Reverend Washington said loudly, letting passion creep into the solemnity of his voice. 'I would trust him with my money and I would trust him with my life.'

'Amen!' the sister shouted, rising from her seat. 'He's a good man.'

The congregation warmed up. Ripples of confirmation ran through all the women.

'He will conquer this calumny of false accusation; he will be vindicated!' Reverend Washington thundered.

'Set him free!' a woman screamed.

'Justice will set him free!' Reverend Washington roared. 'And he will get back our money and lead us out of this land of oppression back to our beloved homeland in Africa.'

'*Amens*' and '*hallelujas*' filled the air as the congregation was swept off its feet. In the grip of emotionalism, O'Malley appeared in their imaginations as a martyr to the injustice of whites, and a brave and noble leader.

'His chains will be broken by the Almighty God and he will come and set us free,' Reverend Washington concluded in a thundering voice.

The Back-to-Africa followers believed. They wanted to believe. They didn't have any other choice.

'Now we will take up a collection to help pay for Reverend O'Malley's defense,' Reverend Washington said in a quiet voice. 'And we will delegate Brother Sumners to take it to him in his hour of Gethsemane.'

Five hundred and ninety-seven dollars was collected and Brother Sumners was charged to go forthwith and present it to Reverend O'Malley. The precinct station where O'Malley was being held for the magistrate's court was only a few blocks distant. Brother Sumners returned with word from O'Malley before the service had adjourned. He could scarcely contain his sense of importance as he mounted the rostrum and brought them word from their beloved minister.

'Reverend O'Malley is spending the day in his cell praying for you, his beloved followers – for all of us – and for the speedy return of your money, and for our safe departure for Africa. He says he will be taken to court Monday morning at ten o'clock when he will be freed to return to you and continue his work.'

'Lord, protect him and deliver him,' a sister cried, and others echoed: 'Amen, amen.'

The congregation filed out, filled with faith in Reverend O'Malley, blended with compassion and a sense of satisfaction for their own good deed of sending him the big collection.

On many a table there was chicken and dumplings or roast pork and sweet potatoes, and crime took a rest.

Grave Digger and Coffin Ed always slept late on Sundays, rarely stirring from bed before six o'clock in the evening. Sunday and Monday were their days off unless they were working on a case, and they had decided to let the hijacking case rest until Monday.

But Grave Digger had dreamed that a blind man had told him he had seen a bale of cotton run down Seventh Avenue and turn into a doorway, but he awakened before the blind man told him what doorway. There was a memory knocking at his mind, trying to get in. He knew it was important but it had not seemed so at the time. He lay for a time going over in detail all that they had done. He didn't find it; it didn't come. But he had a strong feeling that if he could remember this one thing he would have all the answers.

He got up and slipped on a bathrobe and went to the kitchen and got two cans of beer from the refrigerator.

'Stella,' he called his wife, but she had gone out.

He drank one can of beer and prowled about the house, holding the other in his hand. He was looking inward, searching his memory. A cop without a memory is like meat without potatoes, he was thinking.

His two daughters were away at camp. The house felt

like a tomb. He sat in the living-room and leafed through the Saturday edition of the *Sentinel*, Harlem's twice-weekly newspaper devoted to the local news. The hijacking story took up most of the front page. There were pictures of O'Malley and Iris, and of John and Mabel Hill. O'Malley's racketeer days and prison record were hammered on and the claim he had been marked for death by the syndicate. There were stories about his Back-to-Africa movement, bordering on libel, and stories of the Back-to-Africa movement of L.H. Michaux, handled with discretion; and stories of the original Back-to-Africa movement of Marcus Garvey, containing some bits of information that Garvey hadn't known himself. He turned the pages and his gaze lit on an advertisement for the Cotton Club, showing a picture of Billie Belle doing her exotic cotton dance. *I've got cotton on the brain*, he thought disgustedly and threw the paper aside.

He went to the telephone extension in the hall, from where he could look outdoors, and called the precinct station in Harlem and talked to Lieutenant Bailey, who was on Sunday duty. Bailey said, no, Colonel Calhoun's car had not been found, no, there was no trace of Uncle Bud, no, there was no trace of the two gunmen of Deke's who had escaped.

'The *noes* have it,' Bailey said.

'Well, as long as the head's gone they can't bite,' Grave Digger said.

Coffin Ed phoned and said his wife, Molly, had gone out with Stella, and he was coming over.

'Just don't let's talk about crime,' Grave Digger said.

'Let's go down to the pistol range at headquarters and practise shooting,' Coffin Ed suggested. 'I've just got through cleaning the old lady.'

'Hell, let's drink some highballs and get gay and take the ladies out on the town,' Grave Digger said.

'Right. I won't mind being gay for a change.'

The phone rang right after Coffin Ed hung up. Lieutenant Bailey said the Back-to-the-Southland people were assembling a group of colored people in front of their office for a parade down Seventh Avenue and there might be trouble.

'You and Ed better come over,' he said. 'The people know you.'

Grave Digger called back Coffin Ed and told him to bring the car as Stella had taken his. Coffin Ed arrived before he had finished dressing, and they got into his gray Plymouth sedan and took off for Harlem. Forty-five minutes later they were rapidly threading through the Sunday afternoon traffic, heading north on Seventh Avenue.

A self-ordained preacher was standing on the sidewalk outside the Chock Full o' Nuts at 125th Street and Seventh Avenue, exhorting the passersby to take Jesus to their hearts. 'Ain't no two ways about it,' he was shouting. 'The right one is with God and Jesus and the wrong one with the devil.'

A few pious people had stopped to listen. Most of the Sunday afternoon strollers took the devil's way and passed without looking.

Diagonally across the intersection the Harlem branch of the Black Muslims was staging a mass meeting in front of the National Memorial Bookstore, headquarters of Michaux's Back-to-Africa movement. The store front was plastered with slogans: GODDAMN WHITE MAN . . . WHITE PEOPLE EAT DOG . . . ALLAH IS GOD . . . BLACK MEN UNITE . . . At one side a platform had been erected with a public-address hook-up for the speakers. Below to one side was an open black coffin with a legend: *The Remains of Lumumba.* The coffin contained pictures of Lumumba in life and in death; a black suit said to have been worn by him when he was killed; and other mementoes said to have belonged to him in life. Bordering the sidewalk on removable flagstaffs were the flags of all the nations of black Africa.

Hundreds of people were lined up on the sidewalk in a packed mass. Three police cruisers were parked along the kerb and white harness cops patrolled up and down in the street. Muslims wearing the red fezzes they had adopted as their symbol were lined in front of the bookstore, side by side, keeping a clear path on the sidewalk demanded by the police. The shouting voice of a speaker came from the amplifiers: 'White Man, you worked us for nothing for four hundred years. Now pay for it . . .'

Grave Digger and Coffin Ed didn't stop. As they neared 130th Street they saw the parade heading in their direction on the other side of the street. They knew that within five blocks it would run head-on into the Black Muslims and there'd be hell to pay. Already some of O'Malley's Back-to-Africa group were collecting at 129th Street for an attack.

Police cruisers were parked along the avenue and cops were standing by.

The detectives noted immediately that the parade was made up of mercenary hoodlums, paid for the occasion. They were laughing belligerently and looking for trouble. They carried knives and walked tough. Colonel Calhoun led them, clad in his black frock coat and a black wide-brimmed hat. His silvery hair and white moustache and goatee shone in the rays of the afternoon sun. He was calmly smoking a cheroot. His tall thin figure was ramrod-straight and he walked with the indifference of a benevolent master. His attitude seemed that of a man dealing with children who might be unruly but never dangerous. The blond young man brought up the rear.

Coffin Ed double-parked and he and Grave Digger walked over to the raised park in the center of Seventh Avenue and assessed the situation.

'You go down to 129th Street and hold those brothers and I'll turn these soul-brothers here,' Grave Digger said.

'I got you, partner,' Coffin Ed said.

Grave Digger lined himself opposite a wooden telephone post and Coffin Ed crossed to the sidewalk and stood facing the concrete wall enclosing the park.

When the parade reached the intersection at 130th Street, Grave Digger drew his long-barreled .38 revolver and put two bullets into the wooden post. The nickelplated pistol shone in the sun like a silver jet.

'Straighten up!' he shouted at the top of his voice.

The parading hoodlums hesitated.

From down the street came the booming blast of two shots

as Coffin Ed fired into the concrete wall, followed by his voice, like an echo, 'Count off!'

The mob preparing for the attack on the parade fell back. People in Harlem believed Coffin Ed and Grave Digger would shoot a man stone cold dead for crossing an imaginary line. Those who didn't believe it didn't try it.

But Colonel Calhoun kept right ahead across 130th Street without looking about. When he came to the invisible line, Grave Digger shot off his hat. The Colonel slowly took the cheroot from his mouth and looked at Grave Digger coldly, then turned with slow deliberation to pick up his hat. Grave Digger shot it out of his hand. It flew on to the sidewalk and with slow deliberation, without another glance in Grave Digger's direction, the Colonel walked after it. Grave Digger shot it out into 130th Street as the Colonel was reaching for it.

The hoodlums in the parade were shuffling about, afraid to advance but taking no chances on breaking and running with those bullets flying about. The young blond man was keeping out of sight at the rear.

'Squads right!' Grave Digger shouted. Everyone turned but no one left. 'March!' he added.

The hoodlums turned right on 130th Street and shuffled towards Eighth Avenue. They went straight past the Colonel, who stood in the center of the street looking at the holes in his hat before putting it on his head. Midway down the block they broke and ran. The first thing a hoodlum learns in Harlem is never run too soon.

The mob at 129th Street turned towards Eighth Avenue to head them off, but Coffin Ed drew a line with two bullets ahead of them. 'As you were!' he shouted.

The Colonel stood there for a moment with three bullet holes in his hat, and residents who had come out to see the excitement began to laugh at him. The blond young man caught up with him and they turned back to Seventh Avenue and began walking towards their office, the jeers and laughter of the colored people following them. The Black Muslims had looked but hadn't moved.

Then the mob herded by Coffin Ed relaxed and started laughing too.

'Man, them mothers,' a cat said admiringly in a loud jubilant voice. 'Them mothers! They'll shoot off a man's ass for crossing a line can't nobody see.'

'Baby, you see that old white mother-raper tryna git his hat? I bet the Digger would have taken his head off if he'da crossed that line.'

'I seen old Coffin Filler shoot the fat offen a cat's stomach for stickin his belly 'cross that line.'

They slapped one another on the shouders and fell out, laughing at their own lies.

The white cops looked at Grave Digger and Coffin Ed with the envious awe usually reserved for a lion tamer with a cage of big cats.

Coffin Ed joined Grave Digger and they walked to a call box and phoned Lieutenant Bailey.

'All over for today,' Grave Digger reported.

Bailey gave a sigh of relief. 'Thank God! I don't want any riots up here on my tour.'

'All you got to worry about now are some killings and robberies,' Grave Digger said. 'Nothing to worry the commissioner.'

Bailey hung up without commenting. He knew of their feud with the commissioner. Both of them had been suspended at different times for what the commissioner considered unnecessary violence and brutality. He knew also that colored cops had to be tough in Harlem to get the respect of colored hoodlums. Secretly he agreed with them. But he wasn't taking any sides.

'Well, now we're back to cotton,' Coffin Ed said as they walked back towards their car.

'Maybe you are; I ain't,' Grave Digger said. 'All I want to do is go out and break some laws. Other people have all the fun.'

'Damn right. Let's put five bucks on a horse.'

'Hell, man, you call that breaking the law? Let's take the ladies to some unlicensed joint run by some wanted criminal and drink some stolen whisky.'

Coffin Ed chuckled. 'You're on,' he said.

17

The telephone rang at 10.25 a.m. Grave Digger hid his head beneath the pillow. Stella answered it sleepily. A brisk, wide-awake and urgent voice said, 'This is Captain Brice. Let me speak to Jones, please.'

She pulled the pillow from over his head. 'The captain,' she said.

He groped for the receiver, experimentally opening his eyes. 'Jones,' he mumbled.

He listened to the rapid staccato voice for three minutes. 'Right,' he said, tense and wide-awake, and was getting out of the bed before he hung up the receiver.

'What is it?' she asked in a tiny voice, frightened and alarmed as she always was when these morning summonses came.

'Deke's escaped. Two officers killed.' He had put on his shorts and undershirt and was pulling up his pants.

She was out of the bed and moving towards the kitchen. 'You want coffee?'

'No time,' he said, putting on a clean shirt.

'Nescafé,' she said, disappearing into the kitchen.

With his shirt on he sat on the side of the bed and put on clean socks and his shoes. Then he went into the bathroom and washed his face and brushed his short kinky hair. Without a shave his dark lumpy face looked dangerous. He knew how he looked but it couldn't be helped. He didn't have time for a shave. He put on a black tie, went into the bedroom and took his holstered pistol from a hook in the closet. He laid the pistol on the dresser while he strapped on his shoulder sling and then picked it up and spun the cylinder. It always carried five shells, the hammer resting on an empty chamber. The shades were still drawn, and the long nickelplated revolver glinting in the subdued light from three table lamps looked as dangerous as himself. He slipped it into the greased holster and began stuffing his pockets with the other tools of his trade: a leather-covered buckshot sap with a whalebone handle, a pair of handcuffs, report book, flashlight, stylo, and the leather-bound metal snap case made to hold fifteen extra shells he always carried in his leather-lined side coat pocket. They also kept an extra box or two of shells in the glove compartment of their official car.

He was standing at the kitchen table, drinking coffee, when Coffin Ed blew for him. Stella tensed. Her smooth brown face grew strained.

'Be careful,' she said.

He stepped around the table and kissed her. 'Ain't I always?' he said.

'Not always,' she murmured.

But he was gone, a big, rough, dangerous man in need of a shave, clad in a rumpled black suit and an old black hat, the bulge of a big pistol clearly visible on the heart side of his broad-shouldered frame.

Coffin Ed looked the same; they could have been cast from the same mold with the exception of Coffin Ed's acid-burned face that was jerking with the tic that came whenever he was tense.

Yesterday, Sunday afternoon, it had taken forty-five minutes to get to Harlem. Today, Monday morning, it took twenty-two.

Coffin Ed said only, 'The fat is in the fire.'

'It's going to burn,' Grave Digger said.

Two white officers had been killed and the precinct station looked like headquarters for the invasion of Harlem. Official cars lined the street. The commissioner's car was there, and cars of the chief inspector, the chief of Homicide, the medical examiner and a D.A.'s assistant. Police cruisers from downtown, from Homicide, from all the Harlem precincts, were scattered about. The street was closed to civilian traffic. There was no place inside for all the army of cops and the overflow stood outside, on the sidewalks, in the street, waiting for their orders.

Coffin Ed parked in the driveway of a private garage and

they walked to the station house. The brass was assembled in the captain's office. The lieutenant on the desk said, 'Go on in, they want to see you.'

Heads turned when they entered the office. They were stared at as though they were criminals themselves.

'We want Deke O'Hara and his two gunmen, and we want them alive,' the commissioner said coldly without greeting. 'It's your bailiwick and I'm giving you a free hand.'

They stared back at the commissioner but neither of them spoke.

'Let me give them the picture, sir,' Captain Brice said.

The commissioner nodded. The captain led them into the detectives' room. A white detective got up from his desk in the corner and gave the captain a seat. Other detectives nodded to Grave Digger and Coffin Ed as they passed. No one spoke. They nodded back. They kept the record straight. There was no friendship lost between them and the other precinct detectives; but there was no open animosity. Some resented their position as the aces of the precinct and their close associations with the officers in charge; others were envious; the young colored detectives stood in awe of them. But all took care not to show anything.

Captain Brice sat behind the desk and Grave Digger perched a ham on the edge as usual. Coffin Ed drew up a straight-backed chair and sat opposite the captain.

'Deke was being taken to the magistrate's court,' the captain said. 'There were thirteen others going. The wagon was drawn up in the back court and we were bringing the prisoners from their cells, handcuffed together two by two as customary. Two officers were standing by, supervising the loading – the driver and his helper – and two jailers were bringing the prisoners from the bullpen through the back door and herding them downstairs to the yard and into the wagon. Deke's Back-to-Africa group had collected in the street out front, a thousand or more. They were chanting, "We want O'Malley . . . We want O'Malley," and trying to break through the front door. They were getting unruly and I sent the extra officers out into the street to herd them to one side and keep order. Then they began getting noisy and started rioting. Some began throwing stones through the front windows and others began battering the gate to the driveway with garbage cans. I sent two men from out back to clear the driveway to the street. When they opened the gates to go out they were mobbed and disarmed and the mob streamed into the driveway. Deke had just come from the back door on his way down the stairs, handcuffed to a suspected murderer, one Mack Brothers, when the mob came in sight and saw him. Six prisoners had already been loaded. Then, from what I've been told by a trusty looking out a jail window – all the officers were out front trying to contain the riot – the jailers slammed and locked the door, leaving the two officers alone with the wagon. And at that moment the two gunmen came up from both sides of the high back wall and shot the two officers dead. The gunmen were dressed in officers' uniforms so at first they didn't attract much attention. Then they jumped down inside, put Deke in the wagon and closed the door and got into the front seat – and took the wagon out of the yard.' He stopped and looked at them to see what they would say but they said nothing. So he went on. 'Some of the mob had jumped astride the hood and onto the front bumpers and others were running along beside it. They were shouting, "Make way for O'Malley! Make way for O'Malley!" and they rode the wagon out into the street. The rioters went wild and the officers could only use their saps and billies. They couldn't shoot into those thousand people. The wagon got through. We found it parked a block away around the corner. There must have been a car waiting. They got away. We captured the other prisoners in a matter of minutes.'

'What about the one he was handcuffed to?' Coffin Ed asked.

'Him too. He was wandering in the street. He had been sapped and the cuffs were still on him.'

'It was organized all right, but it needed luck,' Grave Digger said.

'The mob seemed organized too,' the captain said.

'Probably, but I doubt if there was a connection.'

'More likely some planted agitators. They wouldn't have to

know an escape was planned. They might have thought of freeing O'Malley by numbers,' Coffin Ed said.

'A holy crusade,' Grave Digger amended.

The captain looked sour. 'We got three hundred of them in the bullpen. You want to talk to them?'

Grave Digger shook his head. 'What are you holding them for?'

Captain Brice reddened with anger. 'Complicity, goddammit. Assisting criminals to escape. Rioting. Accessories to murder. Two officers were killed. And I'll arrest every black son of a bitch in Harlem.'

'Including me and Digger?' Coffin Ed grated, his face jumping like a live snake in a hot fire.

The captain cooled. 'Hell, goddammit, don't be offended,' he threw out the left-handed apology. 'These goddamned lunatics help in a planned escape without knowing what they're doing and cause two officers to get killed. You ought to be mad too.'

'How mad are *you*?' Grave Digger asked. He felt Coffin Ed look at him. He nodded slightly. He knew Coffin Ed read his thoughts and agreed.

'Mad enough for anything,' Captain Brice said. 'Shoot a few of these hoodlums. I'll cover you.'

Grave Digger shook his head. 'The commissioner wants them alive.'

'I'm not talking about them,' the captain raved. 'Shoot any of these goddamn hoodlums.'

'Take it easy, Captain,' Coffin Ed said.

Grave Digger shook his head warningly. The room had become silent. Everyone was listening. Grave Digger leaned forward and said in a voice only for the captain's ears, 'Are you mad enough to let us have Iris, Deke's woman – if she hasn't gone to county?'

The captain sobered instantly. He looked cornered and annoyed. He wouldn't meet Grave Digger's eyes. 'You're asking for too much,' he growled. 'And you know it,' he accused. Finally he said, 'I couldn't if I wanted to. Her case is on the docket. I'm responsible to deliver her. If she doesn't appear it's officially an escape.'

'Is she still here?' Grave Digger persisted.

'Nobody's gone out,' the captain said. 'All the hearings have been postponed, but that makes no difference.'

Still leaning forward, Grave Digger whispered, 'Let her escape.'

The captain banged his fist on the desk. 'No, goddammit! And that's final.'

'The commissioner wants Deke and the two cop killers,' Grave Digger whispered urgently. 'You had two nights and a day to find those boys – you and the whole Force. And they weren't found. We're only two men. What do you expect us to do that the whole Force couldn't do?'

'Well,' the captain said, expelling his breath. 'Do the best you can.'

'We can find them,' Grave Digger kept on. 'But you got to pay for it.'

'I'll speak to the commissioner,' the captain said, starting to rise.

'No,' Grave Digger said. 'He'll only say *no* and that will be the end of it. You've got to make the decision on your own.'

The captain sat down. He thought for a moment, then looked up into Grave Digger's eyes. 'How bad do you want Deke yourself?' he asked.

'Bad,' Grave Digger said.

'If you can get her out of here without my knowledge, take her,' the captain said. 'I won't know anything about it. If you get caught, take the consequences. I won't cover for you.'

Grave Digger straightened up. Veins stood out on his temples and his neck had swelled like a cobra's. His eyes had turned blood-red. He was so mad the captain's image was blurred in his vision.

'I wouldn't do this for nobody but my own black people,' he said in a voice that was cotton-dry.

He wheeled from the desk and Coffin Ed fell in beside him and they walked fast out of the room and softly closed the door behind them.

They got their official car from the garage and drove up

to Blumstein's Department Store on 125th Street and went into the women's department. Grave Digger bought a bright red dress, size 14, a pair of dark tan lisle stockings and a white plastic handbag. Coffin Ed bought a pair of gilt sandals, size 7, and a hand mirror. They put their packages into a shopping bag and drove up to Rose Murphy's House of Beauty on 145th Street, near Amsterdam Avenue, and bought some quick-action black skin dye and some make-up for a black woman and a dark-haired wig. They put these into their shopping bag and returned to the precinct station.

All the brass had left but the chief inspector in charge of homicide. They had nothing to say to him. Many of the police cruisers had been assigned to special detail and had gone about their business. But the street was still closed and heavily guarded and no one was permitted to enter the block or leave any of the buildings without police scrutiny.

Grave Digger parked in front of the station house and he and Coffin Ed went inside, carrying their shopping bag. They kept on through the booking room and past the captain's office and the detectives' room until they came to the head jailer's cubicle at the rear.

'Send Iris O'Malley down to the interrogation room and give us the key,' Grave Digger said.

The jailer reached out languidly for the order.

'We haven't got any order,' Grave Digger said. 'The captain's too busy to write orders at this time.'

'Can't have her 'less you got an order,' the jailer insisted.

'She'll keep,' Grave Digger said. 'It just holds up the investigation, that's all.'

'Can't do it,' the jailer said stubbornly.

'Then give us the key to the bullpen,' Coffin Ed said. 'We'll start in the Back-to-Africa group.'

'You know I can't do that either 'less you got an order,' the jailer protested. 'What's the matter with you fellows today?'

'Hell, where have you been, man?' Grave Digger said. 'The captain's busy, can't you understand that?'

The jailer shook his head. He didn't want to be the cause of any escapes.

'Call the captain for goddamn's sake,' Coffin Ed grated. 'We can't just stand here and argue with you.'

The jailer got the captain's office on the intercom, and asked if he should let Jones and Johnson interview the Back-to-Africa group in the bullpen.

'Let them see who they goddamn want,' the captain shouted. 'And don't bother me again.'

The jailer looked crestfallen. Now he was anxious to co-operate to keep in their good graces. 'You want to see Iris O'Malley first or afterwards?' he asked.

'Well, we'll just see her first,' Grave Digger said.

The jailer gave them a key and called his underling on the tier where Iris was celled and instructed him to take her down to the 'Pigeons' Nest'.

They were there waiting when the jailer brought her in and left, and they locked the door behind him. They put her on the stool and turned on the battery of lights. Her scratches were healing and the swelling was almost gone from her face but her skin was still the colors of the rainbow. Without make-up her eyes were sexless and ordinary. She wore a dark blue denim uniform but without a number, since she hadn't been bound over to the grand jury.

'You look good,' Coffin Ed said levelly.

'Tell it to your mother,' she said.

'Deke got away,' Grave Digger said.

'The lucky mother-raper,' she said, squinting into the light.

Grave Digger turned down all the lights except one. It left her starkly visible but didn't blind her.

'How'd you like to escape?' Grave Digger asked.

'I'd like it fine,' she said. 'How'd you like to lay me? Both of you. At the same time.'

'Where?' Coffin Ed asked.

'How is the question,' Grave Digger said.

'Here,' she said. 'And let me worry about *how*.'

'All joking aside—' Grave Digger began again, but she cut him off.

'I'm not joking.'

'All sex aside then. Do you know Deke's hideout?'

'If I knew I wouldn't tell you,' she said. 'Anyway, not for nothing.'

'We'll clear you,' he said.

'Shit,' she said. 'You can't clear your own mother-raping selves, much less me. Anyway, I don't know it,' she added.

'Can you find it?'

A sly look came into her eyes. 'I could find it if I was out.'

'I'm reading your mind,' Grave Digger said.

'And it don't read good,' Coffin Ed said.

The sly look went out of her eyes. 'I can't find him from here, and that's for sure.'

'That's for sure,' Grave Digger agreed.

They stared at one another. 'What's in it for me?' she asked.

'Freedom, maybe,' he said. 'When we get Deke we're going to drop the load on him. His two boys are going to fry for cop killing and we're going to fry him for killing Mabel Hill. And you get the ten per cent reward from the eighty-seven grand if we find it.'

They watched the thoughts reflected in her eyes and Coffin Ed said, 'Steady, girl. If you try to cross us there won't be room enough for you in the world. We'll hunt you down and kill you.'

'And don't think you'll be lucky enough to get shot,' Grave Digger added. His lumpy unshaven face looked sadistic from behind the stabbing light, like the vague shadow of a monster's. 'Want me to spell it out?'

She shuddered. 'And if I don't find him?'

He chuckled. 'We'll arrest you for escaping.'

She was consumed with sudden rage. 'You dirty mother-rapers,' she mouthed.

'Better to be dirty than dumb,' Coffin Ed said. 'Are you on?'

She blushed beneath her rainbow color. 'If I could only rape you, you dirty bastard.'

'You can't. So are you on?'

'I'm on,' she said. 'You son of a bitch, you knew it all the time.' After a moment she added, 'Maybe if I don't find Deke you'll rape me.'

'You'll have a better chance if you find him,' he said.

'I'll find him,' she promised.

18

'Make yourself into a black woman and don't ask any questions,' Grave Digger said. 'You'll find everything in there you'll need – make-up, clothes and some money. Don't worry about the dye; it'll come off.'

He turned on the bright lights and he and Coffin Ed went out and locked the door behind them. She found the mirror and went to work. Coffin Ed stood outside the door and listened for a time; he didn't think she'd yell and try to draw attention, but he wanted to make sure. Satisfied she was tending to the business, he went upstairs and waited for Grave Digger to come with the keys to the bullpen. They went inside and interrogated the sullen prisoners until they found a young black woman about Iris's size and age, named Lotus Green. They filled out a card on Lotus, then took her down to the Pigeons' Nest for further questioning.

'What you want with me?' she protested. 'I done tole you everything I know.'

'We like you,' Coffin Ed said.

She shocked the hell out of him by blowing coy. 'You got to pay me,' she said. 'I don't do it with strangers for nothing.'

'We ain't strangers by now,' he said.

He stood outside, listening to her explain why he was still a stranger while Grave Digger went inside to get Iris. She was ready, a fly black woman in a cheap red dress.

'These shit-skin sandals are too big,' she complained.

'Watch your language and act dignified,' Grave Digger said.

'You're a churchwoman named Lotus Green and you hope to go back to Africa.'

'My God!' she exclaimed.

He took her out past the real Lotus while Coffin Ed took the real Lotus inside.

'We're going to put you in the bullpen and when the officer comes for Lotus Green you come out with him,' Grave Digger instructed. 'Just act sullen and don't answer any questions.'

'That won't be hard,' she said.

Coffin Ed locked the real Lotus in the place of Iris, assuring her that he was going to get some money, and joined Grave Digger. They went to the captain's office and asked permission to take out Lotus Green, one of the Back-to-Africa group.

'She saw where the woman went who was robbed that night, but she doesn't know the number,' Grave Digger explained. 'And that woman might have seen all the hijackers.'

The captain suspected some kind of trick. Furthermore he wasn't interested in the hijacking, he just wanted Deke. But it put him on the spot.

'All right, all right,' he snapped. 'I'll send for her and you can take her from my office. Just don't forget your assignment.'

'It's all the same thing,' Grave Digger said. 'Here's the report on her,' and gave him the card.

They went back to see the head jailer. 'We're going to try Iris once more and if she doesn't give we're going to leave her in the dark for a spell. We'll fix it so she can't hurt herself and don't get edgy if someone hears her screaming. She won't be hurt.'

'I don't know what you fellers do down there and I don't want to know,' the jailer said.

'Right,' Grave Digger said and they went down and stood outside the bullpen. When they saw a jailer taking Iris, disguised as Lotus, to the captain's office, they went downstairs and got the real Lotus Green and took her back to the bullpen.

'I waited and I waited,' she complained.

'What else could you do?' Coffin Ed said and they went back upstairs to the captain's office and walked out of the station with Iris between them. They got into their car and drove off.

'We're on our own now,' Coffin Ed said.

'Yeah, we've jumped into the fire,' Grave Digger agreed.

'Well, little sister, where do you want to get out?' Coffin Ed asked the black woman on the back seat.

'Let me out on the corner,' she said.

'What corner?'

'Any corner.'

They pulled to the curb on Seventh Avenue and 125th opposite the Theresa Hotel. They wanted all the stool pigeons in the neighborhood to see her getting out of their car. They knew no one would recognize her, but they were marking her for themselves – just in case.

'This is what you do,' Coffin Ed said, turning about to face her. 'When you contact Deke—'

'*If* I contact Deke,' she cut in.

He looked at her for a moment and said, 'Just don't try getting cute because we sprung you. That ain't going to make any difference if you try a double-cross.'

She didn't answer.

He said, 'When you contact Deke, just say you know where the bale of cotton is.'

'*The what!*' she exclaimed.

'The bale of cotton. And let him take it from there. Then when you get him located, keep him waiting and contact us.'

'Are you sure you mean a bale of *cotton?*' she asked incredulously.

'That's right, a bale of cotton.'

'And how do I contact you?'

'Call either of these two numbers.' He gave her the telephone numbers of their homes. 'If we're not there, leave a number and we'll call back.'

'Shit on that,' she said.

'All right, then call back in half an hour and you'll be given a number where to contact us. Just say you're Abigail.'

Grave Digger muttered, 'Ed, you're giving us a lot of trouble.'

'What do you suggest that's better?'

Grave Digger thought about it for a moment. 'Nothing,' he confessed.

'Bye-bye then,' Iris said, adding under her breath, 'Blackbirds,' and got out. She walked east on 125th.

Grave Digger eased into the traffic on Seventh Avenue and drove north.

Iris stopped in front of a United Tobacco store and watched their car until it passed from sight. The store had five telephone booths ranged along one wall. Iris chose one quickly and dialed a number.

A cautious voice answered: 'Holmes Radio Repair Shop.'

'I want to talk to Mr Holmes,' Iris said.

'Who's calling?'

'His wife. I just got back.'

After a moment another disguised voice said, 'Honey, where are you?'

'I'm here,' Iris said.

'How'd you get out?'

Don't you wish you knew? she thought. Aloud she said, 'How would you like to buy a bale of cotton?'

There was a long pregnant silence. 'Tell me where you are and I'll have my chauffeur pick you up.'

'Stay put,' she said. 'I'm dealing in cotton.'

'Just don't deal in death,' the voice sounded a deadly warning.

She hung up. When she stepped outside she looked up and down the street. Cars were parked on both sides. Crosstown traffic flowed from the Triborough Bridge headed towards the West Side Highway and the 125th Street ferry and vice versa. There was nothing about the black Ford to set it apart from any other car. It was empty and looked put for some time. She didn't see the two-toned Chevrolet parked down the street. But when she started walking again, she was being tailed.

Grave Digger and Coffin Ed drove their official car, the little black car with the hopped-up engine that was so well known in Harlem, into a garage on 155th Street and left it for a tune-up. Then they walked up the hill to the subway and rode the 'A' train down to Columbus Circle at 59th Street and Broadway.

They walked over to the section of pawnshops and second-hand clothing stores on Columbus Avenue and went into Katz's pawnshop and bought black sunglasses and caps. Grave Digger chose a big checkered cap called the 'Sportsman' while Coffin Ed selected a red, long-billed fatigue cap modelled after those worn by the Seabees during the war. When they emerged, they looked like two Harlem cats, high off pot.

They walked up Broadway to a car rental agency and selected a black panel truck without any markings. The rental agent didn't want to trust them until they put down a large deposit. He took it and grinned, figuring them for Harlem racketeers.

'Will this jalopy run?' Grave Digger asked.

'Run!' the agent exclaimed. 'Cadillacs get out of its way.'

'Damn right,' Coffin Ed said. 'If I owned a Cadillac I'd get out of its way too.'

They got in and drove it back uptown.

'Now I know why the world looks so vague to weedheads,' Grave Digger said from behind the wheel.

'Too bad there isn't any make-up to disguise us as white,' Coffin Ed said.

'Hell, I remember when old Canada Lee was made up as a white man, playing on Broadway in a Shakespearean play; and if Canada Lee could look like a white man, I'm damn sure we could.'

The mechanic at the garage didn't recognize them until Grave Digger flashed his shield.

'I'll be a *mother*,' he said, grinning. 'When I saw you coming I locked the safe.'

'Just as well,' Grave Digger said. 'You never know who's in a panel truck.'

'Ain't it the truth?' the mechanic said.

They had him take their radio-telephone from their official car and install it temporarily in the truck. It took forty-five minutes and Coffin Ed called home. His wife said no one named Abigail had called either her or Stella, but the precinct station had been calling every half-hour trying to get in touch with them.

'Just tell them you don't know where we are,' Coffin Ed said. 'And that's the truth.'

When they left the garage they were able to pick up all the police calls. All cars had been alerted to contact them and order them back to the station. Then the cars were instructed to pick up a slim black woman wearing a red dress, named Lotus Green.

Coffin Ed chuckled. 'By this time that yellow gal has damn sure got that dye off, much as she hates being black.'

'And she ain't wearing that cheap red dress, either,' Grave Digger added.

They drove over to a White Rose bar at the corner of 125th and Park Avenue, across the street from the 125th Street railroad station, and parked behind a two-toned Chevrolet. Ernie was sitting in a shoeshine stand outside the bar, facing Park. The sign on the awning read: AMERICAN LEGION SHOE SHINE. Two elderly white men were shining colored men's shoes. Across the avenue, seen between the stanchions of the railroad trestle, was another shoeshine, its awning proclaiming: FATHER DIVINE SHOE SHINE. Two elderly colored men were shining white men's shoes.

'Democracy at work,' Coffin Ed said.

'Down to the feet.'

'Down *at* the feet,' Coffin Ed corrected.

Ernie saw them go into the bar but gave no sign of recognition. They stood at the bar like two cats having a sip of something cold to dampen their dry jag, and ordered beer. After a while Ernie came in and squeezed to the bar beside them. He ordered a beer. The white barman put down an open bottle and a glass. Ernie wasn't looking when he poured it and some sloshed on to Grave Digger's hand. He turned and said, 'Excuse me, I wasn't looking.'

'That's what's on all them tombstones,' Grave Digger said.

Ernie laughed. 'She's at Billie's, the dancer, on 115th Street,' he said under his breath.

'Don't pay no 'tention to me, son, I was just joking,' Grave Digger said aloud. 'Stay with it.'

The bartender was passing. He looked from one to the other. *Stay with it*, he thought. Stay with what? As long as he'd been working in Harlem, he had never learned these colored folks' language.

Grave Digger and Coffin Ed finished their beers and ordered two more and Ernie finished his and went out. Coffin Ed used the bar phone and telephoned his home. There had been no call from Abigail, but the precinct station had been calling regularly. The bartender was listening furtively but Coffin Ed hadn't said a word. Then finally he said, 'Stay with it.' The bartender started. Nuts, he thought looking vindicated.

They left their beers half finished and went around the corner and sat in their truck.

'If we could tap the phone,' Coffin Ed said.

'She's not going to phone from there,' Grave Digger said. 'She's too smart for that.'

'I just hope she don't get too mother-raping smart to live,' Coffin Ed said.

Billie was alone when Iris knocked with the brass-hand knocker on the black and yellow lacquered door. She opened the door on the chain. She was wearing yellow chiffon lounging slacks over a pair of black lace pants and a long-sleeved white chiffon blouse fastened at the cuffs with turquoise links. She might as well have been naked. Her slim, bare, dancer's feet had bright red lacquered nails. As always she was made up as though to step before the cameras. She looked like the favorite in a sultan's harem.

Through the crack she saw a woman who looked too black to be real, dressed like a housemaid on her afternoon off. She blinked. 'You've got the wrong door,' she said.

'It's me,' Iris said.

Billie's eyes widened. '*Me* who? You sound like somebody I know but you sure don't look like anybody I'd ever know.'

'Me, Iris.'

Billie scrutinized her for a moment, then broke into hysterical laughter. 'My God, you look like the last of the Topsys. Whatever happened to you?'

'Unchain the door and let me in,' Iris snapped. 'I know how I look.'

Billie unchained the door, still laughing hysterically, and locked and chained it behind her. Then suddenly, watching Iris hurry towards the bath, she called, 'Hey, I read you were in jail,' running after her.

Iris was already at the mirror, smearing cleansing cream over her face, when Billie came in. 'I'm out now, as you can see.'

'Well, how 'bout you,' Billie said, sitting on the edge of the bathtub. 'Who sprung you? The paper said you lowered the boom on Deke and now he's escaped.'

Iris snatched a clean towel and began frantically rubbing her face to see if the black would come off. Yellow skin appeared. Reassured, she became less frantic. 'The monsters,' she said. 'They want me to help 'em find Deke.'

Billie looked shocked. 'You wouldn't!' she exclaimed.

Iris was slipping out of the cheap red dress. 'The hell I wouldn't,' she said.

Billie jumped to her feet. 'I certainly won't help you,' she said. 'I always liked Deke.'

'You can have him, sugar,' Iris said sweetly, peeling off the lisle stockings. 'I'll swap him for a dress.'

Billie left the room, looking indignant, while Iris shed to the skin and began removing the black in earnest. After a while Billie returned and threw clothes across the side of the tub. She looked at Iris's nude body critically.

'You sure got beat up, baby. You look like you've been raped by three cannibals.'

'That'd be a kick,' Iris mumbled, smearing her face more thoroughly with the cleansing cream.

'Here, use Pond's,' Billie said, handing her a different jar. 'That's Chanel's you're wasting on that blackening and this is just as good for that.'

Iris exchanged the jar without comment and went on smearing her face, neck, arms and legs.

'Did you really kill her?' Billie asked as though casually.

Iris stopped applying the cream and turned around and looked at her. 'Don't ask me that question. There never was a man I'd kill for.' There was a warning in her voice that frightened Billie.

But she had to know. 'Were you and her—'

'Shut up,' Iris snapped. 'I didn't know the bitch.'

'You can't stay here,' Billie said bitchily, showing her disbelief. 'They'd lock me up too if they found me.'

'Don't be so fucking jealous,' Iris said and began kneading in the cleansing cream again. 'Nobody knows I'm here and not even Deke knows about us.'

Billie smiled with secret pleasure. Mollified, she asked, 'How do you expect to get to Deke after you've ratted on him?'

Iris laughed as at a good joke. 'I'm going to cook up a good story about where to find the money he's lost and see what he'll pay me for it. Deke will forgive anything for money.'

'The Back-to-Africa money? Honey, that money has gone with the wind.'

'Don't think I don't know it. I just want to get something out of that two-timing mother-raper any kind of way.'

Billie had her secret smile again. 'Baby, how you talk,' she said, adding: 'You can wipe it off now,' referring to the cream. 'I'll make you up in tan so you'll look brand-new.'

'You're a darling,' Iris said absently, but in the back of her mind she was thinking furiously why Deke would want a bale of cotton.

Billie was looking at her nude body lustfully. 'Don't tempt me,' she said.

19

The Monday edition of the Harlem *Sentinel* came out around noon. Coffin Ed picked up a copy at the newsstand by the

Lexington Avenue Subway Kiosk at one-thirty for them to read with their lunch. There had been no word from Abigail, and Paul had just ridden past giving the high sign that Iris was still put.

They wanted to eat some place where it was unlikely they'd be spotted, and where they wouldn't look out of place in their black weedhead sunglasses. They decided to go to a joint on East 116th Street called Spotty's, run by a big black man with white skin spots and his albino wife.

After years of bemoaning the fact that he looked like an overgrown Dalmatian, Spotty had made a peace with life and opened a restaurant specializing in ham hocks, red beans and rice. It sat between a store-front church and a box factory and had no side windows, and the front was so heavily curtained the light of day never entered. Spotty's prices were too moderate and his helpings too big to afford bright electric lights all day. Therefore it attracted customers such as people in hiding, finicky people who couldn't bear the sight of flies in their food, poor people who wanted as much as they could get for their money, weedheads avoiding bright lights, and blind people who didn't know the difference.

They took a table in the rear across from two laborers. Spotty brought them plates of red beans, rice and ham hocks, and a stack of sliced bread. There wasn't any choice.

Coffin Ed wolfed a mouthful hungrily and gasped for breath. 'This stuff will set your teeth on fire,' he said.

'Take some of this hot sauce and cool it off,' one of the laborers said with a straight face.

'It cools you off these hot days,' the other laborer said. 'Draws all the heat to the belly and leaves the rest of you cool.'

'What about the belly?' Grave Digger asked.

'Hell, man, what kind of old lady you got?' the laborer said.

Grave Digger shouted for two beers. Coffin Ed took out the paper and divided it in two. He could barely see the large print through his smoked glasses. 'What you want, the inside or the outside?'

'You expect to read in here?' Grave Digger said.

'Ask Spotty to give you a candle,' the laborer said with a straight face.

'Never mind,' Grave Digger said. 'I'll read one word and guess two.'

He took the inside of the paper and folded it on the table. The classified ads were up. His gaze was drawn to an ad in a box: *Bale of cotton wanted immediately. Telephone Tompkins 2 – before seven p.m.* He passed the paper to Coffin Ed. Neither of them said anything. The laborers looked curious but Grave Digger turned over the page before they could see anything.

'Looking for a job?' the talkative laborer asked.

'Yeah,' Grave Digger said.

'That ain't the paper for it,' the laborer said.

No one replied. Finally the two laborers got tired of trying to find out their business and got up and left. Grave Digger and Coffin Ed finished eating in silence.

Spotty came to their table. 'Dessert?' he asked.

'What is it?'

'Blackberry pie.'

'Hell, it's too dark in here to eat blackberry pie,' Grave Digger said and paid him and they got up and left.

Coffin Ed called his home from a street booth, but there was still no word from Abigail. Then he called the Tompkins number. A southern voice answered, 'Back-to-the-Southland office, Colonel Calhoun speaking.' He hung up.

'The Colonel,' he told Grave Digger when he got back in the truck.

'Let's don't think about it here,' Grave Digger said. 'They might be tracing our calls home.'

They drove back past the 125th Street railroad station and found the Chevrolet parked near the Fischer Cafeteria. Ernie gave them the sign that Iris was still put. They were driving on when they saw a blind man tapping his way along. They pulled around the corner of Madison Avenue and waited.

Finally the blind man came tapping along Madison. He was selling Biblical calendars. Coffin Ed leaned from the truck and said, 'Hey, let me see one of those.'

The blind man tapped over towards the edge of the sidewalk, feeling his way cautiously. He pulled a calendar from his bag and said, 'It's got all the names of the Saints and the Holy Days, and numbers straight out of the Apocalypse; and it's got the best days for births and deaths.' Lowering his voice, he added, 'It's the photograph I told you about night before last.'

Coffin Ed made as though he were leafing through it. 'How'd you make us?' he whispered.

'Ernie,' the blind man whispered back.

Satisfied, Coffin Ed said loudly, 'Got any dream readings in here?'

Passersby hearing the question stopped to listen.

'There's a whole section on dream interpretations,' the blind man said.

'I'll take this one,' Coffin Ed said and gave the blind man a half-dollar.

'I'll take one too,' another man said. 'I dreamed last night I was white.'

Grave Digger drove off, turned east on 127th Street and parked. Coffin Ed passed him the photograph. It showed distinctly the front of a big black limousine. A blond young man sat behind the wheel. Colonel Calhoun sat next to him. Three vague white men sat on the rear seat. Approaching the car was Josh, the murdered junkyard laborer, grinning with relief.

'This cooks him,' Grave Digger said.

'It won't fry him,' Coffin Ed said, 'but it'll scorch the hell out of him.'

'Anyway, he didn't get the cotton.'

'What does that prove? He might already have the money and the cotton might just be evidence. He might have killed the boy just to keep from tipping his hand,' Grave Digger argued.

'And advertise for the cotton today? Hell, let's take him anyway, and find the cotton later.'

'Let's get Deke first,' Grave Digger said. 'The Colonel will keep. He's got more than eighty-seven thousand dollars behind him – the whole mother-raping white South – and he's playing a deeper game than just hijacking.'

'We'll see, said the blind man,' Coffin Ed said and they drove back to the White Rose bar at 125th and Park. Paul was waiting at the bar, drinking a Coke. They pushed in beside him. He spoke in a low voice but openly. 'We've been assigned to another case. Captain Brice doesn't know we've been working for you and we won't tell him, but we have to report to the station now. Ernie's waiting for you to take over. She hasn't moved but that doesn't mean she hasn't phoned.'

'Right,' Grave Digger said. 'We're on the lam, you know.'

'I know.'

The bartender approached with a wise, knowing look. These nuts again, he was thinking. But they left without ordering. He nodded his head wisely, as if he'd known it all the time. They drove over to 115th Street and found Ernie parked near the corner watching the entrance of the apartment house through his rearview mirror while pretending to read a newspaper. Coffin Ed gave him a sign and he drove off.

There was a bar with a public telephone on the corner of Lenox Avenue. So they parked down towards Seventh Avenue, opposite the entrance, so they would be behind Iris if she came out to telephone. Grave Digger got out and began jacking up the right rear wheel, keeping bent over out of sight of Billie's windows. Coffin Ed walked towards the bar, shoulders hunched and red cap pulled low over his black weedhead sunglasses. He looked like one of the real-gone cats with his signifying walk. They figured she had to make her move soon.

But it had turned dark before Iris left the apartment. By now the tenements had emptied of people seeking the cool of evening, and the sidewalks were crowded. But Iris walked fast, looking straight ahead, as though the people on the street didn't exist.

Her skin was a smooth painted tan without a blemish, like the soft velvety leather of an expensive handbag. She wore silk Paisley slacks and a blue silk jersey blouse of Billie's, and one of the red-haired wigs Billie used in her act. Her hips were pitching like a rowboat on a stormy sea, but her cold, aloof face said: Your eyes may shine and your teeth may grit, but none of this fine ass will you git.

This puzzled Grave Digger as he pulled the truck out from the curb a half-block behind her. She wanted to be seen. Coffin Ed had the telephone covered but she didn't look towards the bar. Instead she turned north on Lenox, walking fast but not looking back. Grave Digger picked up Coffin Ed and they followed a block behind, careful but not cute.

She turned east on 121st Street and went directly to O'Malley's church, The Star of Ham. The front door was locked, but she had a key.

Grave Digger parked just around the corner on Lenox and they hit the pavement in a flat-footed lope. But she was already out of sight.

'Cover the back,' he said, and ran up the stairs and tried the front door.

There was no time for finesse. Coffin Ed jumped the iron gate at the side and ran down the walk towards the back.

The front door was locked. Grave Digger studied the windows. Coffin Ed studied the back door and found it locked too. He hoisted himself up on to the brick wall separating the backyard of the apartment next door for a better view.

From the hideout underneath the rostrum, all three distinctly heard her key in the lock, heard the lock click, the door opening and closing, the lock clicking shut, and her footsteps on the wooden floor.

'Here she is now,' Deke said with relief.

'It's a goddamn good thing for you,' the oily-haired gunman said. He had a Colt .45 automatic in his right hand and he kept slapping the barrel in the palm of his left hand as he looked down at Deke.

Deke was tied to one of the two straight-backed tubular chairs and sweat was streaming down his face as though he were crying. He had been tied in that position, with his arms about the chair's back, since Iris had first telephoned, seven hours previous.

The other gunman lay on the couch, his eyes closed, seemingly asleep.

They were silent as they listened over the electronics pickup to Iris's footsteps tripping across the floor above, but their attention was alerted when they heard another sound at the front door.

'She's tailed,' the gunman on the couch said, sitting up.

He was a stout, light-complexioned man with thinning straight brown hair, slitted brown eyes and a nasty-looking mouth as though he dribbled food. He spat on the floor as they listened.

The footsteps rounded the pulpit and stopped on the other side and there was no more sound from the front door.

'She's on to it,' Deke said, licking the sweat trickling into his mouth, 'She's going out through the wall to lose them.'

The gunman on the couch said, 'She better lose them good, baby.'

They heard the secret door through the wall into an apartment in the building next door being opened and closed and then silence.

The gunman standing slapped the Colt against the palm of his hand as though perplexed. 'How come you trust this bitch when she's ratted on you before?'

The sweat stung Deke's eyes and he blinked. 'I don't trust her, but that bitch likes money; and she's always going to keep this secret for her own safety,' he said.

The gunman on the couch said, 'It's your life, baby.'

The gunman standing said, 'She'd better come back soon or it's gonna be too late. It's getting hotter all the time.'

'It's safe here,' Deke said desperately. 'You're safer here until we get the money than being on the loose. Nobody knows about this hideout.'

The gunman on the couch spat. ''Cept Iris and the people who built it.'

'White men built it,' Deke said. He couldn't keep the smugness out of his voice. 'They didn't suspect a thing. They thought it was to be a crypt.'

'What's that?' asked the standing gunman.

'A vault, for dead saints maybe.'

The gunman looked at him, then looked around as though seeing the room for the first time. It was a small square room with soundproof walls, and access from above through the back of the church organ. There was a niche in one wall with a silver icon flanked by prints of Christ and the Virgin. Deke had furnished it with a couch, two tubular chairs, a small kitchen table and a refrigerator which he kept well stocked with prepared food, beer and whisky. Soiled dishes on the table attested to the fact they had eaten there at least once.

One entire wall was taken up by the electronics system with pickup and amplifier that recorded every sound made in the church above. When turned up full volume even the footsteps of a mouse could be heard. On the opposite wall was a gun rack containing two rifles, two sawed-off shotguns and a submachine gun. Deke was proud of the place. He had had it built when reconditioning the church. He felt completely safe there. But the gunman was unimpressed.

'Let's just hope them white men don't remember,' he said. 'Or that she don't bring a police tail back here. This place ain't no more safe than a coffin.'

'Believe me,' Deke said. 'I know it's safe.'

'We sprang you, baby, to get the money,' the sitting gunman said flatly. 'We figured we'd spring you and then sell your life to you for eighty-seven grand. You get the picture, baby. You going to buy it?'

'Freddy,' Deke appealed to the sitting gunman but got nothing from his eyes but a blank deadly stare. 'Four-Four,' he appealed to the oily-haired one standing with the Colt in his hand and drew another blank stare. 'You've got to trust me,' he pleaded. 'I've never let you down. You've got to give me time . . .'

'You got time,' Freddy said, standing up and going to the

icebox for another can of beer. He spat on the floor, slammed shut the box. 'But not all of it.'

From atop the brick wall in back of the church, Coffin Ed got a glimpse of Iris's face peeping from behind the curtains of the back window of a first-floor apartment. It came more from a sixth sense than actual sight. There was only a dim light in back of her, outlining a mere shadow, and the light from outside was filtered from surrounding windows. And she was visible for only a moment. It was the timing more than anything which told him. Who else in the vicinity might be peering furtively from a back window at just that moment.

He knew automatically she had got through the wall. How, he didn't care. He knew she had not only recognized him then, but had made them both from the start. A smart bitch – too smart. He debated whether to burst in on her openly, or take cover and let her make her move. Then he decided to go back and confer with Grave Digger.

'Let her go,' Grave Digger said. 'She can't hide for ever, she ain't invisible. And she's made us now. So let her go, let her go. Maybe she'll contact us.'

They walked back to the truck and drove up to a bar, and Coffin Ed telephoned home. His wife Molly said Abigail hadn't called but Anderson was on duty now and he wanted them to call him.

'Call him,' Grave Digger said.

Anderson said, 'Bring in Iris while I'm on duty and I'll try to cover for you. Otherwise you're certain to be picked up by tomorrow and you'll be finished on the Force – probably face a rap. Captain Brice is furious.'

'He knows about it,' Coffin Ed said. 'He promised to lay off.'

'That's not the way he tells it. He's reported to the commissioner that you've abducted her and he's seeing red.'

'He's mad just because we tricked him; and he's covering himself at our expense.'

'Be that as it may, he's mad enough to break you.'

They sat silent for a moment, tense and worried.

'You figure she might try to take a powder?' Coffin Ed said.

'We got enough to worry about without that,' Grave Digger said. 'And we ain't got time for it.'

'Let's go to Billie's.'

'She's left there for good. Let's go back to the church.'

'That was just to shake us,' Coffin Ed argued. 'She's finished with the church.'

'Maybe, maybe not. Deke wouldn't put in an escape door for nothing. There must be something else there.'

Coffin Ed thought about it. 'Maybe you're right.'

They parked on 122nd Street and cased the back of the church. The backyard was separated by the high brick wall from the garbage-strewn backyards surrounding it. They scaled the wall and examined the back door. It had an ordinary Yale snap lock with an iron grille covering its dirty panes but they didn't touch it. They peered through a window into the vestry back of the choir but it was black dark inside.

Then they went down the narrow walk alongside the church. It was a brick structure and in good condition and on that side two arched stained-glass windows flanked a stained-glass oval high in the wall. The other side of the church was built flush with the apartment house.

'If they got a hideout in there they got some kind of hearing device for protection,' Grave Digger reasoned. 'They can't have a lookout hiding all the time.'

'What do you want to do, wait outside for her?'

'She'll return through the wall, or she might already be in there.'

They looked at one another thinking.

'Listen—' Coffin Ed began and explained.

'Anyway, it beats a blank,' Grave Digger said, as he stopped in the darkness to take off his shoes.

They stood behind the gate and watched the street until it was momentarily empty. Then they scaled the iron gate and hurried up the stairs to the church door, and Coffin Ed began picking the lock. If anyone had passed they would have been taken for two drunks urinating against the church door. When it was open, Grave Digger sat astride Coffin Ed's shoulders and they went inside and closed the door behind them.

The tableau in the hideout was much the same. Deke was still tied to the chair and the oily-haired gunman, Four-Four, was letting him drink from a can of beer. Beer was spilling from his mouth onto his pants and Four-Four said irritably, 'Can't you swallow, goddammit?' slapping his own thigh with the barrel of the Colt. Freddy was lying on the couch again as though he were asleep.

Suddenly they froze at the sound of the front door lock being picked. Four-Four took the beer can from Deke's mouth and put it atop the table and changed the Colt to his left hand, flexing his right. Freddy swung his feet over to the floor and sat up, listening with his mouth open. They heard the door swing open and someone step inside and the door being closed.

'We got a visitor,' Freddy said.

They heard the footsteps come down the center aisle.

'A dick,' Four-Four said, appraising the walk.

Freddy stepped over to the gun rack and casually took down a sawed-off shotgun. They listened to the steps move around the choir and the pulpit and approach the organ. Freddy looked at the access ladder as though in a trance.

'A big boy,' he said. 'Big as two men. Think I ought to go up and cut him down to size?'

'Let him stick his head in, ha-ha,' Four-Four laughed.

'You're not going to leave me tied up!' Deke protested.

'Sure, baby, that or dead,' Freddy said.

The heavy man's footsteps passed the organ, paused for a moment as though he were looking around, then moved on slowly as though he were examining everything. Through the electronics pickup they could hear his heavy breathing.

'A fat baby with a heart,' Four-Four said.

'Guts too,' Deke said. 'Coming here alone.'

'I got something for his guts,' Freddy said, swinging the sawed-off shotgun.

The footsteps circled the pulpit, stopped for a moment, then went down into the auditorium and moved along the walls. They could hear knuckles sounding the walls. The footsteps moved slowly as the man encircled the walls, sounding for a false door. Ear-shattering bangs suddenly shook the small hideout as the man began sounding the wooden floor with his pistol butt.

'Cut that damn thing down,' Four-Four shouted. 'The mother-raper will hear himself upstairs.'

Freddy turned it down until the tapping on the floor became muted. It went on and on until seemingly every inch of the floor was covered. There was silence for a long time as though the man was listening. Then they heard the faint click of his pocket torch being turned on. Finally they heard his footsteps moving towards the door. Half-way they heard him stop and put what sounded like the palms of his hands on the floor.

'What the hell's he doing now?' Four-Four asked.

'Damned if I know,' Freddy said. 'Probably planting a time bomb.' He laughed at his own humor.

'It wouldn't be so damn funny if you got your ass blown off,' Four-Four said sourly.

They heard the imagined dick open the snap lock on the front door and pass out, closing the door behind him.

'It's time for that bitch of yours to be showing,' Four-Four said disagreeably.

'She's coming,' Deke said.

'She'd better come ready,' Freddy said. 'If she don't know where the money is, you can preach both of youse funerals.' He chuckled.

'Dry up,' Four-Four said.

20

Iris came in with perfect assurance. She knew she hadn't been tailed. She had shaken Grave Digger and Coffin Ed and she wasn't afraid. She knew where the cotton was and how they could get it. She knew with this information she could handle Deke. And she had confidence that Deke could handle his gorillas.

Deke and his gunmen heard her when she entered.

'That's her now,' Deke said, sighing with relief.

Freddy got up from the couch and took down the shotgun again. Four-Four jacked a shell into the chamber of his .45 automatic and slid back the safety. Both were tense but neither spoke.

Deke was listening to her walk. He could tell from the rhythm of her steps she was walking with assurance.

'She got it,' he said with a confident look.

'She'd better have it,' Freddy said dangerously.

'I mean the information,' Deke said hurriedly for fear they might mistake his meaning.

Neither answered.

Grave Digger lay face down between two benches, breathing into a black cotton handkerchief, his hand on his pistol underneath his body. His black suit blended with the darkness and she didn't see a thing as she passed. He waited until he heard her footsteps ascending the rostrum, then scuttled down the center aisle on hands and knees to open the front door for Coffin Ed, hoping the sound of her footsteps would cover whatever sound he made.

But they heard it anyway.

'What the hell's she got with her?' Four-Four said.

'Sounds like her dog,' Freddy said and started to laugh, but the look from Four-Four cut it off.

They heard the soft tap on the organ pipe that was the signal for entrance. Four-Four pushed a button and a panel in the back of the organ raised, revealing a small square space beneath the pipes. He pushed the second button and a heavy steel trapdoor opened upward. He raised the ladder and her gilt high-heeled sandals and legs encased in Paisley silk slacks came into view as she descended. He pushed the buttons closing the door behind her when her enticing buttocks showed. Then he raised the cocked .45 automatic and levelled it towards her back.

Her feet touched the floor and she turned around. She looked into the muzzle of the .45 and it looked like the head of a Gorgon. Her body turned to stone. Only the lids of her eyes moved as they continued to stretch as though her eyeballs were squeezed from her head. Slowly, without breathing, her eyes sought the face of Freddy and saw no pity; they slid off and she saw Deke tied to the chair, looking at her with raw anxiety, sweat streaming from a face contorted with terror; next they took in the shotgun in Freddy's hands and finally his nasty-mouthed sadistic face.

Nausea came up in her like the waves of the ocean and she gritted her teeth to keep from fainting. Her terror was so intense it became sexual – and she had an orgasm. All her life she had searched for kicks, but this was the kick she never wanted.

'Who was with you?' Four-Four asked.

She swallowed twice before she could find the handle to her voice, then it came in a husky whisper: 'No one, I swear.'

'We heard something strange.'

'I wasn't tailed, I know,' she whispered. Sweat beaded on her upper lip and her eyes were limpid pools of terror. 'I'm clean, please listen to me,' she begged. 'Don't just kill me for nothing.'

'Tell them, baby, tell them quick,' Deke babbled in terror.

'It's in the cotton,' she said.

'We know that,' Four-Four said. 'Where's the cotton?'

She kept swallowing as though choking. 'I'm not going to tell you just to get killed,' she whispered.

With a sudden movement that made her start, Freddy whipped the second straight-backed chair around behind Deke and said, 'Sit down.'

Four-Four stuck his pistol in his belt and took a coil of nylon clothesline from the floor beneath the gun rack. 'Put your hands behind you, in back of the chair.' She was slow in obeying and he slapped her across the face with the rope. She did as ordered and he began tying her methodically.

'Tell them,' Deke begged piteously.

'She'll tell us,' Freddy said.

Four-Four was tying her chair back to back with Deke's when they heard someone whistling in the street. They froze, listening, but the whistling stopped and there was silence. Four-Four finished tying them together on the two chairs back to back, then they all started nervously as they heard the front door of the church being opened. There was a soft sound like the padded feet of an animal and the door closed softly.

'We better look,' Four-Four said. His voice stuttered slightly and his eyelids blinked rapidly as with a tic.

Freddy's nasty-looking mouth seemed breaking apart and his lips trembled. He got another .45 automatic from beneath the couch, jacked a shell in the chamber and slid off the safety. His motions were jerky but his hands were steady. He stuck the pistol in his belt and held the shotgun in his right hand. 'Let's go,' he said.

Grave Digger and Coffin Ed were deploying along opposite walls when Freddy came from behind the organ, searching quickly with the muzzle of the shotgun like a rabbit shooter. Coffin Ed went down out of sight but Freddy saw the moving shadow. The church exploded with the heavy thumping boom of a twelve-gauge shell of buckshot firing and the heavy charge took a section out of the back of the bench beneath which Coffin Ed had flopped. Grave Digger threw a tracer bullet and in the lightning flash from the trajectory saw the bullet burn through Freddy's sport-shirt collar as he dove towards the floor, and the outline of Four-Four coming from in back of him full speed with the .45 searching.

Grave Digger went down himself, scuttling like a crab, as bursts from the .45 splintered benches above his head. For a moment there was stealthy movement in the dark with no one visible. Then the side of the organ began to burn where the tracer bullet had punctured it.

When Coffin Ed peeped up five rows away from where the shotgun charge had knocked a hole in the back of a bench, the rostrum was deserted and no one was in sight. But he saw the top of a head coming around the front bench on the center aisle and threw a tracer bullet at the round mop. He saw the bullet go through the bushy hair and penetrate the front of the platform supporting the rostrum and the choir. The scream was commencing as he ducked.

A figure with burning hair looked in the flickering red light from the burning organ with a .45 searching the gloom and Grave Digger peeped. The shotgun went off and splintered the back of the bench in front of him and the church quivered from the blast. Grave Digger fell belly down and began crawling fast, shaken by his narrow escape. Forty-five bullets were breaking up the benches all around him and he didn't dare look. He lay on his belly beneath the benches, looking towards the sound, and made out the vague outline of trousered legs limned against the platform that had caught on fire. He took careful aim and shot a leg. He saw the leg break off like a wooden stick where the tracer bullet hit it dead center, and saw the trouser leg catch fire suddenly. Now the screaming slashed into the pool of silence like needles of flame and seared his nerves.

The burning shape of the body issuing these screams fell atop the broken leg, on the floor between two benches, and Grave Digger pumped two tracer bullets into it and watched the flames spring up. The dying man clawed at the book rack above him, breaking the fragile wood, and a prayer book fell on top of his burning body.

The burning-headed gunman was down beneath a bench, rubbing his oily hair with blistered hands, while Coffin Ed was peeping above the benches, searching for him with his long-barreled .38 in the red glare from the brightly burning organ.

The smoke had penetrated the hideout below, and the prisoners tied back-to-back on the two chairs had gone crazy from terror. They were spitting curses and accusations, and trying desperately to get at each other.

'You're a pimp for your mother and sister, you money-sucking snake,' Iris screamed with face distorted and eyes terrified like the eyes of a burning horse.

'You two-bit stooling whore, I'll kill you,' Deke grated.

Their legs were tied together like their arms but their feet touched the floor. They were straining with arched bodies and gripping feet to push each other into the wall. The chairs slid on the concrete floor, back and forth, rocking precariously. Arteries in their necks were swelled to bursting, muscles stretched like frayed cables, bodies twisting, breasts heaving, mouths gasping and drooling like two people in a maniacal sex act. Her make-up became streaked from sweat and her wig fell off. Deke doubled forward on his feet tied to the chair's legs, trying to bang Iris sideways against the gun rack. Her chair rose from the floor and bloodcurdling screams came wetly from her scar-like mouth as his chair tilted forward from his superhuman effort and they turned slowly over in a grotesque arc. He fell forward, face downward, striking his forehead on the concrete floor, as she came overtop in her chair. The momentum kept them turning until her head and forehead scraped on the concrete in turn and he was lifted from the floor. They landed up against the wall, her feet touching it, his chair on top supported only by the angle of hers on the floor. She kept trying to use her feet to push back from the wall, while he twisted violently, trying to rub her face against the concrete. The motion rocked them from side to side until both chairs fell sideways with a crash and they were left on their sides on the concrete floor between the gun rack and the table, unable to move. The thunder of the gunfight above that had shaken the room had quieted to darkening with smoke. Both were too spent to curse, they remained still, gasping for breath in the slowly suffocating smoke.

Upstairs in the church, light from the burning gunman on the floor lit up the figure of the gunman with his head on fire crouched behind the end of a bench ahead.

On the other side of the church Coffin Ed was standing with his pistol leveled, shouting, 'Come out, mother-raper, and die like a man.'

Grave Digger took careful aim between the legs of the benches at the only part of the gunman that was visible and shot him through the stomach. The gunman emitted an eerie howl of pain, like a mortally wounded beast, and stood up with his .45 spewing slugs in a blind stream. The screaming had risen to an unearthly pitch, filling the mouths of the detectives with the taste of bile. Coffin Ed shot him in the vicinity of the heart and his clothes caught fire. The screaming ceased abruptly as the gunman slumped across the bench in a kneeling posture, as though praying in fire.

Now the entire platform holding the pulpit and the choir and the organ was burning brightly, lighting up the stained-glass pictures of the saints looking down from the windows. From outside came a banshee wail as the first of the cruisers came tearing into the street.

Grave Digger and Coffin Ed ran barefooted through the flame and kicked in the back of the organ with scorched feet. But they couldn't budge the steel trapdoor.

When the first of the police arrived they had reloaded and were shooting into the floor, trying to find the lock. Screams were heard coming from below and a dark cloud of smoke enveloped them. More police arrived and all worked frantically to open the door, but it wasn't until eight minutes later, when the first firemen arrived with axes and crowbars, it got opened.

Grave Digger pushed everyone aside and went down first with Coffin Ed following. He grabbed the chairs with the two figures and righted them. Iris was facing them and she was strangling in the smoke and tears were streaming down her face. Before moving to release her, he leaned down and looked into her face.

'And now, little sister, where's the cotton?'

Firemen and policemen were crowding around, coughing and crying in the dense smoke.

'Let them loose, take them out of here,' a uniformed sergeant ordered. 'They'll suffocate.'

Iris looked down, thinking furiously, trying to figure an angle for herself.

'What cotton?' she said, to give herself time.

Grave Digger leaned forward until his face almost touched hers. His eyes were bright red and veins stood out in his temples. His neck swelled and his lumpy unshaven face contorted with rage.

'Baby, you'd have never come here if you didn't know,' he said in a cotton-dry voice, gasping and coughing for breath. He raised his long-barreled .38 and aimed it at one of her eyes.

Coffin Ed drew his pistol and held back the policemen and firemen. His acid-burned face was jumping as though cooking in the heat and his eyes looked insane.

'And you'll never leave here alive unless you tell,' Grave Digger finished.

Silence fell. No one moved. No one believed he would kill her, but no one dared interfere because of Coffin Ed; he looked capable of anything.

Iris looked down at Grave Digger's burned stockinged feet. Fearfully her gaze lifted to his burning red eyes. She believed it.

'Billie's doing a dance with it,' she whispered.

'Take them,' Grave Digger said, as he and Coffin Ed turned, hurrying off.

21

The dance floor of the Cotton Club stood on a platform level with the tops of the tables and also served as a stage for the big floor-shows presented. At the back were curtained exits into the wings which contained the dressing-rooms.

When Grave Digger and Coffin Ed peered from behind the curtains to one of the wings, they saw the club was filled with well-dressed people, white and colored, sitting about small tables with cotton-white covers, their eyes shining like liquid crystals in faces made exotic by candlelight.

A piano was playing frenetically, a saxophone wailing aphrodisiacally, the bass patting suggestively, the horn demanding and the guitar begging. A blue-tinted spotlight from over the heads of the diners bathed the almost naked tan body of Billie in blue mist as she danced slowly about a bale of cotton, her body writhing and her hips grinding as though making easy-riding love. Spasms caught her from time to time and she flung herself against the bale convulsively. She rubbed her belly against it and she turned and rubbed her buttocks against it, her bare breasts shaking ecstatically. Her wet red lips were parted as though she were gasping, her pearly teeth glistened in the blue light. Her nostrils quivered. She was creating the illusion of being seduced by a bale of cotton.

Dead silence reigned in the audience. Women stared at her greedily, enviously, with glittering eyes. Men stared lustfully, lids lowered to hide their thoughts. The dance quickened and people squirmed. Billie threw her body against the cotton with mad desire. Bodies of women in the audience shook uncontrollably from compulsive motivation. Lust rose in the room like miasma.

The act was working to a climax. Billie was twisting her body and rolling her hips with shocking rapidity. She worked completely around the bale of cotton, then, facing the audience, flung her arms wide apart and gave her hips a final shake. 'Ohhh, daddy cotton!' she cried.

Abruptly the lights came on and the audience went wild with applause. Billie's smooth voluptuous body was wet with sweat. It gleamed like a lecher's dream of hot flesh. Her breasts were heaving, the nipples pointing like selecting fingers.

'And now,' she said, slightly panting when the applause died down, 'I shall auction this bale of cotton for the actors' benefit fund.' She smiled, panting, and looked down at a nervous young white man with his girl at a ringside table. 'If you're scared, go home,' she challenged, taunting him with a movement of her body. He reddened. A titter arose. 'Who'll bid a thousand dollars?' she said.

Silence fell.

From two tables back someone said in a level southern drawl, 'One thousand.'

Eyes pivoted.

A lean-faced white man with long silvery hair, a white moustache and goatee, wearing a black frock coat and black string bow, sat at a table with a young blond white man wearing a white tuxedo jacket and a Dubonnet-colored bow.

'The mother-raper,' Coffin Ed said.

Grave Digger gestured for silence.

'A gentleman from the Old South!' Billie cried. 'I'll bet you're a Kentucky Colonel.'

The man stood up, tall and stately, and bowed. 'Colonel Calhoun, at your service, from Alabama,' he drawled.

Someone in the audience clapped. 'A brother of yours, Colonel,' Billie cried delightedly. 'He's attracted by this cotton too. Stand up, brother.'

A big black man stood up. The colored people in the audience roared with laughter.

'What you bid, brother rat?' Billie asked.

'He bids fifteen hundred,' a voice cried jubilantly.

'Let him bid for himself,' Billie snapped.

'I don't bid nothing,' the man said. 'You just asted me to stand up, is all.'

'Well, sit down then,' Billie said.

The man sat down self-consciously.

'Going,' Billie said. 'Going. This fine bale of natural-grown Alabama field cotton going for one thousand – and maybe I'll go with it. Any other bids?'

Only silence came.

'Cheapskates,' Billie sneered. 'You're going to close your eyes and imagine it's me, but it ain't going to be the same. Last chance. Going, going, gone. And look how many actors will benefit.' She winked brazenly, then said, 'Colonel Calhoun, suh, come forward and take possession of it.'

'Of what?' some wit cracked.

'Guess, you idiot,' Billie sneered.

The Colonel arose and went forward to the platform, a tall, straight, confident white man, and handed Billie ten one-hundred-dollar bank notes. 'I deem it an honor, Miss Billie, to purchase this cotton from a beautiful nigra girl who might also be from those happy lands—'

'Not me, Colonel,' Billie interrupted.

'—and in so doing benefit many deserving nigra actors,' the Colonel finished.

There was a scattering of applause.

Billie ran and pulled handfuls of cotton from the bale and the Colonel tensed momentarily, but as quickly relaxed when she came running back and showered the strands of cotton on to his silvery head.

'I hereby ordain you as King of Cotton, Colonel,' she said. 'And may this cotton bring you wealth and fame.'

'Thank you,' the Colonel said gallantly. 'I'm sure it will,' and then signaled to the stage door opposite Grave Digger and Coffin Ed.

Two ordinary-looking colored workmen came forward with a hand truck and took the bale of cotton away.

Grave Digger and Cotton Ed hurried towards the street, limping like soul-brothers with duck feet. The truckmen brought out the bale of cotton and put it in back of an open delivery truck, and the Colonel followed leisurely and spoke to them and got into his black limousine.

Grave Digger and Coffin Ed were already in their panel truck parked a half-block back.

'So he found his car,' Coffin Ed remarked.

'One gets you two it was never lost.'

'That's a sucker's bet.'

When the truck drove off they followed it openly. It went up Seventh Avenue and drew to the curb in front of the Back-to-the-Southland office. Grave Digger drove past and turned into the driveway of a repair garage, closed for the night, and Coffin Ed got out and began picking the lock of the roll-up door as though he worked there. He was working at the lock when the Colonel's limousine pulled up behind the truck across the street and the Colonel got out and looked about. He got the lock open and was rolling up the door by the time the Colonel had unlocked the door to his own office and the truckmen began easing the bale of cotton down onto the sidewalk. Grave Digger drove the panel truck into the strange garage and cut the lights and got out beside Coffin Ed. They stood in the dark doorway, checking their pistols, and watched the truckmen wheel the bale of cotton into the brightly lighted office and drop it in the center of the floor. They saw the Colonel pay them and speak to the blond young man, and when the truckmen left, the two of them spoke briefly again and the blond young man returned to the limousine while the Colonel turned out the lights and locked the door and followed him.

When they drove off, Grave Digger and Coffin Ed hurried across the street, and Coffin Ed began picking the lock to the Back-to-the-Southland office while Grave Digger shielded him.

'How long is it going to take?' Grave Digger asked.

'Not long. It's an ordinary store lock but I got to get the right tumbler.'

'Don't take too long.'

The next moment the lock clicked. Coffin Ed turned the knob and the door came open. They went inside and locked the door behind them and moved quickly through the darkness to a small broom closet at the rear. It was hot in the closet and they began to sweat. They kept their pistols in their hands and their palms became wet. They wanted to talk but were afraid to risk it. They had to let the Colonel get the money from the bale of cotton himself.

They didn't have long to wait. In less than fifteen minutes there was the sound of a key in the lock. The door opened and two pairs of footsteps entered and the door closed.

They heard the Colonel say, 'Pull down the shades.'

They heard the sounds of the shades covering the front windows and the door being pulled to the bottom and latched. Then there was the click of the light switch and the keyhole in the closet had sudden dimensions.

'Do you think that'll be enough?' a voice questioned. 'Anyone can see there's a light on inside.'

'There's no risk, son, everything is covered,' the Colonel said. 'Let's don't be too secretive. We pay the rent here.'

There was the sound of the bale of cotton being shifted, probably being turned over, Grave Digger thought.

'Just give me that knife and keep the bag ready,' the Colonel said.

Grave Digger felt in the darkness of the closet for the doorknob, and squeezed it hard and pulled it. But he waited until he heard the sound of the knife cut into the bale of cotton before turning it. Soundlessly he opened the door a crack and released the knob with the same caution.

Now through the crack they could see the Colonel engrossed in his work. He was cutting through the cotton with a sharp hunting knife and pulling out the fibers with a double-pronged hook. The blond young man stood to one side, watching intently, holding open a Gladstone bag. Neither looked around.

Grave Digger and Coffin Ed breathed silently through their mouths as they watched the hole grow larger and deeper. Loose cotton began piling up on the floor. The Colonel's face began sweating. The blond young man looked increasingly anxious. A frown appeared between his eyes.

'Have you got the right side?' he asked.

'Certainly, it shows where we opened it,' the Colonel said in a controlled voice, but his expression and his haste expressed his own growing anxiety.

The blond young man's breathing had become labored. 'You should be down to the money,' he said finally.

The Colonel stopped digging. He put his arm into the hole to measure its depth. He straightened up and looked at the blond young man as though he didn't see him. For a long moment he seemed lost in thought.

'Incredible!' he said.

'What?' the blond young man blurted.

'There isn't any money.'

The blond young man's mouth flew open. Shock stretched his eyes and he grunted as though someone had hit him in the solar plexus.

'Impossible,' he gasped.

Suddenly the Colonel went berserk. He began stabbing the bale of cotton with the hunting knife as though it were human and he was trying to kill it. He slashed it and raked it with the hook. His face had turned bright red and foam collected in the corners of his mouth. His blue eyes looked stone crazy.

'Gawdammit, I tell you there isn't any money!' he shouted accusingly, as though it were the young man's fault.

Grave Digger pushed open the closet door and stepped into the room, his long-barreled, nickelplated .38 revolver leveled on the Colonel's heart and glinting deadly in the bright light.

'That's just too mother-raping bad,' he said and Coffin Ed followed him.

The Colonel and the young man froze, suspended in motion. Their eyes mirrored shock. The Colonel was the first to regain his composure. 'What does this mean?' he asked in a controlled voice.

'It means you're under arrest,' Grave Digger said.

'Arrest? For preparing a bale of cotton to exhibit during our rally tomorrow?'

'When you hijacked the Back-to-Africa meeting you hid the money in this bale of cotton during your getaway, then lost it. We wondered what made this bale of cotton so important.'

'Nonsense,' the Colonel said. 'You're having a pipe dream. If you think I had anything to do with that robbery, you go ahead and arrest me and I'll sue you and the city for false arrest.'

'Who said for robbery?' Coffin Ed said. 'We're arresting you for murder.'

'Murder! What murder?'

'The murder of a junkyard laborer named Joshua Peavine,' Grave Digger said. 'That's where the cotton fits in. He took you to Goodman's junkyard looking for this cotton and you had him murdered.'

'I suppose you're going to have this Goodman identify this cotton,' the Colonel said sarcastically. 'Don't you know there are seven hundred million acres of cotton just like this?'

'Cotton is graded,' Grave Digger said. 'It can be identified. There were fibers from this bale of cotton left in Goodman's junkyard where the boy was murdered.'

'Fibers? What fibers?' the Colonel challenged.

Grave Digger stepped to the pile of cotton on the floor

and picked up a handful and held it out to the Colonel. 'These fibers.'

The Colonel paled. He still held the knife and hook in his hands but his body was controlled with great effort. The blond young man was sweating and trembling all over.

'Drop the gadgets, Colonel,' Coffin Ed said, motioning with his gun.

The Colonel tossed the knife and hook into the hole in the bale of cotton.

'Turn around and walk over and put your hands to the wall,' Coffin Ed went on.

The Colonel looked at him scornfully. 'Don't be afraid, my boy, we're unarmed.'

The tic came into Coffin Ed's face. 'And just don't be too mother-raping cute,' he warned.

The white men read the danger in his face and obeyed. Grave Digger frisked them. 'They're clean.'

'All right, turn around,' Coffin Ed ordered.

They turned around impassively.

'Just remember who're the *men* here,' Coffin Ed said.

No one replied.

'You were seen picking up the laborer, Joshua, by the side of the 125th Street railroad station just before he was murdered,' Grave Digger continued from before.

'Impossible! There was only a blind man there!' the blond young man blurted involuntarily.

With a quick violent motion the Colonel turned and slapped him.

Coffin Ed chuckled. He drew a photograph from his inside pocket and passed it to the Colonel. 'The blind man saw you – and took this picture.'

The Colonel studied it for a long moment, then handed it back. His hand was steady but his nostrils were white along the edges. 'Do you believe a jury would convict me on this evidence?' he said.

'This ain't Alabama,' Coffin Ed said. 'This is New York, and this colored man has been murdered by a white man in Harlem. We have the evidence. We'll give it to the Negro press and all the Negro political groups. When we get through, no jury would dare acquit you; and no governor would dare pardon you. Get the picture, Colonel?'

The Colonel had turned white as a sheet and his face looked pinched. Finally he said, 'Every man's got his price, what's yours?'

'You're lucky to have any teeth left by now, or even dentures,' Grave Digger said. 'But you asked me a straight question, and I'll give you a straight answer. Eighty-seven thousand dollars.'

The blond young man's mouth popped wide open again and he flushed bright red. But the Colonel only stared at Grave Digger to see if he was joking. Then disbelief came to his face, and finally astonishment.

'Incredible! You're going to give them back their money?'

'That's right, the families.'

'Incredible! Is it because they are nigras and you're nigras too?'

'That's right.'

'Incredible!' The Colonel looked as though he had got the shock of his life. 'If that's true, you win,' he conceded. 'What will it buy me?'

'Twenty-four hours,' Grave Digger said.

The Colonel kept staring at him as though he were a four-headed baby. 'And will you really keep your bargain?'

'That's right. A gentleman's agreement.'

A flicker of a smile showed at the corners of the Colonel's mouth.

'A gentleman's agreement,' he echoed. 'I'll give you a cheque drawn on the committee.'

'We're going to wait right here behind drawn shades until the banks open in the morning and you send and get the cash,' Grave Digger said.

'I'll have to send my assistant here,' the Colonel said. 'Will you trust him?'

'That ain't the question,' Grave Digger said. 'Will *you* trust him? It's *your* mother-raping life.'

22

Tuesday passed. Colonel Calhoun and his nephew had disappeared. So had Grave Digger and Coffin Ed. The entire police force was searching for them. The panel truck had been found abandoned beside the cemetery at 155th Street and Broadway, but no trace of their whereabouts. Their wives were frantic. Lieutenant Anderson had personally joined in the search.

But they had simply ditched the panel truck and limped over to the Lincoln Hotel on St Nicholas Avenue, operated by their old friend, took adjoining rooms and went to bed. They had slept around the clock.

Now it was Wednesday morning, and they had come down to the precinct station in a taxi, wearing bedroom slippers on bandaged feet, to turn in their report.

At sight of them the captain turned purple. He looked on the verge of an apoplectic stroke. He wouldn't speak to them, wouldn't look at them again. He gave orders for them to wait in the detectives' room and telephoned the commissioner. The other detectives looked at them and grinned sympathetically, but no one spoke; no one dared speak, they were hotter than a pussy with the pox.

The commissioner arrived and they were called into the captain's office. The commissioner was distinctly cool, but he had himself well under control, like a man just keeping from biting his nails. He let them stand while he read their report. He leafed through the eighty-seven thousand dollars in cash they had turned in.

'Now, men, I just want the facts,' he said, looking about as though searching for the facts he wanted. 'How was it possible that Colonel Calhoun escaped while you were guarding him?' he asked finally.

'You haven't read our report correctly, sir,' Grave Digger said with great control. 'We said we were waiting for him to come back so we could catch him red-handed taking the money from the bale of cotton. But when he started to unlock the door his nephew said something and they rushed back to their limousine and took off. That was the last we saw of them. We tried to chase them but their car was too fast. They must have had some gadget on the lock to tell them if it had been tampered with.'

'What kind of gadget?'

'We don't know, sir.'

The commissioner frowned. 'Why didn't you report his escape and let the force catch him? Obviously, we have departments better equipped for it – or don't you think so?' he added sarcastically.

'That's right, sir,' Grave Digger said. 'But they didn't catch the two gunmen of Deke's and they had two full days before these same gunmen show up here, in the precinct station, and kill two officers and spring Deke.'

'We figured we'd have a better chance of getting him by ourselves. We figured he'd come back for the money sooner or later, so we just hid there waiting for him,' Coffin Ed added with a straight face.

'For one whole day?' the commissioner asked.

'Yes, sir. Time didn't matter,' Grave Digger said.

The captain cleared his throat angrily but said nothing.

But the commissioner reddened with anger. 'There is no place on this Force for grandstanding,' he said hotly.

Coffin Ed blew up. 'We found Deke and his two killers, didn't we? We gave back Iris, didn't we? We found the money, didn't we? We've got the evidence against the Colonel, haven't we? That's what we're paid for, isn't it? You call that grandstanding?'

'And how did you do it?' the commissioner flared.

Grave Digger spoke quickly, heading Coffin Ed off. 'We did what we thought best, sir,' Grave Digger said amenably. 'You said you'd give us a free hand.'

'Umph,' the commissioner growled, scanning the report in front of him. 'How did this girl, this dancer, Billie Belle, get hold of the cotton?'

'We don't know, sir, we haven't asked her,' Grave Digger said. 'We thought they'd get it out of Iris, they had her all yesterday.'

The captain reddened. 'Iris wouldn't talk,' he said defensively. 'And we didn't know about Billie Belle.'

'Where does she live?' the commissioner asked.

'On 115th Street, not far,' Grave Digger said.

'Get her in here now,' the commissioner ordered.

The captain sent two white detectives for her, glad to get off so easily.

Billie didn't have time for her elaborate onstage make-up and she looked young and demure, almost innocent, without it, like all lesbian sexpots. Her full soft lips were a natural rose color, and without mascara her eyes looked brighter, smaller and rounder. She wore black linen slacks and a white cotton blouse and she looked like anything but a sophisticated belly dancer. She was relaxed and slightly on the flip side.

'It was just a whim,' she said. 'I saw Uncle Bud sleeping in his empty cart when I was driving down beneath the bridge to see about my yawt, and somehow his nappy white head made me think of cotton. I stopped and asked him if he could get me a bale of cotton for my cotton dance; I don't know why, just 'cause if he cut his hair it'd make a bale, I suppose, and he said, "Gimme fifty dollars and I'll git you a bale of cotton, Miss Billie," and I gave him the fifty right then and there, knowing I'd get it back from the club. And sure enough, that same night, he delivered it.'

'Where?' the commissioner asked.

'At the club,' she said, lifting her eyebrows. 'What could I do with a bale of cotton in my home?'

'When?' Grave Digger asked.

'I don't know,' she said, becoming impatient with these senseless questions. 'Before I came at ten. He had left it in the stage entrance where it was in the way and I had it moved to my dressing-room until I wanted it on the stage.'

'When did you see Uncle Bud again?' Grave Digger asked.

'I had already paid him,' she said. 'There wasn't any need of seeing him again.'

'Have you ever seen him again?' Grave Digger persisted.

'Why ever should I see him again?' she snapped.

'Think,' Grave Digger said. 'It's important.'

She thought for a moment, then said, 'No, that was the last time I saw him.'

'Did the bale of cotton look as though it had been tampered with?' Coffin Ed asked.

'How the hell would she know?' Grave Digger said.

'I'd never seen a bale of cotton before in my life,' she confessed.

'How did Iris find out about it?' the commissioner asked.

'I don't really know,' she said musingly. 'She must have heard me telephoning. I saw a want ad in the *Sentinel* for a bale of cotton and called the number. Some man with a southern accent answered and said he was Colonel Calhoun of the Back-to-the-Southland movement and he needed a bale of cotton for a rally he was planning to have. I thought he was some smart alec making a joke and I asked him where this rally was taking place. When he said on Seventh Avenue, I was sure he was joking then. I said I was having a cotton rally on Seventh Avenue myself, at the Cotton Club, and he could come to see it, and he said he would. Anyway, I know I was joking when I asked him for a thousand dollars for my bale of cotton.'

'Where was Iris when you were talking on the telephone?' the commissioner persisted.

'I thought she was still in the bathroom, soaking, but she must have come into the dining-room in her bare feet. I was in the sitting-room lying on the divan with my back to the dining-room door and I didn't hear her. She could have just stood there and eavesdropped and I wouldn't have known it.' She had her little secret smile on again. 'That would be just like Iris. Anyway, I would have told her all about it if she had asked, but she would rather eavesdrop.'

'Didn't you know she had escaped from prison?' the commissioner asked softly.

There was silence for a moment and Billie's eyes stretched. 'She told me that detectives Jones and Johnson had let her out to look for Deke. I didn't approve of it but it wasn't my business.'

Dead silence reigned. The commissioner looked hard at the captain, but the captain wouldn't meet his gaze. Coffin Ed grunted, but Grave Digger kept a straight and solemn face.

Billie noticed the strange looks on everyone and asked innocently, 'What was so important about the bale of cotton?'

Coffin Ed said jubilantly, 'It had the eighty-seven thousand dollars hijacked from Deke's Back-to-Africa pitch hidden inside of it.'

'Ohhhh,' Billie gasped. Her eyes rolled back. Grave Digger caught her as she fell.

Now a week had passed. Harlem had lived notoriously on the front pages of the tabloids. Saucy brown chicks and insane killers were integrated with southern colonels and two mad Harlem detectives for the entertainment of the public. Lurid accounts of robberies and killings pictured Harlem as a criminal inferno. Deke O'Hara and Iris were dished up with the breakfast cereal; both had been indicted for conspiracy to defraud and second-degree murder. Iris screamed in bold black print that she had been double-crossed by the police. The Back-to-Africa movement vied with the Back-to-the-Southland movement for space and sympathy.

Everyone considered the dead gunmen as good gunmen and Grave Digger and Coffin Ed were congratulated for being alive.

Colonel Calhoun and his nephew, Ronald Compton, had been indicted for the murder of Joshua Peavine, a Harlem Negro laborer. But the State of Alabama refused to extradite them on the grounds that killing a Negro did not constitute murder under Alabama law.

The families of the Back-to-Africa group of O'Malley's who had gotten their money back staged an outdoor testimonial for Grave Digger and Coffin Ed in the same lot where they had lost it. Six hogs were barbecued whole and the detectives were presented with souvenir maps of Africa. Grave Digger was called upon to speak. He stood up and looked at his map and said, 'Brothers, this map is older than me. If you go back to this

Africa you got to go by way of the grave.' No one understood what he meant, but they applauded anyway.

The next day Harlem's ace detectives were cited by the commissioner for bravery beyond the call of duty, but no raise came forth.

Undertaker H. Exodus Clay was kept busy all week burying the dead, which turned out to be so profitable he gave his chauffeur and handyman, Jackson, a bonus which enabled Jackson to marry his fiancée, Imabelle, with whom he had been living off and on for six years.

It was a quiet Wednesday midnight a week later and Grave Digger, Coffin Ed and Lieutenant Anderson were gathered in the captain's office, drinking beer and shooting the breeze.

'I don't dig Colonel Calhoun,' Anderson said. 'Was his object to break up the Back-to-Africa movement or just to rob them? Was he a man with a cause or just a thief?'

'He's a dedicated man,' Grave Digger said. 'Dedicated to the idea of keeping the black man picking cotton in the South.'

'Yeah, the Colonel thought the Back-to-Africa movement was as sinful and un-American as bolshevism and should be stamped out at any cost,' Coffin Ed added.

'I suppose he thought it was the American thing to do to rob those colored people out of their money,' Anderson said sarcastically.

'Well, ain't it?' Coffin Ed said.

Anderson reddened.

'Hell, you don't know the Colonel,' Grave Digger said pacifyingly. 'He intended to give them back the money if they went south and picked cotton for a year or so. He's a benevolent man.'

Anderson nodded knowingly. 'It figures,' he said. 'That's why he hid the money in a bale of cotton. It was a symbol.'

Grave Digger stared at Anderson and then looked over at Coffin Ed. Coffin Ed didn't get it either.

But Grave Digger replied with a straight face, 'I know just what you mean.'

'Anyway it made it easier for me and Digger to find,' Coffin Ed said.

'How?' Anderson asked.

'How?' Coffin Ed echoed. The question threw him.

'Because it was still there,' Grave Digger said, coming to his rescue.

Anderson blinked uncomprehendingly.

Coffin Ed chuckled. 'Damn right,' he said, adding under his breath, 'That throws you too.'

Grave Digger said, 'I'm hungry,' breaking it up.

Mammy Louise had barbecued an opossum especially for them and with the fat yellow meat she served candied yams, collard greens and okra, and left them to themselves to enjoy it.

'It's a damn good thing those southern crackers gave Colonel Calhoun enough money to spend to get us back south or we'd still be looking for the Back-to-Africa loot,' Coffin Ed remarked.

'Be a lot of trouble, anyway,' Grave Digger agreed.

'How you reckon he figured it out?' Coffin Ed asked.

'Hell, man, how you think he was going to miss seeing the bale had been tampered with,' Grave Digger said. 'As much cotton as he's handled in his lifetime.'

'You think we should go after him?'

'Man, we've already recovered the stolen money. How're we going to explain another eighty-seven grand?'

'Anyway, let's find out where he's gone.'

Two days later they got a verification from *Air France* that they had flown a very old colored man with a passport issued to Cotton Bud of New York City by way of Paris to Dakar.

They wired the prefecture in Dakar:

WHAT DO YOU HAVE ON OLD COTTON HEADED U.S. NEGRO . . . NEW YORK TO DAKAR BY AIR FRANCE . . . Jones, Harlem Precinct, New York City.

SENSATIONAL STUPENDOUS INCROYABLE . . . M. COTTON HEADED BUD BUYS 500 CATTLE HIRES 6 HERDSMEN 2 GUIDES 1 WITCH DOCTEUR . . . TOOK TO THE BRUSH . . . WOMEN FAINTED . . . THREW SELVES INTO SEA . . . M. le Prefect, Dakar.

FOR MILK OR MEAT ... Jones, Harlem.

MONSIEUR QUELLE QUESTION ... FOR WIVES WHAT ELSE ... Prefect, Dakar.

HOW MANY WIVES WILL 500 CATTLE BUY ... Jones, Harlem.

M. COTTON HEADED BUD ALSO HAS MUCH MONEY ... M. BUD HAS BOUGHT 100 WIVES OF MOYEN QUALITE ... NOW SHOPPING FOR BEST ... WANTS LA MEME NUMERO AS SOLOMAN ... Prefect, Dakar.

STOP HIM QUICK ... HE WILL DROP DEAD BEFORE SAMPLING ... Jones, Harlem.

SHOULD HUSBAND DIE WIVES MAKE BEST MOURNERS ... Prefect, Dakar.

'Well, at least Uncle Bud got to Africa,' Coffin Ed said.

'Hell, the way that old mother-raper is behaving, he might have come from Africa,' Grave Digger said.

Blind Man with a Pistol

Preface

A friend of mine, Phil Lomax, told me this story about a blind man with a pistol shooting at a man who had slapped him on a subway train and killing an innocent bystander peacefully reading his newspaper across the aisle and I thought, damn right, sounds just like today's news, riots in the ghettos, war in Vietnam, masochistic doings in the Middle East. And then I thought of some of our loudmouthed leaders urging our vulnerable soul brothers on to getting themselves killed, and thought further that all unorganized violence is like a blind man with a pistol.

CHESTER HIMES

Foreword

'Motherfucking right, it's confusing; it's a gas, baby, you dig.'

A Harlem intellectual

I know what you want.
How you know that?
Just lookin at you.
Cause I'm white?
Tain't that. I got the eye.
You think I'm looking for a girl.
Chops is your dish.
Not pork.
Naw.
Not overdone.
Naw. Just right.

'Blink once, you're robbed,' Coffin Ed advised the white man slumming in Harlem.

'Blink twice, you're dead,' Grave Digger added drily.

1

On 119th Street there had been a sign for years in the front window of an old dilapidated three-storey brick house, announcing: FUNERALS PERFORMED. For five years past the house had been condemned as unsafe for human habitation. The wooden steps leading up to the cracked, scabby front door were so rotten one had to mount them like crossing a river on a fallen tree trunk; the foundation was crumbling, one side of the house had sunk more than a foot lower than the other, the concrete windowsills had fallen from all the upper windows and the constant falling of bricks from the front wall created a dangerous hazard for passing pedestrians. Most of the windowpanes had long been broken out and replaced with brown wrapping-paper, and the edges of linoleum could be seen hanging from the roof where years before it had been placed there to cover a leak. No one knew what it looked like inside, and no one cared. If any funerals had ever been performed within, it had been before the memory of any residents then on the street.

Police cruisers had passed daily and glanced at it unconcernedly. The cops weren't interested in funerals. Building inspectors had looked the other way. Gas and electric meter readers never stopped, for it had no gas and electricity. But everyone on the street had seen a considerable number of short-haired, black nuns clad in solid black vestments coming and going at all hours of day and night, picking their way up the rotting stairs like cats on a hot tin roof. The colored neighbors just assumed it was a convent, and that it was in such bad repair seemed perfectly reasonable in view of the fact it was obviously a jim-crowded convent, and no one ever dreamed that white Catholics would act any different from anyone else who was white.

It was not until another innocuous card appeared in the

window one day, requesting: 'Fertile womens, lovin God, inquire within,' that anyone had given it a thought. Two white cops in a cruiser who had been driving by the house on their normal patrol every day for the past year were proceeding past as usual when the cop beside the driver shouted, 'Whoa, man! You see what I see?'

The driver stamped on the brakes and backed up so he could see too. 'Fertile womens . . .' he read. That was as far as he got.

They both had the same thought. What would a colored convent want with 'fertile womens'? Fertile womens was for fools, not God.

The inside cop deliberately opened his door, stepped to the sidewalk, adjusted his pistol in its holster and unbuttoned the flap. The driver got out on the street side and came around the car and stood beside his buddy, while performing the same operations with his own pistol. They stared at the sign without expression. They looked at the brown-papered windows. They examined the façade of the whole crumbling edifice as though they had never seen it before.

Then the first cop jerked his head. 'Come on.'

The second cop followed. When the first cop planted his big foot on the second stair with assured authority, it went on through the rotting wood up to his knee. 'Jesus Goddamn Christ!' he exclaimed. 'These steps are rotten.'

The second cop didn't see any need in commenting on the obvious. He hitched up his holster belt and said, 'Let's try the back.'

As they picked their way around the house through knee-high weeds dense with booby traps of unseen bottles, tin cans, rusted bed springs, broken emery stones, rotting harness, dead cats, dog offal, puddles of stinking garbage, and swarms of bottle flies, house flies, gnats, mosquitoes, the first cop said in extreme disgust, 'I don't see how people can live in such filth.'

But he hadn't seen anything yet. When they arrived at the back they found a section of the wall had fallen from the second floor, leaving a room exposed to the weather, and the rubble piled on the ground formed the only access to the open back door. Carefully they climbed up the pile of broken bricks and plaster, their footsteps raising a thick gray dust, and entered the kitchen unimpeded.

A fat black man naked to the waist glanced at them casually from muddy eyes which seemed to pop from his wet black face and went on with what he was doing. The old rusted iron floor from a Volkswagen had been placed on four bricks on one side of the warped board floor and a brick firebox had been raised in its center. Sitting on top of a charcoal fire in the firebox was a huge iron pot, blackened by smoke, of a type southern mammies use to boil clothes, filled with some sort of stew which had a strong nauseating smell, being stirred with slow indifference by the sweating black man. The torso of the black man looked like a misshapen lump of crude rubber. He had a round black face with a harelip which caused him to slobber constantly, and his grayish skull was shaved.

Large patches of faded ochre wallpaper, splotched with rust-colored stains and water marks, hung from gray plaster. There were several places where the plaster had fallen off, revealing the brown wooden slats.

'Who's the boss around here, Rastus?' the first cop demanded.

The black man kept stirring his stew as though he hadn't heard.

The cop reddened. He drew his pistol and stepped forward and jabbed the black man in the blubber over his ribs. 'Can't you hear?'

Without an obvious change of motion, the ladle rose from the stew and rapped the cop over the head. The second cop leapt foward and hit the black man across his shaved skull with the butt edge of his pistol. The black man grunted and fell onto the old car floor beside the firebox.

A black nun came from another open door and saw the black man lying unconscious beside the stew pot and two white cops standing over him with drawn pistols and screamed. Other black nuns came running, followed by what seemed to be a horde of naked black children. The cops were so shocked their first impulse was to run. But when the first one leapt through the back doorway his foot gave way on the pile of rubble and he slid down into the high weeds of the back yard on the seat of his pants. The second cop turned about in the open doorway and held back the mob with his gun. For a moment he had the odd sensation of having fallen into the middle of the Congo.

The cop outside got up and brushed himself off. 'Can you hold 'em while I call the station?'

'Oh, sure,' the second cop said with more confidence than he felt. 'They ain't nothing but niggers.'

When the first cop returned from radioing the Harlem precinct for reinforcements, a very old man dressed in a spotted long-sleeved white gown had come into the kitchen and cleared out the nuns and the children. He was clean shaven, and his sagging parchment-like skin which seemed but a covering for his skeleton was tight about his face like a leather mask. Wrinkled lids, looking more like dried skin, dropped over his milky bluish eyes, giving him a vague similarity to an old snapping turtle. His cracked voice had a note of mild censure: 'He didn't mean no harm, he's a cretin.'

'You ought to teach him better than to attack police officers,' the cop complained. 'Now I smell like I've been ducked in shit.'

'He cooks for the children,' the old man said. 'Sometimes it does smell strange,' he admitted.

'It smells like feces,' the second cop said. He'd attended City College.

One of the nuns entering the kitchen at just that moment said indignantly, 'It is feetsies. Everybody ain't rich like you white folks.'

'Now, now, Buttercup, these gentlemen mean no harm,' the old man chided. 'They but acted in self-defense. They were ignorant of the reactions of Bubber.'

'What they doin' here anyway?' she muttered, but a look from him sent her scampering.

'You the boss man, then?' the first cop said.

'Yes, sir, I am Reverend Sam.'

'Are you a monk?' the second cop asked.

A smile seemed to twitch the old man's face. 'No, I'm a Mormon.'

The first cop scratched his head. 'What all these nuns doing here then?'

'They're my wives.'

'Well, I'll be Goddamned! A nigger Mormon married to a bunch of nigger nuns. And all these children? You running an orphanage too?'

'No, they're my own children. I'm trying to raise them as best the Lord will permit.'

The cops looked at him sharply. Both had a strong suspicion he was playing them for fools.

'You mean grandchildren,' the cop suggested.

'Great-grandchildren, more like it,' the first cop amended.

'No, they're all from the seeds of my loins.'

The cops stared at him goggle-eyed. 'How old are you, uncle?'

'I believe that I am about a hundred to the best of my knowledge.'

They stared at him openmouthed. From the interior of the house they could hear the loud shouting and laughter of children at play and the soft voices of women admonishing them to silence. A feral odor seeped into the kitchen, over and above the smell of the stew. It was a familiar odor and the cop racked his memory to place it. The other cop stared fascinated into the milky bluish eyes of the old man, which reminded him of some milkstones he had seen in a credit jewelry store.

The fat black man was beginning to stir and the cop drew his pistol to be prepared. The fat man rolled over on to his back and looked from the cop to the old man. 'Papa, he hit me,' he tattled in a voice made barely distinguishable by his slobbery drolling.

'Papa will send away the bad mens, now you go on playing house,' the old man croaked. There was a strange note of benevolence when he addressed the cretin.

The cop blinked. 'Papa!' he echoed. 'He your son too?'

Suddenly the second cop snapped his fingers. 'The monkey house!' he exclaimed.

'God made us all,' Reverend Sam reminded him gently.

'Not them fifty little pickaninnies, according to you,' the cop said.

'I am merely God's instrument.'

Suddenly the first cop remembered why they had stopped in the first place. 'You got a sign in the window, uncle, advertising for fertile women. Ain't you got enough women?'

'I now have only eleven. I must have twelve. One died and she must be replaced.'

'Which reminds me, you got another sign in your window saying "funerals performed".'

The old man looked as near to being surprised as was possible. 'Yes, I performed her funeral.'

'But that sign's been there for years. I've seen it myself.'

'Of course,' the old man said. 'We all must die.'

The cop took off his cap and scratched his blond head. He looked at his partner for advice.

His partner said: 'We better wait for the sergeant.'

The reinforcements from the Harlem precinct station, headed by a sergeant of detectives, found the remainder of the house in much the same repair as the kitchen. Potbellied coalburning stoves on rusted sheets of metal in the hallways on each floor supplied heat. Light was supplied by homemade lamps without shades made from whiskey bottles. The wives slept on homemade individual pallets, six to a room, on the top floor, while Reverend had his own private room adjoining furnished with a double bed and a chamber pot and little else. There was a large front room on the second floor with all of its windows papered shut where the children slept on loose dirty cotton, evidently the contents of numerous mattresses, which covered the floor from wall to wall about a foot thick.

At the time of their arrival the children were having their lunch, which consisted of the stewed pigsfeet and chitterlings which Bubber, the cretin, had been cooking in the washing pot. It had been divided equally and poured into three rows of troughs in the middle room on the first floor. The naked children were lined up, side by side, on hands and knees, swilling it like pigs.

The detectives counted fifty children, all under the age of ten, and all seemingly healthy. They looked fat enough, with their naked bellies poking out, but several of their burred heads were spotted with tetter, and most of the boys had elongated penises for children so young.

The nuns were gathered about a large bare table in the front room, all busily counting their cheap wooden rosaries, and chanting verses in musical voices which produced a singularly enchanting harmony, but with such indistinct pronunciation that no one could make out the words.

The cretin lay flat on his back on the splintery kitchen floor, his head wrapped in a dirty white bandage stained with mercurochrome, sleeping soundly to the accompaniment of snores that sounded like loud desperate shouts coming from under water. Numerous flies and gnats of all descriptions were feeding on the flow of spittle that drooled from the corners of his harelipped mouth, in preference, seemingly, to the remains of stew in the pot.

In a small room across the hall from where the nuns were sitting, which Reverend Sam called his study, he was being questioned sharply by all twelve cops. Reverend Sam answered their questions politely, looking unperturbed. Yes, he was an ordained minister. Ordained by who? Ordained by God, who else. Yes, the nuns were all his wives. How did he account for that, nuns had made sacred vows to lives of chastity? Yes, there were white nuns and black nuns. What difference did that make? The church provided shelter and food for the white nuns, his black nuns had to hustle for themselves. But religious vows forbid nuns to marry or to participate in any form of carnality. Yes, yes, rightfully speaking, his nuns were virgins. But how could that be when they were his wives and had given birth to, er, fifty children by him? Yes, but being as they were police officers in a sinful world they might not understand; every morning when his wives arose they were virgin nuns, it was only at night, in the dark, that they performed the functions for which God had made their bodies. You mean they were virgins in the morning, nuns during the day, and wives at night? Yes, if you wish to state it in such manner, but you must not overlook the fact that every living person has two beings, the physical and the spiritual, and neither has ascendancy over the other; they could, at best, and with rigid discipline, be carefully separated – which was what he had succeeded doing with his wives. All right, all right, but why didn't his children wear clothes? Why, it was more comfortable without them, and clothes cost money. And eat at tables, like human beings, with knives and forks? Knives and forks cost money, and troughs were more expedient; surely, as white gentlemen and officers of the law, they should understand just what he meant.

The twelve cops reddened to a man. The sergeant, doing most of the questioning, took another tack. What did you want another wife for? Reverend Sam looked up in amazement from beneath his old drooping lids. What a curious question, sir. Shall I answer it? Again the sergeant reddened. Listen, uncle, we're not playing. Neither am I, I assure you, sir. Well, then, what happened to the last one? What last one, sir? The one who died. She died, sir. How, Goddammit? Dead, sir. For what reason? The Lord willed it, sir. Now, listen here, uncle, you're just making it hard on yourself; what was her disease, er, ailment, er, the cause of her death? Childbirth. How old did you say you were? About a hundred, as far as I can determine. All right, you're a hundred; now what did you do with her? We buried her. Where? In the ground. Now listen here, uncle, there are laws about burials; did you have a permit? There are laws for white folks and laws for black folks, sir. All right, all right, but these laws come from God. Which God? There's a white God and there's a black God.

By then, the sergeant had lost his patience. The police continued their investigation without Reverend Sam's assistance. In due course they learned that the household was supported by the wives walking the streets of Harlem, dressed as nuns, begging alms. They also discovered three suspicious-looking mounds in the dirt cellar, which, upon being opened, revealed the remains of three female bodies.

2

It was 2 a.m. in Harlem and it was hot. Even if you couldn't feel it, you could tell it by the movement of the people. Everybody was limbered up, glands lubricated, brains ticking over like a Singer sewing-machine. Everybody was ahead of the play. There wasn't but one square in sight. He was a white man.

He stood well back in the recessed doorway of the United Tobacco store at the northwest corner of 125th Street and Seventh Avenue, watching the sissies frolic about the lunch counter in the Theresa building on the opposite corner. The glass doors had been folded back and the counter was open to the sidewalk.

The white man was excited by the sissies. They were colored and mostly young. They all had straightened hair, conked like silk, waving like the sea; long false eyelashes fringing eyes ringed in mascara; and big cushiony lips painted tan. Their eyes looked naked, brazen, debased, unashamed; they had the greedy look of a sick gourmet. They wore tight-bottomed pastel pants and short-sleeved sport shirts revealing naked brown arms. Some sat to the counter on the high stools, others leaned on their shoulders. Their voices trilled, their bodies moved, their eyes rolled, they twisted their hips suggestively. Their white teeth flashed in brown sweaty faces, their naked eyes steamed in black cups of mascara. They touched one another lightly with their fingertips, compulsively, exclaiming in breathless falsetto, '*Girl . . .*' Their motions were wanton, indecent, suggestive of an orgy taking place in their minds. The hot Harlem night had brought down their love.

The white man watched them enviously. His body twitched as though he were standing in a hill of ants. His muscles jerked in the strangest places, one side of his face twitched, he had cramps in the right foot, his pants cut his crotch, he bit his tongue, one eye popped out from its socket. One could tell his blood was stirring, but one couldn't tell which way. He couldn't control himself. He stepped out from his hiding place.

At first no one noticed him. He was an ordinary-looking light-haired white man dressed in light gray trousers and a white sport shirt. One could find white men on that corner on any hot night. There was a bright street lamp on each of the four corners of the intersection and cops were always in calling distance. White men were as safe at that intersection as in Times Square. Furthermore they were more welcome.

But the white man couldn't help acting guilty and frightened. He slithered across the street like a moth to the flame. He walked in a one-sided crablike motion, as though submitting only the edge of his body to his inflamed passion. He was watching the frolicsome sissies with such intentness a fast-moving taxi coming east almost ran him down. There was a sudden shriek of brakes, and the loud angry shout of the black driver, 'Mother-raper! Ain't you never seen sissies?'

He leapt for the curb, his face burning. All the naked mascaraed eyes about the lunch counter turned on him.

'Ooooo!' a falsetto voice cried delightedly. 'A lollipop!'

He drew back to the edge of the sidewalk, face flaming as though he were about to run or cry.

'Don't run, mother,' someone said.

White teeth gleamed between thick tan lips. The white man lowered his eyes and followed the edge of the sidewalk around the corner from 125th Street down Seventh Avenue.

'Look, she's blushing,' another voice said, setting off a giggle.

The white man looked straight ahead as though ignoring them but when he came to the end of the counter and would have continued past, a heavyset serious man who had been sitting between two empty seats at the end got up to leave, and taking advantage of the distraction the white man slipped into the seat he had vacated.

'Coffee,' he ordered in a loud constricted voice. He wanted it to be known that coffee was all he wanted.

The waiter gave him a knowing look. 'I know what you want.'

The white man forced himself to meet the waiter's naked eyes. 'Coffee is all.'

The waiter's lips twisted in a derisive grin. The white man noticed they were painted too. He stole a look at the other beauties at the counter. Their huge tan glistening lips looked extraordinarily seductive.

To get his attention the waiter had to speak again. 'Chops!' he whispered in a hoarse suggestive voice.

The white man started like a horse shying. 'I don't want anything to eat.'

'I know.'

'Coffee.'

'Chops.'

'Black.'

'Black chops. All you white mothers are just alike.'

The white man decided to play ignorant. He acted as though he didn't know what the waiter was talking about. 'Are you discriminating against me?'

'Lord, no. Black chops – coffee, I mean – coming right up.'

A sissie moved into the seat beside the white man, and put his hand on his leg. 'Come with me, mother.'

The white man pushed the hand away and looked at him haughtily. 'Do I know you?'

The sissie sneered. 'Hard to get, eh?'

The waiter looked around from the coffee urn. 'Don't bother my customers,' he said.

The sissie reacted as though they had a secret understanding. 'Oh, like that?'

'Jesus Christ, what's going on?' the white man blurted.

The waiter served him his black coffee. 'As if you didn't know,' he whispered.

'What's this fad?'

'Ain't they beautiful?'

'What?'

'All them hot tan chops.'

The white man's face flamed again. He lifted his cup of coffee. His hand shook so it slopped over on the counter.

'Don't be nervous,' the waiter said. 'You got it made. Put down your money and take your choice.'

Another man slipped on to the end stool next to the white man. He was a thin black man with a long smooth face. He wore black pants, a black long-sleeved shirt with black buttons and a bright red fez. There was a wide black band around the fez with the large white-lettered words, BLACK POWER. He might have been a Black Muslim but for the fact Black Muslims avoided the vicinity of perverts and were hardly ever seen at that lunch counter. And the bookstore diagonally across Seventh Avenue where Black Muslims sometimes assembled and held mass meetings had been closed since early the previous evening, and the Black Muslim temple was nine blocks south on 116th Street. But he was dressed like one and he was black enough. He leaned toward the white man and whispered in his other ear, 'I know what you want.'

The waiter gave him a look. 'Chops,' he said.

As he leaned away from the black man, the white man thought they were all talking in a secret language. All he wanted was to get with the sissies, the tan-lipped brown-bodied girl-boys, strip off his clothes, let himself be ravished. The thought made him weak as water, dissolved his bones, dizzied his head. He refused to think more than that. And the waiter and this other ugly black man were destroying that, cooling his ardor, wetting him down. He became angry. 'Let me alone, I know what I want,' he said.

'Bran,' the black man said.

'Chops,' the waiter said.

'It's breakfast time,' the black man said. 'The man wants breakfast food. Without bones.'

Angrily the white man reached back and drew his wallet from his hip pocket. He pulled out a ten-dollar bill from a thick sheaf of notes and threw it on to the counter.

Everyone all up and around the counter stared from the bill to the white man's red angry face.

The waiter had become absolutely still. He let the bill lie. 'Ain't you got nothing smaller than that, boss?'

The white man fished in his side pockets. The waiter and the black man in the red fez exchanged glances from the corners of their eyes. The white man brought out his hands empty.

'I haven't any change,' he said.

The waiter picked up the ten-dollar bill and snapped it, held it up to the light and scrutinized it. Satisfied, he put it in the till and made change. He slapped the change down on to the counter in front of the white man, leaning foward. He whispered, 'You can go with him, he's safe.'

The white man glanced briefly at the black man beside him. The black man grinned obsequiously. The white man picked up his change. It was five dollars short. Holding it in his hand, he looked up into the waiter's eyes. The waiter returned his look, challengingly, shrugged and licked his lips. The white man smiled to himself, all his confidence restored.

'Chops,' he admitted.

The black man got up with the vague suggestive movements of an old darky retainer, and began to walk slowly south on Seventh Avenue, past the entrance to the Theresa building. The white man followed but in a short pace he had drawn even with the black man and they went down the street conversing, a black-clad black man in a red fez announcing BLACK POWER and a light-haired white man in gray pants and white shirt, the steerer and the John.

Interlude

Where 125th Street crosses Seventh Avenue is the Mecca of Harlem. To get established there, an ordinary Harlem citizen has reached the promised land, if it merely means standing on the sidewalk.

One Hundred and Twenty-fifth Street connects the Triborough Bridge on the east with the former Hudson River Ferry into New Jersey on the west. Crosstown buses ply up and down the street at the rate of one every ten minutes. White motorists passing over the complex toll bridge from the Bronx, Queens or Brooklyn sometimes have occasion to pass through Harlem to the ferry, Broadway or other destinations, instead of turning downtown via the East Side Drive.

Seventh Avenue runs from the north end of Central Park to the 155th Street Bridge where the motorists going north to Westchester County and beyond cross over the Harlem River into the Bronx and the Grand Concourse. The Seventh Avenue branch of the Fifth Avenue bus line passes up and down this section of Seventh Avenue and turns over to Fifth Avenue on 100th Street at the top of Central Park and goes south down Fifth Avenue to Washington Square.

Therefore many white people riding the buses or in motor cars pass this corner daily. Furthermore, most of the commercial enterprises – stores, bars, restaurants, theaters, etc. – and real estate are owned by white people.

But it is the Mecca of the black people just the same. The air and the heat and the voices and the laughter, the atmosphere and the drama and the melodrama, are theirs. Theirs are the hopes, the schemes, the prayers and the protest. They are the managers, the clerks, the cleaners, they drive the taxis and the buses, they are the clients, the customers, the audience; they work it, but the white man owns it. So it is natural that the white man is concerned with their behavior; it's his property. But it is the black people's to enjoy. The black people have the past and the present, and they hope to have the future.

The old Theresa Hotel, where once the greatest of the black had their day in the luxury suites overlooking the wide, park-divided sweep of Seventh Avenue, or in the large formal dining-room where dressing for dinner was mandatory, or in the dark cozy intimacy of the bar where one could see the greatest of the singers, jazz musicians, politicians, educators, prize fighters, racketeers, pimps, prostitutes. Memory calls up such names as Josephine Baker, Florence Mills, Lady Day, Bojangles Bill Robinson, Bert Williams, Chick Webb, Lester Young, Joe Louis, Henry Armstrong, Congressmen Dawson and De-Priest, educators Booker T. Washington and Charles Johnson, writers Bud Fisher, Claude MacKay, Countee Cullen, and others too numerous to mention. And their white friends and sponsors: Carl Van Vechten, Rebecca West, Dodd, Dodge, Rockefeller. Not to mention the movie actors and actresses of all races, the unforgettable Canada Lee and John Garfield.

3

Motorists coming west on 125th Street from the Triborough Bridge saw a speaker standing in the tonneau of an old muddy battered US Army command car, parked in the amber night light at the corner of Second Avenue, in front of a sign which read: *CHICKEN AUTO INSURANCE, Seymour Rosenblum.* None had the time or interest to investigate further. The white motorists thought that the Negro speaker was selling 'chicken auto insurance' for Seymour Rosenblum. They could well believe it. '*Chicken*' had to do with the expression, 'Don't be chicken!' and that was the way people drove in Harlem.

But actually the 'chicken' sign was left over from a restaurant that had gone bankrupt and closed months previously, and the sign advertising auto insurance had been placed across the front of the closed shop afterwards.

Nor was the speaker selling auto insurance, which was farther from his thoughts than chicken. He had merely chosen that particular spot because he had felt he was least likely to be disturbed by the police. The speaker was named Marcus Mackenzie, and he was a serious man. Although young, slender and handsome, Marcus Mackenzie was as serious as an African Methodist minister with one foot in the grave. Marcus Mackenzie's aim was to save the world. But before then, it was to solve the Negro Problem. Marcus Mackenzie believed brotherhood would do both. He had assembled a group of young white and black people to march across the heart of Harlem on 125th Street from Second Avenue on the east to Convent Avenue on the west. He had been preparing this march for more than six months. He had begun the previous December when he had returned from Europe after spending two years in the US Army in Germany. He had learned all the necessary techniques in the army. Hence the old command car. One commanded best from a command car. That was what they were designed for. Kept you high off the ground, better to deploy your forces. Also it would carry all the first-aid equipment that might be needed: plasma, surgical instruments, cat gut for sutures, snakebite medicine which he felt would be just as effective for rat bites – which were more likely in Harlem – rubber raincoats in case of rain, black greasepaint for his white marchers to quickly don black faces in an emergency.

Most of the young men waiting to make formations of squads wore tee shirts and shorts. For now it was July 15th. Getaway day. Nat Turner day. There were only forty-eight of them. But Marcus Mackenzie believed that from little acorns big oaks grew. Now he was giving his marchers a last pep talk before the march began. He was speaking over a portable amplifier as he stood in the tonneau of the command car. But many other people had stopped to listen, for his voice carried far and wide. People who lived in the neighborhood. Black people, and white people too, for that far east on 125th Street was still a racially mixed neighborhood. The elderly people, for the most part, were the heads of families; the younger people in their twenties might be anything, black and white alike. There were many prostitutes, pederasts, pickpockets, sneak thieves, confidence men, steerers, and pimps in the area who served the 125th Street railroad station two blocks away. But Marcus Mackenzie had no tolerance for these.

'*The greatest boon to mankind that history will ever know can be brotherly love,*' he was saying. '*Brotherhood! It can be more nutritious than bread. More warming than wine. More soothing than song. More satisfying than sex. More beneficial than science. More curing than medicine.*' The metaphors might have been mixed and the delivery stilted, for Marcus was not highly educated. But no one could doubt the sincerity in his voice. The sincerity was so pure it was heart-breaking. Everyone within earshot was touched by his sincerity. '*Man's love for man. Let me tell you, it is like all religions put together, like all the gods embracing. It is the greatest . . .*'

No one doubted him. The intensity of his emotion left no

room for doubt. But one elderly black man, equally serious, standing on the opposite side of the street, expressed his concern and that of others. 'I believe you, son. But how you gonna get it to work?'

'We're going to march!' Marcus declared in a ringing voice.

Whether that answered the old man's question or not was never known. But it answered Marcus Mackenzie's. He had given a lot of thought to the question. It seemed as though his whole life had been lived only to supply this answer. His earliest memory was of the Detroit race riot in 1943, right during the middle of the United States' fierce fight against other forms of racism in other countries. But he had been too young to comprehend this irony. All he remembered was his father going in and out of their apartment in the ghetto, the shouting and gunshots from the unseen street, and his elder sister sitting in the front room of their closed and shuttered flat with a big black revolver in her lap pointed at the door. He had been four years old and she seven. They had been alone all the times their father had been out trying to rescue other black people from the police. Their mother was dead. When he had become old enough to know the difference between the 'North' and the 'South' he had become terrified. Mainly because Detroit was about as far north as one could go. And it had seemed as though he had suffered all the same restrictions there, the same abuses, the same injustices, as his black brothers in the South. He had lived all his life in a black slum, had attended jim-crowed schools, and after graduating from high school had got the customary jim-crow job in a factory. Then he had been drafted into the army and sent to Germany. It was there he had learned the techniques of the march, although for the most part he had served as an orderly in the women's maternity ward of the US Army hospital in Wiesbaden. He had been very much alone as there were no other Negroes working in the hospital at the same hours. He read only the Bible and he had lots of time to think. He was treated well by the white staff and expectant mothers who, in his ward, were wives of officers, most of whom were from the South. He knew there was little social integration in the army and what there was among GIs was rigidly enforced. The Negro Problem existed there as it had everywhere else he had ever lived. But still he was treated well. He came to the conclusion that it was all a matter of black and white people getting to know each other. He was not a very bright boy and he never knew he had been selected for the job because of his neat, clean-cut appearance. He was tall and slender with sepia skin and a long softly angled face. His eyes were brown. His black hair, worn very short, was straight at the roots. He had always been very serious. He was never frivolous. He seldom smiled. By the time he had served two years, mostly in the company of white people who treated him well, a great deal alone, reading and studying the Old and New Testaments of the Bible, he had come to the conclusion that plain Christian love was the solution to the Negro Problem. But he had learned plenty about marching. For a time he entertained the grandiose idea of returning to the States and imbuing all the inhabitants with Christian love. But he soon discovered that Doctor Martin Luther King had beat him to the idea and he sought about in his mind for something else.

After his discharge he went to Paris to live until his money ran out, as did a great number of other discharged GIs. He got a room with another young brother in a hotel on Rue Chaplain, around the corner from Boulevard Raspail and Montparnasse, almost within hailing distance of the *Rotonde* and the *Dôme*. It was a hotel very popular with discharged Negro GIs in Paris, partly because of its location and partly because of the army of prostitutes who cruised from there under a strict discipline similar to that they'd just left. He knew no one but other discharged GIs, all of whom recognized one another on sight, whether they had met before or not. They comprised an unofficial club; they talked the same language, ate the same food, went to the same places – usually to the cheap restaurants by day and the movie theater – *Studio Parnasse* – down the street, or Buttercup's Chicken Shack over on Rue Odessa at night. They gathered in each other's rooms and discussed the situation back home. Mostly they talked of the various brothers back home who had struck it rich and made the bigtime via the Negro Problem. Most of them had no trade or profession or education in any specific field, if indeed any at all. As a consequence, whether they admitted it or not, most of them were resolved to get a foothold in this bonanza. They felt if they could just somehow get involved in the Negro Problem, the next step up the ladder would be good paying jobs in government or private industry. All they needed was an idea. 'Look at Martin Luther King. What's he done?' ... 'He done got rich. That's what.' But Marcus had no patience for cynicism. He felt it was sacrilege. He was pure in heart. He wanted the Negroes to arise. He wanted to lead them out of the abyss into the promised land. The trouble was, he wasn't very bright.

Then one night at Buttercup's he met this Swedish woman, Birgit, who was famous for her glass. She had dropped in to look over the brothers. She and Marcus found their affinity immediately. Both of them were serious, both were seeking, both were extraordinarily stupid. But she taught him brotherly love. She was hipped on brotherly love. Although it didn't mean the same thing to her as it did to him. She had had a number of brothers as lovers and in time she had become enthusiastic about brotherly love. But Marcus had the vision of Brotherhood.

The same night he met her, he gave up on the idea of plain Christian love. Buttercup was sitting at a big table where she could oversee the entrance, the bar and the dance floor at the same time, surrounded as usual by a number of sycophants, like a big fat mother hen with a brood of wet chicks and ugly ducklings, and she had introduced Marcus to Birgit, seeing as they were both serious, both seeking. At one end of the same table a fattish erudite white man vacationing from his teaching post in Black Africa was holding forth on the economy of the new African states. Feeling the man was getting too much of Birgit's attention, as he had just met her and didn't as yet know about her brotherly love, Marcus sought to steer the conversation away from Black African economy to the American Negro Problem where he could shine. He wanted to shine for Birgit. He didn't know he already shone to her satisfaction. Suddenly he interrupted the man. He held forth his Bible, dangling the gold cross. He was absorbed by Christian love. 'What does that mean to you?' he challenged, pointing to the cross, preparing to expound his brilliant idea. The man looked from the cross to Marcus's face. He smiled sadly. He said, 'It don't mean a damn thing to me, I'm a Jew.' Right then and there Marcus dropped his ideas on Christian love. He was ready for brotherly love when Birgit took him home. But he was serious.

Brigit took him to live with her in the South of France. She had a good business in glassware and was famous. But she was more interested in the welfare of the American Negro than in glass. She was a perfect foil to the wild ideas of Marcus. They spent most of their waking hours discussing ways and means to solve this problem. Once she declared she would become the richest and most famous woman in the world and then she would go to the American South and call a press conference and let it be known that she lived with a Negro. But Marcus didn't think much of that idea. He felt she should be in the background and he should take the lead. It was inevitable that two such wildly enthusiastic people would have some misunderstandings. But the only serious one they had was about the correct way to stand on one's head. She did it her way. He said it was wrong. They argued. He was stubborn. She pointed out that she was older than he was, and heavier. He left her and went back to Detroit. She hopped on a plane and went to Detroit and took him back to France. It was after then that he became convinced of the efficacy of Brotherly Love. He woke up one morning with a vision of Brotherhood. In this vision he saw it solving all the problems of the world. He already knew about the March. That much the US Army had taught him. Put the two together and they'd work, he concluded.

The next week he and Birgit arrived in New York and took a room in the Texas Hotel near the 125th Street station and went into the business of organizing the 'March of Brotherhood'.

Now the moment had arrived. Birgit took her place beside him in the command car. She pulled up her large striped cotton dirndl skirt made by her fellow national, Katya of Sweden, and looked around with an excited smile. But to onlookers it was more like the strained expression of a Swedish farm woman in a Swedish outhouse in the dead of a Swedish winter. She was trying to restrain her excitement at the sight of all those naked limbs in the amber light. From the shoulders up she had the delicate neckline and face of a Nordic goddess, but below her body was breastless, lumpy with bulging hips and huge round legs like sawed-off telegraph posts. She felt elated, sitting there with her man who was leading these colored people in this march for their rights. She loved colored people. Her blue eyes gleamed with this love. When she looked at the white cops her lips curled with scorn.

A number of police cruisers had appeared at the moment the march was to begin. They stared at the white woman and the colored man in the command car. Their lips compressed but they said nothing, did nothing. Marcus had got a police permit.

The marchers lined up four abreast on the right side of the street, facing west. The command car was at the lead. Two police cars brought up the rear. Three were parked at intervals down the street as far as the railroad station. Several others cruised slowly in the westbound traffic, turned north at Lenox Avenue, east again on 126th Street, back to 125th Street on Second Avenue and retraced the route. The chief inspector had said he didn't want any trouble in Harlem.

'Squads, MARCH!' Marcus shouted over the amplifier.

The black youth driving the old Dodge car slipped in the clutch. The white youth sitting at his side raised his arms with his hands clasped in the sign of brotherhood. The old command car shuddered and moved off. The forty-eight integrated black and white marchers stepped forward, their black and white legs flashing in the amber lights of the bridge approach. Their bare black and white arms shone. Their silky and kinky heads glistened. Marcus had been careful to select black youths who were black and white youths who were white. Somehow the black against the white and the white against the black gave the illusion of nakedness. The forty-eight orderly young marchers gave the illusion of an orgy. The black and white naked flesh in the amber light filled the black and white onlookers with a strange excitement. Cars slowed down and white people leaned out the windows. Black people walking down the street grinned, then laughed, then shouted encouragement. It was as though an unseen band had struck up a Dixieland march. The colored people on the sidewalks on both sides of the street began locomotioning and boogalooing as though gone mad. White women in the passing automobiles screamed and waved frantically. Their male companions turned red like a race of boiled lobsters. The police cars opened their sirens to clear the traffic. But it served to call the attention of more people from the sidelines.

When the marchers came abreast of the 125th Street station on upper Park Avenue, a long straggling tail of laughing, dancing, hysterical black and white people had attached itself to the original forty-eight. Black and white people came from the station waiting-room to stare in popeyed amazement. Black and white people came from nearby bars, from the dim stinking doorways, from the flea-bag hotels, from the cafeterias, the greasy spoons, from the shoe-shine parlors, the poolrooms – pansies and prostitutes, ordinary bar drinkers and strangers in the area who had stopped for a bit to eat, Johns and squares looking for excitement, muggers and sneak thieves looking for victims. The scene that greeted them was like a carnival. It was a hot night. Some of them were drunk. Others had nothing to do. They joined the carnival group thinking maybe they were headed for a revival meeting, a sex orgy, a pansy ball, a beer festival, a baseball game. The white people attracted by the black. The black people attracted by the white.

Marcus looked back from his command car and saw a whole sea of white and black humanity in his wake. He was exultant. He had made it. He knew all people needed was a chance to love one another.

He clutched Birgit's thigh and shouted, 'I've made it, baby. Just look at 'em! Tomorrow my name will be in all the papers.'

She looked back at the wild following, then she gave him a

melting look of love. 'My man! You're so intelligent. It's just like Walpurgisnacht.'

4

The Negro detectives, Grave Digger Jones and Coffin Ed Johnson, were making their last round through Harlem in the old black Plymouth sedan with the unofficial tag, which they used as their official car. In the daytime it might have been recognized, but at night it was barely distinguishable from any number of other dented, dilapidated struggle buggies cherished by the citizens of Harlem; other than when they had to go somewhere in a hurry it went. But now they were idling along, west on 123rd Street, with the lights out as was their custom on dark side streets. The car scarcely made a sound; for all its dilapidated appearance the motor was ticking almost silently. It passed along practically unseen, like a ghostly vehicle floating in the dark, its occupants invisible.

This was due in part to the fact that both detectives were almost as dark as the night, and they were wearing lightweight black alpaca suits and black cotton shirts with the collars open. Whereas other people were in shirt sleeves on this hot night, they wore their suit coats to cover the big glinting nickel-plated thirty-eight-caliber revolvers they wore in their shoulder slings. They could see in the dark streets like cats, but couldn't be seen, which was just as well because their presence might have discouraged the vice business in Harlem and put countless citizens on relief.

Actually they weren't concerned with prostitution or its feeder vices, unlicensed clubs, bottle peddlers, petty larceny, short con and steering. They had no use for pansies, but as long as they didn't hurt anyone, pansies could pansy all they pleased. They weren't arbiters of sex habits. There was no accounting for the sexual tastes of people. Just don't let anyone get hurt.

If white citizens wished to come to Harlem for their kicks,

they had to take the venereal risks and the risks of short con or having their money stolen. Their only duty was to protect them from violence.

They went down the side street without lights to surprise anyone in the act of maiming, mugging, rolling drunks, or committing homicide.

They knew the first people to turn on them if they tried to keep the white man out of Harlem after dark would be the whores themselves, the madams, the pimps, the proprietors of the late-hour joints, most of whom were paying off some of their colleagues on the force.

For such a hot night, Harlem had been exceptionally peaceful. No riots, no murders, only a few cars stolen, which wasn't their business, and a few domestic cuttings.

They were taking it easy.

'It's been a quiet night,' Coffin Ed said from his seat by the sidewalk.

'Better touch wood,' Grave Digger replied, lazily steering with one hand.

'There ain't any wood in this tin lizzie.'

'There's the baseball bat that man was beating his old lady with.'

'Hell, bats are made of plastic these days. Too bad we ain't got his head.'

'Lots of them around. Next one we come to I'll stop.'

'How about that one?'

Grave Digger looked ahead through the windscreen and saw the back of a black man in a black ensemble with a red fez stuck on his head. He knew the man hadn't seen them as yet nevertheless he was running as though he meant it. The man was carrying a pair of light gray pants over one arm with the legs blowing in the breeze as though they were running too, but a little faster.

'Look at that boy picking 'em up and laying 'em down like the earth was red-hot.'

'Reckon we ought to ask him?' Coffin Ed said.

'What for? To hear him lie? The white man who owned those pants ought to have kept them on.'

Coffin Ed chuckled. 'You said the next one we came to you'd stop.'

'Yeah, and you said it was quiet too. Let's keep it that way. What's unusual about a black brother stealing a whitey's pants who's laying up somewhere with a black whore?'

They were relaxed and indifferent. It wasn't their business to rescue the pants of a white man who was stupid enough to let them be stolen. They knew of too many cases where the white John went in the room and left his trousers draped over a chair by the door – with his money in them.

'The first thing to learn about whore-chasing is what to do with your money while screwing.'

'That's simple,' Grave Digger said. 'Leave what you don't need at home.'

'And let your old lady find it? What's the difference?'

They let the fez-headed man get out of sight while they shot the bull. Suddenly Coffin Ed blurted, 'It ain't quiet no more.'

A bareheaded white man had materialized suddenly from the darkness into the dim pool of yellow light spilling from a street lamp, trying to run in the direction taken by the black man. But he staggered on wobbly legs as though drunk. They could see his legs plainly because he didn't wear any pants. In fact he didn't wear any underpants either and they could see his bare white ass beneath his white shirttail.

Grave Digger switched on the headlamps and the next instant he stepped on the accelerator. The car pulled to the curb beside the staggering man with the scream of tires on pavement, and both big double-jointed detectives emerged from opposite sides of the car like hoboes alighting from a moving freight. For an instant there was only the sound of flat feet slapping on concrete as they converged upon the tottering white man from fore and aft. Coming up from the front side Grave Digger drew his torch. It was a rapid dangerous-looking motion until the light hit the white man's face. Grave Digger drew up sharp. Coffin Ed, coming from the rear, pinioned the white man's arms.

'Hold him steady,' Grave Digger said, fishing out his shield and turning the light on it. 'We're policemen. You're safe.'

Even while saying it he thought it was a stupid thing to say. The front of the white man's shirt was covered with blood. More blood spurted from the side of his throat where his jugular had been cut.

The white man shuddered convulsively and began sinking to the ground. Coffin Ed held him up. 'What's the matter with him?' he asked. He couldn't see from behind.

'Throat cut.'

The white man's mouth was clamped shut as though he were holding in his life. Blood spurted from the wound at every third or fourth heartbeat. Drops trickled from his nose. His eyes were beginning to glaze.

'Lay him on his back,' Grave Digger said.

Coffin Ed lowered the body full-length on its back down the dirty pavement. Both of them could see that life was going fast. He was not a pretty sight stretched out in the headlight glare. There was no chance of saving his life. That urgency had passed. Now there was a different urgency. It sounded in Grave Digger's voice as he bent over the dying man, thick, constricted, cottony dry:

'Quick! Quick! Who did it?'

The glazing eyes of the dying man gave no sign of comprehension, only the grim, clamped mouth tightened slightly.

Grave Digger bent closer to hear should the clamped lips open. Blood spurted from the man's cut throat into his face, suddenly nauseating him with its sweet, sickish scent. But he ignored it as he tried to hold the man on to life by his eyes.

'Quick!' Urgent, dry, compelling. 'A name? Give us a name!' His jaw muscles rippled over gritted teeth.

A last brief flicker of comprehension showed in the white man's eyes. For an infinitesimal instant the pupils contracted slightly. The man was making a tremendous effort to speak. The strain was visible in a slight tightening of the muscles of the face and neck.

'Who did it? Quick! A name!' Grave Digger hammered, his black face bloody and contorted.

The white man's tightly clamped lips trembled and suddenly opened, like a seldom used door. A liquid, gurgling sound came out, followed instantly by a gush of blood in which he drowned.

'"*Jesus*,"' Grave Digger echoed as he slowly straightened his bent figure. '"*Jesus bastard!*" What a thing to say.'

Coffin Ed's face was like a thundercloud. 'Jesus, Digger, Goddammit!' he flared. 'What you want him to say, Jesus hallelujah? The mother-raper got his throat cut for a black whore—'

'How you know it was a black whore who did it?'

'By whoever!'

'All right, let's call the precinct,' Grave Digger said thoughtfully, playing his flashlight over the dead man's body. 'Male, fair hair – blue eyes; jugular vein cut, dead on 123rd Street—' Glancing at his watch. '3.11 a.m.,' he recited.

Coffin Ed had hurried back to the car to get the precinct station on the radio. 'Without his pants,' he added.

'Later.'

While Coffin Ed was transmitting the essential facts over the radio-phone, colored people in various stages of undress began emerging from the black dark tenements alongside. Black women in terrycloth robes with their faces greased and their straightened hair done in small tight plaits like Topsy; brownskinned women with voluptuous breasts and broad buttocks wrapped in bright-colored nylon, half-straight hair hanging loosely about their cushion-mouthed sleepy-eyed faces; high yellows in their silks and curlers. And the men, old, young, nappy-headed, conk-haired, eyes full of sleep, faces lined where witches were riding them, mouths slack, wrapped in sheets, blankets, raincoats, or just soiled and wrinkled pajamas. Collecting in the street to see the dead man. Looking inexpressibly stupid in their morbid curiosity. A dead man was always good to see. It was reassuring to see somebody else dead. Generally the dead men were also colored. A white dead man was really something. Worth getting up any time of night. But no one asked who cut him. Nor why. Who was going to ask who cut a white man's throat in Harlem? Or why? Just look at him, baby. And feel good it ain't you. Look at that white mother-raper with his throat cut. You know what he was after . . .

Coffin Ed gave Lieutenant Anderson a brief description of the dead body and a more detailed description of the black man in the red fez they had first seen running down the street with the pants over his arm.

'Do you think the murdered man had some extra pants?' Anderson asked.

'He didn't have *any* pants.'

'What the hell!' Anderson exclaimed. 'What the hell's wrong with you? What are you holding back? Let's have it all.'

'The man didn't have any pants or underpants.'

'Mmmm. All right, Johnson, you and Jones stay put. I'll call homicide, the District Attorney and the Medical Examiner and have them send their men, and I'll put out a pickup for the suspect. You think I should seal up the block?'

'What for? If the suspect did it, he'll be to hell and gone by the time you get the block sealed off. And if anybody else did it they were already gone. All you can do is take in a couple loads of these citizens for questioning if we can determine exactly where it was done.'

'All right, in time. Right now you and Jones stay with the body and see what you can learn.'

'What'd the boss say?' Grave Digger asked when Coffin Ed rejoined him beside the body on the sidewalk.

'Just the usual. The experts are coming. We're to dig what we can without leaving our friend.'

Grave Digger turned towards the silent crowd collecting in the shadows. 'Any of you know anything that might help?'

'H. Exodus Clay is the name of an undertaker,' a brother said.

'Does this look like a time for that?'

'To me it does. When a man's dead you got to bury him.'

'I mean anything that might help find out who killed him,' Grave Digger said to the others.

'I seen a white man and a colored man whispering.'

'Where was that, lady?'

'Eighth Avenue at 15th Street.'

People in Harlem always drop the 'one hundred' from the designation of their streets, so that 10th Street is 110th, 15th is

115th and 25th is 125th. That wasn't very near but it was close enough.

'When, lady?'

'I don't remembers 'zactly. Night 'fore last, I thinks.'

'All right, forget it. You folks go to bed.'

A little shuffling followed but no one left.

'Shit!' someone exclaimed.

'Those car cops must be sleeping,' Coffin Ed said impatiently.

Grave Digger began a cursory examination of the body. There was a cut across the back of the left hand and a deep cut in the palm of the right hand between the index finger and thumb. 'He tried to ward off the knife first, then he grabbed the blade. He wasn't very scared.'

'How you make that?'

'Hell, if he'd been trying to run, ducking and dodging, he'd been cut on the arms and back if his throat hadn't been cut to start with, as you can see it hadn't.'

'All right, Sherlock Jones. Then tell me this much. How come his privates ain't been touched? If this was a sex fight that's the first thing they go for.'

'How we know it was a sex fight? It was probably plain robbery.'

'Well, buddy-o, you can't overlook the fact the man ain't got no pants.'

'Yeah, there's that, and this is Harlem, if you want to add it up that way,' Grave Digger said. 'I just wish these mother-rapers wouldn't come up here and get themselves killed, for whatever reason.'

'Iss bad enough killing our own,' a voice said from the dark. It was followed by a sudden indistinct babble as though the spectators were arguing the point.

Coffin Ed turned on them and shouted suddenly, 'You people better get the hell away from here before the white cops come in, or they'll run all your asses in.'

There was a sound of nervous movement, like frightened cattle in the dark, then a voice said belligerently, 'Run whose ass in? I lives here!'

'All right,' Coffin Ed said resignedly. 'Don't say I didn't warn you.'

Grave Digger was staring at the stretch of sidewalk where the body lay in a widening pool of blood. The headlights of their car starkly lighted the stretch down past the street lamp and the front steps of a number of crumbling houses on that side of the street that had been private residences of a sort a half-century previous. The people who had collected stood along the other side of the street and in back of their car so their dark faces were in the shadow but a row of rusty bare legs and splayed black feet with enormous toes were visible. A Harlem sidewalk, he thought, black feet and purple blood, and a man lying dead. This time he happened to be white. Most times he was black like the legs and feet of the people who stared at him. How many people had he seen lying dead in the street? He couldn't remember, only that most of them had been black. Lying dead and without dignity on the dirty sidewalks. Lying in the coins of dried spit, sticky ice-cream and candy wrappers, wads of chewed gum, stained cigarette butts, newspaper scraps, small bones from cooked meat, dog shit, urine stinks, beer bottles, hair-grease tins; stinking, gritty dirt blowing over them by every puff of wind.

'Anyway, no used condoms,' Coffin Ed said. 'They don't like it if there ain't no risk.'

'Damn right,' Grave Digger agreed. 'All you got to do is look around and see how many times they've lost.'

The first of the sirens sounded.

'Here they are,' Coffin Ed said.

The spectators moved back.

Interlude

'Like him?' Doctor Mubuta asked.

'He's beautiful,' the white woman said.

'Wrap him up and take him with you,' Doctor Mubuta said, coming as near to leering as he had ever done.

She blushed furiously.

Doctor Mubuta motioned to the cretin, who had no compunction about wrapping up the sleeping beauty in the bed sheet.

'Take him out and put him into the back of her car,' Doctor Mubuta directed. Then, turning to the blushing, speechless Mrs Dawson, he said, 'He is now your responsibility, Madame. And I trust that as soon as you have thoroughly investigated this miracle and convinced yourself of its authenticity, you will remit the balance of payment.'

She nodded quickly and left. They all watched her leave. No one said anything. No one on the street gave a second look at the black harelipped cretin placing a sheet-wrapped figure into the back compartment of an air-conditioned Cadillac limousine. It was Harlem, where anything might happen.

5

'You've been trying to outsmart the white folks, and you found that didn't do no good 'cause they're smarter than you are,' Doctor Mubuta was saying in his singsong voice, his heavy jaw moving with the lecherous twist of a big black whore shaking her butt. His voice was as solemn as his expression and his eyes were as humorless as those of a religious fanatic.

'Yeh!' The obscene twist of his jaw was caught, like one buttock aslant, then it resumed its suggestive grind: 'And you've been trying to out-lie the white folk, only to discover it was the white folks who invented lying.'

The teen-aged white girl broke out of her hypnotic trance and giggled like she'd been caught out.

Everyone else was staring at him with open mouths as though he were exposing himself.

'Yeh! And you've been trying to out-Tom the white folks, and you're surprised to find the white folks is stealing your talent, like they has stole everything you has invented.'

Mister Sam's old rheumy eyes opened at that and he peeped

at Doctor Mubuta. But he shut them immediately as though he didn't want to see what he saw. Dick's head moved slightly and an expression of pained cynicism flickered across his face. A subtle smile tugged at the corners of Anny's mouth. Intolerable outrage took hold of Viola's expression. Sugartit's stretched black eyes remained unchanged as though she weren't tuned in. Van Raff seemed to be smoldering at the incredible theft. The teen-aged white girl giggled again and tried to catch Doctor Mubuta's eye. Suddenly he looked directly at her; his vision lost its vague sightless scope and focused on her; his bright red eyes stripping off her clothes and looking directly between her thighs.

'Yeh!' He might have said, 'Yeh, man!'

The ejaculation made her start guiltily. She closed her legs and blushed.

Mister Sam seemed to be sleeping, or else dead.

Then they were all listening again, like passengers in a runaway bus, not knowing where they were going but expecting momentarily to run off the edge of the earth.

Doctor Mubuta's expression went vacant again as though he had made his point, whatever it was.

'Yeh! You've been trying to out-yes white folks, but the white folks is yessing you so fast nowadays you don't know who's yessing who.'

'Shit!' Until then the speaker had been so inconspicuous he had passed for a gray shadow in the brightly lighted room.

The word was heard distinctly but not one hypnotized gaze switched from Doctor Mubuta's belly-dancing under-jaw.

'Hear those shots?' asked Doctor Mubuta, ignoring the ejaculation.

The question was theoretical. They had been hearing the sound of sporadic shooting for some time and they all knew black youths were rioting on Seventh Avenue. It required no answer.

'Throwing rocks at the police,' Doctor Mubuta said in his same singsong voice. 'Must think those white police is made of window glass.'

He paused for a moment as though inviting comment. But

no one had anything to say; no one knew where it was leading to; they all knew white police were not made of window glass.

'I have the one and only solution for the Negro Problem,' Doctor Mubuta exclaimed, his heavy black belly-bumping jaw suddenly throwing it to the wind.

That was the one for someone to challenge him, but no one did.

'We're gonna outlive the white folks. While they has been concentrating on ways of death, I has been concentrating on how to extend life. While they'll be dying, we'll be living forever, and Mister Sam here, the oldest of us all, will be alive to see the day when the black man is the majority on this earth, and the white man his slave.'

The teen-aged white girl stared at Doctor Mubuta as though she took it personally, and was even anxious to give it a try.

But not so with Mister Sam's chauffeur, Johnson X, the invisible man. He could hold it no longer. 'Shit!' he cried. 'Shit!' One couldn't tell whether it was an order or an exclamation. 'Shit! Does anyone in their right state of mind, with all their pieces of gray matter assembled in the right way in they haid, with no fuses blowed in they brain, with they think-piece hitting on all cylinders – you dig me? Anyone – you – me – us – they – we – them – him or her – anyone – you dig me? believe that shittt?' His loose lips punctuated each word with a spray of spit, flapped up and down over white buck teeth like the shutter of a camera photographing missiles shot into space, curled and popped over the tonal effect of each sound, and pronounced the word 'shit' as though he had tasted it and spat it out – eloquent, logical and positive.

'I believe it,' Mister Sam croaked, peeking at Johnson from his old furtive eyes.

'You!' Johnson exploded. It was an accusation.

Everyone stared at Mister Sam as though awaiting his confession.

'Niggers'll believe anything,' Viola spluttered. No one contradicted.

Johnson X looked scornfully at Mister Sam from thick-lensed spectacles with heavy black frames. He was a tall angular man dressed in chauffeur's livery. His small shaved skull merging into his wide curved nose gave him the appearance of a snapping turtle, and with the spectacles he looked as though he were trying to pass himself off as human. He might have been disagreeable but he wasn't stupid. He was Mister Sam's friend.

'Mister Sam,' he said, 'I tells you right here and now to your face – I think you is nuts. You has lost whatever sense you was born with.'

Mister Sam's eyes closed to slits of milky blue in his shrunken face. 'Folks don't know everything,' he whispered.

'I helps the old and the sick,' Doctor Mubuta jawed. 'I rejuvenates the disrejuvenated.'

'Shit! Get yo'self in hand, Mister Sam. Look yo' life in the face. Here you is ninety years old . . .'

'More than that.'

'More than ninety, with almost all of yo'self in the grave, been diddling all kinds of women for sixty-five years.'

'Longer than that.'

'Been pimping and running whorehouse ever since you learned the stuff would sell—'

'Jes business. Buy low and sell high. It's Jewish.'

'Been surrounded with women all yo' life, and ain't satisfied yet. Here you is nearmost a hundred years old and wants to go against the ordained order of creation.'

'Tain't dat!'

'Tain't dat!' Johnson X controlled himself. 'Mister Sam, does you believe in God?'

'Dat's it. I been believing in God for sixty-nine years. That's 'fore you was born.'

Johnson X looked stumped. 'Come again, I don't dig you.'

'God helps them who helps themselves.'

Johnson X's eyes popped, his voice became outraged. 'Old and wicked as you is, as much sin as you has sinned in yo' life, as many people as you has cheated, all the lies you has told, all the stuff you has stole, you means to lie there and say you is expecting some help from God?'

'Nothing takes the place of God,' Doctor Mubuta said in his

singsong voice, sounding as pious as possible, then added as an afterthought, as though he might have gone too far, 'but money.'

'Pick up that there Gladstone bag,' Mister Sam croaked.

Doctor Mubuta lifted the Gladstone bag that sat on the floor beside his doctor's bag.

'Look in it,' Mister Sam ordered.

Doctor Mubuta opened the bag dutifully and looked into it, and for the first time his expression changed and his eyes seemed about to pop from his head.

'What you see?' Mister Sam urged.

'Money,' Doctor Mubuta whispered.

'You think that's enough money to take the place of God?'

'Looks like it. Looks like an awful lot to me.'

'It's all I got.'

Van Raff stood up. Viola turned bright red.

'And it's yours,' Mister Sam informed Doctor Mubuta.

'No, it isn't,' Van Raff shouted.

'I'se going for the police,' Johnson X said.

'Sit down,' Mister Sam croaked evilly. 'Jes testing y'all. Ain't nothing but paper.'

Doctor Mubuta's face closed like the Bible.

'Let me see it,' Van Raff demanded.

'Is I is or is I ain't?' Doctor Mubuta demanded.

'I think someone ought to stop this,' Anny said apologetically. 'I don't think it's right.'

'Tend to your own business,' her husband snarled.

'Excuse me for living,' she replied, giving him a furious look.

'He ought to be put in the 'sylum,' Viola said. 'He's crazy.'

'I'm going to look at it,' Van Raff declared, moving forward to take the bag.

'And I found y'all out,' Mister Sam said.

'Now you've all had your say, can I proceed with the procedure?' Doctor Mubuta said.

'Leave it be,' Johnson X said to Van Raff. 'It ain't going nowhere.'

'It sure ain't,' Van Raff declared, sullenly returning to his seat. Neither of the teen-aged girls had spoken.

In the strained silence, Doctor Mubuta opened his bag and extracted a quart-size jar containing a nasty-looking liquid and placed it atop the bed table beside Mister Sam's bed. Everyone leaned forward to stare incredulously at the milky liquid.

Mister Sam stretched his neck and popped his old glazed eyes like a curious old rooster with a bare neck.

'Is that the stuff?'

'That's the stuff.'

'Gonna make me young?'

'That's what it's for.'

'What's that milky stuff floating around in it?'

'That's albumin. The same stuff as is the base for semen.'

'What's semen?'

'What you ain't got.'

All of a sudden the teen-aged white girl became hysterical. She doubled over laughing and choking and her face turned bright red. Everyone stared at her until she got over it, then turned their attention back to the jar of rejuvenating liquid.

'What's them black balls floating around?' Mister Sam asked.

'Just what they look like, black balls, only they is taken from a baboon, which is the most virile two-footed animal known.'

Mister Sam's lids flickered. 'You don't say. Taken from a live baboon?'

'Live when they was took, and rearing to go.'

'Ain't that sompin. Bet he didn't like it.'

'No more than you would 'ave fifty years ago.'

'Uhm! And what's them things that looks like feathers?'

'They is feathers. Rooster primaries. From a fighting rooster what could fertilize eggs from a distance of three feet.'

'Reminds me of a man I knew what could look at womens and knock 'em up.'

'He had a concupiscent eye. One of them is in there too.'

'You ain't missed nothing, is you? Balls and feathers and eyes and summon. What's all them other strange-looking things?'

'All of them is mating organs of rabbits, eagles and shellfish.'

Doctor Mubuta uttered these pronouncements without the

flicker of an eyelash. His audience stared at him with their eyes popping out. Within the frame of reference – light, heat and Harlem – at some time during the recitation they had all passed the line of rational rejection. It wasn't hard. It wasn't any harder to believe in rejuvenation than to believe equality was coming.

'You sho' got some mixture there, if they all start working at the same time, I'll say that much,' Mister Sam conceded admiringly. 'But what's that black slimy stuff at the bottom?'

'That's the secret,' Doctor Mubuta replied, as solemn as an owl.

'Oh, that's the secret, eh? Looks like hog shit to me.'

'That's the stuff which invigorates the other stuff which charges the genital glands, like charging a rundown battery.'

'Is that what it does?'

'That's what it does.'

'What's it called?'

'Sperm elixir.'

'Sounds mighty fancy. You sure it gonna work?'

Doctor Mubuta looked down at Mister Sam contemptuously. 'If you didn't know this elixir would work, you wouldn't have me here giving you none, cheap and stingy as you is.'

'All I know is what I've heard,' Mister Sam admitted grudgingly.

'What you has heard,' Doctor Mubuta said scornfully. 'You has seen people it has worked on. You has been sneaking around asking questions and spying on my clients ever since I have been back from Africa.'

Johnson X was indignant. 'I'm ashamed of you, Mister Sam. Ashamed! You used to have the reputation of being a real big sport, you enjoyed your pleasure and didn't grudge nobody. And now here you is, sitting on a fortune you has made from the sinning of others, and you is so envious of the pleasures of others you is gonna give all yo' money to be able to sin again yo'self – and it ain't really yo' own money, as old as you is.'

'Ain't that,' Mister Sam protested. 'I wants to get married again.'

'Ise his fiancy,' the teen-aged white girl said. Her flat

unemotional announcement, spoken in a jarring voice straight out of the cotton fields of the South, exploded in the room like a hand grenade, causing far more repercussions than the exposing of the rejuvenating elixir.

So much blood rushed to Viola's head it looked like a gorged bedbug. 'You beast,' she screamed. Which one she meant, no one knew.

'Don't worry, he can't do nothing,' Van Raff consoled her, trying to shake down the blood in his own head.

But it was Anny who looked so ashamed. Noticing, Dick said harshly, 'He gonna be young, ain't he? Don't go back on your race now!'

And for an instant the mask slipped from Doctor Mubuta's face and he looked more stupid than ever. 'Huh! You going to marry this here, uh, young missy?'

'What's the matter with her?' Mister Sam asked challengingly.

'Matter with her! Ain't nothing the matter with her – it's you I is thinking about. You is going to need more of this here elixir than I has figured.'

'You think I ain't thought of that.'

'And what is more,' Doctor Mubuta went on. 'If I heard you correctly, and if what is common knowledge all over Harlem is the truth, you already has one wife, who is here present in this here room and two wives is too many for this elixir at yo' age.'

'Give her some too, so she be young as me, and can peddle her pussy.'

The teen-aged white girl became hysterical again.

Viola popped open a switchblade knife from her purse and charged the girl. Van Raff was caught by surprise and couldn't move. The white girl ran behind Mister Sam's bed as though he could help her. Viola changed directions and headed toward Mister Sam with the open blade. Doctor Mubuta clutched her about the waist. Johnson X started forward. Van Raff jumped to his feet. Viola was trying to stab Doctor Mubuta and his hand was getting slashed as he grabbed for the knife.

He was reaching for the Gladstone when Van Raff came up from behind, shouting, 'Oh, no, you don't!' and snatched it out of his hand. Simultaneously Viola stabbed him in the back. It wasn't enough to hamper him and he wheeled on her in a red-eyed rage and clutched the blade with his bleeding hand as though it were an icicle, and jerked it from her hand. Her gray eyes were stretched in fear and outrage and her pink mouth opened for a scream, showing a lot of vein-laced throat. But she never got to scream. He stabbed her in the heart, and in the same motion turned and stabbed Van Raff in the head, breaking the knife blade on his skull. Van Raff looked a sudden hundred years old as his face fell apart in shock, and the Gladstone bag dropped from his nerveless fingers.

With blood coming out of his back and hand as though his arteries were leaking, Doctor Mubuta snatched up the bag and headed for the door. Dick and Anny had disappeared and Johnson X was standing in the door like a cross to keep anyone from entering. Doctor Mubuta ran up behind him and stabbed him in the back with the broken knife blade and Johnson X went out into the dining-room as though a rocket booster had gone off. Doctor Mubuta left the knife in his back and made for the kitchen door. The door opened from the outside and a short muscular black man in a red fez came in. The man had an open knife with a six-inch blade in his hand. Doctor Mubuta drew up short. But it didn't help him. The short muscular man handled his knife with authority and stabbed Doctor Mubuta to death before he could utter a sound.

6

The speaker standing on an upturned barrel at the intersection of 135th Street and Seventh Avenue was shouting monotonously: 'BLACK POWER! BLACK POWER! Is you is? Or is you ain't? We gonna march this night! March! March! March! *Oh, when the saints* – yeah, baby! We gonna march this night!'

Spit flew from his looselipped mouth. His flabby jowls

flopped up and down. His rough brown skin was greasy with sweat. His dull red eyes looked tired.

'Mistah Charley been scared of BLACK POWER since the day one. That's why Noah shuffled us off to Africa the time of the flood. And all this time we been laughing to keep from whaling.'

He mopped his sweating face with a red bandanna handkerchief. He belched and swallowed. His eyes looked vacant. His mouth hung open as though searching for words. 'Can't keep this up,' he said under his breath. No one heard him. No one noticed his behavior. No one cared.

He swallowed loudly and screamed, 'TONIGHT'S THE NIGHT! We launch our whale boats. Iss the night of the great white whale. You dig me, baby?'

He was a big man and flabby all over like his jowls. Night had fallen but the black night air was as hot as the bright day air, only there was less of it. His white short-sleeved shirt was sopping wet. A ring of sweat had formed about the waist of his black alpaca pants as though the top of his potbelly had begun to melt.

'You want a good house? You got to whale! You want a good car? You got to whale! You want a good job? You got to whale! You dig me?'

His conked hair was dripping sweat. For a big flabby middle-aged man who would have looked more at home in a stud poker game, he was unbelievably hysterical. He waved his arms like an erratic windmill. He cut a dance step. He shuffled like a prizefighter. He shadowed with clenched fists. He shouted. Spit flew. 'Whale! Whale! WHALE, WHITEY! WE GOT THE POWER! WE IS BLACK! WE IS PURE!'

A crowd of Harlem citizens dressed in holiday garb had assembled to listen. They crowded across the sidewalks, into the street, blocking traffic. They were clad in the chaotic colors of a South American jungle. They could have been flowers growing on the banks of the Amazon, wild orchids of all colors. Except for their voices.

'What's he talking 'bout?' a high-yellow chick with bright red hair wearing a bright green dress that came down just below her buttocks asked the tall slim black man with smooth carved features and etched hair.

'Hush yo' mouth an' lissen,' he replied harshly, giving her a furious look from the corners of muddy, almond-shaped eyes. 'He tellin' us what black power mean!'

She opened her big green eyes speckled with brown tints and looked at him in astonishment.

'Black power? It don't mean nothing to me. I ain't black.'

His carved lips curled in scorn. 'Whose fault is that?'

'BLACK POWER IS MIGHTY! GIVE FOR THE FIGHT!'

When the comely young brownskinned miss presented her collection basket to a group of sports of all sorts in front of the Paradise Inn, repeating in her soft, pleasant voice: 'Give for the fight, gentlemen,' one conk-haired joker in a long-sleeved red silk shirt said offensively, 'What mother-raping fight? If Black Power all that powerful, who needs to fight? It ought to be giving me something.'

She looked the sports up and down, unperturbed. 'Go back to your white tramps; we black women are going to fight.'

'Well, go 'head and fight then,' the sport said, turning away. 'That's what's wrong with you black women, you fights too much.'

But some of the other young women collecting for the fight were more successful. For among the holiday-makers there were many serious persons who understood the necessity for a fund for the coming fight. They believed in Black Power. They'd give it a trial anyway. Everything else had failed. They filled the collection baskets with coins and bills. It was going anyway, for one thing and another. Rent, religion, food or whiskey, why not for Black Power? What did they have to lose? And they might win. Who knew? The whale swallowed Jonah. Moses split the Red Sea. Christ rose from the dead. Lincoln freed the slaves. Hitler killed six million Jews. The Africans had got to rule – in some parts of Africa, anyway. The Americans and the Russians have shot the moon. Some joker has made a plastic heart. Anything is possible.

The young ladies dumped their filled baskets into a gilt-painted keg with the banner BLACK POWER on a low table to one side of the speaker's barrel, presided over by a buxom, stern-faced, gray-haired matron clad in a black dress uniform lit up with gilt buttons and masses of braid who looked like an effigy beginning to burn on that hot day. And then they went back into the crowd to fill them again.

The speaker raved: 'BLACK POWER! DANGEROUS AS THE DARK! MYSTERIOUS AS THE NIGHT! Our heritage! Our birthright! Unchain us in the big cor-ral!'

'Joker sounds like he's shooting craps,' one brother whispered to another.

The few white motorists threading their way through the crowd, going north on Seventh Avenue in the direction of Westchester County, looked curiously at the crowd, opened their windows and heard the words, 'BLACK POWER,' and stepped on the gas.

It was an orderly crowd. Police cars lined the streets. But the cops had nothing to do except avoid the challenging stares. Most of the patrol-car cops were white, but they had become slightly reddened under the hysterical ranting of the speaker and the monotonous repetition of 'BLACK POWER'.

A black Cadillac limousine, shining in the sun like polished jet, whispered to the curb in the no-parking zone for the crosstown bus stop, within touching distance of the orator's barrel. Two dangerous-looking black men clad in black leather coats and what looked like officers' caps in a Black Power army sat in the front seat, immobile, staring straight ahead with not a muscle twitching in their lumpy scarred faces. On the back seat sat a portly gray-haired black man between two slender, sedate, clean-cut brownskinned young men dressed as clerics. The gray-haired man had smooth black velvety skin that looked recently massaged. Despite his short-cropped gray kinky hair, his light-brown eyes beneath thick glossy black eyebrows were startlingly clear and youthful. Long black eyelashes gave him a sexy look. But there was nothing lush about his appearance, still less about his demeanor. He was dressed in dark gray summer worsted, black shoes, dark tie, white shirt, and wore no jewelry of any sort, not even a watch. His manner was calm, authoritative, his eyes twinkled with good humor but his mouth was firm and his face grave.

The leather-coated flunky next to the chauffeur jumped to the curb and held open the back door. The cleric on the inside stepped to the pavement, the gray-haired man followed him.

The speaker stopped abruptly in the middle of a sentence and descended from his barrel. He approached the gray-haired man with a diffidence that didn't become the masterful exhorter of Black Power. He made no attempt to shake his hand. 'Doctor Moore, I need a relief,' he blurted. 'I'm beat.'

'Carry on, J,' Doctor Moore commanded. 'I'll send L to relieve you shortly.' His voice was modulated, his enunciation perfect, his manner pleasant, but it held an authority that brooked no contradiction.

'I'm awfully tired,' J whined.

Doctor Moore gave him a sharp look, then he softened and patted his shoulder. 'We are all tired, son, carry on just a little longer and you will be relieved. If just one more soul,' he added, shaking his finger to emphasize his point, 'gets the message our labors will not be in vain.'

'Yes, sir,' J said meekly and hefted his wet flabby belly back on to his barrel.

'And now, Sister Z, what have you for the cause?' Doctor Moore asked the buxom black-uniformed matron presiding over the gilt keg of BLACK POWER.

She grinned a smile of pure gold; it was like seeing Mona Lisa break into a laugh. 'The keg is most near filled,' she said proudly, rows of gold teeth, uppers and lowers, flashing in the light.

Doctor Moore looked at her teeth regretfully, then nodded to the cleric, who opened the trunk of the car and undid a large leather suitcase. The leather-coated flunky took the keg of money and dumped it into the suitcase, which was already half-filled with similar coins and bills.

The onlookers watched this operation in a petrified silence. From down the street the white cops in front of the 135th Street precinct station looked on curiously but didn't move. None took notice that the limousine was parked illegally. No one challenged Doctor Moore's authority to collect the money. No one seemed to think there was anything strange about the entire procedure. But yet there were many black people among the crowd and most of the white cops in the police cars who didn't know who Doctor Moore was, who had never seen him or even heard of him. He had such a positive air of authority it seemed logical that he would collect the money, and it was taken for granted that a black Cadillac limousine filled with uniformed black people, even though two of the uniforms were clerical, was connected with Black Power.

When they had taken their respective seats again, Doctor Moore spoke into the speaking-tube, 'Drive to the Center, B,' then as he glanced at the back of the chauffeur's head, corrected himself: 'I believe you're C, aren't you?'

The front seat wasn't partitioned off and the chauffeur turned his head slightly and said, 'Yes, sir, B's dead.'

'Dead? Since when?' Doctor Moore sounded mildly surprised.

'It's more than two months now.'

Doctor Moore leaned back against the cushions and sighed. 'Life is fleeting,' he observed sadly.

Nothing more was said until they arrived at their destination. It was a middle-class housing development on upper Lenox Avenue, a large U-shaped red-brick apartment building seventeen storeys high. The front garden was so new the grass hadn't sprouted and the freshly planted trees and shrubbery looked withered as from a drought. There was a children's playground in its center with the slides and seesaws and sand-boxes so new they looked abandoned, as though no children lived there.

Across Lenox Avenue, on the West Side, toward Seventh Avenue, were the original slums with their rat-ridden, cold water flats unchanged, the dirty glass-fronted ground floors occupied by the customary supermarkets with hand-lettered ads on their plate-glass windows reading: 'Fully cooked U.S. Govt. Inspected SMOKED HAMS 55c lb . . . Secret Deodorant ICE-BLUE 79c. . . . California Seedless GRAPES 2 lbs 49c. . . . Fluffy ALL Controlled Suds 3 lbs pkg. 77c. . . KING CRAB CLAWS lb 79c. . . . GLAD BAGS 99c.' Delicatessens advertising: '*Frozen Chitterlings and other delicacies*' . . . Notion stores with needles and buttons and thread on display . . . Barbershops . . . Smokeshops . . . Billboards advertising: *Whiskies, beers* . . . 'HARYOU' . . . *Politicians running for Congress* . . . 'BEAUTY FAIR by CLAIRE: *WIGS, MEN'S HAIR PIECES, "CAPILISCIO"*' . . . Funeral Parlors . . . Nightclubs . . . '*Reverend Ike; "See and hear this young man of God; A Prayer For The Sick And All Conditions in Every Service; COME WITH YOUR BURDENS LEAVE WITH A SONG"*' . . . Black citizens sitting on the stoops to their cold-water flats in the broiling night . . . Sports ganged in front of bars sucking marijuana . . . Grit and dust and dirt and litter floating idly in the hot dense air stirred up by the passing of feet. That was the side of the slum dwellers. The ritzy residents across the street never looked their way.

The black Cadillac limousine drew to the curb in front of the unfinished lawn. Miraculously the banner across the back which had previously proclaimed BLACK POWER now read: BROTHERHOOD. The two black-coated, black-capped men in front got out first and stood flanking the rear door. Away from the motley crowd at 135th Street and Seventh Avenue, with that quiet, pretentious apartment building in the background, they looked larger, tougher, infinitely more dangerous. The bulges beneath their leather coats on the left sides were more pronounced. There, on the quiet, shady side of the old, wide, historic slum street, they looked unmistakably like bodyguards. The well-dressed people coming and going from and to the apartment entrance gave them a wide berth. But no resentment was shown. They were familiar. Doctor Moore was a noted personage. The residents held him in high esteem. They admired his efforts at integration; they commended his nonviolent, reasonable approach. When Doctor Moore himself alighted, standing between his two clerics, passing residents tipped their hats and smiled obsequiously.

'You boys come with me,' he said.

He walked briskly into the building with his retinue at his heels. There were both confidence and authority in his bearing, like that of a man with a purpose and a will to achieve it. Residents passing through the foyer bowed. He smiled amiably but didn't speak. The doorman kept an empty elevator waiting for him. He rode it to the third floor, where he dismissed his bodyguards and took his clerics inside.

The entrance hall was sumptuously furnished. A wall-to-wall carpet of a dark purple color covered the floor. On one side was a coat-rack with a full-length mirror attached and beside it an umbrella stand. On the other side a long low table for hats, with twin shaded lamps at each end, flanked by straight-backed chairs of some dark exotic wood with overstuffed needlepoint seats. But Doctor Moore did not linger there. After a brief glance into the mirror he turned right into the salon along the front of the building with two wide windows, followed by his clerics. Except for translucent curtains and purple silk drapes behind white venetian blinds, the salon was as bare as Mother Hubbard's Cupboard. But Doctor Moore kept on through to the dining-room with his clerics at his heels. It was equally bare as the salon with similar blinds and curtains. But Doctor Moore did not hesitate, nor did his clerics expect him to hesitate. Into the kitchen they marched in single file. Not a word had been spoken. And as yet still without speech, his clerics shed their coats and clerical collars and donned white cotton jackets and cooks' caps while Doctor Moore peered into the refrigerator.

'They're some neckbones here,' Doctor Moore said. 'Make some neckbones and rice and you'll find some yellow yams somewhere and maybe there's some of those collards left.'

'What about some corn bread, Al?' one of the cook-clerics said.

'All right then, some corn bread, if there's any butter.'

'There's some margarine.'

Doctor Moore gave a grimace of distaste. 'Tap the trunk,' he said, 'A man's got to eat.'

He went quickly back into the hall and opened the door to the first bedroom. It was empty except for an unmade double bed and an unpainted wardrobe.

'Lucy!' he called.

A woman stuck her head out of the bath. It was the head of a young woman with a smooth brownskinned face and straightened black hair pulled aslant her forehead over her right ear. It was a beautiful face with a wide straight nose and unflared nostrils above a wide, thick, unpainted mouth with brown lips that looked soft and resilient. Brown eyes magnified by rimless spectacles gave her a sexy look.

'Lucy's out; it's me,' she said.

'You? Barbara! Somebody with you?' his voice came out in a whisper.

'Shit, naw, do you think I'd bring 'em here?' she said in a softly modulated voice which jarred shockingly with the words.

'Well, what the fuck are you doing here?' he said in a loud coarse voice that made him sound like another man altogether. 'I sent you to work the cocktail party at the Americana.'

She came into the room with the waft of woman smell. Her voluptuous brown body was covered loosely by a pink silk robe which showed a line of brown belly and a black growth of pubic hair.

'I was there,' she said defensively. 'There was too much competition from the high-society amateurs. All those hincty bitches fell on those whitey-babies like they was sugar candy.'

Doctor Moore frowned angrily. 'So what? Can't you out-project those amateurs? You're a pro.'

'Are you kidding? Against all those free matrons? You ever see Madame Thomasina with a hot on for whitey?'

'Listen, whore, that's your problem. I don't pay to send you to these cocktail parties to let these high-society bitches beat you at the game. I expect you to score. How you do it is your business. If you can't collar a whitey John with them all about, I'll get myself another whore.'

She went up to him so he could smell her and feel the woman coming from her body. 'Don't talk to me like that, Al baby. Ain't I been good all along? It's just these matinees when these bitches are free. I'm sure I'll score tonight.' She tried to embrace him but he pushed her away roughly.

'You better, girl,' he said. 'I mean business. The rent isn't paid, and I'm behind with my Caddy.'

'Ain't your own pitch paying nothing?'

'Peanuts. It's split too mother-raping thin. And these Harlem folks ain't serious. All they want to do is boogaloo.' He paused and then said reflectively, 'I could make a mint if I could just get them mad.'

'Jesus, can't your apes do that? What you got them for then?'

'No. They're useless in an operation like this,' he said meditatively. 'What I really need is a dead man.'

7

The assistant Medical Examiner looked like a City College student in a soiled seersucker suit. His thick brown hair needed cutting and his hornrimmed glasses needed wiping. He looked as humorless as befits a man whose business is the dead.

He straightened up from examining the body and wiped his hands on his trousers. 'This was an easy one,' he said, addressing himself to the sergeant from the homicide bureau. 'You got the exact time of death from these local men, they saw him die. The exact cause is a cut jugular vein. Male, white and approximately thirty-five years old.'

The homicide sergeant wasn't satisfied with such a small capsule. He looked as though he was never satisfied with Medical Examiners. He was a thin, tall, angular man wearing what looked like a starched blue serge suit. He had reddish hair of the most repulsive shade, big brown freckles that looked like a bowl full of warts, and a long sharp nose that stuck out from his face like the keel of a racing yacht. His close-set, small blue eyes looked frustrated.

'Identifying marks? Scars? Birthmarks?'

'Hell, you saw as much as I did,' the assistant M.E. said, accidentally stepping into the pool of blood. 'Son of a Goddamn bitch!' he cried.

'Jesus Christ, there's not a thing on him to tell who he is,' the sergeant complained. 'No papers, no wallet, no laundry mark on this one garment it's wearing—'

'How 'bout the shoes?' Coffin Ed ventured.

'Marked shoes?'

'Why not?'

The assistant D.A. gave him a slight nod, whatever it meant. He was a middle-aged man with a white unhealthy look and meticulously combed graying hair. His doughy face and abrupt paunch along with his wrinkled suit and unshined shoes gave him the look of a complete failure. Gathered about him were the ambulance drivers and vacant-faced patrol-car cops as though seeking shelter of his indecision. The homicide sergeant and the assistant M.E. stood apart.

The sergeant looked at the photographer he had brought with him. 'Take off his shoes,' he ordered.

The photographer bridled. 'Let Joe take 'em off,' he said. 'All I take is pictures.'

Joe was the detective first grade who drove for the sergeant. He was a square-built Slav with crew-cut hair that bristled like porcupine quills.

'All right, Joe,' the sergeant said.

Wordlessly Joe knelt on the dirty pavement, unlaced the dead man's brown suede oxfords and drew them from his feet, one after another. He held them to the light and looked inside. The sergeant bent to look into them too.

'*Bostonian*,' Joe read.

'Hell,' the sergeant said disgustedly, giving Coffin Ed an appraising look. Then he turned back to the assistant M.E. with a long-suffering manner. 'Can you tell me if he's had sexual intercourse – recently, I mean?'

The assistant M.E. looked bored with it all. 'We can tell by the autopsy whether he's had sexual intercourse up to within an hour of death.' Sotto voce, he added, 'What a question.'

The sergeant heard him. 'It's important,' he said defensively. 'We got to know something about this man. How the hell we going to find out who killed him?'

'You can take his prints, of course,' Coffin Ed said.

The sergeant looked at him with narrowed eyes, as though suspecting him of needling. Of course they were going to take the body's fingerprints and all other Bertillon measurements needed in identification, as the detective well knew, he thought angrily.

'Anyway, it wasn't with a woman,' the assistant M.E. said, reddening uncontrollably. 'At least in a normal way.'

Everyone looked at him, as though expecting him to say more.

'Right,' the sergeant concurred, nodding knowingly. But he would have liked to ask the assistant M.E. how he knew.

Then suddenly Grave Digger said, 'I could have told you that from the start.'

The sergeant reddened so furiously his freckles stood out like scars. He had heard of these two colored detectives up here, but this was the first time he had seen them. But he could already tell that a little bit of them went a long way; in other words, they were getting on his ass.

'Then maybe you can tell me why he was killed, too,' he said sarcastically.

'That's easy,' Grave Digger said with a straight face. 'There are only two reasons a white man is killed in Harlem. Money or fear.'

The sergeant wasn't expecting that answer. It threw him. He lost his sarcasm. 'Not sex?'

'Sex? Hell, that's all you white people can think of, Harlem and sex – and you're right, too!' he went on before the sergeant could speak. 'You're right as rain. But sex is for sale. And all the surplus they give away. So why kill a white sucker for that? That's killing the goose that lays the golden egg.'

Color drained from the sergeant's face and it became white from anger. 'Are you trying to tell me there are no sex murders here?'

'What I said was there were no white men killed for sex,' Grave Digger said equably. 'Ain't no white man ever that involved.'

Color flowed back into the sergeant's face, which was changing color under his guilt complexes like a chameleon. 'And no one ever makes a mistake?' He felt compelled to argue just for the sake of arguing.

'Hell, sergeant, every murder's a mistake,' Grave Digger said condescendingly. 'You know that, it's your business.'

Yes, these black sons of bitches were going to take a lot of getting along with, the sergeant thought, as he grimly changed the conversation.

'Well, maybe I should have asked do you know who killed him?'

'That ain't fair,' Coffin Ed said roughly.

The sergeant threw up his hands. 'I give up.'

Including the patrol-car cops, most of whom were white, there were fifteen white officers gathered about the body, and in addition to Grave Digger and Coffin Ed, four colored patrol-car cops. All laughed from relief. It was a touchy business when a white man was killed in Harlem. People took up sides on racial lines, regardless of whether they were police officers or not. No one liked it, but all were involved. It was personal to them all.

'Anything else you want to know?' the assistant M.E. asked.

The sergeant looked at him sharply to see if he was being sarcastic. He decided he was innocent. 'Yeah, everything,' he replied, waxing loquacious. 'Who he is? Who killed him? Why? Most of all I want the killer. That's my job.'

'That's your baby,' the assistant M.E. said. 'By tomorrow – or rather this morning – we'll give you the physiological details. Right now I'm going home.' He filled out a DOA tag, which he tied to the right big toe of the body, and nodded to the drivers of the police hearse. 'Take it to the morgue.'

The homicide sergeant stood absently watching the body loaded, then looked slowly about from the idle car cops to the congregated black people. 'All right, boys,' he ordered. 'Take them all in.'

The homicide department always took over investigations of homicide and the highest-ranking homicide detective on the scene became the boss. Detectives from the local precinct and patrol-car cops who took instructions either from the precinct captain or a divisional inspector didn't always like this arrangement. But Grave Digger and Coffin Ed didn't care who became boss. 'We just get pissed-off with all the red tape,' Grave Digger once said. 'We want to get down to the nitty-gritty.'

But there were formalities to protect the rights of citizens and they couldn't just light into a group of innocent people and start whipping head until somebody talked, which they figured was the best and cheapest way to solve a crime. If the citizens didn't like it, they ought to stay at home. Since they couldn't do this, they began to walk away.

'Come on,' Coffin Ed urged. 'This man will have us picked up next.'

'Look at these brothers flee,' Grave Digger noted. 'They wouldn't listen to me when I warned them.'

They went only as far as the littered paved square strewed with overflowing garbage cans beside the front stairs to the nearest rooming house where they could watch the operation without being seen. The smell of rotting garbage was nauseating.

'Whew! Who said us colored people were starving?'

'That ain't what they say, Digger. They just wonder why we ain't.'

As the first of the onlookers were loaded in the police wagon, other curious citizens arrived.

'Whuss happening?'

'Search me, baby. Some whitey was killed, they say.'

'Shot?'

'Washed away.'

'They got who done it?'

'You kidding? They just grabbing off us folks. You know how white cops is.'

'Less split.'

'Too late,' said a white car cop who thought he dug the soul brother, taking each by the arm.

'He thinks he's funny,' one of the brothers complained.

'Well, ain't he?' the other admitted, looking expressively at their arms in his grip.

'Joe, you and Ted bright the power lamps,' the sergeant called above the hubbub. 'Looks like there's a blood trail here.'

Followed by his assistants with the battery-powered spot lamps, the sergeant stepped down into the garbage-scented courtyard. 'I'll need you men's help,' he said. 'There must be a blood trail here.' He had decided to adopt a conciliatory manner.

People gathered on the adjoining rooming-house steps, trying to see what they were doing. A patrol car drew to the curb, the two uniformed cops in the front seat looking on with interest.

The sergeant became exasperated. 'You officers get these people out the way,' he ordered irritably.

The cops got sullen. 'Hey, you folks get over there with the others,' one ordered.

'I lives here,' a buxom light-complexioned woman wearing gilt mules and a stained blue nightgown muttered defiantly. 'I just got out of bed to see what the noise was all about.'

'Now you know,' the homicide photographer said slyly.

The woman grinned gratefully.

'Do as you're ordered!' the car cop shouted angrily, stepping to the sidewalk.

The woman's plaits shook in outrage. 'Who you talking to?' she shouted back. 'You can't order me off my own steps.'

'You tell 'em sister Berry,' a pajama-clad brother behind her encouraged.

The cop was getting red. The other cop climbed from beneath the wheel on the other side and came around the car threateningly. 'What was that you said?' he challenged.

She looked toward Grave Digger and Coffin Ed for support.

'Don't look at me,' Grave Digger said. 'I'm the law too.'

'That's a nigger for you,' the woman said scornfully as the white cops marched them off.

'All right, now bring the light here,' the sergeant said, returning to the dark purple pool of congealing blood where the murdered man had died.

Before joining the others, Grave Digger went back to their car and turned off the lights.

The trail wasn't hard to follow. It had a pattern. An irregular patch of scattered spots that looked like spots of tar in the artificial light was interspersed every fourth or fifth step by a dark gleaming splash where blood had spurted from the wound. Now that all the soul people had been removed from the street, the five detectives moved swiftly. But they could still feel the presence of teeming people behind the dilapidated stone façades of the old reconverted buildings. Here and there the white gleams of eyes showed from darkened windows, but the silence was eerie.

The trail turned from the sidewalk into an unlighted alleyway between the house beyond the rooming house, which described itself by a sign in a front window reading: *Kitchenette Apts. All conveniences*, and the weather-streaked red-brick apartment beyond that. The alleyway was so narrow they had to go in single file. The sergeant had taken the power light from his driver, Joe, and was leading the way himself. The pavement slanted down sharply beneath his feet and he almost lost his step. Midway down the blank side of the building he came to a green wooden door. Before touching it, he flashed his light along the sides of the flanking buildings. There were windows in the kitchenette apartments, but all from the top to the bottom floor had folding iron grilles which were closed and locked at that time of night, and dark shades were drawn on all but three. The apartment house had a vertical row of small black openings one above the other at the rear. They might have been bathroom windows but no light showed in any of them and the glass was so dirty it didn't shine.

The blood trail ended at the green door.

'Come out of there,' the sergeant said.

No one answered.

He turned the knob and pushed the door and it opened inward so silently and easily he almost fell into the opening before he could train his light. Inside was a black dark void.

Grave Digger and Coffin Ed flattened themselves against the walls on each side of the alley and their big long-barreled .38 revolvers came glinting into their hands.

'What the hell!' the sergeant exclaimed, startled.

His assistants ducked.

'This is Harlem,' Coffin Ed grated and Grave Digger elaborated:

'We don't trust doors that open.'

Ignoring them, the sergeant shone his light into the opening. Crumbling brick stairs went down sharply to a green iron grille.

'Just a boiler room,' the sergeant said and put his shoulders through the doorway. 'Hey, anybody down there?' he called. Silence greeted him.

'You go down, Joe, I'll light your way,' the sergeant said.

'Why me?' Joe protested.

'Me and Digger'll go,' Coffin Ed said. 'Ain't nobody there who's alive.'

'I'll go myself,' the sergeant said tersely. He was getting annoyed.

The stairway went down underneath the ground floor to a depth of about eight feet. A short paved corridor ran in front of the boiler room at right angles to the stairs, where each end was closed off by unpainted paneled doors. Both the stairs and the corridor felt like loose gravel underfoot, but otherwise they were clean. Splotches of blood were more in evidence in the corridor and a bloody hand mark showed clearly on the unpainted door to the rear.

'Let's not touch anything,' the sergeant cautioned, taking out a clean white handkerchief to handle the doorknob.

'I better call the fingerprint crew,' the photographer said.

'No, Joe will call them; I'll need you. And you local fellows better wait outside, we're so crowded in here we'll destroy the evidence.'

'Ed and I won't move,' Grave Digger said.

Coffin Ed grunted.

Taking no further notice of them, the sergeant pushed open the door. It was black and dark inside. First he shone his light over the wall alongside the door and all over the corridor looking for electric light switches. One was located to the right of each door. Taking care to avoid stepping in any of the blood splotches, the sergeant moved from one switch to another, but none worked. 'Blown fuse,' he muttered, picking his way back to the open room.

Without having to move, Grave Digger and Coffin Ed could

see all they wanted through the open door. Originally made to accommodate a part-time janitor or any type of laborer who would fire the boiler for a place to sleep, the room had been converted into a pad. All that remained of the original was a partitioned-off toilet in one corner and a washbasin in the other. An opening enclosed by heavy wire mesh opened into the boiler room, serving for both ventilation and heat. Otherwise the room was furnished like a boudoir. There was a dressing-table with a triple mirror, three-quarter bed with chenille spread, numerous foam-rubber pillows in a variety of shapes, three round yellow scatter rugs. On the whitewashed walls an obscene mural had been painted in watercolors depicting black and white silhouettes in a variety of perverted sex acts, some of which could only be performed by male contortionists. And everything was splattered with blood, the walls, the bed, the rugs. The furnishings were not so much disarrayed, as though a violent struggle had taken place, but just bloodied.

'Mother-raper stood still and let his throat be cut,' Grave Digger observed.

'Wasn't that,' Coffin Ed corrected. 'He just didn't believe it is all.'

The photographer was taking pictures with a small pocket camera but the sergeant sent him back to the car for his big Bertillon camera. Grave Digger and Coffin Ed left the cellar to look around.

The apartment was only one room wide but four storeys high. The front was flush with the sidewalk, and the front entrance elevated by two recessed steps. The alleyway at the side slanted down from the sidewalk sufficiently to drop the level of the door six feet below the ground-floor level. The cellar, which could only be entered by the door at the side, was directly below the ground-floor rooms. There were no apartments. Each of the four floors had three bedrooms opening on to the public hall, and to the rear was a kitchen and a bath and a separate toilet to serve each floor. There were three tenants on each floor, their doors secured by hasps and staples to be padlocked when they were absent, bolts and chains and floor locks and angle bars to protect them from intruders when they were present. The doors were pitted and scarred either because of lost keys or attempted burglary, indicating a continuous warfare between the residents and enemies from without, rapists, robbers, homicidal husbands and lovers, or the landlord after his rent. The walls were covered with obscene graffiti, mammoth sexual organs, vulgar limericks, opened legs, telephone numbers, outright boasting, insidious suggestions, and impertinent or pertinent comments about various tenants' love habits, their mothers and fathers, the legitimacy of their children.

'And people live here,' Grave Digger said, his eyes sad.

'That's what it was made for.'

'Like maggots in rotten meat.'

'It's rotten enough.'

Twelve mailboxes were nailed to the wall in the front hall. Narrow stairs climbed to the top floor. The ground-floor hallway ran through a small back courtyard where four overflowing garbage cans leaned against the wall.

'Anybody can come in here day or night,' Grave Digger said. 'Good for the whores but hard on the children.'

'I wouldn't want to live here if I had any enemies,' Coffin Ed said. 'I'd be scared to go to the john.'

'Yeah, but you'd have central heating.'

'Personally, I'd rather live in the cellar. It's private with its own private entrance and I could control the heat.'

'But you'd have to put out the garbage cans,' Grave Digger said.

'Whoever occupied that whore's crib ain't been putting out any garbage cans.'

'Well, let's wake up the brothers on the ground floor.'

'If they ain't already awake.'

8

'You're assuming that I'm a criminal because I'm married to a Negro and living in a Negro neighborhood,' Anny said tremulously. She still wore the dazed look from too much nigger and too much blood and the two black detectives weren't helping it any. She was down in the pigeon's nest on the bolted stool with the bright lights pouring over her, like any other suspect, but she'd already had a taste of this eye-searing glare and that didn't bother her as much as the indignity.

Coffin Ed and Grave Digger stood back in the shadow beyond the perimeter of the glare and she couldn't see their expressions.

'How does it feel?' Grave Digger asked.

'I know what you mean,' she said. 'I've always said it was unfair.'

'We're holding you as a material witness,' he explained.

'It's after midnight now,' Coffin Ed said. 'By eight o'clock this morning you'll be sprung.'

'What he means is we've got to get such information as we can before then,' Grave Digger explained.

'I don't know much,' she said. 'My husband's the one you ought to question.'

'We'll get to him, we got to you,' Coffin Ed said.

'It all came from Mister Sam wanting to get rejuvenated,' she said.

'Did you believe in that?' Grave Digger asked.

'You sound like his chauffeur, Johnson X,' she said.

He didn't dispute her.

'All colored people sound alike,' Coffin Ed muttered.

A slow blush crept over her pale face. 'It wasn't so hard,' she confessed. 'It was harder for my husband. You see, I have come to believe in a lot of things most people consider unbelievable.'

Grave Digger continued the questioning. 'How long had you known about it?'

'A couple of weeks.'

'Did Mister Sam tell you?'

'No, my husband told me.'

'What did he think about it?'

'He just thought it was a trick his father was playing on his wife, Viola.'

'What kind of trick?'

'To get rid of her.'

'Kill her?'

'Oh, no, he just wanted to be rid of her. You see, he knew she was having an affair with his attorney, Van Raff.'

'Did you know him well?'

'Not well. He considered me his son's property, and he wouldn't poach—'

'Although he wanted to?'

'Maybe, but he was so old – that's why he wanted to be rejuvenated.'

'To have you?'

'Oh, no, he had his own. One white woman was the same as another to him – only younger.'

'Mildred?'

'Yes, the little tramp.' She didn't say it vindictively, it was just descriptive.

'Anyway, she's young enough,' Coffin Ed said.

'And he figured his wife and his lawyer were after his money?' Grave Digger surmised.

'That's what started it,' she said, and then suddenly, as the memory washed over her, she buried her face in her hands. 'Oh, it was horrible,' she sobbed. 'Suddenly they were savaging one another like wild beasts.'

'It's the jungle, ain't it?' Coffin Ed growled. 'What did you expect?'

'The blood, the blood,' she moaned. 'Everyone was bleeding.'

Grave Digger waited for her to regain her composure, exchanging looks with Coffin Ed. Both were thinking maybe hers was the solution but was it the time? Would sexual integration start inside the black ghetto or outside in the white community? But it didn't seem as though she would regain her composure, so Grave Digger asked, 'Who started the cutting?'

'Mister Sam's wife jumped up to attack Mister Sam's little tramp, but suddenly she turned on Doctor Mubuta. I suppose it was because of the money,' she added.

'What money?'

'Mister Sam had a satchel full of money under the bed which he said he was going to give to Doctor Mubuta for making him young.'

The detectives froze. More blood was shed for money in Harlem than for any other reason.

'How much?'

'He said it was all he had—'

'Have you heard about the money?' Grave Digger asked Coffin Ed.

'No. Homicide must know. We'd better check with Anderson.'

'Later.' He turned back to Anny. 'Did everyone see it?'

'Actually it was in a Gladstone bag,' Anny said. 'He let Doctor Mubuta look into the bag, but didn't anyone else actually see it. But Doctor Mubuta looked like it was a lot of money—'

'Looked like?'

'His expression. He seemed surprised.'

'By the money?'

'By the amount, I suppose. The attorney demanded to see it. But Mister Sam – or maybe it was Doctor Mubuta – shut the bag and put it back beneath the bed, then Mister Sam said it was just paper, that he was joking. But everything seemed to change after that, as though the air got filled with violence. Mister Sam told Doctor Mubuta to go on with the experiment – the rejuvenation – because he wanted to be young again so he could marry. Then Mister Sam's tramp – Mildred – said she was his fiancée, and Mister Sam's wife, Viola, jumped up and took a knife out of her bag and ran towards the tramp – girl – and she crawled underneath Mister Sam's bed, so Mister Sam's wife turned on Doctor Mubuta, and Mister Sam drank some rejuvenating fluid and began to howl like a dog. I'm sure Doctor Mubuta didn't expect that reaction, he seemed to turn white. But he had the presence of mind to push Mister Sam down on the bed, and shout to us to run—'

Grave Digger broke the spell of his absorbed fascination and asked, 'Why?'

'Why what?'
'Why run?'
'He said the "Bird of Youth" was entering.'
Grave Digger stared at her. Coffin Ed stared at her.
'How old are you?' Coffin Ed asked.
Her mind was so locked in the terrifying memory she didn't hear the question. She didn't see them. Her vision had turned back to that terrifying moment and she looked as though she were blind. 'Then when Johnson X, Mister Sam's chauffeur, began to howl too – until then he had seemed the sanest one – we ran . . .'
'Up to your apartment?'
'And locked the door.'
'And you didn't see what happened to the bag of money?'
'We didn't see anything else.'
'When did Van Raff come upstairs?'
'Oh, sometime later – I don't know how long. He knocked on the door a long time before we opened it, then Dick, my husband, peeped out and found him unconscious on the floor and we brought him in—'
'Did he have the bag of money?'
'No, he had been stabbed all over the head and—'
'We know all that. Now who were all the people at this shindig?'
'There were me and Dick, my husband—'
'We know he's your husband, you don't have to keep on insisting,' Coffin Ed interrupted.
She tried to see his face through the curtain of shadow and Grave Digger went over to the wall and turned the lights down.
'That better?' he asked.
'Yes, we're black cops,' Coffin Ed said.
'Don't insist,' she said, getting back some of her own. 'I can see it.'
Grave Digger chuckled. 'Your husband—' he prompted.
'My husband,' she repeated defiantly. 'He's Mister Sam's son, you know.'
'We know.'
'And Mister Sam's wife, Viola, and Mister Sam's attorney,

Van Raff, and Mister Sam's chauffeur, Johnson X, and Mister Sam's tramp – fiancée – Mildred—'

'What you got against her? You changed your race?' Coffin Ed interrupted.

'Leave her be,' Grave Digger cautioned.

But she wasn't daunted. 'Yes, but not to your race, to the human race.'

'That'll hold him.'

'Naw, it won't. I got no reverence for these white women going 'round joining the human race. It ain't that easy for us colored folks.'

'Later, man, later,' Grave Digger said. 'Let's stick to our business.'

'That is our business.'

'All right. But let's cook one pigeon at the time.'

'Why?'

'You're right,' Anny said. 'It's too easy for us.'

'That's all I said,' Coffin Ed said, and having made his point, withdrew into the shadow.

'And Doctor Mubuta,' Grave Digger said, taking up where she had left off.

'Yes, of course. I haven't got anything against Mildred,' she added, reverting to the question. 'But when a teen-aged girl like her takes up with a dirty old man like Mister Sam, just for what she can get out of him, she's tramp, that's all.'

'All right,' Grave Digger conceded.

'And Sugartit,' she said.

'She was the one sent to the hospital? What's her name?'

'I don't know her real name, just Sugartit.'

'She was the teen-aged colored girl – whycome she ain't a tramp?' Coffin Ed said.

'She just wasn't, that's all.'

'I have a daughter they used to call Sugartit,' he said.

'This girl's not your daughter,' Anny said, looking at him. 'This girl's sick.'

He didn't know whether she meant it as a jibe or a compliment.

'Is she a relative of Mister Sam's?' Grave Digger asked.

'I don't think so. I don't know why she was there.'

'Doctor Mubuta?'

'Maybe, I don't know. All I know about her is what people say, that she's "covered". It seems she's the girl friend of the Syndicate's district boss – if that's what he's called. Anyway the top man.'

'How'd you get to know her?'

'I didn't really know her. She'd wander into the flat sometimes – always when Dick was out. I think it might have been when the Syndicate boss was seeing Mister Sam downstairs.'

Grave Digger's head moved slowly up and down. An idea was knocking at his mind, trying to get in. He looked at Coffin Ed and saw he was disturbed by a nagging idea too. The Syndicate didn't have any business in a joke like this. If an old man with a cheating, scheming wife wanted to risk his life with a charlatan like Doctor Mubuta, that was his business. But the Syndicate wouldn't have a lookout staked unless there was more to it than that.

'And the last you saw of the Gladstone bag full of money was when Doctor Mubuta put it back underneath the bed?' he asked. Coffin Ed gave a slight nod.

'Oh, it was there all the time, when Viola rushed at Mildred and when she turned on Doctor Mubuta and it was there when he yelled for us to run—'

'Maybe the "Bird of Youth" took it,' Coffin Ed said.

'You know he was killed too – Doctor Mubuta?'

'Yes.'

'Who told you?' he shot the question at her.

'Why, you did,' she said. 'Don't you remember? When you brought me and Dick here? You asked him were we present when the doctor was killed.'

'I'd forgotten,' he confessed sheepishly.

'I hated for him to be killed more than anyone,' she said. 'I knew he was a fake—'

'How'd you know it?'

'He had to be—'

'Earlier you said—'

'I know what I said. But he touched me.'

Both of them looked at her with new interest.

'How so?' Grave Digger asked.

'When he was telling Mister Sam he'd discovered the solution for the Negro problem was for Negroes to outlive the white people.'

They looked at her curiously. 'You're a strange woman,' Grave Digger said.

'Because I was moved by the idea?' she asked surprisedly. 'I was just ashamed.'

'Well, he's found the final solution now,' Grave Digger said.

Next they interviewed Dick. He answered their questions with a lackadaisical indifference. He didn't seem affected by either the death of his father or his stepmother, and he couldn't care less about the others. Sure, he knew Doctor Mubuta was a con man, all the hepcats in Harlem had him made. Of course his father knew, he and Doctor Mubuta were in cahoots. They probably staged the act for Mister Sam to cache some money away. His father was senile but he wasn't a square, he knew his wife and Van Raff were teaming up on him. The way he figured it, it looked like Doctor Mubuta crossed the old man, he felt certain the Gladstone bag was filled with money. But he couldn't figure what went wrong at the end, there had to be another person.

'Who?' Grave Digger asked.

'How the hell do I know?' he answered.

He'd never had any part in Mister Sam's rackets. All he knew was his old man fronted for four numbers houses; he would appear at the houses when the tallies were made and the hits paid off. But other people ran the show. The numbers were like a Wall Street brokerage these days. There were girls with calculators and clerks operating adding machines and a supervisor at each house directing the business. The runners collected the plays from the writers and collected the hits from the house and paid them back to the writers who paid off the players and the staffs at the houses never saw the players. In fact they were like high-paid clerks; they bought big cars and houses on credit and lived it up. His father was just a figurehead and a fall guy in case someone had to take a rap, the Syndicate was the real boss. He didn't know whether his father got a salary or a commission, anyway, he did all right for himself considering his age, but the Syndicate took forty per cent of the gross.

'Good picking,' Grave Digger said drily.

'Multimillion-dollar business,' Dick agreed.

'Why didn't you take a cut?' Coffin Ed asked curiously.

'I'm a musician,' Dick said as though that were the answer.

He didn't know anything about Sugartit, he said. He saw her the first time at the seance, if that's what you want to call it. The only way he knew her name was hearing Anny call her Sugartit.

'Does you wife know much about the Harlem scene?' Grave Digger asked.

For the first time Dick gave a question thought.

'I don't really know,' he confessed. 'She's at home alone a lot. Most nights she catches the show at The Spot and we go home together. But I don't know what she does with her days. I'm generally asleep or out. Maybe Viola came to see her, I don't know who she saw; it was her time and she had to fill it.'

'Did you trust her up there with all the soul brothers?' Coffin Ed asked curiously. 'Smalls almost just around the corner and sharp cats cruising up the Avenue all day long in their Cadillacs and Buicks red-hot for a big Southern blonde.'

'Hell, if you got to worry about your white chick, you can't afford her,' Dick said.

'And you never saw Sugartit before last night?' Grave Digger persisted.

'If you so worried about this mother-raping chick, why don't you go and see her?' Dick asked peevishly.

Coffin Ed looked at his watch. 'Three-fourteen,' he announced.

'It's too late tonight,' Grave Digger said.

Dick looked from one detective to the other, perplexed. 'You guys working on this murder case?' he asked.

'Nope, that's homicide, baby,' Grave Digger said. 'Me and Ed are trying to find out who incited the riot.'

Dick's hysterical outburst of laughter seemed odd indeed from so cynical a man.

'Man, that's how you get dandruff,' he said.

Interlude

Good people, your food is digested by various juices in the stomach. There is a stomach juice for everything you eat. There is a juice for meat and a juice for potatoes. There is a juice for chitterlings and a juice for sweet potato pie. There is a juice for buttermilk and a juice for hopping John. But sometimes it happens these juices get mixed up and the wrong juice is applied to the wrong food. Now you might eat corn on the cob which has just been taken out of the pot and it's so hot you burn your tongue. Well, your mouth gets mixed up and sends the wrong signal to your stomach. And your stomach hauls off and lets go with the juice for cayenne pepper. Suddenly you got an upset stomach and the hot corn goes to your head. It causes a burning fever and your temperature rises. Your head gets so hot it causes the corn to begin popping. And the popped corn comes through your skull and gets mixed up with your hair. And that's how you get dandruff.

Dusty Fletcher at the Apollo Theater on
125th Street in Harlem

9

A man entered The Temple of Black Jesus. He was a short, fat, black man with a harelip. His face was running with sweat as though his skin was leaking. His short black hair grew so thick on his round inflated head it looked artificial, like drip-dry hair. His body looked blown up like that of a rubber man. The sky-blue silk suit he wore on this hot night glinted with a blue light. He looked inflammable. But he was cool.

Black people milling along the sidewalk stared at him with a mixture of awe and deference. He was the latest.

'Ham, baby,' someone whispered.

'Naw, dass Jesus baby,' was the harsh rejoinder.

The black man walked forward down a urine-stinking hallway beneath the feet of a gigantic black plaster of Paris image of Jesus Christ, hanging by his neck from the rotting white ceiling of a large square room. There was an expression of teeth-bared rage on Christ's black face. His arms were spread, his fists balled, his toes curled. Black blood dripped from red nail holes. The legend underneath read:

THEY LYNCHED ME.

Soul brothers believed it.

The Temple of Black Jesus was on 116th Street, west of Lenox Avenue. It and all the hot dirty slum streets running parallel into Spanish Harlem were teeming with hot dirty slum-dwellers, like cockroaches eating from a bowl of frijoles. Dirt rose from their shuffling feet. Fried hair melted in the hot dark air and ran like grease down sweating black necks. Half-naked people cursed, muttered, shouted, laughed, drank strong whiskey, ate greasy food, breathed rotten air, sweated, stank and celebrated.

This was *The Valley*. Gethsemane was a hill. It was cooler. These people celebrated hard. The heat scrambled their brains, came out their skulls, made dandruff. Normal life was so dark with fear and misery, a celebration went off like a skyrocket. *Nat Turner* day! Who knew who Nat Turner was? Some thought he was a jazz musician teaching the angels jazz; others thought he was a prizefighter teaching the devil to fight. Most agreed the best thing he ever did was die and give them a holiday.

A chickenshit pimp was pushing his two-dollar whore into a dilapidated convertible to drive her down to Central Park to work. Her black face was caked with white powder, her mascaraed eyes dull with stupidity, her thick lips shining like a red fire engine. Time to catch whitey as he slunk around the Lagoon looking to change his luck.

Eleven black nuns came out of a crumbling, dilapidated private house which had a sign in the window reading: FUNERALS PERFORMED. They were carrying a brass four-poster bed as though it were a coffin. The bed had a mattress. On the mattress was a nappy, unkempt head of an old man, sticking from beneath a dirty sheet. He lay so still he might have been dead. No one asked.

In the Silver Moon greasy-spoon restaurant a whiskey-happy joker yelled at the short-order cook behind the counter, 'Gimme a cup of coffee as strong as Muhammad Ali and a Mittenburger.'

'What kind of burger is that?' the cook asked, grinning.

'Baby, that's burger mit kraut.'

To one side of the entrance to the movie theater an old man had a portable barbecue pit made out of a perforated washtub attached to the chassis of a baby carriage. The grill was covered with sizzling pork ribs. The scent of scorching meat rose from the greasy smoke, filled the hot thick air, made mouths water. Half-naked black people crowded about, buying red-hot slabs on pale white bread, crunching the half-cooked bones.

Another old man, clad in his undershirt, had crawled onto the marquee of the movie, equipped with a fishing pole, line, sinker and hook and was fishing for ribs as though they were fish. When the barbecue man's head was turned he would hook a slab of barbecue and haul it up out of sight. Everyone except the barbecue man saw what was happening, but no one gave him away. They grinned at one another, but when the barbecue man looked their way, the grins disappeared.

The barbecue man felt something was wrong. He became suspicious. Then he noticed some of his ribs were missing. He reached underneath his pit and took out a long iron poker.

'What one of you mother-rapers stole my ribs?' he asked, looking mean and dangerous.

No one replied.

'If I catch a mother-raper stealing my ribs, I'll knock out his brains,' he threatened.

They were happy people. They liked a good joke. They believed in a Prophet named Ham. They welcomed the Black

Jesus to their neighborhood. The white Jesus hadn't done anything for them.

When Prophet Ham entered the chapel, he found it filled with black preachers as he'd expected. Faces gleamed with sweat in the sweltering heat like black painted masks. The air was thick with the odors of bad breath, body sweat and deodorants. But no one smoked.

Prophet Ham took the empty seat on the rostrum and looked at the sea of black faces. His own face assumed as benign an expression as the harelip would permit. An expectant hush fell over the assemblage. The speaker, a portly black man in a black suit, turned off his harangue like a tap and bowed toward Prophet Ham obsequiously.

'And now our Prophet has arrived,' he said with his eyes popping expressively. 'Our latterday Moses, who shall lead us out of the wilderness. I give you Prophet Ham.'

The assembled preachers allowed themselves a lapse of dignity and shouted and amened like paid shills at a revival meeting. Prophet Ham received this acclaim with a frown of displeasure. He stepped to the dais and glared at his audience. He looked indignant.

'Don't call me a Prophet,' he said. He had a sort of rumbling lisp and a tendency to slobber when angry. He was angry now. 'Do you know what a Prophet is? A Prophet is a misfit that has visions. All the Prophets in history were either epileptics, syphilitics, schizophrenics, sadists or just plain monsters. I just got this harelip. That doesn't make me eligible.'

His red eyes glowed, his silk suit glinted, his black face glistened, his split red gums bared from his big yellow teeth.

No one disputed him.

'Neither am I a latterday Moses,' he went on. 'First of all, Moses was white. I'm black. Second, Moses didn't lead his people out the wilderness until they revolted. First he led them into the wilderness to starve and eat roots. Moses was a square. Instead of leading his people out of Egypt he should have taken over Egypt, then their problems would have been solved.'

'But you're a race leader,' a preacher shouted from the audience.

'I ain't a race leader neither,' he denied. 'Does I look like I can race? That's the trouble with you so-called Negroes. You're always looking for a race leader. The only place to race whitey is on the cinder track. We beats him there all right, but that's all. And it ain't you and me who's racing, it's our children. And what are we doing to reward them for winning? Talking all this foolishness about Prophets and race leaders.'

'Well, if you ain't a Prophet and ain't a race leader, what is you?' the preacher said.

'I'm a soldier,' Prophet Ham said. 'I'm a plain and simple soldier in this fight for right. Just call me General Ham. I'm your commander. We got to fight, not race.'

Now they had got that point settled, his audience could relax. He wasn't a prophet, and he wasn't a race leader, but they were just as satisfied with him being a general.

'General Ham, baby,' a young preacher cried enthusiastically, expressing the sentiment of all. 'You command, we obey.'

'First we're gonna draft Jesus.' He held up his hand to forestall comment. 'I know what you're gonna say. You're gonna say other black men, more famous and with a bigger following than me, are employing the Jesus pitch. You're gonna say it's been the custom and habit of our folks for years past to call on Jesus for everything, food, health, justice, mercy, or what have you. But there're two differences. They been calling on the white Jesus. And mostly they been praying for mercy. You know that's the truth. You are all men of the cloth. All black preachers. All guilty of the same sin. Asking the white Jesus for mercy. For to solve your problem. For to take your part against the white man. And all he tell you is to turn the other cheek. You think he gonna tell you to slap back? He's white too. Whitey is his brother. In fact whitey made him. You think he gonna take your part against his own creator? What kind of thinking is that?'

The preachers laughed with embarrassment. But they heard him.

'We hear you, General Ham, baby ... You right, baby ...

We been praying to the wrong Jesus . . . Now we pray to the Black Jesus.'

'Just like you so-called Negroes,' General Ham lisped scornfully. 'Always praying. Believing in the philosophy of forgiveness and love. Trying to overcome by love. That's the white Jesus's philosophy. It won't work for you. It only work for whitey. It's whitey's con. Whitey invented it, just like he invented the white Jesus. We're gonna drop the praying altogether.'

A shocked silence followed this pronouncement. After all they were preachers. They'd been praying even before they started preaching. They didn't know what to say.

But the young preacher spoke out again. He was young enough to try anything. The old-fashioned praying hadn't done much good. 'You command us, General,' he said again. He wasn't afraid of change. 'We'll give up the praying. Then what'll we do?'

'We ain't gonna ask the Black Jesus for no mercy,' General Ham declared. 'We ain't gonna ask him for nothing. We just gonna take him and feed him to whitey in the place of the other food we been putting on whitey's table since the first of us arrived as slaves. We been feeding whitey all these years. You know that's the truth. He grown fat and prosperous on the food we been feeding him. Now we're gonna feed him the flesh of the Black Jesus. I don't have to tell you the flesh of Jesus is indigestible. They ain't even digested the flesh of the white Jesus in these two thousand years. And they been eating him every Sunday. Now the flesh of the Black Jesus is even more indigestible. Everybody knows that black meat is harder to digest than white meat. And that, brothers, *IS OUR SECRET WEAPON!*' he shouted with a spray of spit. 'That is how we're going to fight whitey and beat him at last. We're gonna keep feeding him the flesh of the Black Jesus until he perish of constipation if he don't choke to death first.'

The elderly black preachers were scandalized.

'You don't mean the sacrament?' one asked.

'Is we gonna manufacture wafers?' another asked.

'We'll do it, but how?' the young preacher asked sensibly.

'We're gonna march with the statue of the Black Jesus until whitey pukes,' General Ham said.

With the image of the lynched Jesus which hung in the entrance in their minds, the preachers saw what he meant.

'What you need for the march, General?' asked the young black preacher, who was practical.

General Ham appreciated this practicality. 'Marchers,' he replied. 'Nothing takes the place of marchers for a march,' he said, 'but money. So if we can't find the marchers we get some money and buy them. I'm gonna make you my second in command, young man. What is your name?'

'I'm Reverend Duke, General.'

'From now on you're a Colonel, Reverend Duke. I call you Colonel Duke. I want you to get these marchers lined up in front of this temple by ten o'clock.'

'That don't give us much time, General. Folks is celebrating.'

'Then make it a celebration, Colonel,' General Ham said. 'Get some banners reading "Jesus baby". Give us a little sweet wine. Sing "Jesus Savior". Get some of these gals from the streets. Tell 'em you want 'em for the dance. They ask what dance? You tell 'em *the* dance. Wherever gals go, mens follow. Remember that, Colonel. That's the first principle of the march. You dig me, Colonel?'

'We dig you, General,' said Colonel Duke.

'Then I see you-all at the march,' General Ham said and left.

Outside on 116th Street, a lavender Cadillac Coupe de Ville convertible, trimmed in yellow metal which the black people passing thought was gold, was parked at the curb. A buxom white woman with blue-dyed gray hair, green eyes and a broad flat nose, wearing a décolleté dress in orange chiffon, sat behind the wheel. Huge rose breasts popped from the orange dress as though expanded by the heat, and rested on the steering-wheel. When General Ham approached and opened the door on his side, she looked around and gave him a smile that lit up the night. Her two upper incisors were crowned with shining gold with a diamond between. 'Daddy,' she greeted. 'What took you so long?'

'I been cooking with Jesus,' he lisped, settling into the seat beside her.

She chuckled. It was a fat woman's chuckle. It sounded like hot fat bubbling. She pulled out in front of a bus and drove down the crowded street as though black people were invisible. They got the hell out of her way.

10

Sergeant Ryan came up from the cellar to take over the questioning. He brought along his photographer, Ted, who had finished taking pictures, to get him out of the way of the fingerprint crew who were still at work.

The rooms were small. Each was equipped with a built-in washbasin and clothes closet and a radiator, and furnished with a double bed and dressing-table of oak veneer. All the shades were drawn on the windows on the other side, and the rooms were hot and airless as though sealed. All were alike with the exception of the front room which had a second window on the street, from which the tenant could have stolen the hats from the heads of passersby to go along with all his suits and shirts. With the addition of four detectives they were crowded.

A couple by the name of Mr and Mrs Tola Onan Ramsey occupied the front room. Tola was a presser at a downtown cleaners and his wife, Bee, ironed shirts at the laundry next door. Tola said the suits and shirts were his own which he had bought and paid for with his own money, and he didn't need any hats. The local detectives kept quiet, but they wondered why the Ramseys paid the extra rent for the front room when any of the back rooms would have served them just as well. All they were doing was stealing from their bosses and the extra front window was an unnecessary expense. Bee called Coffin Ed aside to ask him if he wanted to buy some shirts cheap, while Tola was denying to Sergeant Ryan seeing anything, hearing anything or knowing anything. He and Bee had been in bed sound asleep, as hard as they had worked all day, and they hadn't even heard the neighbors in the hall or the people on the sidewalk who, as a rule, sounded as though they were passing through their room.

Sergeant Ryan soon gave up on them. They were too innocent for him. They were the most law-abiding, hard-working, know-nothing colored people he had ever seen. Neither Grave Digger nor Coffin Ed batted an eye.

The couple in the middle room called themselves Mr and Mrs Socrates X. Hoover. He was a tall, lanky black man with buck teeth and dusty-colored burred hair. His stringy muscles jerked like dying snakes beneath his sweating black skin and his small red eyes glowed with agitation under the scrutiny of the detectives. He sat on the edge of the bed clad only in the dirty jeans he'd slipped on hurriedly to open the door for the law, while his woman lay naked beneath the sheet, which she had drawn up to her mouth. She was a big yellow woman with red hair, straightened by a pressing-iron, sticking out from her head in all directions.

He said there was no need of them sniffing so mother-raping suspiciously, that smell came from the cubebs he smoked for his asthma. And she had been straightening her hair, she added, as they could oughta tell from the iron on the dresser. When Grave Digger continued to look skeptical, she flew salty and said if they smelled where she'd been making love with her own husband, that was only natural. What kind of minds did they have? Far as she knew, only white folks knew how to make love without its smelling.

Sergeant Ryan turned bright red.

Socrates said he made an honest living parking cars at the Yankee Stadium. Last winter? He hadn't been here last winter. Sergeant Ryan dropped it and asked what she did. She said she kept appointments. What kind of appointments? Do they have to be some special kind? Just appointments, that's all. Sergeant Ryan tried to catch the eye of one of the colored detectives, but they refused to be caught.

About what had gone on outside their room that night, or any other night, they knew less than their neighbors at the front. They always kept their shades drawn and their window closed to keep out the noise and the smells and they couldn't hear anything inside, not even their neighbors. Sergeant Ryan was silent for a moment while they all listened to the sound of a drawer being opened and the exchange of voices in the adjoining room, but he didn't pursue it. What about when one of them went to the toilet? he asked instead. Poon became so agitated she sat up in bed, exposing two big drooping breasts encircled by deep red marks where her brassière had cut her and tipped by tough brown teats like the stalks of pumpkins cut from the vine. Go to the crapper? What for? They weren't children, they didn't pee in bed. Grave Digger glanced at the washbasin with such obvious suggestion her face swelled with indignation and the sheet flew from the rest of her, revealing her big hairy nest. Suddenly the room was flooded with the strong alkaloid scent of continuous sexual intercourse. Sergeant Ryan threw up his hands.

When things had calmed down he listened to them deny any knowledge of the cellar at all. They might have noticed the door at the side, but neither remembered. If they were directly over the cellar and boiler room, they had never heard any sounds from down there. They weren't living there in the winter. They didn't know who had lived there before them. They never saw anybody going or coming from around the side. No, they had never seen any strange white men in the whole neighborhood. Nor strange white women either.

By the time the sergeant got to the tenants in the last room he was well browned off. These people called themselves Mr and Mrs Booker T. Washington. Booker said he was the manager of a recreation hall on upper Seventh Avenue. What kind of recreation? Recreation, where people play. Play what? Play pool. So you're a hustler around the pool hall? I'm the manager. What's the name of it? Acey-Deucey's? What's that? Onesy-twosy's. Oh, you said ace and deuce's. Nawsuh, I said Acey-Deucey's. All right, all right, and what's your wife's name? Madame Booker, she answered for herself. She was another big-titted yellow woman with straightened red hair. And he was lean, black and red-eyed like his neighbor.

The sergeant wondered what it was about these lean, hungry-looking red-eyed black men that these big yellow women liked so well. And what did Madame Booker do for her living? She didn't have to do nothing but look after her husband but she told fortunes ever now and then just to pass away the time 'cause her husband worked at nights. The sergeant looked at the television set on the deal table and the transistor radio on the end of the dressing-table next to the bed. But he let it go. Who were her customers – clients? People. What kind of people? Just people is all. Men? Women? Men and women. Did she have any white men among her clients? No, she never told white men's fortunes. Why, were the augurs bad in Harlem? She didn't know whether the augurs were bad or good, just none had ever asked her.

Further questioning elicited the facts that they had seen, heard, and knew even less than both their neighbors put together. They didn't have anything to do with the other people who lived in that house, not that they were hincty, but there were some bad people who lived there. Who? They didn't know exactly. Well, where, then? On this floor? The second floor? The third floor? They couldn't say exactly, sommers in the building. Well, how did they know they were bad if they didn't know them? They could tell by looking at them. Sergeant Ryan reminded them that they had just claimed they never saw anyone. What they meant was going sommers; 'course they saw people in the hall but they didn't know where they were going or where they had been. And they never saw any white men in the hall going somewhere or coming from somewhere? Never, only once a month the man came around for the rent. Well, what was his name? the sergeant asked quickly, thinking he was getting somewhere. They didn't know. Did they mean to tell him they paid a man the rent whom they didn't know? They meant they didn't know his name but they knew he was the man, all right; he was the same man who had been there ever since they had been there. And how long had they been there? They had been there going on for three years. Then they had been there during the winter? Two winters. Then they knew about the cellar? Knew what about the cellar? That there was one? Their eyes popped. 'Course there was a cellar, how else could the superintendent fire the boiler if there wasn't no cellar? It was a question, the sergeant admitted. And who was the superintendent? A West Indian named Lucas Covey. Is he colored? Colored? Whoever heard of a white West Indian? The sergeant admitted they had him there. And did this, er, Mr Covey live in the cellar? Live in the cellar! How could he? There wasn't no place for him to live there, 'less it was 'side the boiler. What about the empty room? Empty room! What empty room? Well, then when was the last time they had been in the cellar? They hadn't never been in the cellar, they just knew there had to be one to hold the boiler 'cause they had central heating, and it came from somewhere.

The sergeant took out his handkerchief to wipe the sweat from his face, but remembered he had used it to open the bloodstained door in the cellar and put it back into his pocket, wiping his forehead with his coat sleeve instead.

Well, then, where did Mr Covey live if he didn't live in the cellar? he asked desperately. He lived in his other house on 122nd Street. What was the number? They didn't know the number, but it was a brick house just like this one only it was twice as wide and it was the second house from the corner of Eighth Avenue. He couldn't miss it, the name was over the door. It was called *Cozy Flats.*

The sergeant figured he'd had enough of that. He saw no reason to take any of them in as yet. The next thing was to find Lucas Covey. But when they got out in the hall the photographer discovered his pocket camera was missing. So they started over with the Washingtons. But they hadn't seen his camera. Then they went back to the Hoovers.

'Bless my soul, I wondered where this Kodak came from,' Poon said. 'I was reaching for a cigarette and found it lying there on the floor.'

The red-faced photographer took his camera and put it back into his pocket and opened his mouth to state his mind, but Grave Digger cut him off.

'That could get you ninety days,' he told Socrates.

'For what? I ain't done nothing.'

'Oh, hell, skip it,' the sergeant said. 'Let's get out of here.'

They stopped on the street to wait for the fingerprint crew who were just coming up from the cellar, and he asked the colored detectives, 'Do you believe any of that horse manure?'

'Hell, it ain't a question of believing it. We found them all at home, in bed, asleep for all we know. How do we know they heard, saw or know anything? All we can do is take their word.'

'I mean that shit about their occupations.'

'If you're worried about that you may as well go home,' Coffin Ed said.

'Well, it's half-true, like everything else,' Grave Digger said pacifyingly. 'We know Booker T. Washington hangs around Acey-Deucey's poolroom where he earns a little scratch racking balls when he hasn't snatched a purse that paid. And we know that Socrates Hoover watches parked cars at night on the side streets around Yankee Stadium to keep them from being robbed of anything he can rob himself. And what else can two big yellow whores do but hustle? That's why those sports make themselves scarce at night. But Tola Ramsey and his wife do just what they say. It's easy enough to check. But all you got to do is look at all those suits and shirts which don't fit him.'

'Anyway, none of them work in white folks' kitchens,' Coffin Ed said gruffly.

Faces turned red all over the place.

'Why would anyone live here who was honest?' Grave Digger said. 'Or how could anyone stay honest who lived here? What do you want? This place was built for vice, for whores to hustle in and thieves to hide out in. And somebody got a building permit, because it's been built after the ghetto got here.' He paused for a moment. They were all silent. 'Anything else?' he asked.

The sergeant let the subject drop. He ordered the fingerprint crew to stick around and they followed his car in their car while Coffin Ed and Grave Digger brought up the rear. The three cars of detectives descended on 122nd Street like the rat exterminators, but not a soul was in sight, not even a rat. Coffin Ed checked with his watch. It was

3:37. He buzzed Lieutenant Anderson at the precinct station.

'It's me and Digger, boss. You find any fez-headed men?'

'Plenty of them. Seventeen to be precise. But none with extra pants. You still with Ryan?'

'Right behind him.'

'Find out anything?'

'Nothing that can't keep.'

'All right, stick with him.'

When he had rung off, Grave Digger said, 'What did he think we were going to do, go fishing?'

Coffin Ed grunted.

Take two crumbling, neglected, overcrowded brick buildings like the one they had just left, slam them together with a hallway down the middle like a foul-air sandwich, put two cement columns flanking a dirt-darkened glass-paneled door, and put the words, COZY FLATS, on the transom, and you have an incubator of depravity. There one could find all the vices of Harlem in microcosm: sex perversions, lesbians, pederasts, pot smokers, riders of the LSD, street hustlers and their cretinistic pimps sleeping in the same beds where they turned their tricks, daisy chains, sex circuses, and caterers to the society trade: wife-swappers, gang-fuckers, seekers of depravity – name it, they had it.

But all the detectives found were closed doors, bedroom and toilet odors, the nose pinching smell of marijuana, the grunting and groaning of skin poppers and homosexuals, the muted whine of old blues played low.

The graffiti on the walls of the ground-floor hall gave the illusion of primitive painting of pygmies affected with elephantiasis of the genitals. A sign over a small green door beneath the staircase read: SUPERINTENDENT.

Sniffing the smells suggested by the graffiti, the sergeant said cynically, 'Sin made easy.'

'You call this easy?' Grave Digger flared. 'You mean *hot!*'

Five minutes of hammering brought the superintendent up the stairs to open his door. He gave the appearance of having been asleep. He was clad in an old blue flannel robe with a frayed belt worn over wrinkled cotton pajamas with wide, violently clashing red and blue stripes. His short kinky hair was burred from contact with the pillow and his smooth black skin had a tracery of lines as though the witches had been riding him. He held a blued steel .45 Colt automatic in his right hand and it was pointed on the level of their stomachs. He raked them with furious red eyes.

'What you want?'

The sergeant hastened with his shield. 'We're the police.'

'So what! You woke me out of a dead sleep.'

'All right,' Grave Digger said roughly. 'You've made your point.'

Slowly the man returned the automatic to the pocket of his robe, still holding it.

'You're Mr Covey, the superintendent?' the sergeant verified.

'Yeah, that's me.'

'You always answer your door with a pistol?'

'You never know who's knocking at this time o' morning.'

'Back up, buster, and let us in,' Grave Digger said.

'You're the law,' the man acknowledged, turning to precede them down the flight of brick stairs.

Grave Digger's first impression was he looked too arrogant to be the super of a joint like this, unless he had all the tenants working for him, like a sort of black Fagin. In which case, his being black would account for his arrogance.

To the average eye he was a thin superior-acting black man with a long smooth narrow face and a cranium that was almost a perfect ellipsoid. His thick-lipped mouth was as wide as his face and when he talked his lips curled back from even white teeth. His eyes had a slight Mongolian slant, giving his face a bitsa look, a bit of African, a bit of Nordic, a bit of Oriental. He was proud and handsome but there was a bit of effeminacy in his carriage. He looked very sure of himself.

The only thing missing was the sleep in the corners of his eyes.

Flinging open the door of his bedroom, he said, '*Entrez.*'

The bedroom held a three-quarter bed that had been slept

in; a rolltop desk with a green blotter, telephone, and desk chair; night-table with ashtray; television set on its separate stand and overstuffed leather armchair facing it, dressing table with black and white dolls flanking the mirror. Beyond the boiler room was a room used for a kitchen-dining-room and a shower room off from it with a toilet.

'You're fixed up cozy enough,' Sergeant Ryan said. He had brought a fingerprint man and his photographer with him, and they grinned dutifully.

'That bother you?' Covey challenged.

The sergeant dropped all pleasantries, and began asking questions. Covey said he had been to the Apollo Theater and seen a gangster film called *Double or Nothing* and a stage show which had The Supremes and Martha and The Vandellas and television comedian Bill Cosby, along with the house orchestra. Afterwards he had stopped at the bar of Frank's Restaurant and had a bean and cornbeef sandwich and had walked home down Eighth Avenue.

'You can check that?' Ryan said to the precinct detectives.

'Not easily,' Grave Digger admitted. 'Everybody goes to the Apollo and Frank's bar is so crowded at that time of night only celebrities stand out.'

Covey hadn't seen anyone on entering the apartment and he lived alone so that once he was down in his hole he didn't see anyone until he came up the next day. If it wasn't for the garbage stinking if he didn't put it out, he could be down here dead for weeks and no one would notice. Didn't he have other duties besides putting out the garbage? In the winter he fired the boilers. Didn't he have any relatives? Sure, plenty, but they were all in Jamaica and he hadn't seen any of them since he had come to New York three years previous. Friends? Money was a man's only friend. Women? 'What a question,' Coffin Ed muttered, looking at the dolls. The sergeant reddened. Covey got on his dignity. There were women everywhere, he said. 'Damn right,' Grave Digger said. The sergeant dropped it. Who cleaned up, then? The tenants cleaned in front of their doors and the wind blew the dirt off the street. Well, all right, did he know about the cellar in the other house? Cellar?

Basement? What about the basement? About the furnished room? Naturally he knew about the furnished room, he was the superintendent, wasn't he? Well, then, who did he rent it to? Rent it to? He didn't rent it to nobody. Who lived in it, then? Didn't nobody live in it in the summer; the company built it for a helper to sleep in in the winter – someone to fire the boiler. What company was that? The owners, Acme Realty; they owned lots of buildings in Harlem. Was he the superintendent for them all? No, just these two. Did he know the officials of the company? No, just the building manager and the rent collector. Well, where were they located? They had an office on lower Broadway, in the Knickerbocker Building, just south of Canal Street. And what were the names of the men he knew? Well, Mr Shelton was the building manager and Lester Chambers was the rent collector. West Indians too? No, they were white. The sergeant dropped it. Well, to get back to the room in the other basement, could anyone live there without his knowing it? Not hardly, he was over there every morning to put out the garbage. But it was possible? Everything was possible, but it wasn't likely anybody would be living there with him not knowing; 'cause first they'd have to get in and the outside door had a Yale lock and he had the only two keys. He went across the room and took a large ring of keys from a hook on the wall beside the door and exhibited two brass Yale keys. And if they was to break in, he would see it first thing he got there to put out the garbage. But they could have had a key made? the sergeant persisted. Covey ran a hand over his burrs. What was he trying to get at? The sergeant asked his own question in reply. He had looked into the basement recently? Covey looked around impatiently; his gaze met Coffin Ed's; he looked away. What for? he countered. The place was only used in the winter; it was kept closed and locked in the summer to keep young punks from taking girls down there to rape them. He was a mighty distrustful man, the sergeant observed. Meeting people at the door with a pistol in his hand, thinking of teen-agers as rapists. The colored detectives joined Covey in a condescending smile. The sergeant noticed it, but passed it by. Did he, Covey, know what kind of people lived in these buildings he served? Naturally, he was the superintendent; all respectable, hard-working, honest, married people, like all Harlem tenants of Acme Realty. The sergeant's face was a picture of incredulity; he didn't know whether Covey was making fun of him or not. Coffin Ed and Grave Digger kept their faces absolutely blank. Well, someone had been living in the furnished room of that other basement, the sergeant announced abruptly. Impossible! Covey denied promptly. If anyone had been down there all the tenants on the ground floor would know about it for you could hear through that floor as good as you could hear through those walls. Then somebody was lying, the sergeant said, because not only had someone been living there but a man had been killed there only a few hours ago. Covey's eyes widened slowly until all the other features looked disarranged in his narrow face.

'You kidding, aren't you?' His voice was a shocked whisper.

'I'm not kidding,' the sergeant said. 'His throat was cut.'

'I was just by there yesdiddy morning.'

'You're going back this morning. Now! Put your clothes on. And give me that gun.'

Covey moved in a daze, handing over the pistol docilely as he might have passed a plate. He looked stunned. 'It ain't possible,' he kept muttering to himself.

But sight of the bloody furnished room changed that quickly to rage. 'Them mother-rapers upstairs know about it,' he raved. 'You couldn't cut a man down here without them hearing him scream.'

They took him upstairs and confronted him with each of the three couples. Other than the vilest language that he had ever heard, the sergeant learned nothing new. Covey couldn't shake the tenants' story that they hadn't heard anything, and they couldn't shake his that he hadn't known about the room.

'Let's make an experiment,' the sergeant said. 'Ted, you and this man – what's your name? Stan. You and Stan go down in the basement and yell, and the rest of us will stand in each of the rooms up here and see if we can hear you.'

Putting their ears to the floor they could hear faintly in the middle room, occupied by Socrates and Poon Hoover, but they doubted if they could hear lying in the bed, although they didn't try. But they couldn't hear in the front and back rooms, nor in the kitchen which they tried too. But they could hear quite clearly in the hall and strangely enough they could hear in the john.

'Well, that narrows it down to everybody who was awake in the whole of Harlem,' the sergeant said disgustedly. 'You people go back to bed.'

'What you want us to do with this one?' the white detectives who were flanking Covey asked.

'Hell, we'll take him on back and call it a day. None of these people can get anywhere, and maybe by tomorrow my brains won't be so fuzzy.'

When Covey had disappeared through the entrance of the Cozy Flats, Coffin Ed got out of the car beside Grave Digger, and called, 'Hey, wait a minute; I left my sound meter in your flat.' But Covey didn't hear him.

'Go and get it,' Grave Digger said. 'I'll wait for you.'

The white detectives looked at each other curiously. They hadn't seen Coffin Ed's sound meter either. But it wasn't anything to work up a sweat about; they all wanted to get home. But the sergeant wanted to have a word with the colored precinct detectives before he turned in so the fingerprint crew drove off and left him with his two disgruntled assistants, the photographer, Ted, and his driver, Joe.

Coffin Ed had been slightly surprised to find Covey's hall door unlocked, but he didn't hesitate. He went down silently and opened the door of Covey's bed-sitting-room without knocking and went inside.

Covey was leaning back in his desk chair with a wide, taunting grin. 'I knew you'd follow me, you old fox. You thought you'd catch me telephoning. But I don't know nothing 'bout this business. I'm as clean as a minister's dick.'

'That's too mother-raping bad,' Coffin Ed said, his burn-scarred face twitching like a French version of *the jerk*, as he moved in with his long nickel-plated, head-whipping pistol swinging in his hand. 'Your ass pays for it.'

Grave Digger didn't want to talk to the sergeant at that

moment, so he radio-phoned Lieutenant Anderson at the precinct station.

'It's me, Digger.'

'What's new?'

'Count me ninety seconds.'

Without another word, Anderson began, 'One, two, three ...' Not too fast, not too slow. At '... ninety ...', Grave Digger slid across the seat and got out on the sidewalk and went towards the entrance of the Cozy Flats, loosening his pistol as he went.

'Hey ...' the sergeant called, but he made as though he didn't hear him and went through the entrance and down the front hall.

When he entered Covey's bedroom, he found him lying sideways across the bed, a red bruise aslant his forehead, his left eye shut and bleeding, his upper lip swollen to the size of a bicycle tire, and Coffin Ed atop him with a knee in his solar plexus, choking him to death.

He clutched Coffin Ed by the back of the collar and pulled him back. 'Leave him able to talk.'

Coffin Ed looked down at the swollen bloody face beneath him. 'You want to talk, don't you, mother?'

'Rented to a business man – salesman – nice man—' Covey gasped. 'Nice – wanted place to rest – afternoons – John Babson – nice man ...'

'White man?'

'Seal brown. Brown-colored man ...'

'What's his pet name?'

'Pet name – pet name—'

'His loving name, mother-raper?'

'I – tole you – all ... I know ...'

Coffin Ed drew back his right fist as though he would hit him and his left hand flew to his mouth. Hitting at him from beyond, from where he was standing at the head of the bed, with the long heavy barrel of his pistol, Grave Digger struck with such force he knocked the back of his hand into his mouth so hard that when he pulled it away screaming, three of the front teeth that Coffin Ed had loosened previously, were embedded in the carpal bones of his hand. '*Jesus Baby!*' he gasped.

The sergeant burst through the door, followed by his wide-eyed assistants. 'What the hell!' he exclaimed.

'Fascists!' Covey screamed when he saw the white men. 'Racists! Black brutes!'

'Take this mother-raper before we kill him,' Grave Digger said.

11

Captain Brice was waiting for them when they came up from questioning Dick. He sat in his own chair, leaning back with his polished black oxfords atop the desk. With his thick torso encased in a dark blue Brooks Brothers mohair suit, along with his carefully parted hair and knotted blue silk tie, he looked for all the world like a midtown banker just returned from the annual stag party. Anderson sat submissively in the visitor's chair across the desk from him.

'How was the champagne, sir?' Grave Digger needled.

'Not bad, not bad,' Captain Brice replied, not to be outdone. But everyone knew he hadn't come to the district at three o'clock in the morning just to pass the time of day.

'Lieutenant Anderson tells me you've been interrogating the two star witnesses in that family slaughter on Sugar Hill,' he went on, taking a serious tone.

'Yes, sir, it was a rejuvenation pitch, but you probably know more about it than we do,' Grave Digger said.

'Well, there's nothing new about it. Did you find out where the pitch originated?'

'Yes, sir, it originated with Christ,' Grave Digger said with a straight face. 'But there are a couple of things about this particular shinding up there that need answering.'

'Let homicide answer them,' Captain Brice said. 'You're precinct men.'

'Maybe they ought to state it,' Anderson interjected.

'There's been too much of that now, interfering in homicide's business,' Captain Brice said. 'It's given our precinct a bad rep.'

'I booked them as material witnesses and we're holding them here until the magistrate's court sets bail,' Anderson said, standing up for his men. 'I had them question the witnesses.'

Captain Brice decided he didn't want a run-in with his lieutenant. 'All right,' he conceded, turning back to Grave Digger. 'What needs answering that homicide doesn't know?'

'We don't know what homicide know,' Grave Digger admitted. 'But we'd like to know what's become of the money.'

Captain Brice took his feet from the desk and sat up. 'What money?'

Grave Digger reported what his witnesses had said about a Gladstone bag filled with money.

Captain Brice leaned forward and stared dogmatically, 'You can forget about the money. Sam didn't have any money unless he stole it, and if that's the case it'll come out.'

'Did either of the witnesses actually see the money?' Anderson persisted.

'No, but both of them believed for other reasons – which I will tell you if you want to hear them—' Anderson shook his head – 'that the bag was filled with money,' Grave Digger continued.

'You can forget the money,' Captain Brice repeated. 'Do you think I could have been Captain for this precinct as long as I have and not know who owns what in my bailiwick?'

'Then what's happened to the Gladstone bag?'

'If there was one. You only have the word of two witnesses and they were involved – one his son and the other his daughter-in-law; and now they're the heirs of his estate if it is found that he had any estate.'

'If there was a Gladstone bag, it'll turn up,' Anderson said.

Captain Brice took a fat cigar from a leather case in his inside pocket. No one offered him a light. They watched him bite off the end and roll the cigar between his lips. They let him search through his pockets until he found a book of paper matches and they watched him light the end of his cigar. Anderson took out his pipe and filled it with the same deliberation but Coffin Ed stepped forward and held a lighted match for him. Captain Brice reddened, but otherwise acted as though he hadn't noticed. Grave Digger gave his partner a reproachful look. Anderson hid behind a cloud of smoke.

'What's the other question?' Captain Brice asked coldly.

'Who killed Doctor Mubuta?'

'Goddammit, the chauffeur killed him. Don't try to make a mystery out of this nigger mess.'

'Johnson X couldn't have killed him,' Coffin Ed contradicted, more from the pleasure of contradicting the Captain than from any reasoned conclusion.

'Homicide is satisfied with him,' Captain Brice stated, trying to avoid an argument with the two colored detectives.

'They'd be satisfied hanging the rap on anybody called X,' Coffin Ed went on.

'Anyway, it's too early to tell,' Grave Digger entered a conciliatory tone. 'I suppose homicide is having the fluid analysed?'

'That's obvious,' Anderson said. 'I smelt it myself. It's cyanide.'

'Not even colored folk's poison,' Coffin Ed muttered.

'It served its purpose,' Captain Brice said harshly. 'Sam was a pain in the ass.'

'Fronting for the Syndicate? Why'd you let him? It's your bailiwick, as you just said,' Grave Digger questioned.

'He had a licensed loan and mortgage business. He had a legal right to operate as many so-called offices as he wished. There was nothing I could do.'

'Well, Doctor Mubuta has solved that; now you only got the Syndicate to deal with,' Grave Digger observed.

Captain Brice banged his fist so hard on his desk top the cigar flew from his fingers and landed on the floor at Coffin Ed's feet. 'Goddamn the Syndicate! I'll have the numbers out of Harlem before a week's gone by.'

Grave Digger looked skeptical.

Coffin Ed picked up the Captain's cigar and returned it to

him with such elaborate politeness he seemed to be poking fun. The Captain threw his cigar into the spittoon without looking at it. Anderson peered around his smoke screen to see if the land was safe.

'What you want us to do at night?' Grave Digger asked pointedly, reminding him that the numbers for the most part were a daytime racket.

'I want you two men to keep on this riot bit that the lieutenant assigned you to,' he said. 'You're my two best men and I want you to clean up this precinct. I feel like the lieutenant that these brush-fire riots are being instigated and I want you to nab the instigator.'

'Cleanup campaign, eh?' Coffin Ed sneered.

'It's about time, isn't it?' Anderson said.

Captain Brice looked meditatively at Coffin Ed. 'You don't like it?' he challenged.

'It's a job,' Coffin Ed said enigmatically.

'Why don't you let us talk to the other witnesses, Captain?' Grave Digger intervened.

'The D.A.'s got a homicide bureau for his own use in collecting evidence on homicides,' Captain Brice pointed out patiently. 'They're attorneys and detectives and laboratory technicians – the whole shooting lot. What do you think you two precinct detectives can uncover that they can't?'

'That very reason. It's our precinct. We might learn something that wouldn't mean a damn thing to them.'

'For instance, who's the instigator of these chickenshit riots.'

'Maybe,' Grave Digger said.

'Well, I'm not going to have it. I know you two guys. You go off cracking heads and shooting people on just a theory, and when it turns out wrong, which is just as liable as not, the commissioner cracks down and the press gets on my ass. It might not bother you two tough customers, maybe you can take it, but it's a black eye for me. I come up for retirement next year and I don't want to leave here with a cloud over my head and a couple of trigger-happy dicks subject to shoot anybody anytime. I want to leave a clean precinct when I leave and a disciplined staff willing to take orders and not try to run the goddamn precinct themselves.'

'You mean you want us to lay off before we discover something you don't want discovered?' Grave Digger challenged.

'He means he wants you fellows to lay off status quo before you get all of us into trouble, and yourselves too,' Anderson said.

Grave Digger gave him a you-too look.

Captain Brice said, 'I mean for you to work on the assignment the lieutenant gave you, and let people better prepared for it handle the homicides. Your assignment is a damn tougher assignment, if you just have to satisfy your yen for being tough, and before you're finished with it you won't feel so darned inclined to make trouble.'

'All right, Captain,' Grave Digger said. 'Don't complain if we come up with the wrong answer.'

'I don't want the wrong answer.'

'The right answer might be the wrong answer.'

Captain Brice glared at Anderson. 'And I'm holding you responsible, Lieutenant.' Then he turned and looked from one detective to the other. 'And if you were white men I'd suspend you for insubordination.'

He couldn't have said anything which would have infuriated the black detectives more. They understood at last he meant to muzzle them for the duration. It looked like a two-way play. Anderson, their friend, had given them this impossible assignment; all the Captain had to do was follow it up. Anderson was in line when the Captain bowed out, no doubt with his pockets full of loot. There never was a precinct captain who died broke. And it was to his interests as much as to the Captain's that they didn't rock the boat.

'You don't have no objections to us going and eat?' Grave Digger asked sarcastically. 'Plain licensed food?'

The Captain didn't answer.

Anderson glanced at the electric clock on the wall back of the Captain's desk and said, 'Check out while you're at it.'

They went upstairs to the detectives' room and signed out and went out the back exit past the cop on guard and down the stairs into the brick-walled court where the garage was located. Anderson was waiting for them. The courtyard was brightly lit since Deke O'Malley had escaped that way and Anderson looked frail and strangely vulnerable in the vertical glare.

'I'm sorry,' he said. 'I saw it coming.'

'You sent it,' Coffin Ed accused flatly.

'I know what you're thinking, but it won't be for long. Have a little patience. The Captain doesn't want to leave here with the precinct in a turmoil. You can't blame him.'

The two black detectives looked at one another. Their short-cropped hair was salted with gray and they were thicker around their middles. Their faces bore the lumps and scars they had collected in the enforcement of law in Harlem. Now after twelve years as first-grade precinct detectives they hadn't been promoted. Their raises in salaries hadn't kept up with the rise of the cost of living. They hadn't finished paying for their houses. Their private cars had been bought on credit. And yet they hadn't taken a dime in bribes. Their entire careers as cops had been one long period of turmoil. When they weren't taking lumps from the thugs, they were taking lumps from the commissioners. Now they were curtailed in their own duties. And they didn't expect it to change.

'We don't blame the Captain,' Grave Digger said.

'We're just envious.'

'I'll be taking over soon,' Anderson sought to console them.

'Damn right,' Coffin Ed said, rejecting the sympathy.

Anderson reddened and turned away. 'Eat happy,' he called over his shoulder, but didn't get a reply.

12

They stood on tiptoe, strained their eyes.

'Let me look.'

'Well, look then.'

'What you see?'

That was the question. No one saw anything. Then, simultaneously, three distinct groups of marchers came into view.

One came up 125th Street from the east, on the north side of the street, marching west towards the Block. It was led by a vehicle the likes of which many had never seen, and as muddy as though it had come out of East River. A bare-legged black youth hugged the steering-wheel. They could see plainly that he was bare-legged for the vehicle didn't have any door. He, in turn, was being hugged by a bare-legged white youth sitting at his side. It was a brotherly hug, but coming from a white youth it looked suggestive. Whereas the black had looked plain bare-legged, the bare-legged white youth looked stark naked. Such is the way those two colors affect the eyes of the citizens of Harlem. In the South it's just the opposite.

Behind these brotherly youths sat a very handsome young man of sepia color with the strained expression of a man moving his bowels. With him sat a middle-aged white woman in a teen-age dress who looked similarly engaged, with the exception that she had constipation. They held a large banner upright between them which read:

BROTHERHOOD! Brotherly Love Is The Greatest!

Following in the wake of the vehicle were twelve rows of bare-limbed marchers, four in each row, two white and two black, in orderly procession, each row with its own banner identical to the one in the vehicle. Somehow the black youths looked unbelievably black and the white youths unnecessarily white.

These were followed by a laughing, dancing, hugging, kissing horde of blacks and whites of all ages and sexes, most of whom had been strangers to each other a half-hour previous. They looked like a segregationist nightmare. Strangely enough, the black citizens of Harlem were scandalized.

'It's an orgy!' someone cried.

Not to be outdone, another joker shouted, 'Mama don't 'low that stuff in here.'

A dignified colored lady sniffed. 'White trash.'

Her equally dignified mate suppressed a grin. 'What else, with all them black dustpans?'

But no one showed any animosity. Nor was anyone surprised. It was a holiday. Everyone was ready for anything.

But when attention was diverted to the marchers from the south, many eyes seemed to pop out in black faces. The marchers from the south were coming north on the east side of Seventh Avenue, passing in front of the Scheherazade bar restaurant and the interdenominational church with the coming text posted on the notice-board outside:

SINNERS ARE SUCKERS! DON'T BE A SQUARE!

What caused the eyes of these dazed citizens to goggle was the sight of the apparition out front. Propped erect on the front bumper of a gold-trimmed lavender-colored Cadillac convertible driven by a fat black man with a harelip, dressed in a metallic-blue suit, was the statue of the Black Jesus, dripping black blood from its outstretched hands, a white rope dangling from its broken neck, its teeth bared in a look of such rage and horror as to curdle even blood mixed with as much alcohol as was theirs. Its crossed black feet were nailed to a banner which read: THEY LYNCHED ME! While two men standing in the back of the convertible held aloft another banner reading: BE NOT AFRAID!

In its wake was a long disorganized procession of a startling number of thinly-clad black girls of all shapes and sizes, clinging to the ebony arms of more tee-shirted young men than had ever been seen outside the army. Teeth shone in black faces, eyes flashed whitely. Some carried banners which read: BLACK JESUS BABY. Others read: CHOKE THEM BABY. They were singing: 'Be not afraid . . . of the dead . . . keep your head, baby, keep your head.' They seemed inordinately happy to be following in the wake of such a hideous Jesus. But bringing up the rear was a shuffling mass of solemn preachers with their own banner reading:

FEED THEM JESUS! *They'll vomit every time!*

A devout Christian drunk coming out of the Scheherazade looked up and saw the black apparition being propelled by what looked to him like a burning chariot being driven by the devil in a fireproof suit, and gave a violent start. 'I dreamed it,' he cried. 'That they'd do it again.'

But most of the holiday-makers were startled into silence. Caught between a spasm of nausea by the sight of the apparition of the Black Jesus and the contagious happiness of the sea of black youths, their faces twisted in grotesque grimaces for all the world like good Harlem citizens trying out a new French dance.

They were saved from proceeding any further with this new kick by the sound of thunder coming from that section of Seventh Avenue north of the intersection. The marchers from the north were led by two big rugged black men clad in belted leather coats, looking for all the world like Nazi SS troopers in blackface. Behind them marched the two silent clerics who had been seen cooking in Doctor Moore's unfurnished apartment. Behind them came the sweating tallow man who had last been seen atop a barrel at the intersection of 135th Street and Seventh Avenue, raving hysterically about Black Power. Following at a safe distance, two powerful-looking men bared to the waist were pushing a contraption on two wheels greatly resembling the boiler of a locomotive, which rumbled and boomed with the sound of thunder while light flashed from within, lighting up the white crescents of the black men's eyes, the ivory shields of their teeth, and the gleaming black muscles of their naked torsos, like kaleidoscopes of hell. A large white banner, held aloft by two men on their flanks, was also hit by the flashing light, and trembled in the sound of thunder, reading:

BLACK THUNDER! BLACK POWER!

In their wake followed a packed mass of men and women, dressed in black, who, upon closer inspection, looked of extraordinary size. Their banners read simply: BLACK POWER. In the dim light they looked serious. Their faces looked grave. If Black Power came from physical strength, they looked as though they had it.

The weedheads in front of the pool hall north of 126th Street were the first to comment.

'Baby, them cats is full of pot,' one said. 'Make me high just to look at 'em.'

'Baby, you is already high.'

'Higher. But they so quiet. How come that?'

'How I know? Ask 'em.'

'Hey, babies!' yelled the first weedhead. 'Say something.'

'You babies got any left?' yelled the second weedhead.

'Ignore those fools,' the tallow man said.

'Come on, babies. Talk some Black Power language,' the first weedhead cajoled.

A husky parader stepped out to reply. 'I tells y'alls something, disgraceful dopefiends. I whip y'all's ass.'

'Black Power!' a woman laughed.

'Thass right. I show 'em. I power their behinds.'

'Be calm!' the tallow man admonished. 'It's whitey what's the enemy.'

'Stingy mothers!' the weedhead yelled. 'Keep your old pot. It gonna cause your furnace to explode.'

The people within earshot laughed, they were good-humored. It was all just a big joke. Three different kinds of protest parades.

'Like my Aunt Loo saying three bands play march music at my Uncle Boo's funeral,' a soul sister said laughingly.

It was all really funny, in a grotesque way. The lynched Black Jesus who looked like a runaway slave. The slick-looking young man with his foreign white woman, riding in a car built for war service, preaching brotherhood. And last, but not least, these big Black Power people, looking strong and dangerous as religious fanatics, making black thunder and preaching Black Power.

Best show they'd had in a month of Sundays. 'Course the serious people frowned on these monkeyshines, but most citizens, out celebrating the day, were just amused.

Two big black men who looked as though they should have been with the Black Power marchers, instead sat watching them in the front seat of a small battered sedan parked at the curb in front of the African Memorial Bookstore. The small dirty black car looked out of place among all the shiny bright-colored cars out that night. And any two people doing nothing but sit on the sidelines and look, when there was so much to do that night, looked downright suspicious. What was more they wore dark suits and black slouch hats pulled so low they could barely be seen in the dim light filtering through the windshield, much less recognized unless one knew them. To the average incurious citizen they looked like two thugs waiting to stick up the jewelry store.

A slight dignified man standing beside them on the sidewalk volunteered, 'These ain't all; there are two more.'

'More what?' Coffin Ed asked.

'Parades.'

Coffin Ed got out onto the sidewalk, and stood beside the little man, dwarfing him. Grave Digger got out from behind the wheel on the street side. They could see the parade coming up Seventh Avenue.

'Hell, that's a float,' Grave Digger said.

At that moment Coffin Ed saw the old command car pass the corner of the jewelry store. 'That ain't no float.'

Grave Digger saw it and chuckled. 'That's the general and his lady.'

Coffin Ed spoke to the little man beside him. 'What's this carnival all about, Lomax?'

'It ain't no carnival.'

'Well, what the hell is it then?' Grave Digger asked loudly from across the car. 'It's your neighborhood. You're in with everything.'

'I don't know these groups,' Lomax said. 'They ain't from around here. But they look serious to me.'

'Serious? These clowns? You see more than I see.'

'It ain't what I see. It's what I feel. I can feel they're serious. They ain't playing.'

Coffin Ed grunted. Wordlessly Grave Digger clambered up the left fender and stood on the hood in order to see the parades more distinctly. He looked from the image of the lynched Black Jesus tied to the front of the Cadillac convertible to the face of the young man in the back of the old command car. He saw the first lines of the black and white marchers under the banner of Brotherhood. He saw the harelipped driver of the Cadillac and the laughing faces of the young black couples following beneath their banners of BLACK JESUS BABY. He looked at the leather-coated troopers across the street leading the Black Power procession. He heard Lomax exclaim excitedly, 'They're gonna run head-on into each other.'

Coffin Ed was climbing up the front fender on the other side. Fearing that the hood wouldn't hold them both, Grave Digger climbed on top of the body.

'What the hell's got into these people all of a sudden?' he heard Coffin Ed asking.

'It ain't been sudden,' Lomax said. 'They been feeling a long time. Like all the rest of us. Now they making their statement.'

'Statement? Statement saying what?'

'Each of them got a different statement.'

Grave Digger heard one of the leather-coated troopers shout, 'Let's beat the shit out them sissies,' and called down to Coffin Ed: 'What they say is there's going to be some trouble if they start any shit. You better call the Lieutenant.'

Ordinarily he would have shot into the air and waved his big pistol at the Black Power troopers, but they had strict orders not to draw their pistols in any circumstances except in the prevention of violent crime, the same as had been given to all the white cops.

Coffin Ed jumped down and climbed back inside. He couldn't get through to the precinct right away. In the meantime the two leather-coated troopers, followed by a group of hefty black men, had jumped over the concrete barrier around the park down the center of Seventh Avenue, and were racing toward the line of black and white youths approaching down 125th Street. Grave Digger jumped to the ground and ran to head them off, throwing up his hands and yelling, 'Get back! Straighten up!'

From the sidelines some comedian trumpeted, 'Fly right!'

At the moment Coffin Ed got through to the Harlem precinct. 'Lieutenant? It's me, Ed!'

Simultaneously the police cars began to move. Engines revved, sirens screamed. Seeing the police cars in action the people on the sidewalks began to scream and move into the street.

The metallic voice of Lieutenant Anderson rose into a scream. 'I can't hear you. What's happening?'

'Call off the cops! The people are panicking!'

'What's that? I can't hear you. What's going on?'

Coffin Ed heard pandemonium breaking loose all around him, topped by the screaming of the police sirens.

'Call off the dogs!' he shouted.

'What's that? Everybody's calling . . .'

'Call off the cops . . .'

'What's that? What's all that noise? . . .'

'The white cops—'

'Work with the cops . . . keep calm . . .'

'. . . use our pistols . . . emergency . . .'

'. . . right . . . no pistols . . . keep order . . .'

'ARE YOU DEAF?'

'. . . COMMISSIONER . . . INSPECTOR . . . BE THERE . . .'

'Hell's bells!' Coffin Ed muttered to himself, switched off the radio and leaped into the street. Down in the middle of the intersection he saw men rolling in the street like a free-for-all scramble. Two of them wore leather coats. One looked like Grave Digger. He broke in their direction.

Men from the Black Power parade were fistfighting in knots with the bare-limbed white and black youths from the Brotherhood. Several of them had surrounded the command car and dragged the two youths from the front seat. Others were trying to drag the white woman and colored man from the back seat. The young man was standing up kicking at their heads. The woman was lashing about with a wooden pole.

'Leave them biddies be,' a fat woman was screaming.

'Whip they asses.'

The white and black youths were fighting back side by side. Their opponents had the weight but they had the skill. The Black Power brothers were bulling ahead, but reaping black eyes and bloody noses on the way.

The mob of celebrants had overflowed into the street and stopped all the traffic. The police cars were stuck in a sea of sweating humanity. These people weren't taking sides in the main fight, they just wanted to chase the white cops. The cops were reluctant to leave their cars without the use of pistols.

Assisted by a group of laughing black girls, the harelipped man was endeavoring to drag the statue of the Black Jesus in the path of the police cars. But the cars couldn't move anyway and Jesus was slowly being dismembered in the crush of bodies. Shortly the crush had become so great, the police couldn't open the doors of their cars if they had wanted to. One rolled down his window and stuck his head out and was immediately swatted in the face by a woman's pocketbook.

The only fighting which showed any purpose was between the Black Power and the members of the Brotherhood. And when the Black Power fighters penetrated the defenses of the Brotherhood and came upon the interracial mob of followers, the result was a rout. They looked for sissies and prostitutes to beat. And they beat them with such abandon it looked indecent.

But the serious fighting was being done by Grave Digger and Coffin Ed against the leather-coated troopers, the silent clerics, and a number of other Black Power sluggers. The detectives had been down at first, but had taken advantage of their opponents, kicking to get their feet tangled up. They had got to their own feet, their clothes torn, noses bleeding, knots springing out from their heads and faces, and had begun fistfighting their opponents, back to back. Their long holstered pistols were exposed, but they had orders not to draw them. They couldn't have drawn them anyway, in the rain of fists showering over them. But they had one advantage. Every time a brother hit one of the pistols, his fist broke. They were hammering all right. But no one was falling down.

'One . . .' Grave Digger panted.

After an interval Coffin Ed echoed, 'Two . . .'

Instead of saying 'three', they covered their heads with their hands and broke for the sidewalk, ploughing through a hail of fists. But once through, having gained the sidewalk in front of the jewelry store, no one tried to follow. Their opponents seemed satisfied with them out of the way, and turned their attention to the youths of the Brotherhood trying to protect the command car.

Lomax still stood beside their parked car. While watching the fight with interest he had been joined by a group of Black Muslims from the bookstore. They watched the detectives approach their car, noticing every detail of their appearance: swelling eyes, knotty heads, bruised faces, bloody noses, torn clothes, hard breathing and holstered pistols. Their eyes were fixed, their faces grave.

'Why the hell didn't you shoot?' Lomax said as they came abreast.

'You can't shoot people petitioning,' Grave Digger said harshly, fishing a handkerchief from his pocket.

'Praise Allah,' a Black Muslim said.

'Petitioning my ass,' Lomax said. 'All of them people are phoney.'

'Funny,' a Black Muslim said.

'That's a point of view,' Grave Digger argued.

'Come on, let's beat it,' Coffin Ed said. 'Time's wasting.'

But Lomax wanted to argue. 'What point of view?'

'They want justice like everybody else,' Grave Digger contended.

Lomax laughed derisively. 'Long as you been in Harlem, you believe that shit. Do those clowns look like they're looking for justice?'

'For Christsake, Digger! You argue with this stooge,' he shouted furiously, getting into his seat and slamming the door. 'All he's trying to do is hold us.'

Grave Digger hurried about the car and climbed beneath the wheel. 'He's the people,' he said defensively.

'Screw the people!' Coffin Ed said, adding: 'And justice ain't the point. It's order now.'

Before the car took off, Lomax called with sly malice, 'Anyway, they beat the shit out of you.'

'Don't let it fool you,' Coffin Ed grated.

'We'll come up behind them,' Grave Digger said, referring to the fighting groups.

The only traffic lane open was the one to the north. He had decided to drive north to 130th Street, which he thought would be open, then east to Park Avenue, and follow the railroad trestle back to 125th Street and approach Seventh Avenue from that direction.

But as he pulled away from the curb he caught sight in his rearview mirror of the command car being driven by the leader of the Brotherhood group running wild into the remnants of the Black Power group. It had pushed ahead with the engine racing north on the left side of Seventh Avenue, scattering the Black Power marchers, and had jumped the curb and ploughed through the midst of the spectators in front of the cigar store and was headed toward the plate-glass front of the pool hall and the fleeing weedheads. The white woman in the rear seat was clinging on for dear life.

But he and Coffin Ed had no way of going to their rescue. So he raced north and turned east into 130th Street on crying tires, hoping they'd get back in time. In the middle of the block between Seventh and Lenox Avenues they passed a panel delivery truck going in the same direction. They looked at it from force of habit and read the advertisement on the side: LUNATIC LYNDON ... I DELIVER AND INSTALL TELEVISION SETS ANY TIME OF DAY OR NIGHT AND PLACE Telephone Murray Hill 2 ... Coffin Ed turned around to look at the license number, but he couldn't make it out in the dim street light. All he could see was that it was a Manhattan number.

'My people,' he said. 'Buying a television set in the middle of the night.'

'Maybe the man's taking one back,' Grave Digger said.

'The same thing.'

'Hell, Lunatic ain't no fool. People got to work in the daytime to pay for them.'

'I wasn't thinking about that. I was thinking night's the time for business in Harlem.'

'Why not? They black, ain't they? White people do their dirt in the day. That's when they're most invisible.'

Coffin Ed grunted.

The looting broke out on 125th Street at just the moment they were turning into Park Avenue beside the railroad trestle. The runaway command car had precipitated such confusion the white cops had struggled from their cars and begun shooting in the air. A number of adventuresome young men took advantage of the distraction and began breaking the store windows in the block and snatching the first thing they could. Seeing them running with their arms filled with loot, the spectators stampeded in wild-eyed panic to get away from them.

13

'That's it. A mother-raping white man gets himself killed up here trying to get his kicks and here we are, two cops of the inferior race, stuck with trying to find out who killed him,' Grave Digger held forth as he drove to the precinct that night in his private car.

'Too bad there ain't a mother-raping law against these freaks.'

'Now, now, Ed, be tolerant. People call us freaks.'

The grafted skin on Coffin Ed's face began to twitch. 'Yeah, but not sex freaks.'

'Hell, Ed, it ain't our business to worry about social morals,' Grave Digger said placatingly, easing up on his friend. He knew folks called him a black Frankenstein, and he felt guilty because of it. If he hadn't been trying so hard to play tough the hoodlum would have never had a chance to throw the acid into Coffin Ed's face. 'Leave 'em get dead.'

The night before they had gone straight home from the Cozy Flats and hadn't seen each other since. They didn't know what had happened to Lucas Covey, the building superintendent, whom they had beaten half to death.

'Anyway, the Acme folks probably got him out by now,' Coffin Ed said in answer to their thoughts.

'Just as well, he'd done all his talking.'

'John Babson! Hell, you think that's a name? I thought Covey was just blabbing.'

'Maybe. Who knows?'

It was ten minutes to eight p.m. when they stopped in the detectives' locker room to change into their old black working coats. They found Lieutenant Anderson sitting at the Captain's desk, looking extremely worried as usual. Part of this was due to the fact that the Lieutenant was indoors so much his skin remained an unhealthy white, like that of a man who has been sick, and part due to the fact that Anderson's face was too sensitive for police work. But they were used to it. They knew the Lieutenant didn't worry as much as he seemed to, and that he was hip.

'It's a damn good thing the commissioner don't like pederasts,' he greeted them.

Grave Digger looked sheepish. 'Did the joint get steamed up?'

'It boiled over.'

Coffin Ed was defiant. 'Who was beefing?'

'The Acme Company's lawyers. They cried murder, brutality, anarchy, and everything else you can think of. They've filed charges with the police board of inquiry, and if they don't act they threaten to file a petition in the common pleas court.'

'What the old man say?'

'Said he'd look into it, winking at the D.A.'

'Woe is us,' Grave Digger said. 'Every time we brush a citizen gently with the tip of our knuckles, there's shysters on the sidelines to cry brutality, like a Greek chorus.'

Anderson bowed his head to hide his smile. 'You shouldn't play Theseus.'

Grave Digger nodded in acknowledgement, but Coffin Ed's thoughts were on other matters.

'You'd think they'd want the killer caught,' he said. 'Being as the man was killed on their property.'

'Who was he, anyway?' Grave Digger asked. 'Did the boys downtown make him?'

'Yes, he was a Richard Henderson who had an apartment on lower Fifth Avenue, near Washington Square.' Suddenly Anderson had become completely impersonal.

'Couldn't he find anything he wanted down there?' Coffin Ed put in.

'Married,' Anderson continued as though he hadn't heard. 'No children—'

'No wonder.'

'A producer of new plays in off-Broadway theaters. For that, he had to have money.'

'All the more reason they'd want to find his murderer,' Grave Digger said thoughtfully.

'If by *they*, you mean the commissioner, the District Attorney and the courts, *they* do. It's the slum owners who're beefing. They don't want their employees killed in the process, it ain't worth it to them.'

'Well, boss, it's as the French say, you can't make a ragout without cutting the meat.'

'Well, that doesn't mean grinding it into beef hash.'

'Ah, well, the more it's ground, the faster it cooks. I suppose our boy was well cooked?'

'Too well cooked. They took him out the pot. They got him out this morning on a writ of habeas corpus. I think they took him to a private hospital somewhere.'

Both detectives looked at him solemnly. 'You don't know where?' Grave Digger asked.

'If I knew, I wouldn't tell you. Lay off. For your own good. That boy spells trouble.'

'What of it? Trouble is our business.'

'Trouble for everyone.'

'Oh, well, homicide will get him. They need him.'

'Anyway, you can have a go at the other witnesses.'

'Don't throw us no bones, boss. If any of those people picked up last night had known anything, they would have been to hell and gone away from there.'

'Then you can have the men with the red fezzes.'

'Lieutenant, let me tell you something. Most black men in Harlem who wear red fezzes are Black Muslims, and they're the most bitterly against this shit. Or else they're playing like they're Black Muslims, and they'd be risking their lives running down the street with a stolen pair of pants.'

'Maybe, maybe not. Anyway, be discreet. Don't rake any more muck than necessary.'

Grave Digger's neck began to swell and the tic went off in Coffin Ed's face.

'Listen, Lieutenant,' Grave Digger said thickly. 'This mother-raping white man gets himself killed on our beat chasing black sissies and you want us to whitewash the investigation.'

Anderson's face got pink. 'No, I don't want you to whitewash the investigation,' he denied. 'I just don't want you raking up manure for the stink.'

'We got you; white men don't stink. You can depend on us, boss, we'll just go to the public gardens and watch the pansies bloom.'

'Without manure,' Coffin Ed said.

Nine p.m. found them sitting at the lunch counter in the Theresa building, watching the Harlem citizens pass along the intersection of Seventh Avenue and 125th Street.

'Two steak sandwiches,' Grave Digger ordered.

The prissy brownskinned counterman with shiny conked curls gave them an all-inclusive look and batted his eyes. It was only two steps to the grill but he managed to swish on the way. He had a slender graceful neck, smooth brown arms and a wide ass in tight white jeans. He grilled two hamburgers and put them between two toasted buns on paper plates and placed them daintily before his customers. 'Kraut or ketchup?' he asked seductively, lowering long black lashes over liquid brown eyes.

Grave Digger looked from the hamburgers to the counter-man's lowered lashes. 'I ordered steak sandwiches,' he said belligerently.

The counterman fluttered his lashes. 'This is steak,' he said. 'Ground steak.'

'Steak in one piece.'

The counterman regarded him appraisingly through the corners of his eyes.

'And I mean steak off the steer,' Grave Digger added. 'I ain't talking no doubletalk.'

The counterman opened his eyes wide and looked straight into Grave Digger's eyes. 'We don't have steak in one piece.'

'Don't ask him,' Coffin Ed cautioned out the corner of his mouth.

The counterman gave him a wide, white, scintillating smile. 'I dig you,' he murmured.

'Then dig up some ketchup and black coffee,' Coffin Ed grated harshly.

Grave Digger winked at him as the counterman switched off. Coffin Ed looked disgusted.

'It wasn't a bad idea to call this Malcolm X Square,' Grave Digger said aloud, to divert the counterman's attention.

'Could have just as well called it Khrushchev Place or Castro Corner,' Coffin Ed replied, falling in with the maneuver.

'No, Malcolm X was a black man and a martyr to the black cause.'

'You know one thing, Digger. He was safe as long as he kept hating the white folks – they wouldn't have hurt him, probably made him rich; it wasn't until he began including them in the human race they killed him. That ought to tell you something.'

'It does. It tells me white people don't want to be included in a human race with black people. Before they'll be included they'll give 'em the whole human race. But it don't tell me who you mean by *they.*'

'*They*, man, *they*. They'll kill you and me too if we ever stop being colored cops.'

'I wouldn't blame them,' Grave Digger said. 'It'd bring about a hell of a lot of confusion.' Noticing the counterman listening with rapt attention, he asked him, 'What you think, Sugar Baby?'

The counterman lifted his upper lip and looked at him scornfully. 'My name ain't Sugar Baby, I got a name.'

'Well, what is it then?'

The counterman grinned slyly and said teasingly, 'Don't you wish you knew?'

'Sweet as you are, what you need with a name?' Grave Digger needled.

'Don't hand me that shit. I know who you mother-rapers are. I'm here tending strictly to my own business.'

'Good for you, Honey Baby; it'd be a damn sight better if everybody did that. But our business is to meddle into other people's business. That's why we're meddling into yours.'

'Go ahead, I won't scream; see anything green, lick it up clean.'

Grave Digger was stumped for the moment, but Coffin Ed took over for him.

'What Black Muslims eat here?'

The counterman was stumped. 'Black Muslims?'

'Yeah, what Black Muslims you have as customers?'

'Those squares? They only eat their own food 'cause they claim all other food is dirty.'

'You sure it ain't because they object to something else?'

'What do you mean by that?'

'It seems strange they wouldn't eat here when your food's so cheap and clean too.'

The counterman didn't get it. He had a sneaking notion that Coffin Ed meant something else and he frowned angrily because he didn't understand and turned away. He went down the counter to serve a customer on the 125th Street side. There were only three of them at the counter, but he stayed away from the two detectives. He looked into the faces of the passing people; he stared at the passing traffic. Then suddenly he switched back and placed himself directly in their faces and put his hands on his hips and looked straight into Coffin Ed's eyes.

'It ain't that, it's their religion,' he said.

'What?'

'Black Muslims.'

'That's right. You must see a lot of jokers who look like Black Muslims.'

'Sure.' He raised his gaze and nodded toward the bookstore diagonally across the street. Several black men wearing red fezzes were gathering on the sidewalk. 'There're some now.'

Coffin Ed glanced around and looked back. 'We don't want those, we're looking for fakes.'

'Fake what?'

'Fake Muslims.'

The counterman broke into sudden laughter. His long-lashed eyes regarded them indulgently. 'You policemen, you don't know what you want. Coffee? Pie? Ice cream?'

'We got coffee.'

The counterman pouted. 'You want some more?'

Their attention was diverted by two women in a foreign sports car that turned the corner from 125th Street and passed at a crawl south on Seventh Avenue. Both were large amazonian types with strong bold features and mannish-cut hair. Their brownskinned faces were handsome. The one driving wore a man's shirt of green crêpe de chine and a yellow silk knitted tie; while the other one beside her wore a sun-back dress without shoulder straps and the front so low she looked stark naked sitting there. They stared in the direction of the lunch counter.

'Friends of yours?' Grave Digger asked.

'Those queers?'

'Didn't look queer to me. One was a man; a good-looking man at that.'

'Man my ass, they were lesbos.'

'How do you know? You been out with them?'

'Don't be insulting. I don't associate with those kind of people.'

'No Beaux Arts ball? No garden parties?'

The counterman curled his upper lip. He was good at it. 'You're so crude,' he said.

'Where's everybody?' Coffin Ed asked to get Grave Digger out of trouble.

Willing to call quits, the counterman replied soberly, 'It's always slack at this time.'

But Coffin Ed wouldn't let him off. 'That ain't what I mean.'

The counterman stared at him hostilely. 'What do you mean, then?'

'You know, *everybody.*'

Then suddenly the counterman flew coy. 'I'm here,' he cooed. 'Ain't that enough?'

'Enough for what?'

'Don't play square.'

'You're forgetting we're policemen.'

'I like policemen.'

'Ain't you scared?'

'Why, I ain't been caught.'

'Policemen are brutes.'

The counterman raised his eyebrows superciliously. 'I beg your pardon?'

'BRUTES!'

'You're just fanning his interest,' Grave Digger said.

He looked at Grave Digger with a smirk. 'You know everything, tell me what I'm thinking?'

'When do you get off work?' Grave Digger countered.

His eyelashes fluttered uncontrollably as he went all unnecessary. 'Twelve o'clock.'

'Then you weren't here last night after twelve?'

His face fell. 'You sadistic son of a bitch!'

'So you couldn't have seen Jesus Baby when he stopped by?'

'Come again?'

'*Jesus Baby?*'

Neither detective caught a flicker of recognition in his demeanor. 'Jesus Baby? That someone?'

'A friend of yours.'

'Not mine, I don't know no one named Jesus Baby.'

'Sure you do. You're just scared to admit it.'

'Oh, *Him!* I love *Him*. And he loves me too.'

'I'm sure of it.'

'I'm religious.'

'All right, all right, now cut out the bullshit. You know exactly who we mean. The colored one. The one who lives right here in Harlem.'

They noticed a subtle change in his manner but they couldn't tell what it meant. 'Oh, *him?*'

They waited suspiciously. It was coming too easy.

'You mean the one who lives on 116th Street? You don't go for him, do you?'

'Where on 116th Street?'

'Where?' The counterman tried to look hip. 'You know where. That little door beside the movie; between it and the lunch counter. You kidding me?'

'What floor?'

'You just go straight on through. You'll find him.'

They had a strong suspicion they were being taken, but there wasn't any choice.

'What's his straight name?'

'Straight name? *Jesus Baby*, that's all.'

'If we don't find him, we'll be back,' Coffin Ed threatened.

The counterman gave him his most seductive smile. 'Oh, you'll find him. And give him my love. But come back, anyway.'

They found the door all right just where he had said; it was the entrance to a tenement six storeys high, the iron fire escape along the front descending to the plate-glass window of the luncheonette where pork ribs were barbecuing before an electric grill. But they overcame the temptation and went inside. They found the usual tenement hall, walls scratched with graffiti, urine stink coming up from the floor, food and last week's air. The hall led to The Temple of the Black Jesus. Hanging by the neck from the rotting plaster ceiling of a large square room was a gigantic plaster of Paris image of the Black Jesus. There was an expression of teeth-bared rage on the black face. The arms were spread, the hands were balled into fists, the toes were curled. Black plaster blood dripped from red-pointed nail holes. The legend underneath read: THEY LYNCHED ME.

They went inside. A man stood inside the doorway examining the people who entered and collecting the price of admission. He was a short, fat, black man with a harelip. Sweat ran from his face as though his skin were leaking. His short black hair grew so thick on his round inflated head it looked like nylon pile. His body looked blown up like that of a rubber man. The sky-blue suit he wore glinted like metal.

'Two dollars,' he said.

Grave Digger gave him two dollars and went ahead.

He stopped Coffin Ed. 'Two dollars.'

'My friend paid.'

'That's right. That was for him. Now two dollars for you.' Spit sprayed when he spoke.

Coffin Ed backed away and gave the man two dollars.

Inside there was so little light and so much unrelieved blackness in the walls, the people's clothes, their skins, their hair, they could only distinguish the white crescents of eyes, hanging in the dark like op art. And then they saw the metallic glitter of the harelipped man as he took the rostrum and began to harangue: 'Now we're gonna feed him the flesh of the Black Jesus until he choke—'

'Jesus baby!' someone cried. 'I hear you!'

''Cause I doan have to tell you the flesh of Jesus is indigestible,' the metallic man went on. ''Cause they ain't even digested the flesh of the white Jesus in these two thousand years, an' they been eating him every Sunday . . .'

They turned around and went back the way they had come. Because they had time to kill before midnight, they stopped at the lunch counter and had two servings of barbecue apiece, with coleslaw and potato salad.

It was midnight when they returned to the lunch counter in Malcolm X Square and the scene had changed. The street was filled with people from the late show at the Apollo and the double feature at Loew's and RKO. The streets were crowded with motor traffic, going all ways. The lunch counter was filled with hungry people, men and women, couples, straight people who wanted to eat. There was an additional counterman on duty and two darkskinned waitresses. The waitresses looked evil, but there wasn't anything queer about them but their reasons for looking evil because they had to work. The new counterman looked prissy, too, and they would have liked to talk to him but their counterman spotted them and came over and stood before them with one hand on his hip. He was going off duty and had already taken off his apron and unbuttoned his white coat so that his breasts were almost showing. He licked his lips and fluttered his eyelashes and smiled. They noticed he had already applied some tan lipstick.

'Did you find him all right?' he asked sweetly.

'Sure, just like you said,' Grave Digger replied.

'Did you give him my love?'

'We couldn't. We forgot to get your name.'

'That was too bad. I didn't tell it to you.'

'Tell us now, baby? Your straight name? The one you have to give to policemen who don't like you.'

He blinked his eyes. 'Oooo, don't you like me?'

'Sure we like you. That's why we came back.'

'John Babson,' he said coyly.

The detectives froze.

'John Babson!' Coffin Ed echoed.

'Well, John Babson, baby, put on your prettiest panties,' Grave Digger said. 'You got company, honey.'

14

The panel delivery truck drew up before the front of the 'Amsterdam Apartments' on 126th Street between Madison and Fifth Avenues. Words on its sides, barely discernible in the dim street light, read: LUNATIC LYNDON . . . I DELIVER AND INSTALL TELEVISION SETS ANY TIME OF DAY OR NIGHT ANY PLACE.

Two uniformed delivery men alighted and stood on the sidewalk to examine an address book in the light of a torch. Dark faces were highlighted for a moment like masks on display and went out with the light. They looked up and down the street. No one was in sight. Houses were vague geometrical patterns of black against the lighter blackness of the sky. Crosstown streets were always dark.

Above them, in the black squares of windows, crescent-shaped whites of eyes and quarter moons of yellow teeth bloomed like Halloween pumpkins. Suddenly voices bubbled in the night.

'Lookin' for somebody?'

The driver looked up. 'Amsterdam Apartments.'

'These is they.'

Without replying, the driver and his helper began unloading a wooden box. Stenciled on its side were the words: Acme Television 'Satellite' A.406.

'What that number?' someone asked.

'Fo-o-six,' Sharp-eyes replied.

'I'm gonna play it in the night house if I ain't too late.'

'What y'all got there, baby?'

'Television set,' the driver replied shortly.

'Who dat getting a television this time of night?'

The delivery man didn't reply.

A man's voice ventured, 'Maybe it's that bird liver on the third storey got all them mens.'

A woman said scornfully, 'Bird liver! If she bird liver I'se fish and eggs and I got a daughter old enough to has mens.'

'... or not!' a male voice boomed. 'What she got 'ill get television sets when you jealous old hags is fighting over mops and pails.'

'Listen to the loverboy! When yo' love come down last?'

'Bet loverboy ain't got none, bird liver or what.'

'Ain't gonna get none either. She don't burn no coal.'

'Not in dis life, next life maybe.'

'You people make me sick,' a woman said from a group on the sidewalk that had just arrived. 'We looking for the dead man and you talking 'bout tricks.'

The two delivery men were silently struggling with the big television box but the new arrivals got in their way.

'Will you ladies kindly move your asses and look for dead men sommers else,' the driver said. His voice sounded mean.

''Scuse me,' the lady said. 'You ain't got him, is you?'

'Does I look like I'm carrying a dead man 'round in my pocket?'

'Dead man! What dead man? What you folks playing?' a man called down interestedly. 'Skin?'

'Georgia skin? Where?'

'Ain't nobody playing no skin,' the lady said with disgust. 'He's one of us.'

'Who?'

'The dead man, that's who.'

'One of usses? Where he at?'

'Where he at? He dead, that's where he at.'

'Let me get some green down on dead man's row.'

'Ain't you the mother's gonna play fo-o-six?'

'Thass all you niggers thinks about,' the disgusted lady said. 'Womens and hits!'

'What else is they?'

'Where yo' pride? The white cops done killed one of usses and thass all you can think about.'

'Killed 'im where?'

'We don't know where. Why you think we's looking?'

'You sho' is a one-tracked woman. I help you look, just don't call me nigger is all.'

The delivery men had got the box halfway up the front steps and had stopped to get their breath. 'We could use a little help,' the driver said. 'Being as you're spreading it around.'

No one really believed in the dead man, but the television set was real. A big burly brother clad in blue denim overalls stepped from the ground-floor window. 'All right. I'll help. I'm the super. Where she go?'

'Third-storey front. Miss Barbara Tynes.'

'I said it!' a woman cried triumphantly.

'Why ain't you gettin' one then?' the scornful woman said. 'You got the same thing she is?'

'He-he, must not have,' a new female voice observed.

'Leave my ol' lady be,' a man's voice grumbled from the dark. 'She get everything she need.'

'Says you.'

A slim silhouette in a luminous white shirt emerged from the dark entrance hall. 'I'll give you a hand.' Hair like burnished metal gleamed on an egg-shaped head.

'You sniffing at the wrong tuft, Slick, baby,' said a sly female voice from somewhere above. 'She like chalk.'

'We got some'pm in common then,' Slick said.

'All right, mens, all together now,' the driver said, putting his weight to the box.

The four men slid it up the front stairs and lifted it over the sill into the front hall.

The big burly super was the first to complain. 'This here set must be made of solid lead.'

'You been doing too much night work,' the driver joked. 'Yo' old lady taken yo' strength.'

'Maybe it ain't a television set, maybe it's gold bars,' a spectator cracked. 'Maybe her business is booming.'

'Let's open it and see,' suggested some unseen agitator.

'We gonna open it when we get it up, and all of youse can see it,' the driver said. 'We got an old one to take back.'

'I declare, I never heard of such a thing, changing television sets in the middle of the night.' The woman sounded as though personally affronted.

'Ain't it a sin?' someone needled.

'I ain't said that,' the woman denied. 'Who she getting it from anyway?'

'Lunatic Lyndon,' the driver replied.

'No wonder,' the woman said in a mollified voice. 'Delivering a new set up here in Harlem this time of the night.'

The elevator was out of order, as usual, and the four men had to carry the heavy box up the stairs, sweating and grunting and cursing, with the curious spectators trailing behind like they expected to see a phenomenon.

'Whew! Let's set it down for a while,' Slick said when they reached the first landing. He looked around at the gaping followers and sneered with contempt. 'You people! A man can't open his fly in this town before you nosy people crowding about to see what he gonna pull out.'

A man chuckled. 'Can you blame us? He might pull out a knife.'

'We're ranking Slick's play,' another man said.

'Well, I ain't got no knife in mine,' Slick said.

A woman sniggered. 'Better had. Where you going?'

'If he 'spects to do any cuttin',' the second man cracked.

The woman from the street who had announced she was looking for the dead man spoke up. 'Here you niggers is talking under y'all's clothes when there is one of usses laying dead somewheres.'

'Aw, woman, look in the undertaker's, thass where dead mens is.'

'That woman needs a live man to shut her up.'

'Good an' alive.'

'All right, buddies, let's go,' the driver said encouragingly, attacking the heavy box like it was a Japanese wrestler. 'All this confabulating ain't getting us nowhere.'

'Listen to the 'fessor sling that jawbreaker.'

But the suggestion of a superior intelligence quieted them for a moment and by then they'd got the box to moving again. When they'd got it into the third-storey hall, the driver checked his delivery book again.

'It'd be funny if he got the wrong address,' a woman said.

Ignoring her, the driver rapped on an oakstained door.

'Who is it?' a female voice asked from within.

'Lunatic Lyndon. We got a television set for Miss Barbara Tynes.'

'That's me,' the voice admitted. 'Just wait a minute while I put something on.'

'You don't need to,' a male spectator said.

A laugh tinkled inside. Grins broke out.

'Get yo' knife ready, Slick, baby,' someone said.

'It stay ready,' Slick said.

'All right, folks, gather 'bout,' the driver said. 'We gonna open her and look for them gold bars.'

'I was just joking,' the gold-bar man backtracked.

The driver gave him an evil look. 'Damn right. Like half the people in the cemeteries.'

The top of the box was stenciled: THIS SIDE UP. The driver took a short crowbar from beneath his uniform and pried off the boards on the side facing the spectators. A dark glass screen was revealed.

'That a television set?' the big burly super exclaimed. 'It look more like the front of a bank.'

'She get tired of looking at it she can go inside it and look out,' a spectator said.

The delivery men looked as proud as though they'd produced a miracle. All thoughts of a dead man were forgotten.

The lock clicked in the oakstained door. The door began to open. Everyone looked. The red-nailed fingers of a woman's hand held the door open. The head of a woman peered around the edge. It was the head of a young woman with a smooth brownskinned face and straightened black hair pulled tightly aslant her forehead over her right eye. It was a good-looking face with a wide, thick unpainted mouth with brown lips. Brown eyes, magnified behind rimless spectacles, became larger still at sight of the gaping spectators. From her side she couldn't see into the box; the screen was not visible to her. All she saw was the boarding on the floor and the leering man.

'My TeeVee!' she exclaimed and pitched forward onto the green carpeted floor. The pink silk robe, pulled tight about her voluptuous hips, hiked up from the smooth brown length of legs to show a heavy patch of curly black hair.

Eyes bugged.

The delivery men leaped into the room and pounced on her like vicious dogs on a juicy bone.

'Heart attack!' the driver shouted.

The spectators winced.

'Give her air!' the helper cried.

The spectators surged pell-mell into the room.

A long sofa stretched across the front window. A glass-topped cocktail table sat in front of it. On one side was an armchair. On the other a white-oak television stand. Out in the center of the room was a deal table with four straight-backed chairs. Floor lamps stood about, all lit. A man's straw hat lay on the sofa, but no man was in sight. Four other doors led somewhere, but all were closed.

'Somebody call a doctor!' the driver cried.

The spectators looked about for a telephone, none was in view.

'Where the hell is the medicine cabinet?' the helper asked in a panic-stricken voice like a peacemaker at sight of a cut throat.

The spectators rushed about to look. They found all doors but the front door locked.

Only the big burly super had the presence of mind to ask, 'What you take for these attacks, lady?'

The others were too busy looking at her crotch.

Maybe she heard him. Maybe she didn't. But suddenly she gasped, 'Whiskey!'

Relief fell over the assemblage. If whiskey could save her, she was saved. In a matter of minutes the room looked like a whiskey store.

She clutched the first bottle she saw and drank from the neck as though it were water. Her face took on different expressions, one after another, then she gasped, 'My TeeVee? It's bursted.'

'No, mam!' the driver cried. 'Oh, no, mam, it ain't busted. I just opened it.'

'Opened it? Opened my TeeVee. I'm going to call the police. Somebody call the police.'

The spectators melted away. Maybe they went for the police. Maybe they didn't. One minute the room was filled with them. Offering her whiskey. Staring at her crotch. The women for comparison. The men for other reasons. The next minute they were gone.

Only she and the delivery men were left. The delivery men closed and locked the door. A half-hour later they unlocked and opened the door. They began to take away the wooden television box. It had been boarded up again. One was at the front and one at the back. It didn't seem any lighter than before. They staggered beneath the weight.

No one came to help them. No one appeared to look. No one appeared at all. The upstairs hall was empty. The staircase was empty. The downstairs hall was empty. They encountered no one on the sidewalk or on the street. They didn't seem surprised. The word *police* has the power of magic in Harlem. It can make whole houses filled with people disappear.

15

'Sit down between us, baby,' Grave Digger said, patting the seat beside him.

John Babson looked from him to the towering figure of Coffin Ed beside him, and said playfully, 'This is sociable, it isn't an arrest?' He was resplendent in a long-sleeved white silk shirt with a Russian collar and glove-tight skin-colored cotton satin pants that glowed like naked skin. He didn't think for a moment it was an arrest.

Grave Digger eyed him interestedly from behind the wheel.

'Go on, get in,' Coffin Ed urged, taking his arm like he would a woman's. 'You said you liked policemen.'

He got in exactly like a woman and moved close to Grave Digger to make room for Coffin Ed.

'Because if it is, I want to call my lawyer,' he continued with his little joke.

Grave Digger paused in the act of pressing the starter button. 'You got a lawyer?'

He was tired of it. 'The company has.'

'Who?'

'Oh, I don't know. I haven't ever needed him.'

'You don't need him now, unless you prefer his company.'

'He's an ofay.'

'Don't you like ofays?'

'I like y'all better.'

'You'll like us even better later on,' Grave Digger said, starting the car.

'Where y'all taking me?'

'A place you know.'

'You can come to my place.'

'This *is* your place.' He drove to the front of the building where the white man had been killed.

Coffin Ed got out on to the sidewalk and reached in

to help John out. But he drew back against Grave Digger in alarm.

'This *isn't* my place,' he protested. 'What kind of place is this?'

'Go on and get out,' Grave Digger said, pushing him. 'You'll like it.'

Looking puzzled and curious, he let Coffin Ed pull him to the sidewalk.

'It's a basement,' Coffin Ed said, taking his arm as Grave Digger came around the car and took his other arm.

He shook himself but he didn't struggle. 'How about this!' he exclaimed softly. 'Is it clean?'

'Be quiet now,' Grave Digger whispered suggestively as they walked him down the narrow, slanting alleyway to the green door halfway down. They found the door locked and sealed.

'It's locked,' John whispered.

'Shhhh!' Grave Digger cautioned.

A voice from an open window in the building next door whispered hoarsely, 'You niggers better get away from there. The police is watching you.'

John stiffened suddenly with suspicion. 'What you trying to do to me?'

'Ain't this your room?' Coffin Ed asked.

The whites of John's eyes showed suddenly in the dark. 'My room? I live on Hamilton Terrace. I ain't never seen this place.'

'Our error,' Grave Digger said, holding firmly to his arm. He could feel the trembling of his body coming through his arm.

'Maybe he'll like the Cozy Flats,' Coffin Ed said. He intended to sound persuasive, instead he sounded sinister.

John's excitement suddenly left him. He felt deflated and a little scared. He was finished with the adventure.

'I ain't interested,' he said crossly. 'Just let me alone.'

'Leave that boy alone,' the voice from the darkened window said. 'You come with me, baby, I'll protect you.'

'I ain't interested in none of you mother-rapers,' John said, his voice rising. 'Just take me back where you got me.'

'Come on then,' Grave Digger said, steering him back to the sidewalk.

'I thought you said you liked us,' Coffin Ed said, bringing up the rear.

John felt safer back on the sidewalk and he tried to shake himself loose from Grave Digger's grip. His voice was louder too.

'I ain't said no such thing. What you take me for? I ain't that way.'

Grave Digger turned him over to Coffin Ed and went around the car.

'Just get in,' Coffin Ed said, applying a little force.

Grave Digger slid beneath the wheel and reached over and pulled him down on to the seat. 'Don't struggle, baby,' he said. 'We're just going to drive by the Cozy Flats and then we'll take you home.'

'Where you can feel relaxed,' Coffin Ed added, pushing in beside him.

'I don't want to go to the Cozy Flats,' John screamed. 'Leave me out here. Do you think I'm gay? I ain't gay—'

'Merry then.'

'I'm straight. I just got a happy disposition. Girls like me. I ain't queer. You're making a mistake.'

'What are you getting so hysterical about?' Grave Digger said hotly, as though he were annoyed. 'What's the matter with you? What you got against the Cozy Flats? Is there somebody there you don't want to see?'

'I ain't never heard of the Cozy Flats, nor nobody lives there, far as I know. And turn me loose, you're hurting me.'

Grave Digger started the car and drove off.

'I'm sorry,' Coffin Ed said, letting go his arm. 'It's just because I'm so strong.'

'You ain't exciting me,' John said scornfully.

Grave Digger brought the car to a stop in front of the Cozy Flats.

'Recognize this place?' Coffin Ed asked.

'I ain't never seen it.'

'Lucas Covey is the super.'

'What about it? I don't know no Lucas Covey.'
'He knows about you.'
'Lots of people know me who I don't know.'
'I'll bet.'
'He said he rented you the room,' Grave Digger said.
'What room?'
'The one we just left.'
'You mean that basement what was locked up?' He looked from one hard black face to the other one. 'What's this? A frame? I should'a known there was something wrong with you mother-rapers. I got a right to call my lawyer.'
'You don't know his name,' Grave Digger reminded him.
'I'll just call the personnel office.'
'There ain't nobody there this time of night.'
'You dirty sadistic bastards!'
'Don't lose your pretty ways. We got nothing against you, personally. It was Lucas Covey who told us about you. He said he rented the room to a seal-brown young man named John Babson. He said John Babson was beautiful and sweet. That describes you.'
'Don't hand me that shit,' John said, but he preened with pleasure. 'You're making that up. I ain't never heard of nobody named Lucas Covey. You take me in and I'll confront him.'
'I thought you didn't want to go inside,' Coffin Ed said. 'With us, anyway.'
'Maybe by another name,' Grave Digger said.
'Why can't I confront him?'
'He ain't there.'
'What's he look like?'
'Slender black man with narrow face and egg-shaped head. West Indian.'
'I don't know nobody like that.'
'Don't lie, baby, I saw the recognition in your eyes.'
'Shit! You see everything in my eyes.'
'Ain't you pleased?'
'But the man you described could be anybody.'
'This one is gay, like you.'
'Don't make a fool out of yourself; I told you, I ain't gay.'

'All right, but we know you know this man.'

John became appealing. 'What can I do to convince you?'

'I thought you said you weren't gay.'

'I didn't mean that.'

'All right, let's negotiate.'

'Negotiate how?'

'Like the East and the West. We want information.'

John grinned and forgot to be bitchy. 'You're the West then; what do I get?'

'There's two of us, you get double the price.'

He broke up as though he would cry. Every time he tried to play straight they wouldn't let him. He would succumb to desire, but he wasn't sure. It all left him frustrated and a little frightened.

'Shit on both of you, you sadistic mother-rapers,' he said.

'Listen, baby, we want to know about this man, and if you don't tell us, we'll whip your ass.'

'Don't excite him,' Coffin Ed cautioned. 'He'd like that.' Turning to John, he said, 'Get this, pretty boy, I'll knock out your pretty white teeth and gouge your bedroom eyes out of shape. When I get through with you, you'll be known as the ugly fairy.'

John got truly frightened. He put his hands between his legs and squeezed them. His voice was pleading. 'I don't know nothing, I swear. You bring me here to places I ain't never seen, and ask me about a man I ain't never heard of who looks like anybody—'

'Richard Henderson, then?'

John broke off in mid-speech and his mouth hung open.

'I see that name scored.'

He was ludicrous trying to get himself together. He couldn't follow the sudden switch. He didn't know whether to be relieved or terrified; whether to admit he knew him or deny all acquaintance.

'Er, you mean Mr Henderson, the producer?'

'That's the one, the white producer who likes pretty colored boys.'

'I don't know him that well. All I know about him is

he produces plays. I had a part in a play he produced on downtown Second Avenue called *Pretty People.*'

'I'll bet you were the lead.'

He smiled secretly.

'Just wipe that smirk off your face and tell us where we can find him.'

'At his home, I suppose. He's got a wife.'

'We don't want to see his wife. Where does he hang out by himself?'

'Any place in the Village, although this time of night he might be somewhere on St Marks Place.'

'Where else is there on St Marks Place except The Five Spot?'

'Oh, plenty places for the cognoscenti, you just got to know where they are.'

'All right, you show us.'

'When?'

'Now.'

'Now? I can't. I got to go home.'

'You got someone waiting?'

He fluttered his lashes and looked coy again. He had beautiful eyes and he knew it. 'Always,' he said.

'Then we'll have to kidnap you,' Grave Digger said.

'And keep your mother-raping hands away from me,' Coffin Ed snarled.

'Square!' he said contemptuously.

The drove down through Central Park and turned over to Third Avenue on 59th Street, passing first the exclusive high-rent, high-living district around 59th Street and Fifth Avenue, and then the arty, chichi section of antique shops, French restaurants, expensive pederasts on Third Avenue in the fifties and upper forties until they reached the wide, black, smooth paved expanse that passed through Cooper Square, and they had come to the end of their journey. They remembered the days of the Third Avenue elevated, the dark cobblestoned street underneath, where the Bowery bums pissed on passing cars at night, but neither spoke about it for fear of distracting John from the strange, glittering excitement that had overcome him. As far as they could see, St Marks Place itself was no cause for excitement. Externally, it was as dreary a street as one could find, unchanged, dirty, narrow, sinister-looking. It was the continuation of 8th Street, which ran between Third and Second Avenues. On the west side, between Fifth and Sixth Avenues, 8th Street was the heart of Greenwich Village, and Richard Henderson had lived in the new luxury apartments on the corner of Fifth Avenue. But St Marks Place was something else again.

Jazz joint on one corner, open for business, The Five Spot. Delicatessen on the other, closed, beer cans in the window. White Mercedes drives up before The Five Spot, white-coated white woman with shining white hair driving. Black man beside her with bebop beard, clown's hat. Kisses her, gets out. Goes into The Five Spot. She drives away. 'Rich white bitch . . .' John mutters. On other corner in front of beer cans in delicatessen window, two black boys in blue jeans, gray sneakers, black shirts. Faces pitted with smallpox scars. Hair nappy. Teeth white. Faces scarred from razor slashes. Cotton hair, matted, unkempt. All young, early twenties. Three white girls looking like spaceage witches. Young girls. In their teens. Witches are children in this age. Long unkempt dark brown hair. Hanging down. Dirty faces. Dark eyes. Slack mouths. Stained black jeans. All moving in slow motion, as though drugged. It made the detectives feel woozy just looking at them.

'Who was your daddy, blacky boy?' a white girl asks.

'My daddy is a cracker,' the black boy answers. 'But he got a job for me.'

'On his plantation,' the white girl says.

'Ole massa McBird!' the black boy says.

They all burst into loud unrestrained laughter.

'Wanna go to The Five Spot?' John asked.

'You think he's in there?' Grave Digger asked, thinking, *If he is, he's a mother-raping ghost.*

'Richard goes there sometimes, but it's early for him.'

'Richard? If you know him all that well, why don't you call him Dick?'

'Oh, Dick sounds so vulgar.'

'Well, where else does he go, by any name?'

'He meets people all around. He picks up lots of actors for his plays.'

'I ain't a damn bit surprised,' Grave Digger said, then pointed to a building next to The Five Spot, asked: 'What about that hotel there? You know it?'

'The Alicante? Home away from it all? Nobody lives there but junkies, prostitutes, pushers and maybe some Martians too from the looks of them.'

'Henderson ever go there?'

'I don't know why. Nobody there he'd want to see.'

'No *Pretty People*, eh? He wasn't on the shit?'

'Not as far as I know of. He just took a trip now and then.'

'How about you?'

'Me? I don't even drink.'

'I mean have you ever been there?'

'Goodness no.'

'It figures.'

John grinned and slapped him on the leg.

Next to it in the direction of Second Avenue was a steam-bath establishment calling itself the Arabian Nights Baths.

'That a fish bowl?'

John batted his eyes but didn't reply.

'Does he go there?'

He shrugged.

'All right, let's go see if he's there.'

'I better warn you,' he said. 'The markees are there.'

'You mean maquis,' Grave Digger corrected. 'M-a-q-u-i-s.'

'No, markees, m-a-r-q-u-i-s-e. Bite each other!'

'Well, well, that is what they do? Bite each other?'

John giggled.

They went up steps from the street and passed through a short narrow hall lit by a bare fly-specked bulb. A fat, greasy-faced man sat behind a counter in a cage at the front of the locker room. He wore a soiled white shirt without a collar from which the sleeves had been torn, sweat-stained suspenders attached to faded, stained seer-sucker pants big enough to fit an elephant. His head went down in sweat-wet folds of fat into a lump of blubber with arms. His face was only black-rimmed thick lenses holding magnified cooked eyes.

He put three keys on the counter. 'Put your clothes in your locker. Got any valuables, better leave them with me.'

'We just want a look,' Grave Digger said.

The fat man rolled cooked eyes at John's getup. 'You got to get naked.'

John's hand flew to his mouth as though he were shocked.

'You don't understand me,' Grave Digger said. 'We're the law. Policemen. Detectives. See?' He and Coffin Ed flashed their shields.

The fat man was unimpressed.

'Policemen are my best customers.'

'I'll bet.'

They meant different things.

'Tell me who you looking for; I know everybody in there.'

'Dick Henderson,' John Babson said.

'Jesus Baby,' Grave Digger said.

The fat man shook his head. The detectives moved toward the steam room.

John hesitated. 'I'll take off my clothes, I don't want to spoil them.' He looked from one detective to the other. 'It won't take but a minute.'

'We don't want to lose you,' Grave Digger said.

'Which might happen if you show your shape,' Coffin Ed added.

John pouted. In the familiar scene he felt he could say what he wished. 'Old meanies.'

Naked bodies came out of white steam as thick as fog; fat bodies and lean bodies, black bodies and white bodies, scarcely different except in color. Eyes stared resentfully at the clothed figures.

'What they do with the chains?' Grave Digger asked.

'You're awfully square for a policeman.'

'I've always heard it was twigs.'

'That must have been before the markees.'

If John saw anyone whom he knew, he didn't let on. The

detectives didn't expect to recognize anyone. Back on the sidewalk, they stood for a moment looking down toward Second Avenue. On the corner was a sign advertising ice cream and chocolate candies. But next door was a darkened plate-glass front of some kind of auditorium. Cards in the windows announced that Martha Schlame was singing Israeli Folk Songs and Bertolt Brecht.

'The Gangler Circus is generally here,' John said.

'Circus?'

'You got a dirty mind,' John accused. 'And it ain't the kind with lions and elephants either. It's just the Gangler Brothers and a dog, a rooster, a donkey and a cat. They got a red and gold caravan they travel in.'

'Leave them to the sprouts and let's finish with this,' Coffin Ed said impatiently.

Down here the people were different from the people in Harlem. Even the soul brothers. They looked more lost. People in Harlem seem to have some purpose, whether good or bad. But the people down here seemed to be wandering around in a daze, lost, without knowing where they were or where they were going. Moving in slow motion. Dirty and indifferent. Uncaring and unwashed. Rejecting reality, rejecting life.

'This makes Harlem look like a state fair,' Grave Digger said.

'Makcs us look like we're from the country too.'

'Feel like it anyway.'

They crossed the street and went back down the other side, coming abreast a big wooden building painted red with green trimmings. The sign over the entrance read: *Dom Polsky Nardowy.*

'What's this fire hazard, sonny?'

'That horror? That's the Polish National Home.'

'For old folks?'

'All I ever seen there was Gypsies,' John confessed, adding after a moment: 'I dig Gypsies.'

Suddenly they were all three fed up with the street. By common consent they crossed over to The Five Spot.

Interlude

'I take it you've discovered who started the riot,' Anderson said.

'We knew who he was all along,' Grave Digger said.

'It's just nothing we can do to him,' Coffin Ed echoed.

'Why not, for God's sake?'

'He's dead,' Coffin Ed said.

'Who?'

'Lincoln,' Grave Digger said.

'He hadn't ought to have freed us if he didn't want to make provisions to feed us,' Coffin Ed said. 'Anyone could have told him that.'

'All right, all right, lots of us have wondered what he might have thought of the consequences,' Anderson admitted. 'But it's too late to charge him now.'

'Couldn't have convicted him anyway,' Grave Digger said.

'All he'd have to do would be to plead good intentions,' Coffin Ed elaborated. 'Never was a white man convicted as long as he plead good intentions.'

'All right, all right, who's the culprit this night, here, in Harlem? Who's inciting these people to this senseless anarchy?'

'Skin,' Grave Digger said.

16

From where they sat, the rioting looked like a rehearsal for a modern ballet. The youths would surge suddenly from the dark tenement doorways, alleyways, from behind parked cars and basement stairways, charge towards the police, throw rotten vegetables, and chunks of dirt, and stones and bricks if they could find them, and some rotten eggs, but not too many because an egg had to be good and rotten before it went for bad in Harlem; taunting the police, making faces, sticking out their tongues, chanting, 'Drop dead, whitey!' Their bodies moving in grotesque rhythm, lithe, lightfooted, agile and fluid, charged with a hysterical excitement that made them look unhealthily animated.

The sweating, red-faced cops in their blue uniforms and white helmets slashed the hot night air with their long white billies as though dancing a cop's version of *West Side Story*, and ducked from the flying missiles, chiefly to keep the dirt out of their eyes; then it was their turn and they chased the black youths who turned and fled easily back into the darkness.

Spokesmen from the 125th Street offices of the NAACP and CORE were mounted on Police Department sound trucks appealing to the youths to go home, saying their poor unhappy parents would have to pay. Only the white cops paid any attention. The Harlem youths couldn't care less.

'It's just a game to them,' Coffin Ed said.

'No, it ain't,' Grave Digger contradicted. 'They're making a statement.'

While the police were diverted momentarily to a group of boys and girls launching a harassment on 125th Street, a gang of older youths charged from the shadows toward a supermarket in the middle of the block with beer bottles and scraps of iron. The glass shattered. The youths began darting in to loot, like sparrows snitching crumbs from under the beaks of larger birds.

Coffin Ed looked sideways at Grave Digger. 'What's that statement say?'

Grave Digger straightened in his seat. It was the first time either of them had moved. He noticed the red-faced white cops turn in that direction. 'Says there's gonna be some trouble if they start that shit.'

A cop drew his gun and shot into the air.

Until then the older people on the edge of the sidewalk had been looking on indifferently, some stopping to watch, most going calmly about their business, showing disapproval chiefly by refusing to take sides. But suddenly all movement among them stopped and they became engaged.

The youths fled back into the shadows of 124th Street. The cops followed. There was the sound of garbage cans being thrown into the street.

Another shot rang out from the darkness of 124th Street. The older people began to drift in that direction, seemingly without purpose, but now everything about them showed disapproval of the police.

Grave Digger put his hand on the handle of the door. He was sitting on the curb side, away from the ruckus across the street, and Coffin Ed was beneath the wheel.

Four skinny black youths converged on the car from the sidewalk.

'What you mothers doing here?' one challenged.

In the shadow of the doorway across the sidewalk behind them, Grave Digger saw a squat, black middle-aged man wearing a dark suit and a red fez affected by the Black Muslims. He drew his hand back from the door.

'We's just sittin',' he said.

'We run out of gas,' Coffin Ed added.

Another youth mumbled, 'You mothers ain't funny.'

'Is that a question or a conclusion?' Grave Digger said.

Not one of the youths smiled. Their solemnity worried the detectives. It seemed that most of the other youths engaged in cop baiting were enjoying it, but these had a purpose.

'Why ain't you mothers out there fighting whitey?' the youth challenged.

Grave Digger opened his hands. 'We're scared,' he said.

Before the youth replied he looked over his shoulder. Grave Digger didn't see the slightest motion by the man in the fez but the youths moved off without another word.

'Something tells me there's more behind this little fracas than meets the eye,' Grave Digger said.

'Ain't there always?'

Grave Digger got the Harlem precinct station on the radio. 'Gimme the Lieutenant.'

Anderson came on.

'We're getting some ideas.'

'We want facts,' Anderson said.

Grave Digger's gaze wandered across the street. The elderly people were collecting in little knots on both corners of the intersection of 124th Street, the white cops were backing slowly from the shadows, empty-handed, but wary. The blazing arc of a Molotov cocktail came down from a tenement roof. The bottle shattered harmlessly in the street. Burning gasoline blazed briefly for a moment and dark figures sprang momentarily into vision, faces shining, eyes gleaming, before sinking back into the gloom like stones into the sea as the blaze flickered and went out.

'There ain't gonna be any facts,' Grave Digger informed Anderson.

'Something will break,' Anderson said.

Coffin Ed looked across at Grave Digger and shook his head.

'Well, you want we should move around a little and see what we can pick up?' Grave Digger asked.

'No, just lay dead and let the race leaders handle it,' Anderson said. 'We want the nitty-gritty.'

Grave Digger stifled an impulse to say, 'What dat?' and caught Ed's eye. Anderson made them hilarious with what he thought was hep-talk, but they had never let him know it.

'We dig you, boss,' Grave Digger gave a reply equally as square but Anderson didn't get it.

When he had switched off the radio, Grave Digger said, 'Ain't that some shit! Here they got a riot and a thousand cops scattered all over the streets and they don't know how it started.'

'We don't neither.'

'Hell, we weren't here.'

'The Lieutenant wants us to sit here until the answer turns up.'

A black stringbean wearing a floppy white hat came cautiously from 125th Street with a huge brown woman in a sleeveless dress. They moved as though they were crossing no-man's-land. When they drew abreast they peeped furtively at the two black men sitting motionless in the parked car, peeped across the street at the line of white cops, and drew in their eyes.

Police cruisers and mounted cops were prodding the traffic on. Voices came from the sound trucks. Jokers were crowded in the doorway of a bar. Inside, the jukebox was braying folk songs.

'It ain't much of a riot, anyway,' Coffin Ed observed.

'Too late in the season.'

'In this mother-raping country of IBM's I don't see what they need you and me for anyway.'

'Hell, man, IBM's don't work here.'

Coffin Ed followed Grave Digger's gaze. 'He's gone.' They were looking for the man in the red fez.

Suddenly a scuffle broke out on their side of the street. The five youths who had challenged the detectives previously reappeared from the direction of 125th Street, propelling a sixth youth before them. One held the youth's arm twisted behind him and the others were trying to take off his pants. He twisted about, trying to break free, and butted his attackers with his buttocks. 'Lemme go!' he cried. 'Lemme go! I ain't chicken.'

A couple of grown men stood in burrhead silhouette beneath the corner lamps, watching avidly.

'Less cut off his balls,' one of his torturers said.

'And give 'em to whitey,' another added.

'Man, whitey wants dick.'

'Less cut that off too.'

'Turn him loose,' Grave Digger said, like an elder brother.

Two of the youths stepped back and snapped open chivs. 'Who you, mother?'

Grave Digger got from the car and freed the youth's arm.

Three more blades glinted in the night, as the youths spread out.

The sound of the other car door opening broke into the silence, drawing their attention for a moment.

Grave Digger moved in front of the youth under attack, his big loose hands still empty.

'What's the matter with him?' he asked in a reasonable voice.

The gang stood undecided as Coffin Ed strolled on to the scene.

'He's chicken,' one said.

'What you want him to do?'

'Stone whitey.'

'Hell, boy, those cops got guns.'

'They scared to use 'em.'

Another youth exclaimed, 'These them mothers said they was scared.'

'That's right,' Coffin Ed said. 'But we ain't scared of you.'

'You scared of whitey. You ain't nothing but shit.'

'When I was your age I'da got slapped in the mouth for telling a grown man that.'

'You slap us, we waste you.'

'All right, we believe you,' Grave Digger said impatiently. 'Go home and leave this kid alone.'

'You ain't our Pa.'

'Damn right, if I was you wouldn't be out here.'

'We're the law,' Coffin Ed said to forestall any more argument.

Six pairs of round white-rimmed eyes stared at them accusingly.

'Then you on whitey's side.'

'We're on your leader's side.'

'Them Doctor Toms,' a youth said contemptuously. 'They're all on whitey's side.'

'Go on home,' Grave Digger said, pushing them away, ignoring the flashing knife blades. 'Go home and grow up. You'll find out there ain't any other side.'

The youths retreated sullenly and he kept pushing them down toward 125th Street as though he were suddenly angry. A police cruiser pulled to the curb and the white cops appeared anxious to help, but he ignored them and went back to join Coffin Ed. For a moment they sat untalking, scanning the sullen Harlem night. All the rioters in their vicinity had disappeared, leaving the sanctimonious citizens hobbling along with prime self-righteousness beneath the hot-eyed scrutiny of the frustrated cops.

'All these punks ought to be home doing their homework,' Coffin Ed said, bitterly.

'They got a point,' Grave Digger defended. 'What they gonna learn to cancel what they already know?'

'Roy Wilkins and Whitney Young ain't gonna like that attitude.'

'Sure ain't, but it's still putting butter on their bread.'

From behind drawn curtains of a storefront synagogue the black face of a grizzly-bearded rabbi peeped furtively at them. They didn't see him because some heavy object landed on top of their car and sudden flame was pouring down all windows.

'Sit still!' Grave Digger shouted.

Coffin Ed was opening his door and dove barehanded to the sidewalk, scraping the heels of his hands on the concrete while rolling over in the same motion. Some flaming gasoline had dripped on the calves of Grave Digger's trousers but when he undid his belt and ripped open his fly to tear them off he saw Coffin Ed coming around the front end on the car with the back of his coat on fire. He stood straight up with leg power only and clutched the collar of Coffin Ed's coat when he came within reach. In one swift movement he ripped the blazing back out of Coffin Ed's coat and flung it back into the street, but his own pants had fallen around his ankles and were burning smokily with the stink of burning wool. He did a grotesque adagio dance getting his feet clear and stood in his purple shorts examining Coffin Ed to see if he was still burning. Coffin Ed had stuck his pistol in his belt and was frantically freeing his arms of coat sleeves.

'Lucky for your hair,' Grave Digger said.

'These kinks is fireproof.'

They looked like two idiots standing in the glare of the blazing car, one in his coat, shirt and tie, and purple shorts above gartered sox and big feet, and the other in shirt-sleeves and empty shoulder holster with his pistol stuck in his belt.

From across the street foot cops and cruisers were converging on them and someone was yelling, 'Stand clear! Stand clear!'

With one accord they moved away from the burning car and searched the nearby rooftop with stabbing gazes. The tenement windows had suddenly filled with Harlem citizens watching the spectacle but no one could be seen on the edges of the roof.

17

From the outside, The Five Spot was unpretentious. It had plate-glass windows on both St Marks Place and Third Avenue, flush with the sidewalk like a supermarket. But there was a second wall, recessed from the windows, containing irregular-sized elliptic openings, giving Picasso-like glimpses of the interior, the curve of a horn, white teeth against red lips, taffy-colored hair and a painted eye, a highball glass floating from the end of a sleeve, stubby black fingers tripping over white piano keys.

On the inside these openings were covered by see-through mirrors, in which the guests could see nothing but reflections of themselves.

But it was soundproof. Not a dribble of noise leaked in from the street unless the door was opened. And no one outside could hear the expensive sounds that were being made within. Which was the point. Those sounds were too expensive to waste.

When the two rough-looking black detectives entered with their little friend, no sounds were being made except the hot eccentric modern rhythm by the angry-faced musicians. The guests were as solemn as though attending a funeral. But it wasn't the sight of two black men with an extroverted pansy that brought on the silence. The detectives knew enough about downtown to know that white people dug jazz in utter silence. However, not all the guests were white. There was a heavy seasoning of dark faces, like in the Assembly of the UN. But these black people had caught it from the white people. Silent people surrounded them.

A blond man in a black lounge suit, who was something in the establishment, ushered them to a ringside seat under the gong. The seat was so conspicuous they knew instantly it was reserved for suspect people. They smiled to themselves, wondering how he figured their little friend. Did they look that much like the kind, they wondered.

But no sooner were they seated than the excitement began. The two women who had driven by the lunch counter uptown in a little foreign sports car earlier in the evening, whom their little friend had called 'lesbos', were seated at a nearby table. As though their entrance had been a signal, one of the lesbos leaped atop her table and began doing a frantic belly dance, as if spraying the audience with unseen rays from a gun hidden beneath her mini-skirt. The skirt wasn't much bigger than a G-string. It was in gold lamé, looking indecent against her smooth chamois-colored skin. Her long, unmuscular legs were bare down to silver lamé anklets and flat-heeled gilt sandals. Her midriff was bare, her navel winked suggestively, her breasts wriggled in gilt fishnet like baby seals trying to nurse.

She was slimmer than she had looked in the sports car. Seen up from under, she was unblemished, tall, voluptuous, like a sculptured sea dream. Her heart-shaped face pointed to thick audacious lips. Her short curly hair gleamed like blued steel. She wore sky-blue eye-shadow above her long-lashed amber-colored eyes encircled in black mascara. She had gone so far with the sex image she had stumbled on indecent exposure.

'Throw it to the wind!' You knew a colored man said that. A white man wouldn't want to throw all that fine stuff to the wind.

'Go, Cat, go!' And that was a friend. Probably a white friend. Anyway, someone who knew her name.

She had unzipped her mini-skirt and was shaking it down. His face averted, their little friend jumped to his feet. They looked at him, startled. As a consequence they didn't see the other lesbian at the stripteaser's table get up at the same time.

'Excuse me,' he said. 'I got to see a man about a dog.'

'It figures,' Coffin Ed said.

'Can't you take it?' Grave Digger taunted.

He made a face.

'Let him go,' Coffin Ed growled. 'Just envious is all.'

Foolishly the blond man in the black suit was trying to

push the mini-skirt back into place. The guests whooped with laughter. The stripteasing woman hooked a long brown leg around his neck, encasing his head with the mini-skirt, and pushed her crotch into his face.

The angry-faced musicians didn't bat an eye. They played on, beating out a modern rhythm of 'Don't Go Joe', as though a blond man's head caught in a brown woman's crotch happened all the time. In the background, the pianist was walking around the platform in a long-sleeved green silk shirt, orange linen pants, with a red and black plaid Alpine hat atop his head, and every time he passed the piano player he reached over his shoulder and hit out a chord.

The place had become a madhouse. Those who had had dignity lost it. Those who hadn't became hilarious. Everybody was happy. Except the musicians. The management should have been happy too. But instead there was a bald-headed longfaced man rushing to the rescue of the blond man with his face caught in the stripteaser's crotch. It was debatable whether he wanted to be rescued. Whether he was enjoying it or not, the other white people in the audience were emitting gales of laughter.

The baldheaded man clutched a hot brown leg. Immediately she hooked it around his neck. Then she had both their heads beneath her mini-skirt.

'At the trough!' someone yelled.

'Divide her,' another said.

'But leave some,' a third voice cautioned.

The stripteasing woman became hysterical. She began shaking her hips from side to side as though trying to crack the heads beneath her mini-skirt against one another. With a concerted effort they pulled free, red as boiled lobsters. The mini-skirt fell to the table top. The brown legs stepped out of it, the redfaced men backed away. With one deft motion the sweating brown woman took off her black lace panties, triumphantly waving them in the air. Tight black curls ran down to her crotch, forming a patch the size of a fielder's glove against the lighter tint of her belly skin.

People roared, shouted, applauded. 'Hurrah! Olé! Bravo!'

The door to the street was opened. Suddenly the loud urgent screams of police sirens poured into the room. Grave Digger and Coffin Ed jumped to their feet and looked around for their little friend. All they saw were people on the edge of panic. The happy music played by angry musicians suddenly ceased. The naked stripteaser screamed, 'Pat! Pat!' From many throats came a wail like a cry of anxiety – a new sound. Even before they had reached the street, Grave Digger said, 'Too late.'

They knew. Everyone seemed to know. Pretty boy, John Babson, lay dead in the gutter, curled up like a foetus, cut to death by the lesbian, Pat, who had followed him into the street. He had been cut so many times he bore little resemblance to the exhibitionist pansy of a few minutes before.

The woman was being put into an ambulance backed up to the curb. She had been cut too, about the arms and face. Blood leaked in streams over her black sweater and slacks. She was a big woman, darker than her sidekick, built like a truck driver who could double for a wet-nurse. But she had lost so much blood she was weak. She moved as though in a daze. Two ambulance attendants had clamped the major cuts and were laying her full-length atop the wheel stretcher inside the ambulance.

Police cruisers were parked along the curb on Third Avenue and St Marks Place. People had come from everywhere; from within the houses, from the streets, from private cars stopping in the street. The intersection was jammed, traffic was stopped. Uniformed police screamed and cursed, frantically blew their whistles, trying to clear the way for the Medical Examiner, the DA's assistant, the man from homicide, who had to come and record the scene, gather up the witnesses, and pronounce the body dead before it would be removed.

Grave Digger and Coffin Ed followed the ambulance to Bellevue, but they weren't permitted to interview the woman. Only a detective from the homicide bureau was allowed to speak to her. All she would say was, 'I cut him.' The doctors took her away.

The detectives went back to the Cooper Square precinct station on Lafayette Street. The body had been taken to the morgue but the witnesses were being questioned. When they offered themselves as witnesses, the precinct captain let them sit in on the questioning. The five young people they had noticed on their arrival, the two black boys and the three white girls who looked like spaceage witches, made the best witnesses. They had been returning up St Marks Place from Second Avenue when he came out of the rear of The Five Spot and set off down the street, switching his ass. They had known he was heading for The Arabian Baths. Where else? He walked like it. Then she came out the rear of The Five Spot too, running after him like an angry black mother bear, shouting, 'Police fink . . . stool pigeon . . . sissy spy . . .' and other things they couldn't repeat. What things? About his sex habits, his mother, his anatomy – they could guess. Nothing that shed more light. She had just run up behind him and cut him straight across the ass with all her might. His ass had popped wide open like a sliced frankfurter. Then she had slashed him as far as she could and by the time he had drawn his own knife and turned to fight her off, it was too late.

'She turned him every way but loose,' one of the black boys said in awe.

'Cut him two-way side and flat,' the other corroborated.

'Why didn't you two boys stop her?' the questioning lieutenant asked.

Grave Digger looked at Coffin Ed but said nothing.

'I was scared,' the black boy confessed guiltily.

'You don't have to feel ashamed,' his colored friend assured him. 'Nobody runs betwixt a man and a woman knife-fighting.'

The lieutenant looked at the other black boy.

'It was funny,' he said simply. 'She was chivving his ass like beating time and he was dancing about like an adagio dancer.'

'What you boys do?' the lieutenant asked.

'We go to school,' the black boy said.

'NYU,' a white girl elaborated.

'All of you?'

'Sure. Why not?'

'We called the police,' the other girl volunteered.

The stripteaser was next, back in her mini-skirt. But she sat with her legs so close together they couldn't tell if she had put her panties back on. She looked cold, even though it was hot. She gave her name as Mrs Catherine Little, and her address as the Clayton Apartments on Lenox Avenue. Her husband was in business. What kind of business? The meat-packing industry, like Cudahy and Swift. He made and packed country sausage for sale to retail stores.

She and her friend, Patricia Davis, had come from a birthday party at the Dagger Club on upper Broadway and they'd stopped by The Five Spot to catch the Thelonius Monk and Leon Bibb show. Grave Digger and Coffin Ed knew the joint, in Harlem it was called the 'Bulldaggers' Club; but they said nothing, they were there to observe. Nothing had happened there to shed any light on why her friend cut the man; there hadn't been any men present; it had been a closed affair for the 'Mainstreamers' – that was the name of their club. She had no idea why her friend had cut him, he must have assaulted her, or maybe he insulted her, she added, instantly realizing how silly the first had sounded. Her friend had a high temper and was quick to take offense. No, she didn't know of any case where she had cut anyone before, but quite often she had seen her pull her knife on men who insulted her. Well, the kind of insults men usually threw at women who looked like her, as if she could help how she looked. It was her own business how she dressed, she didn't have to dress to please men. No, you wouldn't call her mannish, she was just independent. No, she personally didn't know the victim, she didn't remember ever having seen him before. She couldn't imagine what exactly he had said or done to have started the fight, but she felt certain Pat hadn't started it; Pat – Patricia – would flash her knife but she wouldn't cut anybody unless they made her. Yes, she had known her for a long time; they had been friends before she was married. She'd been married nine years. How old she was? That'd be telling, besides, what difference did it make?

The uptown detectives asked only one question. Grave Digger asked her, 'Was he *Jesus Baby?*'

She stared at him from wide, startled eyes. 'Are you kidding? Is that a name? *Jesus Baby?*'

He let it pass.

The lieutenant said he'd have to hold her as a material witness. But before they had time to lock her up her husband appeared with a lawyer and a writ of habeas corpus. He was a short, fat, elderly black man with a night tan. His skin had grown lighter and become a shade of mottled brown from the absence of sunlight. He had a bald spot in the back of his skull, around which his kinky mixed gray hair was cut short. His dull brown eyes were glazed, like candied fruit, with thick wrinkled lids. He looked out at the world from these old, half-closed, expressionless eyes as though nothing would surprise him any more. His wide, thin-lipped, sloppy mouth connected with a sharp-angled jaw like a hog's and stuck out like an ape's. But some of his flabbiness was concealed by the very expensive-looking double-breasted suit he wore. He spoke in a low, blurred, Negroid voice. He sounded positive and uneducated; and his teeth were bad.

18

When Grave Digger and Coffin Ed arrived at Barbara Tyne's apartment in the Amsterdam Apartments, they found she had been housecleaning. She had a green scarf tied about her head and was wearing a sweaty pink silk robe when she opened the door. She had a dishcloth in her hand.

They were as startled at sight of her as she was at sight of them. Coffin Ed had said they could clean up at his wife's cousin's; he didn't expect to find Barbara looking like a charwoman. And Grave Digger didn't believe his wife had a cousin who lived in the Amsterdam Apartments, much less one who looked like this and smelled so unmistakably of her trade. She smelled of sweat, too, which was plastering her pink silk robe to her voluptuous brown body, and of a perfume that fitted both her trade and her sweat.

Seemingly, her steaming femality had no effect on Coffin Ed. He was just startled to find her scrubbing in the middle of the night. But at sight of her, sexual urge went off in Grave Digger like an explosion.

She had never seen Grave Digger and for the moment she didn't recognize Coffin Ed. The acid-burnt, terrifying face, with its patchwork of grafted skin, was there, but it was out of context. It was beat up, bloody, bruised. It had a body with torn clothing. It was accompanied by another man who looked the same at first glance. Her eyes stretched in terror. Her mouth flew open, showing the screams gathering in her throat. But they didn't get past her lips. Coffin Ed poked an uppercut through the crack in the door and caught her in the solar plexus. Air exploded from her mouth and she went down on her pratt. Her pink silk robe flew open and her legs flew apart as though it were her natural reaction to getting punched. Grave Digger noticed that the pubic hair in the seam of her crotch was the color of old iron rust, either from unrinsed soap or unwashed sweat.

Coffin Ed snatched a half-filled bottle of whiskey from the cocktail table and held it to her lips. She strangled and blew a spray of whiskey into his face. But she didn't see because her eyes had filled with tears and her glasses misted.

Grave Digger entered the room and closed the door. He looked at his partner, shaking his head.

At that moment, Barbara said, 'You didn't have to hit me.'

'You were going to scream,' Coffin Ed said.

'Well, Jesus Christ, what you expect? Y'all ought to see yourselves.'

'We just want to clean up a little,' Grave Digger said, adding unnecessarily: 'Ed said it'd be all right.'

'It's all right,' she said. 'You just ought to warned me. 'Tween you and them pistols you don't look like the Meek twins.' She didn't show any inclination to get up from the floor; she seemed to like it there.

'Anyway, no harm done,' Coffin Ed said, making the introductions. 'My partner, Digger: my wife's cousin, Barbara.'

Grave Digger looked as though he'd been insulted. 'Come on, man, let's wash up and split. We ain't on vacation.'

'You know where the bathroom is,' Barbara said.

Coffin Ed looked as though he'd like to deny it, but he just said, 'Yeah, all right. Maybe you can loan us some clean shirts of your husband's too.'

Grave Digger gave him a sour look. 'Cut out the bullshit, man; if this girl's got a husband, so have I.'

Coffin Ed looked like his feelings were hurt. 'Why not? We ain't customers.'

Ignoring all their private talk, she said from her position on the floor, 'You can have all his clothes you want. He's gone.'

Coffin Ed looked startled. 'For good?'

'It ain't for bad,' she said.

Grave Digger had stepped into the kitchen, looking for the bath. He noticed the black and white checked linoleum had been recently scrubbed. Beside the sink was a pail of dirty suds, and standing beside it a long-handled scrub brush wrapped in a towel that had been used for dry. But it didn't strike him as strange in that kind of pad. A whore was subject to do anything, he thought.

'This way,' he heard Coffin Ed call and found his way to the bath.

Coffin Ed had hung his pistol on the doorknob and stripped to the waist and was washing noisily in the bowl, splashing dirty water all over the spotlessly clean floor.

'You make more mess than a street sprinkler,' Grave Digger complained, stripping down himself.

When they'd finished, Barbara led them to a built-in clothes closet in the bedroom. Each chose a sport shirt in candy-colored stripes and a sport coat in building-block checks. There weren't any other kinds. But they were big enough to allow for the shoulder holsters and still have enough flare from the side vents to look like giant grasshoppers.

'You look like a horse in that blanket,' Coffin Ed said.

'No, I don't,' Grave Digger contradicted. 'No horse would stand still for this.'

Barbara came back from the sitting-room. She had a dust cloth in her hand. 'They look just fine,' she said, studying them critically.

'Now I know why your old man left you,' Grave Digger said.

She looked puzzled.

'It's a hot night to be housecleaning,' Coffin Ed said.

'That's why I'm cleaning.'

It was his turn to look puzzled. ''Cause it's hot?'

''Cause he gone.'

Grave Digger chuckled. They had gravitated into the sitting-room and upon hearing a Negroid voice saying loudly, 'Be calm—' they all turned and looked at the color television. A white man was shown standing on the platform of a police sound truck, exhorting his listeners: 'Go home. It's all over. Just a misunderstanding . . .' At just that moment he was shown in closeup so all one could see were his sharp Caucasian features talking directly to the television audience. But suddenly the perspective changed, showing all of the intersection of 125th Street and Seventh Avenue with a sea of faces of different colors. Except for the prevalence of so many black faces and such bright clothes, and the cops in uniform, it might have been a crowd scene from any Hollywood film about the Bible. But there aren't that many black people in the Bible. And no cops like those cops. It was a riot scene in Harlem. But no one was rioting. The only movement was of people trying to get before the cameras, get on television.

The white man was saying, '. . . no way to protest in justice. We colored people must be the first to uphold law and order.'

The cameras briefly showed the spectators booing, then switched quickly to other sound trucks, occupied by colored people who were no doubt race leaders, and various white men whom Grave Digger and Coffin Ed recognized as the chief inspector of police, the Police Commissioner, the District Attorney, a Negro assistant police commissioner, a white congressman, and Captain Brice of the Harlem precinct, their boss. They didn't see Lieutenant Anderson, their assistant boss. But they noticed three people in one truck who looked like types of Negroes in a wax museum. One was a black harelipped man in a metallic-blue suit, another a narrow-headed young man who might have been demonstrating Negro youth lacking opportunity and the third, a well-dressed, handsome, whitehaired, prosperous-looking man who was certainly the successful type. All of them looked vaguely familiar, but they couldn't place them just at the moment. Their thoughts were on other things.

'Wonder the big boss ain't beating up his chops about that ain't-the-right-way and crime-don't-pay shit,' Grave Digger said.

'Ought to be,' Coffin Ed said. 'He'll never have as full a house again.'

'I see they left little boss man to hold down the fort.'

'Don't they always?'

'Let's go down and buzz him.'

'Naw, we'd better go in.'

On their way down the stairs, Grave Digger asked, 'Where'd you find that?'

'In trouble. Where else?'

'You been holding out on me.'

'Hell, I don't tell you everything.'

'Sure don't. What was the rap?'

'Delinquency.'

'Hell, Ed, that woman ain't been a delinquent since you were a little boy.'

'It was a long time ago. I straightened her out.'

Grave Digger turned his head but it was too dark to see. 'So I see,' he said.

'You want her to scrub floors?' Coffin Ed demanded testily.

'Ain't that what she been doing?'

Coffin Ed snorted. 'You never know what a whore'll do after midnight.'

'I was thinking about you, Ed.'

'Hell, Digger, I ain't Chinese. I just saved her from a juvenile rap, ain't responsible for the rest of her life.'

They emerged on to the street looking like working stiffs trying to play pimps, filled with complaints about their broads.

'Now to get back to the station before someone makes us,' Grave Digger said, as he walked around the car and climbed beneath the wheel.

'Just don't go by the riot is all,' Coffin Ed said, sliding in beside him.

Lieutenant Anderson came into the detective room as they were searching their lockers for a change of clothes. He looked startled.

'Don't say it,' Grave Digger said. 'We're the last of the end men.'

Anderson grinned. 'Be seated, gentlemen.'

'We ain't beat our bones yet,' Grave Digger added.

'We lost our bones,' Coffin Ed elaborated.

'All right, Doctor Bones and Doctor Jones, stop in the office when you're ready.'

'We're ready now,' Grave Digger said and Coffin Ed echoed:

'As we're ever going to be.'

Both had finished transferring the paraphernalia of their trade to the pockets of their own spare jackets. They followed Lieutenant Anderson into the Captain's office. Grave Digger perched a ham on the edge of the big flat-top desk, and Coffin Ed propped his back against the wall in the darkest corner as though holding up the building.

Anderson sat well back of the green-shaded desk lamp in the Captain's chair, looking like a member of the green race.

'All right, all right, out with it,' he said. 'I take it from those smirks on your faces that you know something we don't.'

'We do,' Grave Digger said.

'It's just that we don't know what is all,' Coffin Ed echoed.

The brief dialog about the prostitute had attuned their minds to one another, so sharply they could read each other's minds as though they were their own.

But Anderson was accustomed to it. 'All joking aside—' he began, but Coffin Ed cut him off:

'We ain't joking.'

'It ain't funny,' Grave Digger added chuckling.

'All right, all right! I take it you know who started the riot.'

'Some folks call him by one name, some another,' Coffin Ed said.

'Some call him lack of respect for law and order, some lack of opportunity, some the teachings of the Bible, some the sins of their fathers,' Grave Digger expounded. 'Some call him ignorance, some poverty, some rebellion. Me and Ed look at him with compassion. We're victims.'

'Victims of what?' Anderson asked foolishly.

'Victims of your skin,' Coffin Ed shouted brutally, his own patchwork of grafted black skin twitching with passion.

Anderson's skin turned blood red.

'That's the mother-raper at the bottom of it,' Grave Digger said. 'That's what's making these people run rampage on the streets.'

'All right, all right, let's skip the personalities—'

'Ain't nothing personal. We don't mean you, personally, boss,' Grave Digger said. 'It's your color—'

'My color then—'

'You want us to find the instigator,' Grave Digger contended.

'All right, all right,' Anderson said resigned, throwing up his hands. 'Admitted you people haven't had a fair roll—'

'Roll? This ain't craps. This is life!' Coffin Ed exclaimed. 'And it ain't a question of fair or unfair.'

'It's a question of law, if the law don't feed us, who does?' Grave Digger added.

'You got to enforce law to get order,' Coffin Ed said.

'What's this, an act?' Lieutenant Anderson asked. 'You said you were the last of the end men, you don't have to prove it. I believe you.'

'It ain't no act,' Coffin Ed said, 'Not ours anyway. We're giving you the facts.'

'And one fact is the first thing colored people do in all these disturbances of the peace is loot,' Grave Digger said. 'There must be some reason for the looting other than local instigation, because it happens everywhere, and every time.'

'And who're you going to charge for inciting them to loot?' Coffin Ed demanded.

19

The Harlem detectives knew him well. They looked at him. He looked back through his old glazed eyes. No one spoke. They kept their record straight.

Jonas 'Fats' Little came to Harlem from Columbus, Georgia, thirty years before at the age of twenty-nine. It had been an open city then. White people had come in droves to see the happy, exotic blacks, to hear the happy jazz from New Orleans, to see the happy dances from the cotton fields. Negroes had aimed to please. They worked in the white folks' kitchens, grinning happily all the time; they changed the white folks' luck and accepted the resulting half-white offspring without protest or embarrassment. They made the best of their ratridden slums, their gingham dresses and blue denim overalls, their stewed chitterlings and pork bones, their ignorance and Jesus. From the very first, Fats was at home. He understood that life; it was all he'd ever known. He understood the people; they were his soul brothers and sisters.

His first job was shining shoes in a barbershop in the Times Square subway station. But the folks uptown in the rooming house where he lived on 117th Street loved the down-home sausage he made for Aunty Cindy Loo, his landprop, from pork scraps he got from the pork concessionaires in the West Forties around the NYC freight line, Saturday afternoons when they shut for the weekends. Other landprops and soul folks running home-cooking joints heard about his sausages, which were dark gray in color from pepper and spices, and melted in the mouth like shortening bread when fried. His landprop put up the capital and provided her kitchen and meat grinder, and they went into business making the original 'Cindy Loo Country Sausage', which they sold in brown paper sacks to Harlem restaurants and pork stores and professional sponsors of house rent parties. Soon he was famous and sporting a La Salle limousine with a crested hog's head painted on each of the front doors, a yellow diamond set in a heavy gold band. He was known throughout Harlem as the 'Sausage King'. That was long before the days of angry blacks and civil rights and black power. A black man with a white woman and a big car was powerful enough. But Fats didn't have any white women – he liked boys.

It was only natural that he became a policy banker. When Dutch Schultz was rubbed out, every sport in Harlem who had two white quarters to rub together opened a policy house. The difference in Fats' was he succeeded, mainly because he didn't stop making sausage. Instead he expanded, taking over the premises of a coal and wood shed on upper Park Avenue, under the NYC railroad trestle, for his factory. And when Cindy Loo died, it was all his own. And he lasted longer than most of the other brothers because he came to terms immediately with the Syndicate, and handed over forty per cent of his gross take to the white man who let him live, without argument. Fats had the advantage over other ambitious brothers, because he always knew who he was. But the Syndicate took all of the hard out of the dick, and soon Fats was earning more from his sausage than his numbers. But the Syndicate didn't want to lose a good man like Fats, who didn't make trouble and knew his place, so they made him their connection in Harlem for horse. That was when he had married that tall tan lesbian chick then working in the chorus line at Small's Paradise Inn, who was still his wife. What with his other affairs, keeping his boys apart and out of the way of his lesbian wife, supervising the manufacture and sales of his sausages, the cutting and distributing of heroin for all the Harlem pushers was too risky; and he got out just one jump ahead of the feds by dumping the shipment for that month into the meat grinder with his sausage moments before they broke in the door. Fats knew his heart wouldn't stand too many capers like that so he looked around for something less hectic and had got in on the LSD trade at the start. Now the extent of his carousing was to take a trip with his favorite boy.

He comforted himself like a respectable and dignified citizen. But he was never caught in a police station without his lawyer. His lawyer, James Callender, was white, brisk and efficient.

Attorney Callender handed the writ of habeas corpus to the Lieutenant and Fats said, 'Come on, Katy,' and took the tall mini-skirted, naked-looking, hot-skinned, cold sex-pot by the elbow and marched her toward the door. They looked like Beauty and the Beast.

The detectives, Grave Digger and Coffin Ed, testified that they'd brought the deceased downtown, hoping he might be helpful in tracing a deviate called Jesus Baby. But they had found no trace of Jesus Baby, nor could they think of any reason for John Babson to be killed, Grave Digger, who was the spokesman for the two, confessed. They were unaware that the man and his murderer were acquainted; he had denied knowing her and she had given no sign of knowing him except looking. They hadn't noticed her leave The Five Spot for their attention had been diverted by the woman who called herself Mrs Catherine Little doing a striptease. It was obvious she did it to cover her friend's exit, but how could you prove it? Or whether she knew her friend was going to attack the victim, or even guessed it? All they knew for sure was that John Babson was dead; cut to death by the woman, Patricia Bowles, who had confessed the crime. But whether it was self-defense or deliberate homicide was anyone's guess until the woman was pronounced sufficiently out of danger to be questioned by the police.

They were instructed to appear next morning at the magistrate's court to give their testimony, and sent back to their home precinct in Harlem.

Grave Digger and Coffin Ed went back to their home precinct. Lieutenant Anderson was sitting in the Captain's office, scanning the morning tabloids. They carried a flash of the latest killing as well as a trailer on the Henderson homicide.

An editorial titled THE DANGEROUS NIGHT charged the Harlem police with dragging their feet in searching for the murderer of the white man.

'I have to read the papers to find out what you're doing,' the Lieutenant greeted.

'All we're doing is losing leads,' Grave Digger confessed. 'We're as bad off as two Harlem prostitutes barefooted and knocked up. First there's Lucas Covey, who we think rented the room where Henderson was killed, sprung on a writ and now inaccessible. There's John Babson, who had the same name as the man Covey said he rented the room to, dead now himself; cut to death by a knife-toting lesbian who'd been runnnng around with the wife of Fats Little, a notorious Harlem racket man and sex deviate himself. None of whom we're allowed to say as much as good morning to. And the papers crying about "dragging feet". It's a drag all right.'

'That's why we have detectives,' Anderson said. 'If all people came forward and confessed their crimes all we'd need is jailers.'

'That's right, boss, that's why detectives have lieutenants, to tell them what to do.'

'Haven't you got stool pigeons?'

'This is another world.'

'Every world's another world. You men have been too long in Harlem is all. Crime is simple here. All of it is violent. If you were on a midtown beat you'd have a dozen worlds of crime.'

'Maybe. But that's neither here nor there. Who killed Charlie is our problem. Or Charlotte? And we need to see our witnesses. What ones that're living.'

'I'm beginning to suspect you fellows hate white people,' Anderson said surprisingly.

They froze as though listening for a sound so vague it might never be heard again but which warned of such great danger it was imperative they hear it. Anderson had their full attention now.

'It's the fashion,' he added sadly.

'Don't bet on it,' Grave Digger warned.

Anderson shook his head.

'Then why can't we have Covey?' Grave Digger persisted. 'He's got to be shown the body, anyway, whether he likes it or not.'

'You had Covey, remember. That's what the trouble is.'

'That! Hell, he can still see. He should have been shown the body of Henderson.'

'He was shown the pictures of the body of Henderson taken by the homicide photographer, and he said he didn't recognize him.'

'Then have homicide send us some pictures of Babson and we'll take them and have him look at them, wherever he is.'

'No, it's not your job. Let homicide do it.'

'You know we can find Covey if we want – if he's in Harlem.'

'I've told you to lay off Covey.'

'All right, we'll work on Fats Little instead. The woman who killed Babson was with his wife at The Five Spot.'

'Lay off Little and his wife. There's nothing to show she was involved in the knife fight or was even aware of it, from what you told me. And Little stands very high on the political front, higher than anyone knows.'

'We know.'

'Then you know he's one of the congressman's biggest campaign contributors.'

'All right, give us two weeks' vacation and we'll go to Bimini and get in a little fishing.'

'In the middle of these killings? I think that's a bad joke.'

'Hell, boss, we can't work up any sweat over these killings. We're hogtied at every turn.'

'Do the best you can.'

'You sound like a statesman, boss.'

'Just take your own advice, and don't make waves.'

'You can say it, boss, ain't nobody here but us chickens. You mean nobody really wants Henderson's killer brought to trial, it might uncover an interracial homosexual scandal that nobody wishes known.'

Pink came into Anderson's face. 'Let the chips fall where they may,' he said.

Grave Digger's face went scornful and Coffin Ed looked away in embarrassment. Their poor boss. What he had to endure from his race.

'We got you, boss,' Grave Digger said.

They called it a day.

The next morning they went to the magistrate's court and heard Patricia Bowles bound over to the Grand Jury and put in five thousand dollars' bond in her absence. They didn't report for duty at the precinct station that evening until nine o'clock and Lieutenant Anderson greeted them.

'While you were sleeping, the case was closed. Your troubles are over.'

'How so?'

'Lucas Covey came in with his lawyer about ten this morning and said he'd read in the paper that a man named John Babson had been killed and he wanted to look at the body and see if it was the same John Babson he had rented the basement room to where Henderson had been killed. The Captain had them taken down to the morgue and he identified the body as the same John Babson, known as Jesus Baby, who was known to take white men to his room. So the Captain and homicide and everyone concerned are satisfied that he was the one killed Henderson.'

'Satisfied? You mean jubilant!'

'So the case is closed.'

'If you're satisfied, who're we to complain? The woman killed him in self-defense, I suppose?'

'Not as we know of. But she has been released in five thousand dollars' bail put up by Fats Little, and moved out of the prison ward at Bellevue into a private room at forty-eight dollars per day.'

'Ain't that something?'

'The only fly in the pudding is a man named Dennis Holman who came in here about seven o'clock this evening and said he was John Babson's landlord on Hamilton Terrace and John Babson couldn't possibly have killed anyone night before last because John Babson was at home all night and he could vouch for practically every minute.'

'I'll bet.'

'Neither the Captain nor homicide nor any of the others concerned like that very much.'

Grave Digger chuckled. 'Just wished he'd go away and disappear.'

'Something like that. But he's all het up. Says John Babson was like a brother. Says he's had a room in his house for three years and that he's supported his wife and child.'

'Let's get those *he's* straightened out. Who *he* with the wife and child, and who *he* supporting them?'

'Well, the wife and child were John Babson's—'

'He was a wife, himself.'

'Maybe.'

'What maybe?'

'And it was Dennis Holman who was supporting them.'

'With that kind of investment, it don't seem natural he'd let John hustle white men, not even for the money.'

'The Captain and homicide don't agree. You want to talk to him?'

'Why not?'

They went down and took him out of his cell and carried him to the pigeon's nest, a soundproof, windowless room with a floor-bolted seat beneath a battery of lights where suspects were questioned. Dennis had just been down there in the hands of two of the Captain's men and he wasn't happy to be taken back. He was a big spongy man in a sweat-stained white shirt rolled up at the sleeves and black pants hanging low from a paunch; not fat exactly but without muscles, like a slug. He had a round boyish face, smooth black skin with a red underglow, and large popping maroon-colored eyes; he always looked surprised. He wasn't an ugly man, just strange-looking as though he belonged to a race of jelly men. He didn't have a white lawyer to front for him and he had already been pushed around. Grave Digger and Coffin Ed pushed him around some more. They turned up the lights so high he seemed to turn into smoke.

'You don't have to do that,' he said. 'I want to talk.'

He was chauffeur for a very wealthy white man who spent

most of his time abroad, so he had little to do. Once a day, generally around five o'clock after John had gone to work, he checked into his employer's Fifth Avenue apartment to see it hadn't been burgled. But most of the time he was at home, he was a home man. Home was a four-room apartment on Hamilton Terrace and 142nd Street. John Babson rented a room and ate with him when he wasn't at work. He did the cooking and cleaning himself, made the bed – beds – emptied the garbage and such. John didn't like housework, he got enough of it at the lunch counter.

'Too cute?'

'No, he wasn't like that, he wasn't mean; he was a sweet boy. He was just lazy out of bed is all.'

'But you got along?'

'Oh, we got along fine, we were good for one another; we never had an argument.'

'He was married, wasn't he?'

'Yes, he had a wife and child – little girl. But he shouldn't have never married that woman—'

'Any woman.'

'Her in particular. She's a slut, just a chickenshit whore. She'll hop in the bed with anybody with a thing.'

'Is it his child?'

'I suppose so, she says it is anyway. He could make a child, if that's what you mean. He was a man.'

'Was he?'

'In that way anyway.'

'How old is she?'

'Who?'

'His child.'

'Oh, about three and a half.'

'How long had he been living with you?'

'About four years.'

'Then he'd already left her when the child was born?'

'Yes, he'd come to live with me.'

'Then you took him away from her?'

'I didn't take him from her, he came of his own free will.'

'But she knew about you?'

'She knew about us from the first. She didn't mind. She'd have taken him back if he'd gone back to her, or she'd have shared him with me if he'd stood for it.'

'She wasn't very particular.'

'Women!' he sneered. 'They'll do anything.'

'Let's get back to the day Henderson was killed.'

'Henderson?'

'The white man.'

'I read about him.'

'To hell with that.'

'Well, John left for work at four o'clock, as usual. He worked from four to twelve—'

'He was late then.'

'It didn't matter. Four o'clock's a slack time.'

'How'd he go?'

'He always walked, it wasn't far.'

'And you stayed at home?'

'No, I went downtown and checked my boss's apartment and got something for supper – John wouldn't eat that crap at the lunch counter if he could help it—'

'Tender bowels, eh?' Coffin Ed said gratingly.

Dennis shrugged. 'Whatever you like,' he said passively. 'I always tried to have supper ready when he came home after midnight. I'd fixed some blue-claw crabs a friend had given me – a chauffeur out on Long Island – and a West Indian dish made of boiled corn meal and okra that I'd taught John to like.'

The detectives became alert.

'You West Indian?' Grave Digger was quick to ask.

'Yes, I was born in the hills behind Kingston.'

'You know many West Indians here?'

'Noooo, I don't have any reason to see any.'

'Was John?'

'John! Oh, no, he was from Alabama.'

'You know voodoo?'

'I'm from Jamaica! Voodoo is serious.'

'I believe you,' Grave Digger said.

'Tell us why she killed him,' Coffin Ed said.

'I've thought of nothing else,' Dennis confessed. 'An' God be my secret judge, I just can't figure it out. He was the gentlest of persons. He was a baby. He never had a vicious thought. He liked to make people happy—'

'I'll bet.'

'—he wouldn't have attacked anyone, much less a woman or someone dressed like one.'

'I thought he hated women.'

'He liked women – some women. He just liked me better.'

'But they didn't like him, at least this one didn't.'

'The only way I can figure it, it must have been a mistake,' he said. 'Either she mistook him for somebody else or she mistook something he was doing for something else.'

'He wasn't doing nothing but walking down the street.'

'Christ in heaven, why?' he exclaimed. 'I've racked my brains.'

'They fought about something.'

'He wouldn't have stood up and fought her, he'd have run away if he could have.'

'Maybe he couldn't.'

'Yes, after I saw his body I understood. She must have run up behind him without him seeing her and cut him so deep it had crippled him.'

Suddenly he clutched his face in his hands and his spongy boneless body heaved convulsively. 'She's a monster!' he cried, tears streaming from beneath his hands. 'An inhuman monster! She's worse than a blind rattlesnake! She's vile, that woman! Why don't you make her talk? Beat her up! Stomp on her!'

For the first time in memory, the detectives were embarrassed by the anguish of a witness in the pigeon's nest. Coffin Ed backed away as though from a distasteful worm. Automatically Grave Digger dimmed the battery of lights. But his neck had begun to swell from impotent rage.

'We can't get to her because Fats Little has got her covered.'

'Fats Little?'

'That's right.'

'What's his angle?'

'Who knows?'

'Fuck Fats,' Coffin Ed said harshly. 'Let's get back to you. How'd you learn he'd been killed? Someone phone you?'

'I read about it in the morning *News*,' Dennis admitted. 'About five o'clock this morning. You see, when John didn't come home I went by the lunch counter and found out he'd been taken by you people – everyone knows you people, of course. I figured you people had taken him to the station here, so I came here and inquired at the desk but no one had seen you people. So then I went back to the lunch counter but no one had seen you people there either – since you people had left with him. I couldn't imagine what you people wanted with him, but I figured he was safe.'

'What did you think we wanted with him?'

'I figured you people was just looking around, looking into things—'

'What things?'

'I couldn't imagine.'

'Then what'd you do?'

'I checked the Apollo bar and the record shop and places in the neighborhood.'

'Sissy hangouts?'

'Well, if you want to call them that. Anyway, no one had seen you people, so I went home to wait. It wasn't till almost daybreak that it occurred to me that John might be hurt in an automobile accident or something. I was on my way back here—'

'You got a telephone, haven't you?'

'It's out of order.'

'Then what?'

'I bought a morning *News* at the Eighth Avenue subway stop and it was in the late news flashes that someone named John Babson had been killed. After that I don't remember exactly what I did. I must have panicked. The next thing I remember was I was banging on the apartment door on St Nicholas Place where John's wife has a room, and his evil landlady calling through the door that she wasn't home. I don't know why I went there. I must of thought of having her go down and identify the body – they were still legally married.'

'Were you surprised to find her out at that hour?'

'No, it wasn't nothing unusual about her being out all night; it'd have been unusual for her to have been home. It was hard to trick in the room with the little girl there.'

'Why didn't you go down and identify the body yourself?'

'I couldn't bear the thought of seeing him dead. I knew she wouldn't care, 'sides which we were giving her money.'

'You knew the body had to be identified.'

'I hadn't thought of it that way. I just wanted to be sure.'

Then at noon he'd bought another newspaper and standing on the corner of 145th Street and Eighth Avenue – he couldn't remember how he'd got there – he had read where John's body had been identified by some Harlem building superintendent called Lucas Covey. This Covey man had claimed that John was the man called Jesus Baby who he had rented a room to – the room where the white man was killed two nights ago – three nights—

'And you recognized the name?'

'What name?'

'Covey.'

'I don't know anyone called Lucas Covey and I've never heard the name before in my life.'

'Did you call John "Jesus Baby"?'

'Never in my life and I've never heard him called that by anyone. I've never even heard the name Jesus Baby. Jesus Baby and Lucas Covey and the rented room and all that, him being killed by someone named Pat Bowles – I'd never heard of her either, and I'd never heard John speak of her, not to me anyway, and I don't believe he even knew her – I knew then it was a case of mistaken identity. Just a plain mistake that got him killed. She mistook him for somebody else. And then Lucas Covey saying he rented him the room where the white man was killed – either another mistake on Covey's part or he was just plain lying. I was standing there on the sidewalk in the blazing sun and I blacked out. Life is so insecure one can get killed any moment through a mistake. And all the time when whatever it was was going on, he was home in bed.'

'You'll testify to that under oath?'

'Testify under oath? I'll swear on a stack of Bibles nine feet high. There was no question about it, he couldn't have killed anyone that night – unless it was me. I can account for every minute of his time. His body was touching my body every minute of that night.'

'In bed?'

'Yes, all right, in bed, we were in bed together.'

'You were lovers?'

'Yes, yes, yes, if you just got to make me say it. We were lovers, *lovers* – I've said it. We were man and wife, we were whatever you want to call us.'

'Did his wife know all this?'

'Irene? She knew everything. She could have cleared his name of all those charges, murdering a white man and calling himself Jesus Baby. She came by the house that night and found us in bed. And she sat on the edge of the bed and said she wanted to see us make love.'

'Did you?'

'No, we're not – weren't – exhibitionists. I told her if she wanted to watch someone make love, she could fix up a mirror so she could watch herself.'

'Did you find her?'

'Find her?'

'Today.'

'Oh, no. She hadn't come home last time I was by there; her landlady is taking care of her little girl. So I had to go down and look at John's body by myself. That's when I knew for sure the killing had been a case of mistaken identity – when I saw the way he'd been cut. He'd been hamstrung from the back so he couldn't have run and that was the end. The only one who can prove this is the – the person who cut him—'

'We can't get to her.'

'That's what you told me. You can't get to see her and I had a lot of trouble getting into the morgue to see his body when I'm – was – his only friend. That's the way it is when you're poor. The police didn't believe nothing I said – they brought me back here and I been held in solitary ever since. But I can prove every word I said.'

'How?'

'Well, anyway along with his wife. If she'll talk. They'll have to believe her – legally she's his wife. And then legally she'll have to claim his body, although I'll pay for the funeral and everything myself.'

'What about your own wife – if you've got a wife? How does she feel about your love life?'

'My wife? I put her down before I came to the World. She ain't no help. It's John's wife you need.'

'All right, we'll look up John's wife,' Grave Digger said, writing down the address of Irene Babson on St Nicholas Place. 'And we'll have you confront Lucas Covey too.'

'I'll go with you.'

'No, we'll leave you here and bring him to you.'

'I want to go with you.'

'No, you're safer here. We don't want to lose you too, through a mistake.'

Interlude

The word 'LOVE' was scrawled on the door in dark paint.

The room smelled of cordite.

The body lay face down on the carpeted floor, at right angles with the bed from which it had fallen.

'Too late,' Grave Digger said.

'From some gun with love,' Coffin Ed echoed.

It was the last thing they had expected. They were shocked.

Lucas Covey had left the world. But not of his own volition.

Someone had pressed the muzzle of a small-caliber revolver against the flesh of his left temple and pulled the trigger. It had to have been a revolver. An automatic pistol would not have fired pressed against the flesh. The body had pitched forward to the floor. The killer had bent over and put a second bullet into the base of his skull, but from a greater distance, merely singeing the hair.

The TV set was playing. A mellifluous voice spoke of tights that never bagged. Coffin Ed stepped over and turned it off. Grave

Digger opened the drawer of the night table and saw the .45 Colt automatic.

'Never had a chance to get at it.'

'He didn't believe it,' Coffin Ed said. 'Someone he knew and trusted stuck a pistol against his temple, looked into his eyes and blew out his brains.'

Grave Digger nodded. 'It figures. He thought they were joking.'

'That could be said of half the victims in the world.'

Interlude

And then the little orphan boy asked the question in all their minds, 'But why? why? why?

Solemnly he replied: 'It was the God in me.'

20

Other than the caper with the big white sex freak involving a gang called 'The Real Cool Moslems' and some teen-aged colored girls – including his own daughter, Sugartit – Coffin Ed had had very few brushes with juvenile delinquency. The few young hoodlums with whom they had butted heads from time to time hadn't been representative of anyone – but young hoodlums of any race. But this new generation of colored youth with its spaceage behavior was the quantity X to them.

What made them riot and taunt the white police on one hand, and compose poetry and dreams complex enough to throw a Harvard intellectual on the other? All of it couldn't be blamed on broken homes, lack of opportunities, inequalities, poverty, discrimination – or genius either. Most were from the slums that didn't breed genius and dreams, but then some were from good middle-class families that didn't suffer so severely from all the inequalities. And the good and the bad and the smart and the squares alike were a part of some kind of racial ferment: all of them members of the opposition. And there wasn't any damn need of talking about finding the one man responsible: there wasn't any one man responsible.

He admitted his concern to Grave Digger as they rode to work.

'What's come over these young people, Digger, while we been chasing pappy thugs?'

'Hell, Ed, you got to realize times have changed since we were sprites. These youngsters were born just after we'd got through fighting a war to wipe out racism and make the world safe for the four freedoms. And you and me were born just after our pappies had got through fighting a war to make the world safe for democracy. But the difference is that by the time we'd fought in a jim-crow army to whip the Nazis and had come home to our native racism, we didn't believe any of that shit. We knew better. We had grown up in the Depression and fought under hypocrites against hypocrites and we'd learned by then that whitey is a liar. Maybe our parents were just like our children and believed their lies but we had learned the only difference between the home-grown racist and the foreign racist was who had the nigger. Our side won so our white rulers were able to keep their niggers so they could yap to their heart's content about how they were going to give us equality as soon as we were ready.'

'Digger, let them tell it, it's harder to grant us equality than it was to free the slaves.'

'Maybe they're right, Ed, maybe they ain't lying this time.'

'They lying all right, and that's for sure.'

'Maybe. But what saves colored folks our age is we ain't never believed it. But this new generation believes it. And that's how we get riots.'

Lieutenant Anderson could tell by the first look at them when they came to work that they weren't in a very cooperative state of mind, so he sent them over to the bookstore to check out the Black Muslims.

'Why the Black Muslims?' Grave Digger wanted to know.

'If somebody was to shit on the street you white folks would send for the Black Muslims,' Coffin Ed grated.

'Jesus Christ!' Anderson complained. 'Once upon a time you guys were cops – and maybe friends: now you're black racists.'

'It's this assignment. You hadn't ought to have put us on this assignment. You ought to know more than anyone else we're not subtle cops. We're tough and heavy-handed. If we find out there's some joker agitating these young people to riot, and we find out who it is, and if we find him, we're gonna beat him to death—'

'We can't have that!'

'And you can't have that.'

'Just see what you can learn,' Anderson ordered.

It was a Black-Art bookstore on Seventh Avenue dedicated to the writing of black people of all times and from all places. It was in the same category of black witchcraft, black jazz and Black Nationalism. It was run by a well-known black couple with some black people helping out and aside from selling books by black people to black people it served as a kind of headquarters for all the black nationalist movements in Harlem.

There were books everywhere. The main store, entered from Seventh Avenue, had books lining both walls, books back to back in chest-high stalls down the center of the floor. The only place there weren't any books was the ceiling.

'If I had read all these books I wouldn't be a cop,' Coffin Ed said.

'Just as well, just as well,' Grave Digger said enigmatically.

Mr Grace, the short black proprietor, greeted them. 'What brings the arm of the law to this peaceful place?'

'Not you, Mr Grace – you're the cleanest man in Harlem as far as the law is concerned,' Grave Digger said.

'Must have friends on high,' Coffin Ed muttered.

Mr Grace heard him. 'That I have,' he conceded, whether by way of threat or confirmation they couldn't tell. 'That I have.'

'We thought you could help us talk to Michael X, the minister of the Harlem Mosque,' Grave Digger explained.

'Why don't you go to the Mosque?' Mr Grace asked.

'You know what they think about cops,' Grave Digger said.

'We're not trying to stir up trouble. We're trying to simmer it down.'

'I don't know if I can help you,' Mr Grace said. 'The last time I saw Michael X was about a week ago, and he said he was dropping out of sight for a time: the CIA were sniffing around. But he might see you. Just what do you want with him?'

'We just want to ask him if he knows anything about someone stirring up these chickenshit riots. The boss thinks there's some one person behind it, and he thinks Michael X might know something about it.'

'I doubt if Michael X knows anything about that,' Mr Grace said. 'You know they blame him for everything bad that happens in Harlem.'

'That's what I told the boss,' Coffin Ed said.

Mr Grace looked doubtful. 'I know you men don't agree with that. At least I don't think so. You've been on the Harlem scene too long to attribute all the anti-white feelings here to the Black Muslims. But I don't know where he is.'

They knew very well that Mr Grace kept in contact with Michael X, wherever he was, and that he acted as Michael X's seeing eye. But they knew there wasn't any way to push him. They could go down and burst into the Mosque with force, but they couldn't find Michael X and the only reason they wouldn't lose their jobs was because police officialdom hated the Black Muslims so much. It would be too much like taking advantage of their 'in' with whitey. So all they could do was appeal to Mr Grace.

'We'll talk to him right here if he'll come here,' Grave Digger said. 'And if you don't trust us we'll give you our pistols to hold.'

'And you can have all the witnesses you want on hand,' Coffin Ed said. 'And anybody can say anything they want.'

'All we want is just to get a statement from Michael X that we can take back to the boss,' Grave Digger elaborated, knowing Michael X's vanity. 'Me and Ed don't believe none of this shit, but Michael X can state it better than we can.'

Mr Grace knew that Michael X would welcome the opportunity to state the position of the Black Muslims to the police through two black cops he could trust, so he said, 'Come into the Sanctum and I'll see if I can locate him.'

He led them to a room in back of the bookstore which served as his office. There was a flat-topped desk in the center covered with open books, surrounded by dusty stacks of books and cartons of items, many of which they couldn't identify. Aluminum containers for reels of film were scattered among objects which might have been used by African witch doctors or worn by African warriors: bones, feathers, headgear, clothing of a sort, robes, masks, staffs, spears, shields, a carton of dusty manuscripts in some foreign script, stuffed snakes, sets of stones, bracelets and anklets, and chains and leg-irons used in the slave trade. The walls were literally covered with signed photographs of practically all famous colored people from the arts and the stage and the political arena, both here and abroad, and unsigned photographs and portraits of all the black people connected with the abolitionist movement and various legendary African chiefs who had opposed or profited from black slavery. In that room it was easy to believe in a Black World, and black racism seemed more natural than atypical.

The ceiling was a stained-glass mosaic, but it was too dark outside to distinguish the pattern. Evidently the room extended into a back courtyard, and no doubt it had some secret exit and access, the detectives thought, as they sat patiently on two spindle-legged overstuffed straight-backed chairs, from some period or other, probably some African period, and listened to Mr Grace dial one wrong number after another under the impression that he was fooling someone.

After what he deemed was a suitable lapse of time and a convincing performance, Mr Grace was heard to say: 'Michael, I've been trying to locate you everywhere. Coffin Ed and Grave Digger want to talk to you. They're here . . . The chief seems to think there's some one person inciting these riots in Harlem, and I thought it'd be a good idea for you to make a statement . . . They say they don't believe you or the Black Muslims are implicated in any way, but they must have something to tell their chief . . .' He nodded and looked at the detectives: 'He says he'll come here, but it'll take him about half an hour.'

'We'll wait,' Grave Digger said.

Mr Grace relayed the message and hung up. Then he began showing them various curios from the slave trade, advertisements, pictures of slave ships, of slaves in steerage, of the auction block, an iron bar used as currency in buying slaves, a whip made of rhinoceros hide used by the Africans to drive the slaves to the coast, a branding silver, a cat-o'-nine-tails used on the slaves aboard ship, a pincers to pull teeth – to what purpose they couldn't tell.

'We know we're descended from slaves,' Coffin Ed said harshly. 'What're you trying to tell us?'

'Now you've got the chance, be free,' Mr Grace said enigmatically.

Michael X was a tall, thin brown man with a narrow intelligent face. Sharp eyes that didn't miss a thing glinted from behind rimless spectacles. He looked like he could be Billie Holiday's kid brother. Mr Grace stood up and gave him the seat behind the desk. 'Do you want me to stick around, Michael? Mary-Louise can step in too, if you want.' Mary-Louise was his wife: she was taking care of the store.

'As you like,' Michael X said. He was master of the situation.

Mr Grace pulled up another period chair and sat quietly and let him take charge.

'As I understand it, headquarters thinks there's one person up here who's inciting these people to riot,' Michael X spoke to the detectives.

'That's the general idea,' Grave Digger said. They didn't expect to get anything: they were just following orders.

'There's Mister Big,' Michael X said. 'He handles the narcotics and the graft and the prostitution and runs the numbers for the Syndicate—'

'Mister Sam?' Grave Digger asked, leaning forward.

Michael X's eyes glinted behind his polished spectacles. He might have been smiling. It was difficult to tell. 'Who do you think you're kidding? You know very well Mister Sam was a flunky.'

'Who?' Grave Digger demanded.

'Ask your boss, if you really want to know,' Michael X said. 'He knows.' And he couldn't be budged.

'A lot of people are laying it on the Black Muslims' anti-white campaign,' Coffin Ed said.

Michael X grinned. He had even white teeth. 'They're white, ain't they? Mister Big. The Syndicate. The newspapers. The employers. The landlords. The police – not you men, of course – but then you don't really count in the overall pattern. The government. All white. We're not anti-white, we just don't believe 'em, that's all. Do you?'

No one replied.

Michael X took off his already glistening spectacles. Without them he looked young and immature and very vulnerable: like a young man who could be easily hurt. He looked at them, barefaced and absurdly defiant: 'You see, most of us can't do anything that is expected of the American Negro: we can't dance, we can't sing, we can't play any musical instruments, we can't be pleasant and useful and helpful like other brothers because we don't know how – that's what whitey doesn't want to understand – that there are Negroes who are not adapted to making white people feel good. In fact,' he added laughing, 'there are some of us who can't even show our teeth – our teeth are too bad and we don't have the money to get them fixed. Besides, our breaths smell bad.'

They didn't want to argue with Michael X; they merely pushed him as to the identity of 'Mister Big'.

But each time he replied smilingly, 'Ask your boss, he knows.'

'You keep on talking like that you won't live long,' Grave Digger said.

Michael X put on his polished spectacles and looked at the detectives with a sharp-eyed sardonicism. 'You think someone is going to kill me?'

'People been killed for less,' Grave Digger said.

21

It was just the blind man didn't want anyone to know he was blind. He refused to use a cane or a Seeing Eye dog and if anyone tried to help him across a street more than likely they'd be rewarded with insults. Luckily, he remembered certain things from the time when he could see, and these remembrances were guides to his behavior. For the most part he tried to act like anyone else and that caused all the trouble.

He remembered how to shoot dice from the time that he could see well enough to lose his pay every Saturday night. He still went to crap games and still lost his bread. That hadn't changed.

Since he had become blind he had become a very stern-looking, silent man. He had skin the color and texture of brown wrapping-paper; reddish, unkempt, kinky hair that looked burnt; and staring, milky, unblinking blind eyes with red rims that looked cooked. His eyes had the menacing stare of a heat-blind snake which, along with his stern demeanor, could be very disconcerting.

However, he wasn't impressive physically. If he could have seen, anyone would have taken him on. He was tall and flabby and didn't look strong enough to squash a chinch. He wore a stained seersucker coat with a torn right sleeve over a soiled nylon sport shirt, along with baggy brown pants and scuffed and runover army shoes which had never been cleaned. He always looked hard up but he always managed to get hold of enough money to shoot dice. Old-timers said when he was winning he'd bet harder than lightning bumps a stump. But he was seldom winning.

He was up to the dice game at Fo-Fo's 'Sporting Gentlemen's Club' on the third floor of a walkup at the corner of 135th Street and Lenox Avenue. The dice game was in the room that had formerly been the kitchen of the cold-water flat Fo-Fo had converted into a private club for 'sporting gentlemen', and the original sink was still there for losers to wash their hands, although the gas stove had been removed to make room for the billiard table where the dice did their dance. It was hot enough in the room to fry brains and the unsmiling soul brothers stood packed about the table, grease running from their heads down into the sweat oozing from their black skin, watching the running of the dice from muddy, bloodshot, but alert eyes. There was nothing to smile about, it was a serious business. They were gambling their bread.

The blind man stood at the head of the table where Abie the Jew used to run his field, winning all the money in the game by betting the dice out, until a Black Muslim brother cut his throat because he wouldn't take a nickel bet. He tossed his last bread into the ring and said defiantly, 'I'll take four to one that I come out on 'leven.' Maybe Abie the Jew might have given it, but soul brothers are superstitious about their gambling and they figure a blind man might throw anything anytime.

But the back man covered the sawbuck and let the game go on. The stick man tossed the dice into the blind man's big soft trembling right hand, which closed about them like a shell about an egg.

The blind man shook them, saying, 'Dice, I beg you,' and turned them loose in the big corral. He heard them jump the chain and bounce off the billiard table's lower lip and the stick man cry, 'Five-four – *nine*! Nine's the point. Take 'em, Mister Shooter, and see what you can do.'

The blind man caught the dice again when they were tossed to him and looked around at the black sweaty faces he knew were there, pausing to stare a moment at each in turn and then said aggressively, 'Bet one to four I jump it like I made it.'

Abie the Jew might have taken that too, but the blind man knew there wasn't any chance of getting that bet from his soul brothers, he just felt like being contrary. Mother-rapers just waiting to get the jump on him, he thought, but if they fucked with him he'd cost them.

'Turn 'em loose, shooter,' the stick man barked. 'You done felt 'em long enough, they ain't titties.'

Scornfully, the blind man turned them loose. They rolled down the table and came up seven.

'Seven!' the stick man cried. 'Four-trey – the country way. Seven! The loser!'

'The dice don't know me,' the blind man said, then on second thought asked to see them. 'Here, lemme see them dice.'

With a 'what-can-you-do?' expression, the stick man tossed him the dice. The blind man caught them and felt them. 'Got too hot,' he pronounced.

'I tole you they weren't titties,' the stick man said and cried, 'Shooter for the game.'

The next shooter threw down and the stick man looked at the blind man. 'Sawbuck in the center,' he said. 'You want him, back man?'

The blind man was the back man but he was a broke man too. 'I leave him,' he said.

'One gone,' the stick man chanted. 'Saddest words on land or sea, Mister Shooter, pass by me. Next sport with money to lose.'

The blind man stopped at the sink to wash his hands and went out. On his way down the stairs he bumped into a couple of church sisters coming up the stairs and didn't even move to one side. He just went on without apologizing or uttering one word.

'Ain't got no manners at all!' the duck-bottom sister exclaimed indignantly.

'Why is our folks like that?' her lean black sister complained. 'Ain't a Christian bone in 'em.'

'He's lost his money in that crap game upstairs,' sister duck-bottom said. 'I knows.'

'Somebody oughta tell the police,' sister lean-and-black ventured spitefully. 'It's a crying shame.'

'Ain't it the truth? But they might send 'round some of them white mother-rapers – 'scuse me, Lawd, you's white too.'

The blind man heard that and muttered to himself as he

groped down the stairs, 'Damn right, He white; that's why you black bitches mind him.'

He was feeling so good with the thought he got careless and when he stepped out on to the sidewalk he ran head-on into another soul brother hurrying to a funeral.

'Watch where you going, mother-raper!' the brother snarled. 'You want all the sidewalk?'

The blind man stopped and turned his face. 'You want to make something of it, mother-raper?'

The brother took one look at the blind man's menacing eyes and hurried on. No need of him being no stand-in, he was only a guest, he thought.

When the blind man started walking again, a little burr-headed rebel clad in fewer rags than a bushman's child ran up to him and said breathlessly, 'Can I help you, suh?' He had bet his little buddies a Pepsi-Cola top he wasn't scared to speak to the blind man, and they were watching from the back door of the Liberian First Baptist Church, a safe distance away.

The blind man puffed up like a puff adder. 'Help me what?'

'Help you across the street, suh?' the little rebel piped bravely, standing his ground.

'You better get lost, you little black bastard, 'fore I whale the daylights out of you!' the blind man shouted. 'I can get across the street as good as anybody.'

To substantiate his contention the blind man cut across Lenox Avenue against the light, blind eyes staring straight ahead, his tall flabby frame moving nonchalantly like a turned-on zombie. Rubber burnt asphalt as brakes squealed. Metal crashed as cars telescoped. Drivers cursed. Soul people watching him could have bitten off nail-heads with their assholes. But hearing the commotion the blind man just thought the street was full of bad drivers.

He followed the railing about the kiosk down into the subway station and located the ticket booth by the sound of coins clinking. Pushing in that direction, he stepped on the pet corn of a dignified, elegant, gray-haired, light-complexioned soul sister and she let out a bellow. 'Oh! Oh! Oh! Mother-raping cocksucking turdeating bastard, are you blind?' Tears of rage and pain flooded from her eyes. The blind man moved on unconcernedly; he knew she wasn't talking to him, he hadn't done anything.

He shoved his quarter into the ticket window, took his token and nickel change and went through the turnstile out onto the platform following the sound of footsteps. But instead of getting someone to help him at that point he kept on walking straight ahead until he was teetering on the edge of the tracks. A matronly white woman, standing nearby, gasped and clutched him by the arm to pull him back to safety.

But he shook off her hand and flew into a rage. 'Take your hands off me, you mother-raping dip!' he shouted. 'I'm on to that pickpocket shit!'

Blood flooded the woman's face. She snatched back her hand and instinctively turned to flee. But after taking a few steps outrage overcame her and she stopped and spat, 'Nigger! Nigger! Nigger! Nigger!'

Some mother-raping white whore got herself straightened, he interpreted, listening to the train arrive. He went in with the others and groped about surreptitiously until he found an empty seat and quickly sat next to the aisle, holding his back ramrod straight and assuming a forbidding expression to keep anyone from sitting beside him. Exploring with his feet he ascertained that two people sat on the wall seat between him and the door, but they hadn't made a sound.

The first sound above the general movement of passengers which he was able to distinguish came from a soul brother sitting somewhere in front of him talking to himself in a loud, uninhibited tone of voice: 'Mop the floor, Sam. Cut the grass, Sam. Kiss my ass, Sam. Manure the roses, Sam. Do all the dirty work, Sam. *Shit!*'

The voice came from beyond the door and the blind man figured that the loudmouthed soul brother was sitting in the first cross seat facing toward the rear. He could hear the angry resentment in the soul brother's voice but he couldn't see the vindictiveness in his little red eyes or see the white passengers wince.

As though he'd made his eyes red on purpose, the soul

brother said jubilantly, 'That nigger's dangerous, he's got red eyes. Hey-hey! Red-eyed nigger!' He searched the white faces to see if any were looking at him. None were.

'What was that you said, Sam?' he asked himself in a sticky falsetto, mimicking someone, probably his white mistress.

'Mam?'

'You said a naughty word, Sam.'

'*Nigger*? Y'all says it all the time.'

'I don't mean that.'

'Weren't none other.'

'Don't you sass me, Sam. I heard you.'

'*Shit?* All I said was mo' shit mo' roses.'

'I *knew* I heard you say a naughty word.'

'Yass, mam, if y'all weren't lissenin' y'all wouldn't a' heerd.'

'We have to listen to know what you people are thinking.'

'Haw-haw-haw! Now ain't that some sure enough shit?' Sam asked himself in his natural voice. 'Lissenin', spyin', sniffin' around. Say they cain't stand niggers and lean on yo' back to watch you work. Rubbin' up against you. Gettin' in yo' face. Jes so long as you workin' like a nigger. Ain't that somep'n?'

He stared furiously at the two middle-aged white passengers on the wall seat on his side of the door, trying to catch them peeking. But they were looking steadily down into their laps. His red eyes contracted then expanded, theatrically.

This red-eyed soul brother was fat and black and had red lips, too, that looked freshly skinned, against a background of blue gums and a round puffy face dripping with sweat. His bulging-bellied torso was squeezed into a red print sport shirt, open at the collar and wet in the armpits, exposing huge muscular biceps wrapped in glistening black skin. But his legs were so skinny they made him look deformed. They were encased in black pants, as tight as sausage skins, which cut into his crotch, chafing him mercilessly and smothering what looked like a pig in a sack between his legs. To add to his discomfort, the jolting of the coach gave him an excruciating nut-ache.

He looked as uncomfortable as a man can be who can't decide whether to be mad at the mother-raping heat, his mother-raping pants, his cheating old lady or his mother-raping picky white folks.

A huge, lumpy-faced white man across the aisle, who looked as though he might have driven a twenty-ton truck since he was born, turned and looked at the fat brother with a sneer of disgust. Fat Sam caught the look and drew back as if the man had slapped him. Looking quickly about for another brother to appease the white man's rage, he noticed the blind man in the first seat facing him beyond the door. The blind man was sitting there tending to his own business, staring at Fat Sam without seeing him, and frowning as hard as going up a hill at his bad luck. But Fat Sam bitterly resented being stared at, like all soul brothers, and this mother-raper was staring at him in a way that made his blood boil.

'What you staring at, mother-raper?' he shouted belligerently.

The blind man had no way of knowing Fat Sam was talking to him, all he knew was the loudmouthed mother-raper who'd come in talking to his mother-raping self was now trying to pick a fight with some other mother-raper who was just looking at him. But he could understand why the mother-raper was so mad, he'd caught some mother-raping whitey with his old lady. The mother-raper ought to be more careful, he thought unsympathetically, if she were that kind of whore he ought to watch her more; leastways he ought to keep his business to himself. Involuntarily, he made a downward motion, like a cat buzzing to the object Jeff, 'Don't rank it, man, don't rank it!'

The gesture hit Fat Sam like a bolt of white lightning and a ray of white heat, and he jumped on it with his two black feet, as they say in that part of the world. Mother-raper wavin' him down like he was a mother-rapin' dog, he thought. Here in front of all these sneakin' white mother-rapers. He was more incensed by the white passengers' furtive smiles than by the blind man's gesture, although he hadn't discovered yet the old man was blind. White mother-rapers kickin' him in the ass from every which-a-side anyhow, he thought furiously, and here his own mother-rapin' soul brother just as much to say, keep yo' ass still, boy, so these white folks can kick it better.

'You doan like how I talk, you ol' mother-raper, you can kiss my black ass!' he shouted at the blind man. 'I know you shit-colored Uncle Tom mother-rapers like you! You think I'm a disgrace to the race.'

The first the blind man knew the soul brother was talking to him was when he heard some soul sister say protestingly, 'That ain't no way to talk to that old man. You oughta be 'shamed of yo'self, he weren't bothering you.'

He didn't resent what the soul brother had said as much as the meddling-ass sister calling him an 'old man', otherwise he wouldn't have replied.

'I don't give a mother-rape whether you're a disgrace to the race or not!' he shouted, and because he couldn't think of anything else to say, added: 'All I want is my bread.'

The big white man looked at Fat Sam accusingly, like he'd been caught stealing from a blind man.

Fat Sam caught the look, and it made him madder at the blind man. 'Bread!' he shouted. 'What mother-raping bread?'

The white passengers looked around guiltily to see what had happened to the old man's bread.

But the blind man's next words relieved them. 'What you and those mother-rapers cheated me out of,' he accused.

'Me?' Fat Sam exclaimed innocently. 'Me cheated you outer yo' bread? I ain't even seen you before, mother-raper!'

'If you ain't seen me, mother-raper, how come you talking to me?'

'Talkin' to you? I ain't talkin' to you, mother-raper. I just ast you who you starin' at, and you go tryna make these white folks think I's cheated you.'

'White folks?' the blind man cried. He couldn't have sounded more alarmed if Fat Sam had said the coach was full of snakes. 'Where? Where?'

'Here, mother-raper!' Fat Sam crowed triumphantly. 'All 'round you. Everywhere!'

The other soul people on the coach looked away before someone thought they knew those brothers, but the white passengers stole furtive peeks.

The big white man thought they were talking about him

in a secret language known only to soul people. He reddened with rage.

It was then the sleek, fat, yellow preacher in the black mohair suit and immaculate dog collar, sitting beside the big white man, sensed the rising racial tension. Cautiously he lowered the open pages of the *New York Times*, behind which he had been hiding, and peered over the top at his argumentative brothers.

'Brothers! Brothers!' he admonished. 'You can settle your differences without resorting to violence.'

'Violence hell!' the big white man exclaimed. 'What these niggers need is discipline.'

'Beware, mother-raper! Beware!' the blind man warned. Whether he was warning the fat black man or the big white man, no one ever knew. But his voice sounded so dangerous the fat yellow preacher ducked back out of sight behind his newspaper.

But Fat Sam thought it was himself the old man threatened. He jumped to his feet. 'You talkin' to me, mother-raper?'

The big white man jumped up an instant later and pushed him back down.

Hearing all the movement, the blind man stood up too; he wasn't going to get caught sitting down.

The big white man saw him and shouted, 'And you sit down, too!'

The blind man didn't pay him any attention, not knowing the white man meant him.

The white man charged down the aisle and pushed him down. The blind man looked startled. But all might have ended peacefully if the big white man hadn't slapped him.

The blind man knew it was the white man who had pushed him down, but he thought it was the soul brother who had slapped him, taking advantage of the white man's rage.

It figured. He said protestingly, 'What you hit me for, mother-raper?'

'If you don't shut up and behave yourself, I'll hit you again,' the white man threatened.

The blind man knew then it was the white man who had slapped him. He stood up again, slowly and dangerously, groping for the back of the seat to brace himself. 'If'n you hit me again, white folks, I'll blow you away,' he said.

The big white man was taken aback, because he had known all along the old man was blind. 'You threatening me, boy?' he said in astonishment.

Fat Sam stood up in front of the door as though whatever happened he was going to be the first one out.

Still playing peacemaker, the fat yellow preacher said from behind his newspaper, 'Peace, man, God don't know no color.'

'Yeah?' the blind man questioned and pulled out a big .45-caliber revolver from underneath his old seersucker coat and shot at the big white man point-blank.

The blast shattered windows, eardrums, reason and reflexes. The big white man shrunk instantly to the size of a dwarf and his breath swooshed from his collapsed lungs.

Fat Sam's wet black skin dried instantly and turned white.

But the .45-caliber bullet, as sightless as its shooter, had gone the way the pistol had been aimed, through the pages of the *New York Times* and into the heart of the fat yellow preacher. 'Uh!' his reverence grunted and turned in his Bible.

The moment of silence was appropriate but unintentional. It was just that all the passengers had died for a moment following the impact of the blast.

Reflexes returned with the stink of burnt cordite which peppered nostrils, watered eyes.

A soul sister leaped to her feet and screamed, 'BLIND MAN WITH A PISTOL!' as only a soul sister, with four hundred years of experience, can. Her mouth formed an ellipsoid big enough to swallow the blind man's pistol, exposing the brown tartar stains on her molars and a white-coated tongue flattened between her bottom teeth and humped in the back against the tip of her palate which vibrated like a blood-red tuning-fork.

'BLIND MAN WITH A PISTOL! BLIND MAN WITH A PISTOL!'

It was her screaming which broke everyone's control. Panic went off like Chinese firecrackers.

The big white man leaped ahead from reflex action and collided violently with the blind man, damn near knocking the pistol from his hand. He did a double-take and jumped back, bumping his spine against a tubular iron upright. Thinking he was being attacked from behind by the other soul brother, he leaped ahead again. If die he must, he'd rather it came from the front than behind.

Assaulted the second time by a huge smelly body, the blind man thought he was surrounded by a lynch mob. But he'd take some of the mother-rapers with him, he resolved, and shot twice indiscriminately.

The second blasts were too much. Everyone reacted immediately. Some thought the world was coming to an end; others that the Venusians were coming. A number of the white passengers thought the niggers were taking over; the majority of the soul people thought their time was up.

But Fat Sam was a realist. He ran straight through the glass door. Luckily the train had pulled into the 125th Street station and was grinding to a stop. Because one moment he was inside the coach and the next he was outside on the platform, on his hands and knees, covered with blood, his clothes ripped to ribbons, shards of glass sticking from the sweaty blood covering his wet black skin like the surrealistic top of a Frenchman's wall.

Others trying to follow him got caught in the jagged edges of glass and were slashed unmercifully when the doors were opened. Suddenly the pandemonium had moved to the platform. Bodies crashed in headlong collision, went sprawling on the concrete. Legs kicked futilely in the air. Everyone tried to escape to the street. Screams fanned the panic. The stairs became strewn with the bodies of the fallen. Others fell too as they tried senselessly to run over them.

The soul sister continued to scream, 'BLIND MAN WITH A PISTOL!'

The blind man groped about in the dark, panic-stricken, stumbling over the fallen bodies, waving his pistol as though it had eyes. 'Where?' he cried piteously. 'Where?'

22

The people of Harlem were as mad as only the people of Harlem can be. The New York City government had ordered the demolition of condemned slum buildings in the block on the north side of 125th Street between Lenox and Seventh Avenues, and the residents didn't have any place to go. Residents from other sections of Harlem were mad because these displaced people would be dumped on them, and their neighborhoods would become slums. It was a commercial block too, and the proprietors of small businesses on the ground floors of the condemned buildings were mad because rent in the new buildings would be prohibitive.

The same applied to the residents, but most hadn't thought that far as yet. Now they were absorbed by the urgency of having to find immediate housing, and they bitterly resented being evicted from the homes where some had been born, and their children had been born, and some had married and friends and relatives had died, no matter if these homes were slum flats that had been condemned as unfit for human dwelling. They had been forced to live there, in all the filth and degradation, until their lives had been warped to fit, and now they were being thrown out. It was enough to make a body riot.

One angry sister, who stood watching from the opposite sidewalk, protested loudly, 'They calls this *Urban Renewal*, I calls it poor folks removal.'

'Why don't she shut up, she cain't do nuthin'?' a young black teeny-bopper said scornfully.

Her black teeny-bopper companion giggled. 'She look like a rolled up mattress.'

'You shut up, too. You'll look like that yo'self w'en you get her age.'

Two young sports who'd just come from the YMCA gym glanced at the display of books in the window of the National African Memorial Bookstore next to the credit jewelers on the corner.

'They gonna tear down the black bookstore, too,' one remarked. 'They don't want us to have nothing.'

'What I care?' the other replied. 'I don't read.'

Shocked and incredulous, his friend stopped to look at him. 'Man, I wouldn't admit it. You ought to learn how to read.'

'You don't dig me, man. I didn't say I can't read, I said I don't read. What I want to read all this mother-raping shit whitey is putting down for?'

'Umh!' his friend conceded and continued walking.

However, most of the soul people stood about apathetically, watching the wrecking balls swing against the old crumbling walls. It was a hot day and they sweated copiously as they breathed the poisonous air clogged with gasoline fumes and white plaster dust.

Farther eastward, at the other end of the condemned block, where Lenox Avenue crosses 125th Street, Grave Digger and Coffin Ed stood in the street, shooting the big gray rats that ran from the condemned buildings with their big long-barreled, nickel-plated .38-caliber pistols on .44-caliber frames. Every time the steel demolition ball crashed against a rotten wall, one or more rats ran into the street indignantly, looking more resentful than the evicted people.

Not only rats but startled droves of bedbugs stampeded over the ruins and fat black cockroaches committed suicide by jumping from high windows.

They had an audience of rough-looking jokers from the corner bar who delighted in hearing the big pistols go off.

One rugged stud warned jokingly, 'Don't shoot no cats by mistake.'

'Cats are too small,' Coffin Ed replied. 'These rats look more like wolves.'

'I mean two-legged cats.'

At that moment a big rat came out from underneath a falling wall, and pawed the sidewalk, snorting.

'Hey! Hey! Rat!' Coffin Ed called like a toreador trying to get the attention of his bull.

The soul brothers watched in silence.

Suddenly the rat looked up through murderous red eyes and Coffin Ed shot it through the center of its forehead. The big brass-jacketed .38 bullet knocked the rat's body out of its fur.

'Olé!' the soul brothers cried.

The four uniformed white cops on the other corner eastward stopped talking and looked around anxiously. They had left their police cars parked on each side of 125th Street, beyond the demolition area, as though to keep any of the dispossessed from crossing the Triborough Bridge into the restricted neighborhoods of Long Island.

'He just shot another rat,' one said.

'Too bad it weren't a nigger rat,' the second cop said.

'We'll leave that for you,' the first cop replied.

'Damn right,' the second cop declared. 'I ain't scared.'

'As big as those rats are those niggers could cook 'em and eat 'em,' the third cop remarked cynically.

'And get off relief,' the second cop put in.

Three of them laughed.

'Maybe those rats been cooking and eating those niggers is why they're so big,' the third cop continued.

'You men are not funny,' the fourth cop protested.

'Then why'd you sneak that laugh?' the second cop observed.

'I was retching is all.'

'That's all you hypocrites do – retch,' the second cop came back.

The third cop caught a movement out of the corner of his eye and jerked his head about. He saw a fat, black man shoot up from the subway, leaking blood, sweat and tears, bringing pandemonium with him. The other bleeding people who erupted behind him looked crazed with terror, as though they had escaped from the bad man.

But it was the sight of the bleeding, running black man which galvanized the white cops into action. A bleeding, running, black man spelled trouble, and they had the whole white race to protect. They went off running in four directions with drawn revolvers and squinting eyes.

Grave Digger and Coffin Ed watched them in amazement.

'What happened?' Coffin Ed asked.

'Just that fat blacky showing all that blood,' Grave Digger said.

'Hell, if it was serious he'd have never got this far,' Coffin Ed passed it off.

'You don't get it, Ed,' Grave Digger explained. 'Those white officers have got to protect white womanhood.'

Seeing a white uniformed cop skid to a stop and turn to head him off, the fat black man broke in the direction of the Negro detectives. He didn't know them but they had pistols and that was enough.

'He's getting away!' the first cop called from behind.

'I'll cool the nigger!' the front cop said. He was the third cop who thought niggers ate rats.

At that moment the big white man who had started all the fracas came up the stairs, heaving and gasping as though he'd just made it. 'That ain't the nigger!' he yelled.

The third cop skidded to a halt, looking suddenly bewildered.

Then the blind man stumbled up the stairs, tapping the railing with his pistol.

The big white man leaped aside in blind terror. 'There's the nigger with the pistol,' he screamed, pointing at the blind man coming up the subway stairs like 'shadow' coming out of East River.

At the sound of his voice the blind man froze. 'You still alive, mother-raper?' He sounded shocked.

'Shoot him quick!' the big white man warned the alert white cops.

As though the warning had been for him, the blind man upped with his pistol and shot at the big white man the second time. The big white man leaped straight up in the air as though a firecracker had exploded in his ass-hole.

But the bullet had hit the white cop in the middle of the forehead, as he was taking aim, and he fell down dead.

The soul brothers who had been watching the antics of the white cops, petrified with awe, picked up their feet and split.

When the three other uniformed white cops converged on the blind man he was still pulling the trigger of the empty double-action pistol. Quickly they cut him down.

The soul brothers who had got as far as doorways and corners, paused for a moment to see the results.

'Great Godamighty!' one of them exclaimed. 'The mother-raping white cops has shot down that innocent brother!'

He had a loud, carrying voice, as soul brothers are apt to have, and a number of other soul people who hadn't seen it, heard him. They believed him.

Like wildfire the rumor spread.

'DEAD MAN! DEAD MAN! . . .'

'WHITEY HAS MURDERED A SOUL BROTHER!'

'THE MOTHER-RAPING WHITE COPS, THAT'S WHO!'

'GET THEM MOTHER-RAPERS, MAN!'

'JUST LEAVE ME GET MY MOTHER-RAPING GUN!'

An hour later Lieutenant Anderson had Grave Digger on the radio-phone. 'Can't you men stop that riot?' he demanded.

'It's out of hand, boss,' Grave Digger said.

'All right, I'll call for reinforcements. What started it?'

'A blind man with a pistol.'

'What's that?'

'You heard me, boss.'

'That don't make any sense.'

'Sure don't.'

Plan B

Introduction

There is a particular purgatory of esteem reserved for those American artists who have been lionized in Europe while enduring neglect at home . . . For both the voluntary exiles and for those who labored in obscurity at home, the final irony of their relative success abroad was that it seemed to delay their recognition in the United States even further.

Thus writes Luc Sante, in 'An American Abroad' (*New York Review of Books*, January 16, 1992, 8–12), an article that seems to signal Chester Himes's own emergence from this purgatory, at a time when most of his books have finally been reprinted in English-language editions.

Indeed, the story of Himes's literary career overflows with irony. After his complex, realistic novels of race relations met with only moderate success in the United States, he moved to France, where he lived in comparative poverty, if not in obscurity. That is, until Marcel Duhamel, the editor of Editions Gallimard's *Série Noire* detective paperbacks, persuaded him to try his hand at a crime novel set in Harlem. The result, *For Love of Imabelle*, was hailed as a masterpiece by such literary giants as Jean Cocteau and Jean Giono. It achieved the distinction of being awarded the *Grand Prix de la littérature policière* for 1958 – the first time the prestigious prize was awarded to a non-French author.

Chester Himes went on to produce no less than eight other *Série Noire* thrillers in the decade that followed and enjoyed the pleasure (and perhaps the irony, too) of seeing the final entry in the series, *Blind Man with a Pistol*, published in Gallimard's *Série Blanche*. In France, of course, these series titles have nothing at all to do with race. 'Roman noir' means 'detective novel' in French, a fact that accounted for the black covers of that particular series. The white covers that Gallimard used for its prestigious *Du monde entier* series were reserved for *belles-lettres* from all over the world.

Most of Himes's thrillers, which he preferred to call 'domestic' rather than detective novels, were set exclusively in Harlem, with the action shifting from back alley junkyard to Sugar Hill high-rise, from barroom to poolroom, and from church to brothel. They were soon hailed as a 'Harlem human comedy' by French reviewers who compared them favorably to Balzac's *comédie humaine*.

All but one featured Coffin Ed Johnson and Grave Digger Jones, a pair of tough, uncompromising black police detectives. Unlike many such characters, Coffin Ed and Grave Digger were complex personalities who daily faced the paradox of serving the white man's law while attempting to provide a modicum of justice for a race that the law continually excluded or victimized. Their dialog often reflects the bitter irony of their lot and Himes continually uses their voices to denounce racial injustice and the American system that makes it possible.

As the series proceeded, Himes's imagination moved from suckers cheated by 'stings', 'blow jobs', and con games to multi-million-dollar drug traffic; from run-of-the-mill street crime to random psychopathic violence; from the everyday socio-economic woes of the black man in the street to the larger social and political issues that affected, and divided, a nation. *Run Man Run* (first published in French in 1959) features a murderous white police detective as its villain. *The Heat's On* (1961) makes grim sport of the heroin trade. *Cotton Comes to Harlem* (1964) includes a sometimes-comical recasting of Marcus Garvey's Back to Africa movement.

As time went on, Himes's vision broadened to include his disgust for religious leaders who enriched themselves through charlatanry. His increasingly apocalyptic view of racial confrontation artfully illustrated the way the 'We Shall Overcome' chants of peaceful civil rights advocates gave way to the Black Power slogans and Black Muslim disquisitions in the years that followed the 'burning summers' of 1964–1965.

By 1967, Himes seemed to have forgotten his earlier misgivings about involving himself in what he had once considered an illegitimate literary genre. His critical and commercial success in Europe so thoroughly convinced him of the value of this new phase of his career that he came increasingly to believe that the Harlem Domestic Series might well be his greatest and most enduring contribution to world literature.

By then, he was living well, if not luxuriously. He could even, at long last, contemplate the purchase of a house, although he was disappointed that he still could not afford to live in his favorite area, the French Riviera. After months of fruitless searching for a place in Spain, a place where he believed he would like to live, Himes seemed genuinely pleased when he finally wrote to Roslyn Targ, his literary agent, on December 17, 1968, that he had bought a couple of lots in a development called Pla del Mar, down on the tip of the coast jutting out of picturesque Cabo de la Nao, near the town of Javea in the province of Alicante. 'We hope to build our little Spanish house,' he added.

That same month, Himes and his wife, Lesley, took up temporary residence in an old palace on Duque de Zaragoza Street in the city of Alicante. Here, Himes was able to write again. A list of unpublished works compiled by his agent around that time included 'Hurt White Women', a 446-page narrative that was an early stage of his first volume of autobiography; 'The Lunatic Fringe', an all-white murder mystery set in Mallorca that he had been unable to complete for years; and 'Blow, Gabriel, Blow', a short movie script about religious con games in Harlem that he had tried vainly to sell.

He wrote to John A. Williams around that same time that 'I have now commenced on the wildest and most defiant of my Harlem series, which will wind it up and kill one of my two detectives.' The novel may have originated in a short story called 'Tang', that was reportedly completed in 1967. Shortly thereafter, he decided to call the new book 'Plan B'.

Himes began writing it in Alicante while he was designing the plans for his new house. Four months later, he described the book as 'the most violent story I have ever attempted, about an *organized* black rebellion which is extremely bloody and violent, as any such rebellion must be.' As was usual for him when he was writing, he forged ahead with the narrative without making much of a draft and without having much of an outline, with the possible exception of a synopsis of the book's concluding chapters.

Not too much later, he noted that he had lost his sense of where the book was going. 'Anyway, I'm not near finished with it – and then on the other hand it might never be published' (letter to John A. Williams, April 15, 1969). He did, however, complete at least enough of the novel to derive from it a long short story that he called 'The Birth of Chitterlings, Inc.' The story was to have been part of a never-published collection of short stories that was to have been entitled *Black on White.* He wrote in the foreword to the collection that he had written the story while 'contemplating how blacks could get guns into the US to stage a revolution'. Meanwhile, what were apparently two other sections of 'Plan B', a short story called 'Tang' and another called 'Celebration' saw publication in *Black on Black*, a collection of stories and essays that was issued in 1972.

Plan B may well have been supplanted in favor of *Blind Man with a Pistol*, a subsequent novel that tackled the same social and political issues. From the end of August 1969 until near the end of a very rainy November when he returned to Paris suffering from hypertension, Chester Himes stayed in Holland with Lesley. He wanted to visit his Dutch agent and spend the summer there after their Paris sublet expired. In a luxurious house in Blaricum, he and Lesley enjoyed for a time a hitherto unknown degree of comfort.

It was during this stay that they were visited by a younger black expatriate writer named Phil Lomax. One day, Lomax called Chester on 'urgent business' and was told to come right away. What Lomax wanted was to plead forgiveness because he had plagiarized a section of *Pinktoes* into a barely disguised rewrite that he had sold in the Netherlands. Chester was magnanimous. Not only did he forgive Lomax, but he invited him to stay for lunch, during which he spoke freely and at some length to the young writer. As they swapped stories, Lomax related an anecdote about a blind man with a gun who began shooting at random in the New York subway. Exactly why he had done so was not clear. Maybe he'd wanted to pretend to himself that he could see, or perhaps he just wanted to feel that he existed for others.

This story found its way into the new thriller Himes was busily working on. He had already completed many sundry episodes, yet without finding the thread between them. At that stage, he decided that absurdity itself should become the unifying theme. He even took the phrase 'the blind man with a pistol' as the title for his book, and graciously credited Lomax in a foreword to the published novel. In unpublished notes for his autobiography Himes explained:

> By accident I wrote two words: 'the dying man gasped: "Jesus Baby",' and never finished the sentence, but the dying man had intended to say: 'Jesus, Baby, you did not have to kill me.' In Holland, I wrote the end of the sentence: 'You didn't have to kill me,' then took it out because I found another ending: the Blind Man with his pistol. It made a perfect ending for the story because I had launched on to a different kind of story where I could accuse everyone of inhumanity.
>
> Phil Lomax told me a story of the Blind Man with his pistol which was my story of all people: confusion, misunderstanding, confrontation with death at the hands of legality.

Himes added, significantly:

> That was the story of all black people, but I never wrote it. I lost myself in trying to write a successful story about black people: *Plan B.*

If we are to believe Himes, he was still thinking about completing *Plan B* after bringing *Blind Man with a Pistol* to a successful conclusion.

At any rate, in September 1970 Himes sent his agent a new short story called 'Pork Chop Paradise' which corresponds to

'The Birth of Chitterlings, Inc.', and clearly is a section of the uncompleted novel. In October 1972, he trimmed a story corresponding to an early section in the same novel, deleting its first four sections, and called it 'Prediction'. This story made its way into the collection, *Black on Black.* He felt confident that this fifth section was enough to make his point without straining credulity (Letter to E. Varkala, October 23, 1972).

The rest of the manuscript remained in a drawer in his little office in Villa Griot, where his failing health allowed him to repair only infrequently now. It lay there until February of 1982, when the Paris-based Editions Lieu Commun asked Michel Fabre to try and secure for them some unpublished material from Himes. A number of his short stories were still unpublished, even in English, because his 'Black on White' collection had never appeared in the United States. There were also many stories that had originally appeared in American magazines during the 1930s and 1940s that remained uncollected. From this wealth of material, a volume of short stories in French, entitled *Le Manteau de rêve*, was published in 1982. Always eager to read Himes after the success of his early protest fiction and his later detective novels, French critics and readers alike enthusiastically welcomed the new collection.

At that stage, Michel Fabre discovered the typescript of *Plan B*, a few pages of which Himes had recently torn up and thrown away in a fit of rage. His deteriorating health had handicapped him to such an extent that he could no longer write at all. Along with the typescript, Fabre discovered a synopsis of the final section. Seeing that it was written out in an expanded draft form with elaborate dialogs, Fabre realized that it could serve as a proper conclusion. He therefore worked on establishing a version of the novel, a task that required the excision of a few repetitious episodes and a strict adherence to the corrected version. This work served as the basis for the French translation, published in 1983 by Lieu Commun. To provide the present version, Robert Skinner has carefully edited this text, a process that involved the incorporation of more recently-discovered typed and hand-written revisions that Himes had added to his original draft. In this process, he made every effort to ultimately produce a manuscript that reflected a genuine respect for the author's socio-political intentions and stylistic concerns.

In 1983, Chester Himes painstakingly signed his last piece. In September he had received a circular letter from the *International Herald Tribune*, asking him to renew his long-expired subscription. With Lesley's help, he composed a letter which showed that he still retained his devastating sense of humor. It read in part:

> I do not disagree that the *Herald Tribune* is 'the only American international daily'. What I am annoyed about is the fact that they NEVER, NEVER mentioned my books [during] my years of writing in Europe, even when my last book, *Un Manteau de rêve* (sic), received enthusiastic reviews from most important French newspapers and literary magazines . . . I am an American, black and very proud to be both. You have ignored me completely and this is why I borrow my neighbors' papers, FREE, when I feel the need to read your newspaper. Indeed, why pay? . . . Will you 'welcome me into your daily life'? I'm not dead yet and I will have another book out in France in a week or so. It is called *Plan B* . . . It is an unfinished detective story.

Proud and comforted as he now was by the certainty of the book's publication, Himes did not live to see *Plan B* brought out by Editions Lieu Commun and to see it even more widely and enthusiastically welcomed by French critics and readers than was *Le Manteau de rêve.*

Before trying to analyse the contents and tone of the novel, it may be worthwhile to consider some of the reviews that hailed the French publication of this novel, in order to show not only how seriously it was taken, but also to place Himes's literary reputation in its proper international context.

One French critic, who asserted that Himes would go down in history as the greatest black writer of the century, considered *Plan B* a delirious legacy that explored the implacable hatred existing between black and white. The unnamed critic felt that Himes had benefited greatly from his move into detective fiction because he used the form to skillfully explore deeper concerns. Other reviews insisted that the book was a great pleasure to read, even though Himes's detectives died in an effort to solve an insoluble political issue. It was 'vintage Himes, indeed'. Many observed that, although Himes had left the book incomplete, the reader need have no reservations about reading it. Admittedly it was a strange book, unbalanced because it started out in the purest *Série Noire* style then ended as a political tract about the American racial problem, but this did not diminish the passion of Himes's prose.

Jean-Pierre Bonicco regarded Himes's description of the ghetto as hyperrealistic and flamboyant, causing his thriller to turn into a novel of manners. The 'great American writer of immense talents' was a 'literary alchemist' who could transform his bleak story into a kind of literary gold. The reviewer mourned the fact that the deaths of Coffin Ed and Grave Digger spelled the end to the Harlem saga, but he regarded the novel as Himes's bloody farewell to literature and to his legacy of despair ('Le Forum des livres: *Plan B*, par Chester Himes.' *Var Matin*, December 18, 1983).

Maurice Decroix characterized *Plan B* as 'a picaresque, many-hued novel that Himes wrote in the heyday of the Black Panthers and Black Muslims.' He advised readers to rush out to get this book, even if only to read Himes's descriptions of Eighth Avenue in Harlem in the August heat ('Au rayon du polar.' *Nord Eclair* October 27, 1983). Writing for the Paris illustrated weekly *VSD*, Jean-Pierre Enard considered 'the ultimate novel by one of America's greatest authors', as 'strong as a glass of gin, rhythmical as a Charlie Parker solo' ('Livres: *Plan B*, de Chester Himes.' *VSD* November 24, 1983, 21).

The well-known *Le Monde* critic and Himes's regular reviewer, Bernard Géniès, made much of the fact that Himes went on a wholesale killing spree that envelops even his two detectives. Géniès believed that the story, set against a backdrop reminiscent of the ghetto revolts of the 1960s, must be read in that perspective to be fully appreciated. Had Himes wanted to end his series and take revenge upon his cast of characters, he wondered? His many references to slavery were seen by Géniès as evidence of a 'more realistic vision' ('Quand Chester Himes assassine ses héros.' *Le Monde*, October 12, 1983, xii).

In a later piece, 'Retour à Chester Himes', Géniès apparently had second thoughts. He regretted that Himes never managed to dig beneath the surface of his poverty-stricken Harlem backdrop in order to become a second Richard Wright. He insisted, though, that Himes's meeting with *Série Noire* editor Marcel Duhamel had enabled him to attain his own identity as a writer (*Le Monde*, November 4, 1983, xiii).

Speaking of Himes's 'splendid failure', Stéphane Jousni noted that, at his best, Himes had kept his two black detectives aloof from the race issue. In *Plan B*, a novel transformed into a political and racial tract, the pair took sides in the conflict and were killed. She believed that the book should be read for its memorable, surrealistic descriptions of Harlem life. For Jousni, as for Jean Giono, Himes was a writer superior to Hemingway, Dos Passos, and Fitzgerald ('Un admirable "raté" de Chester Himes.' *La Libre Belgique*, October 13, 1983).

The *Le Matin* critic used the French title of an earlier Himes thriller to characterize *Plan B* as an 'Imbroglio negro'. He stressed that the career of protagonist Tomsson Black ran parallel to an apocalyptic increase in violence and an ensuing moral dilemma. 'It would not be fitting,' he wrote, 'to call such gutsy writing baroque.' For him, the novel stood as 'both a testament to Himes's talent and the apotheosis of his career' (*Le Matin*, October 27, 1983, 26).

In the left-wing *La Marseillaise*, Françoise Poignant noted that after a humorous opening, Himes's angriest, blackest novel becomes a nightmare that deteriorates into a blood-bath. She wondered if Himes had been unable to find a proper conclusion to this impasse or if he had become so ill that he could no longer write ('*Plan B*: un livre plein de dureur et de bruit.' November 27, 1983, 6).

Frédéric Vitoux's review, 'Au bout de la nuit: *Plan B* par Chester Himes', at once established a link with Louis-Ferdinand Céline's classic narrative of marginality, *Voyage au bout de la nuit.* Vitoux called *Plan B* a book 'as black as ink, as blood, as stupidity, as memory, as hatred, as slavery, as America in 1969 . . . Himes takes the reader to hell with an almost suicidal relish, then dazzles us with his descriptions of crime, injustice, and rebellion in Harlem.' Vitoux felt that the book was bound to remain unfinished because no logical conclusion could really be derived from such large-scale racial strife. He noted wryly that trips to the end of the world have no real conclusion (*Nouvel Observateur*, November 11, 1983).

Christiane Falgayrettes chose to set the book against a wider background. She stated that Himes preferred scorn and humor to the violence and open hatred evidenced in Wright's and Baldwin's works. She also compared Himes favorably with Ellison, concluding that Himes preferred to act upon the guilty conscience of his white readership (*La Montagne*, July 29, 1984, 6).

Cameroonian academic Ambroise Kom, himself the author of a detailed study of Himes's novels, found that *Plan B* combined the absurdity of *For Love of Imabelle*, the grim overtones of *Blind Man with a Pistol*, and the succulent flavor of *Pinktoes.* Kom expressed the view that the book left unanswered many questions about Himes's own vision of the United States ('Chester Himes *Plan B.*' *Notre Librairie*, No. 77, November–December 1984, 125–126).

A few reactions were intensely political. In *Révolution*, Michael Naudy, undoubtedly thinking of Marx and Engels, claimed that Himes was the legitimate heir to the nineteenth-century revolutionary theoreticians of Central Europe. He said that Himes created such a vast human comedy that he should rightfully be called 'a dark Balzac' ('Le fils légitime.' *Révolution*, November 28, 1984, 39).

In another left-wing publication, *Liberté*, Françoise Poignant also dealt with a new reprint of *The Big Gold Dream* in her review of *Plan B.* She wondered if there was any solution to America's race problem and suggested that Himes's way of coping with it was to write in a picaresque style that resorted to caricature and surrealism. *The Big Gold Dream*, she said, was a successful story filled with non-stop humor. *Plan B*, on the other hand, was a nightmarish description of race hatred that offered overwhelming fury and desperation but proposed no solution ('Harlem au bout de la nuit.' *Liberté*, December 4, 1984).

When Chester Himes died in mid-November of 1984, the entire French press paid him tribute. Obituaries surveyed his career as a convict, writer, and expatriate. They invariably stressed the importance of his detective fiction and of his lively picture of Harlem. Laudatory comments about Himes's talent by younger French detective writers such as Michel Lebrun, Pierre Siniac, and Patrick Manchette were often quoted. Since *Plan B* was just out, many obituaries mentioned it at length.

The critic for the left-wing daily, *La Marseillaise*, noted that Himes had brought nobility to detective fiction by using it to protest America's racist society. *Blind Man with a Pistol* was praised as a 'splendid metaphor' and *Plan B* was described as 'an apocalyptic struggle'. The writer concluded that Himes's tough, authentic novels, all of which were firmly anchored in reality, would leave a lasting imprint on American literature (November 14, 1984).

While readers can't fail to experience revulsion at some aspects of the book, they should be favorably struck by the structure and style. It soon becomes clear that the nonlinear construction with its wildly alternating, and apparently unrelated plots, recalls Faulkner's work in *The Wild Palms.* As is true in Faulkner's work, the twin story lines actually intensify the suspense.

It is interesting to realize that a book that made such an impact on European audiences has yet to be seen by American readers. For years, scholars and fans of Chester Himes's Harlem Domestic Series, piqued by Himes's own remarks, have discussed the possible existence of a 'lost' entry in the series, one that included the tragic deaths of one or both of Himes's two heroes, Coffin Ed Johnson and Grave Digger Jones. The rumors even inspired a novel by African writer Njami Simon, published as *Cercueil et Cie* (Paris: Editions Lieu Commun, 1985) in France and later in the United States as *Coffin and Company* (Berkeley, California: Black Lizard Books, 1987).

During the time he was writing *Plan B*, Himes alluded to his work on it in several interviews, most notably the one conducted by John A. Williams that was published in *Amistad 1* (New York: Random House, 1970). Himes invariably discussed the plot to this book in context with his deep discouragement with the lack of improvement in race relations in the United States.

Over a long period of years he had come to believe that the only way blacks could truly achieve equality in America was through some kind of violent revolutionary behavior. Writing in 1944, Himes suggested that progress can only be brought about by revolution, that revolutions can only be started by incidents, and that incidents can only be created by martyrs. Although his process seems to be a forerunner of Dr Martin Luther King's method of non-violent change, Himes saw things in the opposite light. He stated that Negro martyrs were needed to 'create the incident which will mobilize the forces of justice and carry us forward from the pivot of change to a way of existence wherein everyone is free.' ('Negro Martyrs Are Needed.' *The Crisis*, 51, May 1944, 174).

By the time of his *Amistad* interview, Himes was preaching what would have been considered sedition in an earlier time. As he told Williams, 'I can see what a black revolution would be like . . . First of all, in order for a revolution to be effective, one of the things that it has to be, is violent, it has to be massively violent; it has to be as violent as the war in Viet Nam . . . In any form of uprising, the major objective is to kill as many people as you can, by whatever means you can kill them, because the very fact of killing them and killing them in sufficient numbers is supposed to help you gain your objectives.'

Himes's view of revolution was one in which no prisoners were taken. He went on to say that 'the black people kill as many of the people of the white community as they can kill. That means children, women, grown men, industrialists, street sweepers or whatever they are, as long as they're white. And this is the fact that gains its objective – there's no discussion – no point in doing anything else, and no reason to give it any thought' (p.45). One cannot help but be reminded of

Williams's own *The Man Who Cried I Am* (Boston: Little Brown, 1967), but in reverse. Himes was a great admirer of Williams's fiction and it is possible that he may have been trying to create an equivalent of his friend's 'King Alfred Plan' to destroy the black race.

Whatever his intention, it is clear that Himes saw the black man as a powerful, indomitable presence who could actually bring down the American nation through calculated, suicidal acts of violence, and he attempted to suggest just how this could be done in ways that were so brutal, so graphic, so disgusting, that even at the time he was writing it he said 'I don't know what the American publishers will do about this book. But one thing I do know . . . they will hesitate, and it will cause them a great amount of revulsion, because the scenes that I have described will be revolting scenes' (p.47). Himes realized the power of such writing, but he felt that the writing of violence was natural to the American writer. As he said to Williams, 'American violence is public life, it's a public way of life . . .' (p.49).

An important portion of *Plan B* details an unprovoked attack by a resolute, virile, black martyr who ambushes a parade of policemen with an automatic rifle. Eventually, when conventional methods of subduing him fail, a tank is brought in to actually demolish the building in which he is hiding. This counter-attack is so extreme and so destructive that the stock market falls and the United States begins to disappear as a nation.

'The Birth of Chitterlings, Inc.' sequence is part picaresque tale and partly the adventures of a black master criminal named Tomsson Black. As a prelude, Himes takes the reader far back into American history, to the Alabama swamps of the late 1850s. A rather lengthy digression about the travails of the degenerate Harrison family sets the stage for the development of 'piquant' chitterlings from razor-back hogs fed on a diet of sweet potatoes. This is followed by the complete family tree of the black Lincoln family, to whom Himes introduces us in the pre-Civil War South. Himes describes in detail the adventures of each generation of Lincolns until we finally meet George

Washington Lincoln, who later takes the name Tomsson Black, a name originally given to him in insult, but which he later adopts because it emphasizes his 'blackness'.

Throughout this story, Himes provides us with a rather insistent view that white Southerners are sexually degenerate. His purpose in doing so is not clear, but the space he allots to the presumption makes it impossible to ignore. Himes also uses the character of Tomsson Black to express his oft-stated belief that black sexuality was irresistible to whites, and particularly to white women.

Tomsson Black becomes Himes's mouthpiece for much of the course of the story. Although we discover that Black has deliberately traveled to every communist country hostile to the United States, consorted with the leaders, and learned as much as he could about the violent and clandestine overthrow of governments, Black seems initially to be a rather benign character. His troubles, and his change in personality, come about after he is driven to rape Barbara Goodfeller, a rich and depraved white socialite.

Himes's personal attraction to white women is well known, so it is possible to see parts of him in the character of Tomsson Black. This is particularly evident in Black's mingled desire for and disgust with interracial sex and in his belief that black skin brings out the depraved nature inherent in white women. These ideologies will be familiar to anyone who has read *If He Hollers Let Him Go* and *The Primitive*. As was true for the protagonists of those earlier books, Black recognizes that white women are a trap that he cannot avoid falling into. Neither can he keep from allowing his disgust for white women to degenerate into violence. After the rape and beating of Barbara Goodfeller, Black rages to her effete and ineffectual husband 'There's nothing you can do with a slut like this but beat her. Not if you're trapped. Not if you're black.'

After his imprisonment for the rape (which happens, appropriately enough, in Alabama), Black becomes a brooding presence and gradually transforms into a kind of archfiend/master criminal in the vein of Professor Moriarty or Phantomas. All of his energies go into concocting the public personae of black philanthropist and friend to the white community while secretly plotting the violent overthrow of American society. In this we can see the seeds of Dr Moore, who tells an assistant 'what I need is a dead man' in order to have a more productive riot, and the Prophet Ham, a half-mad preacher who has organized his religious cult for the purpose of ramming the black Jesus down the white man's throat. Each of these characters makes an effective, chilling appearance in Himes's book, *Blind Man with a Pistol*, published in 1969.

How Coffin Ed and Grave Digger, Himes's two indomitable detectives, ended up in *Plan B* is rather puzzling. From the very beginning, Himes seems to have had it in mind to write a story in which not even they could conquer the power of racism. What is particularly interesting about their all-too-brief place in the story is the fact that it is Grave Digger, always the more sensible and thoughtful of the pair, who loses his temper and starts the ball rolling. Normally articulate and rational, Grave Digger's rise to anger and subsequent execution of T-bone Smith are as out of character as his vague statement that the murdered prostitute, Tang, reminds him of his mother.

Although he has traditionally been the most ideologically 'black' member of the detective team, Digger's decision, late in the novel, to throw in his lot with Tomsson Black rather than bring him to justice, seems unnatural and is, perhaps as Himes intended, a surprise. That he would subsequently murder Coffin Ed after each has risked his life for the other in so many other adventures, is also a surprise, and an unpleasant one at that.

Although we will never know just what Himes intended, it seems clear in retrospect that he had come to disbelieve the possibility of simple justice for American black people, just as he had become certain of the necessity of organized and armed black revolution to change the American system. In *Blind Man with a Pistol*, he artfully amplifies these beliefs in an alternative scenario where his normally unbeatable heroes are stopped in their tracks by forces so sinister, so deeply imbedded, that they cannot even see them. Himes's reduction of their status from knights-errant to rat exterminators at the conclusion of *Blind*

Man is a far more powerful comment on the defeat of justice than his symbolic murder of them in the final existing scene of *Plan B.*

Plan B thus remains an incandescent parable of racial madness as well as a retrospective of American racial history. The book begins as a thriller, then races toward a horrible climax. One might characterize it as a black *Apocalypse Now*, and although things are quieter now than they were in the 1960s, Himes's vision still strikes the reader's heart and reminds one of the angry unrest that still lies beneath the exterior of American society. Here, his fundamental pessimism reaches a paroxistic dimension in which sexuality can only be bestial, violence ruthless, and racism absolute.

Concluding the adventures of Coffin Ed and Grave Digger with a bang, *Plan B* brims over with extreme situations and an occasional lewdness that seems at times to parody the Southern Gothic tradition of Erskine Caldwell and William Faulkner. Indeed, Himes must have thought of the antebellum mirage of Sutpen's acres and the decadent intrigues of the Compton family while concocting the genealogies of his protagonists in ways that sometimes seem to mock *Gone with the Wind.* We know that his reverence for the author of *Sanctuary* was deep and lasting, and that he loved the irreverent, unlikely episodes of *The Reivers*, which cheered him up while he was in New York Presbyterian Hospital undergoing tests after his stroke in April of 1964. Still, whatever humor there may be in Tomsson Black's memories of his days in the South, it is thickly overlaid with cold, black rage. Life in Himes's South is a negative image of Faulkner's.

While verisimilitude is often strained to the utmost, there is yet a realistic strain, at times reminiscent of the spare, matter-of-fact personal histories or explanatory genealogies of the five black protagonists of Himes's *A Case of Rape.* It also takes little time to discover that Tomsson's coming of age after the killing of his father by an angry white and the hero's subsequent years in jail only repeat the tragic destiny of many a real black family – whether we think of the killing of Richard Wright's Uncle Hoskins by a jealous West Helena, Arkansas, competitor, or the lynching of Malcolm X's father. Indeed, the figure of Malcolm X looms large in this novel, although it does so symbolically, at second remove. Clearly, though, the growth in political awareness of the intransigent Black Muslim leader (whom Himes had briefly befriended while shooting a documentary in Harlem, and who had made it a point to climb ten flights of stairs in order to talk to Himes in his Latin Quarter apartment) is very much present in Tomsson Black's itinerary.

Like much of Himes's writing, *Plan B* has its autobiographical touch. Those familiar with Himes's own family story and the records that his literary-minded mother, Estelle Bomar, kept of her own ancestry and childhood in 'Old Lick Log', will be able to relate more than one detail of Tomsson Black's parentage, or Alabama life, to Himes's background and to his own early memories at Port Gibson or at Alcorn State College.

Perhaps more than anything else, *Plan B* is a symbolic answer to the questions posed by the Black Power movement. One must observe that Himes did not believe in violence as a solution to anything – that is to say that he did not believe in the power of *unorganized* violence. This is thought to be the reason why Himes left this novel unfinished, that he may have reached an ideological impasse.

An analysis of the function of Coffin Ed and Grave Digger in his Harlem Domestic novels, suggests that, while they fought black crime and white prejudice, they were also symbols of integration. In this novel, Himes goes so far as to kill his duo, after one of them has joined the ranks of radical Black nationalism. This amounts to literary suicide and one can well understand why Himes became stalled and could not carry the book through to publication during the early 1970s.

The deaths of Himes's heroes close out a novel filled with racy episodes and bizarre plot twists and which culminates in a civil war, replete with manhunts and surrealistic escalations of violence. Much of Himes's genius lies in his fleshy descriptions of teeming ghetto life, descriptions that recall the paintings of Bosch or the French illustrator, Dubout. Through his peculiar brand of absurd humor, Himes is able to explore America's worst racial fears without directly confronting them.

Although the reader may be appalled by the bloody atrocities and pervasive conflict in *Plan B*, he may still retain an admiration for Himes's skill as a social analyst. His narrative adventure is, at the same time, an opportunity for him to examine the minds of both blacks and whites under the stress of racial antagonism. This lucid, bitter indictment of both races may leave the reader uneasy, but it is impossible to ignore Himes's virtuosity in his imaginative representation of a racist America. His story begins with the roots of racial evil during the slavery era, then swells into a picture of apocalyptic violence and interracial slaughter during the riots of the 1960s, a period when the prevailing contact between blacks and whites was characterized by mistrust and violence.

Himes's logic and clear-sightedness are frightening, and the result is an angry, violent story. In *Plan B*, Himes creates an insistent image of the black man as a sexual symbol, then reflects it back into white consciousness. This brooding, virile image turns against the white American world the same weapons that were fashioned to subjugate his people. Given such circumstances, Himes's black detectives can no longer represent law and order, even according to their unorthodox interpretation of it. They are foreordained to disappear in a cataclysmic explosion of racial violence.

Plan B is a hard book that leaves the reader with a flinty taste in his mouth. It is 'political' fiction, as well as a preamble to the subtler and ultimately more amusing picture of black and white ways of thinking that Himes achieved in *Blind Man with a Pistol*. Apart from the non-stop action and titillating dialog, *Plan B* remains an excellent example of the peculiar blend of surrealism and humor that Himes used to withstand the torments that he must have felt from a lifetime of facing the injustice of American racial policies.

Michel Fabre
Robert E. Skinner

1

A man called T-bone Smith sat in a cold water slum flat on 113th Street, East of 8th Avenue in Harlem, looking at television with his old lady, Tang. They had a television set but they didn't have anything to eat. It was after ten o'clock at night and the stores were closed, but that didn't make any difference because they didn't have any money, anyway. It was only a two-room flat so the television was in the kitchen. Because it was summertime, the stove was cold and the windows were open.

T-bone was clad only in a pair of greasy black pants and his bare black torso was ropey with lean hard muscles and was decorated with an elaborate variety of scars. His long narrow face was hinged on a mouth with lips the size of automobile tires and the corners of his sloe-shaped eyes were sticky with mucus. The short hard burrs on his watermelon-shaped head were the color of half-burnt ashes. He had his bare black feet propped up on the kitchen table with the white soles toward the television screen. He was white-mouthed from hunger but was laughing like an idiot at two blackfaced white minstrels on the television screen who earned a fortune by blacking their faces and acting just as foolish as T-bone had done for free all his life.

In between laughing, he was trying to get his old lady, Tang, to go down into Central Park and trick with some white man so they could eat.

'Go on, baby, you can be back in an hour with 'nuff bread so we can scoff.'

'I'se tired as you are,' she said with an evil glance. 'Go sell yo' own ass to whitey, you luvs him so much.'

She had once been a beautiful jet-black woman with softly rounded features in a broad flat face and a figure to evoke instant visions of writhing sexuality and black ecstasy. But both her face and figure had been corroded by vice and hunger, and now she was just a lean, angular crone with burnt red hair and flat black features that looked like they had been molded by a stamping machine. Only her eyes looked alive: they were red, mean, disillusioned and defiant. She was clad in a soiled faded green mother hubbard and her big buniony feet trod restlessly about the rotting kitchen linoleum. The tops of her feet were covered with wrinkled black skin streaked with white dirt.

Suddenly, above the sound of the gibbering of the black-face white minstrels, they heard an impatient hammering on the door. They couldn't imagine anyone it could be except the police. They looked sharply at one another and then they looked quickly about the room to see if there was any incriminating evidence in sight, although, aside from her hustling in the area encircling the lagoon, neither of them had committed any crime recently enough to interest the police. She stuck her bare feet into some old felt slippers and quickly rubbed red lipstick over her rusty lips and he got up and shambled across the floor in his bare feet and opened the door.

A young, uniformed black messenger with smooth skin and bright, intelligent eyes asked, 'Mister Smith?'

'Dass me,' T-bone admitted.

The messenger extended a long cardboard box wrapped in gilt paper and tied with red ribbon. Conspicuous on the gilt wrapping paper was the green and white label of a florist, decorated with pink and yellow flowers, and in the place for the name and address were the typed words: 'Mr T. Smith, West 113th Street, 4th floor.' The messenger placed the box directly into T-bone's outstretched hands and before releasing it, waited until T-bone had a firm grip.

'Flowers for you, sir,' he trilled.

T-bone was so startled by this bit of information he almost let go of the box, but the messenger was already hurtling down the stairs, and in any case, T-bone was too slow-witted to do more than stare. He simply stood there, holding the box in his outstretched hands, his mouth hanging open, not a thought in his head; he just looked stupid and stunned.

But Tang's thoughts were churning suspiciously behind her red eyes.

'Who sending you flowers, black and ugly as you is?' she demanded from across the room. She really meant it: *who would be sending him flowers, black and ugly as he was, not to mention lazy, and so arrogant in bed he acted like his dick was made of solid uranium.* Still, he was her man, simple-minded or not, and it made her jealous for him to get flowers, other than for his funeral.

'Dese ain't flowers,' he said, sounding just as suspicious as she had. 'Lessen they be flowers of lead.'

'Maybe it's some scoff from the government's thing for the poor folks,' she surmised hopefully.

'Not unless it's pigiron knuckles.'

She went over beside him and gingerly fingered the white-wrapped box. 'It's got your name on it,' she said. 'And your address. What would anybody be sending to your name and address?'

'We gonna soon see,' he said, and stepped across the room to lay the box atop the table. It made a clunking sound. Meanwhile, the two blackfaced white comedians danced merrily on the television screen until interrupted by a beautiful blonde reading a commercial for *Nucreme*, a product that made dirty skin so fresh and white.

She stood back and watched him break the ribbon and tear off the white wrapping paper. She was practically holding her breath when he opened the gray cardboard carton, but he was too unimaginative to have any thoughts about it one way or another. If God had sent him down a trunk full of gold bricks from heaven, he would have wondered who expected him to brick up some holes in a wall that wasn't his.

Inside the cardboard box they saw a long object wrapped in brown oiled paper and packed in paper excelsior, the way they had seen machine tools packed when they had worked in a shipyard in Newark before she had listened to his sweet talk and had come to Harlem to be his whore. She couldn't imagine anybody sending him a machine tool unless he had been engaged in activities which she didn't know anything about. Which wasn't likely, she thought, as long as she made enough to feed him. He just stared at it stupidly, wondering why anybody would send him something which looked like something he couldn't use even if he wanted to use it.

'Pick it up,' she said sharply. 'It ain't gonna bite you.'

'I ain't scared of nuttin' bitin' me,' he said, fearlessly lifting the object from its bed of excelsior. 'It ain't heavy as I thought,' he said stupidly, although he had given no indication of what he had thought.

She saw a white sheet of instructions underneath the object. Quickly she snatched it up.

'Wuss dat?' he asked with the quick, defensive suspicion of one who can't read.

She knew he couldn't read and a feminine compulsion to needle him because he had been sent something that he couldn't understand inspired her to say, 'Writing! That's what.'

'What's it say?' he demanded, panic-stricken.

She read the printed words to herself: *WARNING!! DO NOT INFORM POLICE!!! LEARN YOUR WEAPON AND WAIT FOR INSTRUCTIONS!!! REPEAT!!! LEARN YOUR WEAPON AND WAIT FOR INSTRUCTIONS!!! WARNING!!! DO NOT INFORM POLICE!!! FREEDOM IS NEAR!!!*

Then she read them aloud. They so alarmed him that sweat broke out over his face; his eyes stretched until they were completely round. Frantically he began tearing the oiled wrapping paper from the object in his hand. The dull blue gleam of an automatic rifle came into sight. She gasped. She had never seen a rifle that looked as dangerous as this. But he had seen and handled such a rifle when he had served in the army during the Korean War.

'Iss a M14,' he said. 'Iss an army gun.'

He was terrified. His skin dried and turned dark gray.

'I done served my time,' he went on, and then realizing how stupid that sounded, he added, 'Efen iss stolen I don't want it. Wuss anybody wanna send me a stolen gun for?'

Her red eyes blazed in a face contorted by excitement. 'It's the uprising, nigger!' she cried. 'We gonna be free!'

'Uprising?' He shied away from the word as though it were a vicious dog. 'Free?' He jumped as thought he had been bitten by a rattlesnake. 'I'se already free. All someone wants to do is get my ass in jail 'cause I'm free.' He held the rifle as though it were a bomb which might go off in his hand.

She looked at the gun with awe and admiration. 'That'll chop a white policeman two ways, sides and flat. That'll blow the shit out of whitey's asshole.'

'Wut?' He put the gun down onto the table and pushed it away from him. 'Shoot a white police? Someun 'spects me tuh shoot de white police?'

'Why not? You wanna uprise, don't you?'

'Uprise? Whore, is you crazy? Uprise where?'

'Uprise here, nigger. Is you that stupid? Here we is and here we is gonna uprise.'

'Not me! I ain't gonna get my ass blown off waving that thing around. We had them things in Korea and them Koreans still kilt us niggers like flies.'

'You got shit in your blood,' she said contemptuously. 'Let me feel that thing.'

She picked the rifle up from the table and held it as though she were shooting an invasion of cops. 'Baby,' she said directly to the gun. 'You and me can make it, baby.'

'Wuss de matter wid you? You crazy?' he shouted.

'Put that thing down. I'm gonna go tell de man fo' we gets both our ass in jail.'

'You going to tell whitey?' she asked in surprise. 'You gonna run tell the man 'bout this secret that'll make you free?'

'Shut yo' mouth, whore, I'se doin' it much for you as I is for me.'

At first she didn't take him too seriously. 'For me, nigger? You think I wanna sell my pussy to whitey all my life?' But with the gun in her hand, the question was rhetorical. She kept shooting at imaginary whiteys about the room, thinking she could go hunting and kill her a whitey or two. Hell, give her enough time and bullets she could kill them all.

But her words had made him frown disapprovingly.

'You wanna stop being a whore, whore?' he asked in amazement. 'Hell, whore, we gotta live.'

'You call this living?' She drew the gun tight to her breast as though it were a lover. 'This is the only thing that made me feel alive since I met you.'

He looked outraged. 'You been lissening to that Black Power shit, them Black Panthers 'n that shit,' he accused. 'Ain' I always done what's best?'

'Yeah, put me on the block to sell my black pussy to poor white trash.'

'I ain' gonna argy wid you,' he said in exasperation. 'I'se goan 'n get de cops 'fore we both winds up daid.'

Slowly and deliberately, she aimed the gun at him. 'You call whitey and I'll waste you,' she threatened.

He was moving toward the door but the sound of her voice stopped him. He turned about and looked at her. It was more the sight of her than the meaning of her words which made him hesitate. He wasn't a man to dare anyone and she looked as though she would blow him away. But he knew she was a tenderhearted woman and wouldn't hurt him as long as he didn't cross her, so he decided to kid her along until he could grab the gun, then he'd whip her ass. With this in mind he began shuffling around the table in her direction, white teeth showing in a false grin, eyes half-closed like a forgiving lover.

'Baby, I were jes playin—'

'Maybe you is but I ain't,' she warned him.

'I wasn't gonna call the cops, I was jes gonna see if the door is locked.'

'You see and you won't know it.'

She talkin' too much, he thought, shuffling closer. 'Baby, lemme show you how to work that thing.'

'What's there to do?' she challenged, dropping her gaze to the trigger guard.

Suddenly he grabbed. She pulled the trigger. Nothing happened. Both became frozen in shock. It had never occurred to either of them that the gun was not loaded.

T-bone was the first to react. He burst out laughing. 'Haw-haw-haw.'

'Wouldn't have been so funny if this thing had been loaded,' she said sourly.

His face contorted from a delayed reaction of rage. It was as though a hole in his emotions left by the dissipation of his fear had filled up with fury. He whipped out a spring blade knife. 'I teach you, whore,' he raved. 'You try to kill me.'

She looked from the knife to his face and said stoically, 'I shoulda known, you are whitey's slave; you'll never be free.'

'Free of you,' he shouted and began slashing at her.

She tried to protect herself with the rifle but shortly he had cut it out of her grasp. She backed around the table trying to keep away from the slashing blade. But soon the blade began reaching her flesh, the floor became covered with blood; she crumpled and fell and died, as she had known she would after she first saw the enraged look on his face.

2

A woman who had witnessed the murder from her kitchen window across the air well had gone down into the street, found a telephone and called the police precinct. The radio dispatcher had ordered the patrol car nearest to the scene of the crime to investigate.

The black Harlem detectives, Coffin Ed Johnson and Grave Digger Jones, had been cruising south on Eighth Avenue from 125th Street, looking for known pushers, and they were approaching the intersection of 113th Street when the alarm was broadcast. They hadn't seen any known pushers, just the streets filled with addicts. It had made them sad. Addiction wasn't a crime, only possession was. And they knew none of the addicts had any of the shit left on them. The pushers kept well out of sight. So they were glad to break it off and investigate a killing for a change. At least the victim was already dead; not just dying on their feet like these mother-raping addicts, whom they could neither punish nor save. So they climbed to the fourth-floor flat of T-bone Smith and found him lying on the dirty pallet in the bedroom, strung out on horse.

The door had been unlocked and after one glance at the body of the woman, which they had expected to find, they had stepped into the dirty, half-lit bedroom and found T-bone stretched out on the bed. He was still clad only in greasy black pants, with his torso bare to the waist. One look at his obsidian eyes, extended to the size of California prunes, and at the needle marks on his bare arms told them he was a main-liner of long standing, and that he had just indulged himself in a massive shot.

Coffin Ed reached down and tried to grip T-bone by the hair, but his hair was too short, so he grabbed him by the wrist and snatched him to his feet.

When Coffin Ed's face came into focus, T-bone muttered, 'I were gonna call y'all, boss.'

The tic began in Coffin Ed's face. He pushed T-bone toward a broken-legged kitchen table and grated, 'Sit down.'

Without speaking, Grave Digger went over and turned off the television.

T-bone looked at the chair and drew back in terror. 'That chair got blood on it.'

'It ain't yours,' Coffin Ed said.

'But I'm gonna add some of his to it if he don't straighten up,' Grave Digger threatened.

Coffin Ed pushed T-bone down into the bloody chair. His face turned gray with terror. He was too high to be terrified of the consequences of his crime, he was merely terrified of the blood.

'Why'd you kill her?' Coffin Ed asked.

'She were tryna shoot me,' T-bone whined. Even in his terror, a sly look of cunning flitted over his face. He thought he knew what to tell the police.

Both detectives turned to look at the mutilated body for the first time. At the sight of the slashed and bloody carcass of what had, a short time before, been some kind of a black woman, their blood boiled with anger and revulsion. The sight of this violent death, following on the heels of a frustrating morning watching junkies, filled both of them with rage. Grave Digger's neck swelled until his collar choked him; Coffin Ed's burned face began to twitch. What kind of life had this black woman lived to deserve this bloody death, they wondered.

Finally they saw the gun spattered with gouts of congealing blood. Coffin Ed stuck the long, nickel-plated barrel of his .38 revolver through the trigger guard and used both hands to lift it onto the table. 'US Army,' he observed. 'But it ain't stamped,' he added, after examining it for a moment.

Grave Digger also examined it with his gaze, but neither of them touched it with the naked hand. 'With this gun?' he asked.

'Yassuh, boss, she aim it at me an' threaten to waste me 'n I cut her trying to 'fend myself.'

'You been in the army?'

'Yassuh.'

'And you thought this gun was loaded?' Coffin Ed asked.

'Where'd she get this gun?' Grave Digger asked.

'It weren't hers, someone sen' it to me.'

'To you?'

'Yassuh, boss.'

'Who?'

'I dunno, boss. A boy in uniform come here 'n knock on de do' an' say they flowers for me. But I knew they weren't no flowers 'cause they was too heavy.'

'Where's the box it came in?'

'Over there, boss, but I knew soon's I felt it, it weren't no flowers.'

In stepping over to retrieve the box from the far side of the room where the woman had knocked it trying to escape, Grave Digger noticed the printed instruction sheet lying on the floor, weighted down with blood. He picked it up and read it, and then passed it to Coffin Ed. After having read the printed message, they gave the box a cursory examination.

'Can you read?' Grave Digger asked T-bone.

Sight of the printed page once again filled T-bone with inexplicable terror. He seemed to be more frightened by the printed word than by the angry detectives and their guns. 'Nawsuh, boss, but she read it to me.'

'I'm going to read it to you again,' Grave Digger said and read aloud the printed words: '*WARNING!!! DO NOT INFORM POLICE!!! LEARN YOUR WEAPON AND WAIT FOR INSTRUCTIONS!!! REPEAT!!! LEARN YOUR WEAPON AND WAIT FOR INSTRUCTIONS!!! WARNING!!! DO NOT INFORM POLICE!!! FREEDOM IS NEAR!!!* You understand that?'

Coffin Ed looked across at Grave Digger. 'Don't push him, Digger,' he cautioned. 'He ain't very bright.'

'He's bright enough to know what I'm asking him,' Grave Digger grated, and again he asked T-bone, 'Did you understand what I asked you?'

'Yassuh, boss, you mean do I unnerstand what it say?'

'That's right, what did it say?'

'Well, it talk about stuff I don' go long wid, boss. She say the uprising, 'n that sort of shit. But I'se a law-abiding man an' I was gonna call the police.'

'You were going to call the police and tell them about receiving the gun?'

'Yassuh, boss, leas' I were gonna go get 'em, 'n tell 'em.' He was relieved to get himself in the right.

'And she tried to stop you?' Grave Digger persisted.

Coffin Ed was watching Grave Digger with disturbed emotions; he didn't know what Digger was trying to get at and he felt confused and uneasy. T-bone had grown uneasy too; at first he thought he had gotten himself in the right, but suddenly he was no longer sure.

'I di'n unnerstand you, boss.'

'I asked you if she tried to stop you from going after the police.'

'Yassuh, boss. Dass wut I sayin', she swore she waste me if I goes.'

'And she aimed the gun at you?'

'Yassuh, boss.'

'But you had been in the army and handled this type of gun and you knew it wasn't loaded.'

'Nawsuh, boss,' he denied vehemently. 'I di'n know it weren't loaded.'

'How'd you find out?'

'She pulled the trigger.'

'And when you found out it wasn't loaded you pulled out your knife and cut her to death.'

'Nawsuh, boss, I were jes' try'na get away to tell the police and she wanna stop me. She call me whitey's slave.'

'What do you do for a living?' Grave Digger asked.

'I been looking for a job.'

'What did she do?'

'She went out 'n did some housework downtown sommers.'

'You mean she hustled around the lagoon in Central Park.'

'Sometimes, maybe.'

The whole of Grave Digger's head had begun to swell and his voice became tight and cotton-dry with rage. The veins in his temples roped as though air had been pumped into them.

'You lived off what this black woman made selling her body to white tramps,' Grave Digger choked. 'You lived off her faith and her sweat and her depravity.'

Coffin Ed was watching him in alarm. He had never seen his partner lose himself in such a rage.

'Easy, Digger,' he cautioned again. 'Easy man. This black mother-raper ain't worth it.'

But Grave Digger's head was roaring with fury and he didn't hear his partner. 'And you wasted her because she wanted to be free.'

T-bone began jerking with terror as though in death convulsions himself. 'I were gonna tell is all,' he whined through lips bone dry. 'It were more for her than it were for me.'

'You can tell her again, mother-raper,' Grave Digger rasped, his throat as dry as T-bone's lips.

'Digger!' Coffin Ed cried as Grave Digger drew back his pistol.

T-bone came up out of his seat like a terrified rat and met

the descending butt of the long, nickel-plated pistol with an inadvertent sense of destiny. His body fell straight into the congealing blood of the woman he'd killed. Simultaneously, Grave Digger let out a long strangled sigh, almost as though he'd had a furious orgasm.

Coffin Ed was the first to break the frozen silence. 'He weren't worth it, Digger.'

Grave Digger looked down without regret at the body of the man he'd just killed and said, 'He ain't now.'

'But you shouldn't have done it, man. The commissioner is going to be on our asses.'

'You ain't involved, Ed. I'll take my own medicine.'

'Ain't involved? I'm here, ain't I? I'm your partner, ain't I? We're a team, ain't we? I'd killed him, too, man. I'd have just done it different is all.'

'No, partner, I'm not going to let you stick your neck out for me. This was my own private feeling, my own private action. I don't ask you to feel like me, man, and I'm not going to let you share in the blame. I did it. I killed this black mother myself, I busted his skull alone, and I'd do it again. I did it because that woman looked something like my ma looked as I remember her, a poor black woman wanting freedom. And I'd kill any black mother on earth that was low enough to waste her for that. But I'm not going to let you share this feeling, man, because this is for my mama.'

'Okay, Digger, it's yours and I ain't gonna try to share it, but you can't stop me from saying he drew his chiv on you, because that's what I'm going to say.'

On sudden impulse Grave Digger put the bloodied instruction sheet in his pocket. 'All I want you to do is just don't say nothing about this, Ed,' he said. 'Let's just keep it to ourselves until we find out more about where it is.'

'Where what is?'

'Freedom.'

'All right, partner, I'll be deaf, dumb, and blind. But it ain't going to be easy.'

'Sure ain't.'

3

Like many great institutions, CHITTERLINGS, INC. had come about by accident. At the beginning of the nineteenth century, the large area of swamp land bordering on Mobile Bay that was later reclaimed for the factory of CHITTERLINGS, INC., was the property of an incompetent English slave owner, named Albert Harrison. Because a large section of the swamp was overgrown with canebrakes, he believed this land would be ideal for the culture of sugar cane that could later be sold to rum distilleries. So Harrison purchased five thousand acres for a pittance from a friend who knew a sucker when he saw one, and with the remainder of his inheritance purchased one hundred infirm, bargain-priced slaves, and built a large white, dreadfully uncomfortable mansion on the banks of the Tombigbee River.

Knowing little about the habits of slaves and even less about the responsibilities of ownership, he put his slaves to work clearing the canebrakes and expected them to feed and house themselves off the land. Before long, though, many of his slaves had joined the tribes of native Indians who gave the river its name and Harrison was left alone in the big uncomfortable house with his young wife and one old, decrepit slave who served as cook, valet, and housekeeper.

Sick with frustration and too ashamed of his ineptitude to face his neighbors, Harrison kept to his gloomy house, brooding all day and copulating with his young wife all night. In ten years they had eleven offspring, seven of them afflicted with congenital idiocy. His final hope of ever recouping his fortune disappeared with the death of his father in England and the subsequent loss of his credit. Finally, even his old Uncle Tom slave retainer vanished into the night. To put the capstone on his misfortunes, he discovered that his wife was dying from cancer of the womb.

One morning he awakened to a cacophony of his idiot children crying in hunger and his wife screaming in pain. He took down his old double-barreled shotgun, loaded it, and began systematically shooting them two at a time. He shot his wife first, not out of any altruism he may have possessed, but simply because she was nearest. The idiot children sat looking at him with open mouths and dull eyes, seeming to wait their turns, but the three girls and one boy who were mentally normal took to their heels in their ragged nightshirts, their little white asses shining in the morning sun. He took a couple of potshots at them as they fled toward the canebrake and winged the youngest, a skinny, freckled, tow-headed little girl of three, before the others got away. She had been shot in the calf of her left leg and couldn't move, so he left her lying in the sun, screaming in agony, while he dispatched the rest of the idiots. Then he walked out into the yard in his nightshirt and blew out her brains. Then came his final achievement in life. He reloaded the gun, sat on the back stairs with it held between his knees and, with its stock resting on the bottom step, pulled both triggers with his big toe, blowing off his face.

The orphaned children were taken in by a sympathetic neighboring family named Macpaisley, who were not much better off then the Harrisons had been, but who had at least been able to hang on to a few imbecile slaves. The eldest of the orphaned Harrisons was a girl nine and a half years old called Hope. The next born was a boy called 'Lovely'. Whether it was his real name or a nickname, no one ever knew, for his parents had been the sole authority on the subject. The other remaining child, the fifth born, was a five and a half year old girl named 'Cotton Tail.' If it was a nickname, it was at least appropriate, because if she hadn't run like a cottontail rabbit, she'd now be dead. All three of them were thin, towheaded children, with peaked, freckled faces and wild, frightened, blue-gray eyes.

The Macpaisleys had nine children of their own, three of them almost grown: Liam, a seventeen year old boy known as 'Lim', Nora, a sixteen year old girl called 'Nookie', and Little, a fifteen year old boy called 'Li'l'. The others were stairstepped down to a nameless infant.

Only the three eldest Macpaisley children showed any interest in the Harrison orphans. Lim, the eldest, kept sniffing around Hope trying to get a chance to 'rut' her like his father did his mother. And Nookie kept taking out Lovely's little thing whenever they were alone and playing with it in the hope of getting it hard enough to stick into her 'nookie', from which she got her name. Li'l, who was the nearest to an idiot of them all, just wanted to copulate with five-year-old Cotton Tail as he had seen the black slave, Jeb, do to a neighbor's sheep one day.

Mr Macpaisley, a huge, red-bearded, bald-pated, pot-bellied dirt farmer of indisputable vigor but little ambition, after unsuccessfully attempting to grow sugar cane as affluent slave owners were doing, had settled on raising yellow yams, razorback hogs, and illiterate, unlovely, and unhealthy children with his wife, known locally as 'Fertile Myrtle'.

He had been fortunate to discover, while still solvent, that sugar cane wouldn't grow in the infertile swampland, but that razorback hogs thrived in the canebrakes on a diet of snakes and bamboo roots. Yellow yams grew wild on the bone-dry patches of arid land. The combination of yams and stringy pork had not only proved salable, but profitable, besides supplying his family with almost their complete diet. His eleven infirm slaves had little to do other than dig up the yams and spear the razorbacks with sharpened sticks, and support his prestige as a slave owner, which was actually their primary task.

Myrtle Macpaisley, a fading, gray-haired woman with lean, sagging breasts and a flabby, spreading figure, still retained her craving for a good 'screw'. She was famous for her proud and uninhibited boast that her husband 'could rut like a nigger'. To be sure, however, it is doubtful that Mrs Macpaisley had ever had the opportunity to discover how a nigger rutted.

The three Harrison orphans grew up in the Macpaisley household where it was accepted that Lovely would inherit his father's swampland property upon reaching the legal age of maturity. Little happened to them during those years except that Hope bore Lim's child, but did not marry him. Lovely was repeatedly raped by Nookie but no offspring resulted, and little Cotton Tail acceded to Li'l's abnormal craving so often she had developed a preference for it to all other forms of copulation.

Yet fate had played a more diabolic joke on Cotton Tail than her volitional conversion to sodomy. She had become the most beautiful girl in the area, perhaps in all the South. At fifteen she was a blonde, blue-eyed dream with a body to stir a dead man. She was the most desirable girl along the entire coast of the Gulf of Mexico, surpassing even the Creole beauties. Handsome young suitors came from as far away as New Orleans to seek her hand in matrimony, many of whom were the heirs of fabulously wealthy estates with more than a thousand slaves.

The elder Macpaisleys were in a constant flutter, trying to arrange the most advantageous marriage for her to the wealthiest and most desirable of these young dandies. They had visions of accompanying her into the world of wealth and prestige, and these pretensions set their impoverished neighbors to comment that, 'They think their shit don't stink no more.'

But Cotton Tail was so cold to the advances of these young swains she soon acquired the reputation of being frigid. They lusted for her like dogs in heat, yet none had the imagination to discern in the spasmodic quivering of her buttocks the invitation so obviously posed. They called her a 'teaser', and swore she masturbated, or copulated with her sisters or the Macpaisley girls. She was angered and frustrated because none had the gumption to take the pleasure she went to such pains to offer. Rebuffed by her scorn and anger, they gradually quit coming, and it was left to Li'l to satisfy the craving he had instilled in her.

The Civil War was in its last year when Lovely came of age and the elder Macpaisleys, finally conceding the failure of their plans for getting Cotton Tail married into wealth, unhesitatingly persuaded the three Harrison orphans to return to their homestead. Their sole possession was the shotgun neighbors had retrieved from their father's massacre. They hadn't returned to the house in seven years. It was like making an expedition to the unknown. Nevertheless, having abandoned all hope of getting Lim to marry her, Hope took her six-year-old daughter, Aslip, with them. This was probably the most sensible course, since Lim was already the father of seven other tots in the area, two of whom were half-breeds, and he couldn't be expected to marry all the mothers.

By then the big, gloomy mansion their father had built on the banks of the Tombigbee was overgrown with foliage and was rotting into dust. The roof was falling in, the house had listed to one side, floorboards had caved in, and nests of cottonmouth water moccasins and sluggish rattlesnakes had made it their home.

The wooden pier Harrison had built into the bay for the transportation of his sugarcane in the days of his hope had rotted and fallen apart. The floorboards had fallen into the water and been washed away. Only the decaying, water-logged timbers of the wooden pier that had been sunk into the river bed remained. The five thousand acres of canebrake and swampland had become impenetrable.

The bloodstains of their murdered mother and little sisters and brothers were still visible on the rotting kitchen floor, the rusted stove, the glass and china and the pots and pans. The sheets, bedcovers, and mattresses, and even parts of the wooden floor had been eaten away by carnivorous insects. The massacred bodies had been removed, whether by kind neighbors or wild animals the orphans never learned. No skeletons remained.

Lovely shot into the nests of snakes, making great gaping holes in the floors and walls, but many snakes were killed and wounded. He battered the heads of the wounded with the gun butt and his sisters removed the bodies and piled them atop a stack of dry bamboo in the front yard and burned them.

They had no light or food and the water in the neglected well was doubtless contaminated. For the first week they worked by day on the old house with borrowed tools to make it habitable and returned to the Macpaisleys' every night.

First they burned sulphur candles in all the rooms and closed and sealed the doors and windows the best they could in order to contain the sulphur fumes. Through this method, they killed all the animal life within the house. The next day they found the floor covered with the bodies of dead snakes, many of which were pregnant, dead rats, bats, flies, ants, moths, and a few birds. They built a giant bonfire to burn the carcasses and for many days following the entire area smelled as though a door to hell had opened.

With a hand saw, hammer, and nails, Lovely patched up the floors and boarded up all unneeded windows. All the rotted bedding and garments were burned, producing such an ungodly odor that it seemed that another door to hell had sprung ajar. Afterward they covered their beds with bamboo leaves. Within a week's time they had made two rooms liveable, but were still without light or water. None of them dared lay down on a bed without Lovely first prodding it thoroughly with a cocked and loaded gun. Snakes still found their way inside occasionally, because snakes seemed to like human companionship.

Finally they learned to safeguard themselves while sleeping by placing shards of mirrors strategically about the floor to trap insects on their surfaces and prepare a feast for any snakes that might invade during the night. They put quicklime into the well to purify the water and Lovely soon became adept at shooting the wild razorbacks and boars that wandered into the clearing. The Macpaisleys gave them a bushel of yams from time to time, and the sisters learned to gather the fresh bamboo shoots early in the morning and boil them with the fresh meat.

Thus, with the occasional help and companionship of the Macpaisleys, they managed to survive. They suffered most from the frustration of their sexual appetites. Finally Lovely hit upon the solution of sleeping with his elder sister, Hope. However, poor little Cotton Tail was left to languish in her depraved misery. It seemed perfectly logical for her brother to copulate with her sister, but she could hardly expect him to satisfy her abnormal lust, too. She suffered so in her caldron of unrequited passion that she was prepared to seduce a black slave, but there were no black slaves about who could be seduced.

Most of the slaves had heard about the Emancipation Proclamation via the grapevine, and many of them had taken to the bush. Those who remained were kept under lock and key by their irate masters. But the canebrakes of the Harrison plantation were too forbidding for the hardiest runaway slave, so Cotton Tail was denied her sexual satisfaction.

4

The Harrison orphans had already lit the lantern and were just about to sit down to a supper of boiled pork, bamboo shoots, and yellow yams when a band of marauding Union soldiers appeared one day. The nine ragged, unshaven, red-eyed, savage-looking infantry soldiers came with loaded rifles into the kitchen from the dusk. The Civil War had been over for three months, but the Harrisons hadn't heard about it.

A glance was enough to tell them that the soliders were the enemies of the South, and that they were bent on rape and plunder. With lightning-quick reflexes, Hope slapped her daughter, Aslip, from the table and hissed at the terrified child, 'Run hide.' The soldiers scarcely had time to realize the child's existence, so quickly did she vanish.

They weren't interested in her anyway. They wanted more mature women to rape and caches of gold and precious jewels to plunder. They had heard all about the fabulous riches of the slave owners and the wild beauty and hot passions of their women, but they had also heard that the slaves would be hidden in the woods, the treasures buried, the plantations neglected, the houses unpainted so as to appear dilapidated, and the women dressed in rags to hide their appeal.

At the Harrison plantation they found no more than they had expected; an overgrown plantation made to look neglected, the bearded young heir who had no doubt fought in the Confederate Army and was now disguised in civilian rags, and the women, maybe his wife and sister, one of whom was extraordinarily beautiful and desirable, both clad in the foulest and most repulsive rags. No one but an actress on the stage wore clothes as ragged as those. They weren't fooled. Doubtless the gold and jewels were buried nearby in the back yard. Since darkness was falling they'd just have time to take their pleasure with the women and force the man to reveal where his treasure was hidden before getting back to their company in Mobile in time to beat the midnight curfew.

They quickly bound Lovely to his kitchen chair and set about raping the two women, one in each room. Despite her unkempt hair and dirty face, Hope was found to be more than acceptable. Her body was white and sturdy, had good movements, gripped strongly, and joyously milked a man until he was thoroughly drained.

Cotton Tail, however, was something else again. When the first soldier approached her, she turned over on her beautiful young breasts and smooth milk-white belly and presented her dimpled buttocks. For a moment, the soldier thought he was back in the barracks, but he had never seen anything so delectable there. He had hoped to rape a virgin, but he took his pleasure where it was willingly offered and enjoyed it more than he thought possible.

From his chair in the kitchen, Lovely could see both of his sisters being raped. He didn't resent the rape of Hope so much, for he knew she welcomed a change. However, he was outraged when he saw his little sister, Cotton Tail, bestially prodded in the rectum as though she were a sheep. So great was his rage that he broke his bonds and leaped across the intervening space onto the back of the rutting soldier, but his mates snatched up their rifles and blew off the top of his head. Blood and brains splattered over the back of the offending soldier and droplets of the sticky goo dripped on Cotton Tail's bare skin.

Although Cotton Tail hadn't seen her brother attack her seducer, the sound of shooting shocked her. She was so terrified when she saw her murdered brother's body rolling across the floor that her limbs tightened convulsively and she experienced such an overwhelming ecstasy that she cried out in a loud, wailing moan.

The soldiers dragged Lovely's body out through the kitchen and threw it into the back yard. After cleaning up the more distracting gouts of blood and brains, they continued with their pleasure. Each soldier ravished both women and greatly enjoyed the contrast.

The women thought nothing of being raped nine times. They were as strong and willing at the end as they had been in the beginning. Their only regret was for the death of their brother, although they couldn't really think about it while being so energetically raped.

After the long session of rape, the soldiers were sated with pleasure. With the cessation of activity, the women began to grieve. The soldiers were straightening up their uniforms and buttoning their flies, preparatory to searching for the hiding place of any treasure when suddenly Aslip, Hope's little girl, burst into the room crying, 'I been snakebit, Ma.'

She looked so appealing with her blue eyes glistening with tears and her face flushed from having run down the back stairs from her hiding place that the soldiers felt a revival of lust. She was certain to be a virgin, they thought, and two of them threw her to the floor. The sisters, outraged by this atrocity, turned on the soldiers and fought them like tigresses. They clawed the soldier's faces, tore at their eyes, and kicked them in the shins, but the soldiers finally overwhelmed them with superior numbers. They were restrained, three men to each woman, while the other three ravished the child in turn, her screams and convulsions exciting them all the more. It was not until a fourth soldier prepared to mount her that they realized she was dying. The soldiers fled into the night, their buttons still undone.

Maddened with grief and rage, Hope flew after them. Cotton Tail was left alone to administer to the dying child. She discovered the bite on the back of the child's left calf and tried desperately to suck out the poison, but it was too late. Aslip was already dead. Cotton Tail found her brother's shotgun and took the lantern upstairs to find the snake, but like the soldiers, it, too, had disappeared.

She thought of her sister then, and armed with the lantern

and the gun, she went into the clearing and called Hope's name, but to no avail. She then followed the path that led to the Mobile road, but could find no sign of her sister or the marauding Union soldiers. She returned to the house and arranged Aslip's body neatly on her mother's bed, then dragged in the body of her brother and arranged it alongside the child. Then she fanned up the fire and made some 'coffee' from dried wild berries that they were accustomed to drinking and sat up all night waiting for the return of her sister.

By dawn Hope still hadn't returned. Cotton Tail at first thought that Hope might have followed her ravishers into Mobile, but that didn't seem likely, considering her state of mind. It was more plausible that she had forced them to kill her. When the sun came up, Cotton Tail walked to the Macpaisleys' farm and recounted the night's atrocities.

Macpaisley tried to get his son, Lim, to come with them to investigate, but Lim refused outright. He didn't want to be killed by the soldiers, too, he said.

Eight of Macpaisley's slaves, taking advantage of the confusion, had fled. Only three, feeble old male slaves, dreading the unknown world, had remained. With these three slaves and Cotton Tail, Macpaisley set out to look for Hope. First they returned to the house to see if she had returned in Cotton Tail's absence, but the house, except for the dead, was deserted. Then the little party set out in the direction of Mobile, searching the woods and gullies flanking the road for her body or some sign of her existence. By the time they had reached Mobile, they had still found nothing. However, they learned there that the detachment of Union soldiers had left at dawn and there had been no woman matching Hope's description among the camp followers.

Returning to the house, Macpaisley put his slaves to work digging graves for Lovely and Aslip, after which he said a prayer over each before they were covered. The slaves made crude crosses of cane to mark their graves. It was while they were thus engaged that they found the first trace of Hope. In gathering dried cane at the fringe of the clearing, one of the slaves noticed a cotton rag clinging to a bamboo stalk that couldn't have been there for any length of time.

Macpaisley got down on hands and knees and studied the ground around the cane stalks. He found there bare footprints entering the canebrake, definitely establishing that Hope had returned from chasing the soldiers. But why had she gone into the canebrake? What could she have been doing? He walked slowly around the clearing, studying the ground inch by inch, but there were no other footprints, suggesting that she had been alone. The conclusion that she was still in the canebrake was a frightening one. No human being could remain alive in the canebrake with its legion of poisonous snakes, dangerous boars, poisonous insects, and the bears and cougars that were rumored to be in there.

'Maybe she was searching for the snake that bit Aslip,' Cotton Tail suggested.

Macpaisley felt the hair rise on the nape of his neck. Definitely, she had gone crazy, he said to himself. All the signs pointed to it, and she had had plenty of reason for it. However, she was a white woman and had to be given a good Christian burial, so he ordered his slaves to go into the canebrake and find her body. The slaves looked at one another in terror and consternation. Their eyes rolled whitely and the black seemed to seep from their skin, leaving it gray-looking. They knew no one could ever have gone into that canebrake and come out alive. Macpaisley saw their hesitancy and aimed his shotgun at them. He threatened to shoot them if they didn't obey.

One of the slaves, braver than his companions, muttered defiantly, 'Usses doan have to, us is free.'

Macpaisley shot him instantly. The two others broke away, but they were old and neither of them was spry and agile enough to escape from any sort of fair shot. Macpaisley brought down one with a well-aimed shot to the base of the spine, but the other got out of sight while he was reloading. He could have run and caught up with him and killed him, too, but since he was a Catholic he decided to let him go.

Angered by the whole situation, he spent his fury and frustration on Cotton Tail. 'Goddamned snotnose whore.

Heah ah is lost all my slaves trying to do you cussed people a Christian service when you probably brought all you got down on yo'selves. Tryna fight off them wild randy soldiers 'bout a li'l pussy. Why didn't you gib 'em a li'l pussy, gib 'em all the pussy they wanted? Were it gonna hurt yuh? Now all but you is dead 'bout some pussy that ev'body got for nuthin—'

'It weren't that,' Cotton Tail interrupted. 'You think we'd get ourselves killed for that? It were 'cause they raped Aslip after she were snakebit and she died while they was raping her.'

'Well hell Godalmighty, why didn't Hope have her out of the way?'

'She were, she come in after she were snakebit.'

'Then how'd Lovely git his ass killed?'

'I dunno, I weren't lookin'.'

'Well, ah ain't gonna let you get my ass killed whilst you ain't lookin'. You jus' take yo' ass somewheres elst.'

So Cotton Tail took her ass to New Orleans where she approached the madam of a whorehouse on Rampart Street.

'I wanna job as a whore,' Cotton Tail said.

'Where's your man?' the madam asked her.

'I ain't got no man.'

'What's your experience, then?'

'You mean as a whore? I ain't got no experience of charging for it.'

'Amateur, eh?' the madam sneered. 'We don't use no amateurs here, else all women would be whores.'

'I can learn to charge,' Cotton Tail said.

The madam looked at her appraisingly. 'You got a specialty?' she asked.

'Oh yes, I got a specialty,' Cotton Tail said.

And she had a specialty, indeed. She became famous throughout all New Orleans and on the ships at sea for her specialty.

'Bess piece of ass I had since my li'l mulatto nigger boy growed up,' one discriminating former slave owner said, expressing the opinion of many other former slave owners with similar tastes, to say nothing of the opinions of others who had never been slave owners.

But after she had been in the whorehouse less than ten years, she was bought by a rich Arab who had made his fortune in the black slave trade. He took her back to his native land and installed her in his harem particularly because of her specialty.

Thus the Harrisons disappeared from the face of America, but the Harrison estate with its five thousand acres of totally useless canebrakes, swamp land, and its rotting, foetid, snake-ridden mansion remained. The place was always known to the end of its existence as the 'Harrison Place'. In the vicinity it gained a reputation for being haunted, and no native in his right mind could be forced within sight of it, even at the point of a gun.

However, a few itinerant tramps, white casualties of the Civil War, and freed slaves with nowhere else to sleep, put up there for short intervals, living off the razorback hogs, steaks from fat snakes, and bamboo shoots. Of course, none of these knew of its reputation as a haunted house.

It remained untenanted and unvisited by ordinary human beings until 1917, when it was surveyed by a crew of engineers to see if it could be converted into a naval drydock. By then, a railroad line connecting Mobile to Montgomery had been built along its western boundary, and a short distance further west a highway had been built to Meridian, Mississippi.

However, the engineers turned it down and, after World War I, it was put up for auction for unpaid back taxes. But no one could be found who wanted it, even for free, so it remained uninhabited until Tomsson Black got out of prison and bought it for the home factory of Chitterlings, Inc., because he had heard stories about the razorback hogs with piquant chitterlings.

5

The next to arrive were crews from the police cruisers which had been dispatched from the precinct. But the detectives outranked all the uniformed car cops and everyone stood around waiting for someone with more authority. If the white cops thought it strange that both the man and woman were dead, none of them said so.

The first man of authority to appear was a bored detective from homicide who fired his questions at the two black detectives because no one else was alive who might know anything.

'Where'd she get the gun?'

'He said it was sent to him.'

'By whom?'

'He said he didn't know. A messenger brought it and disappeared. There is no address of the sender and no name or address of the florist on the box it came in.'

The homicide detective, whose name was Rankin, picked up the florist's carton and examined it. It told him nothing. But inside, packed neatly in the excelsior, he found two hundred rounds of ammunition in four boxes that fitted snug to the bottom of one end.

'Here's the ammunition,' he said unnecessarily.

No one disputed him.

He turned to the automatic rifle.

'Army gun,' he stated. 'Stolen from some camp no doubt.' But on further examination, he added, 'But the camp's stamp is missing.' And still later he observed, 'No marks of any kind. Not visible, anyway. Maybe the lab will find some inside. Mmmm, that's strange,' he mused.

'Sure is,' Coffin Ed agreed.

Grave Digger threw him a warning look, but Rankin ignored him, and turned to the corpse of the man. He bent down and examined him as best he could without touching him. Then he looked from one black detective to the other. 'Which one of you men killed him?'

'We don't have to answer your questions,' Coffin Ed flared. 'We're detectives with the same rank as yours.'

'You'll have to answer someone's,' Rankin warned. 'Because this man was killed after this woman was dead and he didn't hit himself on the head.'

'That's as may be. But we'll report the circumstances surrounding his death to our superior officer in our precinct.'

'And at the same time I'll report my observations to my superior officer at the homicide bureau in the D.A.'s office.'

Grave Digger hadn't said anything.

The M.E.'s assistant arrived, shedding dandruff from his long black hair over the shoulders of a blue flannel suit that had seen better days. He went to work examining the bodies, ignoring everyone, like a medical Hamlet absorbed in his private horror. Causes of death in both instances were obvious, but only one obvious murder weapon had been discovered; it was a springblade knife to which were sticking gouts of congealed purple blood. The blunt instrument responsible for the crushed skull of the male corpse was not discovered.

The Harlem precinct was inclined to handle the killing as just another homicide in Harlem. Lieutenant Anderson accepted the veracity of his two ace black detectives, whose report on the killing of the woman was substantiated by the report of the assistant Medical Examiner and the observations of the homicide detective, Rankin. But Rankin added to his report that the death of the male victim appeared to result from a blow inflicted by one of the arresting officers, and, as such, demanded an investigation at the precinct level.

Captain Brice joined Lieutenant Anderson the following day to listen to the statements of the two black detectives.

'What I want to know is just what happened to cause one of you men to club this man over the head,' Captain Brice said with an open mind.

'Nothing happened,' Grave Digger said tightly. 'I just lost my head and hit the black mother with my pistol butt. I just hit him too hard is all.'

'He attacked Digger with his knife,' Coffin Ed amended. 'He had shot himself full of horse after he had knifed the woman and when we got there he was in a murderous state of excitement. He snatched up the bloody knife and started into Digger who was in front, and Digger just banged him once lightly to cool him down. He just hit him too hard is all.'

'Doesn't know his own strength,' Anderson put in, smiling.

'Sounds to me like an open and shut case of self-defense,' Captain Brice admitted.

He appeared willing to drop the inquiry and accept the self-defense verdict. One more dead nigger meant very little to Captain Brice, and it saved the state the cost of convicting him for the murder of the woman. But Coffin Ed couldn't stop talking.

'Yeah, some of these brothers are dangerous as blind snakes when they get high. And that brother had been mainlining for years.'

But Captain Brice didn't agree with his diagnosis. It wasn't that the captain disagreed with the fact that the brother had gone mad after having killed the woman and had charged an armed detective with the bloody knife. That was ample justification for killing him. He was willing to accept it, whether it was true or not. But he disagreed, on purely technical grounds, that such action could be attributed to a massive shot of heroin.

'Heroin is made from morphine,' he lectured. 'And morphine, like all opium derivatives, is a sedative. So heroin is a sedative and not a stimulant. And if this man took a massive shot of heroin after killing the woman, it was to quiet his nerves, not excite them. And whether he took it for that purpose or not, that is what it would have done. It might have put him to sleep, but it wouldn't have incited him to charge an armed detective with a bare knife.'

Anderson didn't agree. He had come up in the school of the crazed drug addict exploding into fits of incredible violence.

'Johnson doesn't claim the heroin stimulated the man as much as it produced a state of dementia. The man who attacked Jones was demented more than incited.'

'Heroin doesn't make an addict any more demented than excited,' Captain Brice argued. 'Unless, of course, it's been cut with an alkaloid with a toxic content, such as various brands of roach powder; and that could only happen by the addict cutting it himself. Which couldn't happen in Harlem because by the time horse gets up here it has been diluted so thin with sugar of milk you could use it on a breakfast cereal.'

'Well, sir, all that might be true,' the lieutenant conceded. 'But I don't understand what you're trying to get at.'

'I'm just trying to say if Jones busted that nigger's skull,' he went on stubbornly, 'it wasn't because that nigger was charging him with a knife. As long as I've been on this Harlem beat I know that there's no nigger who's going to charge an armed cop with a bare knife because he's had a shot of horse.'

'Well, for whatever reason,' Anderson contended, trying to save the day.

But Captain Brice had grown inflexible about his expertise on black character.

'For any reason,' he concluded flatly.

'What you're saying is that Jones just killed this man without sufficient justification,' Anderson spelled it out.

Captain Brice looked Grave Digger in the eye. 'Yes, that's what I'm saying.'

'In that case, we have no choice but to discipline him.'

'No choice,' the captain agreed.

As a consequence, Grave Digger was suspended from the Force until his case could be reviewed by the commissioner's disciplinary committee.

6

The automatic rifle was sent down to the laboratory at police headquarters. There were no fingerprints on the gun, shells, or packing except those of the corpses and the various police officers who had handled them. That in itself wasn't unusual; no one in their right senses was going to leave identifying evidence on a gun destined to figure in a crime. But there were no manufacturer's marks of any kind on the gun, inside or out, which was more alarming. But the most alarming discovery of all was the lack of manufacturer's marks on the shells. All cartridges carry the manufacturer's trade mark. And they were too well-finished to be homemade. Everything pointed to this gun being made for an assassin.

But what puzzled the political experts was why it was sent to this ignorant black man. It would have made sense if it had been sent to anyone who could have been considered as a potential assassin of the president, or some other well-known politician, who were the only people assassinated in the United States. They could have correlated the fact of it being sent to a potential assassin of a black politician, for in recent years they had moved into the target area, too. But this ignorant, black, Uncle Tom bastard couldn't be considered as a potential assassin on any account. And what was more, he would never have committed any crime of violence where an automatic gun of this type was needed. From what was known of him, he had been a chickenshit drug addict, a halfass pimp, a wholehearted Uncle Tom who would never have injured a white man for any reason, for he considered whitey as his meal ticket; and he was not only non-political, but he was actually afraid of politics, which is the case with many people who can't read or write.

In the end it was this train of thought that dispelled all their budding alarms: whichever way you looked at it, it wasn't anything but a nigger mess, and it had never been intended to be anything else. Whoever had sent this gun to T-bone Smith had other intentions than his assaulting a white man, for T-bone Smith was as incapable of assaulting a white man as he was capable of assaulting his black woman, and in the final analysis, that was all that mattered.

7

It was eleven-thirty one Saturday night in August, on Eighth Avenue in Harlem, ten days after the incident of the murdered black woman, and the unmarked gun which resembled an M-14 US Army infantry automatic rifle.

No one can visualize what Eighth Avenue is like who hasn't seen it. First, none of the residents has gone away on vacation, either to the seashore or the mountains, as is the case with most other New Yorkers. In fact, none of the residents has ever dreamed of going away during his vacation even in the wildest flights of his imagination. A few daring souls might get out to Coney Island, but most of these will be of the younger generation. For the most part the residents just sit in their squalor and swelter. There is no relief. Outside is the same as inside, night time is the same as day time. All the energy is steamed from the sweating, stinking bodies, and the will to move or do something about it, if there were anything to be done, is evaporated from the brain. The only relief which comes plausibly and facilely is to stupefy both body and brain with drink and drugs.

For the squalid Harlem slums do not have the same kind of squalor as the squalor of the black ghettos in the warmer climes, such as those in Rio, Miami, Cape Town, or even Watts. The squalor of the Harlem slums is more comparable to the squalor of the black ghettos of Chicago, Detroit, Cleveland, and Philadelphia. For the slum buildings of Harlem were not designed for blazing heat, but for bitter cold; in fact they were designed for the bitter cold and the matter of the heat was completely ignored. Perhaps as a consequence, the heat of Harlem's slums is far hotter than the slums of Rio. The brick and concrete buildings, the concrete pavements, the macadamized streets, unrelieved by tree or shrub, and even the black skin of the black people, absorbs the heat of the sun, the heat radiations from motor vehicles, the heat generated by strong alcoholic drinks, loud voices, and fatty foods, and stores it up in much the same manner as scientists are endeavoring to store up the heat of the summer sun for use in locations with cold and sunless winters – the difference being that this heat, which is stored in the squalid slum environs and dirty black bodies of the residents of Eighth Avenue, merely serves to sizzle them in the summer when they least need it and vanishes in winter when they suffer from the bitter cold of these same environs.

As a consequence, the residents of Eighth Avenue and its environs come out into the street at night seeking relief in the dark which looks cooler because they can't see the heat radiations of the day. It is a well-known fact that in primitive cultures the dark has always been considered cooler than the light, night cooler than the day. And this is still true in many parts of the world where the sun is the chief source of all heat. In Southern California, Florida, the French, Spanish, and Italian Rivieras, and similar resort areas, there is a tremendous difference in temperature between sunny days and black nights.

But there is no practical difference whatsoever between day and night on Eighth Avenue in Harlem. The difference was made by the residents thinking it. So the residents were out in the streets, hopping from one cheap bar to another, drinking bottled heat and getting hotter. Or they were sitting on the stoops of their slum tenements, or on broken chairs on the sidewalks, propped against the hot, crumbling walls, making themselves hotter for the exertions of their loud voices. Or they were packed like sardines into their many horsepowered jalopies, roaring from block to block, polluting the air with the hot gasoline fumes from exhausts, and sweating in the streams of heat blowing up from the engines. Or if they were young enough, they were heating themselves from their violent games, played between the stinking garbage cans. The coolest of the residents were the junkies, which is where the expression 'Keep cool, fool', came from. The horse in their bloodstreams had calmed their nerves and made them so aloof and 'cool' they didn't notice the heat, or even the squalor. That is why so many of them were junkies.

Unfortunately, it was not only unbearably hot, but it stank. Whether the heat would have been more bearable had it been perfumed is one of those stupid questions like, 'which is more destructive, fire or water?' The fact is, it wasn't perfumed. It stank from rotting food in both garbage cans and kitchen cabinets, from animal offal in the streets and human urine on the stairs and hallways, from half-burnt gasoline and half-burnt hair. It stank from body odor – B.O. to you

– underarm sweat, unwashed vaginas, unclean beds, rotting semen, unflushed feces, from the mating odors not only of black people but from black bugs, gray rats, black cats; it stank from the habitation of the many bugs between the walls – bed bugs, cockroaches, ants, termites, maggots – if you don't think the habitations of bugs stink, you should go to the zoo. It stank from the yearly accumulations of thousands of unlisted odors embedded in the crumbling walls, the rotting linoleum, the decayed wall paper, the sweaty garments, the incredible perfumes, the rancid face creams and cooking fats, the toe jam, the bad breath from rotting or dirty teeth, the pustules of pus. It stank from gangrenous sores, maggoty wounds, untended gonorrhea, body tissue rotten from cancer or syphilis.

The residents thought the air was fresher and cleaner and more pure outside than inside. But this was not so. In fact, as the French would say, *au contraire.* Outside there were all the impurities generated by their worn-out automobiles, their brimming garbage cans, the dog shit and cat shit, the putrefying carcasses of rats and cats and dogs and sometimes of meat too rotten even for the residents to eat, which had been tossed into the gutter for the animals. But some of it was too stinking even for hungry animals. And there were also the additional impurities from all the neighborhood food and merchandise stores, from the bars and restaurants, from the barber shops and beauty parlors.

Nevertheless, the residents thought it was cooler outside and that the air was more pure. 'Honey, I'm going outside 'n sit in the cool for a spell 'n git a bit of fresh air.' Therefore, on this Saturday night in August, they were all outside on the street, enjoying the cool and inhaling the fresh air.

8

That same Saturday, two big, red-faced, uniformed white cops were driving slowly down the middle of the street in a police cruiser to impress these people with the meaning of law and order. It wasn't so much they intended to bring about law and order as it was to frighten these people into respecting it. But since this noble purpose was presumed for them instead of by them, in reality they were thinking less of law and order than the highly amusing sights from the police car. And because this assignment was not only boring but repulsive, they sought diversion in the really funny spectacle of terrified black junkies trying to make themselves invisible, as though they weren't already invisible to the great law-abiding mass of the nation's citizens.

They were new on this particular roving patrol covering the more squalid slum streets of the ghetto, which had formerly been attended by Grave Digger Jones and Coffin Ed Johnson. But Coffin Ed was incapacitated and Grave Digger had been suspended. The day following Grave Digger's suspension, Coffin Ed had fallen into an uncovered manhole while off duty and had injured his knee so severely he could barely stand, much less undergo the rigors of patrolling the kinkier slum streets of Harlem in the late hours of the night. Moreover, since an uncovered manhole might be legally construed as negligence on the part of the city, the officials thought it was best to let sleeping dogs lie, or rather injured dogs limp.

Lieutenant Anderson genuinely sympathized with him for more reasons than his injured knee, and let him take over the telephone complaints of the black citizenry, a job that wasn't very difficult since black citizens had so few telephones. The white detectives in the squad room avoided him as though he had come down with a contagious disease instead of an injured knee, and, sad to say, there was no longer as much good American fun in the squad room as there had been in his absence. Which was a pity, for circumstances were proving that the black citizens of Harlem were as funny as ever.

In fact, the two blond cops in the cruiser, Pan and Van, were laughing to beat all hell as they coasted down Eighth Avenue in the heat of the night.

'I'm going to write a book,' said Van, 'and call it *Niggers is niggers is niggers*.'

'Those black junkies remind me of hermit crabs scuttling to sea,' said Pan.

'If I could put those junkies on the stage in Cape Town, I could make a fortune,' said Van.

'You'd need to give out baseballs to throw at them,' said Pan.

'The only thing is the audience couldn't stand the stink,' said Van.

'Yeah, there's something to be said for the gas chambers,' said Pan.

'The stink blew away,' said Van.

'Give them a burst from the siren,' said Pan.

Instead there was a burst from an automatic weapon from the front window of a third-floor tenement and the windscreen of the police cruiser exploded in a burst of iridescent safety glass. Not to mention the fact that Pan and Van were riveted to their black plastic seats by a row of 7.62-caliber rifle bullets that passed through their diaphragms. If they found anything funny about this 'happening', they never said. But still the cruiser kept cruising slowly down the street and still the rifle bullets rained on it, puncturing the roof, shattering the side windows, pounding the drooping blond heads into splinters of bone and blobs of soft gray brain tissue.

Suddenly the naked torso of a black man holding an army rifle appeared in the window shouting jubilantly, 'I done blowed them goldilocks back to whiteyland!'

'Sweet Jesus!' some black woman screamed, whether in terror or rejoicing no one knew.

The black brothers and sisters out for a breath of 'fresh' air in the 'cool' of the night fled as though from the blazing evil itself, and the bullet-pocked police car with the red and gold corpses of the two bullet-riddled cops kept cruising slowly down the street, as though it were the devil pursuing them.

'Come back, brothers,' the rifle-armed brother yelled. 'They ain't no danger to you.'

But the brothers didn't believe him; no more did the sisters. They ran frenziedly in all directions, hiding in corners, doorways, behind vehicles, underneath parked cars and other dark places they thought to be safe, which had been abandoned a moment before by other brothers who considered them unsafe. No truer words describing their flights of panic were ever said than Joe Louis's immortal observation about Billy Conn: 'He may run but he can't hide.' The black citizens on Eighth Avenue in the environs of the shooting were running to beat all hell, but they couldn't find any place to hide. A black brother had mowed down two white cops. No matter how commendable this extravagant action might be, the plain fact was it cast them all in danger. They felt for him, all right, they prayed for him, but they didn't want to bleed for him. They felt for him but they couldn't reach him. In fact, they couldn't get away from him fast enough, and that was the trouble.

Because other police cruisers were coming like the avengers, their sirens screaming like escaped souls from hell, their red eyes blinking like Martian space ships. At first it was the sight of them that was so terrifying. No police in the history of the world looks as dangerous and acts as violent as the American police. Before a shot was fired, black brothers and sisters were shitting in their pants. All these black people, who had protested in one way or another against being considered invisible by the white citizenry, would have given anything to have been invisible then.

The white cops in the cruisers roared up beside their bullet-pocked mate which had crashed into a wall, and looked at the blood-spattered corpses of their colleagues with half their skulls blown off, then looked around for the nearest black brother to start making him pay.

But the half-naked brother in the third-floor window with the automatic rifle began shooting at the cops as though they were scavenger birds, and knocked three of them down before the others had scrambled for cover. Crouched behind their cruisers, the cops began blazing away in unison with their .38 caliber police specials. But the big 7.62-caliber slugs from the rifle were chopping the police cruisers apart systematically. The cops couldn't get to their wounded colleagues who lay on the pavement bleeding. But they kept peppering away at the windowsill in the tenement, behind which the brother was kneeling, blazing away with his rifle which he had rested on the windowsill.

It was the black citizens who were producing most of the drama. In panic-stricken terror, while the lethal bullets were sailing overhead, they had crawled across the filthy pavements into the equally filthy doorways and hallways and stairways of the hot, airless, filthy tenements, where they lay packed on the dirty floors, smelling stale urine, trembling in the stink of their own terror. Moaning, groaning, praying, and muttering vile curses while the gun battle raged outside, and the graffiti scratched and drawn on the decaying, yellowing walls looked down upon them.

An anthropologist might be more interested in the graffiti inside than in the gun battle outside, or even in the sweating bodies of the black people squirming on the floors. Why do slum dwellers express themselves in graffiti depicting exaggerated genitals? he might ask himself. Why always genitals? Why oversized genitals? Why are black slum dwellers obsessed with these enlarged genitals, penises as big, comparatively, as telephone poles, and heads as small as coconuts? What are they trying to tell themselves? That as humans their heads might be small in the white man's sight but their unseen genitals were as big as field artillery? But within the sound of the gunfire outside, their genitals had actually shrunk to the size of match sticks and peanuts.

By now, there were more than thirty police cruisers parked at all angles about the street, their red beacons blinking, but not a cop was in sight. They were all crawling about the paved street in the lee of the automobiles, shooting around the wheels, the hoods, and the trunks. Several tried to find a way to get inside the tenement from the back, but the tenements had been built back to back with the tenements on Manhattan Avenue without any thought of service or ventilation, and to reach the black maniac on the third floor, the cops would have to enter downstairs from the street. And that would entail crossing the deserted strip of sidewalk between the police cruisers and the doorway, through a hail of 7.62-caliber slugs that were slowly ripping the cars apart in lieu of other targets. After which they would have to walk over the sweating, stinking bodies of the black citizens who were packing the floors of the hallway and stairway from wall to wall. None of the cops opted for this solution, and one could scarcely blame them, in view of the fact that their three colleagues, who had been shot down at first, were by now ripped into shreds.

Some climbed into the windows of the tenements across the street and some to the roofs, but the firepower of the black brother's automatic rifle was so brutal it knocked out the windows, frames, bricks from the wall, and huge stones from the cornices of the tenements where the cops were lurking, so not one was so foolhardy as to show enough of himself to draw a bead on a target. Obviously, they were all outgunned by this one automatic rifle in this black man's hands. They were infuriated and frustrated themselves, for a change. They sent for riot guns, but it did not take them long to discover that ordinary riot guns were ineffective in the face of the brutal weapon this black man had. This weapon had been designed to kill under all circumstances, and the cops were loath to prove the point. They sent for tear gas guns, but none got a chance to use them. As soon as they were pushed into view, they were hit and destroyed and blown out of sight.

9

Lieutenant Anderson and Captain Brice had been at the scene for quite a while, but they had stayed clear of the gunfire and out of sight. Every now and then, Captain Brice's megaphoned voice could be heard issuing instructions that were too dangerous to obey. Coffin Ed sat in the car with them because of his injured knee.

Once Captain Brice asked him, 'What would you do, Johnson?'

'I'd give them better housing,' Coffin Ed began. 'Better schools, higher wages—'

'I mean about this nigger,' Captain Brice snapped.

'If it was me, I'd quit thinking about him as a nigger and start thinking about him as sick,' Coffin Ed replied.

'He's going to be sicker than that shortly,' Captain Brice said. 'He's going to be dead.'

'I'm no good here,' Coffin Ed said, and he climbed painfully out of the captain's car.

'Go back to the precinct,' Lieutenant Anderson said kindly, 'and answer the telephone.'

Shortly Captain Brice was on the telephone to the Chief Inspector down at police headquarters, after which he instructed the cops staked out underneath their cruisers, 'Don't try to get him anymore. I've got help coming. I don't want any more of you men to get injured. Just contain him, that's all, just don't let him get away. If you see any black man trying to get out of those buildings, shoot him on sight.'

The cops heard this order and remembered it. They were literal minded, and they did not see any extenuating circumstances, any kind of mitigating behavior. That was for judges and juries. They were cops, and cops were responsible for law and order; cops were supposed to arrest criminals and offenders of this law and order, shoot them if they resisted or tried to escape. A cop is a cop, not a welfare worker, a city planner, a sociologist. If black people lived in slums, that wasn't the cop's fault; the cop's duty was to see that they obeyed the law and kept the order, no matter where they lived. It was coincidental that rich and educated white people who lived in large, roomy, airy houses, in clean, fresh, well-kept neighborhoods were more likely to keep the law and the order, but cops didn't have so much to do in those neighborhoods.

So when Captain Brice instructed the cops, 'If you see any black man trying to get out of any of these buildings, shoot him on sight,' he must have believed the cops would obey him or he wouldn't have given them the order. Unless of course, he was a fool, a windbag, a jokester, or simply ineffective, none of which precinct captains in New York are apt to be.

There was a lull in the shooting, during which the naked torso of the black man who had been shooting from the third-floor window became vaguely highlighted by the street lamps as he peered cautiously up and down the deserted street, at the pocked and pitted police cruisers, at the darkened windows of the tenements across the street, at the skyline of the opposite roof. He held his rifle loosely pressed to his shoulder, ready to shoot at anything that moved. But nothing moved. Not even the polluted, cordite-stinking air, which had become unbearably hot from the explosions of gunfire. His black features were indiscernible against the background, but the whites of his eyes were shaped like the crescent of a new moon, just like white people say. One couldn't see the shine of his pearly teeth for the simple reason that he kept his mouth shut. But no doubt they were there, hidden behind his red lips and his blue gums. All that could be seen of him was the oily glint of his muscular torso, gleaming like a freshly-cast bronze in a pitch-dark room.

Several of the more venturesome brothers on the floor of the street-level hallway crawled to the doorway and looked out, but from their worm's-eye view, they could see the immobile cops lying beneath the bullet-riddled cruisers and the dark blue-steel gleam of the .38 police specials in their hands. Needless to say, they drew back hastily, like worms sighting birds.

So they didn't see the bug-shaped tank coming up the middle of Eighth Avenue from the direction of downtown, looking about with its one eye at the end of a 105 mm cannon, like some kind of strange insect from outer space. The police had boasted of having a sophisticated weapon which could quell any riot imaginable. If this was it, it didn't look sophisticated in the common usage of the word, but it certainly looked impregnable. No human life was visible within it. It was shaped like a turtle with an insect's antenna. It moved on rubber-treaded caterpillar tracks. It didn't make any noise. It came quickly and silently, as if it knew where it was going and was in a hurry to get there.

When the brother with the 7.62-caliber automatic rifle first noticed it, it was almost level with his window. He peppered it with a startled burst from his brutal gun, but the 7.62-caliber bullets ricocheted off its smooth round shell of bullet-proof alloy without any effect. The brother ducked. And just in time. The 105 mm cannon fired with a sound like artillery in a war, and the shell passed above him and hit the back wall of the darkened room, and blew the wall out, the ceiling out, the wall beyond out, the ceiling beyond out, and laid waste the entire four-room apartment from front to back in a burst of flame as bright as a lightning bolt. The impact shook the flimsy building from top to bottom like the tremor of an earthquake. The half-naked brother was covered with falling plaster and white plaster dust. The flat lay in a shambles of blasted walls, ripped-out ceilings, exposed beams, rubbish-covered floors, as though the wreckers had been at it.

Down below, the noise sounded to the frightened black people lying packed side by side on the floor of the entrance hallway like the clap of doom. From them rose a litany of muffled screams, moans of dread, whines of terror, curses of despair. The plaster and plaster dust showered down over them, splotching them with white, as though they were turning white with terror. William Faulkner would have been vindicated in his description of black skin turning the gray of wood ashes.

En masse, they squirmed toward the back of the hallway, but they couldn't escape by the back door because there wasn't any back door. Nor did anyone attempt to go up because that was where the demolition was coming from. What they wished to do was sink beneath the floor, but even though the jerry-built tenement might crumble beneath the cannon blasts, still the floors were strong enough to keep the black people imprisoned.

Nothing had been seen or heard of the black brother with the gun since the first cannon blast, but the cannoneers deemed it expedient to keep on cannonading, in the scorched-earth tradition of the US Army, until any and all possible opposition had been eliminated. They had no intention of unnecessarily risking the lives of red-blooded American cops to capture one lone black maniac, that's why they had the cannon. So they kept blasting through the front windows with the 105 mm explosive shells until the jerry-built tenement began to crumble and disintegrate, like those enemy strongholds in World War II films being decimated by the artillery of our side.

As the flimsy walls and floors began to crumble and fall, dislocated beams and hunks of wall and flooring began to shower down upon the terrified black people lying on their bellies in the stinking dark of the entrance hallway. The black people bolted in terror out onto the dangerous, deserted street. They came out screaming, mouths stretched open, nostrils flaring, eyes walled with white, black skin splotched with white like patches of war paint, pissing and shitting themselves from fear, fleeing for their lives.

Whether the white cops hiding beneath the scattered police cruisers thought they were painted black savages on the war path, or whether they just thought of Captain Brice's instructions ('If you see any black man trying to get out of any of those buildings, shoot him on sight') is a factor which was never determined. The fact is they suddenly rose up from their hiding places and began shooting the fleeing black people down. White cops could never tell black men from black women, as has been evidenced in the Sharpeville massacre in South Africa.

But as the dead piled up and the shouts and screams of pain and terror could be heard above the roar of the gun-fire, it was then, as a subsequent inquiry established, that the white cops lost their cool and became animals, killing people for the sheer pleasure of killing; killing black people who died with the fatalism of animals.

Either the black brother with the automatic rifle sensed what was happening on the street below or else became crazed by the screams of his terrified brothers – and sisters – for suddenly he leapt to his feet and stood in the open window on what must have been the only section of the flooring left in the room which could hold his weight. Ignoring the rifle in his right hand, which he had discovered was useless against the tank, he beat his chest with his left fist like a male gorilla and shouted in a loud, defiant black voice:

'I'll fight you white motherfuckers; I'll fight you one by one,

I'll fight you with anything you wanna fight with; I ain't scared of you white motherfuckers.'

No sooner had the words left his lips (almost as though the cannoneers had waited politely for him to finish), than he was struck in the chest by a 105 mm shell, and his body exploded. Some of the pieces of bloody flesh and splintered bones and loose teeth were blown out through the front window in which he had been standing and rained down onto the black corpses piled below. And those were the only pieces ever recovered to establish the fact of his existence. And the rifle which he had held was so badly damaged it was found useless for providing clues of any kind.

The immediate horror was so great the mind could not accept it. The mind recoiled from it. Some of the white cops found themselves laughing uncontrollably. But law and order had been restored to the vicinity of Eighth Avenue.

10

Tomsson Black first learned about the razorback hogs with piquant chitterlings from another black convict in for rape, too, who slept next to him on the same Alabama chain gang. Some years previous, this convict, whose name was Hoop, had hidden out for several weeks in the old Harrison place and lived on the only diet possible of pork, snake, and bamboo shoots. At that time, Hoop had killed a redneck in the area named Atmore Macpaisley, doubtless a descendant of the slave-owning Macpaisleys, who had tried to make him fuck a mule in order to prove that a nigger was the only animal who could breed with a mule.

Afterward he had hidden from the posse in the snake-infested canebrakes until it became safe enough for him to come out to the old, dilapidated, rotten, mildewed house. Hoop said he had figured out that the chitterlings tasted so 'strong' – *strong* was his word for them – because razorbacks ate so many snakes and fish. He said he had seen them pick up water moccasins, bite them in two, and continue eating them unruffled with the head of the snake biting them until it was eaten up, too.

It had given him gooseflesh, he said, the greedy way those razorbacks devoured live snakes. But they ate live fish in the same way, he said, just like bears did. Only the razorbacks ate the entire fish, head and all, while bears just bit out the bellies. He swore he had seen these razorback hogs diving for fish in the fetid, shallow swamps the same way pelicans did. He had seen a lot of pelicans fishing in the Okefenokee Swamp of Florida, but the razorbacks on the Harrison place could outfish them two to one.

The razorbacks would duck their heads beneath the scummy water and never come up without a fish, or an eel, or a snake. Hoop said he had seen hogs eat snakes ever since he was a child, but that was the first time he had ever seen hogs eat live fish. ''Course, if you come to think about it, if a hog would eat a snake, it'd eat a fish, or anything else,' he said.

He said the reason he began cleaning and cooking the chitterlings and eating them instead of the meat of the hog was because he was scared of being poisoned by all the venom the snake bites had left in the meat.

Both Tomsson Black and Hoop were serving life for raping white women. But there, the similarity ended. For one thing, Hoop had two or three murder charges waiting for him when he got through serving life for rape.

For another thing, Hoop was an older man with a different background and a different outlook on life. Hoop was forty-five years old, with a sagging belly, powerful, sloping shoulders, and a wet-black, moon-shaped face lit by twinkling white crescents and topped by a shiny bald pate. He had the misleading appearance of childish jollity, but he was neither childish nor jolly. Born and raised in the backwoods of the Deep South, he was a violent, dangerous man, with the sneaky lethality of a cottonmouth moccasin who can bite you to death under water. He was the type of man you'd say had never been a child. He had been raping women and murdering men ever since he left the cradle, or what had passed for one in the sharecropper's shack where he was born. And he had killed more nigger-hating rednecks and peckerwoods in the south than pellagra.

He was quick-witted and a past master at taking insults with a grin. He would skin back his gums and show a peckerwood all thirty-six of his big yellow teeth, and the moment the peckerwood turned his back, he'd cut his throat. He had been sentenced to life for raping this piece of white trash and every day the white hacks at the chain gang beat him unconscious for supper. But when he was alone with Tomsson Black at night in the dormitory, he would laugh about it.

'I were goin' through this scrub cotton country 'round Selma and it were so hot my balls were dryin' up and I stopped at this grimy pine shack to beg for a drinka water. From the looks of it, I thought they was niggers livin' there. But a green-eyed white bitch answered the back door. One look at her, I was ready to run my ass off. But 'fore I could get my feet movin' she shot out a skinny hand and grabbed holda me. 'If'n you run, nigger, I gonna scream,' she say.

'Sweat popped out on my head and I felt my asshole tightenin' up. "I ain't gonna run, lady," I promise, lookin' out the corners of my eyes. "I'se jes movin' my feet 'cause y'all's pullin' my dick so hard." "Git your ass inside," she say, pullin' me in by my dick. "Lady, I just wanna get a drinka water and go," I say. "And if you let go my dick, I'll go without no water." "You can't go now, nigger, you jes' got here," she say. "You gotta fuck me first and if you don't fuck me good, I'm gonna call my old man who's plowing out there in the field and have him come in here and blow your head off."

'I look through the open window and see a sweat-stained peckerwood plowing a two-mule team not a half-field away. And there was I, didn't have no pistol, no knife, nothing but my raggedy ass and that peckerwood had a shotgun tied to the handle of his plow, like he expected niggers every day. I were so scared I fell down on the floor outa his sight. Then this trash lay down on the floor 'side me and pulled up her skirt and spread her naked legs.

'"Shuck off your pants and gimme that black dick, nigger," she say. "Ssssshhh, not so loud," I shushed her, 'cause it looked to me like that peckerwood could hear her from where he was plowing.

'But she jes' raise her head and look out over the window sill and say, "He can't hear nothin' but them mules fart."

'Even looking at that white pussy spread out'n front of me, I were so scared I couldn't get a hard-on, but I 'gan fuckin' her with a limber dick to keep her from screamin' until it 'gan hardenin' up. It musta 'gan gettin' good to her for she start twistin' her bare ass on the wooden floor and cryin' every time it got a splinter. And when I start thinkin' of her ass gettin' all splintered up it 'gan gettin' good to me, too, and I start pumpin' my ass up and down like the fly wheel on a locomotive. Her peckerwood husband musta looked up and seen my black ass risin' and fallin' above the window sill, 'cause he call out suddenly, "What in the world are you doin' with that old automobile tire, Maybelle?" If she had jes' let it go at that, it mighta been all right, but she had to go and say, "It ain't no automobile tire, I polishin' the stove."

'He musta stood there and thought about that and it must notta sounded right for all of a sudden he come in through the back door with his shotgun in his hand. He stood there red as a redbird, aiming that gun at me, and I thought for a moment I were a goner. But he took long enough to say, "I'm gonna blow your brains out, nigger, for rapin' my old lady," and I knew I were safe. I were so 'lieved I said, "I weren't rapin' her, boss. I were jes tryna getta drink of water." And all that peckerwood did was take me into town and have me tried for rape.'

Tomsson Black laughed. 'You must have been lightly dressed,' he observed.

'All I had was my pants coverin' my bare ass,' Hoop confessed. 'But that taught me. Heresomeafter, I'se always goin' to wear drawers when I go walkin'.'

Listening to Hoop, one would think he was amused by the eroticism of white people. But Tomsson Black didn't think it was funny. In his estimation, white people's eroticism was responsible for all lynchings of blacks by whites, and it had done more to alienate the races than all other causes put together. This eroticism had made the whites into liars, cheats, thieves, and hypocrites, and had proved to be more dangerous than their hate. Hoop knew that a black man could handle a nigger-hating cracker, but a nigger-loving crackeress was poison.

11

Tomsson Black had not always been his name. He had been christened George Washington Lincoln by a father who had a valid predisposition for the names of former presidents, for his own Christian name was Thomas Jonathan Lincoln.

This lineage of black Lincolns had its roots in slavery. The first black Lincoln was the chattel of a cotton planter named Hassan Hardy Hargreaves, who owned a large plantation on the delta of the Mississippi River near Port Gibson. At the time of his birth by the lusty black breeder, Gee, the first thing that met the gaze of the overseer as he looked about for a suitable object to name the newborn slave after was the gray moss hanging from the limbs of a rotting oak. Hence the name Moss. Only the overseer knew the father of the newly-born Moss was a field slave called Haw. Moss never knew who his father was, anymore than a heifer knows what bull it was sired by, nor did he ever feel the need for knowing.

The Hargreaves were a very large family. In addition to seven sons and five daughters, Mrs Hargreaves's spinster sister and her bedridden mother and Mr Hargreaves's two orphaned nephews lived with them. They had a very large colonial-style mansion in a park that ran down to the riverbank and more than a thousand slaves to till their fields and do their bidding.

When Moss was considered old enough to work at the age of six he was assigned to help the slave blacksmith, Atlas. The former helper, Piggy, who had become twelve, had been sent to the field to chop and pick cotton. He fanned the forge, collected the horse manure for the roses, and held the horses' reins while Atlas was shoeing them. On occasions when Atlas became too hot, Moss would douse him with water from the bucket used to cool the horseshoes.

Moss had one of his ears bitten off by a recalcitrant mare and several times he was bitten on the face and arms due to his fearlessness with the horses. By the time he was twelve and old enough to be sent to the fields in his turn, he resembled a young black monster. On the very eve of his departure, a horse kicked Atlas in the head, killing him instantly, and Moss found himself elevated to the role of blacksmith. He proved to be a good blacksmith and could control the spirited horses with ease, thanks, as the overseer jokingly put it, to the fear his face inspired in them.

During the Civil War the horses disappeared from the plantation when six of the sons went off to fight in the Confederate Army. A blacksmith was no longer needed and Moss was put in the field. After the war had been in progress for some time, a rumor spread like wildfire among the slaves that they had been freed by a white God called Lincoln, a rumor that turned them from willing workers to recalcitrant ones.

Master Hargreaves suspected that an itinerant peddler of patent medicines, who had passed by several days earlier, had started this rumor. Although he was suffering from anxiety and yellow jaundice, he got up from his sick bed, had a mule saddled, and tracked the innocent peddler to a plantation a hundred miles downriver and shot him dead. Still, the rumor persisted and grew into a fact when emissaries of the Union Army canvassed the plantations to tell the slaves that the war was over and they were free.

The blacks did not know what to do with their freedom and many elected to stay on the plantation for their food and shelter. Moss was among the first to leave. It was then that he took the name of Lincoln, since it was the only name he knew with the exception of 'Bible' that had no association with slavery. As Moss Lincoln wandered through the hostile South of the Reconstruction Era, he survived only through his fleetness of foot, his ability to digest acorns, and his grotesque appearance, which got him odd jobs as the 'wild man' at local fairs.

Because he could not read, write, or count above ten, he did not know his age. Moss was thirty-three years old when he left the plantation a free man. Two years later he met a slave girl when he sneaked up to a kitchen door of a sleeping manor house early one morning to beg food from the cook. She was alarmed by the sight of him, for she thought he was a runaway slave. He looked as though he had been severely punished for running away before. It was three years since the Civil War had ended, but she still didn't know the slaves were free.

He hung about the plantation all day and saw her again that night. By morning they were lovers and he had convinced her that they were free. Tying all of her belongings into a bandanna handkerchief, she left the plantation with him before daybreak. Her name was Pan. Thus began the lineage of the black Lincolns.

Having a wife saved Moss's life several times as they walked across Mississippi toward Tennessee, which they thought was 'up North' where Lincoln was a god. By then, the Ku Klux Klan was the scourge of dark country roads and single black males without a white 'protector' were apt to be hung outright.

They arrived in Memphis in the spring of 1869 and were surprised to find an already-established ghetto of freed slaves, all fighting amongst themselves for existence. Thanks to his muscular physique and ferocious appearance, Moss survived. He got a job as a blacksmith's helper at a livery stable owned by whites in the business section of Memphis. However, he and his wife had to live in the black shantytown under conditions infinitely worse than those of the horses he helped to shoe.

Pan's first three babies were still-born due to a vitamin deficiency caused by a diet of fat meat and home-made corn grits. Finally a male baby lived and the exultant father asked Mr MacDowell, his blacksmith boss, to give him a name. MacDowell, without an instant's thought, said, 'Zachary. The poor bugger's gotta be rough'n ready to survive in that poisonous swamp where you niggers live.'

Five other male babies were born to Pan and were named

in turn by the amiable Mr MacDowell John Quincey, William Henry, Julius Augustus, Caius, and Napoleon. Unfortunately, all but Zachary died – one from Yellow Fever, one from pellagra, one choked to death on a pork bone, and the other was killed by a mad dog that found its way into their shanty. Whether they died because of the brave names Mr MacDowell had given them, or in spite of them, the illiterate, superstitious ex-slave and his suspicious wife never decided, but they agreed to name the next one all by themselves. Unfortunately, there were no others.

Zachary grew up their only child and, in his turn, became a blacksmith, going to work for the same livery stable as his father when Moss died. Zachary married the third daughter of the black preacher who had a church of an unnamed denomination in a rotting, abandoned warehouse on the lower end of Beale Street, where it runs into the Mississippi.

At that time, Beale Street was occupied almost exclusively by white trash who were scarcely better off than the ex-slaves, and Preacher Gus was considered a formidable man for daring to preach there. Preacher Gus was a veritable Hercules who, on his regular job, easily carried the five-hundred-pound bales of cotton on his back from the warehouses down to the pier where they were loaded aboard river boats bound for New Orleans. It was considered equally daring of Zachary to marry one of Gus's grown daughters, since it was rumored that Gus wanted them all for himself.

Their first son was born in 1912 and Mr MacDowell, by then a doddering old man but still official blacksmith of the Main Street Livery Stable, promptly suggested the name of Thomas Jonathan (Stonewall). Zachary's wife, Lucy, could not only read and write, but she had attended a boarding school in Nashville called Fisk Institute, and she knew enough about America's history to know that the name was that of a Confederate Army General who had died in the Civil War defending slavery. She did not think it an appropriate name for a black child, the grandson of slaves.

However, Zachary contended that Mr MacDowell would be angry if they didn't use the name and might very likely fire him. She relented, but would never call her son anything but Jonathan.

Lucy bore three daughters afterward, but in 1917 Zachary was drafted into the US Army, in spite of his being the head and sole provider of a large family. The expeditionary force on its way to France to fight the Hun was desperately in need of blacksmiths to serve both the cavalry and artillery. Unfortunately, Zachary, a non-combatant, was killed by enemy artillery during the Battle-on-the-Marne while his company was being moved from one position to another. Lucy and her four young children were left without a husband and father.

Lucy took her children to live with her aging father, Preacher Gus, who was by then a widower himself. He welcomed back his daughter to cook and clean for him, since all of his other children had left the roost. But Lucy was still young, only twenty-eight, and she had no intention of being her father's housekeeper and nurse during his declining years. She was educated and still lovely, rare in a black woman of that time, living as she did in the Memphis slums of Beale Street. In spite of her four children, there was no shortage of suitors for her hand.

She chose a dock worker in the image of her father, a huge, brawny black who could neither read nor write, to the consternation of other suitors who had lighter skin and better educations. To her intimate women friends, she confessed that she didn't want to take a book to bed and wanted to see her husband naked on white sheets.

His name was Ralph Sherwin and he adored her, but he didn't care too much for her children since he wanted children of his own. The children sensed they were unwanted and, even at their tender ages, began to drift away. Jonathan was eight and the only one attending the jerry-built wooden elementary school that Memphis provided for black children. Shortly he began to play hookey and ended up sweeping the floor and racking balls for a new pool room on Beale Street. The blues were coming into vogue at that time, and often he'd stay out all night hiding in the shadows of some popular gin joint to hear them played and sung.

His two eldest sisters, six and seven years of age, went to live with aunts and eventually became prostitutes. His baby sister, who had only been three when his mother married again, had been accepted by Ralph as a child of his own. During the ensuing thirteen years she was provided with eleven half-brothers and sisters.

'Johnny', as Jonathan was known, turned out to be a ne'er do well. One night he met a light-complexioned, teen-aged girl trying to hustle in a gin joint. He took her home with the intention of becoming her pimp. Two days later, when he was trying to place her in a house run by a tall, raw-boned black woman with a scarred face, he ran into his two sisters who were working there. This shocked him out of his intention. Instead, he married the girl, whose name was Naomi, and got her a job as a laundress and chambermaid for a white family. He shortly joined the domestic staff as a gardener and handyman in self-defense so that he could keep his wife faithful.

When they began to raise a family, their employers gave them the use of a tumble-down cottage that had housed an overseer during slavery. By 1942, five years after their marriage, they had four brown tots, who were called 'those Lincoln pickaninnies' by the white family.

In April of 1942, Thomas Jonathan Lincoln was inducted into the US Army as a private in the infantry. Until then, Jonathan had accepted Jim Crow and segregation as the normal way of life. He did his basic training in Southern Jim Crow camps. In December of that year he was sent to the Pacific Theater and spent the next eleven months in a company of other black laborers building and cleaning out latrines for white servicemen on the Pacific Islands.

During that time he smelled and shoveled so much white shit, not to mention the amount of shit he had to take from the whites, that he developed an intense hatred for all white people. Before then he had never actively hated white people. They lived in a white world and he lived in his black world, dependent on them, serving them, but always indulged by them in the special fashion that white Southerners showed toward their good niggers. But the whites in the army didn't make any allowances for his being black. They worked him like a nigger and treated him like a nigger with no compensating indulgences.

He chopped off the first two fingers of his left hand in order to get discharged. He was discharged, but dishonorably, without any GI or other compensating benefits, and his commanding officer told him he was lucky not to have been imprisoned.

He arrived back in Memphis, broke and discharged, to learn that the news of his dishonor had arrived ahead of him. His wife had quit her job and gone off with another man, taking their children with her. His former employers were infuriated both by his wife's desertion from their employ and by his own disloyalty to his country. They would have nothing to do with him.

No one would lend him any money and a white deputy from the Sheriff's Office suggested that he leave town. In desperation, with no money or possessions but his ragged uniform, he hitchhiked to St Louis. The only people who gave him lifts were, as was to be expected, black. He always stepped off the road when a white motorist came into view if he saw him in time.

He immediately discovered that during the war against Japan, St Louis was no place for an unemployed and friendless black man with a dishonorable discharge from the army. He moved into the suburban University City, using his instinct to lead him to the estates of wealthy whites. He knew they would be short of help and unconcerned about his dishonorable discharge. Secretly, many wealthy and intelligent whites saw no disgrace in a black man getting out of the Jim Crow army by whatever means possible. Plus, he was strong enough and sound enough to do all the chores they could find, despite the missing fingers that scarcely incapacitated him at all.

He got a room on credit in the shanty of a black widow employed as cook and housekeeper by one of the white families in the lovely little town and whose only time off was every Thursday afternoon and evening and every second Sunday afternoon. Mrs Booker's four-room shanty was in the shantytown for black servants located in the swampland along the southern bank of the Missouri River, on the outskirts of University City.

Mrs Booker didn't have time to live in it herself, since most of the black servant women lived in now, and didn't need any outside accommodations since all the able-bodied men were away. Only the aged and the infirm black men were about, and Mrs Booker didn't want any of them as roomers. What she wanted was someone as strong and willing – not to mention eager – as she was herself. It was true that Jonathan had a couple of fingers missing, but he didn't seem to be missing anything otherwise, so Mrs Booker let him have the room on credit, trusting him to be there when she was to pay off his bill.

Much to Mrs Booker's disappointment, however, it didn't turn out that way at all. On his first visit to one of University City's small estates, Jonathan got a day's employment as a much-needed handyman and carpenter, the only occupations for which he was qualified. Soon he was working every day on different estates as a handyman and gardener and when Mrs Booker finally got her Thursday off, all she found at home was a week's rent and the word 'thanks'.

Jonathan discovered that the residents of University City were much in need of his services. He didn't need any tools because each estate had its own. He didn't need any food for at each estate he found a black cook eager to feed him. He did not lack for sexual fulfillment for there were scores of black women to fulfill his every desire. He had no competition, since every able-bodied black man was either in the armed forces or else out of sight.

By the end of 1944, Jonathan found that he was prosperous. And he was in love. For two months he had been sleeping with a lovely black nineteen-year-old chambermaid. When she told him that she was pregnant during the second week of January, 1945, he confessed that he was married but that his wife had run off with another man.

'Well, what's stopping you from marrying me, then?' she

asked. 'You know these white folks aren't going to care if she don't raise no stink.'

So at the end of the month he married Hattie Bourchard and at the beginning of March they set up housekeeping on the top floor of a decaying carriage house on a run-down, neglected estate near the southwest corner of town where the Missouri River empties into the Mississippi. The estate was owned by two spinster sisters in their sixties, who were among the last descendants of a tycoon who had built one of the western railroad empires, Major George Mortimer Purcell. In Major Purcell's day it was used as a summer house. The manor house was a sixty-three-room castle faced with brown stone and garnished with many stained-glass leaded windows. It had three octagonal towers, each comprising a single large room with eight picture windows that overlooked the estate.

Surrounding the castle was the 'green', a velvet-smooth lawn of circular shape. From the drawing-room windows, the lawn sloped down to a marble fountain large enough to serve as a swimming pool, beyond which was a rose arbor the size of a plantation laid out between serried rows of white marble columns on brown granite pedestals. Surrounding all of this was a park that served as Major Purcell's private hunting preserve.

But the upkeep of such a place was very expensive and it couldn't be sold since no one who could afford it wanted it. As a consequence, Major Purcell's heirs simply abandoned it and eventually the Wharton sisters, Major Purcell's grand-nieces, settled there to die. By this time the estate was in a hopeless state of decay. The lawn and rose garden were overgrown with weeds and poison ivy, rutted by gopher holes and soil erosion so far advanced that it was beyond reclamation. The park had reverted into a riverbank jungle and the furnishings of the house were slowly disintegrating from rot, mildew, and the continuous assaults of voracious insects.

The Wharton sisters lived in a small apartment at the back of their house. Their one servant, an old and toothless black hag scarcely worth her keep, slept in the old-fashioned kitchen that was big enough to serve an army.

When the black Lincolns approached them about a place to stay in that big empty castle or one of its outbuildings, the Whartons seized the opportunity. The two old women welcomed the protection to be afforded by having a man about the place, even a black one, although they had been without such protection since they had moved in during the early years of the Great Depression. They realized that he could clear the weeds from the driveway and fix the rattling windows, but declined to have him live under the roof with them, even though that roof covered sixty empty rooms. They rented to him the three empty rooms over an old, unused, scorpion-infested carriage house for fifteen dollars a month, plus doing small chores for them.

This arrangement suited the Lincolns fine. Hattie had begun calling him Tom because his first wife had called him Johnny. Since a bus into University City stopped at the foot of the driveway every hour, Tom was able to get back and forth to his jobs in the city and Hattie was able to shop, cook, and keep house for him. Unfortunately, it didn't work out quite the way they'd planned. The Wharton sisters demanded so much from both of them whenever they were at home that Hattie went back to work as a freelance maid and laundress. She and Tom made it a practice thereafter to stay at their jobs until it was too dark for the Whartons to call upon their services.

It was in that vine-covered carriage house that they shared with hundreds of lizards that their first child was born on August 29th, 1945. Thomas Jonathan Lincoln insisted, over the protests of Hattie, who wished to name him Frederick Douglass Lincoln, that he be named George Washington Lincoln. Tom hated white people but he couldn't do without them and he knew they were instinctively flattered by the fact that more black children were named after George Washington, who kept black slaves, because he was the 'father' of the country, than after Abraham Lincoln, who had freed the slaves.

Little George Washington Lincoln owed the nickname Tomsson Black to his schoolmates. The boy was extremely defensive because his mother washed and cooked at Poro

College. His fellow students wrongly charged that his father did anything the Misses Wharton wished, and called him an Uncle Tom's son. Young Tomsson fought many a battle to defend his father's honor, but the name clung to him. Finally, he decided to keep it.

Indeed, he eventually came to be liked and admired in the black community because of the courage he displayed in every circumstance. When he confronted gangs of white youths and was given the choice of fighting or running away, he was psychologically predisposed to fight. He had always been tall, strong, and athletic for his years, perhaps because he had eaten vast quantities of chitterlings, something his father fancied as much as beer.

At Wendell Phillips High School, he was allowed to join the basketball and baseball teams and to run the hundred-yard hurdles. He learned the art of boxing at the black YMCA and taught himself how to ski and skate in the mountains.

Tomsson Black was about to graduate when his father was shot and killed by an angry white man in a tavern. Insane with rage, the youngster nearly beat to death a white police detective who had come to their home to investigate. He was forced to leave town quickly in order to escape punishment.

He went to Oakland, California, where a friend of his father's was running a nightclub on Seventh Street. For a while, he washed dishes there in order to make a living, then became a waiter in a white boarding school on Telegraph Street in Berkeley, near the University of California campus. He was admitted to the university because of his sports prowess and eventually became a football star and political science graduate. At approximately the same time, he encountered a few Black Panthers in Oakland and joined the organization.

Cutting a splendid figure in his black leather beret and jacket, he became a popular member of the group. However, he found the Panthers badly organized and poorly trained in the basics of self-defense.

He decided to form his own organization, which he named The Big Blacks. During a meeting in a warehouse on the outskirts of Oakland, a militant who was standing watch at the entrance to their headquarters was gunned down by police officers. In a flash of inspiration, Tomsson Black ran outside as he heard the gunfire and took photographs of the dying black man and the white policemen standing over him with their guns in their hands. The photos were proof that the dead man was not armed, although the police insisted that he had drawn his gun first. Tomsson Black charged the police with assassinating a defenseless man and the American press made much of the case.

At that stage in his life, Tomsson Black became attracted to Marxist ideology and began a series of tours to different communist countries. Strangely enough, the Department of State neither tried to prevent his visits to these countries nor bothered to investigate him upon his return.

12

It was obvious that Tomsson Black was a much younger man than Hoop because he had never learned the simple facts of life. Nor had Tomsson Black accepted the realities of his two-faced environment; he had not acquired the stoicism that a black man needs to survive in the modern world. Nor had he learned the art of bald-faced hypocrisy that is so important in life. Tomsson Black was an innocent, still believing that whites could be honest, fair, decent, and just, even though they weren't. He still believed they could make the right choice. There were many other blacks who shared his belief.

He was still so furious with the white woman who had sent him to prison for rape that he couldn't bear to talk about her. He wasn't like Hoop. He couldn't stand to admit why he had raped her. He felt dirtied by her action as though she had covered him with her shit. He was both humiliated and outraged at once. He hadn't forgiven her nor her hypocrite husband. He didn't think getting life imprisonment for what he had done was funny. He promised himself that if he ever got out of prison and found them still alive anywhere on the planet Earth, he was going to cut their white throats to the bone.

It was these thoughts that gave him such a look of perpetual anger. Still, he was careful to be studiously well-behaved. Partly because of his good behavior, and partly because the white woman he had raped had been from the North, the Southern white-trash hacks didn't abuse him. Served her right, they thought, having a nigger on the same boat. Tomsson Black often had the same thought himself – in reverse – served his own ass right for being on the same boat with the teasing, nigger-happy whore.

But strangely enough, it had been inevitable. He had been heading for that white slut's cunt all his life, although he hadn't realized it. He had just moved in that direction faster during the previous year.

He had returned to the US from his highly-publicized world travels in communist countries, where he had acquainted himself with modern revolutionary ideologies and the latest techniques and tactics for planning and executing guerilla warfare, and had found the American State Department reluctant to penalize him. However, he discovered the reason for this was the State Department's understanding that blacks were both psychologically and emotionally incapable of organizing and conducting a coordinated action under the command of a single leader.

What he had known all along had just been further substantiated. Blacks were more individualistic than whites. Too many of them desired to be leaders and too few were willing to serve in the ranks. The knowledge dispirited him. He began to lose hope. He concluded that if blacks wouldn't organize, they'd always remain vulnerable to the whites, they'd always be pissed on by whites, and forever remain second-class citizens.

It was then, as both escape and therapy, that he had begun moving in the circles of Northern white liberals who needed the presence of a black face to prove their liberalism. A single dark face in their company had more social value than a thousand proclamations of racial brotherhood. What was more, black skin titillated the sexual inclinations of whites and incited their eroticism. One look at a black face fanned white desire into every imaginable shape and fantasy, frontside up and backside up, forepart behind and hindpart before, upside down and downside up, coming and going and standing still, in a ball, in a chain, in the air, on the ground, under water, and in the mind.

White women had propositioned Tomsson Black in every way under the sun, so it wasn't naïveté that allowed him to be persuaded into going on a cruise in the Gulf of Mexico on the yacht of a liberal, white millionaire philanthropist named Edward Tudor Goodfeller, III. Eddie Goodfeller had told Tomsson Black that he was descended from the General Goodfeller who commanded the English redcoats fighting against George Washington at the battle of Valley Forge, and he had a painting of a red-coated general astride a white horse hanging in his stateroom to prove it.

Tomsson Black grinned and told him he believed it. Eddie Goodfeller patted him on the back and said, 'Good boy.' Tomsson Black didn't let it affect their friendship because he knew that all Goodfeller wanted was to be loved and admired, especially by blacks and other inferiors, as do all American whites. He wasn't even provoked when Goodfeller told him that one of his ancestors had owned a larger number of slaves than any other single individual, and that this ancestor's success in the rum trade was the origin of the Goodfeller fortune. Tomsson Black said that maybe Goodfeller's ancestor had owned his ancestors, for one of his ancestors had been the champion sugarcane cutter of all the slaves in the South. Goodfeller grinned embarrassedly and patted him on the back. 'Have a rum and coke,' he invited. 'And I assure you this rum wasn't made by my ancestor from the sugarcane cut by your ancestor.'

'All the pity,' Tomsson Black had replied. 'It would have been some damn good rum.'

Edward T. Goodfeller was a robust, ruddy-faced man in his mid-forties. He had wide shoulders, was of medium height, and had a shock of white hair that looked electric. His ruddiness was due more to weather than drink, and his piercing blue eyes were those of a sailor. Only people who were envious and malicious had ever called him a homosexual, for he was the very epitome of robust vitality, virility, and heterosexuality, and had a beautiful young wife to prove it.

His yacht, a schooner of almost two hundred feet in length, was powered by diesel engines, but also had three masts for sailing. It had a crew of twelve and could accommodate an additional twelve passengers. Goodfeller was very proud of it. On this particular trip, there were only eight passengers, including Goodfeller and his wife. Although the trip was purportedly a fishing expedition, it had quickly degenerated into drinking and mate-swapping. All were couples except Tomsson Black and his cabin-mate, a very courteous and correct young white college student, whom Tomsson Black seldom saw. He wondered amusedly if Goodfeller thought he was a homosexual.

Such was definitely not the case with Goodfeller's wife. From the very first, she had put herself out to madden him with her white body. It was the first time she'd had a black man all to herself and she intended to make the most of it. Her husband wouldn't have thought of keeping tabs on her and the other white wives respected her claim and kept to themselves.

Her name was Barbara, but friends called her Babs. She was almost a dead ringer for Cotton Tail Harrison – the same type of corn-silk blonde with big innocent-looking blue eyes that gave the impression that butter wouldn't melt in her mouth, along with a figure that would make a preacher ball the jack. She didn't need any birth-control pills – she was safe, a factor that allowed her to indulge in any depravity that struck her fancy.

Goodfeller indulged her as far as it was possible; he kept out of her way. So they went their separate ways as far as sexual fulfillment was concerned.

When she first saw this tall, handsome young black, nearly bursting out of his swim trunks, she became frantic to seduce him. But it didn't happen. Tomsson Black kept himself to himself.

He and the other single man had a choice cabin adjoining the Goodfellers' suite, which gave Babs a greater opportunity to spin her web. She spent a great deal of time alone in her bedroom walking about stark naked with the passage door open, waiting for Tomsson Black to pass.

But when her opportunity finally arrived, and she had shaken her white ass tantalizingly at him, he got the message. The message had said 'keep away from this screwball or you'll be wearing stripes and they won't be pinstripes from London.'

His seemingly cavalier rejection of her provocative invitation outraged her. Who did this black nigger think he was? A white homosexual? But maybe he was just scared, she reassured herself. She had heard that niggers were scared of naked white women, or at least when they first saw them. She had heard of niggers bursting out in hysterical laughter at their first sight of a white woman's pussy.

But she vowed to get this beautiful black, if it was the last thing she ever did. She waylaid him in the bar, at meals, at dances. Her husband and the other whites stood aside and watched her campaign, not one of them ever doubting the final outcome.

Tomsson Black avoided her as best he could, but he couldn't ignore her entirely. She was his host's wife and he was the lion of the entourage – black lion, true enough, but of the African species, nevertheless.

She insinuated herself into his thoughts until he had nightmares of her white legs spread above him like the Colossus of Rhodes, spurting molten metal that shriveled his penis into a charred and stinking cinder. He'd wake up screaming, frightening the wits out of his courteous young white cabin mate.

The next time he passed Barbara's bedroom and found her revealing all her alluring white nudity through the open passage door, he wheeled into the room and slammed shut the door.

'You slut,' he roared, beside himself with rage as he tore the buttons from his fly. 'You dirty teaser, you vicious jailbait, I'm gonna strangle you with it and see how you like it.' His black face knotted with fury, and his muscles quivered from the violence of passion.

She shuddered with ecstasy as though each epithet lashed her with erotic passion. But when he tried to force himself into her, she held him off. He then tried to pull away, but she wouldn't let him go. Suddenly, as in her dreams, thick, sticky semen was spurting over her naked legs. All the glands of her body opened and released a flood like lava from an erupting volcano. She gave a loud moaning cry of such ecstasy that he hit her in the face.

'Ohhh, beat me, my beautiful black nigger! Beat me and rape me!' she cried.

He was so enraged he kept hitting her in the face until he felt another erection coming on and plunged it so viciously into her that it seemed he wanted to split her apart.

Blood was running from her nostrils and from the corners of her eyes, which had already swollen shut and were beginning to turn black. Her face rapidly ballooned out and began turning all the colors of the rainbow. Even then she was consumed with a passion so intense they both came together in an effluvium of hate and ecstasy.

At that moment Goodfeller walked into the room. 'Well, well,' he cried jovially. 'Success at last.' But when he saw her face he stammered stupidly, 'W-w-what happened?'

She pushed Tomsson Black off of her and said, 'This black nigger beat me and raped me. Get the doctor and have this black bastard put in irons.'

'I can't do that,' he said, but he telephoned for the doctor nevertheless.

'You'd better,' she threatened. 'He'd better be locked up before the doctor gets here and sees me like this.'

Ignoring her, Goodfeller looked at Tomsson Black accusingly. 'You didn't have to beat her.'

'What the hell do you know about it?' Tomsson Black raved. 'There's nothing you can do with a slut like this but beat her. Not if you're trapped. Not if you're black.'

Goodfeller nodded understandingly. 'I know, I know. But you've got yourself in trouble. Now you go to your cabin and lock yourself in and don't discuss this with anyone and I'll do my best to save you.'

'You sissie louse,' Babs lisped through her swollen mouth. 'If you don't have this black animal locked up this instant I'm going to tell everyone on board about him beating me and raping me and you taking his side.'

'Babs, let's not be hasty—' he began, but at that moment the doctor knocked on the door and the decision was taken out of his hands.

The ship's doctor was a thin, ascetic, middle-aged puritan from Newport, where Goodfeller kept his ship berthed, who had a very low tolerance for black people. He gave his services free as the ship's doctor on some of Goodfeller's southern cruises in exchange for his keep. But he had always viewed the sexual promiscuity aboard ship, even when limited to white husbands and wives who were guests, with tremendous disapproval. He had felt shocked and outraged from the very beginning of this cruise by the appearance of a black man among the guests. Now this final disaster was no more than he had expected. He took but one glance at the bruised and battered face of the nude white woman, then leveled his gaze threateningly on the guilty black. From then on, Tomsson Black knew his fate was sealed.

Because the ship was in the territorial waters of the state of Alabama, Tomsson Black was taken into custody and tried in that state. Life imprisonment was mandatory for a black man convicted of raping a white woman there. It was a foregone conclusion that once Mrs Barbara Goodfeller took the stand and pointed out Tomsson Black as her assailant, it was bye-bye blackbird.

She looked him straight in the eye as she described in a loud, clear voice and in graphic detail how he had beaten and raped her, down to the pain of the last blow he had rained upon her face. And when she related her most intimate feelings at the time he had penetrated her, she blushed bright red, as did every other white woman in the courthouse, in sympathy.

When he was sentenced to life imprisonment, Tomsson Black's sex dried up like a plant cut off at the root. However, it was reported that Goodfeller went down into niggertown that night and tried to atone. Afterwards he accused his wife of being a depraved, heartless slut, without honor or morals or even common decency. He accused her of being more callous than any slave-owner's wife or daughter, more monstrous than any of the Gorgon sisters. He could not find the vocabulary to express the full hatred and contempt he felt for her.

But three years later, when she had a change of heart and forced him to spend one hundred thousand dollars to secure for Tomsson Black a full pardon with restoration of citizenship, the hatred and contempt he had felt for her he now turned on the niggers. He came to hate niggers with an intensity only matched by a former nigger-loving liberal. He hated them because their very existence threatened him with exposure as an inhibited white 'mother' for scores of black homosexuals.

13

Tomsson Black was thirty-two years old when he got out of prison. He was six feet, two inches tall, with the bold, heavy features and coarse, straight, jet-black hair of a red Indian, but his eyes were a spectacular shade of brown. His complexion was the hot black of soft coal just beginning to burn, his mouth was wide and shaped for laughter, and his thick, full lips which were several shades lighter than his skin, gave the impression of great passion. All women wanted to be kissed by such lips. When he smiled, which was seldom since he had left prison, his brilliant white teeth lit up his whole black face like a beacon in the night. Tomsson Black had always been handsome, now the premature gray at his temples gave him a look of distinction.

He looked considerably older than his thirty-two years, but that was to be expected after his three years on a southern chain gang. But he comported himself with such dignity and gravity he immediately impressed people with his reliability. From prison he went directly to New York and checked into the Pierre Hotel. His distinguished and reliable appearance was such that he was not requested to pay for his room in advance, as was the general policy toward blacks. Despite his cheap clothing and rough edges, he looked like a man of consequence.

The first thing he did was telephone Barbara Goodfeller and ask her to come to the Pierre and visit him. She was both astounded and impressed by his choice of hotel, but she was more intrigued by the thought that he still desired her. For three long years she had believed this lustful compulsion was hers alone, and it stirred her with excitement to think that he desired her, too. She was enthralled by the thought that his three years of enforced celibacy had left him frantic, and her anticipation was so intense that she gave herself the most thorough make-up ever. However, she took so long a time in her preparations to seduce him that when she finally arrived, she found him simmering with rage.

'I ought to beat you,' he greeted her. 'You haven't changed; still arrogant and tantalizing. Besides which, you'll probably like it so much you'll have me sent back to prison.'

'I'll never let you get away from me again,' she vowed, embracing him, hoping he would smell her.

He smelled her all right, she smelled just right, like expensive perfume of rich, white, hot cunt, and money.

'Baby, I need money more than love,' he said appealingly. 'I need a lot of money because what I've got in mind is going to cost a hell of a lot of it.'

She was disappointed but not defeated. 'I'll give you all the money you want. All I want is you,' she added honestly.

'You don't have the kind of money I need, baby,' he said. 'But I'll take what you got, then go look for some more from someone else.'

'I'll make you rich,' she promised.

'Take off your clothes,' he ordered.

Quick as a flash she undressed and lay on the bed, her milk-white body glowing with lust. He stripped naked and lay on her, his body like a hand-carved black fetish resting on the whitest silk. She clutched him lovingly, moaning in ecstasy and had an orgasm even before he penetrated her.

He looked down on her indulgently, knowing that he had it made. 'Isn't this groovy?'

She smiled and said, 'It'll keep me young and beautiful.'

Amusedly, he thought that all he had to do to please her was be black enough and big enough.

After they had finished again, she mused, 'If slavery still existed, I'd buy you.'

'You don't need the institution of slavery,' he said. 'Just buy me and I'll be your slave forever.'

She smiled complacently; she believed him.

Before taking a shower and dressing, she sat at the writing desk and filled out a check for twenty-five thousand dollars which she presented to him.

'Is that enough for my big handsome bull?'

'For this your bull will always keep you in milk,' he promised, carefully scrutinizing the check.

'Not my milk, your milk,' she corrected.

They found themselves laughing simultaneously.

14

The massacre on Eighth Avenue released a deluge of horror in the white community. Whites were so shocked and horrified by the actions of their own white law enforcement officers, that they completely ignored the fact that five of them had been killed first by a black maniac. White people were so predisposed to the emotion of guilt, that they were blind to the murderous assault of the homicidal black, and assumed the role of murderer, themselves. They were plunged into a guilty bereavement, and were impregnable to objective reason.

The white community sprinkled its blond head with ashes and wrapped its shuddering white limbs in sack cloth. It wallowed in a mud bath of remorse. It indulged in an orgy of expiation. The desire to atone became physical. To expiate for its sense of guilt, not only was the white community willing to sacrifice its women, but anxious; and not only were its women willing to be sacrificed, they were avid. Even the most moral of white women were convinced of the palliative qualities of their sex.

Others were more practical-minded. Knowledgeable committees provided means for white donors to give blood to compensate for the blood the black victims lost in death. So much blood was collected that the committee had no place for it and didn't know what to do with it. Someone suggested that they make blood pudding, but this was considered an offensive suggestion. Nevertheless, the donors felt temporarily relieved, almost as though they had masturbated.

And there were some whites who went about crying publicly, like citizens did the time F. D. Roosevelt died, touching blacks on the street as if to express their suffering through contact, and sobbingly confessing their sorrow and begging the blacks' forgiveness. There were a few extremists who even bent over and offered their asses for blacks to kick, but blacks weren't sure whether they were meant to kick them or kiss them, so in their traditional manner, they cautiously avoided making any decision at all.

Never had the white community been so passionately consumed with masochistic desire. Nothing would satisfy the whites other than suffering pain at the hands of blacks. They begged blacks to curse them, to strike them, to spit on them, to rape them, and reveled in ecstasy while they were beaten and defiled.

Never had the white community projected such mawkish feelings of guilt. White men, crying unrestrainedly, confessed to deeds and emotions they had kept concealed and had denied for centuries. They were heard to confess to beating blacks, oppressing blacks, corrupting blacks, lusting after blacks, and most violently of all, to hating blacks. Middle-aged, intelligent, prosperous, highly-placed white men confessed to having hated black men all of their lives. No doubt some of this was due to alcohol, which the whites are known to consume as an analgesic against guilt. But of course, this made it no less true. And they confessed that they were indeed devils, as certain discredited blacks had contended all along, and declared that they should be punished for their wickedness. And strangely enough, during this period of compulsive confession, it was reported that a white man had been seen beating himself in The Village, but this was not taken seriously for white men had been seen beating themselves in The Village for many years, and some had even been arrested for indecent exposure.

A group funeral for all the dead blacks was held in a church in Harlem, and was attended by the mayor, the governor, the vice-president, many congressmen, and any number of prominent whites from industry and commerce. A white millionaire was seen chauffeuring his black chauffeur for the occasion and it was said that his wife washed the dishes for their black cook that same evening.

Newspapers were bordered in black that day, and public institutions were draped in black. The American flag in front of the United Nations building was flown at half mast for the day, and the windows of Fifth Avenue department stores displayed lone wreaths of white lilies on black bunting. White men throughout the city wore black shirts in concession to mourning, and white women wore black diamonds.

White ministers conducted concurrent funeral services in all the city's white churches, and their churches were packed with weeping whites who joined in prayer for the souls of the dead blacks. At the same time, memorial services were being conducted on all the television and radio stations of the nation.

The citizens of other nations in the world found it difficult to reconcile this excessive display of guilt by America's white community with its traditional treatment of blacks. What the citizens of the world didn't understand was that American whites are a traditionally masochistic people, and their sense of guilt toward their blacks is an integral part of the national character.

However, the official inquiry was conducted by officials whose normal duty it was to prevent blacks from opposing their oppression. The committee, appointed by the mayor, consisted of the police commissioner, the district attorney, the medical examiner, and a black politician who was president of the city council. It was their duty to investigate the incidents leading up to the massacre, and determine whether there was cause for the offenders to be punished.

To protect the white cops involved from hysterical members of the white community, they were locked in the cells of the homicide bureau, attached to the district attorney's office in the court house. After they were made safe from their public, the committee was then free to inquire into the causes and effects of the massacre.

It was learned that the root cause had been a black man armed with an automatic rifle of high caliber who had launched himself upon a course of killing as many white cops as possible. His motivation for such anti-social, homicidal behavior was still to be ascertained, but they admitted among themselves that the urge to kill white cops had been growing in the black community in recent years. A psychiatrist was consulted as the first expert. He testified that in his opinion, such homicidal compulsions in American blacks were easily understandable in the framework of the existing structure of American society – in fact it was inevitable. Blacks had always considered white police as their major enemy. He was surprised that there were so few incidents of this nature. The committee decided to drop that line of inquiry.

The district attorney then took over the questioning, as was his prerogative. The police commissioner, being the expert, took over the answering.

Q: What did this black actually do?

A: The black man stood in a front window of a tenement on Eighth Avenue in Harlem and shot two innocent policemen who were peacefully patrolling the street in a police cruiser. He shot them without warning or for any reason which has yet been discovered. And when other policemen in cruisers came to place him under arrest, he shot three of them dead, wounded seven, then held them off with his high-powered automatic rifle until a police tank was sent to their assistance.

Q: Where were the blacks – as opposed to the participants in the gun battle – until the massacre took place?

A: They were lying on the floor of the entrance hall.

Q: Didn't they feel safe there?

A: Evidently not.

Q: And where were the accused officers?

A: They had taken cover beneath the police cruisers in the street.

Q: That arrangement seems to me to be peaceful enough. How, then, did the blacks get themselves shot?

A: Suddenly they rushed out into the street.

Q: And the officers shot them for that?

A: Well, in view of what had already happened to them, being attacked by the black maniac with the rifle, and already having three of their number killed and several others wounded, they thought the blacks were attacking them. They had come out shouting and screaming like savages on the war path with their faces daubed with white paint—

Q: Paint?

A: Well, it turned out afterwards to be plaster dust, but in the stress and excitement of the gun battle, they couldn't be expected to notice that.

Q: And they shot them in self-defense?

A: They thought they were shooting in self-defense. And then again, the black killer with the rifle hadn't been seen since the first cannon shot and they weren't sure but what they were covering his escape.

Q: Yes, yes, we can understand that. But what caused the blacks to rush suddenly into the street when they had felt safe, and in fact had been safe, in the shelter of the entrance hall?

A: It's hard to say. It's like cattle stampeding. Some minor incident, a sound, a flash of reflected sunlight from a shard of mirror, panics the entire herd and they rush in pell-mell flight to their doom.

'You should have been a poet, sir,' the district attorney observed, smiling.

Experts from the appropriate departments presented the statistics of the damage:

Five police officers killed, seven wounded.

Nineteen police cars damaged to varying extents.

Fifty-nine blacks killed, thirteen wounded.

One tenement building completely destroyed by cannon fire, the two adjacent buildings damaged beyond immediate occupancy.

An estimated five hundred people – between fifty and one hundred families – made homeless.

Those made homeless detained in a hastily constructed stockade in Upper Central Park.

The committee of inquiry ordered that the detainees be interrogated.

It was discovered that not one of them had ever seen or heard of the black man who had killed the white cops. He had never been seen about the building, coming or going, in the tenement flat, on the street, in the window; it was as though he had sprung full-grown from the walls of the tenement with a rifle in his hand.

No one had the slightest idea why he would suddenly attack and kill white policemen, who had always been good and kind to black people. They could not imagine him doing a thing like that; none of them would even think of killing a kindly white cop. Not one of them had seen him fire at the patrol car or at any of the other police cars that appeared subsequently. None of them knew anything, had seen anything, had heard anything, or said anything of importance. It was as though they had spent that night on another planet.

The police laboratory identified the gun as identical to the gun which had figured in the murder of the black woman and the accidental death of the black man which had occurred ten days previous and less than five minutes walking distance from where the massacre had taken place. The gun, almost damaged beyond identity by the cannon blast, held no clues, except for one fingerprint from the black killer, recorded from the fragment of a finger which had been recovered from the debris.

THE MYSTERY GUN, the press called it.

At first a faint chill of uneasiness affected the white community by the thought of mystery guns falling into the hands of homicidal blacks.

Then the uneasiness grew as the press published detailed reports of the wanton killing of five white policemen by the black killer. Visions stirred in the minds of white citizens of blacks running amok with mystery guns, slaughtering whites right and left. Trepidation supplanted their orgy of guilt. Why should they feel so bad about a few blacks being killed by the police when all of their lives were in danger? Trepidation grew to anger. Were they asking too much to feel safe in their own country, their own homes, living their own lives? Hadn't they done enough for the blacks who were imposed on them by their ancestors? Did they bring the blacks here from Africa? Were they responsible for the actions of their antecedents? Civilization would be a shambles if the sins of the fathers were visited on the children to untold generations. They were fed up with these unwanted blacks and their impossible demands.

Inevitably, this resentment aroused strong, exaggerated hostilities on both sides of the color line.

15

An outdoor concert was being presented that warm September Sunday afternoon on the mall at Central Park, and a famous white soprano was singing selections from George Gershwin's 'Porgy and Bess' suite. The tremendous standing audience was held spellbound.

Suddenly, an ignorant-looking black man wearing a soiled tee-shirt, patched Levis, and blue canvas sneakers, standing at the northern fringe nearest to Harlem, yelled out: 'Why don't you white mothers leave go them slavery-time songs about lazy, sinning black people? You think all we do is dodge work 'n lay up 'n fuck like rabbits all day.' He was a red-eyed brother with a liver-lipped mouth and a long, narrow head, and he had a strong, resonant, carrying voice. He was heard at a considerable distance by people in the audience, and he sounded as though he meant it.

But what he meant, exactly, no one knew, and no one cared to draw him out from the general to the particular. Some white people who had heard him expressed their disapproval by glowering. Several laughed. A tarty-looking young blonde woman giggled, as though she thought that wasn't such a despicable life.

But the black people in his vicinity stared at him incredulously, as though he had taken leave of his senses. One black brother expressed the opinion of them all by saying, 'Man, Gershwin wasn't a racist, he was just a thief, man. The music you're hearing is one of our own lullabies.'

'Why don't you tend to your own mother-raping business, man, and go on kissing these white mothers' asses if that's what you want.'

'I'm just telling you, man.'

'Telling me what, man, to kiss these white mother-rapers' asses like you? If I had me a rifle like my real black brother had up on Eighth Avenue that night, I'd stop these white mothers from playing these lo-rating songs.'

'Don't lose your black, man,' the brother advised.

But there was a young white man nearby who was stung to the quick by this black man's reverence for the insane black murderer of five innocent white cops. He had resented his first outburst, but had kept quiet for fear of making a spectacle of himself. But this public adulation for a black murderer of white men was too much; it sounded too much like Malcolm X's reference to President Kennedy's assassination.

'Where's your gratitude, you black son of a bitch,' he shouted angrily. 'If it wasn't for us white people, you wouldn't be alive. You black bastards live on our sufferance. We feed you, clothe you, house you, educate you, and take better care of you than any other white majority has taken care of their black minorities in the history of the world.' He was a tall, clean-cut, crew-cut, blond, blue-eyed young man, obviously from suburbia, and his strong, chiseled features were well-suited for the expression of indignation.

But his suggestion that black people lived on white people's mercy goaded the black man to replying.

'Wouldn't be alive? Why you white murderers would massacre us all if you could find somebody else to clean up your shit.'

Any reminder of the recent massacre grated on a tender spot in all the whites' subconsciousness, and the blond young man was not alone in his fury. He rushed up to the black brother and slapped him sharply across the face. The black people in the vicinity did not understand why the white man had become suddenly enraged because all the black man had done was told the truth, but none of them wanted to become involved in a fracas which they thought would blow over after a few insults were passed.

But the black man retaliated with violence instead of words. He whipped a spring-blade knife from the watch pocket of his jeans and slashed at the white man's throat. The white man jerked his head back in time to save himself from serious injury, but still caught the blade across the tip of his chin. Blood showered over his white shirt and seersucker coat. Women screamed.

A broad-assed cop, paunch hanging down over his cartridge belt, hairy forearms exposed beneath the cut-off sleeves of his blue summer shirt, pushed people aside as he tried to get to the fracas. Black people antagonized him with their hostile stares. Then he saw the slashed white man covered with blood, looking as though his throat were cut, and the black man holding him at bay with his knife slashing through the air. He drew his .38-caliber police revolver that hung from the holster at his hip. Maybe he intended to shoot the black man, maybe not. But another black man thought he intended to do so and knocked the gun out of his hand. The cop swung at him with his left hand and the brother grappled with the cop. They wrestled back and forth for a moment, then fell to the ground. When the cop tried to reach for his revolver, which lay a short distance from his outstretched hand, the black man kicked it out of his reach and they began rolling furiously around on the ground. A black sister saw the revolver lying there and, with a quick, sly motion, picked it up and put it in her purse. What possessed her at that moment, no one ever learned, for she began walking swiftly away. A white woman who had seen her pick up the gun and put it into her purse, ran after her, crying, 'She's got the policeman's pistol . . . She picked up the policeman's pistol . . .' Several white people looked at her undecidedly, looked at the disappearing back of the black woman, then shrugged and returned their attention to the struggles that were taking place.

Other white men joined their blood-stained confederate in seeking to contain the black man with the knife, but, since they were all unarmed, the black man lunged forward and slashed gleefully at them. The white men drew back nimbly and dodged artfully. The combined actions of them all evoked the performance of a spirited adagio dance, in which the black man dances the role of an irate woman who tries to mark her fickle, feckless lovers, the white men, with the sign of infidelity. But it was not a harmless dance, and two of the white men who were not sufficiently artful in their dodging were slashed on their faces.

None of the slashed men were seriously injured, but their rich, red American blood flowed so copiously that it seemed as though they were being hacked to death by a black savage.

The white spectators watching the action were appalled. 'Police! Police!' they cried, much to the amusement of the black spectators who knew from experience that not much blood was actually being lost.

Two of the dozens of cops policing the tremendous crowd had finally become alerted to the scuffle, and were valiantly trying to push through the crowd to do their duty. It may have been a compliment to the popularity of the white soprano – or perhaps to Gershwin – or the arias of the black opera – that they were completely blocked.

Fortunately, a young, athletically-inclined, working-class white man had sufficient presence of mind to slip up behind the black man and tackle him about the legs. He paid for this *beau geste* with a slashed skull, but at least he brought down the black assailant so that he could be disarmed.

'Keep hold of the knife!' cried a white woman. 'Keep hold of the knife!' She was the same woman who had seen the black sister walk off with the first white cop's revolver, and she spoke with authority. 'Keep hold of his knife!'

Not only did the blond young man with the slashed chin take possession of the knife, but he flaunted it in the black man's face and threatened to cut out his nuts and feed them to the squirrels.

But his four companions were not animal lovers, so they let the black man keep his nuts, no doubt to the frustration of local squirrels, and rolled him over on his face so they could tie his wrists together with a tie and bind his ankles with a belt.

Now that the white spectators were relieved to find the white combatants had not been hacked to death, they watched the proceedings with intense fascination. However, the black spectators remained calm, but they found nothing amusing about the spectacle, because it wasn't funny anymore.

The white worker, staunching the flow of blood from his slashed skull with a spare tee-shirt he always carried – perhaps because he always expected the worst – suddenly spied a coil of rope attached to a chair. It was used by the park attendants to secure the park chairs at night, but now it sparked the white worker with a bright idea. 'Let's hang the nigger.'

The other five men of the group had graduated from the hanging class, or more probably had never belonged to it. Nevertheless, they discerned instantly the potential in the suggestion. Here were the ingredients for a tremendous joke: a coil of rope, a tree overhead, and a trussed nigger.

'Sure thing,' agreed the blond with the slashed chin who had appointed himself spokesman for the others. Winking at the white worker, to insure there were no misunderstandings, he added, 'You get the rope.'

The white spectators instantly recognized the joke. Smiles spread over their faces as they anticipated a new kind of minstrel show that parodied a lynching.

The black spectators became sullen and angry at this racist

comedy, and their faces darkened until they were even black enough to suit themselves.

The white worker came forward with the coil of rope, along with the chair to which it was attached, and tauntingly uncoiled it before the black man's gaze. The black was still securely pinioned by the knees of the other white men in his back, but his eyes were glued to the rope like the eyes of a bird being hypnotized by a snake. Slowly uncoiling the rope, draining the last drop of sadism from the scene, the white worker intoned solemnly, 'Got anything to say before we hang you, nigger?'

'Yeah, lemme fuck your mama for the last time,' the black man said defiantly.

Smiling, the white worker began fashioning a slip noose in the end not attached to the chair. 'This'll make you come, nigger.' Then to the others he said, 'Put the nigger in the chair.'

When the black man was lifted into the chair attached to the rope, the smiles left the faces of the white spectators and they shivered with a tremor of apprehension. A stir of protest went through the assemblage, quick bodily movements, half-finished gestures, tentative steps, grimaces of revulsion. But suddenly they were immobilized by the sight of the slip noose being lowered over the black man's head and tightened about his neck.

'That's not funny,' a white woman cried.

The white worker grinned defiantly and threw the other end of the rope over the limb of the tree above them.

'That's gone far enough,' a seedy-looking, middle-aged white man shouted with as much authority as he could muster, and took an indignant step.

Behind the black man's head, the blond man with the slashed chin and bloodstained clothing made a gesture denying that hanging was their real intention and to cap it off, winked reassuringly. Fearing that he might not be understood, he shaped the words with his lips, distorting his face into grimaces as though he were chewing a hunk of alum. 'We – just – want – to – scare – the – shit – out – the – black – sonofabitch.'

The white spectators gave no sign that they were reassured; they continued to look anxious and disapproving.

The black spectators were becoming hostile, but it appeared as though they were restrained from violent action by a hypnotic terror that seemed to envelop them, and stun their brains, and incapacitate their muscles. It was the pure and simple thought of lynching that immobilized them, memories that were deeply ingrained in their subconsciousness.

Ironically, the vast majority of the people in the audience were sublimely ignorant of anything at all that may be happening on the upper fringe of the crowd, other than an occasional boisterous outburst from one of the black residents of Harlem.

And thus the incident would have ended, had it not been for four long-haired, black-clad, outlaw bikers. They simply were not satisfied with leaving it as it was.

They had paused in pushing their Harley-Davidson motorcycles across the grass, in complete defiance of posted orders to the contrary, to watch the mock lynching. The thought occurred to all of them at once, 'What are these buggers playing at?'

On the left breasts of their black leather jackets were stitched yellow labels with the words 'DEATH RIDERS' and on the right breasts Nazi crosses, outlined in luminous paint. Their faces were long and narrow, their eyes deepset and dark with black circles beneath them, and one had a long, scraggling black beard. Each had pimply white skin, deeply ingrained with dirt.

The bearded one, who was evidently the leader, jerked his head in the direction of the trussed black man who had been placed in a chair with a noose around his neck, and said 'Let's give black power a boost.' The others grinned their agreement.

The bearded one pushed his motorcycle underneath the tree and looped the dangling end of the hanging rope about its frame beneath the handlebars. Then, as he mounted it, the three others chanted 'Sieg Heil!'

It was a four-cylinder motorcycle with a 750 cc engine and a frame strong enough to hold a pyramid of twenty-four men. When he gunned the motor, it took off with a shower of grass and gravel, pulling the hanging rope at burning velocity, and jerked the body of the black man into the air so rapidly it was still in a sitting position as it shot upward. Evidently, the hangman's knot had twisted the neck, for the head was dangling to one side when it smashed upward into the limb of the tree. The neck broke with a loud, eerie cracking, like a tree exploding from frost. Probably it was intensified by the sound of the skull bursting.

The biker was flung ass-over-teakettle across the handlebars and rolled several yards across the grass as the rope jerked the motorcycle upright like a rearing stallion and the rear wheel ran out from under it. The loop slipped over the handlebars when the motorcycle fell on its side and wheeled about in concentric circles, knocking half a dozen spectators off their feet.

Screams punctured the air and pandemonium gripped everyone, black and white alike. But the Death Riders kept their cool. While the bearded rider was getting to his feet, his three companions wrestled the loco motorcycle to a standstill, cut the engine, and stood it on its wheels. The rider limped back and mounted it. His companions mounted theirs.

'I sailed him,' the bearded rider boasted, grinning proudly.

'You rocketed him,' a companion testified. Grinning together, they gunned their motorcycles across the grass, left the park, and went across the wide asphalt street of Central Park West, disappearing in the direction of the Hudson River before anyone had noticed what they looked like.

16

The press made the customary furor over the lynching. Probably the type was already set up for just such a contingency. Much indignation. Much consolation for the family of the lynched man. Such stirring condolences. Such touching essays on the rights of man. The press asked pointed questions, too.

Is our society sick? Would a strong, healthy society permit a citizen to be lynched simply for expressing his opinion? Did this not demonstrate the malaise this nation was suffering? And where were the police? The press insisted that more vigilant policing of large public functions was required in view of the state of the nation. All that sort of bullshit.

But in the black community, the lynching precipitated a veritable deluge of reprisals. Black men began running amok and shooting white people right-left-and-center.

A black student at the University of Mississippi holed up in the administration building and shot and killed three members of the faculty and four white seniors – two male and two female – before finally being shot dead from behind by a state trooper who had managed to sneak through a rear window.

A black Baptist minister in Washington, D.C., endeavored to shoot up a number of congressmen, but being ignorant of the customs of congressmen and a pretty poor shot, he only succeeded in shooting five secret servicemen, four of whom survived, and eleven tourists, seven of whom were women, none of whom were killed. He was finally destroyed by a hand grenade that a white visitor from Texas was carrying in his pocket as a defense against black robbers.

A Black Nationalist shooting from the window of a flat beneath a Chinese restaurant at the corner of Sutter and Filmore in San Francisco fired into a parade of the Benevolent Protective Order of Elks as they marched down the hill of Sutter Street. Soon, dead Elks filled the street below. The fusillade was ended when the black was scalded blind by a pot of boiling oil dumped onto his head by the Chinese chef from above, and subsequently hacked into bits by the rest of the Chinese personnel.

A black father of eleven children in the Brownsville section of Brooklyn shot into a group of white elementary school teachers engaged in a lunch-hour confab and killed two and wounded seventeen before being shot dead by the two dozen police assigned to the school to keep order and who, as it happens, had been playing pinochle in an empty classroom when the shooting began.

A black handyman in Susanville, California, shot into a group of Ku Klux Klansmen burning a cross on the front lawn of the boarding house where he was living, killing nine of them outright while one, seriously wounded, escaped. Then, turning the rifle on himself, he squeezed the trigger with his toe, blowing off the top of his own head.

A black doctor, a general practitioner in the black belt in Chicago, drove his Cadillac Fleetwood down to the Loop and parked it opposite the Detective Bureau, calmly unpacked a loaded automatic rifle, rolled the front window halfway down, balanced the gun barrel on the glass, and calmly shot dead every white detective who emerged from the building until a modern English-made tank imported by the Chicago Police for riot control rattled into the Loop, shot, and completely destroyed the black Fleetwood, its black driver, and the entire office building behind it, killing twenty-nine white office workers and injuring thirty-seven others in the process.

A black HEW administrator in Cleveland locked himself in the reinforced ultra-security cell block for convicted murderers in the Cayahoga County Jail and began systematically shooting down anyone with a white face, with the exception of the prisoners, who came within his sight, including prison guards, county officials, state's attorneys, probation officers, not to mention city police. A tank from the Ohio State National Guard was brought in but it could not be maneuvered into effective range and was only destroying sections of the county courthouse with its 105 mm cannon, before it was called off. In the end, officials resorted to bombing, and a B-52 bomber was sent from Wright-Patterson Airfield, and the Cayahoga County Jail was blown out of existence.

It was inevitable that the forces of law and order would over-react to the killers. And as the black maniacs went on shooting sprees in more and more sections of the white community, the uncontrollable tendency by the forces of law and order to over-kill was responsible for five times as many deaths of innocent white people than those killed by the black maniacs themselves. In the end, it became evident to all that the forces of law and order would eventually decimate their own race if not restrained.

But what the white community found more staggering was the discovery that not only did these black maniacs have no particular segment of the white community they wished to destroy, but that they, themselves, were not of the same type and class. There was no common denominator. They were blacks from all classes, from all levels of education, from all walks of life, from all economic levels – the poor, the ugly, the rich and the handsome. And they not only hated the white police, as the white community had long since assumed, they hated whites of all ages and sexes. They hated the white economy, the white culture, the white religion, and white civilization in general. This realization shocked and frightened the white community more than anything.

What was more, these black killers were inconsistent in the selection of their victims. What had congressmen to do with a black minister? What had a Black Nationalist got against white Elks? This wasn't the jungle. He didn't want to eat them. And what had a successful black doctor got against the Chicago Police? He wasn't a civil rights worker. He had never been arrested. He had never even been third-degreed. It was all very confusing.

17

The questions that presented themselves to the forces of law and order were who, why, and how.

In most instances, despite the fact that the black killers were mutilated beyond recognition, they had left sufficient clues to be identified. The question of who they were presented no problem. The police knew immediately who they were, and this information was speedily transmitted to the public: they were black bastards who had gone insane, that's who.

But the question who? precipitated the question why? Why

had these black citizens – an alarming number of whom had been educated, intelligent, affluent, and successful in all the ways success is computed in the American way of life – embarked upon this suicidal, insane course of killing innocent, unengaged, unknown white strangers? If whites had injured them, insulted them, abused them, persecuted them, or offended them in any manner or form, it would have made some kind of sense. But the whites these blacks had killed had been total strangers; they had not had an opportunity to incur any black hatred. They had been bystanders, they had been killed without purpose or point, they had been killed without being known, they had been killed like so many birds flying by a cretin who just liked to hear the sound of his gun.

This information, dutifully transmitted to the public, inspired much soul searching in the white community. What had whites done to incur such murderous hatred by blacks? They had never heard the plaintive song sung by Louis Armstrong: 'What did I do to be so black and blue?' What had they done to be so hated by blacks? There might have been misunderstandings between the races, but not of sufficient virulence to bring on these insane outbursts.

What if they had segregated the blacks? Was that a capital offense? Didn't the blacks want to be to themselves? Weren't many of the blacks even now petitioning for autonomy? Wasn't segregation the same as autonomy? And even to themselves they denied having ever persecuted the blacks or oppressed them. They had been permitted to grow up as blacks, live as blacks, die as blacks. Was that oppression? Could they have lived and died as whites even if they had been permitted? Was it possible? Were not the blacks of this nation better off than blacks in any other nation in the world with a white majority? In fact, were their lives not richer, more purposeful, and happier than even the lives of blacks in Africa with their own governments and societies? A serious study of the comparison of the lives of American blacks to the lives of whites in a majority of the nations in the civilized world might well reveal that American blacks were better off than the majority of all the whites in the rest of the world. Was that oppression?

Why then, had these blacks embarked on such a senseless course of killing whites when it would only lead to death for themselves and untold hardships for their race? What could they possibly hope to gain?

An objective sociologist might have noted that the first case of these unrestrained outbursts of killing by black men had been by an unnamed, unknown, seemingly ignorant black man who had appeared to be completely unemotional about killing and totally indifferent about being killed. That might have told the white community something.

The forces of law and order were not as preoccupied with the question of 'why?' as was the white community as a whole. 'Why?' was the question for the courts of law, the various state and federal legislators. The question which presented itself to the forces of law and order was how? How had these killings taken place? How had these blacks arrived at the actual sites of their outbursts? Had they walked, carrying the guns in their arms? Had they rode? Had they flown? Had they had help? And how had they come in possession of these dangerous guns? That was the question. All the others were incidental.

All the guns were of the same make, unmarked army field rifles similar to the US M-14, shooting a 7.62-caliber cartridge. None carried any clues. Nor were any clues relating to the guns discovered in the residences of the dead black killers. Neither families, wives, children, friends, acquaintances, servants, or neighbors admitted to any previous knowledge of any kind concerning the guns. No one admitted ever having seen them before; no one admitted having seen the delivery of the florist's boxes in which they had come; no one admitted having noticed anything unusual in the behavior, the demeanor, or the habits of the black killers before they had gone on their rampages and been killed. No one admitted to any knowledge or act that may have connected them in any way to the shootings. No one admitted having seen anything, heard anything, known anything, or done anything which could be construed as incriminating.

Law enforcement agencies were baffled but not surprised. Under the circumstances, they hadn't expected anyone would voluntarily testify to any knowledge or behavior which might very well get himself in the soup. As a consequence, they proceeded with their own private investigations.

The assistance of the FBI was requested by a joint petition of all the police departments in cities where the shootings had taken place.

In due course, the FBI interrogated all registered manufacturers of guns and ammunition within the territorial boundaries of the US, and diligently searched for clandestine manufacturers, but none were discovered. The manufacturer and sale of arms and ammunition were sufficiently profitable in the US to discourage its being done illegitimately. But not one firm admitted any knowledge of that particular gun, although the type was familiar enough.

No thefts of such guns had been reported, which was no surprise, since no retailer admitted selling or ever having seen such guns. There was no evidence of their having been smuggled into the US, or even any hints that pointed in that direction.

The CIA undertook to discover where such guns and ammunition may have been produced in other nations, and it did not take long to establish that no such manufacturers existed anywhere in the western world. Of course, the guns might have originated from behind the Iron Curtain or inside Red China, but its spy network was unable to uncover any information in this respect whatsoever.

The CIA passed the ball back to the FBI, which was responsible for internal security. The FBI decided that if they could not discover the original source of the guns, they might at least uncover the means by which they were distributed. It appeared obvious that the distribution was carried out by some agency, for no individual could possibly have the means or organization to undertake such an operation.

But there were many organizations capable of such an undertaking, both politically and physically. Of course, it required a certain type of mentality that was strictly the opposite of the common, patriotic, conformist mentality of the average American. From both a physical and political standpoint, it seemed likely that the organization behind the killings had to be an agency with communist or anti-white orientation, but it was also possible that it might be some misguided group of the extreme right who hated blacks and desired to set them up for extermination.

The first agencies the FBI staked out were the John Birch Society, the Ku Klux Klan, the Communist Party, the Friends of Cuba and North Vietnam Committees, and the American Nazi Party. But they were shortly to establish what they had already suspected: that all these agencies had the same kind of harmless, domesticated natures that an old horse has; primarily gentle and loyal but with an occasional desire to kick out and pretend he is a vicious stallion. None wanted to see the demise of the establishment.

However, the major part of its investigation centered on Black Nationalistic groups and black militant groups which had acquired a political standing. Among these were the Black Foxes, the Black Torchbearers, the Black Avengers, the Black Arts-Culture-History (BACH), the Black World, and a small group of black fanatics that called themselves the Black Death.

Impressive caches of arms and ammunition, explosives, and drugs of a kind known as 'Truth Serums', used for interrogations, were uncovered in the headquarters of most of these groups. Sidearms – pistols and revolvers – hunting guns, a few artillery pieces such as mortars, bazookas, .50-caliber water-cooled machine guns, and enough plastic explosive to blow up the Mississippi River were discovered, but no automatic rifles of the type sought. This surprised the FBI, in view of the fact that there was such an abundance of other weapons.

But the FBI did not reveal its discoveries to the public for fear of disturbing it further, choosing to simply call in armed forces to quietly clean out the arms caches and arrest all blacks in the vicinity. When it finally became convinced that no known black group of political militancy was responsible for the distribution of the 'murder weapons', as the automatic rifles had come to be known, there was only one other well-known American agency left. And it was the toughest kind to investigate, because it was invisible. It was the 'Conspiracy'.

But search as it would, no conspiracy was uncovered. And the source of the guns remained a mystery.

18

The white community was not only disturbed but it was confused. The forces of law and order sworn to protect them from the blacks were, in fact, killing more of them through excesses of over-kill and over-reaction. The deaths of these innocent victims, those killed by the insane blacks and those killed by the over-zealous white police, threw the white community into the same slough of grief and despair as it had suffered at the time of the black massacre. But now, added to their guilt was fear, not only of the blacks and the consequences of containing them, but of themselves, the excesses that they, the normal white majority, might be pushed into committing. And over and above all, apart even from their instinctive racial reactions of guilt, fear, and revulsion, was the emotion inspired by the mystery of the guns. It was an emotion of extreme uneasiness stemming from the suspicion that something might be happening in the world that they didn't know about – happening to them. Where were the guns coming from? Who was arming these irresponsible blacks? And for what purpose? Were they, the American white community, targets of some diabolical communist scheme for weakening the US militarily? Were blacks being used for the destruction of capitalism? Was the attack aimed at Authority, Democracy, or all the pillars of American Society? Were they the victims of a conspiracy by all the blacks who inhabited the earth? The white community knew and feared conspiracies, although most white people had never seen one. Or was Red China the nigger in the woodpile?

But regardless of where the guns were coming from, the first act of self-preservation was to discover who had them. The blacks must be searched one by one for possession. A strategy similar to that of the 'search and destroy' in Vietnam must be undertaken in the US. The black bastards who had guns in their possession must be found and destroyed.

There was an immediate demand for larger police forces. More sophisticated weapons which would not subject the white community to needless danger were needed. Domestic security should take precedence over national security. The white community petitioned Congress to suspend the manufacture and stockpiling of nuclear weapons, continental ballistic missiles, and Polaris submarines, and concentrate on developing atomic bombs that could be used to destroy one black bastard with a gun without subjecting the entire white community to danger. An atom bomb that could be carried in a policeman's pocket with his blackjack and which would not produce any radioactivity when it exploded.

In the meantime, conventional weapons and exercises could be employed to scour the black ghettoes for dangerous weapons and at the same time screen individual blacks for dangerous attitudes. Small armed tanks with the latest in anti-riot devices, such as anti-riot glue to immobilize rioters by sticking them together in balls of ten or twelve each, paralysing gas, sneezing powders to incapacitate rioters with paroxysms of sneezing, sprays to temporarily blind anyone who resisted an order, and electronic devices similar to Geiger counters which reacted only to the combined pulsations from black skin and blue steel, for use in the location of black killers with guns, were all needed by police to patrol the streets. House-to-house searches were made of all black residences, no matter how humble, and no black was safe with a piece of iron larger than a nail cutter, unless he was adroit enough to win the time to talk. And still the white community demanded that local police forces be supported by the national armed forces. At the same time, they deplored any excess which might deprive blacks of their civil rights.

In due time, all blacks were required to register with the

police and were meticulously screened for anti-white attitudes. And woe betide the black who was discovered to resist eating rice or drinking milk because it was white. Blacks found guilty of anti-white attitudes were summarily locked in stockades that had been constructed for that purpose. Those who were listed as doubtful were issued yellow cards that permitted them freedom of the street at certain hours of the day, but at night restricted them to their houses. Only those that the other blacks castigated as 'Uncle Toms' were classified by the police as dependable and given green cards that permitted them as much freedom as they had known before. However, they were required to spy, not only on doubtful blacks, but on one another. From this arose so much suspicion that, superficially at least, the black race appeared to be both deaf and dumb.

And yet the white community continued to suffer such fear, guilt, and insecurity, that the very stability of their society was threatened. Many whites became ill and haggard from emotional insecurity. Others retained their sanity through the therapeutic remedy of nightmares, for during this terrible period, whites experienced a variety of assorted nightmares, all of which featured the enlarged sexual organs of black males.

One white woman dreamed that a black had gouged out one of her breasts and was thrusting his enormous black penis, which had two thick, brutal horns, into the bloody hole.

A middle-aged white advertising executive dreamed that a giant nude black, with testicles hanging from his crotch like huge black bombs, was coming toward him, firing from a disembodied penis as big as a cannon barrel. He could feel each of the big solid bullets as it penetrated his body.

Another white woman, a young matron with two lovely children, dreamed that when she had gone out onto the street, she was engulfed by a squirming mass of black pythons. When she screamed for her husband to save her, he appeared soaring overhead, exploding like a brilliant burst of fireworks. In despair, she quit struggling against the pythons and resigned herself to her fate. When she looked at them again, however, she suddenly recognized them as squirming black penises.

In this atmosphere of intense guilt and fear, blacks became

deathly afraid of the whites' fear. The black man had always feared the white man's fear. Added to it, now, were guilt and insecurity, which rendered it even more dangerous and unpredictable.

Blacks became afraid to pass whites on the sidewalk. Invariably they stepped off into the street. When a tank came down a ghetto street, blacks scurried for cover like rats. Possession of a green card did not quiet their fear of white fear. There was an instinctive quality about this fear, as though it were hereditary and had come down through centuries from generation to generation. Black children acted as though they had been born with it. Blacks who could neither read nor write and knew nothing of the history of the white man were possessed with it. Those blacks who had learned of the exploitation of blacks by whites throughout the centuries had also learned that when they suffered from fear and guilt, whites were as dangerous and undiscriminating as blind rattlesnakes. Black people went underground, the good, the bad, and the ugly.

However, at first there had been a few Uncle Toms who, thinking themselves in the good graces of the whites and wishing to remain so, reported the receipt of guns. They rushed with their guns to the nearest police station and told how the guns had been thrust into their hands by black messengers who had then disappeared. They expected an accolade, a pat on the head, or at least a commendation for being good niggers, but when it was discovered that they could not tell the whites the source of the guns – which none of them knew – the whites turned on them with insensate fury and beat them damn near to death. They were subjected to extensive third degrees and brutal torture. Some had their tongues cut out because they wouldn't tell what they didn't know. Others had their eyes gouged out because they couldn't report what they hadn't seen. Others had their hands chopped off, some were castrated, some were beaten so brutally they never regained their senses. They were stripped of their property, separated from their families, their green cards were confiscated, they were denied work, and deprived of shelter. They scarcely survived on the crumbs they could beg from the uncooperative, sullen blacks who had kept their mouths shut. Thereafter, even the rankest, most obsequious Uncle Tom knew better than to report receiving one of the dangerous guns to the white police.

It was even more dangerous to be caught in possession of one of the offensive weapons. It was worse than being caught with the bubonic plague, or more lethal anyway. The guns were more dangerous as malignant objects than they were as offensive weapons. They were, in some ways, similar to sixteen pounds of radium. Just being near one was dangerous, and the wages of owning one was instantaneous death.

Frantically, blacks began ridding themselves of these deadly objects. They shied and shuddered at the sight of one. They fled from their vicinity, but they soon discovered it was not as easy to get rid of them as it was to get hold of one. The guns had been placed in their possession with ease and subtlety, but getting rid of them was just the opposite.

They were too bulky to hide, too solid to melt. They were too heavy to be painted and camouflaged as a child's toy. In most instances, there was neither an ocean, a lake, a river, nor even a well in which they could be quietly dropped. They were forced to leave them in the streets, in tenement hallways, doorways, basements, and rooftops. They threw them down drains, into manholes, garbage cans, parked cars, and through open windows into other blacks' flats. They broke into other flats to hide them under beds, in closets, behind furnishings, anywhere to get rid of them. It became every man for himself. Some ghettoes became so thick with abandoned guns, that the forces of law and order might have given up hope of ever containing the black population, had the guns remained hidden.

In consequence, blacks became afraid to walk down a deserted street because of the risk of being caught near an abandoned gun. They became afraid to return home for fear of finding another gun abandoned there. Meticulously they searched every room and closet and piece of furniture of any flat they entered. They searched the interiors of cars that had been parked and peered beneath the chassis before driving off. Whenever they found a gun concealed in their dwellings or on their properties, they would quickly dump it somewhere else.

They lived in an atmosphere of fear of the whites and suspicion of each other that had, itself, been caused by white fear. It was like a deadly carousel.

Paradoxically, it was the whites' guilt and fear that eventually saved blacks from extermination. The whites had the means, but they did not have the will. Their guilt would not permit them to exterminate the black race. They were more afraid of their own moral condemnation than they were of the danger blacks posed to them. They would have granted all black demands, but they were afraid of the violent objections of other whites. They had no positive proof that these violent objections existed, but they believed in them like they believed in conspiracies. It was in this belief they persisted.

The white majorities of the other nations of the world, particularly those European nations considered most closely aligned to America's white majority, were appalled by what they considered an irrational approach to an uprising by a black minority. While Americans suffer guilt over black segregation and restriction, in other white societies the assumption of black equality is summarily dismissed. This is why other white majorities treat their black minorities with greater consideration and politeness. They do not fear that blacks will ever attain equality or that they will even request it.

Strangely enough, American blacks don't know this, and probably most whites don't, either.

It was perhaps inevitable that blacks would eventually turn on the mysterious messengers who brought them so much danger and hardship. However, the appearance of the messengers had changed since that fateful rifle had been delivered to T-bone Smith. Now they were not as easy to identify, or even remember, as they had been. As relations between whites and blacks had grown increasingly tense, the appearance of the messengers had gradually metamorphosed from the neatly uniformed, purposeful black youths. First, they appeared as older, slovenly, disinterested men, then gradually to younger men of greater physical agility but little intellectual acuity.

All were dressed in the uniform of the unemployed relief recipient – patched blue jeans, soiled blue tee-shirt, scuffed blue canvas sneakers – in other words, the type who could instantly disappear into a crowd. Had they given it any thought, blacks would have quickly concluded that this had been done to give the messengers greater protection. However, most blacks thought only that they were misled numbskulls bent on getting them all into trouble, and as such, that they could be stopped.

But how? This new crop of messengers proved to be quick, strong, and single-minded. They came out of nowhere, always after dark, when the streets were empty of blacks and when white patrols were slack. They thrust the dreaded guns into their recipients' hands and melted back into the darkness from whence they had come. Woe betide any recipient who should try to stop them. Most times the messenger would simply disable the recipient with a few lightning-quick karate chops and leave him floundering on the floor.

When the recipient was a quick, strong, athletic man, equal to the messenger's physical prowess, the messenger would simply draw a .22-caliber revolver and shoot him dead. Soon it became apparent that there was greater danger in trying to capture the messenger than in receiving the gun. In that case, at least, the recipient had time and darkness in which to dispose of the gun.

Nevertheless, some wildly dramatic scenes ensued as some blacks persisted in trying to capture a messenger. Men dressed in jeans and tee-shirts, seemingly like any other out-of-work black man, were often seen fleeing from mobs of other black men, invariably led by a man bleeding profusely from a variety of wounds until he collapsed. In rare instances, black messengers were captured by their pursuers, and some were summarily lynched by the friends of the men they had killed. However, this was nothing compared to the pain inflicted by the police when one of these messengers was turned over to them.

In these instances, the police were not restrained by public opinion. Messengers were sometimes flayed, layer by layer, until the white bone showed through. Some lost their eyes, one by one, their finger and toe nails, one by one, their teeth, one by one, their sexual organs, their hands and feet. Some of these victims of insensate white rage even lost their heads. It was rumored that the severed heads of black men had been seen on display in front of precinct stations, sometimes accompanied by a severed pair of hands, black testicles hanging from a string, severed black feet paired sedately on a cardboard carton beside the precinct steps.

These were seen only by blacks in the ghettoes. Even had they heard of any such rumors, no white man would have believed them, since suicidal black killers continued to surface. The more the killings continued, the more the white community panicked, and the more ludicrous became their demands. Eventually whites demanded that many large, modern prisons be erected all over the United States, and that all blacks be locked up in them, except for the few needed to look after their food and sanitation. These few had to be carefully screened and only those blacks who could pass a series of stringent tests that proved they were reliable Uncle Toms would be accepted. However, the government rejected this demand on the grounds that too many whites would be deprived of their servants.

19

As soon as Tomsson Black cashed Barbara's check, he moved uptown to Harlem and rented the entire first floor of a new office building on 125th Street. While the seven offices were being furnished with the latest in office equipment, he had all of the doors opening onto the corridor, along with the windows fronting on 125th Street inscribed with the legend:

BLACK FOR BLACKS, INC.
T. Black, President

Afterward, he staffed the offices with young black men and women, all under the age of thirty. As soon as he was established, the blacks of Harlem flocked in to express their support. Not because of the nature of his business, for none of them knew exactly what it was, but simply because he was a big, impressive-looking man, a man of distinction with an undeniable air of confidence. Because he was gregarious and courteous and at home among blacks and approachable by all. Because he had been convicted and sentenced to life for raping a white woman but hadn't let it destroy him. Because after only three years' imprisonment he was back among his own people, rich and purposeful and obviously powerful.

Many of them admired him because they still remembered his revolutionary background and that his doctrine had always been death to the whiteys. But mostly they came to see him because he was black, black as a man can be, black as any of them, and even his name was 'Black'.

There was no one on Tomsson Black's office staff except personable young black people. He knew he was being unfair to the light-skinned and mulatto black people, but he wanted to be surrounded by young people who were as black as himself. It was part of his plan. In time he might work up to employing light-skinned black people. In fact, if his plans matured it would be unavoidable. But he wanted to start with the blackest of the black. The young people in his office might have been the winners of a black beauty contest.

They felt a special respect for him, and they loved and admired him, too. They thought him so handsome and self-assured that they were eager to please him. To him, that was the most important thing.

All of them had been to college. Some had attended all-black schools in the South, others had attended colleges and universities in the North. There were several young men who had attended Columbia University, and several young women who had attended Hunter College, and several of both sexes who had attended City College. But he showed no favoritism.

In the beginning he put them to work researching all of the recorded research on the meat-packing industry in the United

States; its inception and its development, its operation and management, its products and by-products, its waste and its profits. These young blacks loved him and admired him and respected him, but they thought he had gone nuts.

When he gave them their next assignment they were sure of it. This was the researching of all the known processes of land reclamation, the researching and copying of all Alabama State laws governing the ownership of land, title deeds and taxes, Federal laws defining territorial waters that listed the uses and control of such waters as regards fishing and mineral rights, and the regulations applying to navigation.

After studying their findings, he assigned them to draw up a prospectus for the construction and operation of a pig farm and packing house that would employ all modern techniques for breeding and raising pigs, processing and packaging pork products and by-products, and distributing such products to all sections of the United States. They were to include the construction of the buildings, the type and cost of the equipment needed, and the nature of the transport required. The prospectus was to be based on the assumption that one hundred thousand people would be employed in its operation. By then they began to wonder what he had in mind, but no one dared ask.

When they had drawn up the prospectus and mimeographed five hundred copies, he mailed a copy to each of the black leaders in the United States, regardless of their political affiliation, political belief, opinions on the right course for black progress, opinions on each other and on the whites. To each he explained that this project would be non-profit making, and that its sole purpose would be that of employing indigent blacks and taking them off the relief rolls and other forms of white charity.

Without waiting for their replies, he went to Mobile, Alabama, and consulted the county registry of title deeds to ascertain the owner of the old Harrison place. As he had expected, the place was intestate and for many years had been offered for sale at fifty cents an acre to pay the back taxes. He paid twenty-five hundred dollars in cash and had the title deed made out to George Washington Lincoln, his former name.

A crowd of redneck clerks from all the other offices in the courthouse, who were familiar with the place and its reputation, gathered to look at the 'half-witted northern nigger' who had twenty-five hundred dollars to throw away. He didn't even give them the satisfaction of hearing his 'Yankee' speech. He silently pocketed his title deed and walked to the railway station where he entrained to the north and back to Harlem. He had not even taken the time to look at the Harrison place, which he had never seen.

Answers awaited him from most of the black leaders to whom he had sent copies of his prospectus. All expressed enthusiasm about the project that would employ a hundred thousand indigent blacks, but most contained suspicions concerning his motives and intentions. He did not reply to any of them.

His next step was to contact a firm of white engineers in downtown Manhattan and employ a team of ten surveyors and two engineers whom he sent to Mobile with instructions to survey the old Harrison place and mark the boundaries. The two engineers were instructed to make an appraisal of the feasibility and cost of clearing and reclaiming the land, building a pier along the boundary bordering on Mobile Bay, and concrete roads leading from it to the boundary opposite.

They went on their assignment equipped with jungle paraphernalia, including boots and suits resistant to snakebite and other poisons, weapons to protect them from the sharptoothed razorback and boar hogs, pumas, bears, and other wild beasts, anti-toxins and lotions and mosquito net masks and every other protection and medication they deemed necessary for a jungle expedition. The only contingency they had not anticipated were the inquisitive local rednecks who came out *en masse* to stare at them and get in their way as they proceeded about their work.

The surveyors marked the boundaries with concrete posts one hundred yards apart and the engineers estimated it would cost in the neighborhood of five hundred thousand dollars to reclaim the land and to build a pier and the roads that Tomsson Black had proposed. Like all the others in the engineering firm, they thought Tomsson Black represented an organization of blacks who wished to build a housing development for black segregationists.

But he was soon to disillusion them. When they returned from their mission, Tomsson Black presented the firm with his prospectus and asked for an estimate of the total cost of building a pig farm and packing house with facilities for transport, in addition to clearing the land and building the roads. Needless to say, the old white men at the head of the firm were shocked by the nature and the scope of his plan. Nevertheless, they gave him an honest estimate that a minimum of one million dollars would be needed to produce the first cured ham for market.

Incorporating that estimate in the prospectus, Tomsson Black gave his project the name of 'CHITTERLINGS, INC.' and sent it to the Hull Foundation along with an exposition of its purpose to employ indigent blacks, to apply for a one million dollar grant.

20

The Hull Foundation had ten billion dollars at its disposal and was the world's richest foundation. Its director, Henry H. Hopkins, former dean of the Harvard University College of Law, was a tall, spare New Englander, whose ancestors had been active in the 'Underground Railroad'. He had introduced such liberal policies in the operation of the Hull Foundation as to incur the fear and suspicion of many of the nation's leading conservatives. Several right-wing newspaper columnists had gone so far as to call him pink, but he was a fervent apostle of the American way of life and of all its institutions, and he firmly believed the solution to America's 'black problem' lay in the capabilities of blacks, themselves, once they discovered them. He believed that by nature of their inheritance and background, blacks had developed a stronger character than whites, but they had not discovered how to exploit it. His greatest hope was that, during his term as director of the Hull Foundation, he would discover a way to endow blacks with the means to fulfill their destiny. He knew that what they needed most in a capitalistic society was capital, and if it ever became possible he would put the full volume of the capital of the Hull Foundation in their hands and let the conservatives castigate him all they would.

When the prospectus for Chitterlings, Inc. and the application for the grant of a million dollars by Tomsson Black reached his desk, he was alarmed. Because of the urgency of the national problem of what to do with indigent blacks, the application deserved consideration. Tomsson Black's plan for creating a profitless meat-packing industry which would employ more than a hundred thousand of them exhibited imagination and understanding, and the prospectus showed that it was feasible. The million dollars would be a comparatively minor endowment, and in view of the anticipated benefits, the application could not be ignored.

But his reaction to the man, Tomsson Black, himself, was strikingly similar to the reaction of the nation's black leaders. From his point of view, the man's motives and intentions were automatically suspect. In many of the nation's leading establishments, the press, charitable and law enforcement institutions, commerce and industry, there was a secret list of the names of all blacks in the news who were classified as 'suspects', and Tomsson Black's name headed the list. The name of Tomsson Black was notorious in the United States. He had been a member of every white-hating black group. He had been given tremendous publicity for his vicious and unfounded attacks on the police. He had defied the State Department and visited all the communist countries declared out of bounds to US citizens. And finally, he had savagely raped the wife of a white man who had sought to befriend him and had been sentenced to life in the penitentiary. And now he was out, after what seemed like a disgracefully short time, and had the audacity to apply to the Hull Foundation for a grant of a million dollars.

However, Hopkins refused to let his personal prejudice against the man deter him from giving full consideration to a project that had such great potential for the relief of human misery. He would not pretend that he liked the man. He would treat him courteously but sternly. He would force him to reveal his true motives and intentions. And if, during the process, Tomsson Black became displeased and withdrew his application, the project, in itself, was of such great value that the Hull Foundation would not let it go to waste. They would find another black to foster it, someone whom they could support in all good conscience. Unbeknown to Hopkins, Tomsson Black had already foreseen this attitude on his part and had bought the land with his own money and held it in his own name.

First Hopkins contacted the FBI to ask how Tomsson Black had gotten out of prison before the expiration of his sentence. When he was informed that Edward Goodfeller had interceded on his behalf and influenced the governor to grant him a pardon, Hopkins asked the FBI to find out what 'hold' Tomsson Black had on Goodfeller, and what other crimes he had been involved in. The FBI was forced to give Tomsson Black a clean bill of health. Goodfeller had interceded for him solely because his conscience troubled him and he and Mrs Goodfeller had decided that Tomsson Black had paid his debt to society. In point of fact, there were no records of Tomsson Black having ever been involved in any other crime.

Next Hopkins asked the State Department if it had placed any restrictions on Tomsson Black. The State Department replied that he was just listed as 'suspect', as he was with all other federal agencies. The department representative humorously noted that it would not nominate him as an ambassador to South Africa.

Hopkins then had all the black leaders listed as 'responsible' canvassed for their opinions as to the reliability of Tomsson Black as a person, and the sociological value of his project. All the 'responsible' black leaders agreed that as a black individual, Tomsson Black was a disgrace to the black race, but his project had great potential for the improvement of black conditions.

Finally, Hopkins had all the better-known white civic leaders and leading liberal thinkers of industry and commerce canvassed for their opinions as to the value of the project politically and as a service to humanity. The replies from this group were varied. Most agreed that such a project, in reliable hands, would undoubtedly effect a strong rebuttal to communist propaganda against capitalism. Some admitted their inability to assess its value as a service to humanity, but agreed that without a doubt, it would help feed the nation's indigent black population and put them to work. This last opinion afforded Hopkins a sardonic smile. However, the common denominator of all the opinions received was that everyone shared his negative view of Tomsson Black.

Now the time had come to meet Tomsson Black face to face. This meeting between two men so dissimilar in character did not shake the world, but it represented a confrontation between the races in microcosm. The tall, elderly, distinguished-looking white man sat across his wide, polished desk from the much younger, but equally distinguished-looking black man. There the similarity ended. Tomsson Black was dressed in a somber pin-striped black suit of excellent cut, white shirt, black tie, shoes, and socks. Mr Hopkins wore a wrinkled gray herringbone suit, blue shirt, red tie, and brown shoes. As in most instances, the black man was the more elegant of the two.

But the white man was more at ease. Tomsson Black was cognizant of this fact and he silently cursed himself. Hopkins was also cognizant of it, and endeavored to make him more comfortable. Not because he had any sympathy for the man, but because it seemed he had an unfair advantage accorded by tradition. But as a counterbalance against this unfair advantage, Hopkins felt a reluctant sympathy for this black man who had committed a crime that he could understand. Was there ever a virile black man immune to raping a lush, tantalizing white woman who made herself available?

However, Tomsson Black had armed himself with a shield of defensive dignity. He returned Hopkins' direct, penetrating gaze with one that was equally direct and candid.

Hopkins asked him to elaborate on the benefits that he hoped would be derived from his project and how they could be best achieved.

Tomsson Black contended that his project would prove beneficial to all of society by employing and housing the nation's indigent blacks. On the five thousand acres where the multi-tiered pig farm and packing houses were to be located, a large, modern housing development would be built to accommodate all of the workers and their families. This housing development would be a complex of twenty-storied apartment houses built around a park and public swimming pool, and would include boutiques, apartment stores, supermarkets, all types of service shops from dry cleaners to florists, a bank, a post office, library, hospital, cinemas, and an elementary school with a stadium for sports. The workers would pay a nominal rent, based on the income of the firm, and could partake of all the services and entertainments free of charge. Attendance in the elementary school would be compulsory until the age of sixteen or graduation.

Indigent black people would be recruited from all the black ghettos in the nation; relief rolls and the lists of blacks on private charities would be canvassed and even the needy would be taken from the streets. These people, the father or the mother, the husband or the wife, or both, and single men, single women, and unmarried mothers would be given jobs with the firm and their transportation and that of their children and dependants would be paid to the home plant in Mobile, or to wherever they were to be employed, free of charge. Furnished housing would be waiting on their arrival.

He hoped, in time, to incorporate concurrent programs for the assistance and cure of drug addicts and the rehabilitation of ex-convicts, along with the medical facilities and homes for the infirm and aged who had no assistance.

It was his intention to eventually provide all of the nation's indigent blacks, along with those who became indigent in the future, the opportunity for gainful employment and agreeable, rewarding lives, so that their children, if not themselves, could participate in the full, creative, and exciting life offered by the United States.

Mr Hopkins was moved by this exposition.

'The commercial accomplishments of Chitterlings, Inc., although necessary for maintenance, are negligible in comparison to the human contribution we wish to make,' Tomsson Black concluded.

Hopkins knew that Tomsson Black was a risky character and he suspected that deep down he was disloyal to America and anti-white, besides. He could feel vibrations of evil emanating from his person, but he felt himself being persuaded in spite of it. Tomsson Black might have been a snake, and he, Hopkins, a bird. He wondered if this was the way a woman felt when she was being seduced against her will.

Suddenly he asked, 'Do you still bear ill will against Mr and Mrs Goodfeller?'

'I never bore them any ill will, sir,' Tomsson Black replied without any hint in manner or voice that the question had disturbed him. He spoke as though discussing an exercise in sociology. 'I have always considered Mr and Mrs Goodfeller as friends and protectors, even during and after the unfortunate business of rape.'

Hopkins leaned forward with sudden interest and his color heightened. 'Mrs Goodfeller is a beautiful woman, I understand,' he ventured.

'Very beautiful, indeed,' Tomsson Black answered with emotion.

'Tell me, did you get any pleasure out of raping her? I mean sexual pleasure.' Mr Hopkins was not normally ashamed of his curiosity, but sometimes, as now, it disturbed him.

'No sir, I became blindly angry at the sight of her body and I thought, "Is this what so many blacks have been lynched for?" It was just the same as a black woman's body, only the skin was white.'

Hopkins caught himself about to rub his hands together with glee. 'Was this the first white woman you ever raped?'

'Sir, I do not go about raping white women promiscuously, otherwise I would undoubtedly be dead.'

Mr Hopkins chuckled. 'You appear to be a strong, vigorous man.'

'I mean shot dead,' Tomsson Black corrected him.

Suddenly Mr Hopkins returned to his previous character of objective, clinical appraisal. 'Why did you rape her, then? You said that she and her husband were your friends and protectors.'

'She was there,' Tomsson Black said in a flat, unemotional voice. Then, realizing that Hopkins expected a more logical answer, he elaborated, 'She kept walking around her cabin in the nude when she knew I had to pass by. My cabin adjoined theirs.'

'Teasing you.'

'Well, I don't know whether she was teasing or not, or whether she was inviting me. It is said that black men inspire the baser emotions in white women because they don't consider us as human. Therefore, they can indulge in any depravity at all with us because they believe it doesn't count.' His voice had roughened and it was obvious the memory angered him.

'Was she depraved?'

'No sir, but I got angry and began beating her.'

'Before you raped her? Or while you were raping her?' Hopkins was shocked to realize that he was deriving a vicarious excitement from this dialog and he wanted to stop it, but the desire to continue was stronger than his will to stop.

'I don't remember. I just remember she was badly beaten up when her husband came.'

'And yet they interceded to have you released from prison.'

'Yes sir, but I don't find that surprising. I have learned that white people are the only true Christians on earth. And it is a Christian tenet to forgive.'

'And have you forgiven them?'

'Forgiven them for what? It was I who wronged them.'

'But they put the flesh pots in your path that tempted you. They plucked you from your native environment and plunged you into a different life, more sophisticated, more permissive, more amoral in a refined fashion.'

'I didn't notice all of that. I must be very naive, a primitive at heart. I thought Mr and Mrs Goodfeller were just friendly, enlightened people, but very moral and high-principled.'

'Just so. I was endeavoring to put myself in your place to understand your attitude toward white people. Tell me, deep in your heart, do you hate us for the way we have exploited you?'

'You mean, do I hate white people?'

'Yes, just that.'

'No sir, I think at this point in the history of America, the races are even in their debt to one another. You took us from Africa as slaves, but some of us were already slaves in Africa and would have remained slaves until slavery there was abolished.

'It is true, you brought us here as slaves and worked us as slaves and profited by our sweat,' he continued, 'but we learned things from you we would never have learned in Africa. We learned trade, we learned Christianity, we learned English, we learned to grow food and build shelter, and eventually we were freed. Now we have acquired more of the blessings of civilization than any other black people of comparable numbers on earth. We American blacks are better fed, better clothed, better housed, better educated, and are more devout Christians than any other blacks on earth.

'We earn more, spend more, produce more, contribute more, and know more, and therefore we demand more,' Tomsson Black said, 'but despite the fact we have grown in numbers, we haven't grown comparably in wealth. And this is a capitalistic nation, where all life forces derive from wealth. We know this, but most of the wealth of the nation belongs to white people, and as a consequence they control the destiny of our nation. Therefore we protest the unfairness of this. We want our share of the nation's wealth so we can control our own destinies. But that does not mean we hate white people. We have too much to love you for.'

It was this outburst that finally broke down Mr Hopkins' reserve and began to swing the pendulum in Tomsson Black's favor. What had at first been intended for two or three brief interviews at the most, turned into long daily discussions touching upon many topics. Hopkins' greatest interest was in Tomsson Black's opinions on what steps blacks had taken to adapt to a way of life that was principally designed by whites and for whites.

'In most instances we can do no more than imitate,' Tomsson Black confessed. 'We have so little tradition outside the structure of our national society, that we have very few basic innovations to offer. With the exception of jazz music, I do not know of a single contribution we have made to American life from our racial heritage. Of course, there are habits and customs we acquired from our tenure of slavery that have, in recent years, become popularized. But most of them were adapted from the whites and forced upon us for the purpose of survival, such as soul food and spirituals. However, soul food came from vegetables and animals the whites raise for their own food, and merely consisted of the parts they threw away.

'We have taken our language from the whites, our knowledge and education from the whites, our morals and religions from the whites, our definitions of justice, ambition, achievement, clothing, shelter; in fact every aspect of our lives but reproduction, which is common to all life. We do not have any remembered tradition. What we know of the African life of our ancestors comes from information recorded by whites. Even Africans themselves are dependent on these white records to learn of their own past. It is not a question of whether we should adapt to the way of life created by whites for whites, since there is no other way of life to which we can adapt.

'And if we create a way of life for ourselves, the very act of this creation will be an imitation of that of the whites. Whatever tradition the blacks ever had on earth is gone and transplanted by the civilization the whites have imposed on the earth, and it is highly unlikely we would want to go back and live like our ancestors, even if we could. But many admirable tendencies have come from this paradoxical attitude of ours. We have learned that to us, black is beautiful. But this, too, we have learned from the whites, who began terming themselves beautiful when they first began to rule the world. All people in authority must, of a necessity, be beautiful. God is beautiful. All rulers are beautiful. Power endows one with beauty. It is not only natural but essential that people of all races must be beautiful to themselves. We blacks in the US have ignored this obvious fact, for, in the acquisition of all of our other cultural attributes from whites, we have accepted their definition of beauty, too.'

'Black people are beautiful, too,' Hopkins said.

'Of course, sir,' said Tomsson Black. 'That is what I've been saying. "Too" is the operative word. We are human, too; we are intelligent, too; we are worthy, too; but we are not white, too, and that is the problem. We are everything but white in a white-dominated, white-oriented society. The one thing which we lack is white skin. So we must imitate the dominant group, as has every minority group in the history of the world. Unlike most minority groups, however, when we achieve our imitation even to perfection, we can not move over into the majority group and become assimilated because of the barrier of our skin. That makes us different from almost all other minority groups throughout history.

'We must achieve our equality in this society against overwhelming odds. That is why we need a springboard, why we need a beginning. We need capital. The white people had slaves, the wedding of coal and ore, the unlimited grazing plains, the fertile earth, the gold rush, the underground lakes of petroleum. With all that, it didn't require too much creative imagination for this nation to become rich and prosperous. We, however, must start at the bottom, at the chitterling of the hog. We don't own fertile fields and slaves to till them for us, we own no plains, we're too late for the gold rush, we own no oil-bearing land. We own only ourselves, and we can't even hire outselves out to the highest bidder, which is another privilege of the white man. We must take what we are offered for ourselves, and ofttimes that is very little. Of course, we are beautiful, too, but that will get us very little of the capital we so badly need, and it might very well hinder us.'

'If it were up to me, I would see that black people were given equal rights this instant,' Hopkins said sincerely. Lapsing into pragmatic self-derogation, he added, 'But no one ever has the will or the authority to act against the will of the majority. Not even dictators,' he concluded after a moment's comtemplation.

'I am not requesting you to act alone,' Tomsson Black said. 'I hope to persuade the majority of our nation's white people that this project is in their own best interests.'

The interrogation did not end there. Mr Hopkins felt that he owed it to his employer, the Hull Foundation, and the whole of the white majority nation, to explore every facet of this man's mind before granting him the power that he requested. For if this project was to be a success, it would be the first concrete example of black power in the history of the nation. So he kept probing at Tomsson Black's mind until it seemed at times that it afforded him some sadistic pleasure.

'Tell me, Mr Black, what was your honest opinion of Dr Martin Luther King?'

'I thought Dr King was the greatest man who ever lived. I thought he was concerned not only with the welfare of us black people, but with the moral character of the nation as a whole. I thought he was a selfless leader, and I particularly admired his stand against violence. I thought his death was a loss to all men of character in the world, regardless of race, creed, color, or political ideology.'

Mr Hopkins nodded. 'I find that we agree, as we have on so many varied subjects. Dr King was a man among men. And what is your opinion of Roy Wilkins?'

For an instant the name did not register in Tomsson Black's memory. It was as though, unconsciously, he suffered from a block. But suddenly his memory cleared and he smiled with relief.

'I grew up with the feeling that Mr Wilkins, as the head of the NAACP, was the titular leader of our race, and as such, I automatically admired his wisdom and intelligence and took it for granted that he always acted in our best interests.'

'Mmmm, but you have not stated your own private, unrehearsed opinion of Mr Wilkins,' Hopkins said.

'I thought I had, sir. I think he is an intelligent and wise leader. He does not have the personal magnetism, the charisma, that Dr King possessed, but he is a wise and perceptive leader of our people.'

'And Malcolm X? What was your opinion of Malcolm X? I believe you were personally acquainted with him.'

'No, my father knew him but I never met him. All I know of Malcolm X is what my father said, what I have read of him and what he wrote about himself in his autobiography.'

'And what was that?'

'My father was a great admirer of Malcolm X, but I could never understand the logic that made him anti-white. Of course, he grew out of it as he developed, but that was what my father most admired about him.'

'Is your father anti-white?'

'He was, sir.'

'You say "was", then I take it he is dead.'

'He was killed in an accident the year before Malcolm X was assassinated.'

'And is your mother still alive?'

'No sir, she died six years ago when I was abroad.'

'Do you think the loss of your father affected your subsequent life?'

'There is no doubt about it, sir,' Tomsson Black said. 'But I have always felt that its effect was more constructive than adverse. It conditioned me to think for myself and bear the blame for my mistakes instead of trying to shift it onto others. Of a necessity, I had to be self-reliant. I had always to analyse my attitudes and reexamine my decisions. Because of this, despite all my mistakes, I grew and gravitated toward the light. That is the one thing for which Malcolm X won my unadulterated admiration. He never stopped growing.

'He grew from a juvenile life of crime and hatred to become a leader of black people,' Tomsson Black continued. 'It is true that he took some of the hatred with him but he was strong enough to grow out of it. When he was assassinated, he loved all people of all races, despite their shortcomings. I would say that both he and Dr King had arrived at the ultimate point in their love for humanity, although by quite different roads, by the time they were assassinated.'

'Tell me, Mr Black, did you feel – believe – a conspiracy was involved in either of these assassinations?'

'Mr Hopkins, as a black man my emotional reaction to both these assassinations was highly partisan and chauvinistic. I wanted to believe that both of these irreplaceable leaders were victims of conspiracies of white racists. I wanted to believe this. I wanted so badly to believe it that, to accept the proof of public evidence, the judgement of white jurists and the dictates of my own reason to the opposite conclusion, was one of the hardest struggles of my life. One of the privileges that white people have that we don't is their privilege to think what we dare not.'

And so it went, day after day, with Mr Hopkins probing into Tomsson Black's mind and Tomsson Black struggling with all his skill and eloquence to defend his identity. Time and again, when it was least expected, Hopkins would question Tomsson Black's reaction to his imprisonment for rape, and ofttimes he would pose the question of an imposed sense of guilt. Can one avoid a sense of guilt for a crime one has committed, whether he has paid the prescribed debt to society or not? And each time Tomsson Black would reiterate that he no longer felt a sense of guilt for a crime he had paid for.

'I was justly accused and sentenced,' he would repeat. 'I paid my debt to society without complaint. I do not think nor feel that I should keep on paying my debt to society through a sense of guilt. The original meaning of the word penitentiary implied the absolution of sin and the end of penitence. My penitence ended when I was freed from the penitentiary. I believe that Mr and Mrs Goodfeller will support this attitude. Whether they do or not, I am stuck with it, sir. If I still suffered from a sense of guilt I would not be in your office now. I would not have had the vision to conceive this project, nor the necessary assurance to activate it.'

'Mr Black, I must commend you on the eloquence of your appeal,' Hopkins said drily. 'I am inclined to think that if you had pled your own case in court, you would not have been convicted.'

'I thank God I was,' Tomsson Black said passionately. 'It was through my imprisonment that I came to see the light.'

Then at last, Hopkins asked Tomsson Black if he had any objection to being psychoanalysed.

It was Tomsson Black's turn to smile. 'Why, do you think I am crazy, sir?'

'Not at all, Mr Black. But there are people in this world who would think you were, if you walked into their office and asked them for a million dollars, for whatever purpose.'

'I am well aware of that, sir. But I felt from the beginning that the potential benefits to my people outweighed the risks of any adverse opinion of me.'

'Well said, and I assure you that I think you are one of the least crazy persons I have ever met. But I'm curious what your subconscious will reveal about your loyalty and your true attitude toward white people. You have expressed your conscious attitudes on these subjects – and very eloquently. Now I would like to know if your subconscious attitudes will be the same.'

'I would like to know, too, sir,' Tomsson Black said ironically.

However, the discovery of these subconscious attitudes was not to take place. Mr Hopkins succumbed to a heart attack shortly after signing the order to pay to Chitterlings, Inc. the sum of one million dollars.

21

The police parade was headed north up the main street of the big city. Of the thirty thousand policemen employed by the big city, six thousand were in the parade. It had been billed as a parade of unity to demonstrate the strength of law enforcement and reassure the 'communities' during this time of suspicion and animosity between the races. No black policemen were parading for the simple reason that none of them had been asked to parade, and none of them had requested the right.

At no time had the races been so utterly divided, despite the billing of unity given to the parade. Judging from both the appearances of the paraders and the viewers lining the street, the word 'unity' seemed more applicable than the diffident allusion to the 'races'. Only the white race was on view, and it seemed perfectly unified. In fact, the crowd of white faces seemed to deny that a black race existed.

The police commissioner and the chiefs of the various police departments under him led the parade. They were white. The captains of the precinct stations followed, and the lieutenants in charge of the precinct detective bureaus, and the uniformed patrolmen followed them. They were all white, as were all of the plainclothes detectives and uniformed patrolmen who made up the bulk of the parade following. All white. As were the spectators behind the police cordons lining the main street of the big city. As were all the people employed on that street in department stores and office buildings who crowded to doors and windows to watch the police parade pass.

There was only one black man along the entire length of the street at the time, and he wasn't in sight. He was standing in a small, unlighted chamber to the left of the entrance to the big city's large Catholic cathedral on the main street. As a rule, this chamber held the poor box, from which the daily donations were collected by a preoccupied priest in the service of the cathedral at six p.m. each day. Now it was shortly past three o'clock and there were almost three hours before collection time. The only light in the dark room came through two slots where the donations were made, one in the stone front wall that opened on to the street, and the other through the wooden door that opened into the vestibule. The door was locked and the black man had the chamber to himself.

Chutes ran down from the slots into a closed coin box on legs. The black man had removed the chutes which restricted his movements, and he now could sit straddling the coin box. The slot in the stone front wall gave him a clear view of the street up which the policemen's parade would march. Beside him on the floor was a cold bottle of lemonade collecting beads of sweat in the hot, humid air. In his arms he held a blued-steel automatic rifle of the type that had been employed by other black men to slaughter whites. He did not think of them; they were dead. He was only concerned with the living.

The muzzle of the barrel rested on the inner edge of the slot in the stone wall and was invisible from without. He sat patiently, as though he had all the time in the world, waiting for the parade to come into sight. He had all the rest of his life. He had waited four hundred years for this moment and he was not in a hurry. They would come, he knew, and he would be waiting for them.

He knew his black people would suffer severely for this moment of his triumph. He was not an ignorant man. Although he mopped the floors and polished the pews of this white cathedral, he was not without intelligence. He knew the whites would kill him, too. It was almost as though he were already dead. It required a mental effort to keep from making the sign of the cross, but he knew the God of this cathedral was white and would have no tolerance for him. And there was no black God nearby, if in fact there was one anywhere in the US.

Now, at the end of his life, he would have to rely on himself. He would have to assume the authority that controlled his life. He would have to direct his will that directed his brain that directed his finger to pull the trigger. He would have to do it alone, without comfort or encouragement, consoled only by the hope that it would make life safer for blacks in the future. He would have to believe that although blacks would suffer now, there would be those who would benefit later. He would have to hope that whites would have a second thought when they knew it was their own blood being wasted. This decision he would have to make alone. He would have to control his thoughts in order to formulate the thought he wanted. There was no one to shape the thought for him. This is the way it should have been all along, to make the decision, to think for himself, to die without supplication. If his death was in vain, and whites would never accept blacks as equal human beings, there was nothing to live for anyway.

Through the slot in the stone front wall of the cathedral, he saw the first row of the long police parade come into view. He could faintly hear the martial music of the band that was still out of sight. In the front row, a tall, sallow-skinned man with gray hair, wearing a gray civilian suit, white shirt and black tie, walked in the center of four red-faced, gold-braided police chiefs. The black man did not know enough about the police organization to identify the police departments from the uniforms of the chiefs, but he recognized the man in the civilian suit as the police commissioner. He had seen photographs of him in the newspaper. The commissioner wore highly-polished spectacles with black frames that glinted in the rays of the afternoon sun, but the frosty blue eyes of the chief inspectors, squinting in the sun, were without aids.

The black man's muscles tightened, a tremor ran through his body. This was it. He lifted his rifle, but they had to march slightly further before he could get them in his sights. He had waited this long, he could wait a few seconds longer.

The first burst, passing from left to right, made a row of entries in the faces of the five officers in the lead. The first officers were of the same height, and holes appeared in their upper cheekbones, just beneath the eyes and in the bridges of their noses. Snot mixed with blood exploded from their nostrils and their caps flew off behind, suddenly filled with fragments of their skulls and pasty gray brain matter, slightly interlaced with capillaries, like gobs of putty, finely-sculpted with red ink.

The commissioner, who was slightly shorter, was hit in both temples and both eyes, and the bullets made star-shaped entries in both the lenses of his spectacles and the corners of his eyeballs, and a gelatinous substance heavily mixed with blood spurted from the rims of his eyesockets. He wore no hat to catch his brains, and fragments of skull. They exploded through the sunny atmosphere and splattered the spectators with gooey, bloody brain matter, tufts of gray hair, and splinters of skull.

One skull fragment, larger than the others, struck a tall, well-dressed man on the cheek, cutting the skin and splashing brains against his face like a custard pie in a Mack Sennett comedy.

The two chiefs on the far side, being a shade taller than the others, caught the bullets in their teeth. These latter suffered worse, if such a thing was possible. Bloodstained teeth flew through the air like exotic insects. A shattered denture was expelled forward from the shattered jaw like the puking of plastic food. Jawbones came unhinged and dangled from shattered mouths. But the ultimate damage was that the heads were cut off just above the bottom jaws, which swung grotesquely from headless bodies that spouted blood like gory fountains.

The scene was made eerie by fact that the gunshots could not be heard over the blasting of the band and the sound-proof walls of the cathedral. The heads of five men were shattered to bits, without a sound and for no reason that was immediately apparent. It was uncanny. Pandemonium reigned. No one knew which way to run from the unseen danger, so everyone ran in every direction. Men, women, and children dashed about panic-stricken, screaming, their blue eyes popping or squinting, their mouths open or their teeth gritting, their faces paper-white or lobster-red.

The brave policemen in the lines behind their slaughtered commissioner and chiefs drew their pistols and rapped out orders. Captains and lieutenants were bellowing to the plainclothes detectives and uniformed patrolmen in the ranks at the rear to come forward and do their duty. Row after row of captains and lieutenants were shot down with their service revolvers in their hands. After the first burst, the black man had lowered his sights and was now shooting the captains in the abdomen, riddling hearts and lungs, livers and kidneys, bursting pot bellies like paper sacks of water.

In a matter of seconds, the streets were strewn with the carnage. Nasty gray blobs of brains, hairy fragments of skull looking like exotic sections of broken coconuts, bone splinters from jaws, facial bones, bloody, gristly bits of ears and noses, flying red and white teeth, a section of tongue, and slick and slimy with large, purpling splashes and gouts of blood. There were squashy bits of exploded viscera, stuffed intestines bursting with half-chewed ham and cabbage and rice and gravy, lying in the gutters like unfinished sausages before knotting. Scattered about in this bloody carnage were what remained of the bodies of policemen, still clad in blood-clotted blue uniforms.

Spectators were killed purely by accident. They were caught in the line of fire by bullets that had already passed through their intended victims. It was revealing that most of these were clean, comely matrons snugly fitting into their smooth white skins, and little girl children with long blonde braids.

Whether from reflex or design, most mature men and little boys had ducked for cover, flattening themselves to the pavement or rolling into doorways and underneath parked cars in much the same way the blacks had done up on Eighth Avenue during the gun fight between the lone black killer and the police.

Unlike that duel in the dark, the black man now behind the gun had not yet been seen nor had his hiding place been discovered. The front doors of the cathedral were closed and the stained-glass windows high up on the front wall were sealed. The slot in the wall for donations to charity was barely visible from the street and then only if the gaze deliberately sought it out. It was shaded by the architecture of the clerestory so that the dulled blued-steel gun barrel didn't glint in the sun. As a consequence, the brave policemen with their service revolvers in their hands were running helter-skelter with nothing to shoot at while being mown down by the black killer.

The white spectators were fortunate that there were no blacks among them, for had these irate, nervous cops spied a black face in their midst, there was no calculating the number of whites who would have been accidentally killed by them. However, all were decided, police and spectators alike, that the sniper was a black man, since no one else would slaughter whites so wantonly, like a sadist stomping on an ant hill.

In view of the history of all the assassinations and mass murders in the US, it was extraordinarily enlightening that the thousands of white police and civilians would automatically agree that he must be black. Had they always experienced such foreboding? Was it a pathological portent? Was it inherited? Was it constant, like original sin? Was it a presentiment of the times? Who knows? The whites had always been as secretive of their fears and failings as had the blacks.

But it was the most gratifying episode of the black man's life. He experienced an intensity of feeling akin to sexual ecstasy when he saw the brains flying from those white men's heads and fat, arrogant white bodies shattered and cast into death. Hate served his pleasure. He thought fleetingly and pleasurably of all the humiliations and hurts imposed on him and all other blacks by whites. The outrage of slavery flashed across his mind and he could see whites with a strange, pure clarity, eating the flesh of blacks. He knew at last that they were the only real cannibals who had ever existed.

He felt only indifference when he saw the riot tank come rushing up the wide main street from police headquarters to kill him. He was so far ahead that they could never get even now, he thought. He drew in the barrel of his gun to keep his position from being revealed and waited patiently for his death. He was ready to die, because by then he had killed seventy-three whites, forty-seven policemen, and twenty-six men, women, and children civilians, and had wounded an additional seventy-five. Although he would never know the true score, he was satisfied. He felt like a gambler who has broken the bank. He knew they would kill him quickly, but that was satisfactory, too.

Astonishingly enough, though, there remained a few moments of macabre comedy before his death arrived. The riot tank didn't know where to look for him. Its telescoped eye at the muzzle of the 105 mm cannon stared right and left, looking over the heads of the white spectators and the living white policemen as they hopped about the dead who lay all up and down the main street with its impressive storefronts. The cannon seemed frustrated at not seeing a black face to shoot at, and began to shoot explosive shells at the black plaster of Paris mannequins in a display of beach wear in a department store window.

The concussion was devastating. Splintered plate glass filled the air like a sand storm. Faces were split open and lacerated by flying glass splinters. One woman's head was cut completely off by a piece of flying glass as large as a guillotine. Varicolored wigs flew from white heads like frightened long-haired birds taking flight. Many other men, women, and children were stripped stark naked by the force of the concussion.

Seeing bits of black mannequin sailing past, a rookie cop thought the blacks were attacking from the sky and loosed a fusillade from his .38-caliber police special. With a reflex that appeared shockingly human, the tank whirled about and blasted two 105 mm shells into the already panic-stricken policemen, instantly blowing twenty-nine of them to bits and wounding another one hundred and seventeen with flying shrapnel.

By then, the screaming had grown so loud that suddenly all motion ceased, as though a valve in the heart had stopped. With the cessation of motion, silence fell like a pall. Springing out of this motionless silence, a teen-aged boy ran across the blood-slick streets and pointed with his slender arm and delicate hand at the coin slot in the cathedral. All heads pivoted in that direction as though on a common neck, and the tank turned to stare at the stone wall with its eye, also. But no sign of life was visible against the blank stone wall and the heavy, brass-studded wooden doors. The tank seemed to stare for a moment, as if in deep thought, then 105 mm cannon shells began to rain upon the stone. People fled from the flying debris. It did not take very long for the cannon to reduce the stone face of the cathedral to a pile of rubbish. However, it took most of the following day to unearth the twisted rifle and a few scraps of bloody flesh that proved a black killer had existed. In the wake of this bloody massacre, the stock market crashed. The dollar fell on the world market. The very structure of capitalism began to crumble. Confidence in the capitalistic system had an almost fatal shock. All over the world, millions of capitalists sought means to invest their wealth in the communist east.

22

The reaction of whites to the massacre in front of the cathedral was of such murderous intensity that the very structure of their civilization was threatened. The white community had previously accused the police of overreacting to these black killers, but now it was the community, itself, that overreacted, and seemed to take a thorough enjoyment in it.

There was an immediate outcry demanding the use of the armed forces to exterminate the black race, but on second thought, the whites realized that this would deprive them of all menial labor. Who would collect the garbage, mop the floors, wash the dishes, mow the lawns, chop the cotton and hoe the corn? That wouldn't do at all, they reasoned. But what if only the males were exterminated? Better still, what if all black males were castrated? That would drain them of their aggressive tendencies and, at the same time, leave them physically capable of performing all menial chores.

Naturally the armed forces could not debase themselves by performing this act, so various individual racists went ahead with the idea, and offered a bounty for every set of black testicles that were delivered. However, this did not prove very rewarding, since no black male was found willing to stand still while being deprived of his testicles.

Frustrated in their endeavor to create a race of eunuchs, a thing that would have relieved white males of the inferiority they felt from the black males' larger penises, whites next advocated the re-establishment of the institution of slavery.

There was a lot to be said for black slavery, despite the opinions of Lincoln and the Abolitionists, they decided, after an interval of sober thought. Black slaves had been kept in hunger and ignorance, as helpless as knocked-up and barefooted Irish women. After all, white slave owners had had nothing to fear but the envy and fanaticism of other whites. Not only would slavery establish blacks in a permanent condition of animalism and servitude, but it would comply with their demands for meaningful employment and fulfill their desire for separation. The whites were soon to learn, though, that slavery was no longer feasible. Nowhere in modern architecture had allowance been made for the necessity of slave cabins.

Whites became infuriated at the frustrations they found at every turn. No eunuchs, no slaves, and as yet, blacks had not been punished. There was a sudden outbreak of lynching all over the nation, north-south-east-west. Black males were lynched on sight, at busy intersections of main streets in broad daylight, on lonely roads near large farms and ranches, in their own remote and desolate sharecropper shacks. They were lynched in every imaginable manner. Alongside the traditional hanging-and-burning, there were modern innovations. Some were crushed against walls by large, powerful cars. Some were chopped to death by women's stiletto heels. Some were drenched with gasoline and set afire and let free to run and fan the flames. Some were simply beaten to death by whatever blunt instruments were close to hand.

To keep alive, black males went underground. They went to live wherever they felt they would be out of sight of the whites. Their ghetto tenements were periodically invaded by the police and were consequently considered unsafe. Even the basements and cellars of their tenements were not considered safe from the relentless police pursuit and their armies of informers. These places were also just as likely to prove death traps during the systematic searches for guns.

So they went outside of the ghettos to go underground. At first, the favorite underground hiding places, made appealing by black writers, were the sewers and conduits for the various public services, such as electricity, telephones, water, steam, and the like. These places honeycombed the areas beneath the buildings of every large city and were easily reached by numerous manholes.

But these places had various drawbacks, which black males soon discovered. It was difficult and dangerous for black females to bring them food. Any female caught passing a pot of hopping john down a manhole to an unseen recipient was immediately suspect. Because these places had been so highly publicized by the black writers who had made them seem so appealing to blacks, they were consequently one of the first places the whites looked for them.

But blacks were not without their own power. Many of them had taken the dangerous, illicit rifles that they had received into hiding with them. They proved almost invulnerable as they sniped from beneath slightly raised manhole covers. Even the riot tanks were ineffective against these forays. Only bombing was entirely effective, and because so many manholes were located in densely-populated business districts, the bombs had to be limited in size and delivered by midget helicopters, which, themselves, easily fell prey to black sniper fire. Nevertheless, the number of bombs successfully dropped on manholes was sufficient to pit the streets of the big cities like the face of the moon.

Soon, blacks who did not have guns began to take pipe cutters and wire cutters and small acetylene torches with them into hiding so they could cut water pipes, and telephone and electric cables, thereby sabotaging the communications and sanitation of the cities. Highly sensitive and important areas of economic, cultural, and commercial activity, such as Wall Street and the Rockefeller Center, suddenly found themselves without water, lights, and telephones. Thousands of people were trapped in elevators, some of whom died of heart failure. Others committed suicide and a few went mad and killed the others.

Tycoons had their telephone conversations cut when they heard the sound 'F . . .,' in the middle of million-dollar business deals. They had to sweat it out for hours before learning whether they had been told 'Fine,' or 'Fuck you.' Executives were suddenly plunged into black darkness at just the moments they were about to plunge their stiff 'boonies' into their secretaries' wet 'moonies', and instead felt them striking against all sorts of unexpected hazards and even straying into such unlikely things as inkwells, paper cups, and waste baskets. And the absence of water, of course, led to dirty hands, the malfunctioning of plumbing, the discouragement of loitering in the johns, and the pervading, astonishingly permissive odor of shit.

But the continual bombing of manholes influenced many blacks to seek less obvious and more permanent hiding places where they could receive food and have their women visit them, or else do it to each other in comparative privacy and security. They began to move into less obvious places, such as the basements of commercial buildings, storage warehouses, and the isolated housings of dynamos that were protected with the warning, 'DANGER! KEEP OUT!'

White custodians and specialized workers were startled out of their wits upon coming face to face with vaguely-seen blacks in dimly-lit, unlikely places. Some were slain outright, silently strangled. Some dropped dead of fright. Others found themselves seized and their throats and vocal cords bitten out by large, dangerous teeth. Soon it reached the point where no white man was willing to enter a dark, uninhabited area alone, not even his own basement to stoke the furnace.

It was then that a lunatic fringe of white racists organized gangs of vigilantes to hunt the blacks out of their holes as though they were wild beasts. Safaris of hunters armed with hunting guns searched the cities for underground outlets where they could smoke the blacks out and shoot them. At the same time, white women armed themselves with handguns to protect their homes in case a wild black got loose.

But the blacks proved to be more dangerous than jungle beasts. They were more intelligent and they had knowledge and experience of the cities. They were the mental equal of whites and were better armed. Living in the ghettos had made them immune to smoke and stinking gases and they just stayed put in their underground holes, waiting for the whites to come in after them.

So what at first had been a vigilante action was now the most dangerous and exciting of all sports. It became known all over the civilized world as 'THE BLACK HUNT'. Unlike the other game killed by civilized hunters, it was not necessary to give blacks any advantage to even the odds. The black was more cunning than his white counterpart, faster moving, and could run faster and jump further. He was strong and agile, and danger enhanced his frenzy. And above all, when stripped naked, he was almost invisible in the dark.

The element of danger attracted all of the famous white hunters in the world, both professionals with big-game experience who were employed to organize these new safaris, and the millionaire sportsmen grown jaded with shooting insipid lions and tigers, dull-witted water buffalo, clumsy rhinoceroses, and the too-too vulnerable elephants.

Even famous American millionaire philanthropists, known for their advocacy of equal civil rights, who deplored the killing of bulls by toreadors, hares by hounds, horses by butchers, and who at first had been repulsed and outraged by this inhuman manhunt, eventually succumbed to the sheer entrancement of hunting niggers instead of having to hire them, and to the inexpressible exuberance of bagging a big dangerous black buck and cutting off his testicles to have them mounted in the trophy room.

Shortly the greatest hunters alive were engaged in THE BLACK HUNT! Master trackers, schools of beaters, white hunters, blonde nymphomaniacs, and whites with so little knowledge of this most masculine of all sports that they had to brush up on old stories by Hemingway to learn what position to take with their wives.

But still the blacks proved formidable, and if a white hunter dropped his guard for just an instant, he was felled by a right cross to the jaw.

23

Needless to say, the presidential administration was appalled by this deterioration of civilized morality. A conference was called of all members of the cabinet, Supreme Court, leaders of Congress, and white civic leaders who had kept aloof from the exciting sport, to discuss ways and means of putting an end to this barbaric immorality. It was suggested that the blacks should first agree to quit massacring whites before any further commitment was made, for after all, the actions of the whites were merely retaliatory. This had the appeal of first convicting blacks before pleading the mercy of the whites, as was the traditional custom, and was agreed upon by all present.

But how were blacks to be made to stop massacring the whites, especially in view of their aversion to 'THE BLACK HUNT'?

Spontaneously, the name of Tomsson Black, the young black president of Chitterlings, Inc., the only black male still free to come and go as he pleased, sprang to everyone's mind. Tomsson Black, they argued, was the only black who commanded sufficient admiration and trust of other blacks to insure that the plan was listened to. What was more, the whites trusted him, too.

As soon as it was learned that Tomsson Black would appeal to his black brothers to abandon those homicidal impulses which led only to death and disgrace, all of the major television and radio networks, independent stations, local and national and international newspapers and news magazines, all the various media of communications, offered him time and space. The television networks gave him their most effective hour between seven and eight p.m., at the cost of millions of dollars in advertising revenue. The news magazines put his picture on all of their covers and, when he consented to the conference's request, newspapers carried headlines in type the size customarily employed to announce a world war:

TOMSSON BLACK SPEAKS TO THE NATION.

The gist of Tomsson Black's appeal was for blacks to count their blessings, to know their friends, to be orderly and law-abiding, to trust their government and do the right thing.

No one in the white community thought this corn-pone, slavery-time gibberish was strange language for an appeal to insane, homicidal blacks in the last half of the twentieth century. It had worked wonderfully for them for more than a century, so why shouldn't it work for Tomsson Black, who had won the respect and admiration of his people. Furthermore, no sane white person was capable of believing that a sane black person might have a deep-seated homicidal hatred for them.

As a consequence, the white community was amazed beyond measure when black men still kept running amok and killing white people with foreign guns.

EDITORS' NOTE: No formal conclusion exists for Plan B. The following pages are reconstructed from a detailed outline found with the rest of the manuscript.

It was then that the Establishment decided to send trusted black men underground to track down the source of the guns. Grave Digger's suspension was lifted and he was ordered to return to duty with Coffin Ed by Captain Brice.

'Now I want you fellows to get yourselves fired,' the captain instructed them.

'How?' Grave Digger asked. 'I thought I was already fired.'

'Hell, you ought to know how to get yourself fired,' the captain said. 'Take a bribe from a pusher; wreck a police car while you're off duty; get in a brawl downtown outside of your precinct; libel the commissioner—'

'How about beating up on some brothers' heads?'

'Hell, you know we woudn't fire you for that – not really. But you'll find a way, I'm sure,' the captain ventured.

'All right, we get fired. Then what?' Digger asked.

'I'll spread the story, get it in the papers, on TV. Everybody'll know in a week's time. Of course, you'll still be on the payroll, you understand that?'

'Yeah, we understand,' Digger answered.

'Get around the bars, the shooting galleries, the whore houses. With a couple of tough hoods like you boys on the loose, somebody's bound to contact you,' the captain said. 'Play it cool, talk anti-white, let the contact lead. Sooner or later, somebody's gonna want two boys like you with your big, fast guns. Just keep in touch and buzz me what you find out.'

'We hear you, boss,' Digger said. 'Sound just like a hipster. When we find something to spiel, we'll buzz you, boss.'

In a couple of days, they dropped into Small's Bar during

the afternoon. Everybody there knew they had been fired for taking a bribe from the Syndicate's Harlem connection, but no one said a word.

From then on, they hung around pool rooms, bars, shooting galleries, prostitution pads. They acted resentful and ill-used. They gave a very creditable performance of having a hard-on for whitey, of being so anti-white that they wouldn't drink a white cow's milk. They were charged with several assaults against white people, and it became common knowledge that they had beaten many whites mercilessly and had never been caught.

Their behavior was in character and therefore believable. They had worked for the establishment as hatchet men on their race, had kissed the white man's ass, and now that they were considered no longer useful and had been thrown out in the street, they had turned on him with hatred and resentment, venomous and murderous like blind snakes in the heat of August.

However, they didn't find out any more about the source of the guns than was already known. By accident they had caught one of the delivery boys who had just delivered a gun and they tortured him unmercifully, trying to make him talk. Either he didn't know where the gun had come from or else he was resolved to die before he told. He was hospitalized in time for his life to be saved and, surprisingly, the black-cops-turned-vicious-hoodlums escaped punishment. No one identified them, no one testified against them.

In talking it over between themselves, they discovered that each had become convinced, of his own accord, that the only organization of the right size, with enough resources, and with the right contacts in the black community necessary for the acquisition and distribution of the guns was the firm of Chitterlings, Inc.

They contacted Lieutenant Anderson and told him they had something to report. He asked if they had any facts, forcing them to confess that all they had was a theory.

It took Anderson some time to convince the brass to listen to the theory, but they finally agreed to listen. The two black detectives waxed eloquent in their charge that Chitterlings, Inc. was the only organization in all the world that fitted the bill. Hadn't its founder and president formerly belonged to all of the militant, anti-white groups in the US? Hadn't he founded the Big Blacks? Hadn't he castigated the police? Hadn't he visited all the anti-American capitals of the communist world? Wasn't he the only US black anarchist who had had the opportunity to learn about guerilla war from the leading revolutionaries of the world? If the guns were not being distributed by Tomsson Black through Chitterlings, Inc., then the entire episode was a figment of the imagination, they argued.

The police commissioner looked at the district attorney. The chief of the New York office of the FBI nodded toward an official of the CIA.

The CIA official admitted that they had had Tomsson Black under suspicion since the start. They had reviewed his entire career; they had sent agents to many communist capitals to investigate his former activities. There was nothing about his entire life, from the cradle, that the CIA didn't know. And in this case, they were forced to give him a clean bill of health. They had discovered no firm evidence, nor even a suspicion of a connection, between his activities and the distribution of the guns. Their detailed investigation only confirmed their belief that he had had a complete change of heart from his former anti-white period, that he was now a firm and staunch supporter of law, order, and the American way, and that he was as trustworthy a black man as it was possible to find.

The FBI official admitted that they had also thoroughly investigated the firm of Chitterlings, Inc. from both the inside and the outside. They had traced its formation, discovered and interviewed all the original backers, examined its articles of incorporation, interviewed a cross-section of its personnel, and contacted individually all the known police informers who had ever been in its employ. None of them admitted to knowing any more about the guns than what they had read in the newspapers.

The only incident that the FBI found interesting involved a ten-thousand-ton freighter that had become incapacitated in Mobile Bay on the night of the last December 24th. At 4:03 a.m., December 25th, the freighter had broadcast an SOS. Witnesses later testified that they had seen heavy black smoke coming from below and enveloping the upper decks. At 4:15 a.m., radio contact had been made with the Coast Guard in Mobile Bay and a Coast Guard cutter had been quickly dispatched to its rescue. The sleepy crew of the cutter had scarcely retired from Christmas Eve celebrations and it was with an ill will that they set forth into the cold, gloomy morning. By the time they arrived at the disabled freighter, the fire in its engine room had been checked. However, the engines had been damaged beyond repair.

The freighter was flying the Liberian flag but was leased by a textile industry in Hong Kong. The captain and mate were Chinese, the crew a mixture of other Orientals of many varying nationalities. It had delivered a consignment of silk worms with all the necessary food-producing trees and plants for their existence, along with a number of Asiatic experts to supervise their care and propagation in Havana for the Cuban government, which had embarked upon a project of native silk production for its own textile industry. When the fire had broken out, the ship had been en route to the port of New Orleans to pick up a consignment of raw cotton for manufacturers in Hong Kong.

The Chinese skipper, who appeared to be thoroughly Anglicized, admitted that they had been rushing to New Orleans, hoping to be there in time for a Christmas Eve celebration when a boiler had become overheated and caught on fire.

The Coast Guard cutter's captain examined the freighter's papers and found them in order. However, the Coast Guard crew were aggravated by the nationality of the captain and his mate, despite their English courtesy, so they made quick work of towing the freighter into drydock in Mobile Bay, from which it wouldn't be able to put to sea again until the first week in January.

However, thorough investigation proved that not one of the

personnel of Chitterlings, Inc.'s main plant nearby had ever heard of the disabled freighter in Mobile Bay.

So the FBI was in complete accord with the CIA that Chitterlings, Inc. and its president, Tomsson Black, could be declared free of all suspicion.

The district attorney pointedly suggested that black people who tried to publicize unfounded suspicions against Tomsson Black and Chitterlings, Inc. could only be considered as suspect themselves.

The commissioner admitted that he was personally acquainted with Tomsson Black, who had impressed him as a thoroughly loyal and dependable and patriotic black American who had proved beyond all doubt that he was completely rehabilitated.

Captain Brice admitted, 'I'd trust him, too. I'd always thought that he was bought.'

The conversation continued in this vein until the white conferees became so incensed at the black detectives for suspecting their boy, Tomsson Black, that the commissioner dismissed them from the force for real and denied them any benefits from the police pension agency.

Afterward Grave Digger said, 'We should have our heads examined. Even a black child knows better than to suspect a white man's favorite nigger.'

'Funny enough,' Coffin Ed conceded. 'Them's the only mother-rapers who can get away with anything.'

'Yeah, whitey'll trust them when he won't even trust himself.

They were out of their jobs again, but there was something different about it this time. This was for real and the black brothers sensed it.

The two ex-detectives were arrested for wearing their pistols, which they had worn ever since they had been on the Force. Now, however, the pistols are considered concealed weapons. They were taken down to the precinct station by white cops and charged under the Sullivan Act.

Soon a strange black woman appeared, and went bail for the two of them. She was so sexy that at first Grave Digger and Coffin Ed thought she was a high-class hooker looking for a bodyguard. She asked them if they wanted to work for their race and told them that Tomsson Black wanted to talk with them.

She took them to her home in White Plains, where they found Tomsson Black waiting. In an atmosphere of assured privacy, Tomsson Black told the ex-cops that he was greatly concerned about the guns that were continuing to fall into the hands of black maniacs. He wanted to employ them to find out where the guns were coming from.

'That's what the white man wanted,' Grave Digger admitted.

'And you couldn't find out?' Tomsson Black asked.

'Oh, we found out,' Digger answered.

'Why didn't you tell him?'

'We did.'

'What happened?'

'He fired us.'

'Do you object to telling me?'

'No.'

'Who, then?'

'You.'

Tomsson Black smiled. 'You are right,' he confessed. 'They're coming from me. But my calculations went wrong.'

Tomsson Black told them about his plan, which he called 'Plan B', for 'Black'. His plan was to arm all American black males, instruct them in guerilla warfare, and have them wait until he gave the order to begin waging war against the whites.

He had acquired ten million guns and a billion rounds of ammunition, and once they had all been distributed and blacks had become familiar with their use and in the tactics of guerilla warfare, he had intended to issue an ultimatum to the white race: grant us equality or kill us as a race. He planned to demonstrate to the whites that blacks were well-armed and well-trained. However, only a small percentage of the guns had been distributed and their owners were running amok with them.

'I was a fool not to have anticipated it,' he confessed. Why should black men act any different from white men in a similar situation? Did black men value their lives any more than white men? Did black men value freedom any less? What was the difference between a black man and a white man whose antecedents had lived under the same society and with the same values and beliefs for three and a half centuries? Did the black man have hereditary slave compulsions passed down from one generation to another?

Tomsson Black would have liked to have had the time to organize the black race into effective guerilla units, and the units into an effective force, in order to add weight to his ultimatum. He would also have liked to have granted white people the time for reflection and consideration before they made their choice. Somehow it had gotten out of his control. Now all he could do was complete the distribution of the guns and let maniacal, unorganized, and uncontrolled blacks massacre enough whites to make a dent in the white man's hypocrisy, before the entire black race was massacred in retaliation.

In the end, it would all depend on the white man's image of himself. Could the white man reconcile the destruction of the black race with his own image as a just, civilized, and compassionate human? Was he capable of slaughtering twenty million blacks and then continuing to live with himself and enjoy his own society? It had been done before. It was a calculated risk to assume that it could never happen again.

But it was a calculated risk that the black man had to take. There was no longer any point in petitioning through the white man's legal apparatus, appealing to the white man's sense of justice, morality, religion, or compassion. Black men had done this before, they were still doing it. But so far, none of the tactics tried had made a dent in the white man's impenetrable hypocrisy.

'One thing I'll tell you,' Tomsson Black said. 'You'd be surprised at the number of responsible white men who can be bought by a nigger whom they hate. I never tried to keep anything a secret; I just pay, like the white man does.'

'Black, you're a dangerous man,' Coffin Ed said.

'Dangerous for whitey,' Black said, 'but not for you.'

'Maybe after you get all the black people killed here you can go and live in Never-Never Land, but I got to live here with the white man,' Coffin Ed said. 'And all my family and friends got to live here. And you're gonna get us killed.'

'Not necessarily,' Tomsson Black said. 'It's a calculated risk, as I said. The white man may be amenable.'

'But I ain't gonna let you take that risk.' Coffin Ed drew his long, shiny pistol. 'I'm gonna kill you.'

Without warning, Grave Digger drew his own revolver and shot Coffin Ed through his right hand.

'Why'd you shoot me, Digger?' Coffin Ed asked, holding his wounded hand.

'You can't kill Black, man,' Grave Digger explained. 'He might be our last chance, despite the risk. I'd rather be dead than a subhuman in this world.'

'And all your relatives and friends and the rest of the black people killed in the process,' Coffin Ed said, chagrined.

'If that's the way the cat jumps,' Digger replied.

'I don't see it that way,' Coffin Ed said, reaching for his pistol with his left hand. 'I'm gonna kill him so my people can live.'

'Don't touch that pistol, Ed,' Grave Digger warned. 'Don't make me kill you, partner.'

'If you try to save this maniac's life, you're gonna have to kill me, Digger.'

Grave Digger let his gun answer. He shot Coffin Ed through the head. As he stood over the body of his dead friend, Tomsson Black drew a small automatic from a side table drawer and shot Grave Digger through the back of the head.

The beautiful black woman who had brought the two detectives to the house came quickly into the room and found Tomsson Black still holding the automatic in his hand. Evidently she had been eavesdropping.

'But why did you kill this one?' she said, lifting her hand in the direction of Grave Digger's body. 'He was on your side.'

'The risk was insupportable. He knew too much and he had killed his partner,' Tomsson Black answered. 'Whitey would make him talk if they had to take him apart, nerve by nerve.'

She looked at Tomsson Black. 'I hope you know what you're doing,' she said.

Payback Press

is an independent imprint within Canongate Books focussing on black culture and black writing. The list features some of the most neglected but important voices to come out of urban America this century. Below is the full list of Payback titles currently in print.

Fiction

BLACK
Clarence Cooper Jnr. — isbn 0 86241 689 2 — £6.99 pbk

THE FARM
Clarence Cooper Jnr. — isbn 0 86241 600 0 — £5.99 pbk

THE SCENE
Clarence Cooper Jnr. — isbn 0 86241 634 5 — £6.99 pbk

THE HARLEM CYCLE VOLUME 1
Chester Himes — isbn 0 86241 596 9 — £7.99 pbk

THE HARLEM CYCLE VOLUME 2
Chester Himes — isbn 0 86241 631 0 — £7.99 pbk

THE HARLEM CYCLE VOLUME 3
Chester Himes — isbn 0 86241 692 2 — £7.99 pbk

PORTRAIT OF A YOUNG MAN DROWNING
Charles Perry — isbn 0 86241 602 7 — £5.99 pbk

GIVEADAMN BROWN
Robert Dean Pharr — isbn 0 86241 691 4 — £6.99 pbk

THE NIGGER FACTORY
Gil Scott–Heron — isbn 0 86241 527 6 — £5.99 pbk

THE VULTURE
Gil Scott–Heron — isbn 0 86241 528 4 — £5.99 pbk

CORNER BOY
Herbert Simmons — isbn 0 86241 601 9 — £5.99 pbk

MAN WALKING ON EGGSHELLS
Herbert Simmons — isbn 0 86241 635 3 — £6.99 pbk

AIRTIGHT WILLIE AND ME
Iceberg Slim — isbn 0 86241 696 5 — £5.99 pbk

LONG WHITE CON
Iceberg Slim — isbn 0 86241 694 9 — £5.99 pbk

MAMA BLACK WIDOW
Iceberg Slim — isbn 0 86241 632 9 — £5.99 pbk

PIMP
Iceberg Slim — isbn 0 86241 593 4 — £5.99 pbk

THE NAKED SOUL OF ICEBERG SLIM
Iceberg Slim — isbn 0 86241 633 7 — £5.99 pbk

TRICK BABY
Iceberg Slim — isbn 0 86241 594 2 — £5.99 pbk

PANTHER

Melvin Van Peebles — isbn 0 86241 574 8 — £7.99 pbk

ONE FOR NEW YORK

John A. Williams — isbn 0 86241 648 5 — £6.99 pbk

SPOOKS, SPIES AND PRIVATE EYES

Paula L. Woods — isbn 0 86241 607 8 — £7.99 pbk

Not-Fiction

THE NEW BEATS

S. H. Fernando Jr. — 0 86241 524 4 — £9.99 pbk

BORN FI'DEAD

Laurie Gunst — 0 86241 547 0 — £9.99 pbk

BLUES PEOPLE

LeRoi Jones — 0 86241 529 2 — £7.99 pbk

BENEATH THE UNDERDOG

Charles Mingus — 0 86241 545 4 — £8.99 pbk

BLACK FIRE

Nelson Peery — 0 86241 546 2 — £9.99 pbk

BLACK TALK

Ben Sidran — 0 86241 537 3 — £8.99 pbk

SWEET SWEETBACK'S BAADASSSSS SONG

Melvin Van Peebles — 0 86241 653 1 — £14.99 hbk (includes CD)

Call us for a free **Payback Sampler** which gives you more information on all the the above titles. The sampler also contains extracts from our most recent publications together with information about the authors. It is a great little booklet that fits in your pocket and gives you a broader taste of what we publish. Check it out!

Alternatively, if you are hooked up to the internet, look for the Payback Press website where you will find all the latest publication details, extracts from the books and author biographies.

Our books are available from all good stores or can be ordered directly from us:

PAYBACK PRESS
14 HIGH STREET
EDINBURGH EH1 1TE
tel # 0131 557 5111
fax # 0131 557 5211
EMAIL canongate@post.almac.co.uk
WEBSITE http://www.4th-edge.co.uk/payback.htm

All forms of payment are accepted and p&p is free to any address in the UK.

ALSO AVAILABLE FROM PAYBACK PRESS

Spooks, Spies and Private Eyes

edited by
Paula L. Woods

AN ANTHOLOGY OF BLACK MYSTERY, CRIME AND SUSPENSE FICTION OF THE 20TH CENTURY

This superb anthology brings together an eclectic and diverse collection of compelling black writing. Much of it has been long out-of-print, generally unavailable or not published at all. The gathering of these pieces has been a feat of detective work in itself!

In *Spooks, Spies and Private Eyes* Paula Woods reflects the wealth of black mystery, suspense and crime fiction that has been written throughout this century.

The book starts with Pauline Hopkins's classic locked-room mystery story "Talma Gordon", which was first published in 1900. It is anthologised here for the first time. Thereafter it ranges from the work of Rudolph Fisher and Chester Himes to the influential non-genre writers Richard Wright and Ann Petry; from the political thrillers of John Williams and Samuel Greenlee to modern mainstream masters such as Walter Mosley, Barbara Neely and Gar Anthony Harwood. The result is this immensely engaging and important collection.

"A remarkable and entertaining collection"
The Washington Post

isbn 0 86241 607 8 — £7.99 pbk

ALSO AVAILABLE FROM PAYBACK PRESS

The Farm

Clarence Cooper jnr

Published in 1967, Clarence Cooper's final and perhaps finest novel, is a bold and experimental piece of poetic writing that probes deep into addiction, prison life and love. *The Farm* is a challenge. It also remains one of the most honest and unrelenting examinations of what it is to be hooked.

John, the hero of *The Farm*, is serving out time in a federal drug rehabilitation centre. He knows how to work the system , which he does with consummate ease - what he can't fathom is what is going on in his own head. His growing obsession for Joyce, a fellow inmate in the co-ed pen, is made all the more unbearable by the enforced separation of men from women.

Written from behind the wall, Cooper's *The Farm* is a frighteningly authentic and profound piece of prison literature that raises serious questions about society's ability to cage human beings and its success in dehumanising prisoners in the process. It is a work of uncompromising genius.

"One of the most underrated writers in America, a Richard Wright of the revolutionary era."
Negro Digest

isbn 0 86241 600 0 — £5.99 pbk
also by Clarence Cooper Jnr.
Black — sbn 0 86241 689 2 — £6.99 pbk
The Scene — isbn 0 86241 600 0 — £6.99 pbk

ALSO AVAILABLE FROM PAYBACK PRESS

Portrait of a Young Man Drowning

Charles Perry

Opening as a pastiche of Joyce's *Portrait of the Artist as a Young Man*, Charles Perry's only novel proceeds to tell the story of Harold, a young man who gets sucked into Brooklyn's underworld scene, whilst trying to escape the control of his overbearing and suffocating mother. It is a riveting tale of compulsion and murder that is comparable in its inexorability to Jim Thompson's *The Killer Inside Me*.

As Harold climbs through the Brooklyn gangster ranks and leaves behind his juvenile delinquent pals, he becomes increasingly possessed by paranoia and power. Caught in a whirlpool of street crime and Oedipal passion, the schizoid narrator is eventually driven by circumstances out of his mind.

Portrait of a Young Man Drowning was way ahead of its time when it first appeared in 1962. This welcome reissue gives a British audience the first opportunity to check out this cult classic.

"*Portrait of a Young Man Drowning* makes *Trainspotting* look like - well, trainspotting."
The Observer

"One of the most powerful and disturbing novels I've read."
Kay Boyle

Isbn 0 86241 602 7 — £5.99 pbk